Honor
&
Sacrifice

A. S. Koi

ISBN: 0615777031
ISBN-13: 9780615777030

DEDICATION

To my father, for all the model planes.

ACKNOWLEDGMENTS

This section could easily be three pages.

It took me 20 years to get to the point where I could communicate these nightmares adequately and another 15 to write them down. I don't particularly think everyone who helped me find that guiding black light wants a thanks in print connected to these contents, and I'm not that vengeful. Any relation to people living or dead in the objective universe is entirely coincidental or at least not provable in a court of law. This is a book about angry fucking space elves after all.

I will thank my beta readers, the fan artists, the people who supported this endeavor since it was a web comic, and the brave few who will continue to support it through to the end of the three-part novelization. Thank you also to the people who volunteered to edit this monstrosity whether or not they actually did so, and C. Hord who actually did.

And my family, both blood and star blood, who believed in … well, any part of this project. There are better things to come. This part just has to happen first.

Honsad Vittair worried the goggles folded in his pocket, resisting the urge to put them on. The boss emphasized his host's potential offense to anything other than bare eyes, some cultural thing. Focusing on the burning and watering helped distract from the instinctive desire to flee.

When he accepted this task, he decided it was a test from God. This conviction faded with each step deeper into the old tunnel; doing business with devils on unholy ground guaranteed no heavenly seat.

I am doing this for my people, Vittair white-knuckled the goggles in his gloved hands, nearly crushing them. *We've worked too hard too long to turn this planet around and instill values for a healthy civilization. I can't, I won't, let those elf-hugging bastards in the Liberty Party sell us out to those degenerate heathen monsters.* He recalled the recruiter's video reel, the appalling tales of human women taken by the kaffir as sex slaves. *I'm doing this for my wife, dammit.*

Something splashed in the dark. A tall, slender silhouette coalesced through the eerie blue mist. As the figure approached, he observed trace amounts of yellow-green bioluminescence speckling its outfit.

Vittair tried to conceal his shuddering from the advancing entity. No matter how many he encountered, something in the motions of saurtzek set off alarms in his soul. They had a human form, although too tall, too thin, with exaggeratedly angular bone structure. Their joints seemed to bend *wrong,* their movements just a little too fast, too flexible.

He braced for the face. When met on human or neutral territory, they wore breathing apparatus, which constantly misted foul ammoniac gas. This device had the kind side effect of covering their too-wide, fang-filled mouths.

Still, they are better than the Archons, he thought bitterly. Over four months of working with them, the saurtzek had explained how kaffir, the 'first race' of Archos, were genetically their cousins, but they abandoned their faith, became obsessed with fleshly pursuits and dark sciences. They employed these unwholesome technologies to breed with alien lifeforms, irreversibly corrupting their very essence. The 'Archon Empire' employed a front of peace and love, promised security and abundance. There was truth in this, the saurtzek said; humans in Archon society were the best treated livestock.

1

Vittair could not pronounce either name or title of the creature that now towered before him; 'Izzru' was the best he previously managed. Saurtzek all looked the same to him, but he recognized Izzru from a particular piece of jewelry, a necklace set with three orange, shifting, rubbery-looking 'stones'.

Izzru wore this against bare, bluish-grey pectorals, above armor that resembled interlocking bones coated in oily dark-brown latex. This covered from ribs to knees and also encircled his throat, but otherwise he was unclothed. Vittair avoided looking down into the mist; he glimpsed those long, razor-clawed toes once and still had nightmares. He trained his gaze instead upon the attentive black glittering almonds slanted over sharp-angled cheekbones. A tiny amount of pale speckling was visible along his jaw.

"Greetings, Mr. Honsad." The creature clasped hands behind his back as he half bowed. "We appreciate your agreeability in meeting us here."

Vittair bowed nervously in return. He wanted this business over quickly. The anti-nausea drink he consumed before leaving the compound seemed defective and Izzru's smile was far too cheerful and smug. Something was amiss, a detail left out somewhere; anxiety swelled.

"Greetings, Izzru. I brought the signed documents from the Kour-Ma'Da." He passed the tube forward and waited for the saurtzek to open it. "I believe you are to show me some vehicles?"

The long head tilted curiously as he scanned the document, then nodded. "You are to approve them. I see. Come with me."

"Those were my orders, yes." Honsad stepped carefully down into the thin layer of liquid that covered the sloping floor. He followed Izzru to a massive structure barely visible in the dim light, an open cylinder extending from the floor into blackness above. As he approached, he saw it penetrated the ground, could make out fluid seeping into the mist-shrouded opening. A fleshy pavilion hung within.

When did they build all this? They only arrived a few weeks ago. I thought all the kaffir structures had long since rotted away.

Izzru unhooked an unpleasantly bone-like gate and slid inside the canopy, holding open the way for his apprehensive human guest.

The conveyance lurched downward with an organic creak and a rush of liquid. Vittair wretched in his mask, sputtered, swallowed to avoid suffocation.

The lower cavern was oppressively foggy and humid. Lights here and there lent little visibility in the mist. Muffled noises of indistinct origin echoed around high walls. Huge reliefs were carved here which he chose not to scrutinize after a glance. *Those must be from before the first human revolt. Who but kaffir could create such blasphemy at all, much less for décor in a transit tunnel?*

The alien guided Vittair to a several storey tall, oblong chamber. Multitudinous vent-holes drizzled misty streams down the walls; both mist and the effluvium that produced it were cold and sticky. It clung to his clothes. They stopped at a bony ledge from which vapor poured into the space beneath. In the fog below sat several large, uniform conglomerations of what looked to be bone, clear hoses, and cables inundating clustered fleshy cylinders. It was difficult to tell from his position what he really saw, but his impression was giant sculptures of hands – fingers pressed all together at the tips - clad in oddly decorated gloves. He focused his eyes on motion within the mist and made out humanoid forms near the towering 'machines'. These shadowy figures loaded the *things* with objects while others built crates . They scrambled about scaffolding and operated lift devices and small trolleys while sentries looked on.

Vittair gasped, thankful for his gloves as he leaned over the railing but not for the sour stench of bile inside his mask. He squinted as the figures below methodically went about their business. Heaviness came over his heart and dragged at the pit of his stomach as he realized the figures below varied in height; they were not all saurtzek. Vittair struggled to hold a blank expression, but his right eye twitched noticeably. Being a decent man of strong moral fiber, he would rather not have decided the machines resembled squat, noduled, wire-pierced phalluses encircled by monstrous half-cybernetic finger-legs. Thereafter he saw no other shape in spite attempts to shake the vile image. *Why are there other humans down there? Or do they use kaffa slaves?*

One of the workers below dropped a canister, which cracked. Bright orange goo spilled from the breach. A great commotion stirred the mists; from what he could see, workers scrambled away; he identified the forms of saurtzek soldiers incoming. A sizable blanket-like structure, black and plastic, was thrown over the orange mass and two shorter workers who did not move quickly enough. Anguished screams rose as the trapped creatures struggled.

"What in the name of God…?"

The warm hand on his back was anything but comforting. Another wave of nausea rolled over; his feet and tongue felt like lead as the queerly accented, hissing voice crawled into his ears. "Those are your vehicles of war, Mister Honsad. Those are Myzhanzi Self-Ambulatory Decimators. They are not yet alive; their skins will grow as they sleep inside the shipping containers. You could activate them now, you see, but they would not survive a single pulse blast. Shame; I rather enjoy the skinless look. They can take quite a few metallic bullets, though. Primitive ballistics are no match for Ilv'xukzuiy technology."

'll-view-shucker-shoy'? What is that? Clammy sweat ran down his face, into his

3

collar. He fought stammering and staid put, unconvinced he could run if he tried. "So, these are the machines built to kill those Archon bastards, to rip their ships from the sky and kill their horrible insect monsters?"

"Correction," smiled the toothy, slow-talking saurtzek. "These are constructed to fire the devices that will destroy our enemies, while devouring and trampling everything in their paths."

I have to get out of here, to go above the boss to the Theocrat himself, to tell him that the War Council's ideas were wrong. We can't work with these beasts. We have to solve this by ourselves…they aren't any better then the kaffir. "Do you have operation instructions for me to bring back to HQ?"

Izzru's tone patronized. "We sent the information, Mister Honsad, when we sent the documents for your leader to sign. You are not here to take anything back." He displayed his entire hideous mouthful of tiny pointy teeth. "Yet."

"My orders were to deliver documents and approve machines! I have done so and am ready to leave, sir."

"I have a request from the Kour-Ma'Da as well, Mr. Honsad, and it does not involve your return."

I. Getting There First

"Hey! Hey, are you lost?"

A feminine voice, from somewhere to the rear. He was alone in the hall, so it was safe to assume the question meant for him. As a rule, females never spoke to him except to yell; he cautiously turned. "Um, yeah, actually."

"I know this base better than my favorite book. I bet I can help!" The first thing he noticed was the smile: large and infectious, punctuated by short, sharp fangs. Her eyes were true green unlike his stormy viridian-tinged hazel. Thick, orange-yellow curls bounced in pigtails above long, pointed triangular ears. Both hourglass curvy and distinctly athletic, she looked like she could kick the ass of a few marines without breaking one of her blue-polished nails. Her leggings were the pressure-sensitive sort; elaborate self-adjusting tubing trimming the legs was responsible for their common name, 'ladders'. Her sleeveless grey hooded top bore signs it could be laced up for similar functions. Extending a stripy biolon encased arm she introduced herself. "Onzillora."

It took him a moment to respond, fascinated as much by her winning presence as her mix of military kit and street fashion. "Uh, Solvreyil Yenraziir." Seeing her mouth and eyebrows twitch a bit, he added his stock line. "You can call me 'Sol', everyone else does."

She nodded. "That hair's natural, huh? The crimson, I mean. Totally jealous."

Her lack of sarcasm confused him. *She meant that? What am I supposed to do with that?* A fluffy scarf about her neck, turquoise like her nails and ribbons, obscured any ID collar she wore. "I'm looking for Star Assault Recruiting."

She screwed up her face and promptly swallowed whatever she intended to say. Inflection exposed her doubt. "Are you sure that's where you're going?"

"Yeah…" Sol shuffled the fiery, uneven mess she complimented a moment prior, wondering what he said wrong. *Maybe she's a marine? Crap, she's going to kick my ass.*

The contagious smile returned as she grabbed his arm and whipped him around. "Well, silly, you're going the wrong way. The dispensary and the crew lounge are the only things down here. If I hadn't found you you'd be on your way to meeting a really strict security guard."

"Oh, uh, thanks."

As she released his arm, he felt an odd sensation like static between them. Onzillora gave a cockeyed grin and wink and gestured Sol follow her back to the main corridor. "You were close. Too far by one hall."

This wing of Orminos had originally been a space cruiser assembly facility; the halls were vast and uninhabited save for janitorial offices and storage. Plants were the only life for some distance in any direction, growing in displays down the center, hanging on the walls, dwarfed and lonely in the empty, cold, bone white space. Sol found himself drifting off in awe when her voice snapped him back. "Down that one until you see the glass door. It's obvious; everything else is a supply closet."

As she turned to walk away, he noted the angular symbol on her back. "Hey, uh wait, Onzillora, please?"

Pigtails bounced in the low gravity as she looked back. "Yeah?"

"Are you … is that… on your shirt…" *Pull it together, Yen.* "Are you wearing the Haarvakjya?"

Slight eye roll, lip bite. "No, it's a tree. Yes it's the Haarvakjya. Are you high?"

"I just… I didn't think there were women allowed in Star Assault."

"We rarely go out on ships, if we can help it." Onzillora shrugged. "Someone's gotta take care of the boys. That's best done from a distance."

Find something to say, Yen. "Do you march in the parade?"

She made a ridiculous face. "Yeah, you can totally see me spinning a pulse rifle, right? Ffft. Hell no. I watch it from a bar like any sane person."

…

Val's hands shook as he pumped bitter brown liquid into the thermos. Food on this trip had been unkind and his conscience was on his case; his guts churned. He knew better, given the company, but words slipped free. "Man, I hate this…"

Perpetually annoyed to be in anything resembling civilian space, the man waiting for the cup behind him only vaguely held back a snarl. "What? Making coffee?" Relief and relaxation lit his face as the vessel entered his large hands. He pulled a whiff of steam from the coffee and glowered.

Feigning a lack of digestive issues, the smaller man acquired a cup as well. "No, no, sir. I hate recruiting out here. All these lunar farm kids who just want to go to college or move to Archos… seems like a dirty trick, major."

A swig preceded his exaggerated eye roll. "It's your fucking job, captain. Save the bleeding heart shit for your political science dissertation." The big man cringed and his long ears lowered briefly as a hand clapped onto his shoulder.

"I happen to agree with Valdieren's bleeding heart," smiled the grey but well-preserved gentleman. He accepted a cup from the grinning captain without taking his gaze off the major. "We need to staff these ships, regardless of how we feel. We are taking advantage of a weak economic situation to do so."

A short, low alarm sounded. Captain Valdieren pulled a device from his belt and flipped it open. "The six hundred is a bit late, but we don't have anyone else coming so we might as well take him now." He screwed up his face at the screen. "Sirs, I can't even read this name. It's all… Shandrian or something."

"Illiteracy is inexcusable for a knight, Val. Mind if I demote him, colonel?" The major flicked out his own slate, shook his head. Eyebrows cocked as he absorbed data; his inflection changed to read the ancient characters employed to spell: "Solvreyil Yenraziir." His expression was indescribable, but 'trustworthy' was not an adjective one might loan it. "I'll take this."

Already reading his own device, the colonel shook his head. "I appreciate you volunteering, Parthenos, but I think Valdieren should take this one."

Confused but not about to disobey his commander, Val saluted. "Sir! Should I reject him outright, Colonel Kiertus, sir?"

Amused concern tinted the kindly face. "Why would you want to do that, Val?"

"Erm…" The young captain shuffled his feet, regimental posture temporarily abandoned. He struggled to evade the trap less than subtly laid by his superior. "He's classified as 'haki', sir; his mother registered as 'human' on her IGN record, his father as 'haki, half pure'… I… er… won't the ship…"

They stared him down, the major in incredulity and the colonel with a smile.

"No fuckin' way -" Major Parthenos was cut off by a sharp, artful chop to his solar plexus; he grunted as the wind left him. Kiertus, side of his hand stiffly held where it landed, continued to smile beatifically.

"There shouldn't be any sort of problem, Val."

The captain straightened, saluted, and stepped out to the lobby, coffee in hand. The major eyed the colonel with pursed lips as the arm at last retracted. "When did you become such a jerk?"

Kiertus snatched his subordinate's coffee and took a swig before returning it. "Needs more bourbon. Had you forgotten Val's only a gc-3?"

"Not what I meant; I deserved the hit and apologize for nearly breeching clearance." Parthenos stared at the cup. "You should finish this; it's probably flammable from your spit."

With a gracious nod and wink, the colonel relieved him of his cup. "I feel your personal involvement in the situation would hamper your judgment, Auri."

"Not that, either. That kid's nineteen. If he weren't emancipated for service, he wouldn't even be in mandatory. He lists his reason to join as 'money'." He filled a new mini-thermos. "I know you're only down here sorting papers to avoid the blue stripes in your quarters." The major held his slate forward, displaying the cruiser's main security map, as if Kiertus had forgotten his access level. "Making Val take him was cruel."

Kiertus shrugged, looking at the door through which the captain passed. "On his current track, barring any incidents, Val will eventually wear our shoes. He must accustom himself to making difficult decisions about young men's lives."

…

The office was unoccupied, save a life-size mannequin in full Star Assault paratrooper gear, complete with model warrior gen companion. The four-legged, four-winged, four-eyed, blue-green creature was about as long as the elf was tall, posed crouching to leap. *So much larger than I imagined…*

Sol had seen pictures, but one could not usually get close to female gen at their enclosure in the Imperial Zoological Gardens. A group of retired chargers and old drones wandered the general observation area, wingless and docile, but the bulk of the hive lay deep inside a dome. Warning signs around the park cautioned avoidance if females should land nearby, but they mostly flew from the dome into the mountains rather than honor the park guests with a glimpse.

She doesn't seem like a dangerous beast. He shyly touched one of the statue's feelers. *We call them bugs, but they're not anything like* droka *or* lepitoxia*. I read once they were a colonial sentient fungoid that took over the bodies of an unremarkable arthropod, fusing into a new species. So strange.*

Patriotic posters featured uniformed men with rifles or standards. 'Star Assault: We Get There First.' 'History's Finest are Tomorrow's Hope.' 'Fly with the Flag.' The Star Assault unit pendant, the *Haarvakjya* on a high-visibility reddish field, hung on one wall flanked by Imperial flags. On his first pass he failed to notice one of two Imperial flags was reversed; upside down, the 'loving brotherhood' rune meant 'unification', and was a symbol of combat readiness.

In etiquette class we were informed not to do that. I've only seen the flag turned in books on the Mior Wars. I guess I was right. No turning back now, Yen.

The furnishings were unlike any he had seen in military facilities: a sturdy but ornate matched set upholstered in a subdued version of the unit banner's red-violet field. Sol took a seat on a surprisingly voluptuous sofa and waited. *This can't be regulation. It looks antique, like that Shandrian brothel exhibit at the history and culture center. Is this someone's idea of a joke?* A sign on the unstaffed reception desk read: 'Confirmed appts msg #0017.'

Odd. Four digit numbers are code for higher-level officers in Intergalactic Navy. I've never even seen one with a double-ought. His IGN-issue slate was serviceably modest. Sol lacked much of a social life, so his communication device's lameness failed to trouble him. ::Present:: he typed.

Minutes later, a youthful gentleman emerged through the door. He seemed casual for a recruiter, wearing a hooded top like Onzillora's rather than a dress uniform. He had typical sharp Ryzaan features, pale yellow-tinted skin, large red irises with elliptical pupils set off by a two-tone highlight job on his stiffly mudded hair. His only military indicator was a little silvery stylized sea-bat pin.

Pretty young to be a captain. Sol stood. *He could be any Ryzaan student, partying on the Royal Strip on Holtiin because half the people of Archos hate his ancestors. Apparently their entire region's a temperate swamp, oppressive summers, long icy winters. Dad said that's why they felt obliged to conquer the universe: 'Shitty weather, shittier food, you'd be an asshole, too.'*

"Captain Valdieren Karshimziel, 17th Star Assault", he said in the clean, crisp accent of an over-educated homeworlder, extending his hand. Sol suppressed jealousy and awe as he considered reciprocation. He was unsure what custom the man observed: the Shandrian greeting of locking fingers or brushing of knuckles, or the Holtiini farmer tradition of clasping hands and shaking.

At least he didn't do that Ryzaan 'uncomfortably intimate little dance step' thing. Sol apprehensively went with the knuckle brush, which he was relieved to find met by an impressed nod. "Ensign Solvreyil Yenraziir. Intergalactic Navy, Refuge and Rehabilitation Division." He swallowed hard, adding, "but hopefully not much longer."

"We'll see about that, hm." The captain sat on the sofa, gesturing for Sol to join. He swapped attention between Sol's eyes and the slate in his right hand. "You seem a little stunned."

"You're the first captain ever to introduce theirself to me by full name, sir."

A winning smile crept onto his face. "You'll find Star Assault very different." Captain Valdieren folded hands over his slate, settled them in his lap. "Our public face isn't everything; we're not for everyone."

Somberly, Sol acknowledged. "Given this administration's fiscal conservativity, if the 17th were just 'the Flag Corps', they would have been cut, correct, sir?" He watched Valdieren's face shift. *I scored. For some value of scoring that includes signing up to kill people.* "I figure you quietly still serve your historical purpose. Otherwise you wouldn't get away with offering hiring bonuses right now, sir."

Valdieren's lips twitched to a frown. "And you're here for that bonus, ensign?"

"Yes, sir."

Frustration and envy pitched the captain's voice. "You have a full scholarship to study languages at Ryzaa University!" He waved his slate, open to Sol's records. "You would be paid to live in the Archon Empire's most exciting city, all for a grade point average! Studying something you clearly enjoy! And you want to throw yourself in front of Stalkers? Are you fucking insane, ensign?"

Stalker? I think those are Baalphae walking tanks. They're referred to a lot in books about the end of the last war. I thought it was odd there were never photographs. Sol remained mostly calm but poorly hid his displeasure regarding the tirade. "If I do that, captain, my mother will die in pain and alone, sir."

Valdieren's expression eased, his eyes widened and eyebrows rose. "What?"

"My mother, sir," Sol breathed slowly, restraining emotion, "has complications from Czeni syndrome. The new VA Plan won't cover her surgery. With the pay bonus and a few months salary saved, I could move her to a veteran's home in Eshandir, on Archos. She qualifies due to service record and familial status, sir."

The captain stared, his tongue curled to the roof of his mouth as if it could scratch an appropriate response from his slightly feverish brain. "I see." He eyed his slate then set it aside, blinked, shook his head, and returned his gaze to Sol. "With no children at home and two Black Feathers, she can move to Archos. If she lives in Eshandir, she qualifies for Community Coverage, VA qualification notwithstanding, and she's already immunized, since she served. Smart."

He can see the records, then, if he can see her medals. "She's been a wreck since my dad died and my older sister moved to Ryzaa for school, sir. If she were with other vets, she might feel less alone." Sol's resolution failed; his eyes teared up. "She blames me, my birth, for everything, captain. So yes, I would throw myself before enemy artillery if it meant changing that."

Stiff blond chunks of hair partially obscuring his face, Valdieren stared at his slate. He silently scrolled the screen. He did not look all the way up to say, "You are aware that you will be sterilized, correct?"

"Yes, sir. I like children, but I've never been that popular with girls, captain..."

Finally he faced Sol with a sad, sympathetic smile. "Understood."

Sol tried to smile too. "My sister plans on it. My family line, my mother's name, will persist." He toughened up again.

"Are you prepared for immediate transfer?"

His nod bordered on frantic. Shortish, boredom-cut hair wriggled like a cartoon brush fire. "Yes, captain. My duffle's in a locker down the hall, sir."

"Right. The *Irimia* is x-docked clearing a hull infestation." A half-laugh. "Boring damn station to be stranded at for a month. Well, you need to sign some papers; I'll send them to the IGN office. I'll get those and one of my superiors so he can switch your ID. Get your things now or later. Then to the dispensary to order a uniform and you're ready to go." He typed on his slate, thoughtful. "Onzillora will trade in your slate; I'm assiging your new call number. Message me when you board the ship; my handle's 'Bootstrap'. I'll give you a tour."

Valdieren saluted and wheeled to the office before Sol could return the gesture.

....

"Regrettably, sir, I found no reason to deny his request."

Colonel Kiertus looked from his paperwork-strewn magnetic desk. He wore his eyeglasses, which always touched Val strangely. He suspected the attraction fueled more by his need for a father figure than by the striking face or legendary heroics, and the vulnerability the glasses lent increased that.

"Really? None at all?"

Val shook his head. "No, sir. And Onzillora flagged his file while I was talking to him. It's gc-4, though."

"Hm? She did?" Grey hair flopped curiously as the bespectacled head tilted and yellow eyes searched the younger man's face. "Is he still out there?"

The venerable commander was at least as amusing as he was handsome; his clownish qualities just as distracting as the guise of elegance he eased into in certain company. *A charming silly old playboy. Providing one disregards his death tolls.* "Yes, sir."

Kiertus slid the small, stylish frames from his face as he stood. "Well then. Suppose I should go have a chat. Did he mention his mother?"

"Yes, sir. Apparently she's quite ill. That's why he wants the bonus. And yeah, he knows we're not just a parade ornament. Too smart, really." He watched Kiertus retrieve a rank pin from the dress black coat that hung from a wall tentacle. The tentacle retracted to a coil. "Due to our proximity in age, I would like to take charge of his training, sir."

Regarding Val thoughtfully, Kiertus remarked, "You're not experienced enough for your own astrum yet, but I would allow you to walk him through the basics until we find a proper novum."

Val knew better than to be disappointed by the assessment. Someone that young almost certainly needed more than he was willing to give at this juncture. *Yet again the colonel shows sensitivity in word choice. Does he find me so fragile he can't be straight with me? I wonder who he'll end up with? Cute scrappy red head with so many un-squired novum on board; I see an epic SACNet thread on the horizon. Time to stock up on crisps.*

Kiertus still eyed him, bemused; Val straightened and coughed, realizing he never answered. He snapped out a salute as the colonel drifted to the door, graceful in spite his messy hair and casual clothes. "Ah, absolutely, sir. I think it would be a good experience for myself, as well, sir."

Humor decorated his face; his long ears flicked mischievously. "Then you should probably learn to pronounce his name, eh, Val?"

...

He seemed affable... Sol's exposure to Star Assault men had been limited but notable. There were a few fighter pilots stationed on the *Irimia* for emergencies, usually 'clearing debris from the perimeter'. They kept to themselves almost as much as he, so Sol made a point of smiling when he saw them. One in particular shared his habit of late nights at the reading café, and took to turning his terminal over to Sol with time left on it. The man never wore a name tag or spoke, but his log-in was 'Whipsting'.

One night, while Sol served an ice cream reward to a few of his older students, a fight broke out in the lounge. It had not really been a 'fight' for the SA boys; the two of them sat smiling at one another while a group of marines pounded them senseless. No one intervened until Whipsting stood up and was not smiling anymore. They were surrounded by security and escorted to the infirmary. The marines were not harshly disciplined, considering how unfair it appeared. He imagined Captain Valdieren leaning serenely against a wall while gang-punched. *Man, fuck the ICSM. Only Imperial Mil branch for elves with more meat than brains between the long 'n 'pointies. I'd probably flip and kill 'em.*

He chastised himself for speciesist thinking and told his human blood to shut up as he felt eyes and realized a stranger, a tall kaffa in dark clothing, had approached silently. *How long has he been watching? Hope I wasn't talking aloud to myself!*

The man's age was impossible to pin; young and old at the same time, definitely over fifty but in excellent shape. His yellow irises were enhanced by smoky shards; his pupils large and elliptical. Slender triangles emerged from dense, peculiar grey hair. He wore clothing of military design, most likely of non-Imperial manufacture, but on his chest sat a pin shaped like *lepitoxia*, the elaborately beautiful but poisonous butterflies found on Archos and remote parts of Holtiin. It was a symbol of rank only Star Assault used; colonels in other branches wore silver crown badges.

He struggled to remember etiquette, held his head down and saluted as ceremoniously as possible.

"Thank you, but there is no need," intoned the man in a nearly hypnotic voice. He held forth a hand. "Colonel Kiertus Sheriden. You must be Solvreyil Yenraziir."

Sol stuttered as he thoughtlessy shook the colonel's hand. "You'll have to pardon me, sir, I'm not used to, uh, people pronouncing my name correctly."

The handshake, from which Sol retracted with another embarrassed apology, was met by a head tilt and a pleased smile. "I'm sure she told you, but your mother, Solvreyil Niarri, gunned for me in 3rd Mior."

"Really?" Sol could not contain his excitement. "My parents told me nothing about their service! That must not have been Star Assault, then, though, right?"

He laughed, utterly unconcerned about the break in formality. "During times of intergalactic war, Star Assault becomes the *Haarkijetj*, and we command larger vessels. Your mother was IGN, but she took the station on my ship willingly, well aware of the risks."

Sol transferred his gaze from man to floor, floor to man and shook his head. "Wow..." *I can't believe it. My mom fired cruiser cannons? Don't you need a pulse organ for that?*

"Do you have some time for tea? Or does the captain have you on a vicious schedule already?" Such a smile; so beautiful it was criminal. *Where have I seen that face before? His eye and mouth shape are quite distinctive. A history book? Yes. Kiertus. What was it he did? Maybe this is his son?*

Sol scratched the tangled disaster area that topped his short-eared head. "Ah, actually, I'm still waiting on paperwork from him." Both men turned their gaze to the office door.

An unseen individual's husky voice called, "Man at the pot!" Laughter and shuffling followed; a scuffle perhaps, or attempts to throw objects in low grav.

"Excellent!" Kiertus leaned through the doorway. "Val, while you're destroying the organization in my file cabinet, would you kindly make tea for our guest?" There was a protest and laughter from the room. "Oh, the Holtiini fah. And another coffee for me. Extra warm. Thank you. Oh, I'll take those, no worries."

The colonel sat on the sofa, handing Sol a short stack of papers. "Fill these out while we chat. They require little concentration – just documentation that you haven't gone AWOL, mostly. There's a waiver stating you're aware of the potential risks of deep space combat and one for ground combat. Exactly as you'd sign in intergalactic and ground forces, respectively." He licked his lips thoughtfully and said the next part slowly. "The bluish form regards respectful interaction with 'alien and manufactured life forms'... it's apparently an addition ever since Flamethrowers and Armored started letting in human combat troops. Don't feel singled out, please; we only make everyone do it to keep the lawyers busy."

Shuffling through the papers, Sol said, "I see, sir. This is mostly in Ryzaan legalese. Not really one of the languages I speak, just enough to know how annoyed it makes me, sir."

Deep, infectious laughter. "Indeed. I've not been a fan for many years." More serious, the colonel continued his previous story. "Your mother served first on Eave's ship, then mine. She was an amazing shot... she could pick a stalker off from orbit, in a populated area, without civilian casualty."

Sol was suitably impressed. Mom never talked about the war. His father mentioned when Sol was very young that they used to 'work on big ships together' and that was how they met. Papa explained that was where they got the shiny medals in the fancy box they kept in the front room. Sol respected the one stipulation to this brief and undetailed story: 'please never ask about it in front of her, thinking about those times makes your mother very sad.' Of course he had always wanted to know. "Wow, really, sir?"

"Nia knew her stuff. She could calculate damage and impact areas in her head for any projectile weapon on the ship… could even compensate for the error margin of the ship's computers." Kiertus smiled distantly at the memory. "I recall one time in particular, one of the young ladies from 68th Armored got quite competitive with her over a lad they both took a shine to in my paratroop unit. Niarri was supposed to be asleep in her cabin – like most of central gunning while the armor units were a-surface - and I found her in the lower turret, sniping the other woman's targets. From orbit. Couldn't even bring myself to discipline her… just brewed a pot and cheered her on."

My mother? A space ace? My mom who gets in swearing fights with walls trying to hang drapes? "I never would have guessed, sir."

"Eave was angrier about losing her as a gunner to me than she was at losing Kvatchkiir as a tech," chuckled Kiertus. "She even worked some bitching into their vows when she officiated the ceremony."

Who the hell is 'Eave'? "Colonel, are you referring to Cha'atz General Eavrallene Oraska, sir?"

Laughter, closed eyes, a hint of guilt. "Ah, yes, pardon. Yes, the cha'atz general. She was just 'Admiral Oraska' then, mind you."

My parents were married by someone famous? The former ensign signed a few forms in rapid succession. "They never even showed me wedding pictures. I had no idea, sir."

"They were married on a classified vessel; all photographs taken were confiscated by presiding officers. If you wish to see them, make the rank of lieutenant."

You're on, colonel. "I don't understand … isn't a pulse organ required to fire cruiser guns, sir?"

Vexation tinted the older man's face, as if Sol should already know. "She relinquished that when she became a civilian; many Mior veterans did."

"That would make my mother… um…"

"Haki? Yes. Just like you. Her choice to live as a human was hers; I respected it. I changed her species documentation in the official records myself. Did she find acceptance with her human family, ever?"

Sol swallowed hard. "Not really. We were estranged from them; I always thought it was my father that was the issue… I never guessed, but it makes sense now." *The 'rotten deadbeat' who disappeared and never came back, her dad, must have been kaffa.* "I never had a big family. I think it's why I love mentoring so much."

Kiertus eyed him sympathetically. "With Star Assault, you will likely be responsible for orphaned children in a very different way. It can challenge a man's heart. Are you sure this is what you want?"

Very seriously, looking up from his papers, Sol asked, "Can you use me?"

"That is not a question. We can always use men who think fast and are good with languages."

"Like I told Captain Valdieren, I'll do anything to help my mother."

"Even serve to the death the administration that screwed her over?"

"I've considered that, sir. I'm here to serve my people, not 'this administration'." Sol coughed, unsure he should go this far. "No offense, sir, but I don't think Queen Marsura will stay in office much longer, sir."

The colonel smiled slyly. "None taken." Slate held in his right hand, he began to tap codes with his thumb. Valdieren reappeared carrying two cups, handed one to Sol and the other to his boss's waiting left hand. Kiertus did not break focus from the screen until he took a sip. He gestured with his right hand – still clutching the device – to his own collar. "Pull down your neck, please."

"Oh, oh yeah." Catching on, Sol tugged down the turtleneck to expose his blue Intergalactic Navy ID collar. Colonel Kiertus held the sensor end of the device a few inches from Sol's throat tag. A hum emitted from the slate followed by a series of quiet beeps. The redhead shuddered.

Captain Valdieren still stood nearby, watching. "That, Sol, is the feeling of your ESDD being partially armed. Pretty creepy, huh?"

I thought the Emergency Self-Destruct Device was a myth invented by conspiracy wanks. Is he joking?

"Don't worry. It can't be accidentally activated. Do your job right and you'll never find out how it works." The captain's smile was not exactly friendly, although the hint of sympathy remained. "But now it is of the utmost importance that you never try to remove your collar and watch it around other people who'd remove it for you."

Sharp red eyebrows raised in mild alarm. Humming indicated the program still ran, he held his shirt and stayed still. His eyes darted between his new superiors.

A chuckle escaped Valdieren. "Oh, worst that will usually happen if someone does manage to pull it off, say in a bar fight, is you get a nasty scar. The grabber loses fingers or a hand."

"Or their eyes," added the colonel without any change of behavior or motion.

"Oh fuck yeah, I remember that." It was clear the captain was making an attempt to avoid laughter. "Watch out for drunken separatists. Mostly because having your collar blown off makes for awkward situations at security check points."

"Um…" *I am really not sure about this.* The slate went silent as the colonel withdrew his hand. The boy hesitantly let go his neckline.

"Welcome to 17th Star Assault, Astrum Solvreyil."

"Astrum?"

"Technically, you're an 'astrum genova'." Valdieren shrugged as Kiertus and Sol gave him funny looks. "It is a promotion, though. I'll explain later."

The colonel seemed amused. Sol continued to stare and bit his lip as he tried to assemble the hierarchy. 'Astrum' was a pre-unification Shandrian title for low-ranking noble soldiers; it was used in Intergalaxy to designate levels of another rank rather than a free-standing title.

"You'll be working directly under me, astrum. I have things to take care of at the moment, but I can put you to it soon as you're aboard; text me right away. There's lots to get done." Valdieren nodded to Sol then bowed to the colonel and retreated to the office.

"That ad wasn't kidding about 'opportunity for advancement', sir. I could've spent years as an ensign in IGN." Sol fingered his collar, wondering what the black looked like against his gold-tinged tan skin. *If nothing else, it will match more of my civvie clothes.*

"Well," Kiertus sipped the acrid smelling substance in his travel mug. "We don't exactly have 'ensigns' in Star Assault; you can think of it as 'sub lieutenant', if you wish. We are understaffed and in need of competent officers. Don't take that promotion lightly." He jiggled his slate in the air, screen toward the boy. "I have a feeling you'll excel wherever we choose to put you."

"You're basing that on my mother's skills, sir?"

The wide smile stirred up a wrinkle or two and showed a bit of fang. "Ah, you'd be surprised what I can see in your records with a clearance as high as mine, Solvreyil. Your mother is only one third of the equation." Grey brows wriggled above escaping steam as the last of the odd smelling beverage was consumed. Sol hoped that in spite of his being isolated to a cruiser for months he still had enough tan to cover the red he felt washing his cheeks.

"Colonel Kiertus, sir, should I go pick up my uniform, then, sir?"

"You're dismissed, astrum. Might be a good idea to remember your belongings as well, mhmm?"

"Yes, yes of course, sir..." Sol was off the couch and had backed out of the lobby before the second 'yes'. He saluted hastily and headed towards Onzillora's wing, fingers still to his collar.

....

An unassuming sign on the door read, 'Star Assault Dispensary and Post Store'. A smaller, painfully orange placard informed via pictograms that no children, service animals, or uncovered consummables were permitted past the door. The placard's final symbol took him a moment; he had seen it before but never on a space station: the silhouette of a gen head, indicating there were genadri in an area and one should exercise caution.

Sol opened the door and slowly entered. It was large but mostly empty, not unlike a reception area in a public medical office catering to the poor. Pale walls were bare save a few informative fliers; furniture sparse, modest, institutionally sturdy. A young woman at the desk fidgeted irritably as he approached.

"Can I help you?"

"I'm looking for Onzillora." He observed her clothing was simple, not an SA uniform, but military; black tank top, black and grey fatigues. Her arm scars were consistent with removal of tattoos or plug grafts. She wore two black collars but her gear was devoid of rank insignia.

Her tone was hostile and dismissive. "The sarge is busy."

"Well, I'll wait, because that's who Captain Valdieren told me to talk to." Sol glared at her as he dropped his duffel and propelled his bony behind onto a not particularly padded chair. He wanted the emphasis but could have done without the bruises. "Could you tell her Astrum Solvreyil is here under orders?"

With an annoyed look she snapped to her feet, whipped around, and stamped between some shelves toward a door. Before she reached it, she suddenly issued a startled sound, jumped, and ran behind the shelves in the opposite direction. Sol heard peculiar scraping and clicking sounds, and in short order, a large, lanky, wingless gen squatted on the counter. The creature tilted his head and let out a series of low chatters. Its predominantly brown carapace scintillated oddly, as if colored lights were being projected across it. *I've heard that's some kind of communication. Sorry bug, I don't speak chromatophore.*

"Uh, hi," said Sol. "Do you work here?"

The bug oozed off the counter and slunk across the floor, continuing to make queer little noises and display subtle patterns. S held still. Chargers were notably friendly; their tendency to passivity made them easy to capture and train for service. Even trained as a guard, the animal was unlikely to be violent unless triggered by appropriate stimuli.

The boy did a mental checklist of his belongings. He carried no food; the last snack machine he found was out of Nutty Chews. His hygiene supplies were devoid of interesting flavor or scents – Sol was not a fan. By this point, the gen was face-to-face with him, propped on pointed feet above Sol's lap. Slight shifting in the cartilaginous matter that covered the creature's limbs served to remind him of its alien malleability. Four black eyes moved independently, looked him over as feelers tapped around his cheeks and hair, all the while the weird noises continued.

"You're strange," Sol uttered quietly. The bug stopped and lowered his big head. An unpleasant, guttural noise emitted from the animal and the carapace went so brown as to be nearly black. *Maybe I said the wrong thing?* He braced himself, but the gen turned with a cheerful burble and leapt back to the counter.

"Bacon, are you bothering people again?"

Sol stood up and followed the bug. "Sergeant Onzillora!" he called cheerfully.

She looked up from petting her now very pleased looking bug. "Oh, hey, uh…"

"Astrum Solvreyil, now. You can still call me Sol, though."

Onzillora laughed. "Sure, hi Sol. You made it, I guess?"

He watched the gen squirming around on the counter, long blade-like legs periodically sliding off here and there as the entirety of him did not quite fit. "I guess so. Is this bug yours?"

"Yeah, this is Bacon. He was a Star Assault Central Hive stud, but he broke a leg mating and needed to recuperate without other bugs. I had an extra bunk so I took him in. We get along great, somehow." She scratched the strange creature vigorously to a chorus of noises, flailing, and garish scintillation. This looked dangerous to Sol, even if the thing was happy. "You're a big pest aren't you, Bacon? You can pet him if you want, but he does bite sometimes. Not really hard. Just say 'No!' firmly."

Sol had mixed feelings. "Um, I … I've accidentally… uh…" *How do I say this?* "I've pulsed animals before. And hurt them really bad. I… I'll pass."

"Oh, honey, no, you know Star Assault uses genadri because they channel pulse, right?" she said this as if talking to a child (in some ways, she was). "He'll be fine. Not getting any stupider, at any rate."

Tentatively, Sol reached forward and petted the writhing bug. To his amazement and joy, nothing horrible happened. The integument was smooth, with a slight rubbery resilience, pleasant, really. Bacon closed all four eyes and cooed. Sol smiled, relaxed, and continued to stroke while he spoke to the sergeant.

"So, I need a uniform…."

"Yeah, yeah. Here." She dropped a large soft-cover book on the counter. *Vektaar Technology - Uniform and Supply Catalog, IY 646-647.* Onzillora flopped it open to a marked section near the back and pointed at a page, handing him a pen and pad of printed forms with the other. "Star Assault starts here."

As he tried to comprehend the complicated diagrams and images before him, he lost track of the fact he was petting the drooling, gibbering charger. "There aren't any descriptions, just numbers and letters. How do I even know what to order? Augh, it goes on for over twenty pages! What is all this!?"

Onzillora leaned on the counter nonchalantly, flipping back and forth through the pages, pointing out where specific sections were marked. "You need everything on page 207, regardless of what you're going to be doing. Then you'll need some specialty gear and armor. Your specialty?"

"Well …" He was going to mention what Colonel Kiertus had said regarding his potential, but this was interrupted as his left nostril was hooked by a wildly waving foot-scythe. A stifled noise of pain and shock escaped him as he jerked his head with the leg to avoid further injury.

"Bacon!" exclaimed Onzillora. "Bacon, down!" She deftly grabbed the second leg joint to stiffen it so Sol could remove himself. The gen looked confused and made a sad sound, feelers flat to his head, carapace pale, then went limp.

Sol held his nose with one hand, eyes tearing up slightly, as he flipped through the marked pages, noting things down. "Damn, that hurt."

"He rarely makes himself fully rigid so you should be OK but let me look at it, alright?" She leaned in as he moved his hand. "Red, no broken skin, good. I am really sorry. Bacon? Bad bug. Go to your box."

Bacon slithered to the floor, hunkering away with a morose whistling sound.

"Wait, did you say you were just 'astrum' or 'astrum genova'?"

"Um, genova. What's the difference?"

Again, that funny look she gave him in the hall. "Um. You joined Star Assault, and a colonel made you astrum genova, and you have no idea what that is?"

She thinks I'm a complete idiot. "The captain said he'd explain, on the ship." Sol checked the nose hand idly for blood. Just snot, which he wiped on his pants hoping she had not noticed. "Uh. So, does that change my gear somehow?"

Onzillora closed her eyes and jammed two fingers into the bridge of her nose; she either massaged a headache or considered \auto-disoculation. "'Genova' means you're apprenticed to a knight and trained to do everything so you can eventually command ships or bases, if you survive."

Her tone was harsh enough that she suspected he would not. Sol swallowed. "Understood, Sergeant Onzillora."

"So yeah, everything on 207, everything marked with green on the next two pages. Wait until you're actually training as a pilot to get the stuff on 209-210 marked red. Definitely get the three things on the top of page 11 in the weapons catalog supplement that's wedged in at the end."

Sol sniffed, wiggled his nose a bit. "What are these? Biolon socks?"

"You'll get paratrooper training, so you want four pairs right off. They're tough, but you and your bug will destroy them. Trust me." She made an eye roll and affirming hand gesture. "Oh, but, here's the best part." She flipped to the last Star Assault pages, which teemed with souvenir mugs, stickers, buckles, and pins. "Once you get to lieutenant or a specialty, depending on your commander, as long as they're official Vektaar Biolon, you can order socks in any of these colors! That's what my arm warmers are!"

Sol marveled as she held up a stripy forearm.

"Try to get away with this shit as a marine, right? Fashion, one of the privileges of Star Assault!" Onzillora laughed. "Kinda weird, huh? But it's cool. These are badass socks, seriously. Self-healing, self-cleaning, they breathe… short of the abuses of actually being a jumper, they're really tough to wreck."

"These boots are almost as expensive as the carapace armor! Fuck!"

"You'll only need one pair of those. They're the second tier down of Vektaar material from the Haarnsvaar armor: weapons grade, semi-living, puncture resistant, auto-adjusti to pressure and gravitational changes, and they auto-synch with your armor so you can do full-body optical camo. The station staff boots are less high tech, though they're tough. Approved for combat in civilian zones, but they sure don't look military." She pointed down to the comfortable-looking black and grey moccasin-style boots adorning her from just below the knees. "I do recommend them for any occasion where you can't be armed, though. A lot of dress affairs in civilian space, you know," She wiggled her fingers, making a ridiculous face to accompany the vocal mockery, "'Flag Corps!'"

"Maybe on the next paycheck.." Intergalactic Navy was nothing like this. Pants, shirt, jacket from the catalog, plain dark socks from wherever. Dress uniform if one made lieutenant. Patches for specific units. None of this responsive, interactive weaponized footwear and designer socks business.

Onzillora flexed her feet as she continued. "Paratrooper boots are pretty sweet; I own a pair for dancing. Of course, you can only wear them inside military-licensed clubs with correct security, like Wings of Fire at Pachar, the Isolate in Ryzaa…" She squinted at Sol, who was trying to think about anything else than how her body moved when she danced. "You even old enough to get into bars?"

Fortunately, he had no shortage of topics to derail her and a catalog at which to stare. "What about a slate? Captain said you'd issue me a new one? Whoa. What in the…? Is this a shirt? A swimsuit?"

She faced the opposite direction, fishing something from a tower of bins, but knew precisely what entry perplexed him. "That's a brace. Occasionally called 'the Star Assault man bra'. Don't laugh; I've seen men in the infirmary with rib cartilage blown because they couldn't bring themselves to wear one. Also provides an extra layer to keep your bug harness from chafing. And you'll get a bug, hence the 'gen' in 'genova'." There were a little device and a foil bag in her hands when she walked back. "Guys say it actually feels good. Massages the ribs and back as it pressure-adjusts. We get something different here, having boobs, rarely jumping out of jets, and all that…"

"Is this … hair mud?" *Come to think of it, I've never seen an SA guy with short or simple hair.* "So, the long hair thing. And mudlocks? That's a branch thing?"

The sergeant bounced up to sit on the counter. She sipped from a bag with anthropomorphic dahi fruits cartoonishly emblazoned. "We are so not marines." Sol tried not to giggle as she twirled an errant bit of his red fluff between her fingers. "The helmets aren't padded, so you'll want to grow this out."

Pay attention, Yen. You are ordering your uniform. You're an officer for real. "I don't know why, but I thought I'd have to get a high and tight."

Onzillora sighed. "Honey, the only things high and tight in Star Assault are the pilots." Before Sol could respond, she handed him the new slate. It looked top-of-the-line. "So this is your stripped-down Star Assault basic model, which is still better than anything IGN's catalog has by far. This is the Modo Jr. GPS, still and video camera, text, vocal, image communications; runs thousands of applications; can synch up with a bunch of features on your armor and weapons; I loaded yours with the Basic Officer Package and the ID the captain issued. The advantage of the Modo Jr over the slightly less expensive but fancier Modo Telsi is sturdiness. If you'd rather have a Telsi, tell me now but expect to be ordering a new one and on shit-duty for a month while you're out of commission because you busted the screen when your bug dropped you wrong."

Sol blinked. "I guess this is why Captain Valdieren sent me to you." His head whirled with the implications of devices he just ordered.

"With the staffing situation, they can't afford to haze junior officers." She gestured. "Dunno if you're interested, but I threw Librumate 7.1 on it. Default reader sucks. Don't mention it; someone higher ranking might not have it. Don't even know if you read recreationally, but as a genova in the 17th, you'll read lots of articles. It's better. Trust me."

"Do I read?" His excitement was poorly contained as he glanced from slate to her and back. He never had a slate with a good knock-off of Librumate, much less the newest version. The *Irimia's* terminals only had the 5.0 reader. "Is there much of a library on the ship?"

"Mostly treatises and manuals, but one of the wing commanders is a goofy philosophy teacher who collects rare books at junk shops and spends his down time translating and transcribing. He's a dork, but seriously amazing stuff; he upgrades the private library here whenever the 17th docks. This time it was Triiun Dynasty romances. Those Shandrian nobles were quite scandalous by today's standards." Her grin was silly, her voice tinged with laughter. "Don't ask me how a guy like that got to be in command of anything on a war ship."

Oh, how badly I want to talk to you about books. "Are you supposed to say things like that, sergeant?"

"Of course not, but you're not going to tell Kiertus I think one of his jet wranglers is a moon-sized nerdball? No. Even if you did, I don't see how he couldn't be aware of it." She shook her head, laughing.

Sol vividly pictured a pony-tailed, slightly heavy kaffa with flowered hair commanding airmen from a desk piled with old volumes. *Perhaps Star Assault will be more fun than I thought....*

"We shouldn't keep Val waiting. I'd hate to think I fucked up his day more. How are your order sheets coming?"

"I think I've got everything, but I want one of those hoodies, like yours. Where are those? All I found was the 'response hood' that goes with the under-armor."

The sergeant dropped from the counter, taking advantage of the low gravity, easing to the floor as she gathered catalog and forms. "Winter uniform's in the Guild supplement. You get that cookie if you live long enough for a clearance upgrade." With no further explanation, she vanished into the back. He heard a muffled, "Bacon, I'm not mad. Heard me say cookie, huh. We'll discuss that..."

Guild? Imperial Guild? Really? Sol fiddled with his new slate. It booted with an image of the Archon imperial flag waving on a starry field. A snippet of the anthem played electronically. Sol laughed aloud. *Our hardware is cute? No wonder Marines beat us up.* The characters were Shandrian, not contemporary Unified Archon. The latter had absorbed the former, but only someone fluent in the older tongue , like him, would recognize the runes as, 'Honor and Sacrifice'. It switched to Archon with a quiet beep. 'Welcome to SACnet,' it now read.

"Obnoxious little thing, huh?" A stack of rice paper wrapped clothing sat on the counter. "One set ladders, four pairs socks, two sets underwear, brace, response hood, gloves. Don't even try on the latter two until commanded; they amplify pulse and you could accidentally hurt someone. Training required but permitted in your possession with a black collar."

Sol tilted his head. "It's a license to be armed in public?"

"Partially. Carapace, panel kilt, boots, and weapons are being sent out the back; they require clearance. You'll get them from the *Sanjeera's* arms sentinel. Sorry; don't know who that is anymore, it used to be Cheldyne but last time we spoke he'd swapped to the hive. Do you want to sit for a bit before you board? You look pale."

Sol reeled. Hot, spacey, dissociated; he absorbed too much information and experienced many rapid emotion changes in a short time. He took the pouch she offered. "The colonel… gave me tea. From home. I never even drank it."

"Colonel Kiertus? Yeah? What did you think of him?"

Is there another colonel in Star Assault? There's one per war cruiser, right? And there's only the 17th Atmospheric active anymore, I thought? "He seems nice, maybe a little spooky, but very attractive though for… however old he is."

She checked drawer contents, made notes. "He's the closest thing we've got these days to nobility, no matter what people say." Cheerfully, she remarked, "He does have the biggest dick in the imperial military, though!"

Water sprayed from Sol's nose and mouth, droplets drifted to the floor and down his shirt. "Wha?" His face was nearly the same color as his hair. His lips twitched as he blinked and wiped his sleeve over his mouth. "How…?"

"I meant Major Parthenos!" Onzillora laughed deeply. "Sorry, astrum. Your face was worth it."

"I haven't met this major yet." Sol regained his composure. "Parthenos, you say?" *Odd surname. Must be an outer colony name.*

"I won't say it's something to anticipate." She shrugged. "But you're going to work with Val. Consider yourself fortunate. SA has some mean bastards."

"What branch doesn't?"

"Oh, you'll see what I mean…"

27

II. Making Trades

She wasn't kidding about this security guard. The post's Head of Security towered over him, a hand taller at least. Grisly scars dove into her collar and hairline; her long right ear was seamed, as if reattached or wholly replaced with grafted tissue. Her massive canine teeth glistened with eager drool as she barked for ID and a statement of purpose, twice, because he did not respond fast enough. While she wore the black collar of Star Assault, her bicep tattoo was the logo of the Fangs, a small, elite unit to which Sol had no exposure other than people bragging they met one. 'Heavy Armor' marines, apparently, but he was unsure how that worked. Lines beneath her eyes – the only rune of Saurtaf he knew, 'Death' inked beside the left - told him she served in the last war.

He stared at this tattoo, and as he pulled down his neckline so to hit him with a hand-scanner, Sol experienced an unusual recollection from early childhood. *His father was home while his mother was visiting relatives and a guest came to stay. All these were rare occurrences on their own. The man was thin and peculiar, with a pretty face framed by long black braids much like this woman's. He was uncomfortable around children, stepping back when they approached. He and papa spent the night drinking on the landscaped tier on which their rollie house nested. Sol had been drawing with his sister Kali, jealous of the man distracting papa, and he decided he would show dad a drawing even if it meant interrupting adults. As he came out, he heard his slightly drunk father say, "Fuck the Fangs. They think they're a replacement for the 'Kijetj. They couldn't wipe their arses without explosives and a map."*

And the strange, jumpy man laughed and said, "If they wiped their ass with explosives, that would solve everyone's problems, wouldn't it?"

"No, then we'd need the 'Kij full-time. And you fuckers would revolt. That wouldn't be pretty either."

"State your fuckin' purpose already!" snarled the guard. He read her nametag (finally, someone wearing one) and cleared his throat, trusting Onzillora's advice on her specific honorifics.

She's apparently' not a sergeant' but if I call her anything else I will be 'pinned to the wall and kicked soundly'. Here goes... "Sergeant Nabaragi, sir, I am boarding the ISC *Sanjeera*, sir. I am under orders by Captain Valdieren to get right to work, sir!"

28

"Ffffffffft. Ask him how his balls are doing," snorted the head of security.

What? "Excuse me, sir?"

"Nothing, get your skinny ass on board. And ask for extra rations, because you'll freeze like that. Do you even eat? Fucking hell. You're a skeleton."

Sol endured years of such harassment, but it still stung. He tried and suffered for attempting to increase his mass, including not attending a school field trip to Archos four years prior. He shot back, still in formal tone, saluting, "I have no interest in fattening myself up so that you can eat me, sir!"

She laughed and delivered a whack to his bony posterior that sent him floating down the hall toward the dock. "Come back when you've got pubes."

He arrived to a waiting lounge, resembling standard military and commercial docks in other parts of the station, but small, with worn benches and two disused check-in stands between the airlocks. There was no one around. Sol walked to the thick clarithane observation window, surprisingly clean and dust-free given the state of the furnishings, and stared into the blackness. Substantial vessels were docked at other arms some distance away, but only one here: a relatively small but threatening biotechnological warship connected via flexible tube to the right airlock. A changeable sign beside informed, '*ISC Sanjeera*'.

Sanjeera, what was that? An Archon city prior to the empire's foundation, I think. I'll look it up...

In spite technical advances and superficial alterations, this cruiser's silhouette had not changed a millennium, resembling an archaic star whaling vessel. To Sol it seemed a hybrid mollusk-crustacean monster, trailing elegant tentacle-structures from its 'head' down the armored, jointed length. Five smaller outcroppings similar in shape to the overall ship crowned the head above a fearsome chitinous phalanges of descending size. An orb of considerable diameter sat in a track almost to the tail. Once the flexway disengaged, this object would orbit, tethered somehow to the groove as the vessel flew. This satellite was a major component of the ship's 'Ioun drive', apparently related to both the jump propulsion system and some unique armaments. With this portable moon, the *Sanjeera* could move across light years in minutes without a relay gate. This amazing feat was usually limited to more compact vehicles over short distances; Kimetj-class cruisers were the largest active craft with such drives. To anyone without the decades-long education integral to understanding its intricate math, the Ioun drive seemed like magic. The only math course Sol performed poorly in was Introduction to Drive Technology; he switched tracks immediately after his first taste and moved to culture and language studies. *Fuckin' hyper geometry, man. That shit will drive you crazy.*

The relaxed forward arms rippled and shifted, as if moved by ocean current. Sol shook his head and blinked. Something drifted among them, cleaning cyborgs, or survival-suited kaffir, dwarfed by the tentacles, periodically lost in their undulating mass, their shifting textures and hues.

The photographs never really conveyed ... this. Dad told me those were primarily for grappling larger vessels. He rememberd his father pointing at the Kimetj-class cruiser in an old book of military bio-vehicles, demonstrating his explanation via ambush hug. *I get tthere's some hard-core gear hidden inside those; he skirted around explaining and the book was vague. 'Boarding spike' and 'grav hammer' didn't sound as grim back then. I wonder if he had to learn all that in police school?*

Sol looked around for an operator, not wanting to do anything out of line on his first day. En route to the airlock, he passed under a slender archway lined in iridescent rows of variously sized orbs; they flashed in sequence. A pre-recorded voice issued from an unseen address system. "Welcome, astrum. Proceed to airlock and prepare for flexway entry." Another voice followed, in old Shandrian. "Bear the flag with honor, holy and glorious son of Archos."

Holy? In spite his confusion at the word choice, Sol straightened and saluted the door. The proper response to such a message by a living person would have been, 'For Eshandir!' or 'For the Queen!' The former was inappropriate and the latter sat poorly with him, so he managed, "For the Empire!" before stepping through. *Does 'vaurya' have other meanings? Could be a homonym with which I'm unfamiliar, or a traditional phrase no one's changed in a thousand years.*

To his continued fascination and amusement, a subdued instrumental version of the Imperial Anthem played in the airlock between station and flexway. The pressure equalization wait was tedious as ever; he hummed along as he poked through applications on his new communication device. Finally a canned voice said, "Thank you for your patience. Proceed." Sol pushed out and worked his way down the translucent tube using arterial cables that ran its length.

30

Flexways held a horrific fascination for the young haki; they seemed too thin and fragile to keep one safe from vacuum and cold. Consciously, he knew they were nigh indestructible. He learned in Basic they were laboratory-grown imitations of the digestive tracts of *inshan-graehu* – 'star whales' - inundated with insulating polymer that allowed light but prevented any other breathing by the membrane. However, something in his blood, probably from the suspicious human genes, made him extremely nervous to look through the undulating, web-like tube, surrounded on all sides by a whole lot of black oblivion. Since he joined Intergalaxy months ago, he camped out at station terminals three times just to watch departing vessels disconnect, the tubes whipping and deflating as they retracted, then failed to sleep later for having done so.

His new post loomed, tiny for a star cruiser, not a quarter the size of the IGN Rehabilitation vessel, *Irimia*. The *Irimia*, named for the third Queen of the Archon empire, was a city unto herself. Along with military facilities, the ship housed a vast complex of laboratories, schools, gardens, recreation centers, a hospital, and a sizeable refugee colony. In this last place he worked while living in the training barracks. In the company of civilian contractors, he patiently helped children of varying ages improve their use of Unified Archon. Independently, he mentored a few in arithmetic and problem solving as well. He did it all uniform, as his superior, Lt. Okalo, ensured this encouraged trust in the empire regardless of the circumstances that may have led to their being aboard. Technically it was not a 'uniform' position; his work group's 'combat instructions' were 'get students to safety, secure self in quarters.'

Sol enjoyed working with the displaced, alienated children. He identified with them, even though he grew up on an original pact world. They did not treat him like a 'freak' or a 'half-breed' like most of his peers in Framework; they looked up to him. Many were human, but there were hybrids and purebreds too, bonded together by situation. At first he was concerned about accidentally hurting one of his charges with his 'dirty secret', his sporadic body energy explosions, but their presence, admiration, strange gifts and silly jokes took the edge away.

Every time I accidentally hurt an animal, it was because I was afraid of mom. I was afraid she would be ashamed of me, because of what dad said... but I guess, maybe, it wasn't shame he worried about, but bringing back trauma. He ran his palm across the material of the flexway, stopped halfway between his old life and his new. Sol had heard that pulse could be focused and used for things other than violence, that most houses on Archos or in the 'elvish districts' of his home world were more reliant on the occupants' pulse than bio-processing generators for power. Because he grew up in a human neighborhood and attended a largely human Framework school, it was not discussed. *It was feared. Papa told me never to talk about it, to anyone, ever.*

For a few years, the family doctor gave him drugs that made it stop, but they also made him ill. The inability to put on normal weight started then. Still, somehow, he passed the Intergalaxy physical. *Am I going to have to take another physical for the unit transfer?*

Sol tapped the icon marked 'Handbook'. The delightfully elegant Librumate 7.1 made the dry, tedious material of the manual seem brighter. He scanned the unit requirements, somewhat relieved. First, because he was barely out of school, his Junior Physical Equivalency exams still counted. He exceeded the requirements for those as well as the gravitational thrust and 'tolerance' exams in Basic, thereby meeting initial requisites for Star Assault. He wondered if that was some of the 'equation' to which Kiertus referred.

The second thing unsettled him, however. "Prior PsyStat, Corps Eval, TenVal, and/or Siri-Ten ratings will be analyzed by superior officers as necessary for basic placement, but a full Brinks-Vaylen Index must be run by a guild-certified examiner once prospective is in the unit." *Never heard of a 'Brinks-Vaylen' but it's got to be branch-specific. Siri-Ten are how they measure pulse for IGN to see if you'd be a good gunner; I've used my age and mom's listed species to get out of them three times. IGN examiners don't have high enough clearance, I guess?* Sol swallowed hard.

The tube interfaced sucker-like with *Sanjeera*'s side. The airlock's external gate was a series of five shimmering plates resembling polished, purple-veined grey bone. Again, the symbols were Shandrian runes, not the mostly-Ryzaan script adopted as the Archon standard. A sensor detected his presence and the monstrous orifice rotated open. Seconds after entry, it closed. The chamber within was unlike any lock he had encountered; the walls were composed of a dark, furrowed material, rubbery to touch. The floor and ceiling were also dark with a faint traction texture. A red light began to flash above as he waited for the exit to open; the ambient light dimmed out. *This is eerie.*

"Decontamination procedure initiated. Remain armored or clothed. Do not retract expanded weaponry."

"Um, what?"

"Instruction not understood. Decontamination in progress."

The blinking light changed to yellow, then white; other than this, the compartment was dark. A series of whirring hums sounded. With each flash, he noted mist rising from floor vents and what appeared to be holes opening in fleshy wall folds. He swore small tubes snaked from the folds.

What the fuck? Sol's heart rate increased. He sought an override and frantically thumbed the handbook.

"Kimetj and Triotine Class Cruisers: Entry Protocols. Mandatory exam and decontamination occur during each boarding of a Star Assault cruiser for all without Harnsvaar escort. Incompatibility with vessel results in immediate termination and recycling or expulsion into space."

"'Incompatibility with the vessel'?" yelled Sol. "What the flying *shuurn*-fuck does that mean!" His body heat intensified, extremities tingled, mouth dried. Incoherent noise escaped his lips as he released a wave of energy; it crackled in the mist; the walls glowed where it hit and absorbed. Miraculously, his slate went black for a second, not even resetting to the start screen.

"Astrum Solvreyil Yenraazir. You are clean and permitted tier one access. You do not need to hit me. Remain still for rinsing."

"Hit you? I didn't mean to; you were going to gas me and dump me in space!"

"Your genetic code confused me. I found your security evidence before evacuating. Be silent, I can still open the door and the flexway is not attached."

Sol looked around, annoyed and perplexed. The flashing slowed. The light changed to blue. The mist tasted like chlorine and isopropyl, it made his eyes water, but dispersed quickly. Holes shrank and tubes retracted. Another fluid, cool and refreshing, spritzed a few times as the main lights returned.

"You are not a saurtzek but you are a pain. Entered into report. Proceed."

The second gate opened. He stumbled out into a passage, barely keeping hold of his duffel and slate.

"Fucking hell!"

"Never been in an airlock before, noob?" Someone shoved him. "What're you?

A civilian? We don't have a high school here, fucko. IGN is that way."

The venom's source was a wiry man with dingy braids. He wore a brace and ladder pants – no insignia beyond his collar and a spikey wreath tattooed over his six-pack abs. His socks were patterned with red and black checkerboard. *He's high ranking or he's got good connections.* Sol managed a salute in spite insults and recent near-execution. "Astrum Genova Solvreyil reporting, sir."

The blond scowled, wrinkling his scarred left cheek unpleasantly. "What the fuck ever. Gotta be Mullet's new cock puppet. That's the only explanation. Out of my way, meat-sock." A toned forearm heaved Sol at the wall in the relaxed gravity and the man moved on without another word.

He watched after the disagreeable fellow, then texted 'Bootstrap', ::: *Reporting at* ::: Sol checked a sign and added, ::: *G-wing lock* :::

::: *Meet you there.* ::: came the reply. Sol leaned back to wait with a sigh. He hoped the blond would not return and absorbed himself in the handbook in an effort to prevent further electrical panics or rage from the ship. The wall was receptive, resilient in texture, a sort of translucent bluish-violet with other layers beneath. There seemed to be movement in these layers – veins of fluid or little vibrations. As he acclimated to the ambiance, he realized the ship sounded like a living body or the reverberations heard while swimming.

"Kimetj class cruisers are traditional kaffir biological vessels. The use of penetrative devices or solvent adhesives is forbidden in decoration of personal quarters. Likewise forbidden aboard are open flames or electrical coil heating devices not properly constructed for use on such vessels. Substitutions are available in the Star Assault section of the Vektaar Uniform Supply Catalog and supplements. Veterans prescribed fenerettes see Medical immediately.

"While Kimetj class cruisers are self-cleaning and self-maintaining under ordinary circumstances, please show respect and courtesy to the life-forms that comprise and occupy these vessels. This includes but is not limited to: urinating and defecating in appropriate facilities only, picking up food waste, picking up after genadri, keeping foreign objects out of the hive pool, keeping voice and personal device volumes at a moderate level wherever possible, and carefully monitoring chemical disposal."

He touched the wall. "I'm sorry we got off to a bad start. I didn't realize how…

alive you are. I'll behave better from now on." Technically speaking, IGN cruisers were alive too, but most crew and passenger sections were systems of prosthetic enhancements. One could not generally touch living portions of vessels unless one was a technical officer or pilot. "I promise."

"She'll appreciate that," suggested Valdieren. "Did Onzi get you set up?"

Sol adopted a formal posture. "I've got everything but armor and weapons, sir."

"No rush. You'll get all that from Dromarka, after Doc and Sentinel Cheldyne get your ratings squared for calibration. First you're getting a tour. Come on." The captain was in something like a uniform now: full ladder suit, boots, utility belt. To Sol's relief, he led them the opposite direction as the ill-tempered blond.

"The major halls are loops; if you stick to them, you'll end up back where you started. Rungs get you between those ovals – we don't use lifts in crew areas to conserve energy. You'll be miserable the first few weeks but your arms will look great." The captain pulled up his sleeve and flexed with a goofy grin.

"Is the ship powered entirely by bio-recyclers and pulse?"

His guide made an uncomfortable face. "Aside from the Ioun drive and standard bacterial processing system, we have a back-up which involves unstable heavy metals and nuclear reactions; due to wear on the ship and potential harm inherent in transporting the materials required, it's more efficient to," he coughed the last comment into his hand, "harvest colonial insurgents to feed the ship."

"Um... how, um, traditional, sir." *That's entirely vile. Maybe he's kidding?*

"Anyway! The basic layout is like this from tail to head..." Valdieren used both hands in a methodical demonstration. "Aft pipes are over aft grappling system flanked by rear propulsion and ARHGs. You'll have no reason to go any of those places. Hive takes up most of the next section; officers lounge and commander's quarters are above that. Medical runs up the tail from the hive right into the substantial training wing. Ioun drive housing and the friction rollers are outside the juncture of hive and medical; as a side effect, that part of the ship has near planetary gravity. I suggest getting used to walking between those parts; spend a few days doing laps after you start taking *'the schedule'*. That's what we call your regimented prescription doses. Any questions?"

"What's an 'ARHG', sir?"

"Affyg-Rydnar Harpoon Gun, but Colonel Kiertus has us in the habit of calling them 'Anti Reality Guns'. They fire multi-pointed, electrified projectiles, often carrying payloads of contaminated toxic seepage from the propulsion systems, jump drive, or the bio-processing facilities. For a fun guide on the various effects those have on enemy cruisers and their occupants, please see 'Chel's Guide to the Fucking Argh!' on the SACnet archives. Any questions about your drugs? They're different than what you take in IGN."

"Not really; I get that I'll be taking some stuff for combat and regular jumps. I'll deal with them as I go, I think, sir. Feel free to continue the tour, captain."

Valdieren eyed him strangely, shrugged, and continued. "Training wing is flanked by other stuff you'll never have to worry about, the ship's temperature control system and some other things. Main body, where we are now, is three layers of barracks wrapped around and above the bulk of the ship's internal workings. This is flanked by hangars and launch tubes – the Hell Pipes, and yes, command calls it that when giving orders. Once your bed's assigned, we'll spend a few days with a timer seeing how fast you can get from your coccoon to points in the pipes. Above and below here are cannon turrets; you won't get trained on those until you've survived some drop tours. We don't waste gunner training. Next there are some facilities areas – weapons, armor, other gear are stored and repaired here; rations are dispensed here. Forward meeting hall is also here; we'll time you on getting there, too. You'll see in your handbook that is not a mandatory part of training but Major Parthenos is strict about promptness to briefings. What's with the face, astrum?"

"Apologies, but…" Sol deliberated on his verbiage. He did not want to seem like some Star Navy tourist, but needed to verify. "Rations, sir?"

"All the snack bars and pubs on your last cruiser? Yeah, we don't have those. Don't even have a mess hall, I'm afraid. Rations are dispensed based on nutritional need of the individual; you can submit a request form via email to get specific contents based on taste but I will warn you from personal experience that takes a while. If you have a burning need to eat around your fellows, you can figure out that shit on your own." The captain's tone remained uniformly cheerful as the tour continued. "There are smaller officer quarters and then the ship's bridge. Then more weaponry and technical shit from there. You'll care if you become part of CC; otherwise, it's best not to think about. And you don't seem like enough of a chewy nutbar to be Cruiser Control or Operations."

They came to a curve in the hall where floor and ceiling were intersected with tube-shaped passageways adorned with bony rungs. The rungs grew straight from the flesh of the walls, surrounded at their bases by scar tissue. A sign informed medical, hive, and training facilities could be reached nearby if one descended here, with more training and operations above.

"We're headed down one level. Go on, astrum."

With curious trepidation he wrapped his bare hands around the rungs. This gave way to fascination as the slightly shiny surface revealed itself to be smooth, warm, and dry.. The shine seemed to stem from incidental polishing from the repeated grip of oily hands. The ship noises grew louder as he descended.

As Valdieren dropped to join him on the lower level, the captain asked, "You put your earplugs in yet?"

"Earplugs, sir?"

Val shook his head and made a face. "She always forgets them because she doesn't come on ships much. She has a pair installed, too. Get your kit out." As Sol unzipped and rifled his duffel bag, the captain explained. "There should be a little bag with the ladders, might be in your utility belt – right, that. Open that... now put those in."

Sol knelt over his duffel, holding two small, spongy, dark grey objects. They were bullet-shaped but organic in appearance, like strange larvae forced into the form. He squished one down and slid it into his ear canal. A squirmy tickling sensation made him shake his head; all sound shifted. "This is weird, sir."

"They're fusing with your ears. It might hurt for a bit. I'll give you a few minutes to adjust." The captain crossed his arms, smiling as he watched Sol's face contort and the other plug was slipped in. "You should have inserted both at once, I'm telling you…"

There was pain, first in one ear and then the other. It built excruciatingly, and for a moment, there was no sound. The pressure in his head changed and he felt disoriented and nauseous. Sol clenched his eyes and pressed his hands to the warm floor. He bit his lip, trying to keep his small but present canines out of flesh. Slowly, things equalized. He needed to say something to test his hearing. "I … I think they're done, sir."

"Among other things those dampen out one entire frequency, which the gen make a lot. You won't miss it day to day, and you'll be saner without it here." He offered his hand, which Sol accepted even though he did not need it. "Might take a little to get used to their functions. You can have them removed after your service with us, but most don't bother. They prevent infection, limit fluid penetration, some reports say they reduce head cold symptoms. My favorite feature is, once you're used to walking around with them, they auto-equalize air pressure in your ears. No more popping. Just a little sigh in your ear."

Was it just me or did he say that kind of sexy?

"Some combative gases can kill them. Then a surgeon has to pull them; you take some down time before you can get new ones." He walked on in the direction marked 'Training 1-5'. "Doesn't stop some troopers from walking into clouds sans helmets. Get used to guys in the infirmary doing this…"

Valdieren stooped mid-step, hands over his ears, and emitted an agonized scream. Sol was grateful his plugs silenced the higher end of the shriek. "I get it, captain. Thanks for the warning, sir."

The transition from mock agony to chipper tour guide was seamless. "Excellent. So how were the girls for you, back at the base? Anyone give you any trouble?"

"Sergeant Onzillora seems really cool."

Turning back with a beaming smile, Valdieren said, "Yeah, she's freaking awesome. One in a million. Her call sign's 'Glimmer'; look her up on the SACnet forums. She knows what's going on if you've got shore leave. I mean, everywhere. She's like, disco intelligence commando for the universe."

Sol could not help but laugh, although he felt a pang of jealousy over what was obviously more than a professional friendship. "The girl that works under her was a cranky snot, captain."

"I'm guessing since you used the descriptor 'girl' it was Charla instead of Dooveen. Doo is older, chews gum, rolls her eyes a lot. Not her, huh? Yeah. Little, dark hair, scars all over her arms? Yeah, Charla."

They stopped beside a door labeled 'Training 3'. "She had two collars. What's that about, sir?"

Captain Valdieren held his palm over a star-shaped fob on the door; a small panel slid open and a faint beam was directed at his collar for a few seconds. A flat voice said, "Number of trainees?" to which Val responded, "One". The door opened. "That would regard a war crime on my nuts, astrum."

Sol made to question the remark then stalled in awe at bio-ware and other machinery crowding the room. Soldiers in various states of undress were hooked to devices, simulators of various kinds, and there were charts, scoreboards, and a large view screen at one end. Valdieren tinkered with his slate and waited. A few men waved affirmative gestures.

"Hey, Val. Oh new trainee, huh?" Sol initially overlooked the pudgy, curly-haired kaffa who sat amidst disassembled parts to the left of the door. "Gonna tell the crotch story again? I'm out. Do whatever. Throw people out. I don't care. Hi kid, you're screwed." The stranger rose and departed.

"Guess I won't be introducing you to Gyrfru. He's the tech sentinel, which gives him domain over sim rooms. I have the skills for his job, I just hate it, but he'll leave me in charge, obviously. Have a seat." Val gestured at a bench that grew from the wall. Sol set his bag down and acquiesced. The captain remained standing, crossed his arms, watched men in simulators as he began his tale.

"It was a few weeks before my 24th naming day. We were station hopping, big recruiting drive, which is always exhausting but the recruiters get lots of station-side R&R to make up for it.

"We were at Todekki, it was one of my days off. I was sitting in the military-side garden. The *Kelmia* was docked at the same time, so there were marines everywhere. In retrospect, I was an idiot and should have been on the civilian side. But I was on a 'night' schedule, so it was pretty empty, and I wasn't really thinking about anything but planning my party, which was going to be at Pachar.

"So I'm sitting there, listening to music on my slate, enjoying the tree smells, reading about the finer dance clubs and whore houses of Pachar, and all of a sudden, my light is cut off. Right as I look up, this big space marine pulls off my headset and he's yelling at me. I'm surrounded."

"Shit," Sol mumbled. *They say my father died at Pachar; he doesn't need to know that.* "Sorry, sir."

"They're drunk, just ome from the bar at the end of the garden. They start roughing me up, throwing my stuff. I'm not in uniform, but I guess my collar gave me away. Who knows, maybe they would have beat anyone. I'm looking for security, there's no one around. One of them is a girl, a little thing, but she's in Fang boots and jacket, has a lot to prove though, she's drunk as fuck and being verbally abusive. I'm a Star Assault officer, we have some foul mouths, right? I couldn't make my mouth say things like that. It would break."

This thought amused Sol, but he kept the tone serious. "Not to interrupt, but what are Fangs, really? Marines, right, sir?"

"They're the ICSM's armored division on paper but really they're the most elite of the A-corps who train with other specialists for a few years. After the last Mior conflict, a lot of Armor was deemed superfluous. Entire divisions were cut and the Fangs started to draw in younger marines who had hard-ons for tank-suits. The training takes years, not everyone makes the cut. They're supposed to cross-train with us, too, we have to work together in event of a war, but she hadn't yet, was pissed she had to, thought she was a goddess because she could operate an exo, you know."

'Exo' was short for 'exoskeletal mobile armor', biological combat devices not properly vehicles nor armored personnel suits (sometimes requiring multiple operators for a single unit). The troops trained to control them were notoriously elite, cliquish hot shots. They wore distinctive, glittering, garishly-colored collars; Sol's bitter boss at his previous station mentioned under her breath that armor units 'were identifiable from a distance to save the rest of us the trouble of trying to befriend them.' He nodded at Valdieren to continue.

"After they took turns calling me names and punching me in the ribs and gut, they drop me on the ground, she leans in, pretending she feels bad and she's going to help me. I reach up for her hand and she stomps me, square on the junk, with those huge fucking Fang boots." The captain cringed and shuddered at his memory. "Searing white light and I blacked out. Came to in the bartender's office. He came out to switch a compost screen at the exact right time. He was ex-SA; he'd been hanging out with the Haarnsvaar who was on the *Kelmia*."

"Haarnsvaar? Really?" Like any young Archon, the Queen's black-armored guards were a subject of fascination for the boy. Elite men, nine of whom lived in the palace at Ryzaa City, selected from throughout the Archon military and further trained by the Imperial Guild. Most were anonymous; Guild graduation was performed in secret. Traditionally, the Haarnsvaar commander and one or two others would retain names and faces in order to speak before the high council. Although politics interested Sol, he was enthralled by their armored suits, which were composed of a tight colony of individually microscopic engineered organisms. "Why was one of them on the *Kelmia*?"

"It's a unification cruiser, you know? Erm, invasion and colonization. What do they call it in IGN? 'Reclamation'. Ryzaan code for 'take back or destroy'? The Black Squadron comes on every so often, to do reviews or meet with bigwigs, same as us. So one was there, at Todekki, in the garden bar. Star Assault has a good relationship with the Haarnsvaar, traditionally. He found Major Parthenos, who had to be pulled from a brothel and was extra full of angry maggots. The Fang lieutenant who was the girl's immediate superior was some proto-noble rich kid with a Kimetj Vanahar fetish. Wanted to serve in Star Assault but his influential mama wouldn't let him. He handed her punishment to Parthenos. So while the dumb grunts got off with massive demotions and docked paychecks, she got black-tagged and sent to work under the men she'd abused."

Sol sat blinking. Comments swirled in his head, but as he forced them into speech, they fell apart. "Is that even close to proper procedure, sir?"

Captain Valdieren freed one hand from his chest to point up. "We're a 'traditional unit', Sol. One can interpret that to mean 'flying around in old-style ships with no humans and wearing traditional ornamentation', it really refers to the fact we operate under Colonial-era Shandrian Law. It pre-dates Archon Imperial military law and the Ryzaan court system we use federally and civilly."

"Wow, so, royal Shandrian court hierarchy? Consider my mind blown, sir." Shandrian Law, as Sol understood, was a simple, old-fashioned, *elvish* way of dealing with criminal behavior. Accusers brought issues before appropriate regional nobles, who arbitrated based on witness accounts. This only worked in non-integrated society; Shandrian kaffir were renowned for natural innocence and practicality; they lacked a word for 'lie' until they warred with the human nation of Aurmaal. Ryzaans might bend the truth or dance around it for the sake of their egos, but they obsessed over justice. Completely inventing something to cover a truth was a human complication, as much as it shamed Sol to admit it.

"I'm Ryzaan. Trust me; even with multiple broken ribs and my balls on ice, I questioned the fairness. It's my blood. The bartender said I was in shock and put me back to bed." Valdieren shrugged. "Star Assault is a big sideways step from 'the system' that protects us as civilians. Our motto is only 'Always First' in propaganda; a bad Ryzaan translation of a Shandrian phrase. As you may have noticed in the handbook, it's actually, 'Be Always True.'"

Sol turned his gaze to the floor as Val stretched and folded his arms against the wall. "Captain, why do the marines do that? And why don't we fight back, sir?"

Eyes closed, smile subtle but present, head leaned back against his arms, Val enunciated quietly and clearly, "I'll tell you what Kiertus told me: It isn't all Marines. It's young, stupid, angry Marines who hear half a story and see part of a picture. Even though they aren't acting like it, we're on the same side. Our secret techniques designed for efficient mass neutralization or hyper-specific termination. You don't play a card like that on your own team. You hold your hand and let the weak-souled fuckers keep kicking."

"Wow." *This is insane; we have our own private legal system? I seem to recall the Shandrians had different standards for sexual consent and drug abuse policies but were harshly aggressive about punishing what they did abhor.* "So if we act out of accord, we are punished by Shandrian standards, which say not to hurt my own kind, however foolish they may be."

"Hurting another kaffa is punishable by forced servitude in the mines, or death, depending on the leniency of one's nobility. Star Assault doesn't send criminals to mining moons though; they get demoted for low-level offenses, moved to different job classes depending on who likes them et al. Hard offenders get black-tagged, sent to 89th if they're useful, or executed by the top brass if not."

What is '89th' code for? "Our regular collars are black. They look like…"

"Lunar mining prison collars." Val turned with a resigned, affectionate smile. "Welcome to the first tier. It gets pretty dark out here."

A slender, muscular kaffa sporting shoulder-length ginger mudlocks stepped from a pod. His tight, long-sleeved shirt ended at his ribs; the towel thrown over his shoulders covered more. Sweat ran in rivulets down his pale skin to the top of his leggings. Reflective strips on the top flashed as he wiped his brow and waved. Vents opened at the shoulder; *was that blood?* The guy was smiling, but seemed jumpy. *Is he smiling to cover pain, or because of it?*

Sol caught the man's too-wide pupils, watched his fingers flex as if molding invisible clay. He wanted to let go of his own mind and the bad taste in his mouth. "I think that pod's open, captain."

"We're waiting on a standing console." His voice requested patience. "One of the good things Parthenos did was implement the 'FMH' – that's 'Fucking Marines! Help!' - code for the Universal Communications app. Any slate with SACnet enabled within one kilometer of the user will flash a distress signal and the user's coordinates. It's a voice command so you just need your slate turned to VCom. Check the handbook. Apparently gonad stomping was a bit far for even him. He says 'Bearing the Standard' shouldn't mean 'to and from the hospital', and if we must 'suffer this indignant time, we will do so on our feet, not alone'." His eyebrows raised subtly, but his jaw was clenched, his lids remained shut. "Almost makes him sound admirable."

Sol wanted to change the subject. *This is inappropriate. It disturbs me people seem to dislike this major so; his rank gives him legal domain over me. I don't want to judge him before I've met him; that's a surefire way to set myself up for harm.* "Were you well enough for your naming party?"

Resigned sadness and frustration dominated the response. "No. In the infirmary a week before I could work again, apparently was still pretty bad off; got ill when we jumped to Orminos so I had to go on forced leave in the station barracks." Val shrugged. "The up side of that was getting to know Onzillora, who tried to keep grouchy, broken me separate from her new employee. And I got to watch the 89th guys unleash their nasty nothing-to-live-for potty mouths on Charla …worth the price of admission." He stood and shook his arms out as a console emptied. The soldier who left it gave Sol a disparaging look, shook his head, and departed without a word.

He says 89th like it's a unit, like he assumes I know. Maybe it's in the handbook? "She seems like she has a lot of power for just a sergeant."

"Well, her title's actually, 'Regimental Quartermaster Sergeant'." Val grinned at Sol's contorted face. "Star Assault's the only branch that uses that designation. We have lots of those… entire chains of those, in fact. At first it's overwhelming, but you'll get used to it, after you've been here a while. Most of the ranks are obvious, but when you meet someone using 'Sergeant' as a title, glance at your slate or vis-reader if you aren't sure whether you're supposed to salute. Green or white, they're beneath you in relative rank. Yellow they're equal. Gold or brown, straighten your shit and get that hand the fuck up. Blue or purple, hit the floor on your knees, don't look up until they ask."

I look forward to my future as a scrubber of processor traps. "Information appreciated, sir. I got Nabaragi was a specialist too; ward sergeant, correct?"

"Something like that. Nabaragi is technically a 'ward sentinel' but *Sentinel* was a vessel that got annihilated in Mior, and she chooses to be called by a subordinate rank. You'll run into that a bit too, with the old folks." His expression briefly shifted to harried frustration. He sighed and continued. "While you're learning how it works, it's most important to understand the chain you're on and in your case, to stay on it."

Whoa. Intense expression. What the... Sol looked down at Val's hands on either shoulder. "Um, ok, sir."

"You're on the track of knighthood, which is a fancy way of saying 'command' in Star Assault. You serve as a paratrooper first, because you have to know what it's like, because the Shandrians didn't believe a war prince should ever send his men to die in a way he wasn't willing to go. Unlike grunt paratroopers, and many of them will envy or dislike you for this, you are issued a gen to help you not be a statistic. You serve as a gunner and pilot next, because you need those skills. You'll work non-combat positions around the cruiser as your supervisors see fit, and over time, learn how our bases work and the slightly different chain of authority in those. Focus on the bug and gear, for now. When Kiertus tells us who your novum is, he'll probably have a bunch of different stuff to say."

Sol blinked. "Novum genadri. A gen knight? That sounds..."

"Romantic. I know. I laughed when they said that was my eventual title; Major P stared me down to my atoms. Now I am one." Val's hands were in his pockets as he looked away, eyed the blank wide screen. His emotions were not easily read, but 'humor' was not present. He shook his head before turning back. "Captains are your knights. They've done all the heavy training and survived several runs of active duty as a paratrooper and pilot while demonstrating aptitude with group dynamics. Lieutenant is the most common rank in our chain; astra who survive their first 'trial', whatever that ends up being, are awarded that title. You'll know a trial when you enter one, although it might be with no warning. Take any job a knight or prince gives you dead seriously."

"Prince?" *It's too late to run. I think I have fucked myself. I don't understand this feeling I'm having, like I swallowed a block of ice. Am I afraid? Or excited?*

"Prince is a respectful nickname for our top brass, whether they're cruiser or base men. 'Lord' also works but careful as that one can refer to the Haarnsvaar."

The red eyes glared significantly. *I'm missing something; is it because the current commander of the Haarnsvaar is an ex-marine? I hope he never comes aboard, that guy seems like a douche when he's giving speeches. I can't imagine that's what he means, because even if one of them came on board, he wouldn't talk to anyone but top brass, right? I bet this is something I'd totally get if I'd grown up on Archos. If I ask any questions, this dude is gonna think I'm a hick. Oh shit, pay attention, shit.* Sol wrangled his focus back to Valdieren.

"...-or, colonel, and the brigadier are the top orders of cruiser command; everyone answers to them. Treat them like royalty and your life will be both longer and easier; following Shandrian Law, if there's no brigadier general, colonel is the Law itself. He can change rules if he feels like it, and only the cha'atz general or Haarnsvaar can intervene." He scanned Sol's reaction. "We are fortunate for the benevolence of our current master, but we live daily with the threat of a less gentle prince's rule. I am finished with this topic and encourage consulting the handbook."

"Understood, sir." *Are all native Archons this weird? Is it that he's pureblooded and has different emotional states so I just don't know how to read him?* The captain resumed progress toward the available simulator and Sol followed.

Valdieren leaned on the outside of the console and gestured Sol to enter. He patted it as he explained. "This is a state-of-the-art multi-purpose simulation unit. Scroll the program listing there. You'll note different hook-ups and control devices; what you'll need for each will be explained if you hit the arrows to the side of the menu. See? Yeah like that."

Sol scrolled the options, finding himself at ease for the first time since boarding. He was no stranger to games; in spite their relative poverty, there was a fantastic console system in the Solvreyil household while he was growing up. *I suggested to mom we sell it after dad passed, but we couldn't because of it being 'a special kind of second hand'.* "It's like the video games in the *Irimia*'s rec center."

"Basically, yes. You should recognize some. These are training versions, of course; you probably had toned down ones on the *Irimia*. Even the puzzle games are motion-driven so you can get a work out for both body and mind. Trainers such as myself will assign specific programs and track your progress. During downtime, you can play whatever. You get a certain number of hours weekly to use these consoles, and additional hours to access online versions of the games from your slate, based on behavior. Checking scores and reading menus doesn't count towards that time on either device." He watched with amusement as Sol scrolled through options and scores. "This week, time permitting, you'll put about six hours on sky diving and shooting gallery. Get your name on the score charts. You'll have twelve hours total, so if you get your name on the charts sooner, you have more time to experiment."

Sol stared at the screen. "Man, whoever this 'Checkmate' guy is, he kicks the crap out of everyone at fighting games."

"That's Major Parthenos. The only guy who can beat him consistently doesn't play martial arts ones much. Everyone has areas of excellence. Try the close combat weapons game." He waited and watched.

"'Gunsmoke'?"

A wicked grin. "Colonel Kiertus. Play against him sometime. You'll lose, but it's really funny when his cuddly little avatar kills you... with a camping hatchet." Valdieren coughed and straightened. "You'll find my call sign on puzzle games that involve jumping and agility! Careful with math and trivia ones; excellence at them instead of more violent games will draw ridicule from jet boys and paratroopers, unless you can wipe Trauma and Wyvern completely off them. Pro-tip, don't even try. Follow me."

Reluctantly, he abandoned the upright and peered into the pod on which the captain now leaned. The *Irimia's* consoles had nothing on this; it looked like a fully functional bio-vessel plug-integration drive unit. The two seats inside could be moved side by side, back to back, or the often-mocked 'tandem position' wherein the gunner basically straddled the pilot's back.

"This replica cockpit can be configured to simulate most military vehicles, including a Dash dropship, a D-7 fighter jet, a Cyvax exo unit.... It can even simulate a cruiser mono-console. We have all those programs; Star Assault must be ready to take control of situations. You'll start on 'Search and Rescue', the first tier paratrooper sim. That'll count toward this week's twelve."

Twelve hours doesn't seem like much, but being physically hooked in might be more taxing than dinking with a tracking camera or control wand.

Valdieren checked his slate. "I'd like you to get started with training sims right away, but Dr. Laathas needs assistance in medical and you're qualified. While you're there he can go over your ratings, which it looks like you're only partially complete on, however you managed that shit. Man you are one weird kid." The captain looked up at a confused and slightly offended Sol and blinked. "I didn't mean it like that, astrum. You know, if you don't get thicker-skinned…"

I usually am. Weird. "It isn't a problem, sir. So am I headed to medical?"

"Yes. I'll be busy most of the evening, but I'll send you a coccoon assignment in the next few hours, so at least you'll have a bed when Laathas sets you loose. Expect to work late; there's always a backlog down there. Check the handbook and main menu to understand how assignment calendars work. I scheduled a breakfast meeting." Sol followed him from the training room toward the hive.

As they approached medical, the wall colors warmed and softened. Alcohol and menthol replaced the rest of the ship's saline musk. Val's slate buzzed and flashed. He swore and ran in the opposite direction. As he raced up a ladder and out of sight, he called back to Solvreyil, "Laathas' office is ahead on the left!"

A little plaque beside the open door read, "Corporal Laathas Eshonja, Master Surgeon." Sol stood at the entrance apprehensively, staring at a big kaffa leaning over the desk within. His beaded mudlocks were blue-black, shiny as if heavily oiled. The glow of a laptop computer reflected on the sheen of his hair and in the small, round lenses of his glasses as he compared the contents of a clipboard to the display. He did not look up, but a friendly smile pushed the glasses up as he asked, "Gonna stand there all day?"

"Ah, yes, sir. I mean, no, sir!" A little jerkily, Sol entered the room.

The surgeon approached to shake his hand. The wide-shouldered man's presence towered in spite being a hand shorter than Sol. His grip was warm and dry; the shake powerful and confident. "You must be Astrum Solfrya."

Adequate pronunciation, odd accent. No idea where he's from. "Yes, sir."

"What sort of medical experience do you have, young man?"

"I spent my childhood at the physician's, but otherwise, not a damn bit, sir."

A nod shook the shiny, ropy hair in a peculiar way. "That's quite all right as long as you're literate."

"I enjoy reading and I'm conversant in four languages, sir."

"Even better," the surgeon smiled appreciatively. His small fangs glinted. Sol studied the man, fascinated that he could not place his ethnicity.

'Eshonja' sounds Vasiit. I haven't met many Vasiit, but most of them were darker skinned and taller. He's got some breadth to him, could be North Shandrian but the surname is Ryzaan for 'Valley', which implies Eastern Hills heritage... he could be off-world haki, maybe? Or a white Mantzaari? Mantzaari are short and stocky, right? Can albinos have black hair?

Laathas sat at the desk, observed some information on his slate and made a few notes. "The pharmacy is two lefts down the hall. Follow the pictures of pills. You're on inventory." The surgeon looked up a moment. "We're tier two here; the doors won't recognize your signature. You'll have to stand sideways and tilt your head so the eye can scan you. Apologies, we'll fix that soon."

"It doesn't scan from the front, sir?"

"The collar can be scanned from any position, but folks generally agree tilting one's head slightly towards the opposite shoulder is more comfortable than tilting it back for a clear scan."

His hair's so waxed it's like rubber tentacles. Is it twitching? That has to be my imagination. The atmosphere must be fucking with me. Maybe it's the ear plugs.

Laathas continued his work, glanced back and forth from the clipboard as he typed. "There's another laptop in there, you'll track stock on that. It's self-explanatory. Setting up your login now." The motion caused his glasses to slide down his nose. A stray mudlock wrapped around one arm of the frame and tugged them back. "I'll text the info to your slate."

I did not just see that. "Um. Yes, sir! I'll text back if I have questions, sir!"

Boxes and canisters were piled high and haphazardly about the pharmacy. The way to the rear shelves and back door was mostly obstructed. Sol managed to find the computer amidst the chaos. His slate buzzed; the message was from 'Bonesaw'. He entered his login with a grin. The program and labeling system were straightforward and he set to work, absorbed enough in his task that he forgot how nervous he had been. He did not register queer little clicks approaching as anything other than the ship until he felt a nudge.

Startled, he looked from his stool to see a genadri, dark olive in color, a notable bit larger than the recruiting office model, gently butting him with her enormous triangular head. Her ocular membranes opened and closed on all four shiny black eyes. He noticed something dangled from her mouth. "Uh, hi."

The massive gen reared and dropped the object in his lap, tips of her blade-like feet poised delicately on the tiny amount of available space. She continued to stare. Sol examined the object: a foil-wrapped Nutty Chew. He picked it up; she tapped her scythes impatiently then did a tight lap amid the clutter of crates.

"Are you allowed to have things like this?" She danced and chirped as the foil was peeled. *OK I might get in trouble for this but she really seems to want it...*

He broke off a bit of the bar and held it out. The creature extended her proboscis and pulled the chunk into her mouth. Eyes blinked as she sat and masticated. Sol carefully took a bite, relieved she did not attempt to fight him for it.

"How's the work coming, astrum?"

Sol hurriedly stashed the remaining bar and swallowed. "Going well, sir."

Laathas walked through the door with another box. "It's fine to eat down here when there are no open mixtures, Solfrya. I gave her that to share with you."

"Oh, uh, thank you, sir." Sol relaxed and returned to cataloging, breaking a bit more of the bar off for his new friend. "Is she yours? What's her name, sir?"

"Minerva." He sorted crates, picked up a few bearing 'Refrigerate Immediately' pictograms and hefted them through the back door. "Did you get these already?"

"Not that stack yet, sir."

"Atquel, six count cylinders. There should be seven crates of those here, help me find them."

Sol hopped from his stool. "That's these little black Amacor crates, right, sir?" *Atquel? That's the most aggressively controlled stimulant in the empire.*

The voice returned muffled from the walk-in. "Break them open in here, make sure the device on the front hasn't turned orange, shelve 'em there. Packing material goes in that bin for reuse."

"Yes, sir." The crates were heavier than Laathas made them appear. Sol could only manage one. "What about these gold crates?"

"The ones with the Mantzaar seal are synthensin. We have to pop those next." Laathas examined cylinders in the fridge; the boy swore mudlocks held the man's glasses in place when he bent.

Sol stumbled, as much for the continued hallucination of prehensile hair as for the crate contents. "Are you serious, sir? This is enough space-dust and Tears for a couple of prison terms." He shook out his messy red fluff. "Apologies. I intend no disrespect, sir. It's just… my dad served in Rim Patrol. Sorry, sir."

"Really? Hm." The surgeon shelved a few jars. "No offense taken, astrum. Intergalaxy transfers always have that reaction. Our combat drugs must be individually customized; our ratios are stronger, so we get the components and compound here, per prescription." Laathas pointed to a tall unit of small, airtight, alphabetized bins. Many lacked designations. "This is the crew drug locker. Few have access to it, not that anyone would want drugs mixed for someone else in the first place. Those who have access to it, well, they have access to this," he held up a cylinder of high-powered Archon hallucinogens, "and that."

Laathas' free hand indicated complex devices behind heavy windows at one end of the walk-in. Sol stared through high-PSI clarithane and blinked as he shelved canisters and checked them off the list. "What are those contraptions, sir?"

"Isolators, boiler, synthesizer, still. If there's a controlled substance, we can make it. Note the double airlock in case of 'accidents'." Sol observed amusement on his face as Laathas unloaded his next crate. "The sheer amount of drugs we use, scheduled or recreational, is part of the rationale for Star Assault's sterilization. Long-term psychiatric or fertility side effects are inevitable."

So elvishly honest and to the point. "Wow, sir."

"You don't have to say 'sir' every time you address me." He returned to the office for another couple of crates. "You're not in the navy any more. The only guy who expects that treatment is Major Parthenos."

"Taken into consideration, sir." He, too, left the walk-in for another load. The surgeon stopped him on the way, not setting down the crates under his arms.

"Speaking of drug schedules and the navy, your records indicate you got through Framework and several months of Intergalaxy without a rating."

Every sphincter in his slender body clenched. His throat was too dry to swallow.

"That's pretty impressive," Laathas observed, swinging his cargo to the side to let Sol pass to the office. His voice continued from the fridge. "I know how to do it in Framework, although I note you were signed up to two athletic clubs, which is a bit trickier. But, really, getting by as an ensign, doing outreach work? You're slick enough for SecFive."

Section Five of the Imperial Articles provided for a pure intelligence unit capable of public sector operation. Instead of referring to Imperial Military Cross-Branch Intelligence (IMCBI, pronounced 'Impsi'), old folks called it 'SecFive'. *You don't seem that old. I would have put you around 36 or so.*

"Look," said the doctor compassionately as Sol stepped back into the cold. "I know every reason a young man avoids getting rated. Trust me, whichever it is, you're safe here." He deposited his crates and placed a hand on Sol's shoulder. "We can't issue you anything without a full BVSI. You want a bug, right?" At the word 'bug', Minerva poked her head around the corner with a curious trill.

Sol eyed the hand; tattooed across the carpals was the archaic high Shandrian rune for 'Strength'. Lines, calluses, and wrinkles reported a longer life than the kind, smiling face. A beaded black tendrils squirmed over and smoothed Laathas' left eyebrow. Sol shook his head. "I'm really sorry, sir. I'll finish this work, but I think all the stress of this day is getting to me, I feel ill."

He set his palm gently to Sol's temple, then two fingers to his throat. "You don't feel particularly feverish, but you are a little pale. I'm going to proceed with the exam when we're done with these crates."

"Ah. I just... I keep seeing your hair move..."

Laathas laughed. "You aren't hallucinating, Solfrya." He turned from the shelf and undid the band that restrained his ponytail. Locks writhed on his shoulders, clicking when beads hit one another. "I lost my hair to chemical exposure in 3rd Mior. These are experimental animate Vektaar implants."

Sol only stared. *You have weapons-grade hair? Now I've seen everything...*

"You can touch them. They only charge one direction, like Haarnsvaar armor."

Sol reached forward, a tendril greeted him, wrapping about his finger. He giggled. "Wow. I had no idea such a thing was even possible."

"Star Assault is in a unique position in terms of our clearance, function, and isolation. Unusual opportunities for modifications are something of a perk." They arranged the last of the cylinders and recounted. "We lack qualified nurses at the moment. Do you have someone you'd like present during your rating to make you feel more comfortable? A superior officer if not a friend?"

"I've not been in long enough, sir. And I think Captain Valdieren is busy."

"He's with Parthenos, and we don't interrupt that particular situation." Laathas grabbed his slate and tapped a message. "Someone has to be a witness. I'd prefer it was someone who at least didn't make you feel more awkward."

"Not that mean blond guy, please," Sol mumbled half-jokingly.

The surgeon laughed. "You just described a quarter of the crew, you realize."

"I hope it's not out of line for me to ask, but wouldn't this normally be the job of the ship's physician?" Delaying the process was not his first intent with the question, he was just curious, but the side effect was perfectly welcome.

"Yes, well, Doctor Saarkovietj got in a spot of trouble recently... seventeen years in Star Assault and he gets injured on a civilian volunteer mission during leave. He's still in recovery on Pachar, although true to his honor code, he'll be back with us in a few months." Pride faded as he added, "So I'm doing everyone's work. However, given the ship's report, I checked your extended file; with what I can see regarding your heritage, I would choose to do your review myself even if he were aboard."

Sol shivered. "Excuse me, sir? Because my mother is listed as human, sir?"

Laathas mouthed silently for a second before he spoke. "I assume you already knew she was not born thus?"

"The colonel told me as much. I didnt believe him, sir. I realize veterans sometimes do strange seeming things because of trauma, but… "

"I don't have time for all twenty some pages at the moment, but her pulse rating and lineage are right here, in her service records from the war. She got multiple stars as a gunner on a Medderax class… a human could not have survived the drugs necessary to do that, much less actually supply the pulse."

A Medderaxus? That class doesn't even exist anymore! Haarkijetj ultra destroyers. Shit on toast! Do I know anything about my damn family? "Erm, no, sir. Twenty pages?"

"Well at least she held to her clearance. Poor boy. That must have been some upbringing." Laathas sighed and cleaned his glasses again, his face patient and sympathetic. "Your mother is only part of it. Your father…" he cleared his throat; his glasses again concealed his eyes. "Your father had factor n blood. You should look as surprised as you do; someone in that party must've had masterful loophole exploitation talents, not to mention your mother's physical strength in having two children with a factor n mate. Acute *Czenishraaja* syndrome would normally have killed her during the first pregnancy."

"Apologies, sir, but…" Sol withheld the expletive exclamation that lay salty on his tongue. "I had no idea." Czenishraaja syndrome, 'Czeni syndrome' as it was colloquially known, was something Sol grasped poorly despite having researched it. As he understood, it was a systemic mutation induced by intimate prolonged exposure to pulse in a body unused to carrying and diffusing such. While under day to day circumstances, exposure to kaffir radiance posed little danger to humans. Even sexual intercourse – originally thought quite dangerous – seemed low-risk. However, the act of carrying a child with kaffir blood, sharing that blood with the growing fetus, even with its pulse organ undeveloped, increased the risk of reactions, cell damage, or mutation. A partner with factor n present in their genes – and he could not have told anyone what that n stood for – increased that risk exponentially. As a precaution, people with factor n genetics were frequently denied a breeding license within the empire and absolutely prohibited from marrying humans. Sol was stunned stupid, impressed at his mother's fortitude and confused regarding his father's civil disobedience.

"I doubt you'd ever have known if you hadn't come aboard the *Sanjeera*. Few officers in Intergalaxy have enough clearance to read what I just did. I feel you have a right to know, clearance be damned."

"She had a pulse organ, and she used to fire cannons, right? So was it really the pregnancy with me that gave her the disease or…"

"I would not carry excessive guilt regarding it. Her organ removal increased her risks. She may not have known your father was an 'n' carrier… I don't think she knew him at all, if what I'm looking at is true." The surgeon's face was painfully sad a moment. "I apologize. This is a matter for others; I do not mean to pry into your family history beyond the medical issues."

What the hell does he mean? Before Sol could request clarity, the surgeons's slate vibrated loudly.

Laathas eyed the buzzing device and said, "I put out a call for availability. Your options are the colonel or the bug sergeant, looks like. Both are fairly old-fashioned and professional regarding subordinate nudity."

Immediate reality snapped him back from parental revelations. Sol chewed on potential awkwardness before responding. "If it isn't likely to piss him off, I guess the colonel. I've met him, at least."

Under the surgeon's orders, Sol headed to the infirmary proper and stripped in a private examination room. He saw no reason to distrust Laathas, but everything about this current predicament made him uncomfortable. It was as if this test, which he avoided one version or another all his life with his father's encouragement – *and there was little secret why now* - would conclusively determine whether he was more kaffa or more human. It was an irrational thing to dread; his external appearance made him unacceptable to either. Scientific proof of identity could not be more harmful, could it?

Dad was factor n, mom was a gunner on a secured ship. Even if I'm not some kind of biological mutant, the fact I exist at all is abnormal. He eyed his protruding hipbones and visible ribs as he shook his head. He poked the pointy tip of one of his modest ears. *I'm a freak no matter how you cut it, really.*

"Here, you might feel a little better if you put these on. They won't interfere with the examination." Sol turned, startled and embarrassed by the interruption, to find Laathas holding the recently issued briefs and brace from his duffle, which he had left in the office. "I'll be in the room across the hall, preparing the devices. Come over whenever you're ready. Colonel Kiertus is here, just so you're aware."

"Thank you, sir." *Did I just fail a test? He seemed really amused...*

He slipped into his uniform underwear and headed through the door to the exam room when the massaging began. His noise of frustrated, surprised arousal as he gripped the slightly yielding doorframe was audible down the hall.

He could not hear two men waiting beyond. "Ah, I remember that moment," mused Kiertus fondly.

Tentacles gripped glasses in place as Laathas chuckled over the minute adjustments he made to various dials on the output reader. "Poor kid. Suppose we should give him a bit of time?"

"Can't see any reason to hurry." The colonel crossed his legs and returned to reading the well-worn book in his lap. "And before you say, 'I have work I have to get back to', you've been on 32 uninterrupted hours. I order a break after this, Eshonja. Insubordination will win you a trip to the 89th."

Spectacled eyes rolled at the over-used threat. "Look who's talking. What would you do for a medic then, Sheriden? Saark's still on -"

A finger rose above the book, which was not set down. "Ah ah. I hired them a new surgeon over six months ago and Yamiro says he's working out well. I wouldn't have swapped you for that brat Guaer but Draumietj is a fine young gentleman with no criminal record."

"You'd trade me! To those louts?" Laathas spun about with a twinge of real shock, although laughed. He almost added something less appropriate when the blushing astrum came through the door. The surgeon turned. "How are you feeling, Solfrya? Ready?"

Sol was a bit out of breath. "Ready as I'll get, I guess. Sorry for the wait, sirs."

Colonel Kiertus did not look up from his book. "I'll hold Captain Valdieren responsible for the fact you weren't in uniform. Carry on."

Following Laathas' gestures, Sol seated himself in a curved chair that resembled one of the cockpit simulators. There was nothing in front of it, however, and it was fitted with a variety of clamps and straps. He sighed heavily as he shifted against the receptive material.

"You'll be just fine, don't worry," the corporal assured as he fixed sensors to the young man's neck, temples, waist, and thighs. He adjusted the straps and set a syrigun on a walking table near the chair.

To ease his anxiety (and to not look at the syrigun or ponder its function), Sol let his eyes settle on the colonel. He was a little apprehensive of the CO's presence at this exam in spite of Laathas' insistence he was 'professional' about such things. Sol, while excessively formal due to his upbringing and understanding of military hierarchy, never cared much for the opinions of his superiors; this man was different. Kiertus' posture was perfect; his demeanor cool and unconcerned, save barely perceptible variations in his facial expression as he read. *I make faces like that when I'm having trouble with a new language. The shape of the book doesn't look Archon.*

"Excuse me, Colonel Kiertus, sir, but may I ask what you are reading, sir?"

Clearing his throat but not taking his eyes from the page, the old gentleman said, "It's one of the great religious works of the Kourhonoi Theocracy."

Sol was impressed. "I don't even know what language they speak, sir."

"Kourhonoi, of course," smiled the colonel, looking up. His expression was pleasant; he did not seem to mind the view. "Which is an offshoot of Ravasich, which is still spoken on Verraken and has roots in Ryzaan. Both planets were colonized by Ryzaans of the Ravasitj ChemTech Corporation. They brought humans to use as food, chemical test subjects, and for... other objectionable labor. Those who settled on Kourhos had Vasiit slaves and concubines as well so the Kourhonoi language has a strong Vasiit influence."

All worries were forgotten; Sol was in his element now. "I thought those were human colonies, sir. I had no idea, sir."

"You may continue conversing, but I am turning the devices on now. One will stimulate you, the other will collect data. Expect some interruptions to your train of thought. It may hurt a bit, but we will not allow you to suffer any lasting injury so please remain calm." Laathas waited for Solvreyil to nod acknowledgment. "If you lose your composure completely during this exam you may become dangerous; that syrigun is loaded with an emergency suppression shot for our safety."

"That makes sense, corporal, thanks for the explanation, sir." Really, Sol was not too thrilled about the 'may hurt' part, but he had a lot of questions for Kiertus and was not about to lose track. "So, what happened to the kaffir on those worlds?"

Kiertus removed and polished his quaint reading glasses. "Isolation from the central supply chain, disease, revolts, a few wars with the Baalphae, the ability of unchecked human breeding to outstrip resources; a complicated mess of circumstances." He slid the glasses into a hard pouch on his utility belt. "This book selects from and simplifies that information to support a hypothesis of a human-centric universe dominated by a singular anthropomorphic deity."

A tingling through his ribs and across his back made Solvreyil twitch. "Isn't that the sort of thinking that got the Aurmalki exterminated?"

Flashes from the reading device reflected in Laathas' spectacles. "You're doing fine, astrum." He nodded slowly, fiddled with some knobs. "Almost done with the first set. It gets a rougher from here, but I'm sure you'll manage."

"Thank you, corporal."

Kiertus set the book on the chair beside him, crossed his legs and folded his hands in his lap. "Primitive humans across the galaxies have a bad habit of personifying good luck and calling it 'divine providence'. Unfortunately, they are better at rationalizing why luck goes awry within an invented system than admitting that maybe they were wrong about how it worked in the first place."

Suddenly his arms felt weighed down, then as if they had fallen asleep. This annoyed him and he tensed a bit. He felt a tug inside his chest, throbbing, and then a sensation Sol could best have described like threaded needles being pulled through his heart and out his arms. He convulsed and gasped as the restraints dug into his flesh

"Try to stay relaxed. Breathe slowly."

"Easy for you to say, doctor." He was aware of a conversation with Kiertus, but it seemed distant now. Sol was so acutely in touch with his physical body that conscious thought fell secondary. The next several minutes were a haze of tingles, shocks, pain, spasms, unintentional ejaculation for which he could not even summon embarrassment, then a welcome curtain of darkness.

…

"There you are. Don't try to move just yet."

He struggled. As control came back over his limbs and senses, he was aware of stinging in his arms and legs, rubbery weakness in his joints, and a warm, strong set of arms that held him. Sol looked into the big, cat-like yellow eyes of Colonel Kiertus Sheriden and said with as much dignity as he could muster, "Colonel, please put me down, sir."

"Not until I'm sure you aren't going to damage my ship, astrum."

Laathas disinfected scrapes along Sol's limbs as the colonel held him from the floor. "The suppressors should've kicked in so that he's no danger to anyone. Except maybe a mop."

Carefully, Kiertus set Sol on his feet, catching him when his knees buckled. "You sure you're ready to stand up there, *partner*?"

What language was that? Sol pondered as he leaned rather unwillingly on his commander. "I'll be fine, sir. Thank you, sir."

"Understood, astrum. In that case, I'll just stand here, and you can move at your leisure." The colonel's tone was serious, but his expression playful.

His predicament embarrassed him but Sol knew better than to move again. "What… happened?"

"The short form is, I stimulated you to release pulse, and you unleashed a field strong enough to tear Prevek bonds and levitate off the ground. The idiot we call 'colonel' rushed in and diffused it with his own body." Laathas gave a hard look to Kiertus, who smiled graciously with a wink and nod. "Then I shot you with suppressors and here you are, all fucked up and no place to go."

Sol did not know how to react. The colonel led him to a seat. Profound dizziness and nausea recalled the pharmaceutical misery of his childhood. "Am I…"

"Your unboosted pulse rating is way off the Tonser Scale, Astrum Solfrya. You were wise to dodge the exam until you got here. In civilian society or IGN, with the wrong doctors, you'd be en route to quiet euthanasia." The surgeon took his heart rate and temperature with a hand-held device. "You're alright now. I'm going to update your files, send your info to the bug sarge, and work out your pharm schedule. Colonel, I'm taking Gronney back from Droo, unfortunately. I need more hands mixing chemicals and he can at least navigate the math."

"Understood. Go ahead and take him, for now. We'll work something out, as long as you are off the clock and in quarters in the next four hours." Kiertus watched the corporal leave as Sol sat, elbows on knees and fuzzy red head in hands. He slid an arm about the young man's shoulders. "Don't you worry, Solvreyil Yenraziir. A second collar is not the end of the world. In a situation like yours, it's another chance at life."

"I'm really a *conduit*. I'm a monster."

"In Shandrian society that would've made you elligible for entry into several prestigious orders; you'd have been training in martial arts and matter manipulation from the first time you accidentally arced. In Vasiit society you would have been considered a Voice of the Spirits, a good omen, treated as holy, showered with love and gifts. The name itself is a hold over from those beliefs – the conduit of universal energy. The ancients saw it as a gift."

He wanted to look Kiertus in the eye but feared movement would disturb his balance enough to toss his Nutty Chew. "Why didn't the Ryzaans?"

"Oh, many would blame a lack of religion, and maybe that's true on some level, but when it comes right down to it, you just can't afford people running around shedding uncontrolled electrical impulses when you live in a swamp, you're up to your knees in water and mist everywhere, and your economy is dependent on fragile human slaves. Later on, I think they were trying to breed out the

Shandrians and Vasiit, to kill off mixed family lines." Kiertus shrugged gently so as not to upset his pukey young charge. "Laws like that just get stuck because they seem like easy solutions; it only takes one convincing speaker who's had a bad experience to keep it going for another century or three."

Sol sighed. "Colonel Kiertus," he said weakly. "I was really looking forward to starting at the Academy in the spring, sir. The captain said …"

"We're on an independent correspondence study program with the JA, my dear astrum. You don't even have to wait until spring on Holtiin." Kiertus rubbed a hand across his back, emitting a very low level of energy to create soothing heat. "And we'll see what we can do to make sure you attend in person. Other double-black men have, we just need to find your specific loop-hole."

Sol looked up gratefully; tears welled with little desire or motivation to suppress them. "Thank you, sir."

"Killing intelligent, talented young people just because someone somewhere is afraid of them is a senseless waste. There are still quite a few positions in the Imperial Military designed specifically for people with your condition. Many achievements of Archon society would have been impossible without them." The colonel cautiously released him and stood. He handed Sol small paper-wrapped cubes. "You should go lie down in the infirmary until you get used to those drugs. Be sure to drink water if you can"

"What are these, sir?" asked Sol, rolling a papered cube across his fingers.

"Ginger candy. Trust me, it'll help. The moment you are feeling up to it, you should get back to your work in the pharmacy. I'll be coming around to secure your collar in a bit."

Sol saluted as best he could given his spinning head and hand full of ginger chews. "Sir. Yes, sir." And the colonel was gone.

…

He was by no means at his best, but he was out of bed and working in an hour. Laathas seemed surprised to see him stumbling into the pharmacy.

"You're up? Found your clothes, I see. How are you doing?"

"I'll live. I can move boxes and count, just not very fast." Sol turned the abrasive monitor brightness down. "Can you explain the BVSI to me?"

"I don't really have time to go into detail at the moment, but very simply, it's a system for assigning a compatibility score for use of pulse equipment and so on based on your psychiatric exam scoring, pulse rating, and a few other factors."

Woozily, he tilted his head. "If I'm off the charts, how's that work for me?"

"Your pulse is off the standard charts, the Tonser Equivalence. As implied by the 'V' in 'BVSI', we use the Imperial Guild's 'Vaylen' system, ergo I had to keep going past where we would have preferred to stop. As it was, Kiertus turned off the machine before I completed your numbers." He went through a pile of boxes. "Have you seen a container labeled with the Shandrian territorial seal and WhipCo logo?"

"I have the contents here. They're counted; you can have 'em, sir." Sol pointed next to his screen. "So I can have a bug, right, sir?"

Laathas collected the little, rattling boxes. "Bug-compatibility numbers – the Brinks – come largely from the first set collected, plus blood and psychiatric data. You took the optional JPE during your primary screen; it's just five questions short of the HPE we use, so you're actually good."

Sol found amusement in this in spite himself. "That pointless 'personality test' I took in mandatory service has practical applications beyond assigning people to appropriate busy work?"

"They have and will all the way through your career, Sol, and you'll be required to retake them after your first year in Star Assault and every five thereafter. No, those tests aren't funny at all."

Lenses reflected the ambient light and refuted Sol's attempt to observe the corporal's eyes, but the voice expressed sympathy with an uncomfortably serious edge. "Ah. Understood, sir."

"The data is entered into an indexing program to create a chart. Cheldyne takes care of things from there. I would like if you would voluntarily do the pulse rating again once you have better discharge control."

Sol rubbed his eyes. "Really not sure I want to…"

"Think about it, please. With enough data, we might be able to change existing civilian standards; if we can do that, we might save some lives." The surgeon vanished toward the walk-in.

Nausea and weakness slowed time. What seemed like six hours was likely closer to two. A set of fingers rapping on the bony counter in front of him brought his eyes to the colonel's smiling face. Too rapidly for his physical state, Sol saluted and almost fell from his stool. "Greetings, Colonel Kiertus, sir!"

"At ease. Finish up there, astrum. You've a new assignment."

"I'm close to done with inventory, sir. Could you give me maybe half an hour?"

The colonel eyed him sternly. "No. I haven't time. I'll call boxes to you as I stow them; hope you type fast." Without another word, he was on it.

I guess on a tiny combat ship, no one can afford to decide work is 'beneath' them. Is this what they call 'Shandrian military collectivism'?

When all was squared away (less than ten minutes despite Sol's wobbliness), Kiertus flicked a long, black strip from his belt, took his slate in the other hand, and approached Sol. "Stand still. Again, I'm sorry I have to do this. It will be better for all in the long run."

"I take it this one is explosive, too, sir?" Sol twitched from the tingling.

"More so than the other, I'm afraid."

I really don't like the way he said that. He sighed painfully as he looked into Kiertus' sympathetic face.

"When you look up at the night sky from a planet, the universe is full of stars. Outside an atmosphere, the universe is mostly darkness." He stored his slate as Sol reached hesitantly for his new collar. "That darkness can devour the weak. It is important you never lose heart."

Sol squinted at the colonel while tracing his fingers between the pair of sentences he wore. *Was that supposed to be a motivational speech?*

"Follow me to the hive. You're going to be with the bug sergeant the rest of the evening." Kiertus was already on his way out. Sol hurried to catch up.

"Colonel, are shifts normally this long?"

"Twelve hour days and overtime are expected when we're staffed as we are now. We have twenty-five brand new recruits in various stages of training as of the past forty-eight hours." His walk was brisk, purposeful. "No one is getting much sleep. That goes for all of us. Today was one of my days off."

Sol watched warning sign covered doors open before them as the colonel passed the sensor.

The hive was constructed to resemble a natural stone cavern and the gen built their own domiciles within nooks and crannies of faux rock. Glistening waxen tunnels and peculiar papery structures literally hummed with bug activity.

"This is really cool, sir."

Kiertus grinned. "I've long found cruiser hives amusing. We engineer a giant living being. Into the guts of that, we insert a simulated lava tunnel, which another species then colonizes."

"Does seem kind of silly when described that way, sir." Fascinated, he touched the wall. Most of the gen ignored them, but a few sniffed curiously at Sol before chirping and hopping away. "Is it a proper hive, with a queen?"

"Well. That's not quite accurate," the colonel explained as he petted a particularly vocal bug. "Wild gen establish 'war hives', colonies who've lost queens band together under the strongest warrior. They continue to produce or draft drones until the appropriate events facilitate a new queen."

"Oh. Do cruiser hives ever manage that?"

"We usually prevent it, but in the event we're presented with queen-potential larva, we ship her to Life Storage. Someone will eventually need one."

A kaffa of moderate height and build approached. He was on the heavier side for active duty military, but definitely in fighting shape. A dark-colored kerchief restrained shaggy grey-brown mudlocks. A ragged sweater of harvested ('dead') fiber hung threadbare, frayed at the neck to reveal a hideous scar down his throat and chest. Another scar across his nose leant his grumpy demeanor an almost comical appearance.

The man saluted in abbreviated fashion. "Greetings, colonel. This the kid?"

Sol gave a little bow. "Astrum Genova Solvreyil Yenraziir, sir. You must be Sentinel Cheldyne."

"You got one hell of a name, astrum."

But you're a detergent! The boy made an effort not to laugh. "Yes, sir, I do, sir. 'Sol' is fine, sir."

Kiertus clasped Sol's shoulder and looked him in the eye. "I want you to meet me in the Officer's Lounge at 23:00. Until then, do your best." Then he strode off toward his apartment.

Cheldyne looked appreciatively at the slate he wielded. "Nice. Other things that can be said about a pulse level like that aside, it puts you in a great spot on the index as far as bugs go."

"Excuse me, sir?"

"You get an Omyoi Type 1. They're rare animals, intelligent, powerful for their size, strongly loyal, high-bonding. They're hive sub-royalty; queen-potential but workers arrest that during larval feeding. Often in the dominance chain, but usually more concerned with being an elf's best friend."

"That's neat, sir. When can I meet her, sir?"

He made a distasteful hand gesture. "Call me 'Cheldyne'. None of that 'sir' shit. I have to wake her, get her cleaned and ready for you. Until that's finished, I'd like you to take care of a little of filing work for me and read the appropriate sections of the handbook regarding the care of your growing gen."

Sol ached with curiosity and tried to hide his dejection. "Oh. Well, could you show me the wake up process another time, then?"

Cheldyne smiled, an action to which he seemed unaccustomed. "That's a great attitude, kid. You're good at climbing right? Don't worry, doesn't hurt to fall too much where we'll be, a bug'll probably catch you anyway. OK, fuck the filing today. Come with me." A big arm grabbed him. "I really need an assistant. You like bugs, yeah? You're one of Val's, huh? Sweet. He owes me a favor, yeah"

Sol focused to quell nausea and set pace with the sergeant. *This could be the best thing I've heard yet.*

...

A cup of hot tea greeted him when he dragged himself to the lounge. The colonel rose from where he huddled with two gentlemen too absorbed in their laptops to notice the boy. "Have a seat, Solvreyil. You look exhausted."

"It was good work, though, sir. I got to help little bugs."

The colonel chuckled a little as Sol shifted the blanket-covered weight in his arms so he could sit and sip tea. "Looks like you picked up one yourself."

"Yes, sir. The hive infected me with one of its own." He blushed as Kiertus pulled up a chair, further embarrassed by the uncontrollable reddening. *Flushing is a latent suppressor side effect, right?*

"May I see her?" the older man implored quietly.

Sol carefully pulled back a bit of the temperature-adjusting blanket, exposing the creature inside. He passed the bundle over delicately. "She's sleeping, please be gentle, sir."

"No worries there." Kiertus tilted his head and made a tiny, affectionate sound as he looked upon the curled bug. He kept his voice soft. "What's her name?"

"Ozlietsin, sir. I'm going to call her 'Ozzie' for simplicity's sake."

An appreciative glance and nod fell in Sol's direction. "Ozlietsin. One of the great poets of Eshandir. Good choice. 'Let thy soul find wings in blackness'." He returned attention to the wee blanketed bug. Disproportionately large eyes opened to stare back. "Well hello. Welcome to my crew, Ozzie."

Miniature scythes struggled free from the blanket and flailed awkwardly until they made purchase on the colonel's coat and in his hair.

"Oh my, you've got me," he chided with mock horror. "So feisty! You're going to grow up to be a mighty warrior, aren't you?" The little bug chirruped.

"It's hard to believe it only takes them six months to get to full-size. Cheldyne said that because she's an *omyoi* it might only take five. She's so small…"

Colonel Kiertus unhooked her feet with one hand as he held her with the other. "Have fun with all the growth stages. The more you get out of it, the more she'll get out of it. Here you go, little girl. Time to go back to your bond!"

Sol took her back with exhausted joy. "I will, sir. Thank you, sir."

"Since you named your bug that, and since you can read Shandrian, would you like to maybe borrow a book for your down time?"

The young man's eyes lit up. "Oh? Do you have something I haven't read?"

Kiertus laughed. "Probably a few. I'll be right back."

Sol rocked Ozzie back to sleep as he looked over at the strangers. They both wore dressy uniform jackets along with the little billed engineers' caps. Each cap bore the Haarvakja. They remained silently absorbed in their computers, although their sideways glances and twitchy ears indicated nervousness. He smiled awkwardly when one looked his way, then yawned. *Dad had one of those hats, without a unit patch,* he thought sleepily. *I tried to steal it before he left the last time, but he said he needed it 'for good luck'. I really miss Dad…*

By the time the colonel returned, Sol and Ozzie snoozed soundly. Kiertus set down the book and some biscuits and returned to the couch, pleased to no end by the serenely adorable scene. When either engineer would move to speak, he held up a finger and shook his head. Eventually, he walked back and gently squeezed the young man's arm.

"You should probably go find your nest assignment." He watched the boy groggily assess his surroundings as he returned to the jumpy gentlemen. "Can we do it on what we have, Lep?"

There was an uncomfortable pause. Sol helped himself to cookies, eying the group curiously.

One of the men chewed his lips and finally spoke. "We f-figured out two different ch-charts…" The man glanced at his companion. "They both take us th-through…" The man stopped and looked at Astrum Solvreyil. "What's his c-clearance, anyway, sir?"

"You could have said it. He's necessarily increased due to that fashionable neck accessory, eh?"

The nervous engineer gave a nod toward Sol. "F-fuck. S-sorry, kid."

"Um, *lebbaku su-na devuna* I guess?" The phrase– 'One loses as much as one wins' – translated too awkwardly in Archon so Sol kept it in the original Shandrian. The man rolled his eyes and nodded in fervent affirmation. "Colonel, was there a reason you brought me here, sir?"

Kiertus sipped tea calmly as he commandeered Lep's computer. "I wanted to know you survived your first day, astrum. I worry about Intergalaxy transfers, call it an old habit."

A little too tired to fully analyze the comment, Sol nodded in half-understanding. "Thank you, sir, I appreciate your concern."

"Send this set to the bridge, then. I hate it the least and Lash can just deal with it." The colonel looked to Sol. "You seem to be adjusting alright, considering."

"Wh-what w-was he in IG?"

Returning Lep's computer, Kiertus smiled. "Youth counselor and educator."

The other spoke this time, not looking up. "Figures. Not a big leap, between kids and paratroopers."

"That's enough of that," Kiertus reprimanded firmly. "Have a good sleep, Astrum Solvreyil."

Sol rose to leave with a yawn and idly noticed the cover of the book he had been loaned. "Thine Sacred Dust", it read in old Shandrian characters stamped into well-preserved bluish lizard hide. Carefully cut semi-precious stones set in the shape of a moth in flight, a heraldic symbol, glinted as he regarded the ancient tome. "This... has to be a replica..."

"No, it's an original, astrum."

I've always wanted to read this, but the only versions I could find were shoddy translations in Archon and Ryzaan that were reviewed as 'heavily edited'. It's supposedly the greatest epic poem ever, detailing in some kind of florid code how to 'awake the gods within'. I can finally find out what that even means. "Thank you, sir, I'll take excellent care of it." Juggling bug, book, and cookies, Sol backed to the exit.

...

The alarm on Sol's slate went off far too early for the time at which he passed out, half-dressed, in his cocoon-bunk. He nestled little Ozzie in his old station jacket next to his pillow beforehand, but she got loose during the night and slept across the back of his neck. She protested removal as he scolded her lightly for the scratches her tiny scythe feet left behind.

"I'm taking you to the hive nursery, you'll only be there a few hours while I figure out stuff and meet Captain V for breakfast. Shh. Stop that." The protest turned to grumbling and a whistle-whine. Sol cradled her in his arms until she settled. He snagged the remnants of the nutrient gel drink that Cheldyne gave him the night before and let her have it. "I'll have regular food for us both when I come back. Sorry I don't have more now. I just was too tired to go pick up my week's rations when we left the hive."

After dropping her off with a startled looking young man sitting in Cheldyne's office, Sol wandered toward the other end of the *Sanjeera* to pick up his ration kit. He had not caught the name of the man; he was apparently just a temporary assistant signing in baby bugs for daycare during morning procedures. He mentioned he only expected a few and got more like a dozen so far and hoped Chel would return soon. Sol disliked this but had no choice; his initial assignments for the day had rigid age restrictions for accompanying gen.

There were a few others waiting in line when he got to the location marked on his slate map. They were partially dressed, seeming roughly a decade older than him, and probably airmen rather than officers. They all smelled of stale sweat and dirty hair with a pungent undertone of some rank chemical. Still, Sol attempted to smile. They frowned or ignored him. The man at the end of the line looked him up and down grimly, as if about to say something snide, but when his eyes settled on the collars, his brows raised, eyes rolled sideways, and he turned slowly, inching forward in line.

What the fuck. Sol watched as the man before him subtly nudged one of the two in front of him. They stood side by side chatting amicably about something Sol could not really grasp – it was Archon, but very slangy and involved rude hand gestures. After two nudges one turned and gave the guy between himself and Sol a foul look. They exchanged sly non-verbal gestures; different sets of eyes landed on Sol then glanced back at one another. The third man shrugged, mumbling something in Ryzaan. The boy struggled; his Ryzaan was imperfect, but he caught, "just a criminal".

Over 500 years had passed since the first attempts of the Council to forcibly merge commonly spoken Archon languages; the people of Sol's home, Holtiin, willingly relinquished theirs for the improved access to education and trade this would offer the long-oppressed citizenry. The Shandrian regions of Archos proper contributed their 'low' language as the skeleton of Unified Archon and thereby had no difficulty with assimilation. The largely displaced Vasiit peoples of the southern coasts lost so much of their language to Ryzaa's depredations that they welcomed the new tongue. For whatever reason, it was the people of Ryzaa, wherein lay the capitol city of the new empire, who were unwilling to stop teaching their native tongue in schools, side by side with Unified Archon in many cases. Only within the past century had this practice finally been scrubbed. It was still taught in private homes; Sol had learned the rudiments of it in an elective 'cultural history' class in Framework so he could understand the rude remarks of Ryzaan tourists. It was a difficult language to learn and pronounce, having a consonant structure imitative of swamp-animal calls, but an excellent tool for being an insulting prick. *They think they're so clever, pulling a fast one on the backwater yokel. I'll let 'em think that, jerks.*

The response from the first came in Ryzaan as well. "If going 89th, why he get rations?"

"Officer, see? *Astrum genova.*" He was forced to annunciate this Shandrian phrase properly; there was no equivalent. "Too young for murderer. Probably death battery." They regarded him over their shoulders.

Death battery? Ryzaan slang for a conduit, I'm guessing? Ick. No wonder we use the Shandrian term.

"Heard Colonel K got new astrum. Probably this kid? Sick old baby raping fucker."

Rage boiled inside Sol, manifesting as a lightly crackling cloud of energy. In the best Ryzaan he could muster, he snarled, "I fucking understand, insubordinate rat-turds."

"Calm down out there or I'll summon monsters!" snapped the man inside the dispensary cage in clear, crisp Archon. "You can check your locators to see who'd arrive first." He shook his slate. "Oh, look, it's Wyvern! Probably just woke up, too. Anyone? That's what I thought. Shut it, get your shit, and scram."

Sol seethed in the direction of the three airmen who were now pointedly ignored him, pretended to be interested in the week's ration allotment. The young officer breathed heavily, not exactly sure how to get rid of his shroud of static.

"Uh, clap your hands," came a strange voice behind him.

"Huh?"

"Your bladed veil. You're trying to get rid of it, yeah?" The man wore a lieutenant's badge on an opened bathrobe over a brace and ladders. His rich dark brown skin contrasted sharply with the red-swirled yellow of the silky robe. He had a tooth cleaning device hanging out the right side of his mouth, catching on his fangs when he spoke. "Looks light, you can blow it away like that, usually."

Sol clapped hard, once, and the crackle dispersed. "Uh, thanks, sir."

"You're welcome, astrum." He removed the sponge-stick from his jaw. "Aukaldir. This is Linda. Linda? Linda. Quit that."

A long bug with a sharply triangular head came into view as her camoflauge faded. She made a little noise and sniffed Sol, then vanished against the wall.

"She's good at that, sir."

Lieutenant Aukaldir glanced side to side and said quietly, "She don't like meat rockets, yeah?"

It was finally Sol's turn; he was presented a largish, biodegradable sack containing seven days of meal packs and a few similarly degradable cylinders and tubes that seemed to contain fluids. They were labeled in simplified Archon characters – just alphabetic reference sequences, as far as Sol could tell, rather than names. Aukaldir noticed the boy's apparent confusion as he retrieved his own goods. "Your ration pack contents are explained in the handbook, but I'll happily give you a run down for that blue bottle, yeah?"

"Hm. OK, deal, lieutenant."

"Alright. That small box there, that's your ampules. Those are customized to your specs, so no trading those. Your scrips should be in there, too, like when you have to take which color. Got a syrigun?"

"No, sir, not my own. I can use the ones down in the training rooms or at the infirmary, right?"

Aukaldir nodded. "Yeah the little wipe packets in your kit are to clean shared syriguns. Mind you, though, until you have grafts – or until you've asked Eek who not to share with - you should get your own, and learn where to shoot in your arm or your thigh." He pointed to locations on himself to demonstrate. "Ask whoever's working in the dispensary or ask Laathas. They're one item we always have in stock on the ship; you can just take it out of your next check and they don't cost that much. If you have to shoot one before breakfast, you probably should just get a gun right here, yeah."

"Got it." Sol held up another tube. "Why's this moisturizer got a rifle silhouette on it?"

"That's oil for bio-hardware, like guns and plug grafts and stuff."

Sol examined this bottle, laughing. "Oh, I guess that makes sense. Thanks, sir."

"So you got your gun oil, which also makes good sex lube; try to be sparing, it's really important to keep your combat equipment and grafts moist, too. A dry gun will screw your world, yeah? Then that is some supplemental nutrient gel. You or your bug might need that; you get one bottle a month. Keep it somewhere she can't get into it until she's grown some, because a little gen will try and drink it all at once and barf this caustic crap all over your coccoon. And Chel will

71

whoop you for real. This here is mild chemical body wash; officers can bathe in the hive so you can trade that to an airman for something sometime. The green packet has scalp salt and skin oil; that's officers-only hygiene stuff; airmen covet that, too. This little tube of gel is Instant Skin, you can use it on scrapes but most of us just use it for condoms. Gun oil doesn't dissolve it. Yeah? You get all that? Makes sense, yeah?"

"Uh, yeah." Sol arranged the contents back into the bag, wondering how much of what he had just been told would classify as 'abuse of military assets' when he checked the handbook later. *My breakfast came with condoms and lube. Why not, right? They gave out birth control shots to staff on the* Irimia *because deep space trips lead to 'the kaffa cure for boredom', but we were expected to buy our own disease defenses at the ship store. Not that I ever did, but he doesn't need to know that.* "So, what's in that blue bottle with the 'jua' rune?"

Aukaldir winked. "That's your monthly liquor ration, kid. Have a nice day, yeah?" He turned and ambled down the hall toward the hive, tossing the acquisition in the air and catching as he went.

So much for the ship being too understaffed for hazing…

…

While nearly anything would be an improvement on the last option, he was not sure how he felt about this kid being the 89th's new surgeon. Major Ulissarian posted an 'up close and personal' article from GenRider magazine on the crew forums to break the ice. The article referred to the young racer as a 'prodigy' in all his chosen fields.

Shaan regarded the antsy little blonde poking his grafts. He did not care if Draumietj was a 'prodigy' in medicine, an award winning athlete, or the son of popular historians. *This isn't a unit for heroes and superstars. He's a fuck up, I just don't know what kind.*

"Damn, Sentinel Kvatchkiir. Who put these on you? Some A-corps exo suit butcher?"

Well, at least he doesn't live in a vacuum. "Guaer. The surgeon you replaced." He cocked a long red brow. "No offense, doc," he said sarcastically, "but have you read my medical records? And you can just call me 'Shaan'. Really. 'Sarge' is fine, even."

"I would love to, but until my clearance is fixed, I'm flying blind with GC2-Med clearance. Comforting, no? Not for me either. Blame that sandy nutter on the bridge." Draumietj waved his ultra high-end slate, decorated with a gen head, at the substantially older man. "Your age, rank, allergies, a few notes three decades old. Anything I need to know, you're just going to have to answer or pray."

"A few weeks aboard and you're already calling Colonel Ferrox a nutter." The sentinel laughed under his breath. *Maybe I'll get along with this one, after all.*

The surgeon pulled up a series of images on his slate and projected them at the wall behind his patient. "That's what your grafts should look like, and where they should be on your arm; even without a degree in medicine, you can see where yours are wrong. I apologize for the comment, but the dude was cave naked in the recruiting office and uses more bad hill slang than any racer I've ever met, while clearly spending his paychecks on hair and manicures. He also flies bare-grip because he says grafts are 'nasty'. Grafts are nastier than basically fucking a space ship? I'm sorry, but…"

"Get used to it." Shaan shrugged. *You ain't seen nothin' yet, kid.*

"What happened to him? The Guaer guy, I mean?" Draumietj asked conversationally as he prepped a syrigun with local anesthetic. "Hopefully he didn't stay in medicine. Tell me he went into meat packing or mulching…"

Shaan responded flatly as the officer turned back toward him. "He's dead."

The blonde's rather stout Ryzaan ears fell and his lips twitched.

If I say nothing else, he'll assume it happened in combat. "So can you fix them? My grafts, I mean."

Draumietj injected his patient's upper arm, staying on target in spite obvious discomfort. "Yeah, won't be any trouble, a few days down time, tops. Do you just have the two?"

"My forearm plugs are older than you. They still work just fine." Shaan smiled.

"I'd like to see them, if I may."

Obligingly, Shaan slipped off his response sleeves, exposing three small, neat plugs up his outer forearms. The surgeon gently examined these, marveling.

"There's so little scar tissue or shift! What's... hey, do you have subdermals?"

"Classified, Draumietj."

The young doctor rolled his eyes. "I'm a four, man, a couple exams and combat experience short a Vektaar certification. I know subdermal Vektaar implants; I'm learning to install them. I'll be a six when I graduate."

"That's admirable, but you still don't qualify."

His mouth opened and closed like a gasping fish, pondering the clearance discrepaancy as he returned to assembling tools. "Your records say you were a tech liaison between the bridge and engine staff of your station in the big war. Why would a guy with a desk job need cannon plugs, anyway?"

Shaan's smile turned cold and grim. "I know. Funny, isn't it?"

The little blond's response was cut short by a loud chirp from Shaan's belt.

"I gotta take this, that's the major's alarm. You'll get started as soon as I'm done, please? Thanks." He opened the slate and read, barely concealing the shock that crossed his face.

"Everything alright, sentinel?"

"Hm. Yeah, fine. Nothing, let's get this done, alright?" But it was hardly nothing. The message from Major Ulissarian read, *"Solvreyil Niarri's son has entered the 17th. Your sentence will be terminated after two final missions. Survive and you are a free man."*

III Path of Monsters

Sol passed Val's first test of comprehending the scheduling calendar and finding him. They hoped to get some time on the machines before their respective shifts started. Even this early, all were occupied upon arrival, so they partook as leisurely a breakfast as possible given the state of things.

"I don't know about these rations, sir."

Captain Valdieren looked up from his breakfast with a chuckle. "No one joins Star Assault for the food. You'll cultivate a tolerance for it."

Distastefully eying the sagging, padded foil bag he held by one corner, Sol commented, "Eggs and rice should not contain fluid. It should also be warm."

The pragmatic Ryzaan continued chewing with the opposite side of his mouth while he spoke. "Knead the bag before you open it. That will fix both issues."

Distrustfully, Sol began to manipulate the contents of the foil and then stopped. "This is gross, sir."

"We get better rations than any of the ground units, trust me. Save stuff you won't eat – you can almost always trade it. Won't go bad if it stays sealed."

Sol poked in the rest of the pack. There was a drink-bag containing vitamin-enriched water to share with his bug. This he stowed in his utility belt, hoping she behaved with the other gen down in the nursery. There was a suspect flavor pack for the 'entrée'. And there was a non-descript paper-wrapped package stamped, 'CHEESE BISCUIT – 2 CT' in Archon. This bothered him less than 'some assembly required' eggs, so he opened it. Inside were two small, golden brown, puck-like objects that were either cookies or the driest bread ever.

"Oh fuck you're not actually going to eat those are you?" Floppy blond bits bounced comically from Val's shuddering as the boy inserted one into his mouth and nibbled cautiously.

They were not as dry as they seemed, and the blandness was followed by a mild, cheese-like taste that was not horrible. "Why? They're not bad."

The revolted captain scooted backwards, clutching his claw utensil like a ward. "Sick! Ew! You like the dreaded 'it's not really' cheese biscuit? You are a sick, sick man!"

"They're a little dry, so what? They taste OK." *This guy leaps out of drop ships and is freaked out by cheese flavored snack rounds?*

"Man. Everyone jokes those are there just to give to the cruiser. Gross."

"Yeah, I like 'em. Trade you my so-called entrée for your next couple packs." Sol shrugged.

"What were you going to ask before we got distracted by reconstituted egg gel?"

It took Sol a second to answer, as he watched a combat simulation broadcast to the projection screen at one end of the room. A well-built, pale amber skinned kaffa in partial armor swept the ground with energy whips from his forearms, decimating a crowd of human soldiers while they fired on him futilely. Bugs descended to pick off survivors. "Erm, how long have you been in the unit, sir?"

An amused smile wrapped around Val's all-purpose, self-cleaning, unit issue eating utensil. It was shaped somewhat like a slender set of pincers, and could be used as such, or for scooping, cutting, or delicate picking. "Unlike other men of comparable rank on this vessel, I keep my entrance data public." Removing the claw, he added thoughtfully, "I think myself and Laathas are the only ones."

Chewing a cheesy "abomination", Sol flipped open his slate. "Wow…. You look your age, sir!"

"I know, right. Pretty rare in Star Assault!" Laughter indicated no insult was taken.

The record stated Valdieren Karshimziel, born Imperial Year 620, transferred from Ground Forces (Flamethrowers) in IY 640. He rose to captain in less than five years. The only data blocked 'with a 'classified' glyph was his 'initiating novum'. Sol's was listed as 'Kiertus Sheriden'. He assumed it unsafe to ask about Val's knight master as he switched to Laathas.

"Holy fuck!" Biscuit fell into the air and floated gently about. Sol nearly dropped the slate. "I don't even – what – this guy's got more designations than a hazardous materials freighter!"

"Oh, yeah." Val looked up from shoveling breakfast into his face and batted an errant chunk of biscuit to the floor. "We call him 'corporal' affectionately. The designation 'EOTC' is an InterOps rank, meaning he can be called to use his specialty basically anywhere, any level of clearance. He could be working a cushy on-call job in any civilian hospital, even; he doesn't need to be stationed since whoever needs him will handle his travel expenses. We currently provide his regular room and board, because he liked it here and wanted to stay."

What a crazy fucker! "OK, so 'HNG' – Honorable Novum Genadri? Right? That gives him the combat rank of 'captain', technically?"

"With this unit, at any rate, yeah. He played with the bugs and wanted one so Chel and Kiertus humored him… that's how the story goes. As you can see, he's been here over twice as long as me." Val scraped something off his pincers. "He unit hopped before that, acquiring many ranks…"

"Wow, no kidding. He's like, history's most over-qualified field medic. What's a 'VCSS – GRX'?"

Val jammed the flashlight end of his multi-tool into the ration bag. He clicked a code on his slate and made a grim expression. "Ick. I'm sure this is an abuse of the emergency surgical camera function of this thing… Oh, and, astrum? Swallow that next bite before I answer. I already took a crumb hit to the eye."

"Yes, sir! Sorry, sir!" Sol chewed and swallowed rapidly while his instructor used the mini camera and utensil to extract bits of something from his breakfast.

"Vektaar Certified Surgical Specialist simply means he took a course in Anima-Vek graft technology at their corporate HQ. The GCX suffix signifies 'ultimate' level clearance. He can work on Haarnsvaar, in their armor." His tone was blasé as he continued to dig for the offending components.

'Simply' Vektaar certified? Something like one in ten applicants even gets in to take the course. People literally kill themselves over failing it. "No offense, captain, but what are you fishing out of that?"

"Fucking chikkiba! I should've read the shit-cocking ingredients. So gross. "

"Gotta agree with you there, sir," mumbed Sol in disgust. "Who puts chikkiba in eggs?"

"Ryzaans. The Shandrians traditionally put it in civil defense spray."

Val's apologetically toned comment amused Sol, but not as much as the man's put-out expression. *It's probably inappropriate*, thought the astrum, *but I am really starting to like you.*

"Sir? Can I ask you a few more questions?"

He carefully folded his servillette full of abnormally pallid chikkiba chunks and tucked them into his belt. "As your team leader and first stage trainer, I'm here to help you understand this unit. Even if it means not eating all my breakfast before morning review." Val's smile was surprisingly kind for the statement.

"Apologies, sir." He let the man swallow before asking, "Is it normal to have so many high-level brass designated for drop crews?"

"In Star Assault, yes, even when we're not as wildly understaffed. Kiertus hasn't jumped in a while but I've seen him do so in the past." Val scarfed down the rest of his eggs in a single gulp. "You'd never see that in the corps, someone with that many medals directly confronting the enemy. In fact, you ever want to get your ass kicked, mention that off-handedly to a marine major."

"No thanks," Sol grinned. "OK, the bug sergeant... he's just, 'Hive Sentinel Cheldyne'? Isn't that just a domain assignment? And seriously, he's a household cleanser company? I was sure that was a nickname." *I looked him up to message him; his call sign is actually 'Serum'; 'Cheldyne' seems to be some unrelated handle. Confusing!*

"You catch on fast." Friendly sarcasm tinged the comment. "Yeah, he keeps everything under lock and key. You have to be above captain to see his combat ranks and specialty. At least he has a name; some guys in SA are just call signs at all times. I don't him. I know he's been an exo biomechanic and security for Vektaar Corporate, he talks about both a lot." Valdieren shrugged. "Any guy that old in Star Assault is someone not to fuck with."

Vektaar Corporate? What's wrong with these guys that they give up good jobs on Archos and move back out to active duty in space?

Sol opened his mouth for a final inquiry, but was lost in the public address system's horrific hiss. "Flash inspection. All drop ship crews to A Corridor Briefing."

"Oh fuck me," snarled Val, tearing off his civilian over shirt and tossing it at the nearest simulator. "We gotta go, now, stash shit under the bench."

"I don't have my uniform on – should I get it?"

His shirt had not even come to rest yet, his food abandoned, the compact Ryzaan called back as he leapt out the door, "No, just get rid of anything civilian, even if it means showing up naked. Trust me, if the military or your genetics didn't issue it, you don't want it on you. Parth is the hardest of hard asses."

This meant that Sol faced inspection in his brace and ladder trousers. A marshal at the entry questioned him regarding his gen's location then bade him proceed. Upon entry he discovered he was not the only one underdressed; it seemed a common way to sleep. Val was one of the few in full ladders, although Sol suspected it had more to do with sensitivity to cold than respect for rank.

Major Parthenos was the sort of elf that gave all kaffir a bad reputation among humans: he was long everywhere – height, ears, jaw, hair, eyes, fangs – and bore an incinerating scowl. His movements sat on the warring border of 'refined' and 'feral', his build that of a lifetime martial artist. Unlike other officers Sol encountered in his short time aboard, the major wore full formal uniform and carried side arms. Medals and chains on his jacket jingled and his black ponytail cracked like a whip when he snapped around sharply to glare down his crew.

Astrum Solvreyil's human side was pretty sure that if there were no witnesses around, this guy would have made him into a couple of steaks. His kaffa side gave him a stern talk about "specism' and 'respecting superiors'. In order to keep his cool, he held his posture stiff as possible and tuned out the major's raving until it came to him. He was aware they were being told repeatedly how unfit they were as a drop team, how dead they would be if they hit the ground with real enemies, how computer games were no substitute for live combat.

He's a Mior vet? Damn, he looks so young. Sol would not have put the major a day over 29 years, until he noticed the long, soft-looking sideburns. *Elves have to be old to grow those, don't they? What's up with this guy? Oh shit!*

The fuming tower of dissatisfaction stood before him, growling. Parthenos leaned in and hissed, "What's this shit on your face, Red?"

Sol twitched. "It's just some jaw-fluff, sir!"

"Well you should fucking shave it, astrum!"

"There were no razors available at the dispensary, sir!"

Massive, dripping fangs were centimeters from Sol's nose. "That's because there are no humans in Star Assault!" He stepped back a bit and yelled, "What's the function of this unit, Astrum Solvreyil?"

Whoa, he pronounced my name correctly. He shook his head to muster tag lines from the handbook and did his best. "We are a special forces unit designed for specific target detection and elimination, sir!"

The man's expression was dubious. "Anything else?"

What? That wasn't the answer? What else do we do? Think, Yen, think! "It is the responsibility of the 17th's Atmospheric Squadrons to provide support and relief during a crisis, be it military, environmental, or otherwise, sir!"

The major stepped back a little further and scanned the crowd. "Would anyone like to try answering the question without paraphrasing publicly available documents?"

A familiar-seeming man, dark skinned with golden-brown locks to his middle back, clad in the complete ladder suit, stepped forward. "Sir, yes sir!"

"Lieutenant Aukaldir. Please proceed."

"Star Assault is a tactical terror unit, sir!"

Damn that booze pinching bastard, thought the chagrinned astrum.

With an appreciative nod towards the man, Parthenos said, "Thank you, lieutenant; that is correct." He spread his hands as Aukaldir stepped back into the crowd with a salute. "We are a *tactical terror unit*. We are the dark side of the peaceful and loving Archon Empire; we are here to remind those who rebuke Archon protection and salvation why they need it." Still looking about the crowd and holding his proud head high, the major grabbed Solvreyil by a short pointy ear and hauled him forward, gesturing emphatically at Sol's face. "We can hardly inspire terror in our enemies with a *soul patch*!"

Once he had been tossed back into the lines, Sol exclaimed, "Sir! Yes, sir! Point made, sir!"

"So you're going to get that shit off your face then, astrum?"

Sol was more than a little annoyed at being made an example, especially by a man with draping sideburns. "Do you expect me to pluck it, sir?"

The major took his focus back from the crowd and put it on Sol. His eyebrows rose and he stepped back with a hint of a grin. Unhooking a crescent-shaped pulse pistol from his belt, he held it up and gestured to it with the other hand. "Trust me when I say, astrum, that it hurts less than this."

Sol's guts clenched; ice water washed his bloodstream. The major, gun still raised, turned to the man standing next to Sol.

"Captain Valdieren! Show this noob of yours proper depilation technique."

"Sir! Yes, sir!"

He spun towards another section of crowd. "Havlaari. Your entire team looks like shit. Shape it up or I'll see to it your alcohol rations are cut for two months."

"Sir! Yes, sir!"

"Bacharanzin. What the fuck are you wearing?"

"A towel, sir! It's military issue, sir! I was waxing my balls, sir!"

"Too much information, Bachi. Gyrfru. Lose the fucking gut."

"Sir! Yes, sir."

"Where the hell is Myshkor? Who's on his team? Lieutenant Pherrinai?"

"Sir! Yes, sir! Captain Myshkor is in the infirmary! He says you're welcome to come rip him a new one down there but Laathas ordered him to stay in bed, sir!"

"I told him that bet wasn't worth it. Fucking idiot." At last, he addressed the group again. "Everyone in this room needs more fucking training." Parthenos snapped his slate from his belt. "Captains. If I don't see at least two members of your team in the top ten scores on at least one of the combat simulations by the end of the week, I'm going to tear up your asses."

As a group, the captains in the room addressed him back. "Sir! Yes, sir!"

"Dismissed!"

The drop ship teams cleared rapidly from the briefing hall. Major Parthenos' voice froze Sol in his tracks. "Captain Valdieren's team! Hold up."

"Fuck," Sol heard Val mutter. "Sir, yes, sir. Staying right put, sir."

He was behind them. Solvreyil cast a curious, worried look towards his captain. Valdieren only shook his head, subtly yet rapidly and whispered, "Later" out of the corner of his mouth.

"Turn around, boys."

The whole team, minus Sol who had not been gang-playing Lunar Dance Party with the captain for several weeks, spun around in perfect time. They saluted in unison. "Sir! Yes, sir!"

"Well, Val. Looks like you've finally got yourself a white bug. Or maybe I should say red? Hmmm." Parthenos stood before Sol, bent to examine Sol's waistline. "Hmf. What do we have here?"

What the hell? Sol attempted to stay formal, although he could feel the major's breath on his meager abs. "What seems to be the problem, sir?"

Parthenos drew his pistol again. He jabbed one end of the crescent against the top of Sol's pants. "I thought this," he ran the warm, living gun up the little fuzzy red line, "was a scar." He stopped abruptly and hooked the tip of the thing into Sol's navel creating a sensation somewhere both curious and uncomfortable. Unstooping, Parthenos faced Solvreyil again but did not move the business end of the gun. "I appear to have been incorrect."

The slender redhead's voice was meek. "Sir. Yes, sir." *What kind of hole would that put through me?*

In a low, throaty tone, his breath hot on Sol's face, the major informed, "You're going to have to wax that, too, Astrum Solvreyil."

"Sir. Yes. Sir." He swallowed. *Why is he looking at me like that? Could this get more awkward?* "Everything, sir?"

Major Parthenos straightened and stepped back sharply, pulling the gun up fast and hard enough to give Sol a whack to the base of his ribs. His voice returned to normal as Sol struggled not to clutch, stumble, and gasp. "Your kinks are none of my business, but you should probably check the handbook in regards to uniform requirements and body hair."

Sol choked out, "Sir! Yes, sir!" and managed to salute.

"Now you're all dismissed. Get the fuck out of my sight."

Outside the briefing hall door, Valdieren complimented his team on their precision stepping. "Sol, we'll get you caught up," he assured. "Seriously, you guys looked great. Keep it up. Everyone's dismissed but this astrum, here. See you all at 14:00 in Sim 3."

Sol was deeply apologetic. "Sorry I made you look bad, sir."

The captain shrugged. "Feel bad if you want, work to correct issues, but ultimately, keeping my team informed of relevant uniform requirements is my responsibility. You've not been here long enough to read the entire handbook, so I'm giving you a pass. Don't leave me hanging like that in the future."

"Yes, sir." Sol synced his stride with Valdieren's. "Are we headed back to the simulators, sir? We've still got forty five minutes until either of our shifts."

"I was going to take you to the hive and walk you through waxing and auto-electrolysis. But you work in the hive. I hate to shift the responsibility to Chel, but we really should get some practice in on the sims. You are getting along with him, from what I can tell, though, yes?"

"Apparently. I take it that's rare, sir?"

Valdieren shrugged. "He hasn't been really friendly since Tyrnan left, and the less said about that situation right now, the better. Come on, let's make an ass out of Major Furbiscuit."

...

"This shit is a pain in my piss canal," Val muttered as he walked with Sol.

His mind on the situation with Parthenos the previous day, he had to ask, "Which shit, sir?"

"The fact you haven't been issued armor yet. It's making the usual training procedure difficult." His tone was short and cranky. Val breathed deeply and then added, "Apologies, astrum. I'm working on this but our best bet in getting your gear at this point is the same furry fuck we seriously pissed off ... I don't dare ask him for special help right now."

Sol fell back a bit, absorbing the information. "Am I even your problem at the moment, Captain V?"

"Technically, your master is Kiertus. He should be dealing with this, but he's buried in administrative shit he can't delegate because there's no one with credentials to take it. I can handle you. That's his theory anyway." He sighed. "Come on... let's go down to the pipes and I'll slip you into the D-7 pilot training. It'll kill a couple hours a day for you, you'll learn stuff, and I can get back to the armor drills."

I'm missing armor drills? This is fucking lame. "Yes, sir."

"Hey, it's not all bad. You'll be way ahead of everyone else when they're all learning to fly."

They took a shortcut to starboard pipes that Sol did not know. "Don't tell the colonel we took this," Val ordered informally as he used an emergency panel to override a security code. "Your clearance and rank are too low to even walk through this hall and I don't want to hear about how I subverted hierarchal order on the ship. I can't leave you untrained. Keep your eyes down. Don't talk to anyone. Got that?"

"Er, yes, sir."

Solvreyil apprehensively followed the young captain. The hallway's classification remained a mystery; it showed on his map as an air duct. It was dark in both lighting and coloration, strangely pockmarked like the oldest coral specimens at the zoological park. The smell was odd, too – super saline with an undertone of acrid drug sweat. They passed a doorless relief nook. Sol looked away quickly, wondered passingly why the man he saw just squatted in the moss, hands on knees, pissing on his own feet. He heard shuffling and scraping somewhere *above* them; Val's hand yanked his wrist downward.

"Eyes at the floor," Val uttered in stiff old Ryzaan. "We're almost to the rungs into the pipes."

The captain's urgent tone increased Sol's heart rate. He caught up and they descended quickly through a few layers of hatches and through another security lock. On the other side, Valdieren clutched the bridge of his nose a moment, eyes closed, nerves clearly rattled.

Signs nearby in the spacious hallway pointed to the various hangars. Nothing indicated the direction or presence of the corridor through which they came. Sol noticed one sign on the way, during the descent out, and had to ask. He chose Ryzaan, choking on it a little as always: "What are 'Aux Coccoons', sir?"

"Gods dammit." Val uttered in plain Archon, clapping his hand over his eyes. "You saw nothing."

"Request to raise my clearance, please, sir. I won't sleep for a week much less be able to concentrate on video games for this ... shoot off, or whatever it is we're working on."

Val proceeded to starboard hangar three, shook his head, not looking back. "Aux Coccoons are where retrievers sleep. End lesson."

Sol conducted a quick SACnet search. 102 entries contained the term. He fell behind his superior again, slacked his gait enough to read a short post that included the phrase, 'sentenced to retrieval missions' and how this required more drugs and carriage of 'dissection tools'. Sympathy flooded the replies; most were short Shandrian prayers. The poster eventually commented his thread, months later: "Will never be the same. Allowed to retire; please no party. Cannot face you to say goodbye."

Sol stopped and looked at Val, still holding his slate, disturbed to twitching. The captain was standing at the last bulkhead into the bays. "Come on, Sol. I really need to get back to T-4."

He did not look the captain in the face as he stepped into the hangar, but asked under his breath, not expecting an answer, "Why dissection tools?"

"Because," came the barely audible answer, "we cannot allow bio-ware or living units to fall into enemy hands. Honor and sacrifice, Astrum Solvreyil." Valdieren saluted, wheeled, and was gone.

The hangar was an impressive space; D-7 fighters sat stacked on garage-shelves surrounded by pulsing tubes and stretchy webbing. Sol understood these functioned as rotating lifts and the *Sanjeera*'s massive pseudopods would hoist them to the launch chute when necessary. The webbing kept them in place if the ship took a serious impact, but could also be climbed by technicians to service the small craft. All techs and pilots in the vicinity were lined up in several tight rows; Sol rushed to join them.

"Made it just in time," whispered an engineer. "Straighten up or he'll rip you."

Sol followed suit, and seconds later was relieved to have done so as he was confronted by a hoarsely yelling ball of lightning trapped in kaffir form.

His mode of dress was a bit odd; a trashed lightweight sweater and tattered work apron over what appeared to be a pilot's uniform. His dark hair was half-mudded, disarrayed, and seemed "styled" by a heavy application of ship grease prior to falling asleep in a rodent burrow. Circles were visible under his eyes in spite of dark shades; his face was heavily creased and relatively filthy. He seemed capable of speaking without breaking or breathing and Sol fought to catch the lecture. If it were not for the cool-looking pin that hung queerly on the sweater, the symbol he knew as 'wing command', Sol would have assumed someone on a bad drug bender was freaking out at the unit.

"...every single one of these jets needs to be in perfect shape, all the time! When one comes in with a wing blown off, you will bend time and space to generate a new one, do-you-understand? And you can expect if you are the shit what got the wing blown off his jet you are going to feel my fucking wrath, and you will fucking wish you'd been killed in combat! What is your primary function?"

Senior pilots in front responded in unison: "To fight and die with honor, sir!"

"Correct! You are fighter pilots of the Archon Empire! There is no greater honor then to die in service of your people! Except one, and what is that!"

The front row snarled: "To take as many fucking Baalphae out as we can on the way to Glory, sir!"

"DAMN FUCKING STRAIGHT YOU HONORLESS BAGS OF MEAT! NOW GET UP THOSE WEBS AND INSPECT THOSE FUCKING JETS!"

"Sir! Yes, sir!"

They dispersed. Sol winced, fumbled out his slate to check for any sort of assignment before –

"You! With the red hair! Who the fuck are you?"

In his rushed attempt a salute as the frothing beast approached, Sol pitched his slate accidentally across the bay. "Astrum Solvreyil Yenraziir, sir!"

"You're not on my team. What the fuck? Are you a fucking paratrooper?" The vibrating, disheveled man whipped out his slate, alternately looking at it and glaring down Sol. Saliva flecked pale, cracked lips; a nasty set of fangs was visible. He reeked of drugs, bio-ship secretions, and bloody meat.

I swear the temperature is actually dropping. This is fear, I am definitely afraid. Sol found comfort in the fact he hit the nook after breakfast and dumped a load, because it would have been in his ladders otherwise. *What did Val get me into? Does he even know this dude?* Amazingly, the astrum got out his reply without stammering. "Commander, sir, Dromarka locked down my armor, sir, so Captain Valdieren sent me to you because he's doing armor drills today. S-sir." *Ok, almost without stammering…*

Eyes rolled behind dark glasses. "I should have known you were one of Val's."

The strained voice quieted; he seemed amused. "Don't worry; I can put you to work." He pointed sharply up tiers of jets and the rasp hardened again. "See that man up there? Lieutenant Hanajiel. He'll run you through small craft inspection. It's about the same for a D-7 as a Dash, and you need to know that. Lose your bug or fuck up enough with Parthenos and you'll need to know the D-7, too. What are you waiting for? Get the fuck up there and get your fuckin hands dirty! Think you're too good for ship fross? Think again! Up that fucking web before I lash you!"

There was no delay on on Sol's part; he was halfway up to Hanajiel before the word "lash" came from that terrifying mouth. He scrambled to meet his assignment without a look back.

"Hi. Lieutenant Hanajiel, sir? I'm Solvreyil Yenraziir, astrum to Colonel Kiertus. The, um, wing commander … "

The lieutenant had a short, frizzy pile of ash blond hair and a cock-eyed grin. "I see. You're the new toy. People been talkin', about youuuu…" All was sung to the tune of a popular song Sol only knew since it was performed repeatedly at the all-ages cantina on the *Irimia*. He pursed his lips. "What, not into karaoke? Shit, you're a kid, like, for real. Fuck. Always thought that shit about him was a human-tale."

Human tale. He really just said that. The acutely nasty phrase meant a lie told to play up the negative traits of another. *This man outranks you, Yen. Don't pick a fight, no matter how much a shithead he is.*

"Lieutenant, that commander down there said to follow you through an inspection, sir. Do you have a problem with that, sir?"

Hanajiel's snorted laugh was joyless and his expression dire. "Not if Wyvern ordered you, kid. His word is law here; you don't wanna ever break that."

Sol saluted as the lieutenant gestured him over for a tour. His vexation at missing armor training was erased by the realization he would learn to fly a craft he obsessed over since childhood. And while he lacked any particular desire to impress this racist knob, he noted Hanajiel's attitude change as he would call out parts before the lieutenant could name them.

"Did they mix up the trooper training or is it just cuz you're one of K's?"

"Excuse me, sir?" Sol expected another pederasty crack and clenched his jaw.

"You've got two thirds of the ship memorized, at least all the stuff that's not classified. I know you haven't jumped yet, so do they make you study small craft first now?"

"No, sir. My dad flew for Rim Patrol, so he'd bring me model ships or books when he came back from duty. Long stints and all, sir."

An eyebrow rose. "Rim Patrol, huh?" Hanajiel looked at his slate again; his mouth wriggled as if a live animal were caught inside. "Uh, okay. So. Time to stump you! What's this?"

Sol followed the pointed finger to beneath the hump where the tail joined the vehicle's main cabin. He was confused, as no model ship he assembled bore the strange ovoid compartment on which he looked. All he missed up to this point were obscure armaments specific to Star Assault. "Another weapon, sir?"

"Well, it can be, I guess," laughed Hanajiel. "Yeah you are so a Kiertus astrum!"

The hell is he on about?

He thumped the orb. "This is a mini-yun bender, kid. It's the jump system for the ship, it's just shielded. Don't ever stand close when one's open outside appropriate gear unless you're really hard to find out what flavors of cancer you're genetically prone."

"It's a baby Ioun drive? That's fucking wicked, sir."

"OK help me oil the wings." Hanajiel tossed Sol a little tub of odiferous unguent. "Do the left. And duck at five." He scratched the vessel's side as he counted. "One, two, three, four, five! I told you to duck."

Sol took the offered hand to regain his footing from where the expanding wing knocked him, laughing. "So these are alive, like the cruiser? Are they as snotty as the cruiser, sir?"

Hanajiel winked as he slid under the right wing. "Did she sass you? That means she likes you."

"I did not get that out of the ex - holy fucksticks, what is this made of? It smells like someone threw eels in a batch of pohji butter." Sol's eyes watered.

"Synthetic van'ra oil. 'This laboratory fabrication is based on a true fish!'" He chuckled. "You get used to it. Lotta guys like to use it as anal lube, not me; I can't stomach smellin' like I spearfish with my cock."

"Gross, but environmentally sound, I guess."

"Speaking of fish and environmental concerns, what's the primary difference between an unmodified Dash dropship and a D-7?"

"Dash floats, D-7's dive. Only part of my favorite simulation ever, sir."

Hanajiel's face appeared from the nose up over the side of the craft. "You play that sim at home?"

"Yeah, of course I …" *What is that look for?*

"Cuz you sure as shit didn't play it in the IGN lounge. If you ever dive in the meat universe, fire all your harpedos before you even think about firing the pulse guns or the *nemtz'a*. Pulsing underwater presents a large risk to wildlife and you work for elves who give a fuck, my friend. A really big fuck."

"Duly noted. I give that kind of fuck too, sir. Probably the most elvish thing about me, really."

"Then you don't want to hear my story. I was stupid when I was new, and I'm not a captain because of it. Let's leave it at that." He capped his jar. "You done with that wing? You'll know because it'll wriggle –"

Hanajiel froze, held up his finger, and whispered, "Hey, ever seen a ship sprite?"

"Huh? No, but I'd love to!"

The lieutenant waved to Sol to lower his voice. "Shh, there's one in the web to the rear."

Something squeezed its way between the web and outer wall. It was small, compared to them, dark, moving quickly considering the difficult strata it navigated. Sol's eyes widened as it squeezed through a gap in the stretchy webbing and slipped onto the platform.

It was humanoid in shape, but crouched on all fours and moved as if its long limbs were uncomfortably hyper-mobile. It was the size of a slender older child, a bit over a meter tall if it could stand up straight, encased in an oily, dripping, shiny suit, dark brown in color but iridescent from the ship secretions that covered it. Sol was fascinated, but Hanajiel stayed still, looking quite uncomfortable.

It approached in jerkily and sat on its haunches. The facial features were delicate and alien; what little bare skin Sol could see was translucent, pallid, blue-tinged. The thing's mouth was covered by a surgically attached re-breathing unit. Its eyes were blank yellowish-white, lacking irises, with slender black elliptical pupils. There were two slits below each eye, which at first Sol presumed – due to the lack of anything recognizably a nose - to be nostrils but realized with a skipped heartbeat that they were more eyes, clenched shut. It half-hopped toward Sol, then thrust out an arm. Its slender, large-tipped fingers were wrapped about something; as they slowly, mechanically opened, he could see his slate. He reached gingerly and met the creature's gaze as the odd little head twitched curiously. The other sets of eyes opened a little; light seemed to cause it pain. It squinted at him with all six as the head tilted and bobbed.

It's curious about me, too. As he snatched the slate he leaned forward and said, "Thank you, very much," in as appreciative a tone possible. The creature bolted, but turned to give him a long look as it hung in the webbing before it squeezed through and vanished.

"Shit!"

"Excuse me sir?"

"Man," Hanajiel wiped his brow and eyes, still a bit tense. "They never come out of the webbing, except… hooo…"

He seems genuinely freaked out. "Except for what, sir?"

"On behalf of the ship. You know, to clean." The lieutenant laughed nervously, then looked Sol over again, then eyed his own slate. "You didn't come here through the retriever wing did you, boy?"

Sol did not look up from his task, still attempting to oil wing tendrils.

"Look at me when I'm talking to you and don't lie. You're better than your short ears and you know it. I'm agnostic, kid, but I got no beans 'bout tellin' your novum you added links to your chain in Hell." His eyes were severe. "I won't tell no one shit if you just tell me the truth."

'A link in your chain for every false word.' "Yes I did, sir, I didn't even know what it was at the time."

"There's your proof the *Sanjeera* likes you."

"How so?"

Hanajiel dropped beneath the craft to check some vents. "You're alive and standing there."

Did it get colder in here? Sol squatted next to the man, watching. "How did you know where I went?"

"Because the sprites congregate in those tunnels; if they find a visitor interesting, they'll follow him around." He stopped working and took a deep breath. "They do it to Wyvern frequently."

"Does he have to go up there because of being a commander?"

"Yes, but he ran a year on retrieval, voluntarily, when allowed to choose a punishment for extreme insubordination early in his time here." Hanajiel swallowed hard. "I'd like to say that's just a story, but both Parthenos and he made a point of telling me as much. People usually quit after that job because it involves cutting up your dead or dying teammates."

"No disrepect, sir, but I'd like to get this inspection thing done in case he gives me a quiz, sir. I don't want to know if that whipping business is literal, sir."

"Understandable. Don't fucking drop anything else, I don't want to see that thing again, 'kay?" He swung up the side of the ship and thumped open the main hatch. "Inside a D7, ready! Smaller cockpit, no crew area, minimal cargo, pilot and gunner sit back to back in normal mode but the seats can –"

"Be swivelled into 'tandem' position so both can focus pulse into the forward guns at the same time."

"And so the rear can give the pilot a reach-around."

"You're joking."

"I'm not. Not surprised your dad didn't teach you that." He made an indescribable face. "Have a seat and tell me what everything is on the console, then I'll show you how to pull and replace parts as needed."

Sol checked his slate before continuing, having noted messages from Val. He popped up Wyvern's stat file but it was nothing save the obvious call sign and a gruesome bit of poetry.

"For peace, their bodies on the altar/Solace only in faith and mercy/Our sacrifice for love is Love and Life itself/Our freedom is the void of Death."

"Your boss terrifies me, sir. Sorry."

Hanajiel exhaled painfully as he poked the forward console. "He's the scariest thing on the *Sanjeera*. I'd rather sleep naked in the reactor than spend fifteen minutes alone with him. That's all I'm going to say. Find the master cables, ship report says they're overdue to switch. Ship reports' here, by the way, it makes this faster; you can interface the ship records through your slate. I've been showing you how to do it the hard way in case you have to do it on the ground with a punked 'brain'."

I could do without the bigotry, but I guess you're not all asshole. "Oh, I see. Thanks, sir."

"You need to know both; you never want to piss off a wing commander, right? They train as medics for a couple years for anatomy while learning high level ma'at-shi arts. You follow? People say Parthenos is meanest, but they're wrong. He's downright direct, by the book about punishment unless it's personal. Jady'll make you puke, way after the fact, usually in public, awkwardly. On a marine or during an awards ceremony. Mean as hell but you can laugh about it later, right? Wyvern…" He glanced out the cockpit. "He hits you with these… pulse 'ropes' and breaks everything he can that won't kill you outright. I never want to see anyone go through that again."

"Yes, sir, lieutenant! Let's fix all the ships! Right! The first time! Sir!"
….

"Three days now," noted Valdieren as he leaned on the sim-pod opposite Sol. "Learn anything so far?"

It was late. Both would normally be ready for bed if they were not cramming study sessions into all available hours.

"I learned how *nemtz'a* work and how mold cylinders turn ship secretions into caustic glue projectiles." Sol grinned at the clever biological weapon array he knew how to clean, repair, and arm. "And Lieutenant Iekierpin's formation lecture was surprisingly interesting."

Val nodded, smiling through exhaustion. "Eek's a compelling speaker. He was in my debate class last semester at the Academy."

"Oh. Is he the guy that..." Sol's tongue stumbled. He blinked, staring down at the side of the pod. "Dammit. How the hell could I forget her name?"

"Who?"

"The hot sergeant at Orminos."

Val laughed. "Onzillora?"

"Ugh. Damn. Apologies, sir." He took from Val's gesture that it was nothing to worry over. "She told me one of the jet guys was a big history buff who liked to upload rare books to the ship library."

One eyebrow rose. "Naw. Not Eek. His only interest in history is how to use it to get people to agree with him." Val climbed into the pod and motioned for Sol to take the other seat.

"Well she did say the guy was a wing commander. There's no call sign on the uploads. I figured he could've lost rank – "

The captain shook his head as he leaned forward to tinker with the console panel. "Naw. Pretty sure she was referring to Parthenos or Wyvern."

"What? Really? That scary fucker can read?"

"Which one?" Abruptly, Val cleared his throat. "So. You grasped my basic pulse lessons so I decided we should try the Dash sim tonight for a break. You ready?"

Sol could not completely push the images from his head. *Hairy and Scary go to the library? The Terror Twins, tormenting harried antiquarians?* He laughed under his breath as Val poked about the pod.

In response to Val's tinkering, the interior of the pod began to reconfigure around them. Sol watched in fascination as fleshier sections folded, stretched, or crept and chitinous bits popped up or clicked into place or slid into hiding under the "skin".

"I can't believe I forgot her name."

"It's the meds. After an adjustment period the stuff you've lost will come back to you and you'll retain details much better. We probably should start on cognitive exercises soon, that'll help." He selected "Basic Drop Ship (2), Standard Exercises" from the on-screen menu. "Could be worse. I couldn't hang on to my superior's name for the first month on board."

"Do you mean superior like you are to me, or like…"

"Like, my knight-master."

Sol chuckled. "Damn, sir."

"He took to wearing his name tag to keep me from constant shame." Val laughed but cast his eyes sadly down. "You gotten to fly a fighter yet?"

"No. We're doing a formation simulation class tomorrow and then, theoretically, we get to ride rear-gun with experienced pilots. You know, contingent on performance in the sim."

"This will put you ahead of the game, so to speak." The young captain smiled at his accidental pun, clearly unconcerned with its cheesiness.

Not sure this is appropriate but I probably should tell someone. "I was offered 'private flying lessons' off-hours by a couple of the guys. They seemed, um, to be kind of, um…"

"Sleazy?" finished Val. "Yeah, welcome to Star Assault."

"Pardon my extreme naivete, sir, but what am I missing there?" The virginal lad braced himself for mockery, but none came.

"The 'old school', Shandrian way to fly still works in all Star Assault vessels, from a D-7 to the Kimetj cruisers. I guess even the Triotine heavy warships can too, but it would require a veritable orgy. Anyway, the process involves sexual release, ergo the fact D-7s can do tandem, so you can, uh, reach-around… I'm not going to cover that tonight." Valdieren's tone was curtly professional. "They were coming on to you, very likely, but intimate fraternization is encouraged in this unit. The sincerity and lesson value will vary by the individual, of course, but it doesn't hurt to learn things."

The reacharound comment makes more sense now, at least. Biting his lower lip, curious as he was disturbed, Sol quietly remarked, "Wyvern seemed the most, um, sincere."

"No fucking way!" Val blinked and shook his head, sputtering as if in recoil from a surprise slap. "Wow. He never offers that. To anyone. He hasn't... it's been... oh, wow."

"I don't know if the proper response is to feel honored or traumatized, sir."

The captain looked over, amusement clear in his expression. "I would respond 'both' to that inquiry, astrum." He turned his attention again to the reconfigured console. "When you are ready to start the simulation, please activate the main switch to release the safety and allow full energy communication."

"Affirmative, sir." Sol toggled a nubby switch toward the center of the console.

"This unit is currently calibrated high, specifically to assist beginners. We're keeping it set thus because I tend to keep my appointed vessel that way. Generally, it's best if pilot and co-pilot have compatible ratings; you'll get to know who all those people are in the unit as you'll be assigned to work with them most. You and I have relatively compatible ratings; I could calibrate my ship very low and still fly it, but I like to fly in ladders."

Because you're a total wuss about the cold. "Got it, sir."

"You will not feel the transfer too much, due in part to the high calibration but also because it's just a sim pod. We're already transferring now. In a real ship, you would feel it from the moment of activation."

The pod, allowed to feed on their energy, woke up. Rubbery wing-like structures unrolled themselves from the sides of the seats. Val lifted his arms and Sol followed suit, each allowing the fleshy things to wrap about their torsos. The captain flicked a tiny switch on the far lower left of the console and two long, slender, triple-ended tubes snaked out from the base of the seat and coiled up each arm. The tips poked into the vents on his graft sleeves. There was a similar activation panel on Sol's side, which he stared at wondering what to do.

"Obviously, you don't have grafts, so you may or may not want to activate your tethers. I fly grip and graft; some people prefer one or the other, some people lean more heavily on voice commands and use the physically interactive features as a back-up. Eventually, you should try everything to see what suits you best. You'll mostly be gunning today but I do intend to swap control at some point. I will warn you before I do it. Please note that when you inevitably fly with Parthenos or Wyvern, because they are your best BVSI compatibility, that they will do it without any warning to keep you on your toes, and they think you screaming and pissing yourself is high comedy."

Oh for fuck's sake. Those two are my best sync? "Understood, sir." Sol located the switch for the weapon controls; two odd appendages emerged from the sides of the hump between his legs. He flipped the catch on the left one and released it into his hand; vein-like wires connected it to the seat. It fit neatly in his hand as he carefully tested the reach on the various – currently shielded - firing buttons. He released the other into his right and grinned in anticipation, listening as the captain continued his lesson.

"Dropships, like D-7s, are set up so that control of the various functions can be swapped to either person in the cockpit. So why is the 'Master Seat' called that?"

Huh. Never seen an explanation. Here goes with the educated guess. "It's the default position by which the ship auto-adjusts, attuning to the primary pilot's signature."

"Correct. Now, why is it always the left side of the cockpit?"

Never even considered it. "Right arm is the plug arm on most pilots and if he was flying manual he'd hit the side of the cockpit a lot?"

"Committed combat pilots get plugs on both forearms and only noobs from Intergalaxy thump the wall." Val winked as he waggled a finger at Sol. He pointed the finger downward as he continued. "Left is the side of Aur from which we fly."

In civilian zones or IG, I could report you for that. You'd be fined for proselytizing. "Shouldn't you have framed that in a historical context, sir?"

"Did we travel back in time while I wasn't paying attention?"

Uh oh. He's making Serious Officer face. "No, sir."

"It's not in the recruiting literature; secret mystic orders of knighthood don't generally advertise."

'Yen, you are the densest rock in the asteroid belt,' as my sister would say.
"Yes, sir."

On the monitor, their virtual ship was being moved via tentacle to the launch catapult. Val's hands rested patiently near an intake slit. "When the propulsion is underway, I will put my hand in here and give the ship a dose of pulse. On ships set up for voice commands, the phrase 'increase consumption' and 'maintain consumption' will work similarly. If you are flying pure manual, an upward motion with the linked arm does the trick. Any questions?"

"What's a Triotine?"

Val gave a sideways glance, but made no remarks regarding the inappropriateness of the question in terms of his lesson. "The class of cruisers that replaced the Medderaxus. You haven't heard of them because they're too new for gossip and they'll never be pictured in books available to civilians. There are only a few, like Kimetj cruisers, and they're only for use in extreme situations. Also like Kimetj cruisers, only a handful of people are trained in their operation; if the *Lorelei II* activated tomorrow we'd lose Kiertus to it. And you, because you'd probably go with him. I have no idea who the assigned folks are for the other ones I've seen… way past my clearance. I only know about the *Lorelei II* because he told us when he gave it the birth blessing toast at Fenrir."

"Is it particularly slow of me that I did not realize Master Kiertus was so important?"

The captain shrugged. "He doesn't rub it in anyone's face like some guys I could mention, you know, so it's easy to forget. Then you read the books, the articles, and you feel honored. 'I get to work with him.'" He smiled proudly. "He blessed the *Lorelei II* because he was on the first one when it went down."

"Whoa. How did he survive?"

"One of the last centacavians – that's the really scary looking Ilu warship, clusters of flipping bony feet, oh just look one up in the files – got hold of her

98

and they were punctured bad enough that if they'd jumped to escape, everyone likely would have died. So Parth took up the rear propulsion – you know you can separate the rear of a Kimetj, in an emergency, right? Yeah. Parth punched it and Kiertus took a big gamble, blew the Ioun core out into the grappling ship. They saved most of the hive and themselves, nearly everyone else was lost. Those gen make up the brood hive on Holtiin, our bugs are descended from them. The few men who survived that nightmare have Black Wings; most of 'em retired with honors, with the gen… Parth and Kiertus went right back to service on another ship. Hard core, huh?"

Sol let this sink in while he watched Val's simulated flying, paying careful attention to his subtle arm movements. "*Lorelei, Sanjeera, Triotos, Medderax…* are there ships in Star Assault not named after the sites of terrible tragedies?"

"Aside from the name of our class, 'Kimetj', of course, no. *Ishulya, Esimaar… Yetjmaal…*" The expression Val made was peculiarly strained, as if he tried not to physically express something to avoid confusing the Dash. "I'd give you the lesson, but the old veterans do it better. It's certainly no accident. I suggest asking Chel, but if you want to get on Parthenos' good side, you could ask him once this week is over. He survived the incident on Ruahanu after which that class of ships is named, after all. The Siege of Triotos. 'When you want to understand atrocity, ask a Ruhn', the old men always say."

Their virtual drop ship glided with effortless grace through the void. "How do they staff those ships otherwise, I mean, the ones that are too big for just Star Assault?"

"They pull people with high ratings from other units; usually no one young, definitely no one planning on kids. Sometimes volunteers, sometimes conscription." The captain glanced at his gunner a moment. "Are you wondering about your parents?"

"Yes, sir, how could I not? It shouldn't even… I can't even… I…"

"I got curious and read what I could of your mother's files. Because of the chaos in the med lab of her station, I guess there was a big fuck up in the mixes for a bunch of folks, all people with … odd names that were alphabetized wrong I guess? So your mom, and Major Parthenos, and some other folks, I guess, all ended up illegally fertile. Dunno about your dad because I can't see his shit."

"What? Parthenos, too?"

"I only know that because he mentioned the situation in a piece he posted to SACNet about the importance of keeping things organized during a crisis. He will also whip out his junk and show you his vasectomy mark if he feels the need to make a point about commitment to the unit. Won't speak a word about it in casual off hours talk though, so, no pun intended, probably a sore spot."

An alarm sounded inside the pod. Sol analyzed the monitor. "Shit, hostiles? I didn't think this was a combat simulation. I thought we were going to target shoot asteroids."

"These are all combat simulations, astrum. The hostiles are randoms that might not come up in a given instance but they can appear at any time. Just like the real thing. These are almost certain to be verties so blow 'em away soon as they're targetable. That'll be immediately with your pulse level, I suspect."

"Copy that!"

Concentrate, center, release. Sol recited the gun lesson from the prior night in his head as he trained a bead on the middle dot. The console spoke: "Ilu V craft confirmed. Hostile, confirmed. Action?"

"Release cannon locks," proclaimed Val with a nod. "Fire when ready, astrum."

The boy released his stored energy through his hands as he depressed the now unguarded levers along the front of the handles. A set of numbers flashed on the lower right of the screen as two digitized plasmoid projectiles shot from the forward cannons. The middle dot shimmered and was gone; the other two began to move rapidly away from one another.

"Good hit, and nice high intensity there… you're not distributing very well but we'll work on that." Val rolled the ship to maneuver toward one of the escaping dots. "I can't imagine you didn't damage all of them with that one hit. We gotta clean up, though; survivors represent future risks."

Sol breathed hard as he realized both enemy fighters were turning to come at them from different sides. He braced himself and built another round, suddenly concerned. "Sir, I don't know if I've got enough in me… damn suppressors…"

"Shit. Try anyway, astrum!"

The enemies were in range to fire at them now, and Val was dodging their blasts as best he could. With a complex, rapid finger movement, Sol fired both the forward cannons and the rear. One of the forward shots connected and the hostile dot fuzzed out, but the other was just too weak and fell short.

"Hang in there, kid. This could hurt." The captain spun the ship; he held his hands strangely as he concentrated. "Swapping. Try to dodge their blasts."

"Affirmative. I'll be using the manual rollers and hump sliders." The boy was familiar with these – they were like the controls for the civilian version of the video game. "Ready, sir!"

Right as Sol took over the flight controls there was another volley. They did not connect, as whatever Val did seemed to have raised a field around them. The strain on Val's face was severe; he made an upward gesture while keeping his fingers curled, then snapped his arms out – not far enough to hit his gunner or the wall. Sol saw on the monitor a set of numbers on the left and a shimmering web around their craft. His surprising order was yelled through saliva drenched fangs. "Full speed at the target, astrum!"

"What?"

"You heard me!"

Slipping his hands in the intake slits, Sol watched in wide-eyed horror as the vertebra-shaped white ship grew, still firing. It attempted to veer, the AI finally grasping the imminent danger. Val boosted the net-like field and the already damaged enemy ship merely glanced it. Sparks, fire, shrapnel; the pod rocked impressively and damage was being reported on the monitor. The enemies were gone but they were in bad shape. "Shitcock. I hosed the lateral stabilizer and one of the starboard vents. That's what I get for tactical experimentation."

"Not good, sir."

"This is how you summon retrievers." Val pulled a concealed lever beneath the middle console and gave a shrug in Sol's direction. "In real life, we would probably survive, depending on the speed of retrieval and the proximity of anything with gravity. But when you damage a ship this bad in this particular sim, it's game over, because we assume the major or a wing commander beat the starry-eyed fuck out of us and then it's demotion city."

Their score on the completion screen was not as bad as Sol expected. "Maybe if you could have held the field up through the explosion?"

"Yeah, I mean, obviously, huh? That was dumb of me." Val was grinning. "You can totally make fun of me for that, you have every right." He gestured at the monitor. "We got a score that good anyway because we avoided their shots really well and we got a 1:1 encounter to kill ratio. I see you need to work on cultivating and distributing, but your aim and piloting are both pretty good for being new."

"I played this game as a kid, but … well obviously not like…" Sol gestured at the pod. "I very rarely beat my dad, though. He was bad ass at it."

As the captain climbed from the simulator and went to retrieve a drink from his gear, he asked, "Sol, I don't really want to say this, but when your dad told you what he did for a living, what did he say?"

"He said he was in Rim Patrol."

"Did he say that, or something else, specifically?"

Sol tidied up the pod as he thought. "He said he was a 'special policeman who protects the perimeters of Archon society from the bad guys.' Actually, I don't think he ever once said 'Rim Patrol' now that you mention it."

"Yeah. Society, not space, huh?" Val returned his drink to his belt and put the belt back on. He yawned and stretched and looked seriously and sadly at his trainee. "I am headed to bed. I wish you a good night."

The boy stared at Val, confused, wondering what the man had been getting at. "Wait, please; just … what are you implying?"

The captain leaned on the door way with a sigh. "I should not have started this. I apologize."

"Just explain, please, sir."

"I looked up Rim Patrol's rosters for the past 20 years. There is no 'Solvreyil' or

'Kvatchkiir' listed among them. The only 'Kvatchkiir' in any military database I could access was listed as 'Air Defense, secure reserve', and his files are locked down hard beyond that."

"'Secure reserve'?"

Val shook his head. "Even discussing this is a bad idea, Sol. I'm sorry. Goodnight."

….

"Hey. Astrum."

Sol did not want to look up from landing gear he polished. He knew who owned the raspy voice and the filthy, bare, long-toed feet.

"Yes, sir. You have my attention, Master Wyvern." As he saluted, Sol looked up to crossed arms; one hand bore a slate in his direction.

"What's this shit about you leaving my department early today?"

He stood, maintaining his salute with polishing rag still in hand. "Captain Valdieren is giving a course in offensive field use. Unarmored, so I can participate, sir."

The wing commander's tone was somewhat dubious. "Is that so?" He tapped a foot and stared Sol down. "Very well, then. Continue with your assigned tasks until you need to depart."

Wyvern turned and stalked away, a musky drug sweat cloud left in his wake. Sol wiped his watering eyes on the cleanest part of his sleeve and returned to work.

….

"It has been brought to my attention that specific members of this group are behind on field control." Some of the men grumbled, but Valdieren was undaunted. "I was surprised as well, considering a few of you are experienced at ma'at-shi. I have chosen to address this as a group rather than single out the offenders because we are all in this together; the unit functions better if we're all on the same page."

As one of the offenders, Sol was a little red at the cheeks, but felt distinct relief not to be made an example. He could not help his lack of training; he attended school essentially as a human, fudged an atrophied pulse organ using prescriptions given him by a doctor over on the other side of town. *My dad's doctor. He worked out of a nice house instead of the offices that mom's docs did. Dad always dropped me at the library and got the drugs for me; I never went with him to the chemist. All these years I figured he was drinking cider at the club by the pharmacy. He was probably picking them up on the base.*

"A force field can be generated intentionally by concentrating energy around your body. This is easy, so easy that young kaffir often do so by accident. These fields are usually invisible and somewhat pleasant to contact. I have selected partners for everyone; the lowest training levels are with the highest, etc. Your partner assignment is on your slate; find him now."

Solvreyil looked and noted he was with Kamadji. He was around 28 Archon years, a little shorter than Sol, with shoulder-length, green-dyed mudlocks. He was a trencher transfer and had an obnoxious, nervous laugh. He was an astrum, but not "astrum genova'.

"Man. We're together? You must suck," whispered Kamadji in a not entirely joking manner. "I don't understand how they select knights. It's bullshit if you ask me."

Not interested in taking the bait but unwilling to pretend he had not noticed, Sol looked back at his slate. "17698, huh? Never seen that on any of the top tens."

The green haired man looked pissed, but Val's voice commandingly returned over them. "Force fields are one of the natural passive defenses of kaffir. It is common to accidentally project one in situations of extreme stress or trauma; this potentially can save one during a fall or help repel a dangerous beast, but it presents some risk to other living beings, which is why we start training very young to control them."

Sol noted with amusement how the normally crisp-speaking young captain had a pronounced Ryzaan accent when he raised his voice.

"I'm going to walk you through generating and breaking fields. If we can do this in a timely fashion, and you all promise to be good boys and not attempt to emulate the tricks you see, the last twenty minutes of the class or so will be devoted to a ma'at-shi demonstration by two certified instructors."

Appreciative whistles peppered with declarations like "All right!" and "Wicked!" rose from the group. The pairs all rushed to face one another in proper stances, eagerly awaiting instructions. Even Kamadji and Solvreyil managed professional postures and bowed to one another.

"Let's do this right, OK? I want to see who gets on the mat with Cap'n V," admitted Kamadji quietly.

Sol nodded. "Agreed."

"You're going to generate a low field in turns; most experienced person goes first. Ready? Go."

The green-locked man exhaled, closed his eyes, and smiled as he clasped his hands lightly. There was nothing visible around him. Sol glanced about a little; he could not see a field around anyone.

"A gentle field does not arc nor burn. Glowing may occur, but that's usually the aesthetic choice of an experienced user. A light field should be invisible in a lit room." Val strode slowly among the pairs, nodding. "Now I want the less experienced members to insert at least one hand into their partner's field."

Sol eyed Kamadji, looked down at his own right hand, and then cautiously held it out. The man's eyes were open now, but his smile remained. The sensation was curious; a cloud of warmth, a palpable aura of inviting kindness. Sol's surprise must have been obvious, as his partner laughed.

"This tactic has been employed to acquire the trust of the ignorant for as long as kaffa have engaged with other life forms. Some humans refer to such emanations, combined with our naturally strong pheromones, as 'the glamour'."

Sol pursed his lips and chose not to correct Val's inaccuracy. In truth, Shandrians and Vasiit had never used their pulse for individual manipulation before learning how from the Ryzaans. The romantic poetry of occupied Eshandir extolled the use of gentle emanations 'for comfort to the ailing, for pleasure in the bed' and that only 'the thorniest of cruel hearts' would purposefully use it otherwise. *He's a good guy most of the time; I can't hate him for being what he is…*

It was Astrum Bacharanzin, a freckly D-7 pilot recently transferred to train as a proper knight, who raised a hand and questioned the statement. He was in the midst of generating a field that – from his partner snuggling blissfully against his chest – was quite entrancing. "Sir, Master Parthenos says only the Ryzaans used it that way in the beginning, sir."

"True. While Shandrians invented pulse cannons and wiped out entire nations, they refused to use their soft fields for unkind acts. I stand corrected and should not represent all kaffir with Ryzaan behavior."

Ouch! Sol winced. *That was a mean set-up.*

"There are many methods to interrupt or dispel a field," Valdieren continued. "To clear one's own, one can simply cease concentrating on it. On fields held long, or generated due to instinctive self-protection, maintaining the force can be automatic. To break these, one needs to program a self-trigger – a vocal or physical command, for example. Or, one can have outside assistance."

Val was right behind Bacharanzin and his partner, who were engaged in a deep tongue kiss. The captain reached into the field and clapped his hands stiffly on Bachi's shoulders. The sudden disturbance caused the ex-pilot's mudlocks to bounce comically. Bachi was startled then sheepish; his partner confused, disappointed, then sharply assumed saluted. "Astrum, keep your make-out sessions to your own time."

"Sir! Yes, sir!"

The captain continued through the crowd. "The best way to do that is to create an opposing force and interfere. In the example just now, I created a minute resistance field by focusing anger into my hands. Bachi's field was strong, but mine was stronger, and I took him by surprise; he might not be able to do the same to me if I chose to resist. Breaking a field when someone is upset can be far more challenging; maintaining a calm and cheerful disposition when a comrade is experiencing discomfort can take serious work." He stopped at the front of the class. "Anyone still holding, please disperse or retract."

A few students uttered strange sounding words or made rapid gestures; most were silent.

"Great. Now I'd like all the newer trainees to generate a light, gentle field of their own and this time, I'd like the experienced partner to feel the radiance and raise their hand if they notice anything out of the ordinary. I want the fields to stay up until I say otherwise regardless of comments."

Sol had never generated a full-body field on purpose. He just learned how to control flow into his arms, and never had to do anything else. Doctor Laathas said contact with the *Sanjeera* was encouraging constant low-grade field generation and was likely responsible for the several visible force clouds he made since being aboard. Even on suppressors, pulse-driven simulators detected his signature and responded immediately. *This is tricky. I don't want to hurt anyone. I'll think about nice stuff, like how cute Ozzie was this morning, and those sexy pictures on Wyvern's office wall... I'll just pretend they belong to someone else.*

Sol closed his eyes and imagined himself into the picture of the lady with ankle-length mudlocks fixing a Cyvax in her underwear. He laughed at it but Wyvern growled, "You have no idea how hot it was in that cave. You'd have been in your underpants, too." The series, according to Hanajiel, was shot by someone in Star Assault, donated to the Academy Annual, and bought by Mobilife and Vektaar Corp for promotional calendars. Only the images with exo hardware could be used, of course, because Star Assault's presence and equipment were classified. While Sol liked the leggy tanker lady best, he drifted to the exceptional gentleman with black and gold mudlocks cleaning and reattaching guns in another image. He reappeared in a later one, pouring water between the breasts of his female team mate, helping himself to some off the skin just below.

Ensconced in his fantasies, only mildly aware of his sultry aura and throbbing erection, Sol barely noticed Kamadji's hand entering his personal space. He fought to maintain the emanation as he realized the inappropriateness of the placement. *Focus, Yen. Don't lose the field. The hand... belongs to... mmm.*

The voice came distantly, slowly closed in. "Astrum Kamadji, your hand is up? What seems amiss?"

"Yes, Captain Valdieren, sir! Astrum Solbry's ass is bony as fuck, sir!"

Had it only been the rude comment or only been a grievous mispronunciation of his family name, Solvreyil Yenraziir might have kept his cozy, inviting energy field. His ire gave it a sudden, painful boost of intensity, blasting Kamadji harshly aside.

The stunned gentleman stumbled and collapsed. "Fuck, that really hurt," he managed to squeak before the captain stood before them, yelling.

"I don't fucking care that it hurt! Get the fuck up and properly address your superiors!"

Kamadji whined from the floor. "But Captain Valdieren, I could have internal injuries, sir!"

"I told you to get the fuck up! Any injuries you have you damn well deserve." Val's arms were crossed. "Everyone, drop your fields and turn your attention here. Any other concerns can be addressed via private sessions later. My afternoon is open after this class. Everyone tuned in? Great." The captain turned to make sure he had all eyes on the three of them. Sol still radiated, staring down Kamadji with a snarl. "Astrum Sovreyu, you are included; disperse your blades."

Sol closed his eyes, pushed anger out of his mind, conjured any image that might make him laugh: swimming bugs, Kiertus's irreverent sense of humor, Laathas' wacky hair, Eek's tale of Hanajiel puking on the Cha'atz general after arriving late to a drill in the port pipes... how Val could not say his name right when he annunciated like his ancestors... The aura diminished and Valdieren continued.

"Everyone in Star Assault –that's everyone, no matter what your rank, path, or specific department – needs to learn to take a hit as well as give. You must be stronger than pain and injury. It is part of who we are. Never fucking forget it."

To Sol's absolute surprise, Val kicked at Kamadji, who still had not stood. The foot did not connect, but Kamadji winced anyway.

"We also are not rapists. We do not molest our team mates without their consent. We have honor. That is what distinguishes the knights of the flag. That is how we select them. Honor. He who does not know it, who shames or wounds his brethren, shall suffer for it."

Sol leaned to help Kamadji up. "No disrespect, captain, but maybe he should go to sick bay, sir."

"I appreciate your concern for compatriots, but there's no need for him to go anywhere."

Just before he heard the voice, Sol was profoundly aware of drug stench. Otherwise he took no notice of the man's approach.

"Hi," Wyvern said creepily over Sol's shoulder.

The boy jumped. "Greetings, Master Wyvern, sir!"

The raspy laugh was unpleasant at best, but it was at least genuine. The wing commander spoke to Kamadji as he modified a setting on his slate. "Hold still while I scan you." Passing the 'reading' end over the torso of the recently-pulsed man, Wyvern shrugged.

"No sign of internal bleeding. Cold pack to the neck now or you won't move well tomorrow." The scraggly blue-black mess on his head flopped unevenly as he dug in a pouch. "Take one of these, every eight hours, until you run out. Just anti-inflammation pills." Wyvern turned to Valdieren. "He'll be fine for regular shifts tomorrow."

"Great, all I wanted to know. Thanks. Wyvern? Care to join me?"

The two men walked back to the center of the demonstration room. Val gestured for the closest folks to step back, then acquired a silky-looking tunic which he slipped over his ladder suit after removing his utility belt. The man sbeside him was dressed similiarly. It was a traditional ma'at-shi garment, although Sol had never seen one this color. It seemed black at first, but when the wearer moved, it scintillated in purples and blues, with a silvery symbol on the back. Captain Valdieren bowed first, then his wild-haired and ragged looking companion bowed as he was introduced.

"This gentleman is Honorable Novum Wyvern. He has a full Archon name but unless you reach my rank or higher, you'll never have a call to pronounce it. If you feel the need to address him by rank, you may use 'Captain' although he is also the Starboard Wing Commander, so you may alternately call him 'Commander' or 'Sentinel'. Astrum genova should address him as 'Master'. He has stars in five spheres and has kindly agreed to join me in demonstrating advanced field techniques."

The trainees looked at one another and the two men. It seemed to Sol they were impressed and startled as he. *That Wyvern guy is all surprises. Doesn't seem he could figure out pants when you just look at him.*

"Before we start, I reiterate: under no circumstances are you to try these techniques unsupervised - "

Slightly behind and to the left of Val, Wyvern held his forearms flat together, hands loosely clasped, half-grinning and lazy fanged, while the other captain addressed the crowd. Before Valdieren could finish the disclaimer, a barely visible tendril of energy snaked from Wyvern's hands and looped about Val's ankles. With a backwards leap and a whipping motion, the wing commander snared and tossed the other man like a rag doll. Some crowdmembers jumped, having paid more attention to Valdieren than the spooky gent behind him; others laughed at the 'oh shit' look on their trainer's face.

Val broke the attachment and rolled to his back, creating a massive rush of force that hurled Wyvern to the ceiling. He realized his mistake and tried to move as Wyvern grinned and braced to launch. The air pressure intensified in their vicinity. Sol touched curiously at the space. *It's like a huge thunderstorm coming in... like...*

The students watched uncomfortably as the prone captain struggled uselessly on the floor, pinned by invisible force. Wyvern propelled himself violently from the ceiling, angling his elbow mid-flight. Viciously, he checked Valdieren in the solar plexus. There was a shower of sparks as their fields converged and canceled. The grunt of pain from the younger, smaller man was audible throughout the room as pressure returned to normal.

The growling animal laugh came quietly, mostly drowned out by groans of "oh man" and "that had to hurt" from the crowd. Wyvern sat straddling his opponent, grinning ear to ear, as Val tapped the floor. The wing commander hopped up gracefully and extended an arm to assist his cohort. When he rose, the symbol on the tunics was visible: the Shandrian rune for 'mercy' flanked by two gen scythes. It was the unit logo of the 17th, the symbol of the *Sanjeera*'s knightly order.

That one isn't in the regular catalog either. Pretty cool. Wonder how you get one?

"We're going to cut this short, unfortunately," Valdieren said with a hint of strain. "Thanks for attending and as I mentioned, I'll be available for one on ones for the rest of the afternoon; just text me." He turned and shook hands with Wyvern, who half-bowed and then leaned over to say something to Val. Sol could only make out Val's reply, which was accompanied by a smile and head shake. "I'm fine, thank you."

Sol waited until everyone filed out to speak to his superiors, which Valdieren informed him to do outside prior to class. He left out the fact Wyvern would be there, of course. The boy bowed at both men. "Thank you for the fascinating demonstration, sirs," he remarked graciously. "I'm not sure which one of you I should follow out of here, though, sirs."

The captains looked at one another and shrugged. "You've stayed on top of your training and been such a good student, Sol," Val said finally as Wyvern nodded in agreement. "Take the rest of the afternoon to yourself, nap, read a book, play with Ozzie, whatever. Laathas has you latere, but you're good until then."

"Wow, sirs, thank you! I really appreciate it!"

Val continued. "Think nothing of it, you deserve it. I'd like to chat with you for a bit but we're walking the same way if you're headed to the nursery."

Wyvern dismissed himself with a bow. Sol followed Valdieren into the hall and they proceeded toward the cruiser's tail. Sol was going to ask a question about the shiny tunics but his slate buzzed loudly. He uttered a confused, "Huh? Apologies, sir, that's my default sound for hangar brass, gotta check."

"A gen threat buzz? Apropos for them. Does it make Ozzie all crazy?"

Sol laughed as he opened the slate. "Yeah, seriously, she gets frantic and makes this baby version of a growl. It's cu-" He froze. "Ack."

"What's the matter? Hanajiel crudely asking you why you aren't cleaning his ship, 'boy'?" The imitation was a little too good.

"No, it's from Wyvern…'I'd love to throw you around like that sometime.' Does he hit on me just to intimidate me, do you think?"

Captain Valdieren rolled his big crimson eyes with a goofy grin. "Told ya: he gets his rocks off putting the fear of Aur into folks. He probably employs overt sexual tactics because he's savant at figuring out what gets to a person best. You could take it as a serious training opportunity; call his bluff. Make him teach you field propulsion. Fuck, if you get shore leave somewhere planet-side with him, ask him to teach you that barometrinesis shit. Training that's prohibited in controlled atmospheres. I can't quite master it but I bet you could. He's tough to train with because he's ace at simultaneous tricks; his distribution efficiency is mind-blowing. Just what you need."

It was certainly a thought, albeit scary one. "I'm honored you think of me that highly, captain. I hope I live up to your expectations."

"I'm sure you'll exceed them. I'm going to visit Kiertus before my meetings start and get him to watch the security footage from the demo room. I want him to see you owning Kamadji." Val waved cheerfully as he bounded off, leaving Sol with an impatiently hopping Ozlietsin. The captain called back before he was out of ear shot, "Meet me in the o-lounge after your last shift, astrum!"

"What's that? Who'd you trounce? I gotta see that vid, too."

"Hi, Chel. Just some lippy grunt from my training group. It was stupid, I didn't mean to, but… he kinda asked for it. Was she good today?" Sol hoisted Ozzie from the floor and held her as she made excited noises and licked his face.

"Pretty good. Minerva lets her ride her around; I think it helps keep her out of trouble… I do break them up so Oz gets proper exercise." The bug sarge coughed and quietly admitted. "I took some pictures. Almost posted 'em to Bug Funnies on SACNet but they should be in your inbox, you can do it yourself."

"Sir, I was wondering if you had some time. I want to ask you about the way ships are named in our branch… Val said…"

Cheldyne's expression drooped from friendly to sad. "If you wish, come into my office and we'll talk philosophy where there are clean eye-blotting rags. Do not blame me if you do not sleep tonight."

…

The one person in the lounge other than Val was Pherrinai, mouthing silently to headphones plugged into his slate as he moved puzzle pieces about a table. Several officers had collaborated on the fancy jigsaw for the past week. Slowly Sol watched the image develop from piles of colored pieces to a gorgeous city built into living rock and coral, heavily surrounded in foliage, which might have only looked like landscape to the untrained eye. *It's the Stone Steppes of Vyeshaal. Used to be the capitol city of Eshandir. I want to see it in person some day. Mom will see it first. I hope she likes it.*

"How are you? You look kinda bummed, Sol." The captain snacked from a bag of curry crisps. He offered some to the boy. "I know, kinda hard on a guy's guts, but so tasty. So glad you guys restocked tonight. Needed some sodium."

It was pharmacy staff's province to restock the snack machines for the rear of the ship. It was not a huge task, there were only four – two in the officers lounge, one in the waiting and recovery area of medical, and one by the access ladder to the engineers' section. "You're welcome. I love that job, free snacks." Sol sat across from his trainer. "Chel lectured me on the principles of divine atonement and retribution earlier. Occasionally, my heritage is grim. I feel pride, mind you, to be part of that tradition. Just. Grim."

"Mmm. 'Physicians of the universe', that lecture? I prefer it from Parthenos, but I could see why you went to Chel instead." He set down the crisps and wiped his hands on a towel on his belt. Squeak raised her head from the floor beside him and complained; he let her lick them. "Better? I have a feeling we'll both pay for that, but suit yourself, bug. Sadly you just missed something I think would have cheered you up. Funniest thing that happens regularly up here."

"Oh?"

"Wyvern bathing. He was out of the pool a square minute before you left."

Sol blinked, incapable of picturing anything but Wyvern standing in a frothing, foul pool while bugs hissed and ran. "I didn't pass him in the hall, are you pulling my ears?"

"No, dead serious. He works five days on, three days off or so, washes at the end of the work week and coops himself up in secrecy for the weekend. People who've been in SA a while develop eccentricities, just happens, can't even call it strange. Yeah you didn't see him because he can generate an inverted mirror field, basically erases everything in his immediate surroundings from view if you don't know what to look for… a lot of guys can do that with sound, but he can do it optically and olfactorily, too."

I didn't need to hear that. "Quit fucking with me! That spooky fucker does not make himself invisible."

"What if he was standing here right now? You might hurt his feelings, calling him names." Val smirked.

Looking around, more creeped out than ever, Sol sought any difference or interference in his environment. Hair rose on the back of his neck. He felt something brush his arm, a strange but non-threatening heat, and then noticed vibration that glided away without a sound. Ozzie, who had been asleep in her sling on his back, awoke and cooed. She wrestled from the contraption and followed the motion towards the door, trailing her little blanket behind. "Ozzie! Come back here!"

She stopped at the door, looked about, made a dejected, tiny trill and trotted back to Sol, stopping only to retrieve her blanket with her mouth when it fell.

"Told you. He's good at lots of things. He can even move along ceilings on his hands like a ship sprite. His call sign is some legendary monster from the folklore of Kiertus' home… a flying creature, giant sea bat sort of thing, whose wings cause storms, whose effluvium poisons rivers."

Fuck sleep; I am unsure I will ever masturbate again. "Why'd you ask me to meet you tonight, sir?"

"To let you know your progress has been so excellent that we won Parthenos' contest a few days early, Sol. No team could possibly catch up to your scores. You can have a whole three days of free time except for whatever you're doing with Laathas or Chel, and I'll see you with the rest of the crew at the briefing. I would like you to study the armor manual and do the little quizzes at the ends of the first 5 chapters. I sent you something from the Silver Sphere Handbook, about tactics for distribution control; that comes with a quiz, too. But I'm sure you can do all that over a couple cups of coffee some morning. Dismissed!"

Proud and relieved, Sol convinced Ozzie to quit chewing Squeak's feet (an act the older bug slept through undisturbed) and follow him out. He nearly sang, he was so thrilled about his break from intensive combat training. "I'm gonna read that book the colonel loaned me. I promise we'll play a lot too! We'll go up to the observation deck and -"

His slate buzzed. He cringed as Ozzie ran under his feet and howl-barked in either direction at invisible angry bugs. The text, from Wyvern, read

::: I'm not offended, but you don't personally know what kind of 'fucker' I am. Yet. 'Night. :::

....

He's right... it's big and empty and dark... all that emptiness, just gets you lost in your own head. When ships couldn't jump did my ancestors just go insane? Sol stared out the observation window while Ozzie slept on a small ledge that seemed provided for the purpose. *The colonel showed me how we move through unpopulated parts of space on runs like this; if we get too close to a ship or a habited moon or anything, it could be considered a hostile act. Suppose that nervousness is justifiable. Wonder what it's like to fire one of the big cannons, to incinerate an entire space port in a single shot?*

He was completely absorbed in the vast void and failed to notice stealthy movements to his rear. When the fingers jabbed between the half-laced sides of his ladder shirt and into his bony ribs, Sol jumped and emitted a thorny blast that tossed Astrum Bacharanzin backwards. Only low gravity spared the snickering ginger further bruises.

"Fucking hell! What is wrong with you, Bachi?"

Freckly cheeks showed evidence of a massive grin beneath skewed locks. "I would answer that, but I don't even know where to start."

"What are you doing up here, anyway? I thought you were hanging with big P tonight." Sol squatted down next to Bacharanzin rather than help him back up.

"Eh. Someone special came in; he tossed me out for a meeting. 'Nuttin' personal, dude.'" He scooped the locks from his countenance, still amused, although the tone became harder and sarcastic. "Being astrum to the big brass fuckin' sucks sometimes. But I know you know that."

Sol shrugged a little sadly as he let himself settle against the wall. "Yeah. Kiertus keeps canceling what are supposed to be our regular meetings. What do you mean by 'someone special'? Does this have to do with the ship I saw headed towards the aft pipes?"

"Oh, you saw a ship? What kind?"

"Like a Dash, but longer and pointier. It was that shiny color shifting black –
what's that called? I know there's a name for it. You did some visual arts in
school, right?"

"Oilburn, or oil indigo. 'Vektaar black' is the common trade name for tube
pigment that resembles it. 'Imperial black' or 'Imperial indigo' if you don't have
the licensing rights." Bachi fished a silver flask from his belt. It was decorated
with the Haarvakja. As he flipped the straw lid, he stared at the ceiling. "I know
so much useless shit."

"I dunno, I think that kinda stuff is cool. Nice flask. Is that from the catalog?"

"Probably. Parthenos is letting me borrow it because he has nicer one." After
drinking, he handed it to Sol. "So, you say it looked like a Dash. You sure it
wasn't a Razor?"

Sol did not look up from the flask; he traced the harsh edges of the intricately
inlaid symbol. The artisan-crafted object showed signs of age, resembling an
antique more than something recently made. "Naw, I know what a Razor looks
like. I built kit ones from each era as a kid. Never seen anything like this."

"Probably an 'Infiltrator'. They start life from the factory as Dash or D-7 but
before they get woken up, they're taken to Fenrir or Uayavu and modified by
Star Assault bio-techs. They're high end private armored vehicles for the elite,
really. Well, as private a vehicle as anyone in the military can have. A couple
guys in every SA unit and some Guild guys have 'em. Combat functional status
symbols. You gonna drink that?"

"Uh, I dunno, it smells like flamethrower agent mixed with medicine."

Bacharanzin laughed and took the flask back. "Suit yourself. It kind of is." He
looked unusually thoughtful. "What are you doing up here, anyway?"

Thinking about my mother, mostly, but I am not telling you that. "Waiting for
Cheldyne. He's the only person I could find who wasn't doing something else
already tonight."

"Huh. Infiltrator in the aft and Chel free? That narrows our options for who's visiting the Sanj tonight. Could you pick out any details on the tail of it, because I know some of 'em from workin'-"

"Quit talkin' shit, astrum."

A big hand swiped the flask from a startled Bachi. Sol kept his laughter quiet and flipped a small salute.

"Evening, sarge."

Cheldyne took a deep swig before responding. "What've I told you about that formal bullshit when I'm out of uniform?" Displaying impressive nimbleness for his size and age, Cheldyne folded his legs in the air and descended slowly to the floor.

I know he's a vet of this unit, but the fact he can use ma'at-shi tricks kinda blows my mind. He had to get to the position he's got somehow, I guess. "Sorry, man. I just feel weird calling you a detergent…"

Bacharanzin laughed and got an intolerant stare. Cheldyne whistled and his burly bug, Curlotta, trotted up, bearing a furiously protesting little gen gently with her mouth. Curly dropped the flailing Rocket rather unceremoniously in Bachi's direction and mimicked the dreadful look from her bond.

"Go play with your bug, astrum," the hive sentinel said, gruffly.

Perturbation graced his face momentarily, then dejection as he gathered Rocket in his arms and looked down at her. His voice was quiet. "That's the same thing Parth said…"

"If your knight master said it, you should probably treat it like an order, kid."

"Yes, sir. See ya later, Sol."

They watched him leave. Chel turned apologetically to his young friend. "I hope I didn't just ruin your evening. If you'd prefer to hang out with someone closer to your age, grab Ozzie and follow him."

117

"That's OK. I can only deal with him in small doses. I'm trying to raise my tolerance, but uh… yeah."

"Fair enough." Cheldyne regarded the flask. "Who'd he fuckin' steal this from? It looks like Wyvern's."

"He said it was his master's."

The eye roll could not be missed. "Yeah. Auri pinched it from Wy during a briefing to prove a point quite a few years back. Never returned it. Once a year Wy posts it to the 'lost and found' forum to subtly remind that it still belongs to him. Him and Auri don't talk unless they strictly have to for professional reasons. Bad blood there. This is his, I know it; I recognize it from the stone inlay and dent." Cheldyne tapped a mark part way down the container. "Man, *I* don't even want to get caught with this. Would you return it to his office? Auri sets that kid up something fierce. I understand his teaching style, but it makes my skin crawl sometimes."

Sol took the vessel as if it were a sacred artifact. *What a dick move, although I'm not sure if it's shittier towards Bachi or Wyvern. Using your own astrum to taunt your enemy? That's just all around assholishness. Wait, they're enemies? Really? I'd assumed they'd get along.*

"What's up, kid?"

"Sorry, I keep… I think the drugs… make me think too much. I keep finding patterns in stuff and stumbling into my brain and running around in circles…"

The hive sentinel leaned towards Sol's shoulder, whispering, "You need more porn. It helps."

"Are you fucking with me?"

The well-worn face beamed. "Nothin' like your dick to help ya focus!"

Sol sighed and shook his head. "Aren't we like, um, monks?"

"Elvish monks fuck. One another, mostly. You only take a vow of celibacy when you're doing the really fancy Order of Maalek stuff or like, one branch of the Order of Aur. There are specific exception conditions for certain clearances if you have a conditional 'silence' vow, too, but pretty sure they all still get to masturbate." Chel waved a hand. "You're too young for that nosedive. You should be at least thinking about sweaty sack sports a few times a day if not actively pursuing them."

"I dunno, I think I might be too young for the latter. I'm still kinda freaked out by the pictures from the Whole Body Health textbook!" Sol would have been too embarrassed to admit this to other members of the unit. "Not the skin pics, I like pin-ups, and the idea of some stuff, but like, penetrative sex. Some of it looks… painful?"

Greyed brows knitted over sad, strange eyes. "I'm going to have a talk with your master."

Huh? What's he mean by that? He said that so oddly. I'm changing the subject before this gets any more uncomfortable. "You've been in this branch a long time, right?"

"Yup."

"OK, so, call signs are earned after your first risk encounter, right? Well how do the lady members of the branch get them, since they don't usually come on the ships?"

"Depends on the soldier. Some of 'em, like Salda and Nabaragi, were in hard combat units prior to joining and get a 'buy' that way. Not everyone, though. Some have to do ops shit, do a mission only a female can do - rough stuff, usually, harder in a lot of ways than what we have to do… you'll know one of those when you meet one. A woman with a call sign in Star Assault always earned it, though. Respect 'em." Chel regarded him seriously. "Enkashen at Todekki is a full-bore knight, jumper and everything; they happen, they're just rare. It's not that they're barred from the ships. Female bugs get violently territorial; to be a ship-side lady means getting along with the hive alpha. That's tough. Mixed crew ships like the Medderaxus class, hive is separate, only approved gen can leave that section."

"Wow. OK. Thank you." Sol watched Ozzie sleep on the ledge as he thought. "Do you know how Glimmer got hers?"

The older man's smile was peculiar. "You got a crush on her or somethin'? Hey, it's cool, I won't tease ya." Chel scruffed the boy's red mess. "She was stationed with a unit of ground at Pachar during the first revolt, got stuck on 'our' side when shit broke out, was partying at the SA bar there. She couldn't stand watching innocent people get hurt and just jumped in working with our detachment; ended up being one of the hands that put an end to it. We hired her on the spot; she agreed to give up the chance to have a baby of her own if it meant she was working to save lives and prevent future tragedies like that one. She's been nothing but an asset since."

"My... my dad... I think that was the fight he died in... Maybe she –"

"Whoa, kid. Don't even think about bringin' that kinda stuff up to Onzillora, you hear me?"

"Why not? I just - I just want to know..." Sol stared at the floor.

"I know, kid, I know, I hear you. Just, sometimes, memories need to stay in the past. Some things are better off staying unknown." A big hand rubbed Sol's shoulder; he did not lift his head as Chel continued. "You need closure, I get that. I would strongly discourage you from using her as your avenue for that purpose. There are better people and places to go to know what you want."

"You know something don't you? Chel, please tell me..."

"Sol, I'm really sorry, but I –"

The all-call alarm blazed over the public address system. Both men twitched and stared upward as Ozzie woke and squawked at the wall. "Paratrooper units to C Briefing. All paratrooper units to C Briefing. This is a mandatory meeting by order of Major Parthenos. Repeat. Paratroopers to C Briefing."

"Fuck!" Sol leapt to his feet, wiping the mist of welling tears from his eyes. "Timing for shit! It's the middle of the night!"

"Combat doesn't wait for suns to rise, neither does the major." Chel remained on the floor, hitting his own flask as Sol checked his belongings and began to run. "Do you know how to get to starboard pipes from here fast? You should probably ditch that thing before the briefing."

"Good point," the astrum called back. "Thanks."

"I'll watch Ozzie for you! Good luck!"

....

Little impeded his progress to the hangar. He shot down the half-way rungs and down a vent shaft right into the bay. Iekierpin had taught this 'expedited' route to the pipes to increase speed for drills. Most of the pilots slept closer to the area, but in the event they were hanging out with other crew or just up on the observation decks when a dogfight situation occurred, speed would be essential.

The men working on craft or sitting about the 'rest zones' in the hangar paid him no mind as he ran to Wyvern's office. As usual, the door was open.

It's his weekend. I'm safe to not see him. I'll just set this - As Sol attempted to lay the flask on the desk, a force caught it; it would not descend. Warmth filled his immediate space but terror flashed across his heart. He released the flask, bowed, and ran back out, taking a short cut toward C Briefing. In the last leg of the race, he received a text message.

::: Won't ask how you did it. Appreciate having it back. They don't make them like this anymore. Special edition. He's fortunate I'm not one for petty revenge. Thanks.:::

Other troopers ran by as he slowed to read the message. *All things considered, he's pretty classy for a poison-spitting monster. If I weren't such a wuss, I'd make an ally of him. I think I need one.*

Sol braced himself and addressed the marshal to enter. Nothing good could possibly come of a session this suddenly announced, especially one that Parthenos had broken another meeting to call.

IV. A Question of Salvation

At first she thought people were working on the derelict motor carriage that had been parked on the curb for two days, but gradually Celita realized they were stripping any and all items that could be removed from its broken husk. Years prior, long before she sold her private vehicle and begun to take the monorail, she most certainly would have called civic enforcement. Clearly, none of these people owned this or any car; they were stealing, they were salvaging anything they could for resale to get something to eat. Celita stroked the holy pendant at her throat and prayed for the starving and the sick.

These days, with Vittair still gone and rent becoming increasingly difficult to cover, she had abandoned the monorail for the creeper tram, a cheap, rickety train that ran in the old dhol tunnel and through the worst neighborhoods. She cringed at first, rubbing shoulders with the filthy, coughing crowds, the crying snot-faced children, the old ladies on crutches talking to themselves... but now she just kept her eyes to herself, wore her mask, and prayed. It was all she could do.

Thinking of old ladies made her wonder about the woman with the bandaged hands she usually saw walking from the station, to whom she had given her breakfast a few days prior. Unable to afford her birth control drugs meant her cycle started with a cruel frenzy and she could not even smell a savory biscuit much less ride the train without becoming quite ill. About to toss the bag of food, Celita noticed the half-blind beggar woman, always there with her bandages and a battered tin box. Sometimes the woman would sing, and while not always perfect in key, her voice was pretty and her songs were poignant. Bravely, Celita approached and quietly offered her the bag, afraid of offending her, even though she was sitting outside a train station in rags pleading for help. Gratefully, she accepted Celita's breakfast, blessing her in an archaic manner as she did so. It was then Celita looked into the beggar's eyes and realized she had vertical pupils. *Elvish descent. Probably kaffir. The poor woman, cursed by birth with a devil's blood. Why should she suffer, though? Why should anyone?*

Today, however, the woman and her sign – "Homeless and Hungry, Please Help, Bless You" – were gone without a trace. Likewise the man with no legs who pushed himself about on a service trolley and muttered lewd things constantly, and the man with one arm and one eye and slight points to his ears who could not speak, only shook a cup quietly; all were absent. There was someone there outside the station, someone new, a younger woman – a girl, really - in mis-matched, patched, dirty clothing, on her knees praying, a small blanket before her, things on it. *She will be arrested soon, vending isn't allowed on this side of the station... poor dear, she's so young; where are her parents?*

Celita wanted to imagine that someone came along and taken the three familiar faces to a shelter, but she knew in reality the shelters that remained open had been over-crowded for years, and the shelters on this side of the city were distinctly unfriendly to people of elvish descent. She found tears on her face and blamed her period, but something else was not sitting well. For the first time in her life, she doubted the Theocracy, she doubted her faith, she doubted everything.

Seeing Gaelle had probably been a bad idea, but Celita's life had been such a confusing uproar these past five months that she grasped for any familiarity in reach. She had not seen Gaelle since just after graduation, when she agreed to the proposal of Honsad Vittair. Gaelle, a kind and peaceful but irreligious person on the best of days, disliked that Vittair worked for Defense Ministry, a political body of the Great Church that she – and other pacifists of her ilk – accused of inciting hostility from the Archon Empire. Worse, Gaelle's more conspiratorial allegations included the Ministry among those who sponsored 'genetic investigation' of private citizens. Supposedly, a secret faction in the group worked on a long-term ethnic cleansing program; they wished to rid Kourhos and eventually Verraken of every trace of elvish blood. The idea made Celita extremely uncomfortable because it could be backed up with scripture; 'there is no salvation for the devil-blood in their veins. Their only salvation is Death.'

At their tea meeting recently, Gaelle avoided such dismal topics. She kept things light and friendly for the most part – obviously, Gaelle could tell Celita was going through enough as it was, with her husband not coming home and money being so tight. She told stories, mostly, about her new friends from the Universal Peace group. Some of these men had visited places inside the Archon Empire and returned to regale their club gatherings with utterly fantastic stories regarding the way kaffir and humans lived together, women earned as much or more than men, people only got married and shared finances if they were going to bear children together, and even wilder, more sinful or confusing practices.

"You should come to a meeting some time, Celie. It's not like we ask you to quit the Church to just attend. We welcome everyone," Gaelle informed, delicately folding the paper place mat into an elaborate little creature. "I learned this from an Archon book, this is a Shandrian practice, although their paper is better than ours for it. Then again, their paper is made in consideration of the environment, too, everything is. Archon society is so efficient. People can walk around in the streets on Holtiin without breathing masks, that's what Mo said, no masks, no gloves, unless you're sick and afraid of spreading it, and you can drink water from the rivers, and swim in them. Can you imagine?"

But you live with elves, and all the 'machines' are living animals. The train you take to work is a giant worm. Everyone regardless of gender has to serve two years in the military! And religion is against the law! Even if the stories of kaffir eating humans are all myths, that's just insane. How could any human live like that?

"Honsad Celita?"

Snapped from her thoughts, Celita turned to the man who entered the room. She released the pendant she had been nervously caressing, brushed her hands on her dress, and extended her right hand for a brisk shake. "Oh, yes! Apologies. You must be Koener Toemes?"

The smile, perfect straight white teeth, no gaps, damage, crowns, or fangs, could have stopped a freighter. His grip was strong and warm. "Yes, ma'am."

Celita could see now why the other girls in the administrative office of the Ministry of Communication giggled and nudged one another when this gentleman's name came up. He was square-jawed and high cheekboned, with a gorgeous olive complexion and raven hair. He looked surprisingly young; she had been expecting someone closer to fifty and Mr. Koener was clearly not far from thirty. His clothes were immaculate, stylish, and high-end. He was so stylish, in fact, that if he did not seem quite so "together", she would have filed his mode of dress as "unprofessional".

"Please have a seat, Mrs. Honsad." Koener gestured to an open chair and then sat on the edge of the meeting table. "You already have a fairly good job, really one of the best a woman can get in this day and age. Would you care to tell me why it is you'd prefer the opening in my department?"

"The hours are intimidating, Mr. Koener, I'll be honest with you, but the pay scale is better, and I ..." Celita choked a little. She glanced at the floor and tried not to obviously wring her hands in the folds of her dress. "My husband has been away for almost three months. I am having trouble making ends meet. I had to sell my car and am trying to move into a smaller apartment, but at my current wages, with no one else to sign the lease, moving is very difficult..."

His face was sympathetic. "Ah. I see." The words hung in the air a moment. "What kind of a man leaves his beautiful young wife alone during such difficult times?"

"Sir, please be fair. Vittair is a good man; he has never been anything but kind to me. He works for the Ministry of Defense, and he just was promoted, you see, and he went on ... on a business trip... I called them, I tried to ... to contact him through them... they keep telling me he cannot be reached. His bank account is still open... but no paychecks have come into it since..." Saying it aloud was too much; the tears came now. Celita turned her moist eyes to the floor. "Apologies. I..."

Koener Toemes was standing now, his hand on her shoulder. He handed her a soft cloth from his pocket. "There is nothing for which to apologize, Mrs.

Honsad. I understand."

She gently wiped her tears before looking up at the kindly face. "Are you married, Mr. Koener?"

"No, ma'am. My career has always come first; I could not put anyone I cared for second to my work, it would be unfair to her, so I keep my interests to myself and have a rather lonely life. What I am doing is important, though, so I have that." He gestured that she should hang on to the handkerchief when she offered it back to him. "Please call me 'Toemes'."

Celita watched him walk to the window where she stood when he first entered. He stared at the miserable, polluted sky and then down at the back side of the tram station, just as she had. Koener's expression was thoughtfully sad as he returned to the interview.

"Why did you choose to learn Archon in school?"

"I was young and idealistic. I wished to bring the word of God to the kaffir. This was before I discovered that preaching is a criminal offense and I would be jailed if I did such a thing in Imperial space."

"Jailed? Oh no, they don't believe in prisons. I believe the current statute involves a few years mining on an inhospitable rock somewhere for trying to save souls." Koener looked back at the clouds, at the gouts of unpleasant smoke from the last open refinery in Tukodok. "The irony, of course, is that elves have no souls to save."

He turned now, the smile on his face grimly sarcastic, as toxic as the billowing filth beyond the glass.

"Your gender is less important to me than your ability and desire to do the job. If you really think you can handle the hours, I am sure I can find a place for you, Mrs. Honsad."

V. Major Issues

"Evening, gents. Hate to cut into cards night like this; folks who aren't entirely sober please pick a buddy to re-brief you when you're stabilized." Parthenos was tense underneath his fairly casual tone. "Hurry up and sort it out, I'll wait but not long."

There was shuffling, grabbing, and nodding among the crowd. Sol noted that about half the unit was undressed, probably because they had stripped from casual clothes to be appropriate for the meeting, but the rest were in full armor and standing sternly at attention. He felt a nudge from behind; it was Aukaldir, winking drunkenly. A finger poked slightly to the right of his spine, just below his ribs.

Sol turned fully about in hopes of eliminating the somewhat irritating sensation. "Want me to brief you when you sober up from chugging my stolen liquor, sir?"

"I could order you to, you know," slurred the lieutenant, jabbing a finger in and out between the loose lacing of Sol's ladder shirt. "I'll give ya my cheesh bishcuits. Feelsh like you needsh 'em. Nuffin here…"

"Fine. Stop poking me though, sir, or I'll pulse you dry."

Aukaldir's hands went up with a sloppy grin. "Aye aye, ashtrum."

"A'right, troops. Listen up." Parthenos crossed his arms over his chest. Although he was in ladder leggings, he was hardly in uniform. His feet were in moccasin boots and the soft, faded sweater he wore was far too small for his mass. It was stretched thin over his biceps and broad chest and rode a few inches above the waistline of his trousers. A shadow indicated where hair had been removed from the firm abs; an inverted 'v' descended into the tightly fitting ladders and Sol found himself annoyed that he was wondering if the major let it grow out in his off months, and if it was soft...

Fucking asshole is pornographically sexy. It makes me want to punch him in the junk. Dear creator, please let me be even half that hot when I am grown up, no fair making me a bony little red thing, could I at least have some of my dad's genetics other than the high tension syndrome? Thanks.

"We are making another route change due to recently received intelligence. Due to the lack of staff and the subsequent shortage of fuel, we are currently soaring to conserve our reserves. In the next day we'll be back in contested space; a few days after that we will very briefly be in Ilu territory, which we will be jumping out of but only when we reach the optimum location. We'll be arriving at Mengheri Gate and have a stop at Todekki. Unfortunately I can release very few of you to shore leave at this time, but we'll get back to that."

The grumbling from the crowd ceased with a harsh glare and a pronounced cough from Major Parthenos.

"Then we're headed to Kourhos, without a stop at Pachar. There are two sign up sheets with Sentinel Drenjiis in the hall; one is for auxillary coaches and mentors. Officers above lieutenant who do not already have a full workload need to sign up on that one. That's 'need'. If you do not sign up to it please send me your revised schedules with new shifts you picked up – I can tell from the virtual time clock that a bunch of you didn't bother doing that already." He rather pointedly looked over Sol at Aukaldir then returned to his pacing. "Obviously we'll have new recruits from Todekki. Most of these men are already officers of the air squad or base defense and all they'll need is to be familiarized with our cruiser.

"Among these men is Captain Enkashen Liekke, and if you treat her as anything other than an untouchable goddess, I will personally take a layer of skin off your ass before I send you to the 89th for a lesson in non-consensual initiatory practices."

It was as if the threat sucked the breath from all present; the only sounds were those produced by the ship's functions. *Huh… They must be friends. Maybe very special friends? I will admit he's attractive when he isn't angry, but what kinda crazy woman would date this fanged shit-spitter?*

"The other sign-up sheet is for back-up on emergency rescue missions. Anyone can sign up to this one; I'll be selecting the most qualified applicants as needed. Are there any questions?"

The man who raised his hand was a captain, fully armored save for a mask and goggles. His face was unfamiliar to Sol. "Major, are we violating our non-intervention policy with the Theocracy, sir?"

"Not exactly, Myshkor. It seems that some double-crossing bastard from our side sold one of the anti-Theocratic groups some of our weaponry." His gaze moved to Sol this time, and it was far from pleasant.

What the... why is he looking at me like that? What did I do?

"Our intelligence reports a number of potential terrorist attacks which we may be able to prevent. I've already sent a few people ahead to work on that. If we can't prevent them, we can at least show up and offer help after the fact so it's clear these attacks were not condoned by the Empire. It's not like we love the Theocracy, but the situation could do a number on our current negotiations with the Universal Peace and Liberty parties."

"Got it, sir. Thanks, sir." Myshkor saluted.

Parthenos nodded slightly and half saluted; his mannerisms were inappropriately casual but his voice retained its commanding edge. "That all said, due to the extreme risk of where we're flying, minimize recreational drug use during off-hours until further notice. Feel free to party it up tonight once this briefing is over; last hurrahs and all. It is absolutely essential we keep the current training trend rolling.

"Speaking of training, I've been pretty impressed by the progress of a lot of your teams. I'd like to congratulate Captain Myskhor and his team for holding the most top ten spots of any non-disqualified group." Parthenos held his hands behind his back as he paced, arching his spine a little, emphasizing the shapely firmness of his torso. Slight flexing caused an audible cracking sound; a tiny smile graced his lips. He now seemed far more interested in his physical body than in what he was saying. Dismissively, he added, "Captain Valdieren's team has been completely disqualified for cheating, however."

Noises of surprise rose from the assembly. Parthenos stopped directly in front of the clearly confused Valdieren to stare him down. Sol noted the major's pupils were vastly enlarged for the lighting in the audience hall. The glower was fierce but the tone remained distant and casual.

"Captain Valdieren Karshimziel, would you care to explain what happens when you put an individual with high tension syndrome in a high calibrated sim unit?"

The captain tensed, gritted his teeth, and clenched his fists at his sides until his knuckles went white. "Sir. Yes, sir. The continuous emittance from the individual can unbalance the scoring mechanism, sir."

Lids half closed over huge dark eyes. Parthenos' voice lowered with the gaze; had the room been anything but frozen in silence, it would have been inaudible to all but Val and Sol. "Correct. If I thought for one second you had done it on purpose, I'd rip that bat off your chest, bend you over right here, and ball your ass until you prolapsed. Going sheerly on the accuracy numbers and ignoring the output ratings, your team would have come in second. However, I refuse to reward you for failing to train lil Red here. Don't let this leniency fool you; I am seriously pissed off right now."

Val responded woodenly: "Sir, yes sir," as the major turned to pace again.

"In case the other members of Valdieren's team think they're being made to suffer unfairly, let me kindly remind you that any of you could have stepped up and pointed out the error in judgment. As a team, you are all responsible to one another. The blame rests equally on all; before you find fault in another member of your group, look first at yourself." Major Parthenos stopped in front of Sol and wheeled sharply to face him. "Problem individuals are my responsibility."

Apprehensive nausea came over him followed by a curious tingling as he distinctly caught the subtle fragrance of vyddarin in Parthenos' sweat. Alluring warmth spilled from the major in direct contrast to his current demeanor. Laathas had explained that a mix of synthensin and vyddarin without the other additives to make a pilot's 'jump drugs' was frequently employed as a sexual enhancement cocktail. *I should not be hard right now. I should fear for my life. The last thing I should be thinking about is tearing off that sweater and –*

"Astrum Solvreyil, your reliance on tricks and accidents is in need of extreme correction."

"Yes sir, Major Parthenos, sir!" *My erection is in need of extreme action, Major Bastard Asshole, sir.*

"You are to meet me at 20:00 tomorrow in Sim 1. Take your shots, including a full suppression dosage, precisely three hours prior. Come in full uniform. Anyone who is off-duty is welcome to bear witness."

Come in my uniform? No problem Already there. "Sir! Yes, sir!"

"Everyone else, keep that training up. You're dismissed except Captain Valdieren." Parthenos saluted with a flourish and waited as they filed out.

Val turned to Sol. "Astrum, I realize 'sorry' isn't going to help. I failed you."

"No. You don't know what you're doing, sir, I can't blame you at all. I'm not your astrum, I'm a trainee you're stuck with," Sol shrugged.

"I don't have an excuse for doing this shitty of a job. I volunteered you on to my team. I'll fix this if I'm not too late. I only just realized how remedial your -" He gritted his teeth as a cough came from behind Sol. Both men looked towards it.

The major leaned on the wall near the door, a sultry expression on his face, gesturing slowly with his finger. His unusually quiet voice had a sarcastic drawl. "Come on, Karshi. Haven't got all night…"

Val saluted with a look of grim acceptance. "Honor and sacrifice, man. Later."

As he stepped into the hall, Sol wondered what was going to happen, between Parthenos and Val as much as between Parthenos and himself the following day. He noticed Bacharanzin standing pensively near the door. "Sorry about fucking things up for the group…"

Bachi waved his hand. "Nah, it was on all of us. Kamadji and I both got private congratulations for our high scores from the major. We just aren't going to get any group commendation or prizes or anything."

"Why do you look so pissed off then?"

The other astrum made a stifled grunt and stared at the floor, shuffling a bit. "Just… 'cause."

What the hell? "Was it just me or was the major on a boat load of drugs?"

"Yeah, he handles them so well. I couldn't give a serious briefing on all that. That's why he's one of the guys in charge, though, right?" Bachi grinned a little as he looked up. "You're right. I shouldn't be pissed. His night got fucked up too. He could have been way more of a jerk about taking that out on us."

Sol turned his slate back on. He snorted sardonically. "Easy for you to say. I think I'm going to get beaten into cake batter after he sobers up!"

"Hey it could be fun. And think of it this way – you'll be getting a hands-on ma'at-shi lesson from one of the best instructors in the Imperial military!"

"Great, a celebrity ass kicking! Just what I always wanted." He rolled his eyes and shook his head then uttered a not entirely voluntary, "Oh, crap," as he read.

"What's wrong?"

"Chel canceled on me during the briefing. Got pulled into the meeting I guess, going to run late or something. Lame. Maybe I'll just go to bed." Sol started walking toward his coccoon, as Cheldyne mentioned he put Ozzie to bed on his way to the colonel's office.

Bachi followed. "Huh. Maybe I was wrong about whose Infiltrator that is… Jady's probably back. That could be really cool… it would mean some duties would shift and both our knight masters would have more free time."

"I suppose if I survive Major Punishment tomorrow I'll finally get some training from Kiertus." The thought provided some relief. Sol continued to read his messages – mostly they were information from Parthenos to accompany the briefing. "I'm working the first shift in the hive tomorrow. Want to race bugs on my break?"

"I'll put a pack of cheese biscuits and half my liquor ration on Rocket!"

"Deal." Mixed in with the messages was a private transmission from Wyvern. It was in Shandrian; a simple and familiar bit of poetry which Sol only recently realized was a prayer.

"In this cold darkness we have fallen; despair not; the Broken Sun lives within me. Let my companions find comfort in my warmth; let my soul find wings in the blackness; let the star residue of my blood light our way to victory."

"Bachi? How do you close a prayer or invocation in Shandrian?"

"Huh? Um, oh. If it's to Maalek, you say 'faith' or 'glory' and clasp the hand of the person you're praying with or if you're alone you hold your hands together like this? If you are invoking Leviathan, you bow, and you say, 'Kaajya', which I think is 'freedom', sort of? I think you're supposed to do it in the direction of the nearest ocean or volcano or something; if you're on a ship you're supposed to do it facing the ioun core. And don't ask me about Aur, I haven't the foggiest. They're weirdos, all secret rites and shit... why?"

He said that like it was self-explanatory, like I should already know. Clearly I have some reading to do. "Mm. No real reason. See you at the races."

...

He slept poorly, tormented by anxious nightmares and a periodically flailing bug, so when Sol's slate buzzed far too early, he assumed it was his alarm and smacked at it blindly with his palm. Ozzie's warning bark gave him pause, and he fumbled it towards his pillow to read the message.

:::Switch to hangars when your hive shift would normally start. Serum permission already given. Need extra hand on emerg jet prep:::

"Shit, of course." Sol dragged his ladders out from under a snapping Ozlietsin. "We could need the fighters at a moment's notice. I guess honey and wax take a back seat, right girl?"

The gen chirped affirmatively.

"I'll drop you at the hive. Not going to sleep more so might as well get started."

Chel was in his office, amazingly awake and huddled with his laptop, albeit in an open robe that displayed his scarred, tattooed torso and his substantial, not remotely regulation gut. "What's wrong with you this morning, kid? You look like you're on your way to a funeral."

"Yeah, mine possibly." Sol sighed. "Parthenos is going to kick my ass."

"He is the ship's disciplinary officer, it's his job. Do you feel it's deserved?"

"Val and I made an honest calibration error and he interpreted it as cheating."

The sentinel was buried in a run of new recruit indexing. "Hm. That would explain that mail he sent out. Apologies for generally ignoring him; I might have been able to ground him on the launch pad. I can usually tell when he's gunning for Val."

"You think this is about him and Val?"

Cheldyne shrugged, turning towards his young friend. "Eh, it's fifty fifty, Val or you, and you're working for Wyvern too now so it's an extra token against you." He acquired the slate from his desk, deftly tapping something in as he continued. "Don't look surprised, of course you're a target for Auri's derision; you're an astrum of Kiertus. It's one of his duties to make sure you're worth the colonel's investment. Acquiesce to the punishment but make sure no matter you demand witnesses. It's your right."

Sol's response was interrupted by his slate beeping. A nod from Chel indicated he should check it.

"I'm going to get coffee and you should be on your way to starboard pipes. Say hi to Wyvern for me." He squeezed Sol's shoulder on his way out the office after stopping to tighten his robe. "See you later."

The message from "Serum" contained a clearance release and link. As he looked up to ask the sentinel what it was, he noted the man's on screen ID going from blue back to its usual grey. Sol's eyes fell back to the note hovering at the screen's bottom. He followed the link to a document: "Knight's Handbook, 17th Atmospheric Mercy Corps. For rank lieutenant and above only except under authorization by the Imperial Guild."

...

The first time Sol was assigned under Iekierpin, he was genuinely delighted. He still appreciated both Eek's elegant Vasiit good looks and his profound intellect, but was wary of the man's gossip habit. While he found potential in some of the information Eek casually dropped, he also found the bulk of it uncomfortably none of his damn business.

It was through Eek he learned, for example, that Hanajiel came to the unit after internal corruption devasted his Rim Patrol division. He originally trained as a paratrooper, but puking during a bayonet sim led him to becoming a pilot and nearly left him with a callsign of 'Squeamish', rather than the slightly more complimentary 'Spearhead' ('simple but gets the job done'). Further, Sol learned Hanajiel, although substantially older, had been Dromarka's lover since the younger man joined the unit.

Going from paratrooper to pipes seemed pretty common; Wyvern apparently was a wretched bio-mechanic – notoriously so in his Exo unit - but 'preferred the pipes to being a trooper, and no one questioned him', particularly after he had the will to volunteer as a retriever and remain aboard. "He's a bad ass, no doubt about it," Eek remarked. "But he's far better at taking things apart than putting 'em back together."

Sol also learned the *Sanjeera*'s upper level staff massively restructured after a 'violent incident' at a relay gate station about a year prior, although he could not confirm several details, because, "The Aur and Leviathan guys keep it bolted down, but even us down here in the pipes, we can see the rifts between the former majors and the current prime, and the fact we still don't have our own."

Star Assault vessels were supposed to have two majors, the 'M-Prime' who functioned as second in command to the colonel and took care of general executive duties, and 'Wing Superior' whose function was to oversee the commanders of the pipes and maintain order therein. Parthenos had gone from starboard commander to Wing Superior to M-Prime and left a void. The catch of picking a new one involved a stipulation that the Wing Superior needed to be a knight-level paratrooper and a recognized priest of a religious sect; no current commander could fulfill all the pre-reqs, save one who had been "coming and going on Guild business, and he probably refuses the job on principle, having already been M-Prime on two vessels".

"Hey there, hey, watch it, watch the coils – oh good, good." Iekierpin smiled. "You've got good hands, kid. Fast learner, too. Gonna miss you when Droo pulls his head out of his butt."

"Thanks, sir." Sol returned the shielded flaps and secured them, wiping down the underside of the D-7 and turning back to his supervisor to ask if the arms needed review before moving to the next jet. Eek looked down into the bay with consternation. "What's going on there, sir?"

"Don't know yet, not good though, not a good sign, Big P in the hangar…"

"What?" Sol slid from the jet and rolled to peer down from the lift. "Crap."

"Worse, he's making a straight line towards –"

Since Sol arrived, Wyvern had been loading a modified Dash positioned on the launch track. He was terse, hurried, and his delegation of orders seemed shorter tempered than usual. Iekierpin and Hanajiel took the reins smoothly, more than experienced enough to run the pipes without getting in the commander's way. Eek observed the Dash was one of the colonel's, so whatever was afoot was crucial, best not interrupted. Parthenos strode right to this vehicle, yelling something that was drowned out at Sol's level.

"Uh oh." Eek slid back a bit from the edge and gestured that Sol do likewise. "Stay low. Maybe now would be time to run that other set of diagnostics…"

Sol got right to it, trying not to look over his shoulder too often while he updated life readings on the jet's charts. "This one's looking good now, should we go up or left next?"

"Nowhere. Not going to move off this lift while he's down there."

"Don't really want to get his attention myself, sir; he has a boner to smear me like cheap cheese spread."

"Well, he's a rage-cock to all of Sheriden's astra. That's normal. He pushes you to see if you break; he broke Droo, you know, broke the fuck right outta him." Eek sighed and shook his head. "Alshunejol took it like a champ, no one could take him down, he was the kind religious guys should all aspire to be."

"What happened to him, sir?"

"Didn't come back from the relay gate. Beautiful funeral, but the ship's been fucked since." He shook his head again. His voice softened, though there was no way anyone could have heard the conversation. Sol crawled closer to listen as he continued. "P was worst on Wyvern. Guy was such a shit when he got here, though, fuckin' bot jock, snobby rich kid, and a porn star too; like if you went to the Plane of Perfect Ideals, you know, Wyvern was the Perfect Iconic Asshole."

Sol choked a little. "Porn…star?"

"Three Academy Annual appearances, two calendars, two popular vid reels. Civvies love tankers. Kinda sickening, cuz if you know 'em in real life, they're childish hot shots. He was the worst I ever met."

"Gotta say I didn't see that one coming."

"He's from Ryzaa but he's Shandrian, good Shandrian family, keeps his body covered all the time. Apparently except in front of cameras, but you see him in the flight webbing and you'll get it." Eek laughed. "He was such a little prick when he got here though, Parthenos couldn't take it. He knew the guy was top level at ma'at shi, he had civilian level awards, at least, so he said, 'Come at me, you fuck.' And Wyvern kicked his ass. Cleanly, no contest, with witnesses."

"No kidding?" Sol looked to where Wyvern hung half-way out the Dash hatch, being apparently lectured by a tense-seeming Parthenos. *Who the fuck would ever question him, knowing that?*

"He didn't let it go there, though; he bragged about it, mocked P at every chance, sarcastic 'sirs' tacked on to each belittling comment. Big mistake." Long, dark lashes lowered over deep amber eyes. He looked away. "The security cams were disabled, somehow, there were no witnesses to the assault, but it was sexual in nature. He was hospitalized and almost forced into early retirement. P fired off a pulse blast, inside him, I guess? Horrible to think about. He's missing a section of his intestines, ergo all the drugs, all the time, to just stay working, to be able to eat. You may have noticed in the pharmacy..."

"That explains the, uh, protein shots; I thought he was just boosting his muscle mass, like ... gods, that is... I can't, sir. I'm ill."

"Fuck. He's gesturing this way."

Parthenos had his slate in hand, pointing at the lift where Eek and Sol crouched. The boy shuddered as his slate made the sound assigned to the major and colonel. Eyes squinted and jaw clenched, he confirmed a "Front and center" command from Parthenos.

"Good luck, kid. Don't go off the working camera grid. Page Gunsmoke, Serum, or Trauma if he tries to take you anywhere alone. Bonesaw, too. Set up a mass-page single click now. I'm not kidding."

...

He stood before Parthenos on the hangar floor while the rapid business of preparations continued around them. Save Wyvern, who sat on the modified

Dash, staring fiercely at the major's back as he cleaned his shades on his sweater.

"What the shit, Red? Why didn't you come to me? This is my shit, my business, my fucking job, Solvreyil. This is brass business, my fucking business!"

"Sir! Yes, sir! I apologize, sir!"

"Did Bootstrap or Wyvern give you an order to keep this from me?"

"No, no sir, Major Parthenos! Val said he was unlikely to be well-received if he came to you, in light of recent errors, but he gave no order I could not do so. In fact, he said I should have gone to you for the ship name lecture, sir. I assumed going to you would be insubordinate; I was incorrect, sir."

The major slapped his own forehead, dragged his palm down his nose and tugged his sideburns. He stared Sol down. "Astrum, it's taking my entire force of will not to kick your balls into your skull. Do you comprehend?"

Sweat broke out along the boy's hairline. "Sir! Absolutely, sir!"

"Come with me. We're gonna have a chat on the way to setting Dro'markaal in his place." He grabbed Sol by the shoulder as he stormed towards the door, turning the youth about with a snap.

That was a hair's breadth from dislocation. Why did Eek have to tell me that story?

"I happened to be reviewing security footage, on a tip from Chel, and I happened to see you tossing a certain little mouthy douche, and I happened to look up your training records at that point." Snide incredulity flavored his words. "According to those records, you've had one formal ma'at-shi lesson, from Valdieren, that day. Does that remain true?"

"Yes, sir, unless you count gun and ship sims, those are first tier black sphere and silver, correct, sir?"

"Well yes, but I am specifically referring to hand to hand combat, Solvreyil. Don't be pedantic, I will smack you." Parthenos delivered a sideways glance that hung between hostile and amused. "You are a good boy with a Shandrian-style upbringing. You aren't going to lie to me, right, astrum?"

"No, sir! I would not dream of it, sir!"

"Then stop and look me in the fucking eye, astrum." They froze in the hall. Sol noticed as he turned his face to the major that the security eye above them was on, flashing a tiny blue light. Queerly glinting indigo eyes bored into him, searching, serious. "Have you accepted any off-records training from Wyvern or any other wing commander?"

"Sir! No, sir! I have received offers from Wyvern, but have not had time to accept them. Honestly, his pervy text messages scare me shitless, sir!"

Parthenos recoiled, sputtered, shook his head. "Pervy, Red? Did I hear you correctly, you said, 'pervy', like 'perverted', like, he sexually came on to you?"

"Yes, sir?" *Did I just get Wyvern in trouble? I don't want to do that. They have enough problems, clearly, and weird or not, Wyvern seems to look out for me.*

"The guy is a fucking celibate fucking monk, Solvreyil, over twenty years; he was a sacred prostitute before that; he does not 'hit on' people. You sure you're not misreading those messages?"

Celibate? Makes some sense, I guess. "Maybe so, sir. Val seemed to think he was just messing with my head, I guess that would be why … um… sorry, sir."

The major sighed and looked at the ceiling, shook his furry head again. "Typical shitbag thing for him, especially after turning you down as an astrum. Still a prick after all these years. He doesn't learn." He gave an expression best described as 'sympathetic', to Sol's surprise. "As of today, you're in my jurisdiction; you're not working in starboard anymore. If you really like jet work, cool, I'll put you in port when we're done with the paratrooper training."

"Sir! Erm, uh, wait, am I still Sheriden's astrum?"

"Yes." Parthenos started walking again, gesturing him to follow. "He refuses to let me trade Wildfire off and take you. I've asked no less than three times. He offered you to the port commander and the auxiliary, too. I'd be personally insulted except I know why."

"Why doesn't he want me as an astrum?"

"He's old, tired, overworked, and worries too much. He wants you to get the best training possible; he's got a personal obsession with making good men out of conduits."

Like you, huh? You've led a hard life, I think, and I don't want that story Eek told me to be true.

"What about Yndel? I mean, Chel, Serum, whatever he's letting people call him these days. Has he given you any lessons?"

"How to catch myself with a pulse field when I fall. I have sucked at it so far, sir. But that's all, sir. He said most of his skills are way past what I'm ready to learn."

"Probably true, but he hates recruiting for the Sun, which is likely the real reason he's reluctant. Conduits tend to get used hard and thrown away, and he's not going to let that happen to anyone he likes."

"I feel I have the respect of a lot of important people and have done nothing to deserve it, sir."

"You do, Solvreyil. And I get why you think that, but contrary to how it appears, we don't like to waste talent and brains around here. You can see how badly we need it. You're young and inexperienced and that presents obstacles. You're going to get yelled at and hit once or twice. We all did. Some took it better than others."

He's being really forward with me, this is unusual. "Major Parthenos, did you suspect Wyvern was training me in secret to fight you?"

Parthenos glared, slit-eyed and soul-strangling. "You're savvy, Solvreyil, save where learning to shut your fucking mouth is concerned."

Sol coughed and meekly asked, "So, what happens now?"

"I'm taking your training, and I don't have time, so if you suck you're scrubbing traps until someone else can take you. You better show that same fast learning talent. Right now? We're on our way to confront Droo." He produced his slate and tapped furiously. "We're getting your armor. One way or another."

Sol swallowed, consumed by an unfamiliar crushing sensation. Save for an occasional growl, Parthenos was silent until they were arrived.

"I cannot fucking believe this guy, endangering our crew and holding an officer back; he has some nerve." He held the slate out; a huge file lay open, although Sol could not really focus on it save Dromarka's photograph – the cranky blond man from his first moments aboard the *Sanjeera*. There was definitely more available for the major than if he looked it up. "See that? 'Air sergeant', nothing else; he's stuck where he is because he's got the training but won't advance an inch from risk of immediate death while I'm on this ship. It's his fault. I'll show him how far his fucking 'authority' extends, damn right."

Parthenos called a string of explicit orders as they entered, summoning the resident sentinel from an antechamber. After a nerve-wracking wait beside the impatiently smoldering major, the foul-tempered blond appeared.

"Yo, Dro'markaal. Where've you been the past two weeks? I don't recall relieving you of squad duties."

"No, sir, just my bat and command, sir." He scowled, serving the final "sir" came with a side of spit.

"So, this guy right here," Parthenos grabbed Sol's shoulder roughly and shoved him towards Dromarka. "This wee officer is the newest astrum genova of the Blessedly Knighted Colonel Kiertus Sheriden. He's weeks into paratrooper training and hasn't been issued arms. We're flying toward Ilu space. What about that doesn't sound fuckin' right to you?"

Dromarka's mouth moved over half-formed words but issued no excuse or even a coherent sound.

"Armor? Or do I have to go back and get it myself?"

"Major, I'm sure you realize, this kid's a conduit; Laathas is having a difficult time stabilizing him. I'd rather not have him inadvertently blow a hole in the ship, sir." He shuffled a bit but maintained his impenetrable countenance. "I've been waiting for specific autho-"

Like a striking snake, Parthenos' hand shot forward and gripped Dromarka's armor by the chest clasp. Energy crackled around them. "Shelve your personal issues and arm the little motherfucker before you're an airman on the *Esimaar*. Am I being perfectly fucking clear?"

"I question the wisdom of this, Major Parthenos."

A pulse blast from the bigger elf slammed Dromarka to the floor. Sol felt residual waves from it ripple across the hair on his arms and tickle his neck. "Release his gear immediately. I'll take responsibility for what happens thereafter. We cannot have un-outfitted officers in this sector. The very fact he is a conduit increases our urgency to train him."

Solvreyil offered a hand to the downed, stunned sergeant. Dromarka righted himself and dusted off, shoving Sol aside with a grunt. Without a further sound, he returned to the back room.

"Thanks, major, sir," Sol uttered with a little stammer.

"Don't thank me. This fucker is hampering the ship's safety and increasing my workload. It's a serious disciplinary issue." Parthenos fiddled with his slate. "I'm clearing blocks of your schedule for armor training. Refresh your calendar and acknowledge. I'll continue to hold your rifle and cresc until you can do off-ship exercises, but we'll work through helmet, boots, kilt, knife, and carapace in that order."

This was strange and exciting news. "I don't recall ordering a crescent pistol, sir. I thought those were an upper-level officer item only. Was there a mistake, sir?"

The major seemed both amused and annoyed. "No, apparently the colonel thought you should have one due to your performance at Virtual Target Carnival." The side-burned grouch shrugged, remarking dismissively, "Eh, it was on his paycheck. Nothin' I can even say about it. Free gun, right?"

Dromarka reappeared. "Here's everything, major. Do me a huge favor and train him as far from my part of the ship as possible, asshole. Sir."

Gathering the parcels, Parthenos winked and snottily said, "That's what the bulkheads are for, shit bag. We'll start in B-1, maybe you should keep a hand on the override. Have a *great* day, you fuckin' douche."

The sergeant's sarcastic tone followed. "Sir, yes, sir."

"Will I be training directly with you, sir?"

"Not as frequently as I'd prefer; you've got Myshkor for most of your armor basics since he's grounded right now anyway." He waited for Sol to affirm before continuing. "We're going to go over your helmet and response gear now, though, before I have to put my ass into finding a new arms sentinel." Parthenos turned and activated B-1's door, all of one bulkhead off the armory. "C'mon, Red, manhood awaits."

He's calmed down a lot, so I'm less concerned, but did he have to put it like that?

"OK what's Val explained to you so far? You get how the sleeves and hood work, right?"

"Yes, sir, the sleeves help channel pulse for guns or other hardware; hood does the same with the helmet."

He sat casually on the floor, gesturing Sol to join. "You realize of course us conduits don't need either, especially once trained? They can assist in terms of protection, but your armor membranes will do most of that work for you. We can enter combat, in a bio or chem zone, bare ass naked save for kilt, boots, carapace, helmet, and be just fine, technically."

Sol stared at him as he recieved the helmet. "You've done that, sir?"

"Yeah, I was young, and the ship was being boarded. It was straining after a few hours, but I am as you see me – disease free, relatively undamaged. Fuck, only serious scar I got was received fully armored, outside of a declared war." He shrugged. "Kiertus and my high priest both said God watches out for me; they honor different forms of God, so I've wondered. Maybe I'm just lucky, maybe just fast. Point is, in a tight scenario, you don't have to rush the other shit on, you're naturally equipped for emergencies."

Your scars are plenty, I think, just not so physical. "Erm, which way is forward?"

"The default antennae position is angled back."

Sol examined the helmet, enamored with the six strange little optical orbs staring back. The 'antennae' looked more like horns; there were six at least, nearly flat to the chitinous plates that curved back to a tail-like point. "It's... the

142

… the leg things are flexing, sir."

"Well go on and put it on your head, dumb ass."

Fascinated as he was by the technology, Sol had trouble getting over the design. The engineering's base creature was a giant chite, a whale louse or something equally unpleasant; it resembled an armored game-monster version of a scalp parasite. This had not occurred to him previously when he saw them worn. A look at the underside, the part which would contact his head, made it clear. He did not want the major to see him cringe as he raised the squirmy thing up and placed it onto his skull.

They were seated a few feet apart. Parthenos leaned on an arm, slate in his free hand, staring expectantly.

Weird little appendages wriggled in his hair. Sol made a solid effort to remain calm. Then tiny, sharp hooks found their way into his scalp as the helmet-creature found flesh for purchase. Its security was the undoing of young Solvreyil. He lost a bit of skin and a few hairs in the act of ripping the thing free and tossing it with an exclamation of revulsion and pain.

Major Parthenos clutched his sides as he rolled and howled with laughter. The helmet scurried frantically into a wall, backed up, and ran towards Sol, who leapt away from it. It ran about his dancing feet in confusion, slowing down as the cold air put it to sleep. Eventually it stopped moving and floated slightly. Sol continued to curse.

"Man," the major wiped tears from his large dark eyes. "I told ya, ya need to grow your hair out, kid."

"Everyone told me that the helmets weren't padded, sir. They didn't mention the fact that they are giant fucking lice with needles for feet, sir!"

Sprawled on his back, Parthenos chuckled as he regarded his slate. "People still use that line, huh? It's true, they aren't padded. Good old kaffa sin of omission." He pushed himself up a little. "Thirty seven seconds. Not too bad. Grab it again and we'll go over synching. By the way, you're six seconds better than Bachi's first, if you wanna trick the lil fuck into a bet he can't win, I mean, not sayin', just sayin'."

143

My hive shift starts in a half hour and I'm already shot. Parthenos had gone over more than armor synchronization; he managed to cover storage and care as well before releasing the boy to "go straighten your shit before you gotta work". *He's efficient, if nothing else. He does not fuck around as a teacher.*

Reaching his cocoon, he noticed the door ajar, panicked a moment before observing Ozzie cautiously crawling sideways along an adjacent bunk. He looked at her vibrating wings – a few feet above him at a right angle to where he stood - and her determined expression and asked, "Whatcha doin', honey?"

This surprised her and she lost footing, but between the furious flapping and low gravity, she stayed aloft. "Good girl! Go go! Keep it up!" He scrambled up the wall and grabbed her from the air. "We'll have more time to practice that later, though. Come with me to the hive, OK?"

She chirped, squirmed, flailed and got loose, flapped, rolled, and fell than crawled up the wall and hopped off to try again. Sol laughed, texting Chel to tell him: she had flown, a few weeks before expected.

::: She's a prodigy. Told ya she'd be smart, huh?::

He climbed to shut his bunk door, noticing as he did the adult photographic magazine Chel had given him during his last shift. He sat in the opening and eyed it, something not sitting quite right in his brain. *Eek said Wyvern did porn. Parth said he was celibate after being a ... what? A 'sacred prostitute'? Temples still do that? There are organized enough temples to do that, even? Or is someone telling me wrong?*

Curiosity got the better of Sol; he opened the Knight's Handbook and searched for the terms, immediately finding an entry regarding the sanctity of temple rent-men, that some historical sites were entirely funded on the work of such folk, that their discipline was highly respectable, and because many of them were taken as children – conduits or underage criminals or both, rescued by a high-level monk, trained in secrecy – only have consensual sex for money they are not allowed to keep, as they owe their lives to the temple. Following this was information for knights on interacting with such folk, as a client, a trainer, or a comrade. The comrade notes were painfully sensitive, since kaffir friendships, especially within a close unit like Star Assault, but also among civilians, were often highly physical.

I thought I felt bad for Wyvern before, but there but for the grace of being born off the homeworld go I. I know I'm not ready for sex, but when I am, I want it to be because I like the other person and we feel connected. Not because I'm property of a religious society. Man, that's just sad. If I interpret this correctly, ma'at-shi training and bouts are his primary outlet and the only time he's cool to touch someone without money going to his church, probably the Temple of Aur in Ryzaa. *Heavy.*

He climbed down and headed for the hive, flailing knobby petulant bug under one arm.

Sol turned Ozzie loose at the pool, but there were several mature warriors around so he did not go far or let her out of sight. He parked his slender self on an outcropping near the office door and waited for the boss. His buglet rapidly absorbed herself in a game of tag with Rocket and Squeak.

"Howya doin', kid? Ya look deep in thought. Careful. That thinkin' stuff's a killer." Cheldyne squeezed himself onto the damp outcropping beside Sol, his larger derriere nearly forcing the tired astrum from the improvised bench.

Grinning while attempting to hold his balance, the boy quipped, "Damn, sir, do you need a special clearance for that butt?"

Cheldyne smiled as he barked his reply. "Fuck yes and you had best respect it, son. I earned this arse in an exo brigade before you were born!" With a sideways bump of his hips, Sol was on the floor.

"I'm honored to be shoved by a genuine Imperial Armored butt, sir!" Sol saluted in spite his position and both their laughter. Bugs approached to investigate.

"Well look at you, little miss. Buzzin' around like you own the place." Even though she had to land often between brief airborne stints, gravity seemed easier for her to negotiate. Cheldyne masterfully reached up and snatched her mid-flight, held her thorax while her wings vibrated furiously. Antennae darted about and eyes rolled. "You're so cute! I could put you on a lead and walk you around the park!"

Sol leaned on the edge of the outcropping, gazing up at Ozzie. "Is it backwards that she's better in gravity than in low?"

"A little," remarked Chel, releasing the buzzing gen so she could alight upon her

145

bond. "Just means she'll be a really strong flier in the long run, though. They always are when they're backwards like that. You want her to be a strong flier." He looked down sternly at the boy. "Otherwise you're a number for retrievers."

Slender tan arms encircled the cooing bug. Sol had no verbal response.

"I'm sorry you got assigned to new trainers, it's partially my fault. I expect you're a bit angry with me."

"Maybe I should be, sir, a little, I really like Val. And working with jets was cool, and I'll miss the starboard guys, but Parthenos says I can train in port after my armor skills are up to par." He looked over to where two older warriors had a dominance fight. "I'm not excited about this Myshkor guy, he sounds obnoxious. Auk seems to think he's a turdcake. That's his bug, the scarred one?"

"Holiday arbitrarily hates people as a hobby. The scarred one is Tracy, Jady's bug. Myshkor's Liana is the one getting her ass wooped." He stood and gestured for Sol to take the other route around the pool. "Help me break this up. I don't want to deal with their bonds later if Liana gets seriously injured."

"That… looks kinda dangerous, sir."

"Yes. However, Tracy is easily distracted by electronic devices. Open the stupidest, noisiest app you've got, or maybe one of the irritating vid uploads on Bug Funnies. I'll grab Liana. If we time it right, I won't get slashed."

Sol quickly found a loop of animation cuts set to obnoxious music. Apparently uploaded for Wyvern's naming day months prior, the cuts featured Ryzaa City's tourism mascot Tomki Vo. Tomki Vo was an adorable cartoon version of a *vohjaadu*, Archos's remarkably engineered cephalopod-derived transit vehicles. The astrum turned this up as loud as his slate permitted, not particularly wishing to approach the violently thrashing genadri.

To his surprise, Tracy raised her head, disentangled herself and bounded over. *This bug is very large … oh fuck shit fuck no, no, no* – Impact knocked the wind from Sol; he thudded to the damp floor as Tracy snatched away the singing slate and bolted to a niche.

"Well, that did work." Chel stood over him with Liana squirming and nipping in his arms. "You injured?"

"I'll live. Can I just… lie here for a while?"

Chel released Liana, who immediately left the hive toward the officers lounge. "I'll let you, but the chance of getting humped by a bug is strong if you do."

"Dammit." Sol got up. "How am I supposed to get my slate back?"

"Ask her for it. She's just watching her favorite videos, after all." He smiled and pointed to the niche. "She usually doesn't come down here, tends to hang up in ops or with the engineers. Probably got kicked out because people are too busy to play electronic games with her."

"No kidding? That's wild. Pretty smart bug."

"Genius to the point of self-endangerment. Just like her bond." Chel laughed, a peculiar, fond smile on his face. "You'll probably get to work with him in port. He's nuts, but he's a good guy."

"You know, I'm not mad at you for bringing Parth's attention to that video. You probably saved my ass, literally. I'm mad I got involved in their revenge game."

The old elf's eyebrows rose. He nodded solemnly. "Did you read that guide?"

"A good portion of it, sir." *Yes, aside from just temple prostitutes, I'm ass-deep in secretive religious shit.* For example, Parthenos' trademark facial hair signified his standing in the Trench of Leviathan. Ordinary on older male civilians, long flowing cat chops on a career military man were code for 'Tetrarch', meaning the ill-tempered hair farmer was one of four high priests among his sect's soldiers. The only other permission for facial hair in Star Assault was a certain cut of goatee for high-level members of the Order of Maalek. "I have a lot of respect for Parthenos in spite of his reputation. I am honored I will be able to train with him, even if that story Eek told me is true."

"Ah. That story is true. Eek was training in the infirmary when they brought Wyvern in. Parthenos has never fully dealt with his own darkness. He is a man of great accomplishments, nonetheless." Chel sighed, idly stroking the scar at the bridge of his nose. "Everyone's got some demons."

Sol stared at the floor. Ozzie rubbed against his legs before flying over to Tracy.

147

He worried a moment, but the larger bug made a spot for her in the niche and terrible music played from the stolen slate. *The Curry Shack jingle? Why can't my earplugs kill that?* "How literal are these religious orders?"

"Depends on the member and the faith, Sol. Most of us see them as symbolic systems to protect and preserve the arts of our predecessors. Some men believe in literal embodiments of the god-forms, outside ourselves, and some of us believe we are those embodiments." He looked intently into the boy's eyes. "You've a long time to pick a faith, Sol. I gave you that so you'd understand, not to push you any faster."

"I appreciate that, sir." *I don't want to ask how much of Wyvern, Val, and P's 'feud' is actually sectarian in nature. What's the punishment for raping a monk of another sect? How does he still have a career? Ugh no. Even if Chel could tell me, I don't want to get deeper into it*

"You know what will make your day better?"

Every answer in his mind was snide or facetious, so he merely looked at the sentinel.

"Tattoos." Chel gestured for him to follow. "I have a gun in the office; we can do the work in the infirmary where it's more sterile. Come on."

….

Ozzie swam cheerfully with her cohorts while Sol watched from poolside. He wished he found being social as natural as she. He chose to take their bath so late to avoid the funny looks some of the other men gave him. There were a few older men in the lounge who seemed disinterested in activity below, and quite a few bugs clearly tossed from cocoons or stations for interrupting work or sleep, but he had not seen another living being besides. There was even a note in Chel's office, "Out for a fuck, if you page me you'd best have a bug on fire."

Wondering is inappropriate. But… no, Yen, don't look at your locater. Sol splashed his feet in the salt pool. He missed the door opening because of this, and was startled by Valdieren's voice.

"Hey. Surprised to see you here."

"Oh, hi, sir." *Awkward. We haven't spoken since I got reassigned.* "Needed a wash before I could sleep."

"I hear that." The captain sat beside him. "Your hair isn't even wet though."

Sol touched his head, almost as if he did not realize what Val meant. "Yeah, I got tattooed yesterday. Trying to bring myself to get in. Chel says it'll be fine with the salve, but I know it's going to sting."

The captain slid mostly clothed into the pool. "Yeah, it will. Salt and all. Nupril just stops discoloration and drying out, not pain." Val dipped his head and scrubbed salve into his scalp. "If you just do it, you get over it pretty quick. No point in delaying, y'know? What'd you get, if you don't mind me asking?"

"Setting sun." He gestured to his hip, a little shyly. "I thought about getting the unit logo but I'm still not sure how I feel about it; 'scythes of mercy' is kind of ominous. Chel suggested some Shandrian runes, but I don't feel I deserve them yet, either." He watched Val swim, guessing the captain was using his under armor to stay warm. "Do you have any, sir?"

"I'll show you but you have to get in and have to stop fucking calling me 'sir' while we bathe." Val laughed as he half floated, half paddled in the deepest part of the pool.

His hip stung like fire. Sol lanced his lower lip with his diminutive fangs as he pushed to where his superior bobbed. Val swam to the far end, dispersing bugs as he went. Squeak did an exuberant lap before climbing out and shaking a shower down over all. Sol blinked water from his eyes and joined the captain.

Valdieren looked up towards the lounge. "Seen Furface around tonight?"

"He was in Laathas' office earlier, they were getting a supply order together. Computer was all jacked up and P. gave up and went to bed. Why?"

"No reason." Val rested his back against the pool edge, wrestled himself from his shirt. On his left upper arm, just above the graft sleeve, was a stylized sapling in black ink, with small orbs sprouting at the end of seven curving branches, each orb a different color. On examination, Sol realized the earth beneath the tree bore an entwined set of meticulously concealed runes, 'Yl' 'Quel' 'Ktah'.

Does High Shandrian conjugate the same? Is this even what this is? "'Blood of the common ancestor?'"

The captain's gestures and darting red eyes indicated he would prefer Sol lowered his voice. "Yes. Each of the orbs is a species that shares the blood." He continued to cast eyes about as he pointed to one. "Violet for the North Shandrians, blue for the South, um, Aurians, sorry…"

"It's OK, I don't identify with my Archon heritage enough to be offended." Sol was not convinced he could play this game but decided to give it a shot. "Bone for Ryzaans, red for Vasiit – did I pronounce that right? Gold for… for the Huari?"

"Well, all the Islands; from their point of view, that's eight more sub-ethnicities, but yeah. You got all those right…" Eyes swapped between Sol, the main door, and the lounge. "Do you know the top three?"

He thought about the ethnicities of Archos and philosophies of old Eshandir. "Orange is humans?"

"Yep."

The final orbs were green and black. He also noticed a budding branch starting up the black orbed limb, a branch with no orb of its own, as it had just begun to grow. Sol very much did not want to be wrong. "Um, black is… saurtzek?"

Val's crimson eyes half-closed as he looked at the water. "Science's truths are occasionally unpopular among politicians and philosophers."

"I believe the findings that say we're related. The Ruhn claimed viable crossbreeds, right?" Fascinated by the image and in awe of Val's audacity wearing this on a warship full of Mior vets, Sol ran his finger over the branches without even realizing he was touching his former supervisor.

"The Kemshiya people of southernmost Vasa were apparently the first crossbreeds; there's argument regarding how the saurtzek got there – brought back by Shandrians, brought by gen, accidentally crashed a vessel, but there were apparently saurtzek on Archos over 2000 years before the empire. No one will ever know because Ryzaa wiped most of them out. The survivors that escaped to Eshandir destroyed their historical evidence to hide. Supposedly

150

that's why there are blue skinned Vasiit… it's not an accident of covergent evolution."

"Wow." Sol realized his finger was on Val and withdrew. "What about the green?"

"It's obvious, if you think about it." He pushed blond streaks from his face and smiled. "What else have you met in the universe that's sentient?"

Behind Val's head, a few feet away, Ozzie and Squeak tumbled, tugging a sock lifted from somewhere. Sol looked at them and the tattoo and back into the big red eyes. "You have to be shitting me. We can't … they can't… we…"

"Philosophers have long considered them the 7th Race. But." Valdieren was barely audible. "Apparently, both Baalphae and Archon empires conducted experiments, and while artificial insemination is required, and an incubation system is needed to prevent grievous harm to the bearer and/or young, yeah… I don't know how much I'm supposed to know about that. It's better to keep it to philosophy, huh?" He pulled his shirt from the bank and splashed back into it.

Heavy shit. I don't know what to believe. No wonder he pisses people off so much. "Um, dare I even ask about that 8th budding branch?"

The captain hauled himself from the pool without looking back. Before his voice was lost to the noise of the hive, he said, "That is the new growth of Hope. Goodnight, Sol."

VI. The Space between Stars

Myshkor Syvashikki, call sign "Bonespur", continued to seem like a fecally-based baked good to Sol as he read his profile en route to their first meeting. *I've heard enough about you that I've a bad feeling. He's a captain though, and according to gossip, he's kept that rank in spite of 'really stupid shit'. What kind of entitled jerk does mandatory service as Academy campus police? Is that even a real job?* He was a little lost en route to 'Training Fy-2'; according to the map he was there, but he stood in an alcove about a metre from the pharmacy door. Checking who was idly logged in to ask if it was a map error or joke, he noted a small sign with an arrow pointing down a chute.

It's under medical? I've never even been on this level. Thought this was all drive tunnels and shielding down here. Sol hopped onto the rungs; a hatch opened automatically beneath. He dropped through, surprised to find himself in a low, cushioned room, face to face with a lopsidedly grinning man with frayed light brown mudlocks. His pale pinkish-tan complexion was smooth, fine pored, flawless in an almost disturbing way. *If his ears weren't a hair akilter, he'd resemble a mannequin- sculpted by a human who had never met any kaffir, only read about them. Kinda spooky.*

"You found me. Congratulations."

Insignia was absent but his slate indicated this was 'Bonespur'. "I did, sir?"

"Myshkor. Mysh is fine." He extended his hand, smacking the back of Sol's rather than a brush. 'Mysh', like Sol, wore full ladders; his armor lay neatly piled nearby. "Guess Val couldn't train your mutant ass and you're my problem now? Figures. Fine. Let's get to it."

Sol slitted his eyes and considered a text to Parthenos.

"What? You are one; HTS is a mutation. Ffft don't gimme that look, it would be unethical of Parth to give you to me without that information. Just unethical, but not criminal, because I'm a mutant, too. Of course. Now, try to hit me. Like a human, no pulse."

What the fuck. "I can't pulse right now, sir, I'm on a double suppressor dose by P's orders, sir."

"That just reduces charge rate; you still can. Come on, haven't got all day."

Sol braced and swung. They were roughly equal in mass; Myshkor was a bit shorter, thicker boned, wiry but not hyper-conditioned. He moved, however, like a bolt, dodged Sol's punch and delivered a wind-robbing blow to his stomach.

The captain stood above the crumpled astrum, tapping his foot. "See how that didn't work? Can't hit the lazy Ryzaan bastard, huh?" He seemed amused. "You should be faster than me and have better reach, kid, you're skinny but you've got tone and longer limbs. Try again."

I hate you already. Trust me, I'm going to… Sol rolled rapidly from the fetal position and back flipped, feet aimed for the center of Myshkor's mass. This would have surprised the average foe and probably looked badass on the security cams, but Mysh sidestepped non-chalantly, extended an arm, whirled his pointer finger in the air, and spun his would be assailant into the wall.

"Your form's better; I can't move like that from my side or back." Myshkor approached Sol's inverted wreckage, wiping his palms. His grin contradicted his serious tone as he extended an open hand. "Anything feel broken?"

He just dispelled a field. That was pulse, somehow. Sol accepted the help and rose to lean on the wall beside the captain, panting. "Did you really just spin me in the air with one finger, sir?"

"Well, not the finger, the pulse vortex around the finger, but yes." Myshkor laughed. "Haven't watched any of Wyvern's ma'at-shi bouts on the archives, huh? He made me relinquish a whole paycheck to him to teach me that. No idea where he donated it. Fuckin' monks, right?"

Sol just stared, fought to control his breath. "Right, sir."

"Anyway. We'll start with some easier stuff, basic silver and black techniques, improve your blows and movement detection. Lemme know when you're good."

"Captain, I take it you're a conduit, too, sir?" *Sixteen years in the unit, and not a scar on him. Just looks like a New Asrian hustler, honestly, a street rat, not military except the uniform…*

"No, pretty average. Just good at control and management. I'm no Wyvern or Gunsmoke, even, just good." He shrugged, his eyes on the opposite wall.

Not as if I care for you, but I need to know. "Then, is this a punishment for you, the risk, I mean, sir?"

Myshkor turned slowly and issued a growling partial laugh, devoid of joy. "Parthenos put you with me because of my mutation, yes. It's not high tension syndrome, though. Ready?"

"I guess. Are you going to put your armor on, sir?"

"Not yet. Build a field. It'll take a bit on those drugs and you'll need a pretty good one to repel me when I come at you, which is where we'll start. By the end of the day, you'll be able to control the repulsion, aim me at targets." He yawned and stretched.

"Uh, right, OK, here goes, sir." Sol concentrated, watching as the captain stretched his arms and legs, made rude remarks probably to aid Sol's intensity. When the aura was visible and the boy was genuinely irritated, wanting a shot at hitting him again, he realized Mysh was going to hurl himself straight into –

It happened before he could move; there were sparks, the blow knocked both down, Sol on his butt and Mysh on one knee, one hand flat to the floor, the other behind him. Fingers flexed on the non-supporting hand as the captain rose his head slowly. Light burns traced his cheeks, burns which seemed to fade as Sol watched. *Am I seeing things?*

"And that's your answer. My mutation: ultra-accelerated tissue regeneration." He stood, stretched to an audible crack, laughed, and shrugged. "You gotta break my bones to stop me, kid. Try harder next time. Come on, time to go from boy to elf. Build that field and take me down."

If my life didn't depend on learning this, I never could. "Sir! Yes, sir!"

....

Tension was nigh unbearable throughout the ship upon entering Ilu space. Everyone acted different, on edge; more than half the paratroopers stayed in armor constantly and even milder-mannered crew members were cranky and short. Even Lep, the stuttering engineer liason, wore an armored vest and carried side arms. To his relief, Ozlietsin chose to keep close and not stray at all during this time, and when Major Parthenos called the boy into his office for a chat, he complimented them on that behavior.

"That's what she should do. It proves you're bonding." He barely glanced up from a spread of maps and files on the screens covering his desk. "At ease. Although I think the fact you both salute is adorable."

Sol relaxed his posture and turned with some surprise to Ozzie, who had been mimicking the gesture. *I didn't train her to do that. Silly bug.* "Thank you, sir. What did you need, sir?"

"I noticed you hadn't signed up on the search and rescue list." Parthenos raised his head finally. "Care to explain why?"

"I didn't think I qualified, sir."

Sideburns flopped comically as the big elf snorted. "Nonsense. You score excellently in the S&R sim and Laathas and I agree you're getting your pulse adequately under control."

"Th-thanks, sir. I just... Ozzie's not big enough for proper jumping yet so we haven't trained at that..."

"These are human territories, Sol. We wouldn't even be using gen for drops. Either ships will land or you'll be on an analog 'chute. You'd mostly be along as support on any missions and your presence would be more for your training than anything else." He shrugged and double checked his typing. "I'm signing you up, astrum, if you've no further objections. Then I'd like you to hang out for a bit so I can give you a private lesson in using pulse grapplers and sticky bombs."

"Sir! Yes, sir."

"Training with Myshkor going OK for you? His reports show nothing more than vague progress."

Uh, man. Where do I start? "The lessons are contrary to my basic nature. He's verbally abusive so that makes it somewhat easier to try and kill him, sir."

Parthenos remained serious but seemed amused. "Common initial reaction to Mysh. But you can't kill him. Even if you did, I don't know if that would deter him." He smirked. "Mandatory service in the planetside MP force. They train you by beating you until you fight back. When he was your age, he was swamp hash before first call, every day. Star Assault is a comparative luxury cruise."

No thanks. Wait, campus cops are MPs? I'm a judgmental prick. "Are we training in Fy-2 or B-1, sir?"

"C-1, co-op sim. I gotta finish this, first." Parthenos waved his hand, stylus still clutched by a thumb. "Just, I dunno, read a book or some shit. Make coffee while you're at it."

Ozzie flapped over to the little couch on the farthest end of the room from Parthenos and curled up with a small yawn-squawk. Sol formed a protest against the trek to the lounge then realized the waving stylus was pointed to a device on the book shelf. He examined the object and determined it a low-grav, ship-safe hot beverage brewer. It appeared brand new. He whistled appreciatively.

"Naming day gift. Pretty sweet, huh?"

Sol fished out a coffee pod from a labeled canister and inserted it in the machine. "Oh, was that recently, sir? Happy naming, major."

"You clearly missed that thread on SACNet. Try not to live in a vacuum, astrum. Pun fully intended. Stay informed, it's part of your job." He coughed. "Night of that fucking meeting, actually. Thanks."

I use the search feature and try to avoid the ongoing threads and fluff forums… did the major just imply I should be reading the fluff forums? "Oh, that sucks. Sorry to hear, sir." The device made strange noises as it worked. Sol strove to avoid foot tapping and other nervous habits. His eyes fell on assorted photographs above the shelf. One was a starkly breathtaking city on a sheer, icy mountainside. Small craft flew about the upper towers in a light snow. The shot seemed ancient. Sol almost asked, then realized it was probably Triotos and stayed silent. The bulk of the images were Parthenos at various ceremonies, receiving medals or shaking hands with the Cha'atz General (a regal kaffa woman with a black wing pinned into her elaborate hair) or the Haarnsvaar Commander (a tall, stout blond in black armor who seemed grim even when smiling). In the middle were three images in a triptych frame that grabbed Sol's attention. In the first, he could see a fairly young Parthenos in an oilburn robe, on his knees before an altar in an elaborate arched niche. The niche resembled an open, toothy maw, hung with floral vines and strands of shiny stones. Within stood two men in similar robes, faces partly obscured by shadows and hoods. Impressive silvery hair flowed from one cowl and sideburns flanked a half smile. Both held spear-like scepters, crossed over the kneeling man's shoulders.

His knighting ceremony at the Trench of Leviathan? I wouldn't have imagined cameras being allowed at something like that. Then again, anyone who saw this outside this unit would think it was from a live action role playing game. And this one must be from when he was a paratrooper…

The picture on the right of the triptych was Parthenos again, with shiny black mudlocks bound mostly out of his face, the very slight beginnings of sideburns on his cheeks, squatting with a big, happy looking shiny blue-black gen around whom he had an arm. The confusing part was that both appeared to be wearing the garments of a formal Holtiini bridal party – he in a red and gold sash, she with a fluffy corsage on her neck. *I must be imagining that his eyes are red. He really looks like he's been crying. Maybe he's allergic to the flowers? I wonder what happened to his bug? And who the fuck's wedding was he at? The Cha'atz General maybe? He served on her ship a while… Is she Holtiini?*

The middle picture was the strangest. A very young and slender man in a partial racing uniform – the Academy junior team's, if he remembered the colors correct – was struggling against the restraint of three slightly older laughing men. A fifth looked on somewhat disapprovingly in the background. The scene was shot on a street with familiar lighting and scenery – somewhere on the waterfront in New Asria, the city in whose suburbs Sol had grown up. Most of those buildings were still there, although the trees were bigger now. The racer was unmistakably Parthenos Aurgaia, albeit a scrawny, very young Parthenos; there were no tattoos or scars on his exposed ribs.

"You were a gen jockey, sir?"

"I was never good enough for pro, but junior varsity racing was how I got my double-collared ass into college. And that uniform so forgivingly covered the collars, even if it didn't cover much else without the vest on." Parthenos looked over, his expression vaguely snotty. "Recognize anyone else?"

Sol examined further. The oldest looking of the men grappling little Parthenos had a thick mane of steel grey and smiled fearlessly at the camera. He was clad in black and charcoal clothes with a straight, sharp cut and pointy leather boots. Cat-like yellow eyes cleared any doubt. "Wow. Kiertus was buff when he was younger."

"He's still no weakling, but time and trouble have eaten away at him." The voice was nostalgic. A cough and it switched back. "Anyone else?"

A man with gold mudlocks in a shirt bearing the Shandrian characters for 'twenty three', dark blue ladders and tank boots, held Parthenos' hips as if he might yank down the boy's pants. His face read pure mischief. Pulling on the left arm was a man with black and white braids completely overcome by his own laughter. The dourer looking chap in the background had dark brown hair and a slight goatee, blue robe over exo underarmor. "No, I don't think I've ever seen any of these guys in my life."

"Really? Are you sure?"

He said that really creepy. I don't like this all of a sudden. The brown hair grouch could be Chel, but that would make him way older than the '77 years' on his records. No way.

Parthenos was standing behind Solvreyil. He reached under the boy's armpits, around his torso, very careful not to touch, to acquire his coffee. Sol felt the man's radiance through his clothes; short hairs on the back of his neck stood at attention as he stiffened. The low, nearly whispered voice retained the hint of snide superiority and withheld secrets as it dripped down his shoulder. "They were taking me for my first set of mudlocks before formal initiation." He said the final word as if a filthy come-on. "Don't you wonder what that might entail? Isn't it interesting, how you can see the photographer in the tattoo shop window?"

The hot coffee passed Sol's ribs as the major turned and wandered back to his desk, leaving the astrum to stare at the picture. He discerned a faint, reflected image of a muscular young man in fingerless black gloves, wearing the lace-up armored racing vest that should have covered Parthenos, over a pilot's shirt and black ladder leggings. Short copper mudlocks flopped around the camera and the grinning, all-too-familiar jawline. Sol could have been looking in a mirror. He whirled, stammering.

Feathery black brows arched as Parthenos sipped the anti-bubbling straw. "Hm?

Something wrong, Solvreyil Yenraziir? Something... bothering you?"

Sol stumbled on his tongue. *If I don't phrase whatever I say carefully, he'll just fuck with me more. Damn him. I can't win.*

"I suppose we should get to our lessons, then." The major continued to sip as he tossed a semi-cylindrical object and slowly caught it with his free hand. He held it still in the air between his long thumb and forefinger. It resembled a caterpillar. "This is an Archon sticky bomb." Parthenos chucked the rubbery, worm-like thing at Sol, who flailed to catch it. "Don't worry, that one's disarmed."

It wriggled in his hand. "Is it ... alive, sir?"

"Not in the same way as you or me or a gen, or even your helmet, for that matter. We're Archons, not Ilu, for fucks sake." Parthenos scowled and sat on his desk. "To carry those you affix a harness to your belt. Without a harness they can't be activated. The slots on the bottom are the triggers; pulling them off the harness activates both the adhesive release and explosive, although you can set that differently once you learn. Basics, first."

"Of course, sir."

"Ozlietsin, *aanj-y'ta!*" snapped the major sharply. Ozzie jumped to attention on the sofa.

High Court Shandrian commands? I thought Chel was teasing me. Gonna have to review that list again...

The gen hopped-flew to within a yard of Parthenos as the man continued to Sol, "You need to make her sniff it, lick it if she wants; she needs to learn this is a shape she never wants to fetch."

Sol held out the grenade to his symbiote, who perked her feelers curiously and sniffed with her jaw sensors. Almost instantly, Ozzie recoiled as if struck and gave Sol a look as if to ask, "How could you?"

"Sorry girl. You can sit back down." He pointed to the couch but she did not need an order. "What are they made from that they smell so repellant to her, sir?"

"Great question, astrum." Parthenos spoke authoritatively, as if teaching a class; Sol could imagine him as a civilian with a very different, peaceful life. "Their lubrication glands are –"

Alarms blared. Sol had never heard this one in tests or sims and clenched, nearly dropping the grenade. Ozzie leapt to her feet on the couch and screeched.

"White alert. Battle stations This is not a drill. White alert."

"Fuck!" Parthenos exclaimed. He snapped his mini-thermos into a holder on the desk as he grabbed his slate from his belt. "Follow me. Stay fucking close and drop when I say get down."

Sol swallowed hard as the major yanked the bomb from his hand and snapped it onto a pronged fixture at the rear of his utility belt. "What about Ozzie?"

Parthenos was already halfway out the door. "Tell her to stay."

They ran toward the starboard pipes. Sol's heart pounded. His assigned 'battle station' was 'secure the pharmacy and await instruction' but orders from the major overrode prior commands. They were nearly to the pipes when the alarm sounded again. The ship's voice was replaced by that of Colonel Kiertus.

"Alert suspended. All units to stay in place and await instruction. Checkmate to starboard pipes."

The major stopped and looked back at Sol, annoyed. "Stay with me and stay alert, astrum."

Soldiers stood and saluted stiffly as Parthenos and Sol ran by. As they entered the main hangar, Sol observed a ferocious looking Infiltrator and two uniformed people, their hands up, every gun available pointed in their direction. Even nervous Hanajiel was poised on a lift with a bead on the strangers.

"Major!" called a female voice.

"Auri! Great to see you. Help a brother out?" called the other captive.

Long ears twitched and a sigh escaped the big Ruhn. "Unfuckingbelievable." Parthenos turned back to Sol. "Watch and learn."

Shoving a few pilots and troopers aside, the major approached the two people in front of the awkwardly landed vessel. "Keep your guns on them, but let them remove their helmets," he instructed.

Piloting hoods lowered and breathing masks were removed, goggles went up. A man and a woman, both kaffir, both in armored versions of the SA pilot's uniform, purple and blue in color. She wore a captain's pin, and he wore a sharp, long emblem at which Sol squinted. *That's the Triaartja. It's the Haarnsvaar symbol. An Imperial Guild courier, maybe? I thought they had a different uniform?*

"Captain Enkashen, what's the proper procedure for entering a cruiser in hostile space?"

The woman saluted stiffly. "Major Parthenos, sir, the proper protocol is to warn and de-cloak before entering even if one can jump through shields, sir."

"Correct. What part of that did you forget?"

"I did not forget anything, sir, Cadet Lyfforth jumped in before I had cloaking off. I apologize to you and your crew, severely; I will accept any punishment you see fit, sir."

"Lyfforth? You realize I'm going to have to report this?"

"Auri, come on," the man shrugged and patted his fingers near his sternum. "You wouldn't do that to me, would you, bro?" The cadet attempted to walk forward, continuing to gesture with curled, gloved fingers to his heart; he was blocked by a number of rifles. "OK, maybe you would."

Parthenos grabbed the back of Lyfforth's collar and hauled him through the crowd. "Fucking idiot. You're lucky Wyvern's not here. He'd have shot you first." He turned his head back to the group. "At ease. Let her through."

Enkashen hopped down from the boarding platform as various arms lowered; a ripple of silver and blue mudlocks cascaded behind her. "Gods, major, I am so sorry, I really should have – "

"Shut up. That's what you should do. You should shut the fuck up."

"Sir! Yes, sir!" She stood before Parthenos. Captain Enkashen was tall, but he still towered. He released Cadet Lyfforth who held the back of his own neck as if it was quite sore and smiled cringingly.

The major's eyes softened as he regarded her although he was still tense and annoyed. "I'm glad to see you, even if you are a fucking idiot sometimes."

"Thank you, sir." She removed her gloves and cast big pale blue eyes around the hangar and the scads of men who still had not put their weapons away. "Where's Freyr? I was really hoping to see him…"

"Ugh. Not you, too," Parthenos snarled under his breath, rolling his eyes. "Classified, captain. He probably won't be back before you leave, either. Get your ass to medical and get to work. Astrum Solvreyil, please escort her. I'll deal with this moron and confirm all-clear. Behave yourselves, knights."

"Yes, sir." Both Enkashen and Solvreyil saluted at the same time, glancing at one another as they did so. Sol led the way quietly, although he had a lot of questions.

Tucking her gloves into her belt, looking about the hall as they traveled, the captain swore mildly. "Oh, crap. I left all my clothes at the station. I am having the stupidest damn day…"

"If it's any comfort, captain, everyone on the ship is pretty much staying in armor while we're out of Archon territory. You won't be out of place, sir."

"Well, yeah, but … I can fight in plain clothes. I'm like Parthenos. You know. HTS and all that?"

This gave Sol a start. "Really? I mean, really, sir? Me too, sir."

She pulled down the hooded collar of her uniform to display the double black tags. "See? Yeah. Sucks a dirty butt, doesn't it? At least we have some place to go, huh?"

"I bet I have something that'll fit you, sir. My cocoon's up the ladder on the left and just down the corridor, not too far out of our way. Sir."

Enkashen seemed genuinely happy. "Really? This outfit drives me crazy when I'm not flying. Please?"

Politely, Sol climbed to his bunk alone and retrieved an older, long sleeved shirt. He gestured to a nook, saying she could change down in medical when she began stripping in the hall. He looked away quickly and hold out the shirt.

"Uh, what's wrong? Don't you guys all change in front of one another?"

"I guess some of the guys do, I'm not really like that, sir." Sol kept his eyes on the floor, away from her.

"Aw. You must be the kid Wyvern was telling me about." He felt the shirt leave his hand and involuntarily glanced. As she struggled into it, he realized two things: her right arm was partially prosthetic and her chest was scarred as if both breasts had been surgically removed.

She seemed flat; I thought it was the vest. Ack, don't stare! It's rude!

"What? Oh, the scars? I had them removed for combat purposes. I guess women with HTS have higher cancer risk due to confused hormones, too, so it's for the better. I'll never model swimsuits, but hey, fuck that noise. I can hose a vertie in one shot." She winked and made a gun with her left hand. "Pew pew."

Sol smiled. Enkashen looked cute in the worn old mock turtleneck and her collars looked more like a fashion statement than a prison sentence. "So, you're a medic?"

"Yeah, I am now." Her face twitched. "I was a scout. I'm lucky P and Okie let me stay in the unit after I got my arm blown off. But, yeah. I'm going to back you guys up on Kourhos if you need it. The Kourhonoi religion mandates that females can't be touched by males they aren't married to, even doctors, so if you guys recover any injured women, I can attend to them."

"That's stupid, sir." They continued their stroll towards medical.

Enkashen shrugged. "I try not to judge, whatever, that's their beliefs, y'know? Not my problem. Anyway, I came early to help Laathas prep stuff for the graft surgeries he'll do while the *Sanjeera*'s docked at my station. I want to learn the procedures."

"Cool. Do you have a gen, sir?"

"Yeah, *they* live at Uayavu, though; I haven't gotten to see them a while. Too mean for station living." This clearly bummed the captain out. "I hope I can get a transfer back soon. I miss my buggle. And my friends. But mostly my bug!"

"Whoa, you have a 'gold' bug?"

Enkashen smiled hugely. "They are gold, yes, but they're oilburn and blue in default coloration. *Vazu'tki* breed, hyperdrone, with flight. Rare and gorgeous and such a menacey poo! I love my Fiend!" She popped out her slate and opened it to a photographic screen saver: a large shiny blue head that reflected rainbows between enormous glinting black eyes jammed against the camera. "See? My monster baby! Darling, no? There's a whole gallery on the desktop for when I'm sad."

As he flipped through the images, Sol felt impressed and out-classed; he fell back a little as he imagined the massive frightening beauty in combat with the slight, energetic captain. "I love my bug, sir, but I have to admit I'm a little jealous. Aren't those what the Haarnsvaar have?"

"They have *Semjazoi* or type 3 *Vazu'tki*, the ones with the better, more trainable dispositions. Don't be too jealous." She laughed. "That's what Wyvern classifies for... I guess he just doesn't want to stay at Uayavu for ten months training his to be able to come on this ship. Stupid, if you ask me, but don't tell anyone I said that."

Friends with both Wyvern and Parthenos? Seems like a risky spot to sit. "Not to pry, captain, but I did not know conduits could be medics, sir."

"Takes patience, training, and sometimes suppressors, but yes. The mental shift was the difficult part, going from scouting to search and rescue... You're S&R, right?"

"I guess so, sir. Parthenos put me on the roster..."

Enkashen stopped for a moment and her eyes widened on Sol. "That means he respects you. Or he wants you dead." She returned with renewed speed to walking before the final words were spoken.

Sol would prefer not to have heard them at all.

…

ISC Sanjeera cleared hostile space without incident and after a leap, approached Todekki Station. Solvreyil squeezed in extra training hours around his shifts, getting caught up on proper use of all his equipment. With the station dock and subsequent new recruits imminent, pharmacy priorities took over and Cheldyne cut several of his shifts so he could help medical prepare for the influx of troops.

Sol had worked through his usual shift and was pushing into his sleep time, but he was determined to organize the surgery schedule before 'morning' shifts started. Originally his primary motivation to finish this self-imposed project was to have a day without shifts in which to read or sleep as he chose. Hours into the epic disorganization, his determination was personal: to right the clerical errors of the asshole who left it this way in the first place.

Thank whatever intergalactic explorer stole the first coffee plants from whatever backwater crap hole it came from. How did I live without this stuff before Star Assault? Admittedly, he preferred tea for taste, but he found coffee's substance reassuring even while his brain functioned at a marginally higher speed. *I wonder how we afford it. It's grown on mountains in Holtiin, but was so expensive in shops I never even thought to order a cup. Kiertus called it a "military perk" and laughed like that was the funniest joke.*

He he was just over half way done. *This should go quickly now I've figured out Gronney's main error.*

Activity at the main door registered on the monitor. Sol tensed, apprehensive the entrant would be the person who created this nightmare and left it to fester mere days before the surgeries were scheduled to begin. He was relieved to see Doctor Laathas step into the office, relaxed, sipped his beverage, and returned to typing. *Wait a minute.* Sol glanced at the doctor again, shook his head and blinked. The man was wearing a large fluffy blue bathrobe over a loose casual top and ladders. He looked barely awake; some of his hair-tentacles rubbed his cheeks or scratched his scalp.

"Evening, sir. Is everything all right, sir?"

"Are you aware of the time, Solfreya?"

The astrum persisted at his endeavor with a shrug. "Absolutely. It's displayed on my screen, sir."

"Then you are aware it is technically two hours past zero, it is not technically 'evening', and your extended shift ended over an hour ago?"

"Corporal, it is not morning until you come in at four, sir." Sol smirked as he typed one-handed, sipping coffee with the other.

Laathas rolled his eyes. "Your knight master has infected you with his attitude, I see. No cure for that, I'm afraid." He tightened his robe and trotted over to observe Sol's work. "Merging those notes should have taken a half hour. What are you doing?"

"Would have taken a half hour if Gronney hadn't half-assed the alphabet, miscalculated times, and left out meal breaks?" He gestured to the screen as he looked at the man in charge. "Apologies, sir. Once I discovered that I couldn't just leave it. These are graft operations for new recruits, right? It's important to get it done in a timely manner so everyone has maximum recovery before training sessions start, right?"

The older kaffa stifled a yawn. "Fair enough, good job picking it up. I told that boy he needed to quit staring at Enki and pay attention to his work. I'll let Parthenos have a word with him." Laathas pulled up a stool next to Sol and began poking about on his slate, "I'm going to get a cup of brown death from the o-lounge and soak my feet in bug soup. You have anything to address with me before I go to that?"

"Actually, sir," the youth asked thoughtfully, slowing his typing, "I noticed my entry has a question mark on it. Are we still waiting on an all clear, or is that left over from Dromarka?"

"Sorry about his being an ass, but I approved you weeks ago, you realize? His power trips have no effect on my surgical schedule." Sympathy registered on the tired face. "You do not technically need a full set of plugs, due to your high rating. Response gloves and maybe interface salve would be all you'd need to fire a rifle. Now, that's not to say that you wouldn't want the grafts to 'fit in', as it were, or to avoid any unusual discomfort that might occur."

'Unusual discomfort'. I wonder what he's not saying this time? "I see, doctor, I think."

"Other men I've known, who score above the Tonser scale, but with lower Vaylen ratings than yours, do just fine with ships and in the field without grafts. Some, like the current colonel of the 89th, go with the grafts for formality's sake, then change their mind part way through the surgery. Or if you're Wyvern, you go with the grafts for aesthetic reasons and have them modified every few years to improve that value. It's a toss up, really, as to which one might find more comfortable: old-fashioned interface or civilized surgical grafts. I appreciate mine, but I need them." The surgeon shrugged, clapped his slate shut, regarded Sol with more than professional curiosity. "I leave it to you. You have a day or two to read about the procedures and differences on your own – keep your appointment scheduled, though. If you decide against surgery, I'm sure I can make other use of the time."

You're a sly old man. You know I'm going to say hell no to surgery. I'll bring two cups of tea with me when I come in for the appointment. Sol smiled however, appreciating that he was being treated like an adult. "Thanks, sir. This will be done by the time you're out of the bug broth. Would you like it mailed?"

Laathas was headed out the door already, stopping in the open doorway for a moment before he departed. "Eh, just leave it on the system for me to download. I'm intending to enjoy the novelty of a soak without my slate beeping. Get some sleep and do that reading I mentioned; I'll see you in a few days."

…

"When you told me about my mother and father, I wasn't cleared to know that, was I?"

Laathas chuckled as he blew on his tea. "Absolutely not." He held up the cup. "Thanks, by the way."

"So did you know I was going to have a higher GC when I walked out of the office?"

"The ship flagged your reaction in the airlock; she knew first. But it was visible to me on sight… one learns the signs after some time in the field." He used an archaic Ryzaan term for 'field' that could mean both an area of expertise or a physical location where battle might take place. "Did you look up her records, now that you can see some of them?"

"I can get about five pages, and it's mostly black lines. I can't see my dad at all beyond, 'Solvreyil Kvatchkiir Meshaan, deceased'. Even his age is blanked out. Who stays classified after their death?"

The surgeon coughed tea out his nose. "You can't see his blood type or age?"

"No. Black lines. The 'service history' section read 'document expunged'."

"Hm. Well my bad for mentioning anything, I suppose. I expect an earful from Sheriden at some point."

Silence fell. Sol knew he would get no further direct information about his parents fromLaathas, so he switched to his other recent reading topic. "So, Planetary Air Defense is actually a division of Star Assault. Can you explain to me why we don't use that to a publicity advantage?"

The branch-jumping surgeon seemed the best person to ask beside Parthenos, and he never wanted to be perceived as wasting P's time. He watched Laathas' face move thoughtfully as he sipped. His hair continued to disinfect itself with sanitary wipes as he considered his words.

"It's not like you can't see the SA logos on air bases. You've certainly visited the base at Holtiin, yes?"

"Well, yes, of course. I took a tour of the unclassified sections in Framework. I wasn't even consciously aware I saw the Haarvakjya all over until I was reading about Air Defense yesterday. They're understated, not something one would notice unless specifically looking." Sol took a drink of tea, savoring it. The bags were graciously donated from the colonel's personal stock. They chatted briefly in the hive that morning while Sol cleaned around the pool; he finally thanked Kiertus for the crescent pistol, even though he had yet to hold it. "In light of my reading, I get why the tour focused on the IGN and ICSM sections and 'meeting an Air Defender' was about five minutes of him saying how happy he was to be part of the team that kept us safe. No recruitment propaganda. Didn't seem odd at the time; I wonder what answer I'd have gotten if I asked."

"Cagey avoidance or riddles, most likely. Those guides are usually high level base staff in civvies for the day." The surgeon did hand exercises; flex, curl, massage. Flex, curl, massage. "It's less a secret than an elegant dance around an unpleasant subject. The general civilian populace is happier if they don't think about why Air Defense is necessarily trained by Star Assault, why only combat veterans can transfer to that unit... are you following?"

"It's only reasonable rookie D-7 pilots flying in civilian airspace would be discouraged, although it seems to me there would be unpopulated or barren places to train."

"Sure, they could be trained in space first. AD's Sevens are just like the ones on this ship. They can go pretty much anywhere. But even without that fact, you're missing why only combat veterans – not just trained pilots – are employed by Air Defense." Laathas looked up from his hands, picked up his cup for a drink, as Sol shrugged. "Would you really want the civilian populace and the supporting ecosystem of Holtiin, of your home, protected by people who lost their ladders at the sight of verties entering the atmosphere?"

The visual in Sol's mind – vertebra-shaped fighters firing multi-tip propulsor projectiles into screaming crowds in a burning New Asria - churned his guts. He cringed. "I'd say you made that point, doc. A little sorry I asked now."

"On a more positive note, the necessity of these units to train those keeps the 17th alive. Parthenos has pushed before the council to formally change the division name to 17th Atmospheric Crisis Response, since that is one of our functions – getting there first and saving lives – but his even bringing it up started the usual civilian and ex-marine petty politician trash talking and initiated another move to completely cut us from the budget."

"That's insane. Who would pick up the slack? Rim Patrol?"

"Realistically? No one. They say Rim Patrol and the ICSM could, but they'd depend on the 89th to do everything we currently do. They'd never cut the 89th even though they're afraid to invoke the unit name in the council chamber. Even if a single unit could do everything – and as we're all painfully aware, just two units is pushing it – there's a strong question of how they'd keep the 89th from revolt in the wake of executing at least 20 officers."

Sol choked. "Executing?"

"Even though you haven't been here long, please, tell me: are Sheriden and Parthenos men you think would retire on request, passively, and go make farms on some outer colony planet? Do you think they would quietly accept Air Defense jobs, parted out to Mior-knows-where to rot in command of some podunk airbase? Do you think they could watch this ship, to which they've given their lives, dry-docked and hashed for parts? There are some officers in this unit who cannot even re-station; they literally have nowhere else to go. What happens to them?"

He could imagine his knight master quite peacefully tending a small farm, except considering the loss of the *Sanjeera*, the modest house and fluffy herd beasts rapidly transformed to a bar floor. "That's sad to consider, sir. But it also urges me further to ask you, why are you here? Can you even tell me?"

"I could be anywhere I chose. I chose this ship, this crew, and these commanders. When you have served a long time, it is not easy to settle down in civilian space surrounded by strangers with whom you cannot identify. Being home on Archos makes me cry, Solfreya; it is such a beautiful world, and I do enjoy visiting, but I would rather be out making sure nothing ever happens to it, and should I die, I will die beside my friends, protecting paradise to my last breath."

"Apologies, sir. I've never been to Archos." He decided not to amend the statement with the painful truth that he had never experienced friendship on a level where dying near those people would be meaningful. Sol could only abstractly understand the sentiment and felt both blessed and cursed by the intelligence that allowed him to recognize that abstraction. "Not for a lack of desire to do so, though, sir."

The surgeon's eyes were sympathetic as he stood and donned his smock. "But you grew up on Holtiin, which is just as much a part of that paradise. I suppose it's easy to take heaven for granted when you've never been to hell." A firm hand squeezed Sol's shoulder before he departed from the break room.

....

Parthenos called a quick meeting while they were docked at Todekki, informing they would be hanging around a bit to pick up more recruits. The crew was instructed initial terror attempts were thwarted 'by forward operatives of Star Assault and the Imperial Guild' but the danger was not over and all were to remain on alert. While here, however, a few groups were cleared for live fire drills on Gravian, 'a sorry little mining planet' in Todekki's jursidiction. The major personally took Sol aside after the meeting to let him know he was in Dromarka's group with a bunch of newer trainees. "I could put you in Mysh's group instead with men closer to your class, but I trust you to watch and report, understood?"

Deserts were not Sol's thing. Rationally, this cold, stony waste should not have bothered him that much. It was just windy, dusty, and cold, and he was covered completely by ladders, carapace, and additional membranes to prevent exposure. At no part of the day did temperatures soar to an incinerating level, unlike the rocky 'death zones' on Holtiin. The sun was not blindingly bright, instead distant, red, and dismal. He had previously never seen a star he would describe as 'ugly' and felt a little sorry for Ummaxia and this craggy rock that orbited it. He could not imagine anyone wanted to live in alkaline filth, but apparently a group of former miners were trying to establish a permanent settlement here.

I guess just this part of the Bleeding Desert is high alkaline. Laathas mentioned he and Parthenos were coming down here for 'baths' of some kind a few hours before we came in. Rolling in the sand on the other side of that mesa, apparently. I think he was pulling my shaft. How would having a dusty crack be any cleaner than dipping in the hive pool?

Sol shifted again, flexed his torso and stretched his arms as instructed to dump accumulating sediment from armor crevices. The suit's sensitivity was attuned enough, or he was so hyper-aware from his pharms, he felt the buildup well before it could interfere with motion. Some of this week's trainees were not doing as well. Dismayed, he watched them take turns at the targets. This was the third tediously identical session he suffered through this week; eventually Dromarka would have farted around enough with all the newbies and would announce it was time to return. There would be a glib apology and the armory sentinel would continue to hold Sol's rifle, taking full advantage of the fact Parth was far too busy to examine usage and check-in records. *Busy trying to replace you or find an excuse to brig your ass.*

Sol reported during a piss break as he had each previous day. He copied the mail to Myshkor and Parthenos as before, but was surprised not to receive the usual, 'He's working on his Silver Asshole medal, dude!' from Mysh. Parth's silence was typical, but the Infiltrator that materialized and landed certainly was not. The mask hid Sol's smug joy. *Finally! Oh please, be Parthenos. And let the acoustics of this place be in favor of me hearing every word.* Sol laughed, which he buried in a mostly fake cough.

171

Dromarka, bothered by the interruption, halted exercises and approached the elaborately customized craft. He crossed his arms, stared up at the hatch and waited. To the surprise of all present, Colonel Kiertus stepped regally down in full armor, goggles and face guard up, breathing mask down.

"Good afternoon, Sergeant Dro'mr'kaal. I came to watch the rifle drills," he called with a cheerful wave. "Has my new astrum done his yet? Oh? Well fabulous, because I would love to see how he's doing with my own eyes! Carry on, now."

On one hand, Droo will hate me even more. On the other hand, fuck that guy.

The arms sergeant saluted and turned back to the line of soldiers, although he did not get far. A long-fingered, gloved hand fell on his armored shoulder with a clap. "Excuse me, one moment, sergeant. Where is Astrum Solvreyil's rifle?"

Dromarka performed such an excellent imitation of rigor mortis that softer portions of his carapace armor stiffened and flared, then curled inward. "Colonel Kiertus, sir, it is lying against that rock over there, where he left it, sir."

Even at the distance he stood, Sol could feel eyes boring into him and see a single brow arch as the colonel's finger beckoned. He traversed the sand as professionally as possible, in spite a profound urge to skip. Kiertus turned to Dromarka. "Now, Athaaresh, I know you wouldn't lie to me, but I'd like it if you lifted your goggles and lowered your mask. Oh, pardon me, did I call you by your given name, Sergeant Droo'mr'kaal? How disrespectful of me. That's an order, sergeant. Face me in your elven flesh." The smoky voice chilled and sharpened, reminiscent of the wind.

Sol took a position a few steps behind and to the left of Dromarka. He saluted Colonel Kiertus, but his eyes were on the sergeant's back as the man unmasked.

Kiertus crossed his arms and waited. The moment the mask was off, he stared down Dromarka sternly. "Tell me, Armory Sentinel –formerly-Captain Dro'mr'kaal Athaaresh, did Solvreyil abandon his rifle at the rock because he is an inexperienced soldier who does not fully realize the risks inherent in leaving military hardware unattended or because he was ordered not to pick it up by a superior officer?"

Sol wished he could see Droo's expression, particularly when addressed like a child by his full name. 'Dromarka' was an odd Ryzaanization of his mother's Shandrian name, a fact Sol had learned reading what the sergeant kept public. He did not like the Ryzaan character used for both first and final syllables ("ul" in Standard Archon) or the way people were wont to pronounce it. He was raised in Ryzaa and considered himself Ryzaan, he explained, but still could not stomach butchery of his mother's name. The astrum continued to gaze upon his superiors as the long pause became uncomfortable. Finally, Dromarka – Dro'mr'kaal – said, "The latter, sir."

"Thank you for being honest. You are dismissed to your quarters aboard the *Sanjeera* and relieved of all duties until further notice. Lieutenant Aukaldir will fly you back in my vessel. You will have a meeting with Disciplinary Officers Parthenos or Yadzfreyr at their discretion." Kiertus saluted and waited; Dromarka continued to stand before him. "Maybe you missed it, but I definitely said," the colonel spoke slowly, raising his voice for the final word, "'dismissed'."

Dromarka saluted, turned, and boarded the craft. Sol's eyes switched back to the irritable-looking colonel.

"Return to the line, soldier, we haven't got all night," commanded Kiertus with a rushed salute.

Sol spun about, hopped quickly to the rock and acquired his missing piece. It resembled a knee-high sculpture of a serpentine form coiling up a slender tree trunk with a flower on top. The coils looped open at the end opposite the flower, just enough to allow a forearm through. The "sculpture" was rendered in an iridescent rubbery black substance that shimmered when lifted from the ground. The side leaning against the rock featured a dark half-egg shape nestled in the coils near the hole.

He had seen other men arm theirs and done so in simulation, but Sol had never held an actual V-Tek 760. This was exciting, but unfortunately sort of embarrassing in front of his knight master.

Dammit! He slid his arm through the receptive opening and his hand fumbled in the cluster of coils beneath the egg. *Where the hell's the grip? It seems so obvious in mockups. Oh wouldn't it just be rich if after all this my gun was defective and needed to be returned?*

The airman nearest him quietly asked, "Hey, sir, you having some trouble, sir?"

Sol glanced at Kiertus, keeping his voice similarly hushed, smiling as he spoke to make the conversation appear jovial from a distance. "Because of Droo being a cockbite, I've never held a real rifle. I feel stupid; where's the hand grip?"

"Aukaldir said it's different on every one." The airmen looked off, suddenly bashful. "But he said it's like a woman; you gently caress the folds and you'll know the spot when she responds."

"What?!" exclaimed Sol, flustered beyond all belief. His hand shifted on the coils as his body tensed; the spongy folds woke to his pulse and admitted his fingers. Still getting over the disturbing, inappropriate statement and his apprehensions about mishandling expensive bio-weaponry, he buried his hand in the material and grasped. Amidst the spongy substance, covered in a thin layer of rubbery skin, was a bony handle that fit comfortably in his palm. This he recognized, as it was properly imitated on simulators and he had squeezed one many times.

"Yeah, like that, sir!" The man jumped back suddenly as the sculpture reconfigured itself into a proper rifle. This should not have been any shock to him as he held a nearly identical weapon; Sol realized why right as he said, "What the fuck, you don't have any grafts, sir! Colonel!"

Sol could neither express gratitude for the assistance nor order their commander's presence unnecessary; he was caught up in fusion with the aggressive bio-ware. The larger of the lowest coils unfurled and wrapped his upper arm while the barrel telescoped outward with an oily creak. Tubes along either side of the barrel filled with fluid; the "flower" shifted and two small orbs opened near the tip while a red-violet pyramidal crystal emerged from the "petals". Tiny tendrils snaked out from the large one that wrapped his arm and sunk through the semi-permeable membrane at the shoulder of his armor. Sol gasped; they felt like miniscule sharp, sucking mouths. He panted as the sting turned to a burn but could not take his eyes from the gun, feeling pulse hungrily siphoned into the charge chamber. The rifle tightened its grip and the thin black membrane drew away from the glaring red-violet orb. Sol was happy for both the mask that covered his parted, saliva-dripping fangs and the armor kilt that concealed his similarly seeping erection.

The colonel, properly masked and goggled now, looked right at him. "All in order to fire that thing, Astrum Solvreyil?"

"Yes, sir, I can perform my primary function, sir!" *For the love of fuck, let me discharge this!*

"Step forward and sight the target, then, astrum! What are you waiting for? Move it!"

Sol hopped to the front of the line and forward to a marked area. Two other soldiers stepped to position, but Kiertus threw up an arm and yelled again.

"Did I order you airmen to the stage? No? Fall back!" The colonel scanned the line, cast a glance at Sol, and then hastily added, "That goes for the whole unit; fall back ten paces!" As the last soldier hurried into place, Kiertus whipped back toward Sol, pointed at the target and commanded, "Fire!"

Releasing the trigger was akin orgasm, albeit one that knocked the wind from him; he felt the energy sucked from his body, a peculiar prickle that accumulated somewhere around his solar plexus, up his thorax and out his forearm. Sol was so wrapped up in this moment he barely noticed he hit the target wall, and completely missed the arc of sparks that rained off his body.

"Fuck shit man! Wow!" came the voice of a trooper behind him.

The others were in on it too. "Holy fuck, sirs!"

"Pardon my Ryzaan, colonel, astrum, but I can't blame Dromarka for not wanting to give him a gun, sir."

Kiertus approached his astrum, who stood a few inches from where he originally fired. Sol examined his goggles, wondering if they had fogged somehow, as the colonel spoke in a peculiar tone to the buzzing crowd behind. "At ease, boys. Training's over, everyone assemble for pickup."

Airmen grumbled as they shuffled about. "Lame. I wanted to go again, sir…"

"That's not really possible, I fear." Kiertus clasped Sol's shoulder. "Is it, Astrum Solvreyil?"

"Sir? Did I hit the target, sir?"

"The reason you cannot see the target wall, Solvreyil," he leaned in and pointed, "is because it is no longer there. See those fragments of rock? That was the east edge of the wall." He patted the astrum's back, shaking his head. Louder, he called to the crew. "Everyone assemble in the depression near the landing site for inspection. We'll go over cleaning and stripping rifles in the hangar."

"Sorry, I didn't mean to blow it up, sir." Sol looked down, noticing oddly discolored areas on his commander's armor slowly returning to normal, and at their feet, a pronounced ring of black char.

"I can only guess you hit a vein in the rock with the full brunt of the blast. All that red streaking on everything is iron oxide, that's what gives this desert its name… Haven't seen a man shoot with a rifle that wickedly in a gen's age." He gave Sol a shoulder hug, an odd performance in full armor. "There are other walls we can use or set up, it's nothing in particular. You do need to see Laathas, immediately. Meet me for tea when you've finished your shifts. Understand?"

Sol saluted, in a shocked sort of pride. "Yes, sir!"

…

There were a small handful of officers in the lounge, not quite enough to make Sol feel self-conscious but enough that he had to navigate a little to get to the office door. Kiertus waited within, making grave faces at his laptop. Relief dispersed the dourness as he cast a glance toward his guest. "Oh, you're here, fantastic! Have a seat on the sofa, please, just leave the door open, thank you." The colonel retrieved the tea service and poured two cups. "How do you feel?"

"Colonel Kiertus, sir, thank you for the tea, sir. Discharging that rifle was something else, sir. Simulation really does not compare." Sol was still giddy; he blushed and giggled a little, then apologized.

"By all means, it's quite alright. We do have some rather thrilling equipment at our disposal." Kiertus stirred a sweetener stick into the steaming cup in his hand. His smile was peaceful but sly. "Should I dismiss you to go off and have some 'special alone time'?"

Solvreyil gave his commander a funny look. *Does he mean to go masturbate? I already came like four times today.* "Thank you colonel, but I think I'll be alright, sir." He looked into his tea; it was whole-leaf fah, a high grade, subtle and floral, the kind one could never find in Holtiini shops because it was all exported. "Sir, I expect that Dromarka will feel poorly towards me over this incident, well, more than he already did, sir. I am afraid I regret ratting him out, even though it sped up my training. I also regret inconveniencing Major Parthenos and yourself, sir."

"First, the formality is not necessary. We are master and astrum, at the moment. Second, while I cannot speak for Parthenos on this particular matter, I can tell you that were it not for my workload, I would have been more than happy to issue your gear and walk you through each step. Dro'mr'kaal's poor choices were the inconvenience." The long-fingered hand brought the painted cup to his lips, from which a short, frustrated sigh escaped before he drank. Solvreyil could not shake the impression that what he witnessed there was deep disappointment, possibly on the level of 'heartbreak'.

"I still apologize, sir. I feel badly that I snitched on him, sir."

Setting down the cup, the colonel sighed again. "Certain members of my long-term staff have pushed for an official investigation into Dro'mr'kaal for a while, due to what they perceived as sympathy for the Ruhn genocide espoused in posts on SACnet. I personally did not feel the comments warranted a Sec5 investigation or Haarnsvaar involvement. People talk shit and quests to justify senseless atrocity are normal." He drank again, watching Sol's face. "He was seen with GPM materials. Such literature is not illegal to possess, mind you; advanced philosophy courses at the Junior Academy require a thorough examination of a plethora of objectionable viewpoints." His look was apologetic. The Genetic Purity Movement discouraged breeding with humans and viewed haki like Sol to be 'degenerate abominations' not even fit for slavery. "There is no crime in believing in such nonsense, of course, 'long as no recognized or prospective citizen of the Empire should come to harm'. Interfering in the function of a military vessel, however, is treason. I will respect everyone's privacy as regards my ultimate decision, but upon reaching Avenaur, Dro'mr'kaal will no longer be a member of this crew."

Sol almost dropped his lovely little teacup. To quell his vibrating hand, he examined the elaborate painting on the thing; some manner of conveyance floated in the harbor of a fantastic city. It reminded him of photographs of Ryzaa City, but rendered in a style that made everything squatter and blockier. The painting was blue on white, so further detail was not readily apparent. There were glyphs of some sort on the cup, although they were unlike any language he knew. "That's heavy. I guess it explains a lot though. Do you have someone to replace him, yet, sir?"

"Parthenos negotiated a transfer through the Avenaur base, in theory. I'm sure things will be just fine." Kiertus sipped. Silence fall over the room. After a short time, he stretched his legs and inquired, "Is there anything else that has you tense, astrum?"

Yes. I don't even know if I can evem address it. But I can't imagine who else I would speak to if not you…

"Well, colonel," Sol began, finally getting some nerve.

"Sheriden," the colonel corrected. "If the informality really bothers you, try 'Master Kiertus', please."

"Yes, sir. Master Kiertus." *That feels weird, too.* "Will I ever get to work with Val or Wyvern again?"

Kiertus cradled his tea cup and nodded. "Of course. I already had words with Parthenos about your removal from their instruction. I understand his reasoning, but he overrode my decisions without consulting me, and his constant fear of revenge from Wyvern is ludicrous. Don't repeat that, mind you; those wounds are old but they are still quite real and quite mutual."

It disappointed Sol not to have seen or heard from him in some time. "Wyvern sent me a prayer after the major challenged me. I didn't know the proper response, so I didn't say anything. I think I may have offended him. I did not realize, the, uh, depth of his commitment to his faith, at the time."

"Solvreyil, how far have you gotten in that book I loaned you?"

"Not far, sir, shamefully. It's quite dense for poetry. I keep stopping to look up words, and everything is double meanings, at least where I am right now. Would you like it back?"

"No, no… it's by far the best way to explain the intricacies of Shandrian feudal society, I think. Something you need to learn." The tone's gravity was not reduced by the compassionate face; underneath it all was a definite *something*

Sol could not pin down.

"I've read the knight's handbook," Sol offered. "I get some of it, and I've been trying to ask the right people the right questions."

Kiertus seemed a little surprised. "It's possible I should just short cut the process and explain why I loaned you the book. Our schedules are terrible right now, and it could be a long while before –"

The all-call alarm shattered the air. Parthenos' voice crackled over the public address system. "Secure positions. Undocking from station and preparing to jump. Repeat, secure all stations." The ship's voice followed with a series of instructions; she sounded bored reciting them.

Kiertus stared at the ceiling in deep aggravation. "Now? Really?"

"What should I do, colonel?"

"Don't worry about the pharmacy; Enki has it under control. Go to your cocoon and see if you can sleep through the trip. We might need you on the other side. I have to go to the bridge." Kiertus stood. "If you can't sleep, read. Specifically, the poem called, 'The First Prince of the Stars'."

A hand fell on Sol's arm as the man passed him. He looked up. "Yes, sir. Anything you need, please, just tell me, I know I'm not worth much yet –"

"Don't be ridiculous. You're worth plenty. Secure yourself." The hand squeezed and then released and the colonel was gone.

. . .

The book, as Sol understood so far, was the story of a young boy in a fishing village in the northernmost reaches of ancient Aurius. The village was pressed against a range of foothills contested between Aurius, Ryzaa, and Shendiir (the story took place shortly before Shendiir and Aurius unified as 'Eshandir'). Ryzaan troops invaded the village under the belief a mighty weapon was hidden there and burned it to ashes searching. A Shendiir warrior prince, on field exercises with his men, happened upon the razing, routed the invaders and discovered the orphaned boy. The prince returned to his arboreal mountainside manor with the adolescent and educated him in folk-ways. At first Sol viewed the situation as an adoption, but as he caught the subtleties, the prince's

179

intentions were far from fatherly.

Reading this far was labor; the language was arcane and perspective swapped between boy and prince with the only warning being a slight tonal change in the narrative poems. Stranger still, a third perspective was introduced about half way through; when the fairly youthful prince would tell tales of Shendrian folklore, he employed a different, older voice, which Sol identified as some sort of predecessor metaphorically speaking through him. This understanding drove him to re-read many prior parts. Exhaustion was nodding him face first into the aged pages as he reached the recommended poem.

As if dreaming he absorbed in fragments a legend of love and sacrifice, how the entity Maalek annihilated himself to save 'the first elves' and how Aur, his primary lover, collected nine pieces, but his other lover – strangely his rival, also - took four and refused to allow Aur to repair the fallen deity. Wracked with desperation and grief, Aur captured primitive creatures and forced parts into them so each would develop some of Maalek's former talents and he would live on forever in their offspring.

This is single-handedly the most bizarre mythology of my people. Why is it even in this book? And what the fuck is Kiertus trying to tell me? Have kaffir soldiers just been on crazy drugs since time began?

VII. That Kind of Archon.

Buzz, buzz, buzz.

"What? What? Ozzie? Are you …"

Time eluded him, but he could not have been asleep long. More angry buzzing, then Ozlietsin growled. She grabbed the slate furiously in her mouth and shoved it at Sol.

Wyvern's texting me? Where the hell has he been? Oh gods, was I sleep-drooling on that precious book?

::: Meet in starboard pipes, now. Full armor, no bug. Order.::::

He texted affirmative as he scrambled over Ozzie and into his gear. She made an effort to join him, perplexed at his refusal. "You haven't trained to be around humans yet. Sorry. Chew your toys, not the smelly book, OK? Good girl."

…

"Astrum! Over here!" Valdieren's voice originated near a Dash positioned on the launch catapult. Val inspected while Wyvern hoisted canisters of foaming agent into the projectile compartments.

Wyvern did not turn but acknowledged Sol with a wave. "Get in and settled. We'll brief you in a second."

You're too busy for me to tell you how happy I am to see you. "Yes, sir!"

Captain Enkashen was inside, stocking emergency supplies in various compartments. "Give me a hand putting this away. Pharms forward, wound closure supplies in those two bins, extra masks and blankets there." Full paratrooper armor looked peculiar on her slight frame. Sol wondered if he looked that odd in his. Her slate squeaked; she popped it up and cursed. "They just changed my ship assignment. Dammit."

She raced from the vessel and vanished across the hangar as Val slid through the forward hatch. "Looks like you're alone with us unless they toss someone else our way. I thought three captains to one Dash was unbalanced."

"One more coming," Wyvern remarked as he climbed in and took the master seat.

"Copy that." Val watched Sol as he waited. "Have you injected yet? Your armor's being really flashy."

"Aw, shit, sir. My bad, captain." Sol fumbled his syrigun from his belt. "Combat or jump?"

"Combo. Ideally you'll only need the one but …"

Sol nodded as he loaded the proper color of charge. "Understood, sir."

Wyvern secured hatches after Aukaldir climbed in. "What's up, cap'ns?" He fastened himself in next to Sol. "Hey, astrum, shoot me up?"

"Excuse me, lieutenant?"

Val chuckled as the ship started and Aukaldir handed Sol his loaded syrigun. "Shoot me up. I hate doing it myself." He fingered open the vent on his upper sleeve. Sol twitched his lips but knew what to do. His companion's face showed tension, then relief, and finally turned back with a smile. "Thanks."

"Heads up." Val kept his eyes on them but moved towards the cockpit. "Parth and Myshkor are leading the primary relief units, we'll be providing support. We might not have to hit ground at all; depends on the casualty to survivor ratio and overall feasibility of rescues. We've got analog parachutes but shouldn't even need them – we should be able to get close enough to rope-drop or land if we have to go in. The Theocracy's units are occupied and we shouldn't even end up in confrontation." Valdieren slid into the cockpit, sat, and tethered.

"So, I take it our ops didn't get all the terrorists, then, sirs?" Aukaldir asked the cockpit, half smile on his swarthy face.

Wyvern's voice returned in severe perturbation: "No they fucking did not, lieutenant. Would you like to make any other fucking critiques of our extremely strained intelligence and scout units?"

The crooked grin remained but he glanced at Sol and gave him a nudge as he winced and replied, "No, sir, Commander Wyvern, sir, I certainly would not!"

The cockpit door slammed shut. Aukaldir squirmed from quelled laughter.

"Is agitating him wise, lieutenant?"

He responded quietly as he wiped a tear from his eye. "No. It's just funny. Prob'ly pay for it later." He gently nudged Sol's foot with his. "Your drugs kicking yet?"

"Oh, that's what that is. Never done the combo shot before." Sol grinned stupidly.

"Don't worry, that crazy rushing sensation dies down pretty quick." Aukaldir leaned back and closed his eyes. "Try to relax and enjoy. I know it's kinda hard to chill with Freaksauce up there but at least I got him to shut the door, huh?"

Sol wanted to say something in Wyvern's defense, but was profoundly distracted by the sensation of softer extremities – his tongue, his cock, his ear tips – feeling as though they melted. What came out was, "Nggh... rrrngh...?"

Both men laughed. Val's direly serious voice issued from a speaker. "Attention, drugged up jack holes in crew cabin – flaming fruit butt plug, do you copy?"

Sol twisted his face and stared at the door. "Was that some military jargon I should know?"

The lieutenant shook his head. "That's just Cap'n V fucking with you to see if you're paying attention, yeah." He whacked the response button and replied, "Affirmative, Bootstrap. Butt plug, on fire, composed of fruit. Suggested course of action: remove from rectum."

"Preparing to launch." This time it was Wyvern's voice, tinged ever so slightly with amusement.

Sol felt his body move with the ship, as if he were part of it. It was as frightening as it was enjoyable. He breathed a little "Whoa," as they shot into space. His experience flying in a D-7's gun seat had been less pharmaceutical-intensive. His fingers dug into the cushion beneath him.

"It's even more impressive up front." Aukaldir's eyes remained closed as he relaxed against the spongy rear of the bench. Had they carried their bugs, the spongy areas would have given way to allow the genadri to nestle in a nook behind each. "Very different from simulation, no?"

"Completely."

An automated voice reported, "Jumping. In. Five. Minutes."

"Never done this part before…"

"Oh? Well, it's nothing; just relax as much as you can."

'Nothing' was hardly how Sol would have described it. For a moment, he felt as if his entire body was liquefying and running all over the crew cabin. He shut his eyes and tried to follow his companion's advice but he clenched, spasmed, and before he knew it, vomited profusely.

Sol opened his eyes to Aukaldir's smile as he wretched into a suction device the lieutenant held for him.

"Everything alright back there?"

"How you doin', astrum? Stabilized yet?"

Surprisingly, he felt limber and liberated, minus some stray bits on his face. "Think I'm all right, sir?"

Aukaldir released the device; it snapped back to the bench. "All good, Bootstrap." He passed Sol a towel.

Sol wiped his face. He felt great, if a bit embarrassed. "That won't happen every time, will it?"

"No, that's your suppressors fighting with the vyddarin," rasped Wyvern. "Talk to Bonesaw and Checkmate when we're back on the Sanj. If you need back up for the argument, I'll come with."

"Will do, sir. Thank you, sir." *He'd stand up to P … for me?*

"Damn. Dude must like you," whispered the lieutenant after the communicator clicked off. Sol only shrugged. "That would freak me right out, but it's kinda lucky, kinda."

They circled for a time after entering the atmosphere; comments from the cockpit indicated they viewed extensive damage to the city below. The door between them opened.

"This wasn't on the original target list," Sol heard Wyvern say. "I think we missed it because there are no Defense Ministry buildings here…"

Val surveyed monitors, a tone of disturbance in his voice. "What is here? Or was here?"

"Ministry of Communications."

"A major office of it? I can't even find it on the layover map…"

Wyvern leaned over the console just enough to point a location. "Right there. Small office, but apparently involved in the 'cleansing' operation."

The cockpit went silent. Sol saw Val staring down Wyvern dubiously. The younger captain's voice came slowly. "You don't suppose our operatives overlooked a few locations on accidental purpose, do you?"

"What might you be suggesting, there, Bootstrap?" Wyvern's response was cold and dry.

Val's eyes closed as he turned to the monitor and shook his head. "Suppose there are any survivors?"

"Somewhat likely. The people here are tough, even if they do plan their cities for shit." Wyvern called through the door. "This is devastation, as brought by Archon ingenuity in the hands of humans."

A monitor dropped into the crew cabin and came on to show a leveled city. Sol and Aukaldir whistled; there was an appreciable level more sorrow in the noise from Solvreyil.

Wyvern's explanation was emotionless. "Quake charges prey on natural fault lines. They often require a suicide drop into a deep location to set up properly, but the effect, as you can see, is impressive. There seem to have been additional gas charges set up in key buildings; the damage to the buildings triggered those, releasing toxic gas into the already damaged city."

"The particular gas released here is potentially lethal to pure humans. It wasn't originally developed for that." Val on the other hand seemed morose. "It was a Ryzaan bio-agent for crowd control, a fast acting virus that affects muscle tissue, to immobilize groups in a small area. Kaffir have natural defenses to it, especially those raised on Holtiin and Archos; kaffir in units like Star Assault are immunized against it. Pure humans have less to fight it. Most need to treat the symptoms immediately or they suffer system shock or organ failure. It's… unpleasant."

Who would do something this horrible? And why does the Empire still produce something that dreadful? "So um, Checkmate and Bonespur, they're already down there, right?"

"They're in one of the known target cities, Seventy-eight. This is Tukodok."

Ugh being a number is lame. "Affirmative."

"Holiday? We're going to drop you here. There are signs of life around some undamaged buildings in this area. Careful, though; they power part of this city and some of their vehicles with combustible gases and the environment may be unstable. The entire west side of the city up to the river is on fire…"

Wyvern coughed. "River's on fire."

"Um. Yeah. West side up to and including the river is on fire. Holiday, are you go?"

Aukaldir stood and gave Sol a nod and salute. "Affirmative, Bootstrap." He gripped handles along the ceiling and maneuvered to the rear hatch. "Do you trust that roof to rope drop me since I don't have my little killin' machine?"

"I don't trust the roof on any of these buildings. We're going to swing in and drop you on that low thing there; I think it's a warehouse. Most of this sector is abandoned so I'm surprised we're seeing anything resembling life. You fully armed?"

"Affirmative."

Wyvern's voice was tense. "Circling in."

Sol watched on the monitor as wind and heat from the Dash tossed debris around atop the building. Aukaldir gripped a triangular structure cabled to a dispenser in the craft as the hatch opened. He gave Sol a wave and hopped out, using his pulse to create a resistance cushion and break his fall. The cable snapped back into the ship and the door closed. As they lifted away, Sol watched the previously decrepit, now half-leveled neighborhood shrink from view. *'Population crisis within Theocratic states has been aggravated by entire districts becoming unlivable due to pollution, disease, infrastructure issues and crime,' Parthenos' report informed. 'Due to ill-thought subterranean construction, sinkholes and landslides limit access to older, less funded sections of major cities; stranded individuals and even whole communities who could not afford importation of food or potable water are known to have died in atrocious conditions in such locales.'*

Growing up on Holtiin meant Sol had seen cities where ingenious and far-thinking people built structures over and into existing quake damage. *The humans where I lived may sometimes have been afraid, but they learned from the kaffir, at least. We built for survival and adaptability and everyone who doesn't grow his own food has emergency supplies...*

"No way."

"Excuse me, Bootstrap?"

"I'm getting a sign of life in the parking garage near the Ministry building."

Silence fell for a moment before Wyvern remarked, "I'd say that warrants a 'no way'. Maybe even a 'no fucking way'. Seventy-eight, are you ready to lose fear in the face of glory?"

Sol's heart jumped. "Sir! Yes, sir!" *That gas kills humans. I'm only half and I'm immunized, right?*

"We're going to pull over this park, low enough for you to just hop out," Val's cursor lit up on the map. "You'll be headed here. There's a mini-map loaded in your slate but you'll have to depend on its detection abilities; this cursor won't be there. We didn't really have the wherewithal to set all this up optimally. Remember the building shapes. Look out for fires. Mind your pulse around any hissing vents – it could be flammable gas. Your armor should be able to detect it and warn you."

"Understood, Bootstrap."

"Don't trip over any bodies, they're nasty."

Lifting his mask, Sol licked his slightly puke-flavored lips. "Um, duly noted, Wyvern."

"Honor and sacrifice, buddy. Stay alert and keep in touch." Val turned to give him a brave smile through the cockpit door as he backed toward the hatch. As it opened, Sol jumped out, tumbling less than gracefully into dry, sad, reedy grass.

He got to his feet and noted the preponderance of corpses in the park, many huddled together, contorted in agony, blood and dust on their clothes and faces. Sol looked away rapidly and sped as best he could along the fissure that split the road toward the garage. A few stray vehicles were hung across the ledge where the road abruptly became bi-leveled. The drivers were slumped; passengers hung half-way out doors, pools of gore dried around them. *My people made these weapons to kill the other half of my people. I'm not feeling good about this. I have to think about my job. I need to save lives not dwell on dead ones... it's just like the sim...*

Previously he had not looked at the sky; it was dark and grim, like a continuous volcanic ash cloud choked the air. He noticed some of the dead were clutching breathing masks and rags. A good deal of Kourhos was toxically polluted from their ore refining processes and fuel production. Sol watched as the Dash in which he arrived flew towards a fire and disappeared from sight amidst filthy clouds. *Val put out fires before Star Assault. I guess that makes sense, it just seems pointless. There's barely a city left...*

As he approached the garage, he heard something. It was faint, but definitely a voice. He jumped and dodged debris, honing in on the sound. He checked his monitor; behind a fallen beam, in what might be a lift or a supply closet, was someone alive. Sol fiddled with his settings until he could broadcast loud and clear in spite his mask. One of Parthenos' mails included phonetically spelled "phrases of use" in Kourhonoi and Ravasich. *I will give this my best shot. It's like weird Ryzaan. My worst language but I gotta fix that anyhow.*

"I'm here to help! Stay where you are!"

There was movement behind the door as he surveyed the position of the beam to see if he could shift it without anything else collapsing. His slim knowledge of engineering and physics told him 'no'.

"Hello? Hello?" Kourhonoi. Female. Muffled, clearly distressed. "Please help me!"

Sol hit a short string of commands to contact the other team members as he called back at the door. "How many of you are there?"

He could not understand the answer. *Dammit!* Sol switched to Archon for the team call. "How do I tell her to step back from the door?"

As he awaited the reply, he realized he had not turned off his speaker. Archaic, strangely accented Archon was returned. "I get back! I back, I back!"

"Are you away from the door?"

"Yes! Please, please help!"

"Turn to the inner wall, cover your neck!" Sol thrust his hand forward and blasted the metal door with a low arc from his open palm. He heard a scream and his heart pounded. "Are you OK in there! Speak!"

"I alive! Alive! Help!"

Sol backed up and smacked the butt of his rifle into the damaged door. He felt the impact over his whole body but was sure he could not have positioned himself on the beam to kick it flat-footed. Another punch and it fell open. He reached an arm through. "Can you walk?"

"Seventy-eight, is everything all good down there?"

"Survivor, one, female. Trying to get her out of a closet. Seventy eight out." He shut off the broadcast and leaned in. With his goggles and his natural kaffir vision, he could see in the pitch-black room; he realized she could not. The garage was probably dark as well. "I'm here, in front of you. Careful."

Sol lit his armor; she half jumped and half stumbled towards him. He caught the slight figure of the woman and wobbled a bit, pulled her up and out and set her gently in the garage. She backed away from him on her hands, still in a crouch. "You're – you're... don't touch me!"

"What? I'm an Archon, sorry! I figured you knew that!"

"Please, don't hurt me!"

She cowered, shaking. She wore a military issue gas mask in which she panted. Sol knelt beside her, palms up, rifle returned to his back. "I have no plans to hurt you. Keep your mask on, OK? Try to calm down. You're bleeding... what happened to your arm?"

"What! Oh, no... no..." She sobbed and shuddered. "The blood, the blood is from..."

Sol switched the team broadcast back on. "One woman, human I think, injured but alive. Can I get a proper medic? She won't let me near her."

"I'll swing back," came Wyvern's rasp. "Keep talking to her but keep her still once you get her out to the street. You need to get out of that building."

Parthenos interrupted on the final syllable. "I'll come with Wisp. We got it. Trade me places, Wyvern – all survivors here male."

His annoyance was audible, even over mechanical communication. "Affirmative, Checkmate."

"A doctor is coming, a woman, just please stay calm. We should leave here. Can you walk? I won't hurt you. What's your name?"

The woman refused to answer. Unsteadily, she stood up.

"This building isn't safe. Lean on me if you need. I swear I won't hurt you."

Sol escorted her carefully out to the street; she begged to sit on the dirty curb and he allowed it. He heard her weeping inside the mask as she shook. He thought of how frail his mother looked as he left for basic and ached inside.

"You're going to be fine. I promise."

"But you did this, didn't you?" her tone rattled with fear and accusation.

He aimed his goggles at her mask, doing his best to look into her eyes, even though she probably could not see his at all. "No. A human faction against the Theocracy did. We were trying to stop it. They stole the weapons from us. We're not happy about it."

The Dash appeared above them and circled into a landing on the edge of the park. She was reluctant to come with him. "Please no, I – "

Sol threw up his hands. "Fine, stay here in this pile of corpses and ruin, really, if you don't believe me."

The woman looked around in what was to her, the dark; only distant fires lit it. Sol concentrated radiance from himself, illuminating the carnage on all sides. "See? Not that you want to. I don't want to either. Will you just come with us, already? We'll take you somewhere safe."

She sobbed again, masked face in her hands.

Parthenos' voice was irritated. "Take her by force if you have to. We need to get out of here."

"I do not wish to but I will use force if you do not board this ship. Please don't make me."

Sol reached for his rifle but a shaky little hand grabbed his arm. Steadier this time, he took hold and hoisted her through the hatch. Enkashen sat fully masked within. She gently spoke Kourhonoi to the terrified lady, taking over for Sol as he sat her down and the hatch closed. Parthenos leaned from the cockpit, also masked. "Wildfire's got the controls. Everyone stay masked while we pump the air clean. Upper atmosphere is still OK. Take us up, eh?"

"On it, Checkmate."

The wait for the ship to call clear was tense. The woman was unused to flying, nervously gripped the seat then released on realizing how unfamiliar the materials were. Enkashen continued her efforts to comfort as she ran a scan with her slate.

The ship's voice acknowledged, "Air quality high. Optimally breathable for human lungs. Kaffir are recommended moisturizing. Saurtzek are recommended equalizing masks."

Parthenos lowered his mask and regarded the rescued woman. "She doesn't look too bad… off."

"Just a sprained ankle. Blood appears to be someone else's. Needs water and could use something for inflammation and nerves." Enkashen removed her mask and goggles, wriggled her cramped ears.

"You can take off your mask too, miss," noted Sol, releasing his own apparatus. "We cleaned the air for you, even though it won't be really comfortable for us."

Shakily, she worked on the straps. Enkashen offered help. She regarded the kindly elf woman a moment then allowed the assistance. She coughed as the mask came off and Parthenos raced to her side. He spoke Kourhonoi fluently and offered his hands without touching. Reaching into a compartment, Enkashen acquired a water pouch and handed it over, saying, "Just water."

"Thank you," panted the lady as she took a cautious sip.

Parthenos glanced at Sol. "She speaks Archon?"

"Yeah. Couldn't you tell?"

He grunted, reached across the cabin, and smacked Sol lightly up side the head. "Could've said as much."

"Hey, ow, sir! Sorry, Checkmate!"

Parthenos sighed. The woman said something in Kourhonoi and a short conversation commenced. The major put on his best charm, lowered his lashes and kept his eyes down, smiled boyishly, flicked his ears.

"I'm getting the pharmaceuticals." Enkashen stood. She rolled eyes at Parthenos from a perspective only Sol would notice.

The woman gave Solvreyil a thankful look and said in stilted Archon, "I am sorry. My name is Celita. Thank you for getting me out of there."

"Not any trouble, it's my job, miss."

"Ah, I believe that's, 'ma'am'. She's married. You see the bracelet?" The major gestured. "I apologize for my friend. He was raised in a culture that treats marriage differently from yours."

"So I have heard." They continued their conversation in Kourhonoi. Sol watched curiously, trying to pick up anything he could. Something Parthenos said made her blush and look away; the big elf chuckled softly and apologized. Sol noted Enkashen's shoulders and ears tense as she rummaged the drug supply.

The conversation went on a bit, seeming to terminate amicably with a lot of nods as Captain Enkashen returned with a few little packets and Parthenos stood. "I'm gonna help Wildfire get this beast to Pachar. You guys take this from here."

"Pachar?"

"Refugee. We're not leaving her here. That would be cruel." He made his way to the cockpit. "We'll swap ships there to come back for more, probably."

"I guess," Celita said, staring at her feet, "There is a revolt in our capitol city..."

"Broke out last night," Enki offered pills with a brief explanation in Kourhonoi and gestured at the water pouch. "The Theocratic forces are tied up in a number of messes and what little you had of non-military emergency squads either were with the revolt or ..." The captain shook her head. "Just trust us; it will be safer for you at the station."

Sol crossed the cabin to sit beside Celita. "How are you feeling?"

"Hurt, scared... grateful." Celita managed a smile as Enkashen draped a blanket over her shoulders.

Parthenos called back. "Hey, Wisp, they need you at Maanahkouc. Lots of survivors, big mess, major risk. Can you analog in? Don't want to leave the clean air."

"Affirmative, Checkmate." The captain turned to Sol. "Keep her warm; make sure she drinks that water. Knock her with a pink dose if you guys gotta jump." Enki gestured at her neck as if pumping a syrigun.

Sol nodded slightly. "Read loud and clear, Wisp." He switched to Shandrian. "Honor and sacrifice."

"Every day of my life, man, every fucking day." With that she was suited up and out the hatch.

"Well, she fucking hates me right now. Again," sighed Parthenos in Shandrian.

Celita swallowed her pills and looked apprehensively at Sol. "You're just a child," she remarked.

He was taken aback a second. "Only chronologically, ma'am. I'm a soldier of the Empire."

"My husband wanted children; we were waiting…" She stared at the floor, eyes filling with tears. "I'm never going to see him again, am I?"

"I can't say." Sol wanted to hug her but knew better. He emitted the gentlest warmth he could muster, lowered his head to look into her reddened, tired eyes. "We'll get you somewhere where you don't have to worry about survival, at least, on top of everything else. There will be some of your people there…"

He heard Parthenos, agitated but restrained, speaking in Shandrian. The cabin door shut softly. Sol did his best to focus on the refugee, tried to think of something to say.

"God abandoned us," Celita said finally. "Men… came for … for my boss. We ran. He shoved me in the lift as they…" Tears came again. "The blood, the blood is his… I couldn't… do anything…"

"I'm sorry. That's terrible. I wish we had gotten there sooner." Sol meant it but it felt odd to declare. "Were the men revolutionaries?"

She wiped tears as her face contorted. "No, that's the really ... odd... part. They were enforcers, Bureau of Civil Protection, Knights of the Theocracy... security passes to enter building... said they were taking us. Power died when the elevator hit the ground... I don't know when the quakes started or how long I... slept... when I woke, other passengers... were..."

Celita grabbed Sol and bawled into his armored shoulder. His compassion kept his armor soft; but he held it with grim determination. "It's going to be all right. We won't let anything happen to you."

Parthenos' voice came gently, in Shandrian. "I caught all that. We won't be taking her to the Kourhonoi side of the station. We might be walling it off. This is not good but please stay the way you are, don't upset her more. You're doing a great job, kid."

"Thank you, Checkmate."

"I have a feeling she survived the gas not just because she was lucky enough to have that mask. Could you ask her where she got that, by the way? It's Theocratic issue."

Sol reached over for the mask, trying not to contact her in any way that would disturb her as he let her sob on his suit. "This is pretty fancy. Where'd you find something like this?"

"Vittair... my... my husband. Gave it to me to ride public transit when we lost our car." She looked up. "The air got so bad, so many sick people, you can smell their ... diseases. The ... rotting sickness... It smells so terrible. I could afford shots..."

'Several cities in the southern hemisphere, Tukodok included, are infested with a virulently contagious necrotizing illness spread originally from hand contact but ended up in their water system'. That was in Parthenos' briefing reports, too. Something else we're immunized against in basic... but if you don't use certain kinds of cleansers, you usually won't get it anyway because you won't kill the micro-organisms that protect against it. Sick. The trains were full of people with their skin rotting off before they died. I hope I'm all out of puke. 'Nasty' corpses, indeed.

"I'm sorry I brought it up. Do you think maybe you can sleep? It's going to be a while before we get anywhere." To his surprise, she curled up in his lap. *The drugs Enki gave her are working, I guess… Maybe I won't have to pink her.*

"Mister Red?" Celita whispered.

Sol laughed a little. "How can I help?"

"Do you believe in God?"

"I don't know. Sometimes I think I might. But it's probably a different God than yours. Sometimes I think they might all be the same, if there are Gods. I can't really say though."

"Your friend with the black hair … says God sent you to save me. He says he is close to God."

Turning his head towards the cockpit, Sol wondered what Parthenos actually told her. "He is. He's that kind of Archon. Maybe I am, too. I don't think I'll know until I'm older."

"I think," She yawned deeply as her body shuddered from exhaustion. "I think I like that kind of Archon."

As she slept, he watched her breathe. His slate vibrated silently at his hip and he carefully removed it to check a message – from Parthenos – which read: "The ship is monitoring her vital signs. You can sleep too, if you need. Great work."

…

"Wake up, kid. We're here."

Parthenos leaned on his arm on the seat beside Solvreyil. His face was tired although surprisingly pleasant. "Apologies, sir. Oh wait, can I … are we…?" Sol glanced around. They were alone.

"Affirmative, Solvreyil. We're good." Parthenos stood and stretched. "I'm fucking beat. Tempting as it is to crash here while they work on this Dash, there are beds in the base. We can demand quarters, come on, it's one of the little pleasures of this job." He gestured Sol to follow as he hopped out the forward hatch.

The hangar was small, only half filled, mostly occupied by D-7s, a couple escape shuttles, and lots of service equipment. He quickened his pace to join the major up a ramp signed "To Station". Sol stared off at others labeled, "To Hangars 2 & 3", "Hangar Staff Lounge", and "Shortcut to Exo".

"First time here?"

Sol looked around as they proceeded; this was far from the sterilized structures at Orminos. "Yes. I've heard it's huge, sir, but …"

"Yeah, it's massive. A hub of interstellar trade and diplomacy, serving the edges of Archon space and any non-Imperial groups with whom we choose to exchange goods or negotiations." His mouth twitched. "This is Star Assault's wing; we share it with the Guild and that's it."

"Wow." They emerged from a long hall empty save for scanners into another decorated with posters celebrating the Empire's major destinations and cultures and from there into a wider hall decorated with banners hung amidst a myriad of doors. The banners represented current and former Star Assault squadrons and vessels; all were in High Shandrian runes compiled into intimidating sigils.

"It may not have all the comforts of home, but it beats hiding in broom closets to avoid marines." Parthenos strode to a door beside the 17th's unit symbol. He ran his hand over a scanner and the door opened. "Stay behind me; none of these will recognize your information yet."

A tall, slender young man with bleach-tipped dark brown hair in starter mudlocks leaned on a podium. He was confined to a half-body cast but seemed relatively cheerful. "Hey, Major P."

"What are you even doing out of bed, Highnote?"

"Hey, Saark said I was allowed a few hours a day now long as I don't overdo it, sir." A large wingless male gen trotted from an open side door and barked once. "And, see, my time is up and I'm awaiting my replacement. He won't let me stand too long, will ya, Rocky?"

The gen barked again. Parthenos shook his head. "We need quarters. My astrum is finishing checking a refugee in and he'll be here in a few hours… you have anything or should I go ask the Wings?"

"We're good actually. You want three bunks, two, or one?" The gentleman smiled at Sol oddly.

Parthenos turned and regarded the boy as well. "Eh, three. I don't care if they're in the same room, even, I just need to stretch my legs and not get kicked." The trooper in the cast handed him a key card. "While we're at it, can we get some clothes so our armor can sleep?"

"Number five is up and to the left. I'll ask Ayleth to bring over robes. She's at the Wings right now but she can probably pick something up, y'know."

Parthenos headed toward the door from which Rocky entered. "Nice. Thanks. Go the fuck to bed. If my astrum has to sleep outside because your replacement is late I'll kick their butt and not yours."

"Fair enough, sir. Sleep well."

They took a curved, upward sloping hallway. Sol asked, "Does each unit have their own barracks here?"

"No, we all share the general Star Assault and base defense barracks. The check-in entrance just happens to be between the 17th and 23rd's flags because those units contributed the most to the construction."

They reached a cluster of doors and passed through one using the key card. There were four bunks – two per side – each with a bio-fabric mattress, a flattish pillow, and a thin sheet rather than a blanket. A small desk/table and two stools were built into the wall between the half-cocoons. It was not dissimilar to Sol's former accommodations aboard the *Irimia*, save the walls had been grown rather than built, and in a few areas, decorative patterns reminiscent of mountains had been crafted somehow. The boy approached the table and touched the sun setting in the center above it. "Amazing, sir…"

"Traditional Ryzaan art," remarked the major, his voice tired and low. "They used to carve the bones of their food and enemies until they learned to grow this, what we call 'ostrekaal'. Now it's done by putting a frame in the forming analog; it grows over creating a natural looking formation in low relief."

"But the imagery is Shandrian, isn't it, sir? Symbolically speaking, I mean."

"A fusion of millennia of Ryzaan and Shandrian art and culture; the men who funded this project are deeply spiritual and based these rooms on monastic meditation cells." Sol heard armor unfastened slowly behind him. "Mountains for endurance of spirit, for the toughness of the kaffa heart, and for reverence of nature and creation; setting sun for our sacrifice and for the fear we must accept we evoke." A glance back confirmed to Sol his superior was staring at the sun with hand over heart. As Sol turned back to the wall, Parthenos uttered a very quiet, "*Kaajya*."

"*Kaajya*," Sol responded automatically, a little to his surprise. They stood silently a moment longer.

Parthenos lay in one of the lower nooks before removing his footwear. Sol observed and began to follow suit in the opposite bed. "What are you doing? Sleep in the bunk above mine. That's an order."

"Excuse me, sir?"

Carefully, the major arranged his carapace armor and boots at the end of his bunk. Before flopping with his broad back to the room, he explained, "Bachi totally snores. I don't want him above me. Get up there, I know you don't."

Having recently been asleep, however, his mind was active. Sol stared at the ceiling and finally, in a soft tone so as not to rouse Parthenos should he no longer be awake, asked, "Sir?"

"What."

"Is the revolt memorial somewhere I can see it? I mean, with the collars on…"

A long sigh preceded another pause. "Solvreyil, he has a shrine on Holtiin. Your mother has his feather. You're allowed to see her one last time even though she probably has your feather now too. If you need to honor him, do so there, or in your private prayers."

His voice was almost apologetic though he seemed annoyed. *I have to know. I can't keep wondering.* "Why is he in that photograph of you? That was him, wasn't it?" *He'll say no, dad must have had a brother I never met, because that guy would have to be twenty years older than my dad.*

"Your father was a different person, you see, a long time ago. He's had the distinction of dying more than once." Mixed emotions surfaced in the tired voice. "If I'd realized that sooner, you wouldn't be lying up there right now. Rather than allow myself to think about that for another second, I order you to sleep."

Sol stiffly silenced, but sleep was the furthest thing from his mind as he stared at the ceiling. He felt his distance from home. To distract himself and become more comfortable, he slipped his utility belt off (at last count, he noted the major still wore his, side arms, sticky bombs, and all). He fished out and checked his slate. A group message to the rescue team from Val informed he and Wyvern were in room 7 while Enki and Aukaldiir checked in a large number of survivors, mostly haki; there would be a breakfast meeting regarding redistribution of personnel.

Sol returned a private text to Val. ::: Is there any bunk space in 7? Checkmate freaking me out. :::

::: Yes, have snacks, be awake a bit. Wisp has quarters local; Holiday wants room without Wyvern :::

The astrum managed to sneak half way out before Parthenos rolled over. "Where are you going, exactly?"

"Val's room, sir." He held his slate up. "I didn't want to wake you. They have food and I'm starving, sir."

"Huh?" The major slid his hand around on the bed and sat part way up. "Fuck I'm sleeping in my belt, with guns on. Awesome. I hate when I do that." He scratched his scalp and stared at his slate. "Right. I got take out when I dropped off Bachi and the refugee. You weren't awake to ask what you wanted. But you of course do at least have some rations, correct?"

Of course, I've got cured fish and a cheese biscuit. But I would have loved some take away. Dick. "Yes sir, of course, sir."

"Take your gear. Aukaldir's on his way apparently; he can have your bunk." Parthenos flopped back on the nominal mattress.

Room seven was quiet when he arrived, although both men were awake. A few recyclable carry away boxes with still warm contents lay on the built-in. Valdieren sat on a stool, eating dried fruit from a bag. "Hey, Sol. Did you guys come back with just the one refugee?"

"I think so, but, I crashed hard; wasn't even awake when we checked in." He took the bunk across from Wyvern, who read a book, huddled in a robe and self-heating emergency blanket along with the sheet.

Val shrugged as Sol poked at unfamiliar foodstuffs. "Parth called back to the *Sanjeera* for more transports. Mysh's report was bad. Then I guess he was just done. Not my job how to tell him to do his."

Sol expected one of the containers to contain steamed rice or green salad, but found nothing but fried, coated things and pale, over-cooked vegetable matter cut into strands. He picked up a piece of the least bothersomely textured thing; it was small and crispy looking. "What kind of meat is this?"

"Rock lizard," Val said as if he was silly for asking. "It's not spiced at all, that's what the sauce is for."

Wyvern interjected dismissively, "The other thing is runfi and it wasn't skinned properly so if you haven't ever had it, don't try that, or you'll hate it forever."

"Naaza isn't the best Ryzaan but it's ace when I'm homesick.," smiled Val, reaching over to snag a little chunk of runfi.

It's a rodent. It's chunks of salted rodent cooked whole over a fire. Ryzaans solve all their pest problems by making cuisine of them. Don't barf, Yen. It'd be rude. He selected the least recognizable breaded lizard chunk and eyed Val suspiciously. "If it's good at all why are you eating fruit snacks instead of this?"

"It's not instead; there's supposed to be dahi and taapo on the reed salad, but it's kind of expensive to get those fresh in this sector. I'm making do."

The lizard was not bad, although he wondered about the 'breaded and fried' aspect. "I've never had Ryzaan at all, my mom wouldn't set foot in a Ryzaan place and steered us away from those fair stands."

"Not surprised, if your mother identified with her human heritage or she was particularly Holtiini."

Valdieren shot Wyvern a look. Sol caught it (Wyvern did not even look up) but decided not to seek clarification. He slowly chewed another piece of lizard. *The Ryzaans used to eat humans. Sure it was a long time ago, but the food is all chopped up and overcooked and unrecognizable, what isn't the rat anyway, so I kinda get it. I could be eating anything right now...* He stared at the chunk with a bite out of it in his hand and set it down. "Can I have some fruit, please, sir?"

"Oh, no problem, here. Are you sure you don't want to try the salad? It's a little oilier than I like it but it's better than you can get anywhere else out here... and they made it without chikkiba special for me!"

Salad? Salad? It's cooked! What the hell, Ryzaa? "Do you like this stuff, Wyvern, sir?"

"I've eaten worse. At least you can tell the lizard is lizard because they left the bones in. That's the crunchy part, their little bones." Wyvern shuddered visibly, although Sol could not tell if it was over the cuisine or the drugs leaving his system. "That woman you found turned out to be important," the filthy man said, changing the subject. "The Information Department had a lot of questions. Almost feel sorry for Bacharanzin right now... almost."

"Important how?"

"She was a translator for the Ministry of Communication, the Theocracy's propaganda and intelligence division; that's interesting in its own right, not just because that section rarely if ever hires women, but especially because she appears to be haki, although she was not aware." Wyvern marked the musty little book and sipped from his flask as he eyed Sol. "Her husband, Honsad Vittair, worked for the Defense Ministry, was under watch by our operatives until he vanished a few months ago."

Val assembled a box of food and slung into the bunk above Wyvern's. "When you guys are done, please close all that up. I'm totally taking all those leftovers."

He examined the stool, but noted Wyvern had moved his legs to make room. Sol accepted and sat on the bunk's edge. "So, wow, um... is she going to be all right?"

Val chose his words slowly, precisely. "They'll have lots of questions for her before they turn her over. Part of Bachi's job is to make sure she actually goes to an IG refugee facility and is not 'lost' in Info Department... paperwork." Wyvern and Valdieren both coughed. "She's safe with him; he can be a big fool sometimes but when it comes to preservation of detainee dignity, he's got a hard-on for justice."

"Kinda like someone else I know," chuckled Wyvern, looking at the bottom of the bunk above.

"We can't all be double-pay-rolled government dicks. That would defeat the purpose of Star Assault."

"What."

"What."

Sol looked over at Val. "What'd you say, sir?"

"I didn't hear him say anything." Wyvern coughed again.

Val's face appeared upside-down over the side of the bunk. "I said, 'Fuck Wyvern you smell like a *vohjaadu* crashed into a Shandrian whore house'. When was the last time you showered?'"

"Probably about the last time you did, stink bug."

For a moment, Sol considered this; no one showered on the ship, both of these men were sweaty and chemical ridden, but all he could detect in the air was food and a faint musk he identified as the personal scents of "Wyvern" and "Valdieren". *Our armor is Vektaar, after all... I guess the sleeves and carapace are even more efficient at cleaning up body funk than our ladders.*

"Hey, speaking of bugs, how do you not get lice?" Val seemed genuinely curious.

Wyvern took another shot, grinned, and stretched, carefully avoiding kicking Sol. "Ship sprites."

"Are you fuckin' serious dude? You let them pick your hair?"

"Actually, the ship mucus is naturally de-lousing even when it's really clean." His eyes closed as he yawned. The creases around his mouth and eyes moved strangely. "Good for your skin, too. Night, guys. See you at breakfast, maybe."

"Psst. Sol. Flask." Val whispered as he waved his arm about in the air between the bunks. "He won't wake up. Grab it. I'll give it back I just ...Thanks. Come up and drink with me."

"Um, OK, sure." Sol climbed up. He sniffed the flask. It was potent, but definitely not alcohol. "It smells like medicine... wah... what is this?"

"It's a sedative mix. Takes the edge off the pharm come-down and helps you sleep post combat, but not so hard you won't wake for an alarm or have a nasty hangover." The captain caught his concerned expression. "It's safe, Sol, it's prescription, it's just his own blend, because he's like that. As wing commanders go, Wy's the least abusive of his pharmacy access I've ever met. You think he's fucked up you should meet Ythaarin or Jaahyden... or Ilzyatar from the 89th. That guy, that guy is scary."

I can't even imagine. He returned the flask without drinking, suspecting he would hurl fried lizard if he chugged a dose of medicated syrup. "Cap'n V, your slate's buzzing, you gonna get it?"

Val inserted the flask to his mouth and held it there as he flipped the top on his device. "Huh. Aukaldir and Myshkor just went back to the Sanj; orders from Kiertus and the Guild. I guess the Queen doesn't currently back our actions and we're going to run out of funding if we keep it up."

"We tried." Wyvern's voice was less raspy, more sluggish. "We almost had a workable treaty with the Kourhonoi. Month from now, maybe two, we'll be back, but it won't be humans we're fighting. I have almost enough pride to tell Marsura and the Council to eat my shit. If I was the colonel, I might just."

"I know, man. I know. And they'll blame us, and we'll pay for it either way." Val sighed.

"They can't take all our ships. They'll lose the Empire." Not very awake, not commanding, drifting up from below, his voice was nearly hypnotic.

"I feel you, but please don't talk like that." Val half-heartedly passed the flask to Sol again and poked listlessly at his food. Sol drank at last; it tasted like children's nerve tonic and swung like a wrecking ball.

The last words from Wyvern before gentle snoring commenced were spoken like dwindling fluid, almost with that smoky quality of Colonel Kiertus, lyrically beautiful in spite of their slowed-down syllables, so that the implication only hit Sol's brain in full right as the medication pulled the rug from beneath his consciousness. "One Infiltrator jump to the *Esimaar* and two can play that game even if someone has to come between Ferrox and the purification cannons... what's your love worth, Sheriden?"

VIII. Records

Sol was concerned about being a stranger in this lounge; he at least expected to show his collars and state his purpose if not be actively harassed by local hazing specialists. Occasionally he felt as if watched, but noticed no one staring upon looking up from his studies. This kept him self-conscious about moving around so he remained, nervous, at the corner table.

Not like I want to bother anyone else. I just want to look at all the stuff in here…

The furniture was standard issue for any military lounge in the empire but there was art on the walls, flags he had never seen before, and most peculiarly, a wall of shiny clarithane tanks like at the zoological park's aquarium. Each time he threw an eye that way though, people talking in front of them would stop briefly, fidget with their slates, pretend to look at something else…

If someone has a problem with me I wish they'd say as much so I could tell them I'm under orders to be here. He watched a man with pale mud locks and a woman of notable age, both in brown uniforms, chat as they departed. Both wore officer's jackets and rank pins. *I guess if their slates are like ours and they're above 'astrum' all they have to do is look me up in cross-reference. It hadn't occurred to me how creepy and invasive that feature is until now. Why us? Shouldn't only Impsi or the Haarnsvaar or maybe Rim Patrol have that much access to personnel data?*

"Yo." A big hand clapped onto the table on either side of Sol. While somewhat jarring, it lacked the intimidation he suspected was intended

"Greetings, Major Parthenos, sir!" *Awesome, got that salute off without accidentally clocking him in the face. Quit looming over me like that and get on with the disciplinary speech already.*

The hands moved; medals jingled as Parthenos walked away. "Come on, kid."

Sol collected himself rapidly and followed Parthenos, who to his surprise, walked into a niche beside the wall of terrarium-like structures.

The boy hesitated. *Dude you are the second to last person in all Imperial Space I want to follow into a toilet… whoa everyone's staring now, I better go.*

The niche led not to the restroom but instead a corridor illuminated by interior lighting of the terrariums or light filtering through them from the lounge. It made curious patterns on walls and floor. Parthenos stood with a peculiar expression, two thirds the way down the wall, hand flat to the clarithane. Sol examined the one closest. Inside was a beautiful miniature forest under simulated natural lighting. A gentle breeze from a tiny tidal waterway waved through the branches. Rain began to fall.

"These are like the envirariums at the Grand Library, where you can see the Burning Waste and Storm Valley safely. Amazing what Archons can make, sir."

"Yes, but no." Parthenos kept his gaze on the tank where his hand lay. "If you had the means, you could go see Storm Valley. You will probably fly exercises in the Waste, soon, in fact. But these places are lost to us: you will never be able to visit them as they are memorialized here."

A label in simplified Archon on the forested coast tank read, "Ennautuok Inlet, Draujuozaa, Verraken."

"I don't know the history of this place…"

"It's an outer colony, covered in the files on Kourhos. The populace is divided as to whether to fully join the Archon Empire or to join the Kourhonoi as an independent state. They have primitive space travel but would unlikely hold out against the Ilu even if they survived themselves. We are likely headed there soon, so you might want to re-read all that." The major coughed as he raised a brow. The look carried more the weight of a professor's good-natured jab at a lagging student than anything else.

"Understood, sir. I guess I thought that was our territory and it was more like Holtiin. I skimmed that section and will revisit it." Sol gave a curt quarter bow. "But it looks so peaceful and beautiful…"

"Unlike Kourhos, where the Ryzaans lost the revolts fair and square, the brand new Archon Empire at the time gave the slaves independence when revolution brewed. Even without nuclear exchange, the humans failed to manage their resources. Try not to hate your ancestors when you see it now." Parthenos gestured at the tank beside it. "You were just there; doesn't look like this now, does it?"

Dense jungle covered rolling hills, mist rose in the valleys, tiny waterfalls flowed; the array of colors was staggering. "Amboua Hills, Tukodok, Kourhos," read the placard. Sol's stomach clenched as he looked down the row of envirariums. Parthenos returned attention to his original tank; eyes closed and face angled down; his mouth moved silently. Finally he opened a previously concealed door in the wall opposite the tank. "This way," came his dampened yet peculiarly reverberating voice.

"Could we ever restore it? I mean, clearly, we have some of the proper materials, right, sir?" Sol asked hopefully as he hesitated, staring back at the tiny jungle, to the forest to its left, and the rocky valley forested with comparatively massive fungi and looming fog to its right. *Where was that? 'Yetjzmaal, Baalphegor'. At least Archons own their own mistakes...*

Parthenos froze in the doorway, not looking back. "Some of them, maybe not their full former beauty, and not everything. These are only terrain, after all; just symbols to remind us of entire species, cultures and histories, wiped out forever by greed and hatred." Sol looked down the row of tanks one last time; his eyes settled where Parthenos stood on his original approach.

Miniaturized mountains, jagged and ominous in spite their scale, were draped in drifting snow. As the artificial sun rose over them, glaciers glittered in a dramatic rainbow. Tiny ice caves became visible in the changing light and a half-frozen river moved silently at the bottom of a treacherous ravine. *I can't argue the beauty, I get why the pirates who originally settled there chose it, but it seems like a challenging sort of place to build cities and raise families. I wish we'd discussed Ruahanu more in Intergalactic History.*

"Are you coming or not, kid?"

"On my way, sir." Trying not to get lost in the tanks – he wanted to read them all, now - Sol hurried to catch up. Along the new corridor were a cluster of mossy nooks and what appeared to be a few supply closets. The hall curved down and split. The right fork was labeled, 'Security Checkpoint, Shopping Plaza, Food Court'. Parthenos took the unlabeled left.

They stepped into an area with a faux stone floor, benches, and some natural full-sized plants and then through a partly hidden archway. The room beyond was minimally lit with a few tables and benches in alcoves and a long curved bar. Music played at a moderate volume over a sound system concealed in the ceiling. Most of the features were imitation wood and coral in dark colors; the lights resembled mollusk shells and translucent pods. Parthenos proceeded to the bar with an amused glance back at Sol. "Somethin' wrong, Red?"

"Is this supposed to be... a Holtiini theme pub?"

Parthenos chuckled and patted the stool beside his. "I've always had the impression the designer was just homesick, but you could definitely describe it that way, huh?"

Sol sat and scanned the polished surface of the bar. *My first time at a pub counter and I'm with you, that's just weird. At least you're not raping me in a shit closet.* "Never would have known this was here. Is it Star Assault only?"

"Something like that." Large indigo eyes examined the selection, caged in shatter-proof containers with non-grav spigots. "If you went up that stairway to the side there, you'd be in the secured part of the Wings of Fire; if you're still double-tagged next time you're here, that's where you can go to dance. If you dance, that is." A suspicious look fell on him. "You dance, bookworm?"

"Um, I've taken some classes, sir?" *That look was even worse. His eyes are so spooky; his pupils haven't changed in size no matter what the light. I wish he'd look elsewhere.* "I've never really been to a night club before, sir. I'd kind of like to, though..."

As if in answer to the request, Parthenos turned his gaze back to the beverage wall. A wiry man approached on the service side of the counter, wiping his hands on a rag. "Sup, Major P?"

"Hey, Kahner. What's new?"

The man shrugged. "Eh, another day at the Come Down. Almost didn't open for early hours today; heard the 17th was around... seems to be true." He stood before Parthenos, his back to them, watching the major's face in the bar mirror as he checked stock. "Red Eye?"

"Double, please. Only having one today, might as well make it count, right?" The drink was in his hands before he finished speaking. Parthenos smiled and turned to Sol. "Whatever you want's on me –"

"Hey! Is this guy even old enough to be in here? What the fuck, Parthenos?" interrupted the bartender with a scowl of his deeply elvish features. He gestured at Solvreyil.

Sol gagged as the pointer finger of Parthenos' right hand hooked under both his potentially explosive ID collars and snapped his upper body forward over the bar. The major took a swig of his drink as he held the astrum toward Kahner. "Got eyes, Sentinel Syavrasky?"

The boy strained uncomfortably, half pulled across the counter by the wickedly strong arm. He did not want to move a muscle at the risk of damage to his tags. Beads of sweat ran down Sol's forehead as the bartender stiffly responded, "Point taken, sir."

Released, Sol massaged his throat gently and coughed. "I'll have whatever he's having."

"Not on your suppressor dosage." Parthenos looked annoyed for a second then regarded the booze again. "Early Light, make it very light."

"Coming right up, sir." The bartender's voice remained wooden. As Sol watched him mix ingredients from a gun set-up below the counter, he observed Syavrasky's features. His cheekbones were high, his irises large and dark, and his skin tone – although difficult to see in this lighting – was similar to Sol's. His hair was orangey red, a few shades lighter than Sol's father's. This orange spray was cut fairly short save a long slender braid down his back.

The name is Ryzaanized, but he's got to be an Islander with those big nocturnal eyes and that feral face. The photographs I've seen of Huari make them all look so pretty; I'm glad they come in an 'average' version, too. "Thank you for the drink, sentinel."

"Kahner, please, and no problem." The bartender turned to Parthenos again. "Heard you guys are looking for a new arms sarge…"

The major's long feathery black brows lifted as he sipped. "As it happens, yes. Bored of city life?"

"I could… use a change of scenery. That's all." Kahner returned to cleaning, though the place already appeared spotless.

Parthenos glanced over at Sol. "Is the kitchen open by any chance?"

"I can make anything on the menu." He handed the major a laminated card and wandered into the back.

"Here, pick something, I know you missed breakfast." Parthenos shoved the menu at Sol. "Fortunately for you, and more importantly for Wyvern, you weren't essential at it."

"Sorry, sir. I didn't realize what was in that flask would knock me out quite so hard…"

"Of course you didn't and he should've said so." The major shrugged. "It's already been addressed."

He doesn't seem angry, really. Where did Val say Parthenos was when he woke me up and told me to wait in the lounge? 'He's at Civic Affairs swinging his charismatic monster cock on behalf of our righteous cause.' "May I ask how things went this morning after the meeting I missed, sir?"

"It was effortless. The Agricultural Bureau donated two freighters for the Kourhonoi refugee effort and the local civic government – the Pachar Trade Commission, that is – elected to take over the project from us. All we have to do is escort their ships back and forth." Parthenos gave a wide, genuine smile. "Nothin' the civvies around here love like making the Imperial Council look like a bunch of selfish assholes. Course, I can't really cry about us showing up every other branch in one fell swoop either."

"You know what you want?" Kahner reappeared and leaned over Sol.

"The egg cakes, please." He handed the menu over. "Wait, you don't put chikkiba in them do you?"

Sol might as well have spontaneously sprouted a second head. "What the – fucking hell, no, gross. Egg cakes are egg cakes. Fluffy, with gully herbs and sea vegetable. You been eatin' too much swamper food, kid." He snatched the menu, offended. "Anything for you, Parth?"

"Steamed rice and red lichen, please." The major chuckled as he watched the bartender shudder and mumble his way into the back. "Don't complain about the way it's plated, astrum, or I'll smack you."

"No worries, sir. I'm happy to be able to get this close to Holtiini food after last night. I thought ship rations were scary but Val and Wyvern got Ryzaan take away last night…"

Long ears drooped and twitched. "Nuff said." Parthenos' slate squeaked; he pulled it to reply to a text.

Sol stared thoughtfully in the direction of the kitchen. "Sir, do you ever think we'll just be 'Archons' instead of Ryzaans and Shandrians and Islanders and … you know?"

His mouth opened and lips twitched but Parthenos said nothing. He completed and sent the text and finished his drink. "Great discussion question for your Cultural Ethics debate hall."

"Man, I wish." Sol stared at the drink he had barely touched. It smelled and tasted like a semi-sweet stomachic tea with a mild burn to the aftertaste. *Not what I expected for my first drink in a grown up bar, but he has HTS too. He probably spent his teens barfing his breakfast all over spaceships just like me.*

"And…what's stopping you?" The silky black hair escaping the major's pony tail nearly brushed the bar as the man leaned his cheek on his fist and stared patiently at young Solvreyil.

Oh creepy eyes again, dammit. "Even if I could go to the Academy, those kinds of classes are wait-listed and require recommendation. I don't even think I can remember the name of a single professor from Framework whose word would count and I'm sure I made a terrible impression on anyone in my Refuge division if they even noticed me." He looked up from his drink again to note Parthenos' look shifted to 'slightly less patient'. He rolled his free hand at Sol as if to say, 'So? And what else?'

What's he at? Is he just picking on me?

"You applied to the Junior Academy last year, right?"

"Yes, sir, before I left Framework for Basic Training. Don't I have to reapply now though, with the tags?"

There was a strange, too regular glinting as the big indigo eyes rolled. "No. JA apps and admissions stay on file until five years after death, which means long as you get a removal or exemption for the second collar in that time, you're good. With your qualifications, there's probably a formal acceptance letter rotting at one of our mail facilities. They don't email those, you know, JA tradition." Parthenos tinkered with his slate again, one arm still held up his head on the counter. "And look here. You are in the roster for first winter if you want to start correspondence courses. If you want to think positive though, you could wait for *true spring* session and pick your courses as if you'd be attending in person."

Holtiin, by virtue of her somewhat faster and slightly irregular orbit, had two winters in the course of the standardized Imperial Year; the first followed by a brief explosion of new life and heavy rains and an intense, hot summer chased almost immediately by a shorter winter and what was known as "true spring": several beautiful months of mild weather during which the planet's chief industries – tourism and food production – boomed. Institutions planned their sessions accordingly, shutting briefly during the hottest part of summer and the worst winter weather. Junior Academy correspondence courses were held year-round in four session blocks, with those professors being the best paid academics since their only regular breaks were festival days.

Sol watched as the slate was jiggled before his face. Motion aside, he was looking at official Academy records. *What the hell kind of power do you have? Sure it's a military university but...* "Sir, I would love to do that. I suck at most of the scholarship sports. Could I trade my Ryzaa U scholarship for something?"

"Maybe." Parthenos sat up straight again and poked at his slate on the counter with both hands. "Gonna go for true spring then?"

Fuck it, what have I got to lose? "If I find out I can't go for some reason, what's the cut-off to tell them I'm out without penalty?"

"Forty days unless you have Active Deployment on your file, which everyone in the 17th and 89th has automatically. That means you can hold off until the very last minute to play that card and go the next semester with no penalty. Register for everything, including any pre-reqs you want to kill off in correspondence, and you'll have a better chance of getting in to the wait listed stuff."

A good mood makes him an entirely different person. I kind of want to cry and hug him, minus the scary. "I appreciate the advice sir." A sign beside the booze bore the cartoonish image of a mud-locked kaffa with off-kilter ears and an exhausted face. 'Come Down', read the larger font above the head. Beneath it assured in a smaller font, 'We've got you covered.' "You think Kiertus might write me a letter of rec for a few classes? A colonel is good as or better than a noted professor, right?"

"Well probably, but that won't really be necessary." Parthenos scooted his slate across the counter with the side of his hand. Sol picked it up to read.

The screen displayed a mock-up of Star Assault letterhead. The body described why Solvreyil Yenraziir would make an exceptional member to true spring semester's Cultural Ethics debate session. It cited his thoughtful approach to problem solving and his delicate handling of 'sensitive situations' and was signed, 'Major Parthenos Aurgaia, 17th Atmospheric Assault Force' followed by a short but impressive list of abbreviated certifications. Sol could not think of a thing to say; he merely sat, mouth open.

"Before I hit send on that, promise me you will not drop that course and will ride it out even if you decide you hate it and everyone else in it a week in."

"I-I- I promise, Major Parthenos, sir."

"This does not exempt you from the previous challenge; we will fight some day, once you're trained. Don't forget it." Picking up his slate, the major hit 'enter' with a flourish.

"Understood, but, thank you, sir." Sol accepted the plate handed him as the bartender walked past. "Thank you, as well, sir." He took a deep breath over the two fluffy yellowish finger-thick disks, inhaling the fragrant herbs, and waited for utensils. Parthenos, he noted, was already digging into his rice with his claw utensil. The boy followed suit, but stopped part way through a cake. "That woman we picked up, Celita… is she going to be all right, sir?"

"Count on the fact she's valuable and we have no interest in returning her as far as how she will be treated by our empire. Her compliance with questioning and acceptance of her blood are up to her, though." The major chewed his lichen, eyes on the bar mirror. "She's got much to deal with, all alone. Quite a chasm to bridge, waking one day realizing you're the very thing that's given you nightmares all your life."

Sol watched the man eat and worked on his own breakfast, disturbed not only by the statement, but by Parthenos' seeming obsession with the mirror. *He's not looking at himself... he's watching the room behind us. Is there something wrong with his eyes or is he expecting something?*

"How're your cakes?"

"Uh, ah, great, sir, I mean, Kahner." He smiled at the bartender. "Like my dad used to make, really."

Kahner squinted as he leaned toward Sol. "Holy shit, are you Rope-"

"Did someone order a taxi?"

Parthenos whirled around on his stool and saluted before Sol recognized the voice. Kahner, likewise, was at attention, bar rag hastily stuffed in his belt.

"Greetings, Colonel Kiertus!" The sentinel snapped quickly from his salute and, popped a squarish bottle from under the bar as Sol turned to face his master.

"You shouldn't have, Syavrasky, really. Where did you get that? I suppose a shot – " Kiertus rolled his eyes. "At ease, major, astrum; the hard time is unnecessary. We're in the Come Down, for Pete's sake."

Who or what is a 'Peet'? "Should we hurry up our lunch, sir?"

"No need, Solvreyil. I'm going to have a few and make the major drive." Bits of steel grey mop poked over raised goggles as Kiertus slid off his gloves and leaned to Sol. "How many has he had?"

"One double, sir."

"Double *what*?"

Sol eyed Parthenos' vexed expression from the other side of their commander. "Terribly sorry, colonel, but I haven't any idea what he ordered, drink names don't mean much to me, I'm afraid, sir. I had a digestive tea." The boy held the remains of his drink demonstratively. *I hope he can tell I'm not even lying.*

214

"As usual, I should forbid my current astrum from hanging out with any of my former, I see." Kiertus sat beside Sol and took a little container from Kahner. "Still never will be right, doing whiskey shots in low grav glasses. I appreciate the effort anyway, Syavrasky."

"Jady swore it was good, I wouldn't know, tastes like fuel to me and turns my sweat to piss."

Kiertus winked as he downed the entire contents of the little vessel. "That's part of the charm, *pardner*."

"Who's watching the Sanj?" Parthenos asked snidely as he poked his rice. "Gotta shipful of blue up there?"

"Oh, it's in good hands, I assure, but half the ears right here aren't cleared to hear." Kiertus passed the glass back for a refill. "Figured you could use a lift back rather than waiting for Wyvern or Val... or are you going to argue with driving my Infiltrator?"

"No, sir."

"That's what I suspected."

"Are they taking Dro?"

"No. We hand him over at Uayavu. Which'll be tricky unless we get in before the Prince comes home from court." The colonel eyed his second in command grimly. "Can you take the helm when we arrive so Wyvern and I can move him from confinement and get him off the ship?"

Parthenos stared back, slack-jawed. "I'm uncomfortable with this plan, colonel."

"How would you distribute the labor on this, then, Aurgaia?"

The major's jaw ground and brows furrowed. There was a conspicuous pause before he finally replied. "I concede, Colonel, but only because we lack the luxury of deliberation. For the record. Sir."

IX. A Most Difficult Task

"What are you doin' down this way?"

What a strange question, coming from you. "Used to be down here all the time, lieutenant. Trained as a pilot before I trained on armor, sir. Don't think I've seen you down here once, no disrespect, sir."

"Oh, none taken." The familiar mischievously goofy smile lit the lieutenant's face. "You trained over here probably while I was mostly working in the port pipes."

Sol tilted his head as he continued to walk along. "I'm running an errand for the colonel." He waved the little package he carried at Aukaldir, who was heading starboard as well. "I thought you were mostly a paratrooper. I've never looked up your non-com job, though, apologies, sir."

"I'm in administrative; I can work from the lounge if I want most of the time, yeah." Aukaldir laughed. "That gets boring though so I picked up ship tattooing. Chel taught me, you know, didn't think I'd ever get to do it, 'cause he's so good… but I guess he leaves the hive as little as possible, now." Wistfulness tinged the usually carefree voice.

This is a wild guess; I only read his stats the first day I met him, most of it was classified. "Was he your master?"

"I'm impressed, lil man, you called it. You got a pretty close-woven net up there." The lieutenant patted Sol's head. His voice was genuinely sad beneath the hint of amazement. "Do you enjoy working in the hive with him?"

"Yeah, he's a nice guy, and I've learned so much from him about bugs and about the other half of my people, you know, cuz…" Sol coughed embarrassedly.

"I was a Frameworker too, y'know? Surprised, huh? The point of Framework, aside from giving kids from splintered or retired families skills and goals is to make you feel part of a community; that's how I understood it and how it worked for me. Maybe not on Holtiin, huh? Maybe the human – kaffa split is too much deeper than the Ryzaan – Shandrian – Vasiiit split, yeah? Never really thought about that, but that's growin' up on Archos. If you'd grown up there, you wouldn't think about it, because there aren't many humans. You'd be worried about being Shandrian or Islander or whatever, and about too many text messages from girls in the middle of class!"

"No way, sir! Girls act like I'm covered in fire-shooting sores!" Sol laughed.

Aukaldir was at least smiling again. "Red heads like you, even bony ones, are a big hit, especially with that skin tone, yeah? You'd be so rich as a pay-boy in Ryzaa or Maayukoraa or Vyeshaal... phew, man... I can't even imagine, and I did OK."

The lieutenant got a few feet ahead before realizing Solvreyil had stalled in place in the hall. "Hey, you're not weird about prostitutes, are you? Because a lot of the guys do it during their leave months, several of the officers on this ship have other lives as house boys, even. It's - "

"Oh, no, sir, it's not that. My dad said something about being 'Archon candy' when I was a kid that I never got. I think I do now though." Sol laughed in embarrassment. "Shit it's the best profession you can get into, my Framework school, Chenzaanyil, offered Physical Recreation Vocational Studies, I was never old enough and never even thought... man... that's... are you messing with me?"

"Not at all. Your hair's almost dark enough to pass as Mantzaari, yeah? You'd be a hit." They were nearly to the starboard pipes. "You went to Chenzi... I thought you came from a poor family. Damn."

"Same as any imperial metro area schools; qualified applicants native to the locality from serving families get free tuition. That's what we were local to. What's so special about Chenzi?"

Aukaldir walked in silence a step ahead of Sol, apparently in deep thought. As they got to the hangar doors, he turned with a strange smile. "I figured out what's wrong with you, kid."

That's about the smuggest tone in the history of smugness. "And what would that be, sir?"

"Real simple, Solly. You've had privileges all your life, opportunities people literally kill and die for, and you never even knew it, just stumbled blindly on through, thinking you're better than all that and wondering why you've been so wronged." The man shook his head. "That's a combo of human and kaffa traits that is, thankfully, curable."

What the? Is he trying to piss me off? "I don't know what to say to that, sir."

"Well for starters, you can thank Star Assault, yeah? Then you can thank the Empire by serving in it. See ya later, astrum!" The lieutenant saluted and was on his way. "Say hi to Freaksauce for me!"

Sol found he growled under his breath then squinted and sputtered a little. *I didn't tell him I was delivering this package to Wyvern… what the…*

"Is that mail for me?"

Ack! "Sir! Yes sir." *You've been standing behind me the whole time, haven't you? Spook!* "I don't know why he couldn't just deliver it, because he also told me to tell you to meet him at 'soft freeze' whatever that is, sir." *If there's been ice cream on this ship this whole time I'm gonna laugh… then I'm gonna go get some, fuck yeah, ice cream!*

The haggard wing commander frowned as he took the package. "Our prince is a man of many quirks, Astrum Solvreyil. Come with me, please." Wyvern turned and headed to his office.

Sol had almost gotten used to the overtly sexy photographs displayed all over the walls in cling frames. He did his level best to keep from examining the assorted gratuitous anatomy (and trying to figure out which person was a younger, less life-weary Wyvern) as he watched the wing commander open the package, read an enclosed note, tuck the object into his belt, and toss the package for recycling.

"You're coming with me, I guess. This could become extremely dangerous; signals will be issued in Shandrian. Slates will not be used. Are you carrying your re-breather?"

"Damn, no ice cream."

"What?"

"Nothing. Sorry, sir. Yes, I am carrying my re-breather. Val said I always had to since I spend time in the pipes, sir." Sol promptly removed the device from its pouch and held it up. "Should I put it on now, sir?"

"No. You have a fast enough on/off time you can keep it in your pouch and keep the pouch unlatched. Secure your ladders though."

This is my thickest over shirt; how can he tell my ladder shirt is only half-fixed? "Yes, sir." Sol removed the concealing layer and connected the 'snakeheads' so the lacing activated, tightening the suit. The semi-living material was not constricting even when fully secured, but Sol's face displayed his grievance.

"Apologies, sir, I keep it loose because I get so warm in it... I know it's not really useful to my muscles if I walk around like this, sir." As he looked up, he noticed Wyvern smiling, but the face changed instantly on catching his eyes.

"Let me guess, Val instructed you on the proper use of it?"

"Yes, sir."

Eyes rolled. "If you find yourself too hot in it, instead of unlacing it, keep it on and let the heat build. The suit will cool automatically. If it's taking too long, you can trigger it by lightly pinching right behind one of the snakeheads." Wyvern slipped behind a column of magnetic storage receptacles and kept talking. "Or, if you're good with pulse control that way, broadcast to the suit you have a fever and are in pain. It will do the rest. It won't judge you for lying; it is a tool and not the guardian to heaven."

When he stepped back out, Wyvern was in his ladders as well. *I know Eek said he was a proper Shandrian, but I wonder what horrific thing he has tattooed on himself? I want to see his fancy grafts!*

"You ready?"

"Other than the fact I have no idea what's going on, yes, sir."

As they departed the office, Wyvern quietly rasped, "We're going to get Droo and load him on Kiertus' craft." Suddenly he snarled up at the lifts, "Hey, Hanajiel, watch the fuckin pipes, I'm stepping out for a bit, brass business, got it?"

219

"Aye aye, commander, don't fuckin' die, sir."

"Shut your cake hole, lieutenant." Quiet returned. "He's been in solitary confinement, his slate communication ultra limited. He's been allowed one monitored visit and one meal a day. All his food has been drugged. He is under the impression his punishment has a term; this is true. But the end of the term is being shipped to a real prison for processing."

"Processing?" *That word can mean so many things in our culture.* "Isn't he going to the 89th?"

"There's at least one man waiting in the 89th who will kill him immediately on arrival; he has made many enemies in criminal circles. While some people might support that situation, our current colonel is a man who believes in fair treatment and rehabilitative opportunities."

Sol mulled this over a moment. "So what do you mean by 'processing'?"

Wyvern chuckled unpleasantly. "I forget you're Holtiini, you look like such an *'ey'maurefae.*

Yi'ehmohrifeh? That's how that's pronounced? I've only ever seen it in books. He just called me a sea elf. Sol suppressed a giggle. "We use that word for rendering corpses in energy plants. Holdover from…"

"When Holtiin was a prison planet, I know. It's what your family name means, too. 'The solution' or 'solver of problems'; the renderers for the prisons." He looked back and waived his hand dismissively, as if Sol already knew all of this, as if it were common knowledge.

My mother told me it had something to do with distillation. I wonder if he's talking out his ass? "So legal processing, like a competency assessment for trial?"

"If I'd meant the other, well, the ship always needs fuel." Wyvern was silent for a moment. "Do you know what it means to *k'djek*?"

"Not really. That poem about Maalek that the colonel made me read used that expression…"

Wyvern turned, stopped Sol in the hallway, put a hand on either shoulder. Sol glanced at each hand nervously. "Look me in the eye, astrum"

"Yes, sir." Bloodshot as always but a light of intelligence and concern hid in the harsh glare.

"Listen. I won't repeat. To *k'djek* is to throw your field. In its most extreme form, you force all the pulse from your body in one blast. A person can seriously hurt himself without channeling armor on, especially a conduit, do you understand me?"

"Yes, sir." *I think. Anything from a shower of sparks to a massive electrical detonation is theoretically possible; self-immolation maybe, simply expending so much energy your organs fail, OK no he could be talking about all kinds of stuff. I'm lying, I think. Fuck it.*

"Men of the Sun consider *'k'djek'* to be an insulting description. They call the act *'heokier,'* 'to return love'. Men trained in other art forms use *k'djek* as a warning to other soldiers in their sect; either they or someone nearby is about to do it, so others can form a force field to keep from being hurt."

"Got it." *I wonder if I would find this less terrifying if someone else was explaining it to me.*

"Not done." The expression was intense. "I don't throw my field. If I say that, get your mask on as fast as you can and get on the other side of a bulkhead if possible. Remember, if the ship is compromised, a force field can keep you alive in space for a time. Your worst enemies are panic and exhaustion."

Help. "Yes, sir. Understood, sir."

"One last thing. I won't be visible when we approach. Do not talk to me. Talk only to Kiertus when you see him. Do not mention me. Do you understand? This is crucial."

"You aren't even there, sir."

"Good start." Wyvern released him and stepped backwards, slowly dissolving into the background. "Now for the fun stuff."

Sol tried to track Wyvern in the hall as they proceeded to an isolated set of cocoons to the rear of the port pipes. Occasionally, flickering in the air occurred as the wing commander moved between floor and wall, wall and ceiling. His pattern seemed entirely random. *I probably shouldn't be looking at him if I'm to pretend he isn't here. What the hell... there's a ship sprite following him under the dermis of the wall?*

A little bulge moved along barely perceptible beneath the surface. It ran into tubing or other solid structures and attempted different approaches. Eventually it gave up and wobbled off from wherever it came. While he was a little disturbed by it at first, it reminded him of silly things Ozzie would do, and wondered how she faired. *Val said she'd be happy on the bridge with him and Nova... but isn't that where Parthenos is? She doesn't like him...*

"Good day, Solvreyil! It's so good of you to meet me here. How are you doing?"

Sol could not help but smile as he bowed to his master. "Fine sir, thank you for asking. What was it you needed me to do?'

"Quite simple, really, if you wouldn't mind. Stand to the side right here while I open this cocoon. Then we'll escort the chap within to the port pipes." He wore no insignia, no officer's jacket, no heavy armor, and oddest of all, his feet were bare. His toes, clean as they were, had the same beastly appearance as those of Wyvern; long with curved, pointed nails. Even so, Kiertus Sheriden had the grace and bearing of a refined Imperial military gentleman. "Your slate is vibrating."

"Huh? So it is." Sol checked, confused he had not even felt it. "It's Val; he says Nova just let herself off the bridge, sir."

"Auri probably wouldn't make a lap for her." The colonel exhaled in amused frustration. "Well, tell him I have more pressing things at hand and just to keep Ozlietsin and himself there."

Kiertus isn't wearing a slate, his pouch is slack, that's strange. Is he even - Sol looked at his monitor after he replied to the frantic text from Valdieren. *Neither he nor Wyvern shows up in this hall, it's just me and 'Flashpoint' behind the coffin door. This is beyond unsettling and I want it over now.*

The colonel knelt to open the lowest door. His voice was gentle but firm, almost fatherly. "Hello, Ash. Ash? Are you awake? Come now. Well come on, yes, of course you can come out. Careful, there."

Kiertus took the man's arms as he climbed out of the cocoon and into the hall. Dromarka seemed a little weak and shaky. Sol stood at attention nearby.

"Am I going to trial or the 89th?" asked Dromarka in a tired and impatient tone. He was dressed the way he had been when Sol first encountered him – brace and ladders, no shirt, no shoes. His muscles seemed to sag a little and his hair was on the ragged side.

"You are going to trial."

While he spoke to Kiertus, he cast Solvreyil an unforgiving glower. "What's my charge?"

"You have about twenty official charges, Ash, and I can change none of them now. Treason is the important one." The colonel seemed more tired than his prisoner. "I would prefer not to cuff you. But please make it easier for me and turn around."

"You're not telling me something, I can hear it in your speech... where am I going to trial?"

"Fenrir, like any man of your caliber. Please turn around."

Dromarka hesitated then turned. The colonel already had a rubbery mini-noose tie in his hand. As this was looped around his wrists, the former armorer said, "But you're not taking me right to Fenrir, are you? It's too far from where we are now. You're taking me to trade me off to a courier. Where?"

Clenching his teeth, Kiertus secured the tie firmly before he uttered, "Uayavu."

Every muscle in Dromarka's body tensed visibly as he whirled and staggered. "You're lying!" He spat, exhaustion replaced by fury. "You wouldn't give me to Master Okallin! You've set something up!"

"I'm not giving you to Okallin, and I set nothing up."

He sure didn't deny lying or allowing him to be set up, though.

"Parthenos did it then. You let him take care of my sentencing… after everything… I knew it. I knew it!"

A glow surrounded Dromarka. It hissed and crackled. Kiertus merely stood, just barely touched by it, not moving or flinching. "Don't be a fool. If Auri had handled your sentencing, we wouldn't have wasted the rations on you; you'd already be processed aboard the *Esimaar*. Recall your field; you don't want to do this. Each second you delay is a chance we won't make the exchange meeting and trust me; the outcome of that possibility is very poor for you."

Dromarka tensed again; the field waivered but did not disperse. Sol felt something move just above and beside him; suddenly Dromarka lurched and snapped back as if he had come to the end of a tight rope. A painful noise escaped him and his field vanished.

"Nice try, Flashpoint." Wyvern became visible, holding Dromarka's wrists at a harsh angle. "You're not fully suppressed but you're several days without adequate food. Did you think we wouldn't notice that Hanajiel was coming back from your 'conjugal visits' unable to pass a piss test for the jet shop?"

"Fuck that double-crosser and fuck you."

"He did everything willingly, because he cared about you, stupid. It's a crying shame you don't return that favor to anyone who's ever trusted you." On the last syllable, Wyvern shoved Dromarka forward. "Get a move on. I'm not about to let Okie get the last laugh here."

"Let him go, Freyr." Kiertus gestured. "I said, let him go, captain."

Freyr? Is that his real name? Master K controls his emotions astoundingly well, but I can tell he's really unhappy going through with this. So fatherly though…

Wyvern hesitated. His voice was hollow. "Yes, sir." He stepped back a little.

The colonel hooked an arm through Dromarka's crooked right elbow and urged him onward. Wyvern stepped to one side, following at a small distance off to the left. Sol moved to take up the rear. He could hear Dromarka muttering.

"Why don't you just listen to me, all of you are going to die, they don't need Star Assault anymore... the New Sun soldiers will replace us. They already are."

The colonel scowled. "There is no 'New Sun', not on the level you imagine. And it's not what you think."

"They made monsters, out of men, now they can make monsters that aren't even men, and you know it, you know it, you've been there, you've seen it... why won't you listen... "

"I don't make a habit of listening to insanity. You need help, Ash."

The glow began again. Dromarka's voice became more urgent. "You're not taking me to a trial. You're taking me to a reconditioning. You're going to 'end stage' me. What are they going to use me for?" He commenced struggling again. "We're no better than them... you're no better than the Ilu!"

His previously calm demeanor gone, Kiertus hissed into the rising field. The voice contained enormous threat without any real loudness or dark words. Sol could barely make it out above the sounds of the ship and the crackle of Dromarka's force. "You need to be silent or I will make certain of it for you."

"I was so blind. I never should have trusted you... you keep trained saurtzek as pets and you're priming one to advise the throne – you've probably been in their pay since the second war, you fucking monster – and you have the nerve to call me 'traitor' – "

The limit was reached. Kiertus rotated his arm artfully and flipped Dromarka to the floor in a single sharp motion. "Your attempts to get me to kill you here and now have been noted. I think you have forgotten, in your delusion, whom you are fighting."

Dromarka inched backwards, his arms still restrained, a slight look of victory on his face. He generated a visible field, not as crackly as the previous one. "What's my life to you? You've eradicated entire colonies, ships full of your own men. Your single-handed body count is higher than all currently enlisted marines, together. What's one wayward shit-talking student?"

"Enough!"

My knight master has a much larger set of fangs than I realized...

Wyvern moved nearer to Sol; he stood with his feet apart, knees slightly bent, clenching and unclenching his hands as if torn on what to do.

"What's that thing with you anyway, that red-headed thing? Which one of you ordered that made? You think I haven't heard the stories?" Sol strained to hear Dromarka's increasingly quiet voice. "I know, I know what that is... "

"You know nothing." Fire lit amber eyes as Kiertus assumed a combat stance.

"*K'djek*," whispered Wyvern softly as he sprang onto the wall. He headed for the ceiling as Sol moved backwards to the nearest bulkhead, slipping on his mask.

Why was he talking about me like that? What's going on?

"I know enough, by looking with my own two eyes, Sheriden." Dromarka got to his feet and made a point of spreading his arms slowly to show that his wrists bore burns but no trace of the tie. "He more than resembles my trainer in the sound arts. He's a walking replication, only 20 times as dangerous. Something like that doesn't happen on accident." Dromarka assumed a slight crouching posture, held his hands about a foot apart, rotated his wrists slowly and rhythmically; the light about his body was being pulled into the space between. "One wasn't enough; they made a Ropetrick that could take out entire planets!"

Kiertus threw his crossed arms before him, catching the fireball Dromarka threw squarely. A shower of sparks descended. The colonel staggered from the blast but did not give ground. "What did I tell you about speaking? You should really ... stop."

Wow I think a hit like that would have blown me right into the wall in this little gravity... how is he anchoring himself? Sol was just to the other side of the hatchway but saw and heard nearly everything. An alarm sounded; the ship recited instructions to clear this sector including the port pipes. "Orange alert," she said, far too calmly. "Non-essential personnel evacuate highlighted areas. Orange alert."

Dromarka prepared another fireball, but Kiertus simply backed away from him, arms up, hands forward. "Are you, the great War Priest of Aur, afraid of me?

Are you just too old to fight? Too old and cowardly and broken to fight a half-starved, drugged paratrooper, a completely disposable kaffa?"

"It doesn't have to go this way, Ash; you can stop now and go to a fair trial with dignity."

"I don't want your version of a 'fair trial', you homicidal mercenary bastard! What did you do with the saurtzek at Altair station? What did you trade at Yuh'geth?"

The ball of fire would be much larger this time, and Kiertus was cornered. Wyvern was nowhere to be seen. Without thinking, Sol leapt forward. "Master!"

The emergency hatch slammed shut, issuing a creak as it sealed, trapping him in the space. The air was hot and unpleasant. Kiertus braced with his arms before him, concentrating, determined, but not the least bit afraid. Dromarka exhaled and half-jumped, hurled a massive gout of fire forward from his arms.

If there was anything Sol could have done, he was too far away. "Sir! Look out!" he cried into his mask.

The pressure in the room changed; the air felt moist, then dense and visibly wet. The gout of fire collapsed inward on itself and vanished. Dromarka gasped and flailed as Kiertus stood, unharmed, shrouded in a pale aura, his hair and clothes bone dry as Sol and Dromarka became soaked. Wyvern, now also wearing a mask, dropped from the ceiling as if he jumped feet first into a pool. He glowered at the fallen man, who clawed at his own throat, his face discolored. The wing commander knelt, put a finger to Dromarka's lips and shook his head. He snapped his fingers and the moisture reabsorbed into the *Sanjeera*'s walls and dispersed into the air.

Kiertus bridged the gap between them, grabbed Dromarka and flipped him to face the floor in a peculiar wrestling hold before the man could fully draw a breath. He had a weapon at his captive's throat. "Do you really want to die?" said the colonel emotionlessly.

Dromarka growled and struggled and Kiertus repeated the question, more urgently this time.

"Sir. No sir."

"There it is, then." Kiertus brought up his arm rapidly, impacting Dromarka under the nose with the object in his hand. Sol cringed at the visceral crack. The blonde went limp and unconscious as the colonel released him. "Pinch him, Freyr."

Wyvern shrugged and shook his head. He removed something from his belt and fitted it over Dromarka's nose and mouth. He made to speak but an alarm went off. Wyvern looked up and then at Kiertus. "Why wasn't that followed by 'all clear'?"

"Aurgaia has overridden me again, Sheriden," came the ship's voice. "Thank you for preventing my injury, though. Your friend is here. I will let her in."

The bulkhead hatches whooshed open. Nova, Kiertus' aged, massive genadri charged in, burbling furiously. She ran to the colonel and nipped at his sleeve.

"What's the matter with you? When did you get so needy?"

Nova made a perturbed expression and spat out the colonel's slate, which floated to the floor in a little flurry of drool. She squawked impatiently and kicked a scythe at it. He stooped, picked it up, furrowed his brow and remarked, "Shit!" just as the 'jump' alarm began.

"Urgent transfer in… five minutes. Secure positions. Non-essential personnel to stations of refuge."

"What the hell is Parthenos doing!" Wyvern leapt to his feet.

"It's not Parthenos." He showed the wing commander his slate as Sol looked on in confusion. "Imperial orders. On the up side, you and I don't have to take a small craft expedition to Avenaur today." Kiertus shrugged. "You and Nova get him to Laathas and locked down safely. Hard freeze, preferably."

"Yes, sir. You going to the bridge, then?"

"Damn straight." The colonel gestured for Sol to follow as Wyvern draped Dromarka over a somewhat resistant, flat-antennaed Nova.

"You should ice those burns on your arms."

Kiertus made a strange face. "My suit's on it. How'd you even tell? The suit's not damaged."

"Just good at this stuff, I guess. Oh, one more thing," Wyvern reached into the pouch where he earlier deposited the colonel's mystery gift. "I appreciate it, but not today."

"Within reason, under the circumstances, captain." The colonel winked and nodded and began toward the other end of the vessel.

....

"Solvreyil, how much of the argument did you hear?"

For over a minute they walked in silence, interrupted only by alarms and periodic crew rushing in one direction or another. Kiertus seemed unhurried however.

"Pretty much all of it, sir."

"I apologize, then." The colonel stopped and faced him. "There were grains of truth in much of what he said, although filtered through a lot of nonsense not reflected by the world outside his skull."

"I gathered that sir, as unsettling as some of it was."

"I encourage you to ask if you have questions. Don't fill in the blanks alone, that's a slippery slope."

Sol had so much to ask but did not want to approach from the wrong angle. "Why'd he call me a 'thing'?"

Kiertus waved dismissively. "Oh, that's just a manifestation of his particular brand of racism. Human blood invalidates your status as an individual since he considers humans 'herd animals' and haki 'abominations', therefore you get object neutral treatment. There's no way to sugar coat it, I apologize."

"It's fine, sir. But he said I was 'made'. What did he mean by that?"

"It has been repeatedly proven that factor n blood and therefore High Tension Syndrome are more common in kaffa with mixed genetics – human and saurtzek genetics, specifically." Cat-like yellow eyes glanced his way as they walked. "Some say the Ilu attacked Ruahanu not because of their piratical depredations but because the mixed society produced an inordinate number of conduits, and it concerned them… or they wanted to seize and recycle the traits."

How ghastly. "I see, sir."

"Either way, particular enclaves of conspiracy theorists suspect a secret society inside the Archon military is creating conduits intentionally. Sometimes I think that could be true, but I do not think it is true of you. I knew your mother and father; no one forced them to marry." His smile was sweet and sad as he set a hand on Sol's back. "Even if you were a construct, does that make you less an individual, less deserving of love and respect? I do not think so; no true kaffa would."

This did not exactly improve the state of Sol's heart and mind although Kiertus' respect meant a great deal to him. "So ... was Ropetrick my father's call sign?"

"One of the ones he held over the years, yes. I can't tell you much more about him, I am afraid, or I would be looking at more time at Fenrir."

Sol stared at the floor with a sigh.

"So much worrying, especially in one so young, can be toxic over time. Speaking of your age, it is likely the only thing that keeps people from suspecting you are investigating on behalf of Sec5, and that as you grow older, questions about highly classified individuals might raise eyebrows. Instead of asking around so much, one might attempt the tactic of working to increase one's clearance."

Logical, I guess. "Thank you, sir." They stopped in the hall again, staring at the public address system as the ship called jump proximity, realizing they would not make it to the bridge at this pace. Sol's mind still reeled from what he had seen and heard. "Was Dromarka always like that, sir?"

"No. There was some question about parts of his psych profile when he originally joined; Parthenos in particular had objections to his enlistment." Kiertus shrugged. "I can't waste time regretting my decision and wishing I'd listened to him."

The alarm again. Without warning, Sol was plucked from where he rested and hoisted into an alcove in one graceful leap. Kiertus braced his back against one side of the niche, releasing his astrum with a nod. Sol attempted to do similarly in spite of his gangliness and confusion. Their legs tangled in the alcove.

"We need to secure ourselves for jump, so hold on."

Sol grabbed onto his master furiously.

The colonel chuckled. "That's not quite what I meant. Not that I mind." With a wink he gestured his head toward his left hand, which clutched a hold in the wall niche's spongy surface.

"Oh. Uh, sorry, sir." Utterly embarrassed, Sol unglued himself from Kiertus and took a handle.

In a hushed, kindly tone, Colonel Kiertus continued his previous train of thought. "It is part of the duty of Star Assault's highest officers to take young kaffir, people who love and cherish life and living, and teach them to do the opposite. To teach them to optionally turn off their nature in favor of protection or destruction. On every level, this is challenging. Sometimes it is heartbreaking; it is certainly the most difficult part of my job."

Sol stared into sad yellow eyes as the jump warning blared again.

"Dromarka dealt poorly with being a member of my crew; other former astra of mine were distinctly distrusting and unkind to him. I think he expected other things from the experience. He transferred to another unit, and, as luck would have it, became embroiled immediately in drama he would rather not have, so he returned, right as we went to examine an apparent 'tragedy' in a secret installation at Tohdo.

"Again, I can't reveal details. Suffice to say, what we dealt with there was unpleasant; this crew is still recovering from what occurred then. It was the last straw for Dromarka; he simply couldn't cope with no one to blame. He drew connections without much evidence, and again, I simply wanted to believe that because he'd been my astrum, he was better armed – internally, emotionally – to deal with it all. He is my mistake, Solvreyil, and I have been a little distant with you because I don't want to repeat that."

The emergency lights were flashing along the now-dimmed halls. *Even more questions than answers, as usual. Damn all these secrets!* Sol sputtered, searching his master's face, wanting more information while wishing to console him, wishing to assure him, "I'm not like that, I'm tougher! I'll prove it!"

Anything that could have been said was lost in the disruption of time and space around them as the *Sanjeera*'s ioun drive activated. The focus of Sol's existence became not vomiting on the colonel, then simply being part of the ship-creature and of reality and time itself.

As the process reversed and colors, shapes, and sounds reverted to normal, Sol blinked and shuddered, still clinging to the tissues of the alcove as firmly as he could.

"All right there, astrum?" Kiertus asked, only partly eying Sol as he fixed his command pin to his chest.

Is that what he gave Wyvern? "Did you expect… did you think that Dromarka would… Wyvern was talking to me about 'ship compromise', I …"

"There is always a potential, Solvreyil. I like to be sure the crew is prepared in the possible event of my death. Of the three of us, I was least likely to survive; I lured his fire so he wouldn't just blow a hole in her. I wanted to deplete his energy completely before we got to the pipes and he could do real damage."

Sol stammered.

"I know Wyvern told you to stand on the other side of the bulkhead. Why did you disobey him?"

My answer seems pretty stupid now. "I was … worried about you, sir."

"While I appreciate the sentiment, I am an old man; my life has been more good than bad, but the universe might be better and safer without me in it. I am not afraid of atonement." Kiertus leapt nimbly from the alcove and offered Sol his hand. "They wait for us on the bridge."

Mute sadness overcame him as he followed his knight master. After a long, sympathetic glance, the colonel took out his slate and tinkered. Shortly, Sol's vibrated. He squinted at Kiertus as he checked it.

In a mail from "Gunsmoke" was a set of virtual documents. The first was large, labeled, "Condensed Account of Actions at Mior, Kiertus Sheriden, 23rd Star Assault and 17th Star Assault/Ice Invasion Armada". The second much smaller: "Official Court Records and Witness Testimony, Second and Third Mior Wars, in re: Admiral Kiertus Sheriden (defendant)."

"You're welcome to read the long form version in my library any time; I have the out of print copies of the Coloniel Times Library bound collection from immediately after the war as well as accounts printed after the trial." His smile was grim but strangely peaceful as he strode. "A man's best armor is the truth, astrum; here are your first layers."

X. Under Handed

"You dropped this, um, sir." He had not checked his slate, but Sol was surprised to see Hanajiel after his ascent. *It's not like you to be clumsy. It's not my place to ask if you're OK.*

"Oh, thanks for finding this, astrum." Listlessly, he took the tool from Sol and stared back at the Dash on which he labored. "Saved me the trouble of going all the way down."

"No problem, sir." Sol made to descend.

"Hey. Are you in the escort group?"

His hand stopped on the web. "For Dromarka? Yes, sir." *Oh...*

Hanajiel walked over and sat on the lift's edge. He stared down at the slightly modified Dash below, one of Colonel Kiertus' two personally customized small craft. "Should I maybe just go to the lounge for a bit? Is this going to upset me?"

Why would you ask me *that?* "What do you mean, sir?"

"Is ... did they... is he 'pinched'?"

"Um, if you mean they put that weird mask thing on him and took him to Laathas, yes."

The lieutenant shuddered. He did not look Sol in the eye. "I've been in one before, they really hurt."

"Excuse me?"

"Running exercises out in the Burning Desert, training with the Patrol, I got caught in one of those freak down-drafts out there.... What do they call those?"

"Heat-cones is what they call them in school but 'hell-cones' is what my dad called 'em and he flew out there plenty. *Miorjviir* in his language, *diiskony* in my mother's."

233

"Those. Fucking things. Anyway, I didn't react in time. My jet was nearly intact – otherwise I might have just cooked – but I was all fucked up, shattered ribs and sternum, broken collarbones, internal injuries. Ladders and brace kept me alive. The ship itself clung around me and helped hold me together. Wyvern was my first responder, ironically, seeing as I work for him now. He put one of those masks on me, it was all he had in his emergency kit, he said later. But he's kind of a bastard on a good day. Pinch-masks intubate you like a bio-surgical mask but they also bind with your face and throat; you can't take them off yourself even if you try. A surgeon trained in the procedure has to remove it."

"Sorry, sir, that makes it sound like Wyvern saved your life."

"OK, granted, yes; Wyvern and that horrible mask kept my broken body functioning until he could get me to Saark back at the air base." Finally he looked at Sol; his eyes were red and puffy. "It was really uncomfortable though. I won't ever forget how awful it was to wake up with that thing on me and in me, breathing for me…"

I think I get it. "Sorry."

"He fucked up. Trust me that I'm upset about that, too. It was foolish of me to hope he'd come to his senses." Hanajiel sighed. "I still don't want to see him in pain. Not that pain."

"Would you rather he had blown out the port pipes?"

His face aghast, the lieutenant snapped, "Fuck no!"

"Apologies, sir, but I pegged you for a racist, too."

"What? Oh. I'll fully admit to being a racist. Droo decided at some point he was a full-on speciesist, that he believed humans and kaffa were totally separate, that it didn't matter that they can breed with kaffa, that they're 'lesser animals' that are supposed to be slaves or food, and breeding with food is abhorrent."

Sol blinked at the frankness. His voice was flat as he asked, "And what do you believe, then, sir?"

"Humans are just the weakest form of the folk; they've lost their pulse and their connection to nature; that doesn't mean they need to be killed! And eating 'em is still cannibalism and a real bad idea just all over the place. Their bad traits can be trained or bred out, you know that, look at you, you're no cave ape."

This is hardly consoling speech. I think it's intended to make me happy, though, so I'll pretend it does. "Hm. I suppose I can accept that, then, sir."

"I'm Shandrian, kid, even if you think I'm an asshole, I'm Shandrian. We don't eat people. That's Ryzaan and Ilu shit… and even half o' them know better and stopped doing that. I don't really think you can burn the savage out of people though, I think you talk it out of 'em." He looked around, wiped his face on his hand, stood and laughed uncomfortably. "Funny thing for an Assault pilot to say, huh? It's true though, in spite of my job. I only kill when I'm ordered; if I was a good talker like Eek, I wouldn't be a pilot."

Before Sol resumed his climb down to the launch bay, he glanced at his locator then back at Hanajiel. "You might still have a chance to make it somewhere else before they get him here. They're moving really slow from medical." *Come to think of it, why didn't they just land the colonel's Dash in the aft pipes and take him out the hive, anyhow?*

"Naw, I'm just gonna finish these diagnostics…last thing I want is Wyvern to see me obviously running from this. I helped them catch him… too late to be a coward now." The lieutenant saluted and slipped inside the hindered craft as Sol descended to wait for the brass.

***

Mouth held in a dire frown, Major Parthenos sat next to an unwillingly masked and groggy Dromarka in the crew cabin. Wyvern sat, arms crossed, tapping his foot soundlessly on the cabin floor, on the other side of the captive. Valdieren and Bachi sat across from them. Everyone was eerily silent, even Rocket, Squeak, and Ozzie, who all huddled in a pile in the seat between Bachi and Val. It would have been comical if their staring at Dromarka and the two grouches had not been quite so disturbing.

They're making the same faces they make when we have toys they want. Toys… or snacks. Sol turned back to watch Kiertus pilot the drop ship to the surface of Avenaur. Studying the seasoned combat veteran was not proving worth much; the colonel made pulse-enabled flight seem effortless.

"You look like you need to talk, Sol." Kiertus smiled, seemingly relieved to have an excuse to shut the door between cockpit and cabin. "So talk to me."

"You used some wrestling moves I recognized in the fight... will you show me how to use pulse to make those moves stronger?"

"Absolutely. After our little visit here I'll have more time for that sort of thing."

Sol opened his mouth then clammed up and stared down. "Sorry I'm so behind in everything, sir."

"Ah, ah. None of that. You're ten years beneath the average age at which people join this unit. I don't expect you to have a lot of finely honed pulse arts skills. I'm surprised you have none, mind you."

"Dad said he was going to teach me, on my 17th birthday, but..."

The face was sad, sympathetic, but a strange frustration lay there too. Sol wished he could read the old man's mind, then wondered what hidden cost might accompany that knowledge and snipped the thought-line. "You didn't join this unit in part for revenge, did you, Solvreyil Yenraziir?"

"Revenge..."

"On the resistance movement that backed the revolt at Pachar?"

This gave the boy a start. He shook his head rapidly. "Gods! No! No, sir, the thought had never crossed my mind! I mean, now, I see the – oh. I guess, I could see, um, how you'd come up with that, sir."

"I'm glad, because lust for vengeance makes a bad master. You deserve more worthwhile goals." Smiling again, the colonel initiated the landing sequence. On the monitor, a huge plateau rose from a jagged, rocky island in a dingy-colored body of water. Poking here and there from the dreary murk were crooked outcroppings of partially eroded stone. The sky was yellow-grey, not quite dissimilar to Kiertus' eyes. Sticky looking fog hung around the rocks at the water line and obscured any more distant shore. From Sol's perspective, this near-treeless hunk of earth was the only treadable land on this entire planet.

"I've always wanted to see this place, funny as that sounds, sir." Wide-eyed, Sol took in the view, marveling at the brutal-looking peak that towered at the far end of the plateau, sadly amused at what appeared to be green spaces sealed inside small domes in a cluster near the base of it. "My last ship came to this system once, but barely anyone got approved for shore leave."

Kiertus seemed focused on steering the ship and monitoring various details of the process; his response drifted out of him like an exhalation of smoke. "Probably all Armored and Star Assault people, yes? That would be typical. What isn't high-clearance on Avenaur requires harsh environment survival training."

"Oh! Oh. Now I get it. That makes more sense. And here I was all sad about it." Sol laughed at himself. He employed the gunner's mini-monitor to scan the mist and then look over the ominous mountain.

"You want to see an archeoaevis, I bet."

"Well, everything else native to this planet is pretty much extinct or so endangered it might as well be. I'm kinda curious to see some of the invasive species that adapted and took over... but the zoo on Holtiin is probably my best bet for terrapods, huh?"

The colonel simultaneously chuckled and shuddered. Sol merely assumed he had received some pulse stimulation from the Dash and ignored it.

"This is Summit Isle. The Great Convergence is held here in a few months, when the weather is a little... better. All the archeoaevis come here, and the people that care for them and the little communities that support those people can trade with one another. That set of structures on the far end of the plateau, see? Fairground accommodations for the summit."

People! Living on the backs of giant animals in cities grown from their bones! Sol nearly hopped in his seat, he was so excited. He recognized that in theory, the archeoaevis communities were principally the same as a small bio-starship like that in which he currently dwelled. The aesthetic and technical differences, however, enthralled the boy.

"May I make another request?"

The colonel chuckled, otherwise remaining in his flight posture. "Depends. I operate a heavily classified vessel, you know."

"I want to learn how to move across the walls and ceiling, too." Sol looked over the misty muck and its hazardous outcroppings. "Like in that video demo of you and Wyvern fighting… the one Val uploaded and Parthenos pulled, sir."

"Ah, that video." Kiertus flew straight for the horn-like mountain-spire. "Well, yes, but Wyvern can set a better example for you." He coughed. "I cheat a bit."

This came as quite a surprise. "You cheat, sir?"

"I use my claws, astrum." The old man laughed as he steered the Dash into an opening in the tower. "Don't look at me like that; the ship heals quickly."

Sol suppressed all possible remarks regarding the talent. While long toes and heavier nails were common enough at the swimming areas back home, Sol had never seen them unsheathed and 'used'. It had not really occurred to him that "elven claws" were more than a figure of speech. His supposedly "very kaffir" father had not possessed the feet of an enormous hairless forest cat, and he wondered what genetics gifted those talons to his commander or if maybe papa had favored some recessive human genes. The astrum looked at the closed cockpit door and asked, "What's the protocol here, sir?"

Kiertus landed the Dash and switched it to 'rest mode'. "Bugs off first by rank seniority of their companions. Prisoner and escorts last. You'll be third off with your gen; I'm not companioned so I go after you. There is a section on prisoner protocol in the handbook. Today might be a good day to read it, but I won't have your ass over it. It's easy to remember if you think of it as inverse of a combat jump. Without a prisoner, we'd follow standard station docking protocol, where gen go absolutely last with an additional handler. I assume that's what's confusing you?"

"It's seems complicated, sir."

Kiertus opened the hatch and intermediary door; his eyes settled on Dromarka like an unexpected turd in the garden. "Perhaps, but it avoids unnecessary… situations." He gestured for Sol to pass into the cabin. "After you, astrum."

A distinct relief accompanied the fact the forward upper hatch was opened rather than the rear jumping one; Sol did not have to walk past the terror twins and their distressing captive. He waited for Val and Bachi to file out with their

238

bonds. As Valdieren passed, he turned to Sol with eyes down and nodded solemnly. His voice was barely audible and Sol would not have seen his mouth move if he had not been consciously avoiding the area behind the captain. "Check your texts when you get a chance, astrum."

Ozzie hopped up, clearly eager to see where the other bugs went. As usual, she veered away from Parthenos, but she lunged at Dromarka, whose tired eyes bulged as he pulled back in his restraints. Wyvern shot between them, blocking her scythes with a crack of his forearm.

"*J'tu!*" he snapped in his cold iron voice. Ozzie recoiled with a hiss, antennae back, eyes rolling.

"Ozlietsin! Bad! Bad bug! Come here! Sorry, sirs, sorry, I don't know what's gotten into her, sirs."

Parthenos barely looked at them; he had not moved a muscle. Speaking quietly in the direction of the opposite wall – to Sol's surprise, in fluent albeit oddly accented Holtiini – the major said, "Were it up to me, I'd take us back to the Bleeding Desert and let her have him."

Dragging his uncooperative, growling gen out the hatch, Sol took in a breath. "Whoa." Chirping in unison with his astonishment, Ozlietsin's mood changed. The landing bay inside the spire was identical to the *Sanjeera*'s hell pipes, but easily four times the size. Busy technicians and soldiers, many accompanied by wingless worker genadri, scrambled up and down webs, worked on craft, carried cartons of materials, and waited for lift tentacles. Here and there, drop ships and transports moved about slowly on their wing digits. Five uniformed officers and a broad-chested, shirtless man waited on a lighted and labeled exit path. The big man waved as Kiertus slid out the hatch and Ozzie and Sol clambered down to the floor.

"Hoy there, Prince of Cheese! I heard you brought me a present!"

The colonel stood beside Sol, his expression patiently amused. Sol thought he detected a brief eye roll before the man spoke. "Welcome to Uayavu Tower Air Base, otherwise known as 'the Spire'."

A hand on Sol's back coaxed him gently forward. "It's something else, sir." They strode away from their craft; Sol kept a hand hooked into the front edge of

Ozzie's thoracic carapace. "Holy shit, are those exos down there, sir?"

"Maybe a few, yes, I believe, there might be some exoskeletal armor craft here."

I think he's mocking me. The crew of officers they approached interested him more than the good-natured teasing. The shirtless man was heavily tattooed and gruesomely scarred; his smile was broad but his eyes harshly focused on the prisoner and escorts bringing up the rear. The tattoos were mostly monstrous forms drawn into his flesh to appear as if tearing from the near-circular burns – one covered half his ribs, a few smaller ones spattered his chest, stomach, neck, and face. The facial one climbed into his hairline above the left ear, displayed by that half of his head being shaven. The rest of his hair was ragged, long and dark, riddled with grey, some loose, some in mudlocks. His belt was hung with devices whose purposes Sol could only guess. To his left were two men, in full Star Assault dress uniforms – one with red patches on his coat – plus a man in heavily padded SA mechanic gear but a very obvious crown-shaped medal. The two other figures Sol originally assumed male were distinctly not; one was a buff looking brunette in brown mechanic's pants but with violet adorning her jacket. The other was tall and slender, delicate of features from dark eyes to long ears, still and regal. Long black curly hair fell in waves down her back. She wore the dress black of the 17th's highest officers, with combat medals. Sol was terribly curious but did not wish to stare. *Wait. Look carefully before you assign a pronoun. She has breasts, but that's a man's mouth... she's probably a gold. Why does that face seem familiar?*

"Hi, hi, hi there, hello, ah... Astrum Solverileel, is it? Sorry, sorry, that's a tough one, I tried, I tried. Ahah, and this must be Ozlietsin? Hello! Hello, hi there, oh what a gorgeous little omyoi you are, oh my!"

It was the man in the brown padded uniform. His skin tone was bluish-grey, his hair nearly white but reflected the green of the walkway guide-strips. Sol was somewhat confused. "Um, Major...?"

"Oh, I am wearing my crown, not my buggie, aren't I? Sorry, sorry. I'm Tzanshidi. I'm the hive sentinel here; don't worry about the other title. Stupid pins. Haha." He smiled broadly and offered a hand, giving Sol a start with his mouth full of sharp teeth. "Don't worry, I don't bite! I'm a vegetarian."

Their hive sentinel is a saurtzek? Seriously? Aren't they notorious for torturing and mutilating animals? What the fuck. I guess I have to stay open-minded, and

Ozzie seems to like him, but... what the fuck. "Nice to meet you, sir. You did better than most, sir. 'Soul-vrey-il', but everyone just calls me 'Sol'."

The man's odd eyes went wide. "Oh! No no no! Like Solvreyil Niarri! No no no. I am a bad and forgetful man for mispronouncing! One must respect a name that big!" He nodded emphatically, which caused the three bugs standing nearby to begin 'charking'. It was a cheerful noise of excitement, according to Cheldyne, but Sol was happy the earplugs suffocated most of it. "You will pardon me; I must get our winged friends out of here before they become too curious and get into things! Oh yes, the things they would get into! Cannot be having that. Come along, little friends!" The man joined them in hopping and charking for a moment, then stopped sternly, held an arm out straight, and called, "Attention! Forward to the hive, this way, make way, and – march!"

Ozzie, Squeak, and Rocket snapped to it, marching regimentally out of the hangar with their strange guide calling cadence as they went.

"Ya jump the whale and ship out green
To see some places you ain't seen
Tour new worlds and fuck their girls
Then blow it up with big machines!

Sound off, one two!
Sound off, three four!
One two, FUCK YOU
And your dad, we're Armored Corps!"

Staring after, blinking, Sol overheard Wyvern's rasp as the wing commander leaned to Kiertus and said, "Hate to say it, but I miss that dipshit sometimes."

"I know what you mean, captain."

Sol swallowed a little apprehension to turn around and ask, "Can he be trusted with bugs, sirs?" He expected a reprimand regarding racism and braced himself.

"Absolutely." Wyvern gave a sharp nod and returned to Parthenos and the bound captive by the Dash.

"Tzanshidi is a natural citizen of the empire, born here on Avenaur. His family was among refugees who escaped a purge by the current dynasty about a century ago. Those purges have been historically common. Many *Ilu* rulers, ah, Baalphae emperors, have seen certain spiritual and political movements or genetic strains as a threat, and kill off anyone who disagrees with them." So much pain and regret swam in his eyes Sol could hardly maintain the contact. "The question then, of course, is whether our rulers offer them amnesty. His parents were fortunate Aphoisia was in power."

Sol turned away, unable to handle the face any longer, feigning interest in the tattooed man and the elegant gold approaching. "Does he mind fighting his own people, sir?"

"He joined during Third Mior to do just that, but you should talk to him about his feelings on the matter. He knew your mother and held her in high regard." Kiertus performed a curt half-bow at the pair that stood before them. "Greetings, Master Sergeant Schenjaar Tuonandrir, Corporal Liesh'leyen Vahaily."

Boggling over the pronunciations – especially since the Archon standard characters on the name tag of the gold read, 'Lieshlyn' – Sol bowed and saluted. He wondered if their names were like his, pre-dating Imperial standardization, or like the colonel's, originating outside the empire.

The gold spoke with a soft but deep voice. "At ease, Astrum Solfrayell." She was as tall as Sol at least and her face was ideally 'elven'; in a less tight uniform, Sol would have read only 'beauty' and not tried to stamp a gender to this officer. 'She' probably used the all encompassing polite pronouns of Vasa or Northern Eshandiir. But something else bothered him.

I know that voice, that accent... maybe an actor, a singer...? He watched as Colonel Kiertus shook hands with the bare-chested man.

"How's life in exile treatin' you, colonel? Chased any cheese lately, you crazy bastard? New astrum, I see, nice one." The apparent Master Sergeant – he had no insignia hooked to his collar, even - turned to Sol. "Name's Schenjar. Don't forget it. I'm the disciplinary officer for this base; behave and you'll rarely see me. I like it that way. You look like a good kid. Stick with this guy, he's a crazy fucker but he'll teach you respect," Schenjar clapped his hand on Sol's shoulder and leaned in towards his face, "for cheese." Then he strode with Wyvern to meet with the prisoner and Parthenos, who finally came towards them.

"You'll have to pardon Tuoni. He spends a lot of time in his room." Lieshlyn smiled; perfect teeth, dainty fangs, a lineless face that could be any age. "I'm afraid I must go as well, but I needed to see you with my own eyes. You have grown into a fine looking young man, Yen. You look so much like your father back in the day." When the perfect face finally creased with nostalgic sorrow, Sol recognized the man who visited their house, so long ago.

"V…Vahi? Um, I mean, sir?"

Lieshlyn nodded and half-bowed. "It is interesting, the things that time can change. Take care, Yen, or should I say, Astrum Genova Solfrayell Yenratseer." He gestured to Wyvern, a series of hand signs that were lost on Sol. Wyvern nodded and returned with an 'in a short moment' gesture. Lieshlyn gave Sol a strange look and wink and departed, gliding silently toward the upward slope of the forked hall.

"You gonna give me that shit, or what?" he heard Schenjar bellow. The voices of Parthenos and Wyvern remained out of his reach, which seemed strange as they were within normal speaking distance and their body language was not that of people whispering. *It's like an invisible barrier is absorbing the sound. Is this normal? No, I'm thinking, nothing about Star Assault fits civilian definitions of normalcy. I think I need to 'embrace the new experience as the tiny seedling of a great thing', as the old Shandrian explorers proverb goes, or I'm going to go pretty crazy pretty fast.*

Observing the scene from his side, not looking away, Kiertus remarked quietly, "You will learn in time why, but careful around Liesh. Never answer more than he specifically asks no matter what the question or the nature in which it is asked. Remember that." He cleared his throat and continued. "Don't let his disrespectful jostling or rowdy spirit fool you; Tuoni's a good man. Sometimes one develops a character to deal with the less pleasant aspects of his job."

Parthenos and Wyvern held firm in their end of whatever negotiation was afoot. "I guess I understand. I take it the 'cheese' comments refer to something I'm too young to understand, sir?"

"Oh, that." The colonel cough-laughed. "I was born far outside the Archon empire, but my heritage is Kez Mountain, so when I finally visited Archos, I researched my people. I found the closest tribe to which my family line came, and joined it. Many still live as they always have, following throkk herds through the passes – at a safe distance – and adopting weaklings abandoned by the herd or picked up and dropped to them by helpful gen." His amusement seemed out of place given what transpired a short distance away. Wyvern spoke with his hands; lots of pointing up and strongly negative gestures; Parthenos stood like a statue, arms crossed as Schenjar glanced between the slate in his hand and the snarly wing commander. "As a boy, on my home planet, I wrangled steers and ran cattle, ah, herded domestic animals for meat, milk, and hides; I did it from the back of another mammal, a horse, they have some at the Holtiini zoo, have you seen them?"

"Oh, yes, I read people ride those things, sir." *Riding a mammal sounds like a hot and stinky affair. Any culture willing to bend an equine to servitude could just build a dhol train, couldn't they?*

"I had done that, so I figured I would see what all the fuss was about and milk a throkk. Not a big deal, I thought, one of the village throkks, theoretically a 'cripple', not like wrangling a wild, right?"

"The ones at the zoo seem pretty docile and fat, sir, hairy and a bit funny smelling but not really any trouble, sir. I've heard the wild ones can move pretty fast and be somewhat dangerous." Sol squinted. He stared until he made out a hazy vibration in the air before Parthenos and Wyvern. *The barrier is only invisible, I guess, if you don't know how to look?*

"To put it mildly." With half-closed eyes, hands clasped behind his back, rocking on his feet, Kiertus finished his tale. "I was determined, however. Several hours later, with tattered clothes, multiple lacerations, two dislocated shoulders, a fractured knee, and several broken ribs, I limped to the village elder with half a cup of milk, reminded him he promised to make cheese for me himself if I survived. He laughed." He shrugged. "I learned to do it right and spent many years between wars as a throkk handler."

Sol turned at last from the prisoner hand-off and regarded the colonel. *The mythological feral mountain elf, with sharp talons for climbing? My boss, my cultured knight master, a bare-footed, beast-wrestling tribesman? Seedlings, Yen. Seedlings.*

He turned back in time to see Schenjar yank the restraints that held Dromarka, forcing them mask-to-face. "Welcome home, asshole. Can't say I didn't see this coming," hissed the Master Sergeant, tightening his grip. Dromarka's drugged eyes were defiant but displayed intense pain. "Lucky you, your ride's already here; I only get a few hours to 'process' you." He switched to Ryzaan, which Sol struggled to follow. "Extra lucky you, don't get any time with Master O. Just got home, you know, he's right upstairs. Probably on a soak and smoke right now. One fucking slip, piss me off at all - that promise I made Freyr won't mean shit." He shoved the captive harshly toward a downward passage to the right.

Sol glanced around. Parthenos was talking to Wyvern, who rubbed his eyes with thumb and forefinger, arms otherwise clenched close to his chest, shoulders hunched; a posture of exhausted misery. Bachi and Val chatted with the female officer in tech clothes and the gentleman with red patches; they seemed uninterested in the prisoner situation. However, in a subdued voice, in Holtiini, not turning to face his astrum, Kiertus said, "Did you catch all that?"

"What I got I didn't get, sir."

"No concern. I know what I heard. I want your translation." Kiertus turned Sol about to face the end of the hangar where the exo units crouched and walked toward them. He gestured; his speech returned to Archon with a bit more projection. "Oh, well - these are training units, mostly, but several folks here are versed in their use. Perhaps I can secure you a hands-on lesson, if you're interested."

They walked into the noise of lifts and tinkering as Sol repeated what he made of Master Sergeant Schenjar's snarl. The colonel gestured to Parthenos who joined them momentarily. *He moves faster than Wyvern. That's kinda scary.*

"I hate to put you out, but could you secure quarters with the man of the house? I'm going down to the hole to talk Tuoni into a game of cards." He used excessive emphasis on the last few words. After a moment of chin-scratching thought, he added, "If it's not too much trouble, send the winged beastie up to my encampment while I'm downstairs."

The big Ruhn seemed easier going than usual. Tiredness tinged his movements. "Nah, no problem, colonel. Wyvern's fucking shot and I don't think he could handle even half a round of 'drinking with Okie' right now. With Liesh up there, I'm thinking... no. I got this." Parthenos turned to Sol and snapped a question, giving no chance to answer before he wheeled off in the direction of the ascending passage. "How's the burden of that flag goin', kid?"

"Pretty amazing, eh, astrum? Can you actually see the city yet?"

The distant beast lumbered slowly through swampy shallows. He lay on his stomach atop their floating Dash and adjusted his goggles to get a better look. Amidst the folds of the great creature's back nestled a tiered arrangement of towers, villas, and gardens. To avoid ambient noise and overwhelmingly foul air, they communicated via helmet hardware. "It's really something, captain. The scale is awesome, sir."

Valdieren stood below on a moist tussock, squalid reeds crushed beneath his armored boots as he tinkered with an open panel on their craft. "Our people make some amazing things," he remarked without looking up as a fleshy bit of hose popped loose and sprayed him with ill-colored fluid. "I don't count this drop ship among those wonders at the moment. Pass me your utility, astrum."

He swears he learned jet tech level temporary repairs, but I have a lack of faith. I've been shown them, too. I'd rather call for help. "Um, OK, sir. What happened to yours, sir?"

Goggles and mask dripping goo, left arm buried in the ship up to his mid-bicep, the captain irritably replied, "I'm using it as a clamp. No, I didn't drop it in the gunk. This time. Fucking toxic swamp gunk fuck shit. Now, astrum."

Damn, he's almost as moody as Parthenos today. Sol inched carefully to the right and passed his multi-tool down to Val's extended hand. "The readings say it's pretty gross out here, bet it smells even worse than it does from the Spire, huh, sir?"

"It's pretty bad. Keep your mask on, try to not fall in." He worked his other arm into the opening. "And don't be Bacharanzin and swim in it on purpose."

"Gross, sir." *Without a doubt, Astrum Bacharanzin is the biggest wackjob in Wackjobville.* "I assume since he's still with us, he was alright, sir?"

"Severe intestinal and ear canal parasites. Was in the infirmary for a few weeks. Earplugs saved his life; would've got brain worms otherwise. That's what Laathas said, anyway." Valdieren slapped the sticky panel shut and clamored up the side to join Sol on top. "That and I guess you Holtiini dudes have a natural immunity to some of the crap in the slime here, just from growing up drinking the water there."

The archeoaevis trudged into deeper water. As it did, it raised its stubby wing-like fins to shift from walking city to living island. "I've never considered that there might be an advantage to growing up on my home world, captain. I'd always thought of us as 'the Empire's most average'."

"Not hardly, Sol." A cheerful hand patted his back.

While the gesture was certainly friendly, he was more than accustomed to his superior's sense of humor. "Captain, you just covered me in ship spooge, didn't you, sir?"

"Your armor will digest it!" laughed Valdieren.

"And I'll smell like funky meat until then!" Sol withheld the insubordinate urge to shove Val in the muck.

The captain moved toward the upper hatch. "Speaking of which, I need to get back and shower before my meeting with the brass. We should move it."

Bastard. "Yes, sir." Sol took one last look at the archeoaevis swimming from the dingy bog out towards open waters then followed Valdieren into the Dash.

"I'm going to fly back, only because I don't really trust my repair technique."

You're not the only one. I'm trying to remember prayers, because if I second guess you out loud, you'll make my day worse somehow. I'll just stare, blankly.

Val needed no response. "I'm sure Sentinel Salda can do a better job. Spend time with her in the hangar reviewing Dash anatomy. Get Ozzie out of the kennel first, she's got to be bored senseless." The captain spoke as he ran pre-flight. "Can you visit with Squeak a bit? I won't have time until after the meeting."

"Affirmative, sir." He did his best to conceal his annoyance at not being able to shower for several hours more. At least the barracks had proper showers. *Perhaps Salda won't notice how much I reek. After all, she's around this crap all the time.*

…

"Augh, little man, ya stink of rancid ship innards!" The woman had a deep Holtiini accent and used her hands when she talked. This was something of a dangerous proposition as she had a tool in each at basically all times. "What's that lil swamp-cat been doin' to ya?"

Sol saluted. "Using me as a hand-towel, sir!"

"Well since ya already smell like Dash guts, how 'bout givin' me a hand here, eh?" She grabbed him roughly, yanking his slight body toward the flayed open side of a badly impaired vessel.

As Sol approached, he noticed the forward sensors flash in sequence. He remembered Hanajiel explaining for some procedures, ships had to be out of 'rest' mode. "Sentinel, can it feel what you're doing, sir?"

Salda knelt before the grisly opening and returned to her task. "Naw. I got it really doped up. What you're going to be doing is moving and replacing clamps when I ask. And watch this device right here. If that gauge goes red, turn the valve until fluid drains into that canister there, then turn it back when it's gone yellow again. Got it?"

"Um, OK, sir." He was a little daunted at first, but the task was not difficult so much as monotonous. His mind wandered as he monitored the gauge color. He continued to focus his eyes and hands on his duty as he asked, "Sentinel Salda, sir, if these ships can be drugged, doesn't that pose a risk, potentially?"

"Well, you have to be inside 'em to feed 'em or administer drugs, really, so most ordinance to convey those chemicals would pose the more immediate threat of a hull breach." Salda fused two fluid lines with a heat-tool and gently applied salve to the junction. "Not that the Baalphae don't have some nasty devices specifically designed for contamination. Fortunately our updated technology stands up to it all better than it did during First Mior."

Salda gave him a grim wink as she disabled and unhooked the valve contraption. "Climb inside our friend here via the regular way. There'll be a little crusty cube next to the secondary intake on the console. Drop the cube in this," she gestured with the drainage cup, "wait for it to dissolve, then pour it slowly in the intake.

Then we'll let this poor bugger take a good long nap and heal." She followed to observe, approvingly nodding as he performed to the letter of instruction.

"I have two questions, if I may, sir."

"Permission granted, Astrum of Kiertus."

That appellation gave him a feeling somewhere between pride and embarrassment. He could not immediately explain the latter sensation and chose to disregard it. "What put this Dash in your care, sir?"

"Inexperienced pilot and friendly fire during a test run." Frustration haunted her tone despite her professional and authoritarian demeanor. "It happens sometimes. And the other?"

"Your tattoo, sir." Sol demonstrated with a gesture at his left shoulder. Unlike the first time he met her, she wore a sleeveless padded vest and long gloves, no jacket. "Were you in the Rim Patrol, sir?"

As she led him from the ship and into the hangar, she explained with a sad kind of pride, "Yes, Astrum Solvreyil, I served in the RP for twelve years. And yes, I met your father then."

"Really, sir?" *Don't ask questions, even though you want to…*

Salda smiled and scruffed his increasingly lengthy red mop. "Not an easy surname to forget… or a hair color, to say the least." Sol trailed behind as she passed into a small office to acquire tea.

"What was he like, to work with, I mean, sir?"

"Solvreyil-Kvatchkiir Meshaan made an excellent guardian. He served the empire admirably. It was clear he did it for love of his wife and children, and that he missed ya all terribly." She handed him a steaming cup. He did a double take at the open thermos. *Right, not in the* Sanjeera*'s hangar. It's* Avenaur. *There's gravity.* "Kept pictures on his slate, took any opportunity to brag about how cute and smart ya were."

Blushing, Sol said, "Thank you, sir. He was gone so much, I barely even knew him. These things are good for me to hear, sir." He bowed, trying not to spill his tea. He had wished to talk to Corporal Lieshlyn before he left, but found himself corralled by Kiertus' unsettling comments for the entire day and night before the strange soldier departed with Dromarka and the man in red patches. They left in an Infiltrator with Imperial Guild tattoos; Bachi dragged him from his bunk to watch it leave the base. At the time, Sol was not hot to be awake or sneaking from his bunk to the observation deck, but the beautiful, intimidating view was worth the trip.

'That's what happens when you fuck with the Empire,' Bachi muttered as he stared at the ship. 'I never want to stand before the Haarnsvaar unless I'm gettin' a medal. They're scarier than the Baalphae, man.'

Maybe, Sol thought at that moment and again in memory, still smiling over Salda's words as he was, *maybe I never want to know what my father really did.*

"Far as I can tell, he wasn't just a proud father talking shit. Good on ya, there." Salda laughed. Her slate buzzed; she made a confused face before opening it. Sol watched her go through an array of emotions before she said, "I guess you're to meet with the colonel after the meeting lets out. I'll dismiss you to go clean ship gore off yourself, then."

His relief was beyond words; he knew she still needed assistance and she was under no obligation to excuse him. "Thank you, sir." *Minus one thing.*

"Colonel… Colonel Kiertus, sir?"

"No, Okallin. Head of the base here. Now, get on witchya, stinky."

On his way out of the hangar, Sol swung over to the pile of inert bio-ship scraps where Ozzie slept. "Wake up, you. Thanks for being such a good little bug while I was working." The gen, at about halfway through her growth stages, was not all that 'little' any longer. She stirred and chirped curiously then shook and took to air, hovering at about the height of his shoulders. "Nicely done! Come along, now."

The barracks showers were not the finest accommodations (like the hive pool they were communal) but they were the closest things to civilized bathing he had seen for some time. They ran recycled, treated water and could be made somewhat hot. A sign outside warned him to be "mindful" with gen in the facility. "We don't have to pay attention to that sign, now do we, because you're a good girl, right?"

Ozzie chirped affirmatively and followed her bond into the shower. He stripped to his underwear – more a force of habit than anything else – while she took a seat and groomed her antennae. She was in quarantine for several days as part of routine procedure, so this was her first time in the shower, or any shower, for that matter. She was fine until he turned on the water, whereupon she hopped about on her pointed feet and squawked in alarm.

"It's just water!" Sol assured with a laugh. "I'm not in any danger, I promise!" He watched somewhat helplessly from the font as she ran in frantic circles around the perimeter. "Quit being silly. I'm fine."

Concerned Ozzie's little freak out might be streamed to a security station, he waited until she passed close on a lap and hauled her into the stream. She let forth a squeal that would have been painful to anyone not equipped with SA issue plugs but was still no doubt audible several rooms away.

"Damn! People are gonna think I'm torturing you." He scrubbed a oil into his scalp as he watched her finally settle down. "I told you it was just water."

Having deemed 'shower' 'not a threat', Ozzie was not content to share one with Sol. She trotted to the nearest spigot and rammed her nose into the 'on' button, then danced in and out of the stream.

"OK, you do that, but don't waste water. When the timer runs out, no restarting." He continued scrubbing, rapidly now that he realized his timer ought to run down soon.

"Damn...and I thought I was thin," came a voice from behind. Recognizing it as Bacharanzin's, Sol did not bother turning around.

"Fuck off, Bachi."

The other astrum laughed. "So, Parthenos told me we're supposed to train together in tandem runs. You cool with that? I got a high tolerance but don't want you to get all pissy and paste me."

"Order's an order. I don't have much to say about it." The water ran down and shut off and Sol looked for something to dry himself. "I want to get through the exercises fast so I can get back to training with Captain V."

"He's training you to fly atmospheric, right? That's stupid. I've been a pilot longer than Val's even been in this unit. I could teach you and we could do all the exercises then maybe we could get some off time... then maybe I could go see an archeoaevis finally."

Sol looked over in time to catch Bachi's frustrated pout as he turned on his spigot. *He's almost two decades older than me, but he's such a kid sometimes.* "I agree; it doesn't seem efficient." Rather than driers or towels, there was a mossy wall and floor area off to one side of the showers and a sign reading, "PISS OR SHIT HERE AND I WILL GUT YOU, LOVE SCHENJAR". Sol felt a little odd, but he rubbed himself on it anyway. It felt fantastic and he soon rolled around unnecessarily. *Like I've got room to talk. But I* am *a kid. Fuck it.* "I saw one today."

"Aw, for real? Man. Twice now I've been here and not been able to find one."

"I noted the coordinates of the one we found. I bet if we use the trajectory app, we can find it again. It's not like they're super maneuverable." Sol scrunched up his face as he lay in the moss. "You've been here before so you might know... why would Colonel Okallin summon me to his office?"

"Uh, dude." Bacharanzin stopped scrubbing and stared at the wall. In Holtiini, he said, "Because he a dirty old lizard-snatcher. He make Sheriden look a fuckin' jungle scout."

"What? Your Holtiini is terrible, Bachi. I can't believe you're native." Sol sat up, laughing.

"Well, fuck you too. You're supposed to speak Archon. So that's what I spent my energy learning. Oh, and trying to fly commercial space liners and learn station communicator jargon. Seriously, fuck you. Goddamn dilettante Frameworkers. Get a real job." Bachi did not bother drying off. He pulled his ladders on irritably over wet skin.

Solvreyil also clothed himself, still seated in the moss, far more relaxed. "Fuh. Whatever, man. Colonel and Chel both say linguists have tons of career opportunities in the military."

On his way out the door, in a true huff, Bachi stopped by the moss to sneer closely at his half-dressed training partner. "'Career opportunities for linguists' in the Archon military include 'marine interrogator' or 'Impsi operative'. You have your exciting career choice between torturing enemies and torturing 'citizens of interest' on your own side. Knock knock, great opportunity!" Then he stomped away.

....

Sol found the chief's office accidentally on their first day in; he stumbled into it in search of the visitor barracks and was escorted out by an amused administrator. The base was built into the natural rock formation, emulating a wild gen hive in its complex layout and number of exits. According to Colonel Kiertus, this was a traditional aerial assault squadron fortress, exactly as had existed in the border territories of Eshandir prior to the formation of the empire.

Due to repeated problems with warrior gen and the archeoaevis, the hive was more of a kennel and breeding facility. The occupants were provided with a playground of sorts, but boredom and irritability were issues since 'outside' was forbidden to those not trained specifically to be near mobile arcologies. Tzanshidi and his assistants engaged in a noble effort to raise genadri accustomed to the things, but mostly, the bugs wanted to build nests right in the living tissue thereof.

Sol made a circuit around the hive, keeping Ozzie near, and up the spiral to the top. The quarters of the highest-ranking officers were all here, beneath the command center, behind the upper hangars. The door to Colonel Okallin's office was open and no admin was present, so he wandered in and took a seat.

The room resembled a tea house; thick cushions were strewn about the floor (some inert, some wriggling about, variously attracted to his body heat or shying from his strong signature), ornate walking tables rested or paced against the walls, and two low, long divans occupied the space where a desk should sit. He noted, as he sat on a sofa, a small portable computer in a crawling case took a rest on the ceiling. *I've never met this man, but I can tell already: he's a character. Tiny seedlings.*

Ozzie wanted none of the ambulatory furnishings; she hackled and growled, reared and barked at a particularly excitable pillow, even more annoyed when she kicked it away only to have it chase her down. Try as he might to convince her otherwise, she refused to curl up for her next nap anywhere but the couch beside him. She probably felt this was a better defensive vantage point from suspiciously squirmy luxury accoutrements. He gave up pushing for room and fiddled with his slate, squashed into a corner of the spacious couch.

Sol wished he brought a tangible book. The civilian digital library lacked as it mostly contained dense biotechnical husbandry manuals and treatises on pollution and resource management. The periodicals collection was less obscure but dreadfully spotty. Apparently, the scattered survivors of the planet's various catastrophes and the latter relief crews uploaded personal stashes to preserve some cultural continuity and pass time during early stages of the archeoavis project. As a result, there was a random jumble of science journals, comic books, trade publications, romantic serials, and photography annuals in assorted languages; not a complete run in the lot, an average five issues each, uploaded with no particular titular convention. It was an archivist's nightmare; even with the casual approach to thoroughness that caused him to abandon his consideration of the library science field, it made Sol twitch.

They sent biotechnicians, pollution experts, horticulturists, specialized military units, and prostitutes to help in the first waves of the project, but they couldn't be buggered to draft one fucking librarian?

Hunting through the chaos after sexy picture books Bachi swore existed was exasperating enough to send him screaming to his assigned reading archive. 'Analysis of the Causes of the Mior Wars' by Colonel Kiertus Sheriden of Star Assault ('formerly Brigadier of Intergalactic Invasion Armada, Division Ice') and NH Thielassian Zhemhiir ('formerly Rear Admiral of IGN') was more interesting than it sounded. While under most circumstances, tired from a long, if technically hampered, day of flight and gun training, he would avoid a title that dry. The names and especially their connected ranks piqued his interest. He still was not sure if 'NH' was a specialist designation or a typo. *Novum Ha'e? Ha'e what? 'Haarnsvaar'? There was a Haarnsvaar commander named 'Thielassian', wasn't there? Briefly, between wars, because he was a Ruhn and a former pirate or something and it pissed people off?*

It was a heavily academic, dreadfully dark article. From a quick summary of the three most recent conflicts in Mior's troubled system, it delved back into frequently glossed-over history of kaffa and saurtzek interaction. Clarity sank over him as he read about the Kingdom of Ryzaa's claim on Baalphegor, the saurtzek homeworld. He felt solidarity with the Shandrian trader colonists who refused to relinquish their holding there, a saurtzek and Shandrian city, called 'Yetjzmaal', after Ryzaa conquered Eshandir. Even though he knew the outcome from school, he still shed a little tear as Ryzaa solved the problem using Shandrian weaponry to prove a point.

We made them hate us. Thanks, Ryzaa. Thanks a lot. Unfortunately for his interest in higher learning, the boy succumbed to his trying day and was curled up with his gen, slate still in hand, before he could trudge even half way through the long piece.

"He's cute when he's asleep. Oh, you're ruining it!" There was laughter; a hand gently shook his shoulder. It annoyed his half-awake brain, followed immediately by the stark realization he was surrounded by top-ranking officers. The young man snapped upright and saluted, knocking Ozzie from the sofa and elbowing Valdieren's jaw in one fell swoop. "Astrum Solvreyil reporting for duty, sirs!"

Laughter diminished but did not stop. He studiously avoided eye contact with the lot, but heard Colonel Kiertus saying, "At ease, astrum." He lowered his head into a slight nod and relaxed his posture as he noticed they were quite cheerful and wobbly. Even Major Parthenos, who by all reckoning hated being planet-side, any planet, anywhere, smirked with amusement. *Are they all drunk?*

Along with the three men from his own unit, he recognized Tzanshidi, properly attired as an SA major, accompanied by two men in captains' coats and appropriate rank pins, one pale and Ryzaan with long brown mud locks and the other with pitch-black skin and thick grey hair. All the Spire staff wore deep blue-violet, slightly reflective patches on their uniforms where his unit wore black. They leaned on one another and spoke in the local dialect, slurring their speech terribly. *But where is their chief?*

"I'm here to meet with Colonel Okallin, sirs."

Kiertus nodded. "Of course, astrum." He turned to the group and cleared his throat. "Everyone else standing around here has better places to be, actually."

Sol watched each walk (in some cases 'stagger') out while Kiertus remained. He turned to Solvreyil, lay a hand on the novice's arm and said, "He has an offer for you. Consider it wisely." He nodded and left.

The door remained open a moment; a static interference in the air made it clear the colonel was not the last to leave. Wyvern's voice hissed quietly in Shandrian as the door eased shut, leaving Sol alone in the lobby, "Have faith in your heart."

A man emerged from the office. He had long, thin, tannish braids bound into an elaborate holder behind his ears. When he turned, they seemed to shimmer and change color in the light. His skin had a gold undertone like Solvreyil's, albeit paler, and his bone structure spoke of centuries racial mixing on the home world: he could easily pass as any native ethnicity. Long ears twitched subtly as blue-grey eyes regarded the astrum.

"You must be Solvreyil Yenraziir. I am Okallin Teshkanzin. Welcome to my mountain."

Sol bowed, trying to place what accent gifted each "s" and "z" with a slight "th" sound. "Okallin" (and its variants, "Augallin", "Okallo", and "Okolo") was a common family name on Archos, so it was a dead end. He fixated on the man's mode of dress instead and tried not to make that obvious as he replied, courteously, in Old Shandrian, "It is good to make your acquaintance, Honorable Master Okallin."

"You needn't call me that yet, Astrum Solvreyil." The colonel smiled, bringing attention to both his needle-like fangs and the modest, soft-looking doe tail that adorned his chin. "Follow me, please."

Master Okallin, then, same one Dromarka was afraid of...

The opportunity to gawk at the outfit from behind without Okallin's gaze was more than welcome. He seemed dressed for a pre-Imperial military re-enactment or a fancy costume party. Covering his torso was the archaic version of the Star Assault officer's jacket – shorter in front, angled, emulating the unit armor, albeit flattened out with a cape extending from the shoulders in back. The shoulders bore more armor than the modern version. He did not appear to be wearing anything underneath. On his legs were some modified variant of ladders, and his hips were hung with an old-style slightly armored belt with lightweight, layered drapery in the front and back. All were laden with decorative chains and devices, with the colors blue-violet, black, and white instead of the 17th's plain black and silver.

256

On the one hand, that get-up's a disgrace to the Empire. On the other, damn, it's really cool. I 'd rock it..

Okallin's private quarters were similar in décor to the office: pillows and throws on the floor, everything in shades of purple, black, and gold. A low, wide bed sat partially concealed at the chamber's rear. An extensive liquor-and-curio cabinet along one wall and an elaborate shrine in a decorated nook spoke as much of the occupant's wealth as it did of his long occupancy of this space.

"You may sit wherever suits you." The host gestured to the floor as he moved with gracefully toward the cabinet, almost as if he walked in low-gravity. Sol was mesmerized. The man was certainly staged; his face bore no lines but his eyes and the length of his eyebrows, the fact he had facial hair at all in spite indications of pure kaffa blood, indicated his distance from youth. Again Sol was tormented by the sensation of familiarity, but a Star Assault old-timer like this could have had his face in history books.

"How do you take it?"

Solvreyil shook his head rapidly, blushing. "Excuse me, colonel?"

The man raised his eyebrows as he issued a cough-laugh. Lips flexed into a mischievous smirk as he held his tongue and paused before saying, "Your liquor, Solvreyil. How do you like it?"

"Oh, ah, thank you, sir. I don't know, sir." Sol smiled uncomfortably. "Quite new to drinking, I'm afraid, sir. My family didn't consume alcohol at meals and I've been trading my rations. I had something called an 'Early Light' with Major Parthenos at the Come Down; I didn't mind it, sir."

"A senior civilian drink? That boy never changes." Okallin removed two ornate glasses from the cabinet and after a few seconds of deliberation, a simple carafe of blue-tinged transparent liquid. He returned to where Sol sat and explained, "In Star Assault, one is expected to develop a toxin tolerance, and one is expected to consume alcohol at bonding functions."

Accepting the glass, Sol asked, "What if we were attacked, right now, for example, sir?"

The chief seated himself so one leg was arched upright and the other folded beside him. It had the unfortunate side effect of drawing attention to his crotch, and Sol observed (not that he particularly wanted to) the ladders were customized for easy access; they stopped about halfway up the inner thigh. The drape obscured any details; he may have worn underpants, he may not. "Interesting question, Solvreyil." Okallin took a sip of the liquid Sol had not yet touched. "I happen to be confident I can command this base and shoot straight after quite a few drinks. I have that same confidence in Sheriden." He swished his glass thoughtfully and made only the barest eye contact with his guest as he sipped again, "In fact, I've seen him command a fleet, with tact and talent, after downing the better part of a bottle."

Sol looked into his host's eye to avoid his gaze drifting anywhere inappropriate. *That face, I know it, it's one of the men from the picture in Parthenos' office. I'm sure of it. This thing in my hand though, I am really not sure of it.* The irregularly hexagonal tumbler was a pale green, faceted, decorated with dark green cabochons set in a gold filigree encasement. The cabochons had their own swirling inner light; he almost dropped the glass when he realized it was not his imagination. *I bet they're alive in some way.* Within the glass, the blue liquid acquired the green of the vessel, the light from the living gems dancing through it and refracting off the beveled glass. The effect entranced. "These glasses are really something. Do you mind me asking where you got them, sir?"

The reply hung between amusement and irritation. "I will happily tell you if you can give me the courtesy of taking a drink of my best alcohol first."

"Ah! Apologies, sir." Sol sipped cautiously. It burned, but the aftertaste was sweet, tingly, as if happy little flowers blossomed in his mouth. He blinked. "That... that wasn't horrible at all."

"Perhaps I should have started you on something cheaper. You look so Aurian, I figured you for a man of culture." Okallin shrugged and sipped.

The result of this jab was surprisingly visceral. Sol's mouth went dry; he felt pain in the pit of his stomach. He took a deep breath, swallowed hard, suppressed tears and rage. As calmly as possible, he looked the base commander in the eye and said, "I refuse to feel shame for being raised poor in a human community. Unless you should wish me such, sir."

"What a strange thing for your parents to choose to do. Did you ever ask them why?"

He fought to avoid a protocol violation by mentioning his father. Sol shifted and sipped from the glass in his shaking hand. "Things were difficult after the war; our benefits were cancelled by the new administration. My mother wanted a second child more than a comfortable life in Eshandir."

The chief rose, returned to the liquor cabinet, and poured himself a short shot. "That is the reason you grew up in poverty, not a reason to have grown up isolated from your people and their traditions."

Why is he baiting me? "Humanity is just as much my people, sir." He questioned the reality of the statement as he said it, staring into his glass. *At least, they should be.*

Okallin turned, drink in hand, and gestured emphatically but not enough to spill as he spoke. "Look in a mirror, at your pointed ears, the structure of your face, at your fangs – you are no human in their eyes."

I shouldn't mention Dromarka calling me a 'thing'. I don't know the history but they were trying to hide him from this man. I have a feeling I'm bone-fragged no matter what I say. Sol sighed and looked into his drink. "Parthenos once said I don't deserve those pointed ears, sir." *And then he got me into an exclusive course at the Junior Academy. I still don't understand that, either.*

He was startled by a hand on his shoulder. Sol had not heard a sound or been aware of movement. The strangely accented voice was quiet, with a hint of bitterness deep beneath. "Parthenos has his own demons in regards to heritage. Dark stars make sad satellites; let your light be your own."

Turning toward the hand, he observed a stylized sun emblem on it; an orb surrounded by thirteen curling spokes. Nine of the spokes were black, but four were only outlines. The center of the orb held the Shandrian rune *shuh* (representing both "pain" and "education"). The strong drink slowed his response time a little and the man took a seat and spoke again before he could react.

"What would you say to never having to deal with Parthenos as your superior again?" Okallin sipped from his luminescent glass. The other hand also had a sun tattoo, this one with a *ha'a* rune (which represented "death" but could also mean "peace").

"I don't think I'm ready for any promotions at the moment, sir." *Am I slurring my speech?*

Okallin skimmed his fingertips over the glass as he balanced it on one knee. "I'm not talking a promotion so much as reassignment." He let go of the glass completely, keeping his eyes on it. A barely visible arc extended from his knee to the tumbler, apparently keeping it steady. "You would become my astrum and train as an Adept of Maalek."

The facial hair, the tattoos, the old outfit. Of course. He's not a disgrace; he's a tradition. He's what they call a 'Hand' or a 'Tongue', I think. The sun cult was very body oriented, if I remember correctly. Is, I guess, very body oriented. "Colonel Okallin, I am flattered, but I would need time to consider such an offer." Swallowing the last of his drink, Sol remarked, "Would you really be interested in training such an uncouth young man, sir?"

The chief turned slowly and lowered his legs to a folded position before him, leaving the glass hovering to catch in his outstretched hand. His face was a mask of propriety that poorly concealed a hungry beast. "To be sure, Solvreyil Yenraziir, you'd be a fine elvish gentleman by the time I finished with you."

Why am I so ill at ease? Is he doing something to me? Is it the booze? I need to be careful. Play it cool, Yen. Sol admired the tiny light show he held, turning his glass for a kaleidoscopic effect in marine hues. "You never did tell me where you got these glasses."

His smile was a thing of wicked brilliance. "The liquor's recipe is ancient, derived from specific plants still cultivated on the southern shores of Eshandir. The distillation we currently consume is called 'Yashenja', 'sweet water star' in Shandrian, you know this, yes?"

"I know the Shandrian, not the alcohol. Was Prince Azarkin named after a drink?"

"Both liquor and prince were named for the reflection of light on moving water in a dark place. Fairly standard, naming children after natural phenomena; boys after water or sky, girls after plants and weather, either after earth and stone."

The astrum rolled his eyes and slumped a little, mumbling, "Dammit. I knew my mom gave me a girl's name." Then quickly straightened and said, "Sorry, sir.

Go on."

"Correction; she masculinized it, so I would say she complimented your natural beauty by giving you a gold name." Okallin drank before continuing. "This particular distillation became popular among saurtzek separatists who settled on Ruahanu. They appreciated the color, you see, like thinned saurtzek blood or glacial ice. These glasses were made by Ruhn craftsmen of saurtzek descent; they employ unique technology to bring out the visual qualities of the substance." He held aloft his glass to emphasize the point with a nostalgic look. "I bought them there, while training."

Sol nearly dropped his glass. "They must be very valuable, then, sir."

"Indeed, to the right collector. There are people in the current administration of both empires who would rather see such things destroyed."

This reminded Sol of his earlier reading. He sadly contemplated the artful glass, wishing to lose his sorrow in the tiny twinkling ocean. "You trained there during the treaty period before First Mior, sir?"

"Do you know much about Ruahanu?" His inflection was peculiar, as if he expected the answer.

"No, sir, not really. Just the bits in Kiertus' articles, some photographs I've seen, the envirarium on Pachar..." His words stumbled. *This is hitting me really hard. Laathas would say I'm drinking 'for research purposes'... he'd also say, 'Watch your alcohol intake while taking suppressors.' Aw, shit.*

"This saddens me, astrum, as does the fact you'll never see it as long as you serve under Kiertus." He stood and headed back to the cabinet. "Would you like another glass? Or would you perhaps like to try something else, Solvreyil?"

Shit. I can't turn him down. That would be rude, after I asked him to talk politics. "This is a little strong. Perhaps you can recommend something a little weaker but still flavorful? I can't imagine something quite as decorative." His mind rolled around a bit and came back to the original topic. "Wait, why can't I see the ruins of Ruahanu? They're still there?"

"How far have you gotten in those articles anyway, young man? Kiertus and any ship he commands are specifically barred from the Vaursti system by the wording of the Zhynxhai Accord."

He fought valiantly for focus, watched Okallin's back as he poured something translucent and coppery into simple Ryzaan pyramid cups. "That's uh, pretty fucked up, sir."

Okallin turned, drinks in hand. "Yes, the situation was and is, 'pretty fucked up'." He passed one to Solvreyil. "This is *kolzhi*, from Mantzaar. One of the weaker grades as the additives go but I find it is by far the most drinkable."

"Additives?" Sol turned the cup in hand after a sip. There was a hint of synthenzin in the aroma. The cups were emblazoned with the Haarvakjya, understated enough he had not noticed as drinks were poured.

"Well, you're aware the Mantzaari theocratic state has more relaxed laws on recreational sale and use of intoxicants, correct?" Okallin waited for the nod. "The standard recipe for Kolzhi involves euphoric and psychedelic compounds found in plants occurring naturally in that region. Since a combination of those properties can effect sexual arousal while impairing judgment, it is only sold to citizens over 24 cycles with a history of strong mental health, within the empire."

Sol considered the connection of one's mental health records to one's credit with the Imperial Bank to be somewhat invasive if not completely unnecessary. *That's the most sense that set of statutes has ever made to me. I'm absolutely in support of civilians with possible disorders not drinking synthenzin-laced alcohol. So they say, bartenders and pharmacists can't see why you're denied something you're trying to purchase with a UB ID; they can't even see your age...*

Okallin continued matter-of-factly. "It's banned in most non-Imperial human colonies. That bottle there, weak as it is, could be traded on the black market for an amazing array of valuable goods. It only lacks warning labels because it was purchase inside Mantzaar. So what do you think of it?"

"The taste is strong but good. Spicy, but not abrasive." He avoided mentioning how the queer warming sensation running down his throat and into his guts stirred him. Then again, Okallin probably knew.

He sat closer to Sol this time, flipped his head slightly to shift the weight of his braids. "So, Yenraziir, what is it you wish to talk about?"

Using my given name now? I guess it's alright. The color-changing effect of Okallin's braids came from an intricate three-part dye or extension job; a piece of each braid was red, white, or the man's natural light brown. Silvery, gold, and bone beads were integrated throughout the coiffure. *I guess everyone spends his paychecks differently. I imagine it could get really boring on this rock. Focus, Yen.* "Ruahanu. What was it like, before the wars?"

"Beautiful. Cold, but beautiful. Its people were the latter, but not the former. Star Assault favored training there – the steep inclines and strong winds were ideal practice conditions. We had independent treaties with the Ruhn colonists before Archos pulled its collective head out its butt and recognized them. Ryzaa had a few bones to pick about the piracy, but who didn't?" He leaned back and sighed. "We loved their mercenaries, too. Passionate, high output types. Parthenos is a good example, if you can conceive of him sans the bitter moroseness. My novum was Ruhn, my first astrum was Ruhn. It was to be the first planet to openly permit conduits to live past birth since the law Empire adopted the law."

"But weren't a good deal of the settlers pacifists? What use are conduits outside war?" Sol was as surprised that the words came out of his mouth as Okallin seemed.

"Do you really feel that way about yourself?" The master of the Spire looked him over and shook his head at the ensuing silence. "While this may be the safest avenue to train you in this time, there have been plenty of high output kaffir who lived during peace times. The Ilu were for a time deterred by their fear of conduits, and part of the Accord states that the Ryzaan mandate stay in place, and that factor n bloodlines are discontinued. We were the ones who refused to fully ratify it as a treaty, you realize? I won't make peace with a society that tells my civilians how they're allowed to breed."

"But it does already."

"It prohibits criminals, spendthrifts, and unrepentant abusers from establishing families, yes. That's just socially sane. The Zhynxai prohibition is worded against specific inter-species marriages between psychologically healthy, stable, willing adults."

Sol swore he had looked over the Accord in school, but realized it was longer than the Articles; he had never finished reading it. He blinked at Okallin. "It's already happening, isn't it?"

"Yes. There are groups within our current administration who believe it is the road to true peace with the Baalphae. It is, however, the road to enslavement by them. They will not give us peace; they will come at us when our guard is down." Okallin's voice was emphatic, tinged with darkness. He gazed into his cup. "They will take the pure humans first. I have seen it before."

His mind was strangely awake now, indubitably from the synthensin, but his filters were diminished from the alcohol. "So, why don't we just give Baalphegor, at least Yetjzmaal, back to the saurtzek? People live there, it's not uninhabitable. The saurtzek generally live underground. Couldn't we share it?"

Okallin turned so that he was sitting on his right hip, knees folded together, drink held in both hands. "It would be nice if it could work like that. But we've been using the planet for our own ends for over 1000 years. We couldn't 'just give it back' and the religious royal family isn't about to 'share' holy ground." Another sigh; this was a topic he had obviously been over many times. "Vektaar Corporation and Mobilife have extensive R&D divisions on Baalphegor. The research division of our military is largely stationed there."

Sol ruminated on his host's words. "That doesn't seem respectful to their dead." *There is something he left out, can't pin it. The drugs have me thinking in the wrong direction. Or...*

"The current administration of the Ilv'xukzuiy Empire refuses to discontinue their use of fully sentient, natural born beings for slavery and entertainment. They remain in violation of the Zhynxai Accord, with their common citizenry none the wiser. Those against ratification have been using this to stall while they wait for change."

Wow, he actually said the proper name in Saurtaf. "We caught on to them, though. That was the reason for the recent trade embargo, right? But we use prisoners in mines; that's slavery."

"Yes, we caught them 'trading' with independent colonies for live creatures. Kiertus won't tell you about that sting operation, but I still am disgusted with the way he let it play out." Okallin set his glass on the floor near Sol's and edged closer. "We don't call them 'Twisted Folk' because they're grey skinned and double jointed. The saurtzek peoples are capable of creating and using vat-grown tissue and bone or hybridizing specialty beings that don't mind being used, like we do, but the most widely accepted belief system of the Ilu states they are the supreme beings, that none below them has True Consciousness. They view torture as a right and privilege of their supremacy; it amuses them." He swished his glass, staring into it as if seeking to find memories drowned. "They like to use free-born people and animals, to create situations wherein creatures believe they are free and in control, and then take that control with deliberate, violent cruelty."

"I guess that's where those 'animal torturing' legends come from." *Let what play out? What was it Dromarka said about Yuh'geth? Where is that, anyway? Oh my brain. Ugh.*

"Humans are their favorite prey. Originally Ryzaa came between them and that prey because it was a common resource, of course, but the Shandrians changed their minds. Most of their minds, I suppose. Some firmly believe that if we gave up on humanity, traded the humans to the Ilu and let it go, they would leave us alone forever."

"I see." Sol no longer wished to look at his host's eyes. He recalled reading the Baalphae combat technology article and his head flooded with dire images. He gazed into his own cup and took another sip. "I am sorry I asked, Teshkanzin, may we change the subject?"

As if in answer to a prayer, Sol felt a tiny vibration from the pouch on his utility belt that contained his slate. *Bachi inviting me to the card game, I bet. I should really go check.*

There was again a strange, devious look in the colonel's eyes. "Pick your topic."

"I have one, but I need the mossy corner first. Would you kindly show me where you keep it?"

Okallin chuckled slightly. "Behind the division flag to the left of the cabinet." He called out as Sol wobbled upright and off towards the banner. "Enjoy your first opportunity to aim drunk!"

265

When he approached the banner, the astrum stopped and examined for a moment. There were flags just like it at Pachar. It was the same blue-violet of the uniform patches and armor he saw around Uayavu. Along with the Haarvakjya, it had two crossed lightning bolts with the Shandrian runes for 'Death, Hailing' at their intersection, and the number '23' beneath. He paused in alcohol haze for a moment before asking, "Teshkanzin? What happened to your ship?"

"The official story," came the bitter voice behind him, "is the *Ishulya* was 'too old' and a 'hazard to her crew'. They put her on 'donor' status, iced and parted out her salvageable organs and armaments. The 23rd went off the books, but were not disbanded." There was a harsh sigh. "Take your piss already."

The nook was unreasonably huge, a walk in closet solarium with a chimney vent out to a crysta-dome skylight. Plants covered every surface save a lizard-footed walking case – currently suspended from a vine - that probably held books or hygiene supplies. *I thought the restrooms on the* Sanjeera *were posh and old school... a toilet just shouldn't smell this good.*

His father used the euphemism "mossy nook" for the composting closet in their rollie – their old family home, a quake-proof, semi-mobile orb - but the restrooms in Star Assault ships and bases were niches of artificial stone (in this case, actual rock) lined in living mosses and lichens. Moss filtered and processed most of the liquids on its own, producing a not-unpleasant odor, and solids were vacuumed through vents concealed by the lush green fuzz. Similar to the sterile plastic and ceramic commodes of space stations and IGN vessels, discarded matter was then 'digested' by the microbial processor and converted to energy. Sol sort of preferred the stone ones since littering on the bio-ship seemed rude. He realized the ship 'lived' off such waste, but it was the principal of the thing.

As he alleviated himself and looked around, he noted a passageway to the right of the entrance, partially concealed by moss and vines. Through this he stepped to check his messages.

Beyond the floral barrier lay a salty stone chamber. Moss or some sort of blue-green algae (he was too inebriated to differentiate) grew in spots around a short soaking tub hewn straight from the rock along with a shower assembly. Two wall niches held erotic statuary; a man and woman and two men, respectively. He found both fascinating and a hair embarrassing. Sol opened his slate,

266

laughing to himself. *Dirty motherfucker has his own private salt shower. I guess it's good to be Prince of the Spire?*

The message, to his surprise, was from 'Gunsmoke'. *Master Kiertus?*

::: Have you accepted his offer? :::

Sol shook his damp brain out and typed a reply. He almost typed 'sir' but remembered in electronic communications off-ship one was to avoid rank identification.

::: Told him I need more time. Not sure about religion today. :::

While awaiting a response, Sol looked around more. A shiny object twinkled near the statuette of a man and woman embracing; he approached and noticed a silver ring set with a pale blue-green stone, identical to the one Kiertus sometimes wore. Sol had never seen another quite like it. Carefully, he picked it up. It was cold, heavy, real metal, real stone, completely inert. Sol felt wrong snooping about a stranger's bath examining their possessions and as such jumped and nearly tossed the ring when his slate buzzed.

::: If you wish to remain undecided, I recommend against sleeping with him. I will run interference if you would prefer a blow to your pride rather than insulting your host. :::

What the fuck? He set the ring back where he found it to type his reply.

::: I apologize but I don't understand. :::

There was no immediate response this time so Sol returned to the main room. Okallin was up again, pouring a fantastically shaped and faceted crystal bottle into short, odd-angled flutes. The liquid was thick, amber colored, almost glittery. "Is that *luret*, sir?"

"I was fine with my given name, Yen." The man handed him a flute. "This is my own blend, made here in the Spire. No matter how I try, I cannot make it as good as we made aboard the *Ishulya*; I blame my miserably cooped-up bugs. I do apologize."

Sol took the glass and sniffed. Smelled like gen honey with a disinfectant undertone, much like the still on board the *Sanjeera*. "This will be my first try, so I wouldn't know the difference, I'm afraid." He sipped; it was syrupy and heavy with a hot aftertaste; it hit his stomach like a brick. Instantly, he disliked it. *Talk about not wanting to insult my host. I should have told Kiertus yes, just to avoid this.*

"Mind you, it is still some of the best available, even at a pale imitation of its former glory. The premium at which I sell it is responsible for these accommodations."

Looking thoughtfully at the flute, the young man rather tipsily explained, "I believe you. I do not however think luret is going to be a thing I drink often."

"Ah, a shame." Okallin approached, removed the flute from his hand, downing it in one shot with a haughty smile. "It is something of an acquired taste."

The fluid buffer around his psyche insulated his pride from the targeted remark. The older man put a hand on his shoulder that stayed in place as he passed Sol toward the bed, releasing just before it would have been a strain to continue. "Yenraziir, regardless of your response to my offer, you are welcome to spend the rest of your time here training with me, if your superiors permit." He crossed his legs as he sat, exposing a substantial amount of thigh as the drape shifted. Tossing his head just enough to rattle his hair-beads, the colonel continued, "In fact, if you'd like –"

A knock on the door interrupted; Okallin's eyes went to slits. "I wonder who that could be?" An irritated wave of pulse energy followed as he leapt to the cabinet to hit the door remote. "Come in."

It was rare to see Colonel Kiertus in anything that was not military issue. He wore his officer's coat over a pair of worn-in work trousers and a red tank top in a similar state. Across his chest was something in white characters Sol did not recognize. Okallin seemed less than excited by the new guest. "And to what do I owe this visit, Sheriden?"

The tired-looking officer smiled. "I believe I left my ring in your shower, Kanzi. Mind if I look for it?"

His reply was flat. "Go right ahead." The Prince of the Spire looked to Sol like a desert cat stuck out in the rain. "Would you like a night cap as well?"

In place of an answer, Sol heard "Oh! Found it!" called cheerfully from the back. Okallin's eyes rolled and he released air through his nostrils rather than speak whatever thought he percolated.

Kiertus strode out, slipped his ring on, admired it. "Hm, no, thank you. Was already in bed when I noted it missing. Vid-conference call with Eave in the morning, would like to not be bag-eyed for it, hm?"

"Well then. Good night, Sheriden."

Kiertus turned to leave then rotated back on a heel. "Oh, my. Almost forgot something else of mine you incidentally have." His eyebrows rose as he regarded the intoxicated red-head sitting on the floor. "Astrum Solvreyil? Come with me."

"Yes, sir. Right away, sir." Sol missed the furiously thwarted look that flashed across Okallin's face as he righted himself with difficulty and made to follow his knight master. He forced coherence to address his host. "I will consider your offer, Colonel Okallin. I need to," he paused to hiccup, hoping he would not vomit, "go to bed now, I'm afraid." This was his last conscious act.

....

"I appreciate that, Astrum Solvreyil. Goodnight." Okallin glowered at the smugly smiling knight and his charge until a closed portal sat between them. Kiertus remained unconcerned over the chief's irritation.

He escorted the stumbling young man toward the barracks, but after stopping twice to let him barf profusely, Kiertus hefted Sol and carried him to his own temporary quarters in the officers' wing. After settling his charge in the nook, he sat in the doorway. He explained, though he knew it would likely not be remembered, he could not leave the boy to pass out in a communal commode his first time drunk.

"You'll have many years of service in which to experience that particular joy. I would feel partially at fault for the grievous hazing. Let you buy your own liquor before finding out what consummate bastards your mates are."

A 'merp' came from the main room. Ozzie stood, antennae down, head low. Her appearance at his door was the catalyst for his initial text to Solvreyil. "He'll be alright, Ozlietsin. Don't you worry now, lil girl."

She cautiously trotted over and Kiertus gave her a scratch. Her bond heaved and mumble-whined in a distressing manner; she cringed and looked to the colonel. He was happy enough to have her about; Nova disliked the Avenaur base and if she realized where they were headed, she would hide rather than follow him to the Dash. If found at all, she would put up a terrible fight not to go; if made to, she would sulk in a corner until departure. Kiertus had given up pursuing her about the *Sanjeera* this time in less than five minutes. It just was not worth it to force the old bug to do something she hated that much.

"He might do that a while. We are going to sit right here and keep an eye on him, OK? Your loyalty is commendable, my pointy friend."

….

Where am I? Sol blinked, felt around. This was not his cocoon on the *Sanjeera*, nor an infirmary bunk, nor his bunk in the Uayavu barracks. It was a modest divan with an unfamiliar blanket. He tasted mint, then bile when he exhaled. The world swam around as he sat up. *I am really freaking hungry...*

He realized he was clothed, and part of the night before returned. A moment of panic ensued. Sol tossed the blanket aside and turned to leap from the couch, but in turning his head he noticed a quietly snoring Kiertus on the bed across the room. The man was clad in a long, silky bathrobe, lying on his side, head on his arm, with an open book before him. Sol flopped back in relief. *If this sort of thing keeps happening, I could change my stance on religion.*

Ozzie hopped onto the couch, disturbing his reverie. She chirped loud enough to rouse the colonel.

"Ah. You survived. That's good to see." Kiertus closed his robe before he stretched and yawned. "So other than him getting you crap-housed, how did it go last night?"

"He said if I had permission from my superiors, sir, that I could train with him while we're here, even if I don't join his ... become his... do whatever it is Adepts of Maalek do, um, sir." Without consciously realizing, Sol held his bare feet in his hands. The location of his boots was unknown. Ozzie rubbed her head all over him and he had to push back against her to not be knocked off the couch.

The old gent chuckled. "Adepts of Maalek become the Shadows of the Sun."

Mystical rubbish. "Yeah I read that poem, sir. It's very pretty, in a lyrical sense. But light creates shadows; it doesn't have them, sir."

"I beg to differ." Kiertus held the robe shut and closed his book as he rose. "Every star that lights a life supporting world has just as much a dark side as every star that does not."

"Sir, I do not mean to pry, but you have faith, yes?" *I know the answer. What I don't know is how to ask what I really want him to tell me.*

Feline eyes regarded Sol as the graceful form knelt before his duffel bag. "Yes, Solvreyil, I am quite aligned and reverent, if it was not obvious. I belong to a different sub-sect than Okallin, but for a time, we trained with the same master." He stood, folded uniform under one arm, the other kept the robe in place. "You may not understand or believe in the precepts of a faith, but I advise you respect the foci of the Aligned Masters, and when one invites you to train, appreciate that a man of highly refined talent has seen potential in you. I must prepare for a meeting, if you will excuse me. Avail yourself of the biscuits and tea over yonder if you wish." The colonel nodded and slipped into his nook to change. Sol merely stared after him, lost.

…

"You did well tonight." Colonel Okallin set a tray of food between them on the office floor.

He felt a little guilty even looking at it knowing Val and Bachi were stuck below with a choice of rations or the snack machine since the main kitchen was currently closed to guests. He wondered about people like Kahner and Laathas who preferred life aboard SA ships to bases with bars or food courts. *What's so bad about here? Or Pachar, even?* "Thank you, sir. I find your lessons challenging so I'm glad to hear there's been progress."

"Shot of something with dinner or after?"

Mushrooms in a simple sauce over rice-like grain. Simple, but it's warm, didn't come from foil, and contains no obvious rodent parts. "After, please, if you don't mind. I want to make sure I taste and digest as much of this as possible."

Okallin smiled in understanding. "Absolutely. How is it? Good? I only cook for company these days. Why the look? There's a pulse operated oven in the back office." He finally ate as well. "Yenraziir? May I ask you a terribly personal question?"

I should have known that if there were gifts that something of this sort would follow. "Go ahead, Teshkanzin. I can't really refuse you at the moment."

"Is Sheriden giving you a properly old-fashioned initiation into Knighthood?"

Chew, chew, swallow. "Don't quite know what you mean." Bite, chew, chew.

He sipped his water and regarded the food on his utensil before he asked, "Has he fucked you?"

The boy nearly spat partially chewed mushrooms all over the cushions. "No, sir. That would be against the law, sir; he's over 100 years old, isn't he? I'm not even 20!"

"Pfft. That's Ryzaan Law, Yenraziir." He tapped his now clean utensil on Sol's arm, amused. "I know Marsura's little New Civility Brigade has taken all the good books from your schools but you have to know how the Genovum and Haarkijetj carried on in the old days. A lot of great Shandrian literature wouldn't exist without all that religiously-sanctioned pederasty."

Sol stopped eating and gave the old warrior-monk an incredulous stare.

"Initiates of the Sun and the Sea were usually taken by age 15 or so, before the traditional age of Induction." Okallin became more serious. He gestured at his student to please continue eating.

"Induction being ...?"

The colonel swallowed. "Self-initiation into the world of sexual maturity. The point of the family 'house person', besides chores, is to provide a safe, knowledgeable, trustworthy experimentation partner for curious teenagers." He shrugged. "Still is, if you have a family that practices such things. Parents set the minimum age in the original contract agreement; house folk are not allowed to request services from the household, of course, but once the minimum age is reached, adolescents may request from the occupant just as their parents do."

In theory, Sol understood this. No one in his neighborhood had such things, but he read of it. On Holtiin, it was customary for a kaffir family without house folk to get youngish prostitutes for some birthday between 16th and 18th. Human families sometimes also observed this, but it was frowned upon in many communities in spite of prostitution's status as a legal and respectable profession. By his 16th, Sol's father was gone, and his mother was ill and broke. Thinking about this made him uncomfortable. He labored to eat not to insult his host, but his appetite was gone. Listlessly, he finally responded, "So the Knight Master takes the place of the house person?"

"Theoretically, yes." Okallin scrutinized him in a chilling manner. "A man should not come to adulthood stumbling." Passion and annoyance tinged his voice. He looked from Sol to take a few bites and tap the utensil on his dish. Okallin cleared the aftermath, mumbling something about a refrigeration unit as Sol struggled to articulate his mind.

"Shouldn't I have been matched with a younger knight so it wouldn't be awkward or scandalous?"

When the colonel returned, he bore two chilled glasses of ginger-smelling alcohol. He poured some of his remaining water into each, handed one to the boy. "Generally, except you're a conduit and the only men who would take you are those capable of discharging your field." He sat beside Sol, their thighs touched. "Force like yours, uncontrolled, undistributed, during orgasm, for example, could be lethal."

This hit Sol like a slap in the face. He held his cool glass in both hands as if it were the only solid thing in the universe. "Are you serious?"

"Deadly serious, Yenraziir. Women feel your aura of fear stronger than men do, do they not? Never even had a date, huh? Willow girls kinda run from you? Yeah. That's why. Natural sense of the danger, even if they aren't consciously aware of the risk."

'Willow'. That's an old word for people who plan to make a family, isn't it? They say willow for women and coral for men, or something? Sol twitched. He sipped from the glass and set it down slowly so as not to spill. "It really explains

so much."

Doing a mental tally of the only females in his life he had ever been close enough to kiss, even though he never dreamed of making a move, without them becoming flustered and making an excuse to get away, were the female officers he met in this unit. Even his own mother limited her hugs to a few seconds after his 10th birthday. Tears of frustration welled.

"There aren't a lot of men of that ability level floating around outside the Haarnsvaar these days. In the current scheme of things, you are left with Colonel Kiertus Sheriden, Major Parthenos Aurgaia, myself, and Adeptus Tyrnan Avenkiir. That is everyone, in three units of Star Assault, with enough experience and talent to completely initiate you who could do so without a professional conflict."

"Professional conflict?" Sol took from his host's gestures that the question would go unanswered. "Where's... where's this Tyrnan person?"

"89th." Okallin took a drink and did not look at Sol. "You're unlikely to meet him. He will not be in the same star system with Parthenos if he can help it." He sighed and put an inappropriate arm around the younger man, gesturing with his glass. "Lousy, really, since he is a Red Sphere Master and I think you were born to manipulate the Red."

In spite feeling creeped out by the manipulative old pervert's contact, he relaxed. "Really? That's gases and atmospheric pressure, right? It's the one civilian fire crews and Flamethrowers learn, right?"

The arm gripped a little stronger; the chin angled toward his ear. "Yes, Yenraziir, but they only learn up to a few stars. Hearts of the Sun have generally mastered 8 or 9 stars in the Red..."

In a moment of quick thinking, Sol used his excitement over the discussion to pull away and face his instructor. "What... what if I just transfer to the 89th?"

Okallin expressed, just for a second, a sliver of defeat. "You'd never get approval."

"I could," Sol's eyes squinted as he sipped and said, deviously, "I could violate protocol in an epic – "

"No. You wouldn't get kicked to the 89th. Just demoted. I wouldn't push it with Sheri and Aurgaia, either. Trust me. I can't tell you why, but that would be an exceedingly poor idea." The sense of victory crept back to his demeanor. "You could however stay with me. The 89th comes here every quarter."

Sol squinted, swished his drink, and downed the rest. This was certainly something to consider.

XI. Threatened Species

"Good evening, Solvreyil."

The voice gave him a start. He was watching the sun set – a phenomenon with which he had not grown up – thinking about Okallin's last lesson. He tried not to be annoyed waiting for Bachi and Val since he had already put everyone behind by oversleeping.

"Good evening, Master Tzanshidi, sir." Sol half-bowed and saluted, the proper greeting of an astrum to a knight master.

"Ah," smiled the sentinel. "You have been talking to Okie. I can tell. How are you this lovely night?"

Tzanshidi, according to Colonel Okallin, was not only a master of two ma'at-shi spheres, but a multi-degreed bio-scientist. He was the base's second in command although he preferred to spend his time in the hive, working on breeding projects and helping the chief medic make luret.

"I am alright, sir. The double training is hitting heavy, but I feel I'm getting a lot from it, sir."

The hive master joined him in the view alcove, looking out at the stunning pink and purple sky. "It is the sort of thing one can get away with, when one is young." He placed a bluish finger against the clarithane of the window. "There are naarpu out tonight. Be careful with your little bug."

Flimsy looking black shapes drifted near the horizon, like paper caught in the wind.

"They normally do not come into this region. They are probably starving. Should you have to put one down, it is humane to shoot them in the head. That is the shortest part of them, it is not easy."

"Aren't they endangered?"

Tzanshidi sighed sadly. "The council deems we should let them die out; re-establishing their regular prey is impossible until we can clean the scrub forest. Even then, there may be too much flood water. They are 'adapting' to try and eat the citizens of the arcologies. It is not acceptable."

"That is frustrating, sir." Sol watched the creatures soar and dive. *What's it like, to make a decision like that, to prioritize the value of life on such a grand scale?* "Sir, may I ask you a personal question?"

"If it is personal, then I am much likelier to find it in your clearance to know."

Is he imitating Kiertus or does Kiertus get it from him? "Sir, how do you deal with the … anti-saurtzek sentiments people make, all the time, in this unit?"

"I know what they mean - the Ilv'xukzuiy, the Devoted Blood, even if they do not know that. I fault no kaffa or human for lacking the vocal flexibility to utter the proper name. It does not upset me." He stared at the naarpu, one hand flat to the window, even as a bug jammed her head under his free-hanging hand and pushed, demanding to be petted. "Physiological traits not withstanding, I am a kaffa, like you. I have a developed pulse organ and can survive in low-nitrogen environments. Otherwise, the *Sanjeera* would have purged me; I never would have made it to my latter stations. Those ships are made to kill and eat people like my mother. I understand why. I cannot be angry." He knelt down and used both hands to pet the gen, who chirped softly, antennae back. She licked his face. Tzanshidi looked up; Sol saw ages of sorrow in the warm grey (very kaffir) eyes. "I have stood among destruction and misery wrought by the out-of-control ideologies of my mother's blood. It takes strength not to hate. It is the same for you, yes?"

Icy winds ripped into his heart with hurricane force. Sol scraped against them to dredge his memories, but found he could not defend against the comparison.

"My grandparents were pacifists. They raised my mother thus. She tried to raise me so as well, and was displeased when I chose to join the military instead of doing civil service. I think it is wrong of the strong not to protect the weak; I think that Ruahanu could have been saved. It is not a matter to kill people so sick as to create such malevolent chaos. A parasite with consciousness is still a parasite. We are the physicians of this universe, sometimes; we must make choices about life."

He snared me into a lesson. Dammit. Old blue elf is just as bad as old yellow elf.

"Where does it all go, sir? Okallin called it all 'a violent dance, that ends when the music stops'."

"Or when the music is changed." Tzanshidi sat on the floor, leaned against the alcove wall. "Emperor Jyuraxis II is dying. It is not public even to the people of the Ilv'xukzuiy Empire; our surveillance confirmed it. His three sons are all somewhat strong politically; one will continue in his footsteps if allowed, possibly with more aggression. The other two favor peace negotiations with us, to varying degrees." Sol watched as the old gen climbed awkwardly into the man's lap. Portions of her carapace were grayish-white and did not scintillate in as lively a way as the rest.

Scarred and battered but still getting on, like a lot of Star Assault.

"So, could we help eliminate the ... um, bad son, sir, and help one of the others to power?" He could not help kneeling to pet the old bug. She seemed so sweet.

"Cassie is her name," Tzanshidi noted. "Before Aphoisia's death, that was the idea, to manipulate who the succession. At the moment, Prince Rygiel, the youngest, seems to be the most likely successor. He is not popular among the upper castes, but he is savvy and good at dodging assassin's darts. This man could change both empires for the positive; he is not only the hope of the saurtzek peoples but possibly of all intelligent races. Queen Marsura and the current High Council of Archos dislike him and have indicated they would reject his treaty." His voice hushed. "There are many, even in power, even in the military, who would consider separation from Archos if such an attempt at peace was refused. The *Ishulya* is in parts because Brigadier Okallin said as much in front of the Assembly."

Brigadier? As in, the Brigadier General of Star Assault? "I am not calling you a liar, sir, but, what? And they only demoted him to colonel?"

"The news cameras were off, at least. No one calls him 'colonel' outside this station, mind you; we do so out of respect for him, you see? He was stripped down to 'major', in point of fact. Think not less of his talents and wisdom; he is sick of war. Sick enough to risk losing everything."

"Why not just retire, at that point?"

"The Oath of the Sun is for life. His only retirement would be in death. The fact he lives and breathes speaks a volume; one day, you will speak the language to understand it." Tzanshidi looked over to where Val and Bachi stood, Val patiently and Bachi less so. "Watch out for the naarpu, tonight. Show mercy if you cannot avoid them."

As he joined his companions, Sol tried to chip away at the frost forming inside him. *I'm just an astrum. I'm just a kid. Why do I get a feeling I'm being singled out? Or tested?* He stopped and saluted stiffly a few feet from Captain V and his wry amusement. "Apologies, sir. You could have interrupted, sir."

"Oh, no, I really couldn't have, astrum." He was absolutely calm as he walked forward, silencing Bacharanzin's bitching with a harsh hand gesture. "The field he was projecting was like knives."

"I told you, I could've walked into it, sir. We – "

"You can't fly a Dash from the infirmary, Astrum Bacharanzin." His calmness and smile were purely exterior; Sol could see something close to rage peering through. "Maybe you should give a second thought to 'all that ship-board nonsense and religious crap'. Eventually, Major Parthenos will get sick of using you as a jizz receptacle and return you to Wyvern."

Whoa. I'm staying out of this one. Sol fell back to walk with the anxious bugs who stayed a respectful distance, tried not to jump on their bonds, but were excited to get out. They seemed to appreciate the company and settled down.

Bacharanzin tensed, opening his mouth to retort, instead straightening up to salute. "Sir, yes sir."

"It's entirely your choice, to be a worthless spunk bucket, to be a bullet sponge, but I can tell you the major has a low tolerance for people who uphold that reputation after they've chosen the knight path." Vitriol slipped between the gaps in Val's cultivated serenity. "You're not a flyboy anymore and you're not a meat bomb; you're an astrum genova. Fucking act it. If you can't bring yourself to slap on the wacky tattoos and start speaking in riddles, do it for your bug if nothing else."

After a pained, "Sir, yes, sir" from Bachi, the remaining trek was in silence. Sol wondered if he would go the 'wacky tattoos' route. Tzanshidi's voice echoed in his head. *'The Oath of the Sun is for life.' If I survive a couple years of service, will I even want to acclimate to civilian life again? Maybe oaths like that make sense when you've seen places you love razed to the ground and all the people you knew rounded up and butchered. When you've given an order to fire that killed thousands at once… So if my mother gunned for Kiertus, does that mean…?*

"Please take the master seat, Astrum Sol. Bacharanzin, please take the gunner's."

"Sir! Sorry, fell into my own brain, sir."

Val was leaning in the cock pit door frame as they squeezed past and took their positions. "You really don't want to do that in this sector of space, Sol. Can you tell me why?"

"Is this still contested space, sir?"

Bacharanzin laughed, earning a thump on the shoulder from the captain. "Uayavu's not decorative, let's just toss the intergalactic politics lesson and leave it there. When in uniform, what are you?"

"Sir! I am a knight, sir! Star Assault must always be combat ready, sir!"

"Correct, astrum. Forget it and you're shrapnel." Valdieren leaned forward casually, a hand on the back of each seat. "Okay. We're going to fly low-interface, because you're," he poked Sol's upper arm "on a new suppressor dosage and you're," he poked Bachi, "on a whole pharmacy of weird shit for another month at least. So we're going to role play, and the part we're going to play is flying back wounded from heavy combat. Your legs are fucked up, Bachi. Sol, you're sucked dry of pulse, in a lot of pain. Got it? OK. I'm seriously wounded, might be permanently blinded, so even though I'm your superior officer, I cannot fly. Me and these three terribly noisy bugs are your only survivors. Now concentrate, get us out of here, fly to the location indicated on the map. That's our pretend hospital. We'll fly back with roles swapped. Go."

The bugs sat quietly in the crew cabin until Val hopped through and flopped on the floor, howled in mock agony, and shut the cabin door with an emergency switch. The cacophony from the back was suddenly quite rattling as Sol strapped on arm panels and slid switches. *Great I have to think in theatre and pilot now. At least the launch gates are bigger than the Sanjeera's. Upside, if I fuck up, we're in atmosphere. Downside, if I fuck up over anything but water, we're in gravity.*

"Initiatie launch sequence. Hangar Prime, this is 078 of the 17th requesting clearance to launch."

"Prime. Permission granted, 078. Proceed toward the gate."

"Dash, crawl," Sol ordered the ship-creature. It rose up on its wing tips and scuttled. He encouraged an increase in speed by gently rolling a ball within the manual control panel. In a full-interface situation, this would be unnecessary.

Bachi adjusted his monitors and straps as the ship increased its digit crawl into place on the acceleration ramp. He turned to watch Sol talk to the craft. "So this is the like, what, the second or third time you've done this out of simulation, right?"

"Dash, adjust for atmospheric flight." He flicked a switch to reinforce the command. "More like the first."

"Retracting wings. Atmospheric configuration," came the craft's airy voice.

The bay doors opened before them. "Haha, well, right, fine, but you've co-flown with a shit load of people, right? Wyvern and Spearhead, right?"

"Dash, enter launch sequence." This part he knew relatively well; he inserted his hands into a slot beneath the panel, which, like his rifle, was slightly moist and spongy. "Well, no, just Val and Kiertus. I've only ridden rear guns in a D-7."

"Launching in three... "

"You're fucking kidding me!" His co-pilot's eyes bugged. "They don't even use voice commands! You're going to get us –"

Sol had not intended to feed pulse to the ship, although it hardly seemed to mind, hurtling up the ramp and leaping out into the air. Mildly shocked at the accident, Sol pulled back the Dash dove toward the edge of the plateau and the rocks. He rapidly re-inserted his hands, breaking a sweat, urging the vehicle, "Up! Up! Level out, level out, cruise!" as Bachi broke into an impressive multi-lingual expletive stream.

As the ship leveled, Sol relaxed and resumed the manual flight position. "I take it back, Wildfire."

Bachi touched his chest and legs as if to confirm his existence. "Fuck. Take what back?"

"What I said about your Holtiini. You curse in it just fine."

...

"Considering how this started, you guys are doing great. We're gonna run to the plateau once more, fly back, and call it a day. Bachi, I'd like you to pull us out and land this time and Sol, you fly back."

Sol was exhausted, but realized if he held out a little longer, he could get an hour nap before meeting with Okallin. He looked at his co-pilot and nodded. "Affirmative, sir."

For the fifth time they began their game; Bacharanzin's launch was effortlessly smooth and he made it to the vicinity of the 'hospital' site in record time.

"Shitworms! Bootstrap, there's another craft here – were we –"

The communicator flashed. Sol hurried to answer as Bachi slowed down, approaching the black, hovering thing that materialized before them. Some kind of intentional distortion masked the voice. "Present credentials immediately or landing at this site is denied."

I am so thankful you're flying, because I don't have all this hovering and holding down yet… Man am I looking at… is this? It's a Razor. The current model. It has to be. Maalek's scattered blood, that is the most beautiful and ominous thing I have ever laid eyes upon.

"Bootstrap!" Bachi hissed as he reached and held the communicator off a second. "Fucking hurry, you're better at protocol than me."

"Credentials immediately or I will fire."

"Fuck!"

Sol smacked Bacharanzin's hand off the comm and hastily replied, "*Maata maanieja*! Bootstrap, Wildfire, 078, dispensed from Uayavu by the 17th. Three gen, all registered to *Sanjeera*. Scan at will. Over." He gave his training partner a dirty look as he re-pressed the button. "Seems like protocol would be the first thing to learn if you shit your pants in the presence of Haarnsvaar."

Although angry, he said nothing. He pursed his pale lips and concentrated on hovering.

"Cleared to land. Everyone but Bootstrap is to stay in the ship until we give permission. Over."

Val opened the cockpit door after they landed. "You guys keep these bugs still."

"This was planned," Bachi muttered, staring at his knees against the padded console. "I just failed a test."

"Don't take it so hard; if I'd been flying just then I would have smashed us into a rock trying to hover."

"Bootstrap doesn't have a reason to set you up and hit you like a festival dummy right now. Of course you weren't flying for that. Even if that were the case, I could have swapped controls before we bit it." He leaned back and looked hopeless. "Fuck I'm an idiot. I should have stuck my nose in the books when he got on my case about it a couple days ago. I'm the senior pilot here; I should know how Star Assault presents credentials to their fucking bosses."

The hatch opened again. Squeak hopped about but did not break for the exit. Ozzie and Rocket were more excitable. "It's good, boys; you can come out for a break. Maintain behavior, company's heavy duty. If you can't control a bug, leave her here."

Bachi gave Rocket a hug. "You wanna watch the Dash? No, probably not, huh? Oh, guess what I've got… sit nice. No, nice, like, not with your legs all over the place. Oh, good job! Here."

"Wow, where the hell did you get an actual piece of fruit?" Jealously, Sol watched Rocket munch on the gift. She pushed some with her nose at Ozlietsin, who took a cautious bite then happily rubbed on Rocket's thorax with her head before trotting to Sol.

"Wisp gave me a package of them; she's been helping some of the locals with a garden." He smiled kind of funny. "I know she just did it because she's got a stupid hero crush on my master, but she's the coolest girl to ever give me a present."

Ozzie scaled Sol, perched on his back and cooed. "Hey, that's right, you got that right, that's what we're supposed to do… if we were jumping into combat, which we're not, but very good anyway!" He let her stay. Before he stepped from the cabin, he quietly remarked, "Just a crush, huh? I guess I thought they were an item."

"Oh, she wishes. They've done the deed, at least once, when she was pretty new to the unit, before she got her arm blown off. These days he thinks of her like a kid sister; super protective of her but won't touch her like that."

I get it now… poor Enki. That's a raw deal, wounded in combat and rejected. Sol, wearing his gen like a rucksack, hopped out the Dash and onto the hard, rocky earth of the plateau. He eyed the Razor in its unconcealed glory, gleaming eerily against the cloudy night sky.

"Seventy-eight. Fancy that. Congratulations." Cheldyne, in black and bone colored armor, sat on a large rock a bit away from the two craft. Some kind of light followed his hand as he held it to his face and then moved it away. Sol squinted.

"Hey, what are you doing here, Serum?" As he walked over, something smelled horrific, as if someone had set fire to the stinky lichen the pharmacy got in now and then.

"Having a smoke, what's it fuckin' look like?" The big kaffa smiled around his hand-rolled cigarette. "Sheriden makes me use patches on the ship, it's tedious."

Wow people are really prescribed that horrible fenatja *crap? I thought that was some kind of inappropriate joke about illegal drug use.*

"Now now, open flames policy, Serum," Val admonished humorously. He stood closer to the Razor next to an individual Sol had not previously noticed.

The man was taller than Val by a small bit, shirtless, in armored, shiny black leggings and not in ladders. Intricate tattoos graced his shoulders and back; at first Sol had thought he was wearing shoulder armor due to the symmetry of form. He wore an unusual hood – kind of like the hood on the SA pilot uniform, but with tendrils. When he turned in Sol's direction, his face, save for his large, dark eyes, was covered by an elaborate breathing apparatus. Realizing what he observed, Sol saluted and turned his eyes to the ground. *That's probably one of the Faceless, or at least an eligible Guild member. Makes sense, with the Razor and all.*

"At ease," responded the synthetically distorted voice.

Bachi stood near Cheldyne in the opposite direction of the wind from the hive sentinel. "Are you seriously going to fly after puffing that?"

"Yes, Wildfire, I am."

"Is your tolerance just that high or is that thing low on fuel?"

Chel seemed amused, talking out one side of his mouth with the cigarette held by the other side. "I didn't say I was going to jump anywhere in 'that thing'."

The masked stranger made a spooky sound which took Sol a few seconds to identify as chuckling

"Isn't that your first day in the Guild, learning to get puked on?" Val joked.

"No, that's Star Assault." Cheldyne gestured at their Dash with the burning spliff nub. "'Encouraged toxin tolerance' includes being covered in other people's."

Harassing top-level brass seemed Valdieren's comedic specialty. "Is that why wing commanders take medic courses?"

"I thought that was so they could prescribe themselves *fenatja*." Bachi made this remark with no hint of sarcasm but everyone laughed anyway.

Ozzie and Squeak went suddenly frantic. The masked gentleman caught on first. "The naarpu is back," cautioned the Guildsman. "Get your gen aboard the Dash."

This required a bit of wrestling on the part of Sol, who had a headrush and was fairly nauseous for some reason he could not quite pin. Chel, now sans the cigarette but still reeking of it, offered assistance. "I'm gonna get Gunsmoke and come back for it. If anyone on this smudge-ball has the rifle skills to bring that down in a clean shot, it's him."

Sol regarded his friend sadly. "Do you have to kill it?"

"It's starving to death, Seventy-eight. 'Mercy' isn't an idle part of our unit logo."

Ironic, the name of this planet is 'Avenaur'... 'Mercy of the First'... Aur, the embodiment of consciousness and awareness to more primitive kaffa... Oh. "I think I get it, Serum."

"Eventually, when one stops trying, the pieces fall in order on their own."

XII. The Living Example

Okallin seemed unsurprised when the fuming copper-haired beast stormed into his office. An assistant rushed towards Shaan demanding a presentation of credentials but withdrew from the abrasive glare, rapidly realizing confronted the notorious "Ropetrick", merciless Arms Sentinel of the 89th.

The cringing, droop-eared admin was dismissed. Okallin addressed the snarling, double-collared soldier with cool formality. "Adeptus Myentrios. How nice to see you. Please, have a seat."

"You court death from all angles, Whisper." Saliva flecked the fangs in Shaan's open, panting mouth. The violent roar that should have escaped it was silenced with a snap of Okallin's fingers. In fact, everything was silenced; all sound was suppressed. Okallin shook his head and Shaan lunged.

Wide-eyed but otherwise without expression, Okallin Teshkanzin stepped aside and clapped, returning sound to the room, bracing himself slightly. "Stop, please. Your assumption is incorrect."

Tense anger rippled through him. "What did you do to him?"

"Your son? I trained him without consummation and let him go. He left as he came: a young virgin in the treacherous mine field of the 17th." There was a hint of relief in the way Okallin breathed as Shaan's muscles relaxed and his radiation withdrew. "Surprised? I was too. Maybe I'm getting soft. But if I succeeded in coercing him to stay, you could not come here, now could you? You are running out of places you can go in the empire, I would hate to give you one less."

Shaan did not know what to say. He could not bring himself to feel guilty about his incorrect guess, but he also knew he was in the wrong. Grudgingly, he bowed. "Apologies, Prince Okallin."

A tattooed hand carressed Shaan's hair. "I would miss you, you know, even if you seek an excuse to kill me. I do not really blame you." The hand slipped the ponytail free; shining copper cascaded down his cheeks. Okallin knelt. "We do what we have to in this universe of cold and darkness and we hope for the best.

Can you possibly feel worse about him being with me than with Sheriden? Have I not atoned?"

"Not enough." In response to the submissive gesture, Shaan knelt as well. "Nothing personal, but I'd like him to be free of religion and magic, but I guess that's not my choice. If he's going to go that way, I guess I'd prefer he wore wings than suns."

"It is so cute when you call it 'magic'." Okallin smiled, playing with a lock of Shaan's hair. "But he will probably wear everything. He is talented. I tried to make him aware of Sheriden's … flaws… but I do respect his decision."

"Did he give you a reason?"

Their eyes locked a moment, but Okallin closed his as he quoted Sol. "'Papa always said I should never do anything I don't believe in one hundred percent and never follow a path I can't see with both eyes and heart. I might be naïve, but I still think he's right.' I could not argue; his papa learned the hard way."

Shaan's eyes fell to the floor. *I walked willingly into it by your side. If you hadn't gotten us nailed, I'd have nothing to be angry about, and I wouldn't be sitting here having just accused you of dragging my son into it too. My son would be a free man, because we'd have won. Hm, no I do still want to hurt you...*

Okallin continued, "I won't even ask who told you. That young man raised every eyebrow in the Spire. It was not possible to be inconspicuous…"

"I suppose not." He rubbed his eyes, mildly relieved that Sentinal Salda would be in no trouble for her (honestly quite delicate) passing of the sensitive information. Still, Shaan was not entirely settled from his previous rage. Okallin would likely surmise that Lieshlyn had fed him the news under the auspices of getting him to spill in kind, which was half-correct; Liesh had mentioned in a round about way that a 'familiar face' had been at Uayavu when he left. However, Shaan had long since learned that confiding in the 'reborn' Liesh was a high-risk gamble, and simply bribed Salda with imported liquor to drop more clues. "Is he well? In your opinion."

"Ah." Okallin leaned back in the pillows, unconcerned about the current unseemly disarray of his clothing. "He is lovely, thin as they come, ah, conduits on suppressors, I mean, you know. You remember how Auri was in his teens…"

An unpleasant laugh slipped from Shaan's teeth. "Bonier than a Ryzaan buffet? Poor boy."

"Healthy otherwise; nice high endurance; persistant, energetic, charming in his dedication even when he has no idea what's going on. Ah, apologies for comparing your son to Aurgaia, that was not particularly thoughtful of me."

Waving a hand dismissively, Shaan shook his head. "No, the bad feelings there are all on him. His methods are and always have been admirable, if a bit naive. Perhaps he will succeed where others before him, who took the more direct approach failed? Hm?"

The Prince of the Spire leaned on his elbows amid the cushions, one leg up just enough to garnish his elaborately armored but otherwise proudly displayed genitalia. Shaan was unimpressed; he had seen it all before, licked it, and returned it to the storage position, so he focused on Okallin's sly eyes instead. "Who said anyone failed? Have the men before him been hung in a square somewhere that I was not invited? All I see is a trail of feathers, dust, and lies…The sun has not yet truly set for them."

"I suppose not. But it also can't hang over the horizon forever."

XIII. The Gates to Rebirth

For the third time since entering his compartment, Sol awoke suddenly with his barely read book awkwardly flopped open on his chest. This roused him shamefully upright to cursorily examine the spine and pages for damage, then he would commence reading again, struggling to appreciate the complex nuances of its arcane prosaic contents. Inevitably, his exhaustion overtook him, and the fascinating romances of his ancestors were absorbed into another fragmented set of dreams. On the sixth waking, he finally gave up and tenderly folded shut his precious temporary acquisition, setting it into one of the cushioned nooks that lined the vaguely fleshy wall beside him.

Sol rubbed his eyes, pushing back a few stray, shocking-red mudlocks behind his lamentably short ears. "It figures," he sighed, casting a beaten glance at the charmingly bound old volume. "I finally get some quiet time and I'm too pounded to read."

'Quiet'. If one could call the incidental orchestra of barely insulated bio-ship hulls - the vaguely digestive creaks, the weird hiss of minute pressure adjustments, the unsettling huff of oxygen valve aspiration, the constant thrum of the ioun drive, all periodically peppered with the chittering of bored gen - 'quiet'. The resulting laugh from this observation woke his slumbering symbiote. She raised her rounded blue-green pyramid of a head and chirped admonishingly.

"Sorry, Ozzie," he appealed. "Everything's just so ridiculous!" He rubbed her nose with his blanket-covered foot. Her irritation gave way to sleepy nudges and little trills. "I must go for a walk. Pardon me."

Slowly, he extricated his long limbs from the blanket and its extra drape of petulant alien arthropod. His mild sense of guilt over disturbing her sleep and robbing her of his warmth was annihilated by her immediate sprawl across the entire coffin. *When did your legs get so damn long?* He rolled his eyes as he opened the hatch and slid out to the ladder. A smile eased to his lips as he felt the smooth, firm, resilient living bone of the rungs.

Guess I deserve these pointed tips after all, he mused as he stepped into the mossy nook to alleviate himself, apologizing to the *Sanjeera* as always. Of course he could have 'gone' using the built-in vac tube in his sleep coffin, but preferred only to do so in emergencies, as it tended to leave the vague scent of effluence trapped in the space for hours.

On his way back to his compartment, unfortunately more awake, Sol stopped to lean back against the wall, shut his eyes, and just listen to the vessel. He synched his breathing to the rhythm of her monstrously intricate workings, and lost himself in them.

What are things right now? Oh, they're good. I was really stressed this morning but I got good news. I remember now. He was concerned when summed to Parthenos' office in the middle of his hive shift. The major looked stern, and while Sol could not think of any offense he committed, that would not necessarily prevent the major from finding one.

'Astrum Solvreyil, we reviewed your request for shoreleave on Holtiin and found no reason to deny it.' Parthenos' raised finger demanded Sol continue to listen. 'You will be under strict regulation; you will spend each night at the Air Base in specified quarters, an Air Defense medic will administer your shots and monitor you. You are prohibited from sexual encounters with civilians,' a harsh glare accompanied the warning followed by a pause, 'and you are allowed to visit with Solvreyil Niarri under auspices of assisting her relocation, which is approved, managed by the Association of Assault Veterans. Your donation was filtered so it does not appear a personal act.'

'I don't know what to say, major, beyond, 'thank you'.' Sol relaxed as Parthenos gestured 'at ease'. 'Did I provide enough funds for everything?'

'No need to thank me, astrum. Four other members of the unit contributed. Any surviving members of Ice who suffer are our responsibility. Had we known earlier, we could have done more.' The major turned his face to the wall and saluted backwards. 'You are dismissed.'

"Astrum?" The voice of Colonel Kiertus drifted into his ears with its whimsy-tinged wood-fire tone. Sol would not necessarily admit aloud how much he loved the way his commander spoke Archon, how all the Shandrian words sounded in his totally alien accent. *It could be a part of the ship, it's so perfectly strange...*"Astrum! Attention!"

He started and snapped to a decently respectful posture. "Ah! Sir! Yes, sir!"

The intense expression flowed back to its usual wise benevolence. "At ease, astrum. I was just seeing if you were alright."

"I'm fine thanks, Master Kiertus. Just exhausted."

The colonel's expressive, wide mouth curled, revealing tiny creases that betrayed his drug-concealed age as his large eyes half-closed. His ears angled downward with a delicate flick. *You look like a sweet old man when you do that. A sweet old librarian, about to ask me to please take my tea outside…*

"Parthenos and Val like to cram a lot into those last weeks of training. How annoyed they would be to know they had a damned thing in common, eh?" He chuckled. "You're probably looking forward to your time back on Holtiin, hm?"

A single fiery mudlock fell haplessly over one eye, not quite covering the more muted red coloring his cheeks. *What is it, nearly 90 years of age difference? I shouldn't feel like this. It's just wrong.* "Yes, sir, although the ship has started to feel like home, sir."

The wide smile became more appreciative and the lovely eyes were near completely closed, thick eyelashes now emphasized on his pale cheeks. Only his coiffure was not distinctly that of noble kaffir stock - a thick, shaggy, unfashionable graying mop, which just made his appearance that much more disarming. *A sweet but handsome old librarian, responsible for the deaths of thousands.* "I am delighted to hear that, Astrum Solvreyil. I'm rather attached to the *Sanjeera* myself." A long-fingered hand patted the wall. A barely perceptible shift in noises made it seem as though the ship responded. *Two enemy refugee ships hiding in the asteroid belt and an entire inhabited moon, that's what the articles said and Okallin confirmed. It doesn't seem possible.*

'The Butcher of the Belt', as he was referred in less-favorable reports, *reputedly so terrifying 'he gives the Ilu nightmares'. My knight master, my mentor, painfully kind to his crew, erudite, well-traveled, old enough to be my grandsire… and the way he says my family name gives me an erection. Hey, penis? We need to discuss 'professionalism' sometime; you embarrass me. Haven't you gotten over the drugs yet?*

"I wish I had more of a chance to read the book you loaned me before my leave, sir." Sol shifted so his excitement was less obvious.

"I trust you quite well enough with it that I'd let you take it with you, minus the fact that if you were seen with it, someone would certainly question whether you'd lifted it from the library."

The astrum scoffed. "I don't even think they even have this in the New Asria rare collections room."

Grey eyebrows raised in amusement. "Fair enough. Why not take it home, then? Read it during your leave, and hand it over to Acquisitions when you are done. I'd appreciate if you donated it in my name."

Sol was stunned. "Are you serious, sir?"

"Absolutely," smiled the handsome old kaffa. "It's not like I can't go visit it. I have a flat in Sunfield."

Sunfield. The wealthiest neighborhood in New Asria, maybe in all of Holtiin. Sol had taken the above ground dhol train through the borough, with its intricate gardens and private parks. There was no reason to stop there unless one had a residence in the area; any bars or retail establishments were elusive at best. He was impressed to the point of silence. *I guess I shouldn't be surprised. He's a prince, just like Okallin. No, not* just *like Okallin; Okallin is loose-lipped, rebellious, and sleazy.*

Colonel Kiertus leaned forward. "Do you suppose you'll find any personal time around taking care of the stranded veteran mission?"

'Stranded veteran mission'. Not my mother, because I am legally dead or property now, by some archaic law that's still on the books because seventy per cent of the population doesn't even know where to look. "I've been thinking I would go to the Bloom Festival, just to watch…" He turned his eyes from the elliptical-pupiled yellow orbs of his superior.

"Really? Have you ever been?"

"My dad took me for ice cream in the park while it was underway, I was quite young. He said I would appreciate it when I was older." Sol shuffled against the wall. *Virginity is just a detail in my medical records. I shouldn't be ashamed.*

The colonel's face, as always, forgave. The ears flicked again. "May I make a suggestion?"

Sol looked up, drew in breath and exhaled suddenly. His master's expression remained unchanged. "Alright, sir."

"Chel said he gave you the setting sun. Wear it openly. It will save you trouble and pain over time, and in the short term, help prevent violating ground rules."

"Yes, sir." *The Festival is traditionally a way for marriageable people to meet. It's common courtesy to declare a lack of viability. Or low-risk fooling around, according to Chel. He said people who aren't ready to marry like to have flings with SA guys. Not me, not this trip.* "I wouldn't want to hurt anyone, anway."

Kiertus stood too close. Sol felt his breath, smelled decaying forest floor with a salty hint, a scent all unwashed kaffir seemed to dispense. "Go out where there aren't many around. The beach at Lykwa, perhaps. Wait for the rain, and disrobe. Sit in it until you're cold, maybe a bit past that. Return to the barracks for a warm shower, and sleep wrapped in blankets made from natural fibers."

"You mean dead fibers and not bioware."

"I do. You can request such things from the base medics, by the way. If you don't miss it already, you're going to soon enough. All of it." Long, tapered, claw-like fingers stroked his chin. Yellow-grey eyes bored into his. The long-lipped, fanged mouth was mere inches from Sol's more modest set of canines. "You're never going to think of rain the same way again."

Rain? Why rain? Sol parted his lips to ask, but found them buried in moist warmth with an aftertaste of blood, honey, and alcohol. He shivered, unable to move, his tired mind a rush of disjointed things. *At least the 110- year-old war criminal was not my first kiss. Just my second. My life is terminally fucked up.*

"Echo."

"What?" stuttered Sol, completely lost.

"Your call sign. Echo. You are no longer '078'. You should have received it after your mission on Kourhos. I apologize for the substantial distractions between then and now and the fact I only just realized you were still stuck with a temporary number when Parthenos submitted your leave approval today. I asked him who the hell 'seventy eight' even was. Again, you have my sincerest apologies." Kiertus sighed and saluted. "Hail, Echo of the 17th." With that the colonel wheeled around and drifted gracefully down the vibrating hall.

I think I expected a ceremonial kiss of naming to be more chaste, maybe in a shrine, not in the hall by the pissbox. But that's what just happened, I think. Sol stared after his knight master. *I finally have a call sign, which means I've officially graduated from meat grenade to holy page. I want to text someone just to see it on my slate...*

When he brought up the screen to see who was awake and around, he discovered twenty five new messages. Sol blinked and scrolled through; most had arrived while he slept. Someone must have announced the naming on SACnet since he did not recognize all the handles that digitally saluted him. All but four of the messages were some variation on:

::: Hail Echo, welcome to the 17th!:::

Wyvern and Kiertus sent prayers, Valdieren a heart-felt note about how great it was that Sol made it and what an honor it was to have him as a crew mate, and Aukaldir's simply read:

::: Well look who's fucked now! :::

....

Solvreyil Yenraziir had seen 18 true springs in New Asria; all of his years prior to joining the military, he had never seen spring elsewhere. He spent many long, lonely afternoons reading about other planets in the Empire, particularly Archos, 'the homeworld'. He read of giant trees and colonies of land coral, sculpted into living dwellings, and pondered the phenomena called 'sunrise' and 'sunset'. He read of the freckled, shy kaffir of the western island chains. He read of Ryzaa, the Imperial Capitol, 'the City of Bone', staring awed for hours at pictures of jagged, pale clustered towers looming above the Great River. He spent his youth ignoring the beauty of his home – 'cramped tourist traps and farm towns' – envious of the vastness, history, and culture of its sister planet.

Today, however, he leaned back on his elbows in the fluffy jauga that covered the open ground throughout Liberation Park, stared up at the purple and pink foliage of the trees, and listened to the voices and laughter and sounds of the lake. He appreciated the smell and taste of a healthy natural atmosphere as opposed to the artificial and filtered ones he experienced over the past ten months. He paid attention, since he landed at the airbase two days ago, to the way the same species of plants look different when grown in natural atmosphere and gravity. Sol closed his eyes and wriggled his hands amidst the tiny, tough round leaves of the persistent ground cover which saved the hill from erosion in spite heavy seasonal rains and generations of playing children.

A blended fruit juice appealed almost enough to get up from his half-shaded spot just off the lake path. If he was not careful, this would become an impromptu nap, and he would wake up with tiny circular leaf prints on his face. He heard approaching feet and turned, protecting his eyes from the sun – dim as it was - with an open palm.

Civilian clothes and dark shades created a mild distraction, but the two-tone hair and goofy smirk were unmistakable. "Captain V?"

"Heya, Sol." Val half-crouched in the jauga, then cautiously asked, large crimson eyes peering, "I'm not cock-blocking you if I sit here, am I?"

Sol twisted his face in disbelief. "Uh, no?"

"Oh, I just thought, maybe you were… you know…. Her…" The captain gestured to a young lady playing a game of stick-net with a group of friends down the hill. She wore little more than a strip of cloth for a top with a low-slung pair of short pants, a blue IGN collar, and nothing else. Her pointed ears were highly expressive and moved emphatically with every shout and laugh. Her skin was freckled light tan, her hair reddish blond; a Huar Islander, he guessed.

Sol's lips twitched. "She isn't really my type." He had not even noticed her until now. *Just as well… I guess Val doesn't know about my restrictions.*

"Would you like a drink?"

The younger man shook his mudlocks out as if casting something from his ears. "Sure, captain. I can't drink much because of my dosage, but thanks, sir."

Offering an unmarked flask, Valdieren laughed. "You can stop calling me by rank. I'm off duty."

"No such thing as 'off duty' in Star Assault." Sol sniffed the open flask and cocked an eyebrow at his companion. "You know I'm civilly not of age to be drinking *kolzhi*, right?"

Valdieren waved a hand dismissively. "Trust me, you shoot a stronger mix when you do exercises. And yeah, technically, we are always on; we're the first response team. If there was a terrorist attack right now, we'd be obligated to get everyone we could to safety and report to the airbase. But unless there's actually a terrorist attack, can you just call me Karshi?"

Pondering this concept, Sol took a sip. *What got you, the friendly liberal pacifist, to captain so fast while guys like Bachi and Aukaldir, who've been in the unit longer, stay beneath you? Even Myshkor didn't make captain until his 11th year in. Eek said you were one of the team who went to the gate...*

"This tastes great. Did you buy it locally?"

"Huh? Buy it?" The captain looked confused, chuckled a little, and answered quietly, in Ryzaan, "Wyvern's recipe; he gave me this so I'd run an errand for him while we're here."

I suppose I should have guessed that. I don't even want to know what he means by 'errand', though. "Erm, uh, my compliments to the chemist, then."

Valdieren retrieved the flask and took a hard swig, pushing his sunglasses to his hairline as he flopped into the fluff. Compared to the other young folk clustering on the hillside today, including Sol, he was dressed conservatively: unit-issued leggings, light weight moccasins, and a fashionable fitted long sleeve shirt composed of a mix of dark green panels. The shirt was not quite long enough to hit the top of his leggings, exposing both his utility belt (devoid of obvious weapons) and enough of his hips to show his setting sun tattoo. A fringed bandanna was tied loosely around his neck, covering his ID collar.

"You were somewhere with marines this morning?"

"Yeah," smiled Valdieren, fingering the fringe on his scarf. "Doing some TA work at the Academy this week. Just guessed there'd be some in my classes today. I guessed right; glad I wore it."

"The ladders don't give you away?"

"Nah. Flamethrowers wear 'em too, they're pretty easy to get in surplus stores back home." He gestured at Sol with the flask, who accepted graciously. "I like what you're wearing. I'd be freezing in that, even as warm as it is today."

The tradition of the Bloom Festival was that citizens over the age of sexual consent but as yet unmarried dressed in a revealing manner. It was apparently a unique tradition in the Archon Empire; tourism to Holtiin spiked strongly during the season. Sol had always been shy about his lanky body and little patches of blood-red hair, but after a few months of training in what amounted to bio-rubber underwear, an abbreviated leather vest over a mesh shirt and black cut-off pants did not seem so trashy. So people stared? *So what. If I was fully clothed, they'd be staring at the hair on my head, or my collars. Might as well give them something seriously freaky to look at.* "The vest is vintage," Sol explained proudly, feeling the effects of the strong, laced liquor.

"Boots too, huh? What are those? Ground Forces issue, couple decades old?"

"Armored Corps!" The red-head beamed. "Bought it all this morning coming back from the travel agent."

"Be sure and show those boots to Chel, he'll get a kick out of them." Val chuckled at his pun before segueing to the other part of the statement. "Travel agent? Were you arranging a flight for your mother?"

Sol smiled. There was pride and relief in his voice. "She doesn't know yet. She knows I hooked her up with a specialist doctor but she thinks he's on Castoro station. I took her to an appointment yesterday to make sure she was well enough for a jump flight. She passed and we got her on a course of drugs to prep for the trip just to be sure."

"Damn," Valdieren looked up at the violet leaves which filtered Holtiin's perpetual twilight down over them. "This is costing you a fortune, huh?"

"The only reason I had anything left for this outfit was because other unit members anonymously chipped in. And I'm still going to dump a chunk of the next several checks into upkeep on long-term care until she has official community membership. I don't mind though." He was so happy there were tears in his eyes. "She'll be better, and that's what matters."

"How did she react to your uniform?"

Sol shrugged and looked at the ground. "About like you'd expect, I guess."

The old rollie on the upper end of Barrel Court was dark when he entered. He triggered a light sensor and set his bag on one end of the kitchen bench. "Mom? Are you here?"

"Yen? Is that you?"

"Yeah, mom." Sol fidgeted with his locks apprehensively and then tied them back again. Some day he would find something to keep them in place for more than an hour at a time. "What room are you in? Can I bring you anything?"

There was silence, then a light came on in the sitting room. *She started sleeping in there when dad shipped away.* He approached slowly, stopped and shuddered slightly when he viewed her frail form draped with a few thinned blankets, end table beside the sofa littered with pill bottles and injector tubes. The syrigun case was Star Assault issue, although he could not quite make out the faded name runes tattooed upon it. There were a few periodicals nearby. *At least she's been reading, or trying to...*

"How is the service," she said flatly, fumbling with her glasses.

"I'm... I'm not in IGN anymore, mom."

She blinked behind her lenses, clearly having difficulty with her vision. He understood now as never before the shame and frustration this must bring her, 'best gunner in the Imperial military', going blind from a condition that could have been prevented or arrested. *I'm so sorry, Mom.*

Lady Solvreyil's mouth opened upon viewing him, standing there in his ladders and a loose Air Defense Squadron overshirt he borrowed on arrival. He wore it unfastened but his ladders were laced in accordance with pilot regulations; a modesty panel on his utility belt politely draped the logo of the 17th over his crotch. The open mouth closed but the gawk continued. *She needs to stop staring at me like that, she looks like a grumpy douhmet and I'm going to laugh and then I'll really hate myself.* Finally she spoke. "So that other feather I got in the mail was not a mistake."

Black Feathers were a medal awarded to officers who lost comrades in combat, or to those who lost their significant others or children to the same. When a young man entered Star Assault, his parents, if they lived, were always sent a Black Feather. He noticed there were two hanging in her shadowbox of medals now, along with her Silver Star and her rank bars and a little plaque bearing the silhouette of an extinct class of cruiser with the name "Star Destroyer Vol-Hryzrmr ". Leaning on this was an octagonal black metal coin with a stylized wing on it and Shandrian characters – "ISC Lorelei".

Sol wanted to ask about the coin, but asked about the feathers instead. "They sent you one for papa?" He could feel the tears starting at the back of his throat as he touched the edge of the box.

"The declassified report says he fought bravely against the uprising, that he served and died as a soldier, that his body was given honors, processed aboard the *Kelmia*, wrapped in the Imperial flag," she sniffed and sighed, not really having the capacity for tears at that moment. "Yen, will you take me to visit his shrine while you're here?"

This was the first time she had requested that. He walked to the sofa and took her shaking, cold, withered hand. "Yes, mother."

She seemed lost, far away, staring into the wrinkles of the faded blanket hanging on her knees. At last she turned her tired eyes to him and said, with some strain, "That is a great uniform, it has been worn by great men. Don't let anyone spoiled by this administration tell you otherwise. Star Assault are heroes."

As Sol finished his edited version of the story for Valdieren, they killed the flask. "Wow," muttered the captain. "I wasn't expecting that. I came home to my stuff in the garden and when I managed to confront my father he said, 'I have a feather that says my son is dead. I don't know who you are, but his crap's on the stump if you want to go through it.'"

Sol coughed and stared incredulously. "Are you fucking serious?"

"Completely. My parents were both Imperial Corps, you know, marines. I didn't know about that whole 'failure of air support during the Moon Wars' thing." He shrugged, about to say something else when a perky female voice interrupted.

"We have like, one good clear day finally and you guys are just lying in the shade getting drunk." It was the Islander girl. "What unit are you two? Flamethrowers?"

299

The two officers looked at one another, Sol winced slightly and opened his mouth but Valdieren butted in. "You got room in that game?"

Visible disappointment darkened her face as she saw the tattoos. "Of course."

"Let's get in a few rounds before it rains, then," Val said with a hint of drunkenness, reaching to Sol.

"Nah. I think I'll go for a walk down the shore, see if I can't talk the handler out of a skiff." He rose, looked over at the girl, down her slender curves, at the light trickle of perspiration beading on her neck and lower back, then at his mildly intoxicated superior. "Thanks though. Have fun."

He turned from their confused expressions and strode into the woods on a shortcut to the boat rental kiosk. *Thanks, but I have a date with the rain.*

Sol had known Darago the boat-man since childhood. Darago was well into his seventies, grey haired but short on wrinkles, no doubt due to side-effects of regenerative combat drugs. As long as Sol had known him, he lacked a few fingers from each hand. Tell-tale marks of skin grafts recorded a distant past where an unknown device removed most of the right side of his face; his right eye remained absent. Today he wore a patch over the scarred hole and was clad in his usual loose knee-length wrap-pants. Sol was amused that he seemed to have forgotten the shirt he normally wore under his meshy vest.

Aren't you a little old for the Bloom Festival, Darago? Sans shirt, though, tattoos and more skin-graft marks were visible on Darago's arms. *He probably had a full complement of integrated bio-ware at one point, now removed for reasons of comfort or sanitation. What was it Laathas said about removing grafts as part of PTSD treatment?* Suddenly the mischief-enabler of his youth made a lot more sense.

"Yen!" came the familiar voice, waving from the shallows where he dragged a peddle-boat.

This cheered him a little; losing Valdieren to the girl left him grumpy. He wanted to invite the captain swimming at the secret spot out by Dream Island where he used to practice after class. He was not interested in inviting some snobby Intergalaxy willow there. Sol waved back. "Hi Darago!"

"You're looking good! How was Mandatory? What unit you finally end up with?" Shoulder to shoulder he was twice as wide as Sol. He was haki too, and received his bone structure from human genes.

Sol shuffled and cleared his throat, moving the densely-woven neck of the mesh shirt down to show his dual black ID collars. The boat-man nodded knowingly.

"Good choice, I say." Without a word about the second collar, Darago turned and knelt to tie the peddle boat to the dock. Visible through the netting covering his back now was the sigil *haarvakjya*, upper arm and tail elongated and stylized to give the appearance of a bug-winged pulse rifle. Ringed with flames, footnoted with a date in Shandrian script, it was unmistakable: the friendly old man had earned his ink in the Haarkijetj, apparently in the 89th. 'The Invisible Squadron', undiscussed by civilian tongues.

Those scars likely were earned in a Baalphae prison camp. Glad my childhood curiosity never got the better of me. I bet he's still in the system, if I wanted to look him up... I won't, though.

When the boat-man turned back, Sol saluted, quickly and tightly, receiving the same gesture in kind.

"You must be making good money now." Darago sat on the bench beside the dock, rolling something papery between his fingers.

"Yeah, I am, but I dumped it into booking my mom into the Western Sun Veterans Facility in Eshandir."

Darago dropped his cigarette, genuine shock on his face. He retrieved it from the bench before it rolled out a crack and into the water. "No kidding? How is your ma?"

"Worse than I'd like, but better than I thought. Well enough to go to Archos, at least." Sol joined Darago on the bench, even though he hated the smell of fenatja, which was almost certainly what was rolled up in that little blue square of paper. *I wonder if that's prescription or if he just 'has friends'?*

"You should bring her for a boat ride before she moves." The last few words were spoken around the butt of the now-lit cigarette. The reek of burning lichen confirmed Sol's suspicion. *'No shame in fennie for asteroid belt vets,' Laathas had explained. 'Mior is named that for a reason.'*

Sol blinked as smoke hit his eyes. "Yeah, I really should. She'd like that, I think it would be good for her."

"I don't suppose," intoned the scarred man as he idly rolled the butt from his mouth and swapped it between his remaining fingers with deft movements, "you know where to get hold of some good luret?"

"Yeah actually. I have a bottle of *'Che-koshi'*, the *Sanjeera*'s house brand. They say it's the best since the *Ishulya* got iceboxed. It upsets my stomach badly, so I was just keeping it to give as a gift…"

"That is deeply unfortunate for you, Yen. It's the best way to keep from losing your insulating fat layer to combat drugs. Ship's gonna be painful cold if you stay that thin." He took a deep drag, closing his eye before exhaling. Sol held his breath to keep from taking in any second-hand. He had not considered how nauseous the smell would make him after half a flask of decently strong Mantzaari booze.

"Probably true, but I've never noticed cold too much. I will bring you the bottle when I bring mom down." Sol smiled hopefully. "It's about a pint."

Darago looked impressed. "You serious? You gonna give me the whole thing?"

"That was my intention."

"Go ahead. Take a boat for the rest of the day. Whichever one you want. And the ride with your ma is covered too. Go on." The veteran gestured at the dock. "I know you can handle the knots. Go. Before you puke on me."

Sol laughed, but he knew he was visibly pale in the presence of the fennie roll. He slid off the bench and over to a contraption that resembled a hollowed out millipede with pairs of rubbery flippers every other segment. He wanted to take one of these out since he was ten cycles old, but they required pulse signal to operate and his papa had refused to demonstrate. *I've got training, now, how tough could it be?* He arranged himself carefully so as not to tip the boat creature, knees up just as if he were in a pilot's seat, arms nested in little alcoves, hands on the response grips on either side of his thighs. Sol breathed in, closed his eyes and focused.

With a profound undulation, the shiny black and gold thing propelled itself from the cove and onto open water. The creature had a certain cheerful purpose to it, bringing to mind Ozlietsin. As he steered, he wondered how she was getting on in the hive in his absence. *I hope she's not fighting too much with the other bugs or bothering any of the crew. I really miss her. It's funny how attached I've gotten to her. I suppose that's the point. "The better the bond, the better the combat unit.'*

The apparently excitable boat creature moved rapidly, and the lush, perpetually misty vegetation of Dream Island came into view. In fact, they came upon it so fast he realized they would collide with the rock formations that jutted at the shoreline if he did not act quickly. The boat resisted his attempt to swerve. Sol braced, closed his eyes, but opened his mouth slightly to reduce the amount of teeth chipped on impact. The expected impact did not come, and he found himself looking over the side, bewildered, as the boat-creature simply chugged across barely submerged rocks on its flippered segments. On reaching the beach, it unceremoniously dumped him out in the sand and gravel and curled into a ball to take a nap.

Sol got to his feet, picking little bits of grit out of his ears, shirt, navel, and locks, glaring at the snoozing spiral mass that previously served as a boat. "A little warning would have been nice." He spat gravel out nearby. *Maybe I overdrove the poor bugger.* Sympathetically, he leaned down and petted it, at which it tightened its coil and raised a set of heretofore unseen hostile-looking spines. Sol withdrew his hand post-haste. "Point fuckin' taken, boat-dude!"

Ew. Am I picking up someone else's speech habits?

He hiked carefully through swampy tufts to the place where exposed ropy roots of moss-covered marsh willows entwined to form a sort of basket-throne. Here, as a youth, he ruled as the prince of his own imagination for many a lonely vacation day. Into the familiar cradle he climbed, moss and lichen leaving green-blue streaks on exposed skin as he surveyed his misty realm while the amphibians sang.

A gentle wind blew, and Sol was convinced he could feel the trees breathing. *There was a lot of synthenzin in that Kolzhi, lower on vyddarin and alcohol; I think I prefer that recipe.* Tiny rainbows rippled on mist clouds and swirled in dew drops. Halos of light winked in and out as the breeze shifted leaves and branches. *A lot of synthenzin. That wasn't street legal booze, even if I'd been*

303

old enough to buy it. He giggled, an unseemly noise he was perfectly happy no one was around to hear.

The sounds changed again; a cacophony of rubbery squeaks; for a second he thought his memories of the ship had taken over. A small, violet-spotted brown amphibian, it would have fit in his hand, sat beside his head, staring at him with faceted black eyes, periodically washing its face with one of its two stretchy feet. It sang again as he stared. Sol smiled. "Thank you. That's very lovely. It sounds like home."

It sat a moment longer then hopped into the water beneath, tail trailing a second before it disappeared. He pondered the strange life cycle of these animals, who spent most of the year buried in mud, coming out for the brief, colorful explosion of first spring to breed, then burying themselves with their eggs to be devoured by their own young in the burrow. In spite of his past several months of life with Ozzie and constant chemical suppression, Sol was still nervous around animals, considering contact between him and anything with a fragile little heart a death sentence. The *goba* had just been lucky to have caught him fried out of his skull, and he may have injured the flippipede. That thought concerned him, so he climbed out of his basket-throne and nimbly crawled back to the beach.

The boat-creature shuffled about the shore, snuffled among the rocks along the water's edge, examining the clumps of vegetation. He squatted to watch; he was unaware the thing was this alive at first. "Are you alright? You seem alright. Are you hungry or something?"

It undulated toward him, stopped short and reared. He noticed its rows of eyes, like a gen's, only smaller and more numerous. Intelligence, while very alien, was absolutely present. It did not seem to have a voice, but made a sound by flapping feelers against its head and clapping its first few sets of flippers against one another. *No, much more like the ship sprite than it's like Ozzie.*

"I really hope I didn't hurt you. I didn't mean to upset you. My boss got me high then made me mad…" *The explanation is more ridiculous than the situation. As usual. Tiny seedlings?*

The thing lowered its head and looked him square in the eye. *Three to one. It has me beat on that score,* thought Sol in amusement. The flippipede clicked at him, then resumed its hunt. Finally, it found a loose tuft and went beneath, effectively buried save the tip of its head.

"Hey! Come out of there!" It clicked its feelers then folded them up. Just then, rain started to fall. Thunder crackled in the distance. "Oh. I get it."

Sol turned to the lake and looked past New Asria, jutting from the shore in the distance, to the mountains, where the darkest wall of clouds clustered, shot through with periodic flashes. The Bloom Festival would be racing into the community center, merchant plaza, and coffee shops. Every place open to the public with indoor seating would be covered in damp young couples and trios pawing at and kissing one another. *Just as well I'm out here.*

He covered the flippipede's head with his vest before clambering back to his secret mossy lair. He leaned forward with his arms crossed on the jutting roots, chin settled upon them, and watched the distant storm creep over the city. The droka silk of his shirt felt amazing with the pattering rain across his shoulders. Sol smiled. *Silk from custom-bred droka was the greatest Aurian export; when they decided that clothes were something they wore, they wore layers of tunics much like this one.* Sol appreciated the concept of emulating his distant Archon ancestors, most of whom were wiped out when the human continent across the ocean fired ballistic missiles at the Haanouros Island space port. Currents carried fallout over Aurius, decimating the population of the capitol city, Sanjeera, in a matter of weeks. Aurian blood persisted in the universe because some Aurians emigrated prior to the attack to Mantzaar, Ruahanu, or Holtiin.

Sanjeera. My home…

As the frequency of droplets increased, the colonel's words came to mind. *'Trust me, you'll miss it'. It's rain. Isn't rain the same on other planets? It's not like we're all deserts and space stations. We're Star Assault. We go everywhere. It's in the handbook.*

Cold water pelted his shoulders, massaged his slightly itchy scalp. *It'll never be the same.* What was it Cheldyne said? Something, about human colonies coming to be nervous about rain…

'Our ships are alive. They secrete constantly when in atmospheres… it's the only sign prior to an Archon invasion: a gentle but sticky rain, from the hulls and from the gen. Then the lights go out and it's over.'

Was that what Master Kiertus meant? Sol's drugged mind superimposed the memory over the view of the city. He saw Cheldyne, dour expression wrinkling his scarred nose, ragged graying mudlocks askew. He used a scoop to clean hive chambers; Sol listened while he clung to the slippery wall, holding bags of wax. It was distracting. He realized now he had absorbed it all unconsciously.

'True kaffir love rain. It is benevolent, rhythmic, and beautiful. It makes plants grow and cleans things off. Everything shines after the rain, the fungus comes up, and the fish come back.' Scoop, scoop, scoop. 'People who do not see it that way, see the coldness, the breaking of fragile things, the dark clouds, flooding, mudslides… all the bad things that rain can also mean. But soon,' scoop, scoop, scoop, 'you will never see the bad again, you will see purpose and renewal in what others call "bad", because you will become the rain. Rain cannot hate itself for being rain.'

Lightning hit a pole on the old royal palace's highest tower, reverberating across Sol's vision in rainbow waves.

'We are the cleansing rain of the universe. We will heal its wounds, even if we have to drown it first.'

Tzanshidi's face and voice appeared and merged in with Chel's. *"We are the physicians…"*

Sol watched the perpetual half-sun break through clouds over the mountains, illuminating the storm and the city with a fiery, rainbow glory. It was breathtaking, but his soul struggled against a layer of ice. Tears welled up, luminescent in his still enhanced eyes, he thought of the scars and body counts of all those pain-filled gray-haired men, and the stigma about which both his mother and Kiertus warned him. *Was it merely air squads' failure on the moons, or Kiertus' heavy-handed solution to the issue of disputed refugee ships? What kind of 'great men', what kind of 'heroes', are too awful for the public to accept?*

He imagined Celita in an interrogation cell and cringed. Too well-reared to run from obligation and too aware of what desertion could lead to, he relaxed against the damp, mossy elbows and burls. With the acceptance of his fate weighing on his heart, he asked of the distant stars: "Father, what have I done?"

….

To his great surprise, his mother was dressed and upright when he walked up the hill from the dhol stop. "You're already up. And here I came early to help you while we waited for the taxi."

Her voice was slow and weak but still bore admirable confidence. "It's rare I have days where I can do it myself, Yen, so I do."

"Fair enough." He smiled, offering hands to assist her down the ramp to the street.

Niarri hesitated. "Yen, where did you pick up that expression?"

"Um, didn't …" *Parthenos. A lot of the 17th says it, but I picked it up from Parthenos and I think everyone else did, too. I was about to say dad said it a lot.* "A superior officer in my unit."

She stared down Barrel Court, at the slightly overgrown cab stand and the various rollies with unkempt mini-gardens and window boxes, dripping vegetation, the occasional flying pollinator flitting cautiously amidst the aftermath of the morning's storm. Holtiini was less of a labor for her tired vocal cords than Unified Archon. "It's a Ruhn expression, you know? Their chieftains used it when mocking the Ryzaan treaties against piracy and it caught on."

"Do you know much about the Ruhn?" he asked as he escorted her down.

"Rather a bit." Her voice was strained, sad, and distant.

Perhaps this is not a good train of thought for her, and I should change the subject in spite my curiousity. "So the shrine we're going to isn't Enjalphea, it's actually closer, I was surprised."

"Of course his shrine is on the mountain. Honoring a pilot in a cave would be rude."

"Technically, I think it's considered a 'grotto'."

"Cave."

"Grotto!"

"Cave."

"You win."

Her smirk was barely perceptible but the fact it was there at all pleased Sol.

"Do you mind if I call us a military transport instead of a civilian taxi? It'll make the trip up the mountain easier and cheaper."

"I was surprised you didn't just show up in one."

Sol entered the request sequence. "There are staffing issues. I didn't want to make anyone wait if you weren't ready to go." *I also didn't want to upset you.*

The beetle shuttle was an eight-seater capapble of short flights. It was air defense grey and violet; both its armaments and its *haarvakjya* were carefully concealed. The driver did not ask to see Niarri's credentials as a veteran; he simply tipped his hat to her as Sol helped her aboard.

"G'morning, astrum. Where would you be escorting this lovely young lady?"

"Astral Walk, um, the shrines on the other side of the Khyvaar Springs."

The driver seemed vaguely amused as he adjusted the engineer's cap atop black mudlocks. "I am familiar with the Astral Walk; it'd be easier to get there in a Dash honestly but I'll get you as close as I can, on behalf of your skinny legs, of course." The man winked at Sol as he tilted his head back towards Niarri.

There was one other passenger on their silent trek to the mountain. His pale ivory face and long blue mudlocks were a bit scruffy. He wore double collars and a disheveled officer's jacket and stunk of perfumed oil and liquor.

Sol watched his mother – Lady Solvreyil, as he was informed to refer to her during the course of this trip – sleep as the man across the aisle fidgeted. *Red piping, empty space where unit insignia should be, double black tags; 89th for sure. Probably outranks me. Wonder if that expression regards his state or the fact he slept off base against restrictions and he's on his way to demotion? There but for suppressors and discipline go I; I've no room to judge.*

The beetle stopped at the air base and the mysterious officer stumbled off, pausing just as he was about to step out onto firm ground to shudder and exhale once in grim determination. Niarri's voice gave Sol a start as the door shut behind the man.

"Airsharks never change. Comforting to see they're still around, in a way."

He regarded her as the taxi hopped up the road toward Ma'epar Drokaidi, the mountain that held their destination. "If you say so, ma'am." *'Behave as if she is simply an elderly veteran who has hired you as an escort,'* the reviewer *reminded Sol before he left.*

It was not long before the beetle-handler called back, "I'm going to stop at the snack stand over here, it's where I'd normally drop riders headed up the mountain, but I'm willing to take you all the way to the bridge. It'll be a bit bumpy of a ride, but easier by far than hiking up."

"Understood, sir."

They filled travel containers of water at the stand while a bored man with short, blond mudlocks leaned on the wall and whistled badly. Sol observed he was armed, probably only for tradition's sake. 'Source guard' was a time-honored position, ancestral on the homeworld and district-assigned on Holtiin. At least one was stationed at every spring, making sure the water remained uncontaminated and that no one attempted to bottle with intent to charge. For the first time in his life, Sol appreciated his Imperially-mandated Right to Clean Water. *Seems such an obvious thing, but I've been to worlds that don't have anything like it.*

He apologized to the guard as he eyed the snack machine. "I've only enough to tip or buy food, sorry."

"Tip the source guards; they are your life, astrum."

Sol froze, interrupting the exchange between his collar and the machine, disturbed by his mother's tone. "Yes, ma'am." He turned slightly to the blond man, again apologizing. The only reply, through continued whistling, was a raised palm bearing an Air Defense ID number. As he slate-transferred the value of the sea veggie and egg wrap he intended for lunch, he tabbed the guard's profile. A purple bar where his name should have been denoted superior rank and class; his only designation was 'Secure Reserve'.

Where have I seen that before? What does that mean? To stave off the sinking feeling that rapidly came over him, Sol bowed politely to the guard and assisted his mother aboard the beetle. "Sorry I was not better prepared for this journey, Lady Solvreyil."

Niarri shrugged. "I've been living off public care food… wasn't much worth packing a lunch from around the house." She followed this with a sad smile. "Usually too nauseous to eat anyhow."

"Will you mind if I have some of my rations, after we stop? I missed breakfast." Sol poked in his ration pouch. "I'd offer, but I just have a couple fungus protein strips and a pack of cheese biscuits."

"Oh? I happen to love those." They exchanged a surprised look and laughed.

The bridge was an impressive structure, built across a ravine from some manner of heavy duty webbing. Roughly four meters below this was a large expanse of dew-speckled silken web. Sol gazed down at it as he approached the bridge. A sign cautioned droka were present and not to be alarmed.

"Of course there are droka present, but there must be thousands of them for webs like that…"

"*Maava* droka, so only a family. I'd rather not see them, even if they are helpful." Niarri employed both Sol and the bridge 'railing' to support her as she shuffled across.

I want to see one! I've only seen the pair at the zoo! Giant droka! "But don't the gen here…"

"Those little tower things, see, with the beacons?" She gestured meekly at a slender spire of manufactured bone. "The beacon makes a noise repellent to wild genadri and trained ones can theoretically smell the kaffa on them and leave them be."

"I can't hear anything."

Niarri shrugged. "Neither can I, still have my earplugs."

310

"Well, don't look over the side just now if you don't want to see one." The creature somewhat timidly went about its business of tending the web complex below and drinking water collected here and there. Sol wished to take a snapshot but he was warned against camera use during the briefing. "They're not wild animals, huh?"

"No, imported from Archos, bred to adapt to the weather here, specifically to maintain the safety net for this place." She shuddered, resisting the urge to glance at the sizeable eight-legged arthropod below.

"They only eat algae and fungus; they have sucker mouths and can't hurt you."

Her response was abrupt, a sharp reminder she was once a star ship officer. It snipped the conversation off cleanly. "They remind me of stalkers, astrum."

Beyond the ravine stood clusters of natural rock formations, some several storeys tall, worn from time but carved and polished in various ways. The tallest had steps chiseled into them for access to higher levels. Soon they were surrounded on all sides by these; Sol took in a breath in amazement.

"This is beautiful. I had no idea there was such a place on Holtiin."

She seemed to know the precise location of the shrine she wanted. "It is a monument of death, and in the ways of the faith that built this place, it is considered rude to create a visual record of its existence."

Was that a hint of distaste I heard?

"Here," she said softly, stepping down a small ramp into a hewn and glinting alcove.

It was little more than a crevice at the base of a tower covered in such niches, enough room for one or two to sit or kneel before carvings on the smooth wall. Shelves and pockets were cut into stone; faded photographs, strings of beads, incense, clusters of flowers in various states of decay. Imbedded in the rock where Niarri knelt was a photograph transferred onto heavy sheeting. It showed the handsome face of a long-haired man facing down with closed eyes; his nose was larger but jaw and eye shape were quite similar to Sol's. Plants left here, some quite recent, all appeared nibbled on. Casually examining a leaf with an all-too-familiar bite out of it, Sol laughed uncomfortably.

"I see the gen aren't that repelled." He knelt as his mother fished in her pocket to produce some incense.

"Would you light that for me, Yen?"

"Turn away, please." *Let me see if I can actually make fire with my hands*. He concentrated pulse into incinerating heat, focused at the tip of his finger. There were sparks and the incense smouldered.

I finally lit something! Take that, Okie. "There you go, ma'am."

He continued to examine. *I wonder who left all these plants. I guess he had a lot of friends I never got to meet. So many little gifts*. Engraved beside the photograph's nook, in old Shandrian, was the name, "Solvreyil-Kvatchkiir Meshaan. Husband, father." It lacked dates, unit symbols, or other proper details. Other names surrounded it, mostly covered in wreathes and ropes, evergreen cones, seed pods, charms. Not wishing to disturb the shrine before his tearlessly weeping mother, he slipped out to sit facing away from the scene.

....

"Would you like some time alone in this memorial?" came Niarri's weak voice.

"Yes, please. I saved you a cheese biscuit and protein strip, if you're feeling up to it. It's a long trek back." Sol left the food sitting atop a blank stone on his open kit. He returned to the alcove. When he was certain she no longer paid attention, Sol quietly slid garlands and wreaths aside, being gentle so as not to disturb tiny bells amongst them.

The largest memorial plaque read, in archaically styled Shandrian engraving worn down by decades of caressing hands: *'Myentrios Hyrshaanziir, Triotos, Ruahanu, IY 554 – 579. With blessed light we renew the cosmos.'*

Three glyphs followed. The first was 23rd Star Assault's 'hailing death', the second the stylized van'ra teeth and gen wings of the 89th, and the third a sun identical to that tattooed on Okallin's left hand. The niche that should contain a photograph held a small liquor flask bearing the haarvakjya.

He examined the other names on this side; some seemed nicknames or callsigns, some only family names, some had dates or locations, some did not. Most of the

312

engraving was quite old. He recognized a few, the most notable sat above: *'Okallin Teshkanzin, Yihaura, Vasa, Archos. 543–.569. The path of peace is paved in bone.'* A bit beneath Myentrios' name was a niche with a little clarithane box which held a shed antennae casing, floating in viscous fluid. Sol mouthed the High Shandrian characters here: "*P'aar Yrti Niiz*".

That doesn't quite make a name; it's just 'Faith – Justice – Hope'. But it's followed with a city and dates. 'Triotos, Ruahanu, IY 558 – 577.' *What's the rule for those characters, if it was a name, you'd read it like, 'Payer-tee-nyuz... nee-os... Par tee ...'* "Parthenos?"

He had not meant to say it aloud. Outside the alcove, he caught his mother flinch out the corner of his eye. He examined the carvings, realizing most of these men were still alive, only written outside society because they followed the path of knighthood. *'The secret immortality,'* Chel once referred to it.

Touching the edges of his father's photo-plaque, he remembered coming home from the library after reading about Shandrian and Aurmalki temples. He wanted to talk about it because he could not understand why things so pretty and fascinating were abandoned. Papa walked him down to the stream and told him to pick out shapes in the clouds instead. This frustrated the excited little boy, but Shaan's response was to smile broadly and embrace him. *'Why not simply live and enjoy the beauty that is here?'* He gestured to the water and sky and the lush sub tropical foliage. *'Religion is best left to the dead.'*

Maybe I should just let this trail end here. Sol laid his hand on the cold carved stone and stared at the memorial wall. *Whatever the truth is, I still love you, dad.*

XIV. Finding Balance

It was his first 'tea day' since returning from leave. Sol made plans in place of tea since the colonel never seemed able to meet and headed to play a gen race sim with Bacharanzin and Aukaldir. Ozlietsin behaved poorly when they hooked up the simulated male genadri mounts – barking, dominance humping, biting the riders – and until he figured out how to train that quirk out, he would leave her with Val or Chel. As he entered the hive airlock, however, he received a text from Kiertus.

"Well Oz, looks like you're coming to the office with me, and I've got to cancel with Bachi and Holiday. We're actually having tea with our noble master. Will you behave with Nova?"

Waving to Cheldyne and assorted paratroopers using the pool, Sol crossed the hive and ascended to the lounge. To his slight dismay, Parthenos sat with Aukaldir examining spreadsheets on a laptop. "Yo, Red."

"Greetings, major, sir. And lieutenant, sir."

"Hey, Sol. Are we still on?"

"I just texted you." Sol waved his slate at them. "I gotta go see the colonel."

Parthenos grabbed his forearm as he passed. "How was the trip home?"

"Um, surreal, sir." *To say the least!*

"Bein' dead takes some gettin' used to. How did the lady Solvreyil take her reassignment?"

"She yelled a lot." Sol frowned. "I told her she had no choice, she was getting reassigned for treatment, the arrangements were already made, I only acted under orders. The transit ship attendants sedated her. I apologized to them."

The major said nothing about the protocol breach as he released his grip. "Good job, astrum. Thank you."

Sol felt awkward as he entered the colonel's office. Kiertus was seated on his desk, entering something on his slate while periodically glancing at the open lap top clipped into the desk's holder. "Tea or coffee?"

"If you have tea that'll treat an upset stomach, I'd greatfully accept it, master." Sol watched as Ozzie nuzzled against Nova's shoulder and made a sigh of relief as both curled up in a chair together. *If you can be well-behaved one place, I guess this is the best one...*

Kiertus gestured to a sofa. "I understand." He prepared their beverages cheerfully. "I have plenty of connections at Western Sun, you realize; I can keep up with her progress without any violations."

"That... that's good, sir. It makes me feel a little better." *I wonder if he was watching the lounge security camera or is his hearing as good as the rumors say?* "She seemed so angry about losing the house. I feel bad; I know it's all she had for so many years..."

"I would be resistant to that level of change as well." The colonel passed him a steaming cup. "But she will adjust. She is stronger than she seems, even if the past few years have wounded her. I have faith." Kiertus sat beside him and stirred his usual honey stick into his tea. "How was your leave otherwise?"

"I finished reading the book and gave it to the library. I thought the head antiquarian was going to have a seizure. He called out everyone from the back to look at it and me."

Kiertus laughed. "What did you think of it?"

"I think I could have read it several more times and gotten something different from it each instance." Sol was not evading; he simply did not know where to begin. "I am accustomed to the Shandrian habit of presenting history through romanticized symbolism and drama, master; I did play the last prince of Aurius in my school's production of -"

"I know, Yen. I was sitting in the audience on opening night."

Sol nearly choked on his tongue.

"You did a fantastic job, I thought, especially in light of such a wooden Halurashiin to perform against." He shrugged. "It is my favorite Shandrian play; I don't miss a production of it, even amateur ones, if I can find the time."

"Alright, so, you gave me 'Thine Sacred Dust' to read because it presents a model of warrior monk master/astrum relationships, correct?"

"Well, one template thereof, but yes; everything in that book is just as true now as it was then."

This statement bothered Sol a great deal but he could not have explained why without hours and diagrams, so he picked the first detail and ran with it. "Shendiir isn't fighting Ryzaa and Ryzaa isn't raiding Aurius for resources anymore. Archos is unified."

"Tell me that after you've stood an hour on the senate floor."

He's so patient. He didn't even sound sarcastic or raise his voice. I should return the gesture, I guess. He's respectable; I would like to be so, as well. "Fair enough, I suppose. I'm only familiar with Archos from literature. I retract."

"I meant more the purpose of the warrior-monks, the function of the protective societies, our relationship with the genadri, and so forth. Time may change borders and names, but the will to create war, and the subsequent need to stop it in its tracks, that does not change."

"Understood, master." There was uncomfortable silence. *I believe he may have just preached at me. But on whose behalf?* "The harpoon trick. Can anyone on this ship teach me that?"

"It's how we use our bayonets, but masters do not even need an object built specifically for pulse transmission to use it. Mind you, the object rarely survives, but what would you miss more – your favorite foraging knife, or your life?" Again, the broad shoulders shrugged. "I can if we can find time. Mysh is training rookies for a while or he could, Val won't, and Freyr is always busy, more so than me."

"I've been embarrassed to ask, but who is 'Freyr'?"

Kiertus tilted his head and squinted, as if he thought Sol should already know. "One of our wing commanders. He is not consistently aboard due to other career demands." He leaned half turned against the back of the sofa, resting the side of his face on his free hand as the other held his cup. "There is another qualified in the Black Sphere art you wish to learn. He is recently back aboard and not wildly occupied. I offered you as his astrum and he declined, I assume because his last committed combat suicide. He would not admit so, but he's sensitive."

The boy tried to keep his tea and gaze steady as he faced his aged master. "I appreciate that you kept me, sir, even if another astrum was not something you particularly wanted, either."

"Think nothing of it. You are good company. I endeavor to make you one of my successes."

"I do think I've a better understanding of the knightly ideas of honor and death now, though, sir."

"Oh?"

"The day after I finished the book, I escorted my mother, er, 'the Lady Solvreyil', to Ma'epar Drokaidi, to Astral Walk..."

"Ah, *Spider's Cradle*. Amazing place." He inhaled the fragrance before sipping.

"Spaeydair?" *Those are those things, at the zoo, some of them are poisonous, but they look kind of like droka. Even the largest were very small though. Where did those come from? Yrthyi? What's the Archon name for that world? It's just a Ryzaan character sequence, uh, RVN something...* "Are you from the world of spaeydairi?"

"Earth, is what we call it. Similar to the Holtiini word for it, by no accident." Kiertus stretched his legs then folded them onto the couch, keeping his cup steady as he did so. "Yes, that's my home planet. I very much appreciate that you are well-read enough to acknowledge it."

"I should have gone back to the mountain after I took her home. I wanted to see if you had a plaque up there somewhere."

More laughter. "I think I am honored on more than one memorial there. Such is the way of knights."

Sol made a confused expression. "More than one?"

"Those shrine stones are maintained by the heads of the Orders. Each shrine is devoted to specific units, trenches, sub-orders, or situations. One person is the base of the memorial; others of his order or his 'star blood' are honored on the surrounding surface. I have been close to many over the years, so I am named on multiple plaques." Kiertus set his cup on the table and turned toward Sol. "I spend a lot of time there, cleaning mostly, but I enjoy meditating on my novum's shrine."

Which probably has your name on it. "You pray on your own grave?"

"Can you think of a better place?"

Sol sipped his cooling tea quietly, staring at his amused knight master.

"It is no coincidence of geography or poor civic planning that one must go through the air base and show military ID to get there, and no surprise you were unfamiliar. Had you looked for a time, you might have found your own name; at least one member submitted an addition request before we docked at Castoro."

"I guess that explains why there's a small arts center on the airbase grounds and they teach stone carving and ostrekaal sculpting there. That seemed strange to me when I noticed it looking for the mess hall."

Kiertus lifted his face from his fingers to gesture past his eyes toward the ceiling. "Indeed. Fly boys make graves, including their own."

"Can you? Work stone, that is, sir." Sol was amused imagining the colonel with dusty hair and filthy knees grinding away on a misty mountain morning.

"I have taken a course, but it's not really my art of preference. I do carry a pulse-driven worm-stylus and a small manual chisel, in case I'm the last survivor, stranded on some asteroid, and want to spend my remaining oxygen on leaving some lovely poetry for whoever finds the wreckage." He shrugged and resumed a posture more appropriate to consuming tea.

None of that remotely darkened his countenance. As if he didn't even realize what he said was horrifically grim. "If stone carving is not your art, do you have one? Like the prince said in the book, 'a knight needs balance; he should pursue an art or sport beyond his combat prowess'?"

"Absolutely; it's in my profile."

"Sir, there's nothing but a bunch of number and letter designations on your profile, for me, anyway."

His eyes twinkled as his smile produced tiny wrinkles beside them. "IGC? 'Imperial Guild Choir'?"

"Ah! Apologies, master. I'm dense. Wow, that's quite an honor."

"Yes; if you review any recording of the Armed Forces Day Parade from the past several years, you can locate me standing a step down from Councilor Therek singing the anthem before the fireworks. Even with the guild veil on, my hair is distinctive."

I never watch that much of it. My dad always cried during the anthem, even when he sang. And Therek's zealous eyes and wicked fangs gave me the first nightmare I had featuring sexual assault. I've never told anyone about that and I'm not going to start here. "Like the monks in 'Dust' are tree-husbands? Do all knights follow that model, then?"

"The good ones do; obsession with violence makes poor soldiers and worse leaders." Kiertus finished his tea and set his cup down, projecting an aura of perfect calm. "On this ship alone, we have musicians, carnival acrobats, poets, recreational chemists, distillers, tattooists, portrait photographers, illustrators, and at least one impressive erotic dancer. The 89th has all the painters and for whatever reason, the best cooks and horticulturists are in the 23rd."

Sol tried not to giggle as he attempted to match knights to the listed talents. Aukaldir and Cheldyne were tattooists; Aukaldir's sketches and flash designs were in a public folder of the ship's virtual library. He could certainly picture Valdieren as a gymnast, especially noting the activity games at which he held unbeatable scores. Wyvern could easily fall under 'recreational chemist' or 'poet' with no surprise. Myshkor posted photography and videos on SACnet (his 'stupid stunts' mostly involved bodily harm to get better shots) and apparently did musical projects with other team members. Okallin inarguably cooked well. Enki was good with plants… "Erotic dancer, sir?"

Grey eyebrows rose. He paused a moment before speaking in which time Sol made the grave error of taking a drink. "Surprised he did not demonstrate when you were killing time at the Come Down. They have a pole and swing, after all."

Tea sprayed across the table. *Oh, gods, is that why he asked me if I 'danced' with that funny look?* "Apologies, sir. Let me…" Sol reached for the towel on the tea service as the colonel laughed. "I got that everywhere. At least we're in gravity. Did I get any on you?"

"It's quite alright, astrum. I set you up for that. Don't worry about the sofa, but the table is polished coral." Kiertus wandered to his desk and leaned over his computer. "We're approaching the transfer gate, so hurry that up and get to your station. Kourhos in thirty six hours by current calculation. Be prepared for rapid reassignment."

…

Bug snot. That was Sol's first thought on waking. Ozzie needed a bath and decided Sol did too; she dribbled her mucus all over him to prove it. This did not dawn on him as quickly as she would have liked so she increased the output until goo entered his mouth. Sputtering, he flung himself upright, knocking her back, wiping at his face and flailing his arms with an incoherent guttural noise.

Ozlietsin righted herself easily and unleashed a staccato set of squawks and trills. Sol glared back, red locks dripping with slime, eyes sticky slits. "I don't have to be up for another two hours. What the fuck, bug!"

She lowered her head in a perturbed manner, pulling his scrubbing gloves out of their nook with her mouth. She thrust them at Sol with a muffled chirp.

"Fine, we'll take a bath. Little miss high maintenance drool machine wins again. I give up." He slid the door up and swung out; she half-hopped, half-flew to the floor to wait for him, scrubby gloves still dangling from her mouth.

As he climbed, mumbling and cursing, down the ladder, the door to the compartment beneath his opened. "Good morning, astrum," said a sleepy looking kaffa. "Is everything all right?"

Startled, Sol almost lost his grip. "Apologies, Captain Valdieren. Didn't know you were in. In fact, I didn't know I was assigned the coccoon above yours. I was yelling at my bug, sir. She was being nasty, sir."

"I see." The captain rubbed his eyes and checked his flashing slate. "Just as well, I have to report to the major in forty-five. You guys headed to the pool?"

Sol hung there on the ladder, hair dripping with sticky goo. "Nah, cap'n. I was thinking of going to a dance club and trying to pick up ladies."

"Hard not to feel sexy when you're covered in mucus, hm?" The captain grabbed his pants and followed Sol down the ladder. "Careful or you'll turn into Wyvern."

The astrum tried not to eyeball his superior's athletic posterior wriggling above him. The tight black Vektaar-patented briefs emphasized the curvature as he descended. *Star Assault's uniform underwear looks more to me like stripper gear the more I see it.* "Where's Squeak, sir?"

"She's been sleeping on the colonel's bed lately with him and Nova, since her feelers got hurt when we confiscated... uh...."

Sol tilted his head at his Valdieren. "Did I miss something?"

"About a week ago I went out on a mission with Major P. Classified, but we were picking up some stuff, you know, taking care of a mess some permanently stationed ground forces made, again. I don't know where she got it, but she carried back ....um... a body part. Had to chase her all over the ship..." He was sort of pale. "Chel and the colonel thought it was hilarious. They finally helped me catch her though."

"'Body part'". Sol decided not to ask for elaboration. Rumors abounded of gen collecting 'souvenirs'; he recognized some objects were inherently more sanitary than others, and he would probably be just as grossed out if Ozzie decided to bring him some rotting corpse fragment.

They passed through the series of moist airlocks to the grav section of the ship, pausing for short periods between. Somewhere in the midst of this, Ozzie deemed it a good time to drop the scrubby gloves and get a grip on a dangling leg of the trousers Val carried and pull. Slightly off his footing already, attempting to adjust to the change in gravity, he slid down the wall with a startled noise and fell on his ass. His attempt to yank the leggings back instigated tug-of-war game with the large, uppity symbiote.

Sol smacked his forehead, almost as if he could disconnect his overwhelming desire to laugh at his prone superior. The act of smacking his hairline simply resulted in a spray of sticky grime left from her previous antics. His mirth was poorly restrained as he attempted discipline: "Ozlietsin! Bad bug! Bad! Leave the captain alone! Down!"

"You are in some serious trouble, miss!" snarled Valdieren in an increasingly Ryzaan accent, struggling against Ozzie's balance advantage. "Astrum! Do something! If I pulse her, she'll just hit me back! Astrum! That's an order! Control this soldier at once!"

His usually kind, thoughtful demeanor was lost to frustration and humiliation; the bug had him beat and knew it. The final door to the hive opened, turning the last lock into a comedic stage where all within the hive pool chamber could easily see.

It was fortunate to a degree that the only man in the chamber was Colonel Kiertus. He sat peacefully on the pool's edge scrubbing his talon-like toes, singing a song in the tongue of his youth while Nova, Squeak, and Curly played a game in the water. The colonel glanced up at the yelling and growling, sighed, and shook his head with a smile before returning to his pedicure.

Astrum Solvreyil nearly collapsed from laughter, having tried everything he could to get Ozzie to release the ladders. He even attempted a wicked pressure pinch at the thorax/head connection area, but she felt it coming and generated a shield from the malleable substance on her back. "Dammit, bug, you're too good at that." *I'm impressed; I should tell Cheldyne. After I'm done being in a lot of trouble with Val.*

Ensconced in his unsettling toenails, Kiertus called without looking up, "Drop the pants, captain. She'll lose interest."

"What!"

"He said drop your pants, sir!"

Valdieren released his hands and Ozzie staggered, skidded, and flailed out the door, knocking Sol down en route. She regained footing and scampered, leggings in mouth, to an unseen hiding place in the hive.

"Don't chase her, either of you," the colonel ordered with calm matter-offactness. "You'll only encourage her acting out."

Chagrinned, Valdieren came up to the edge of the pool with a sigh. His own gen swam to the far side and submerged all but the top of her head in a submissive gesture. "Aw, come on, Squeaky-beak. I'm not mad anymore. C'mere, girl."

She burbled underwater but stayed put. Sentinel Cheldyne's symbiote, Curly, swam to the captain instead, pushing a toy at him. "At least you don't hate me," he said, accepting the toy and tossing it toward the far end. Curly and Nova pursued it and the three bugs began to play again. Ozzie joined them shortly, pants nowhere to be seen.

"You need to fix this issue with her or it's going to destroy your pair bond, Val." Kiertus meticulously filed and buffed each claw-like nail, still not looking up. He wore only a towel, a hair tie, and his ID collar. Sol stared in mute fascination, switching his myriad tattoos and beastly feet.

"I don't know what to do, colonel. She used to just bring me interesting rocks."

The fanged mouth achieved a quirky expression even though his gaze stayed on his feet. "And you yelled at her for bringing you a rock."

"It was a piece of *uranium*, sir!"

Kiertus looked up, cleared his throat, and calmly stated, "Well, to be fair, that is a pretty interesting rock."

Val made a noise somewhere between groan and sigh and buried his head in his hands. "Why do I have to have the stupid bug?"

"She's not stupid," Colonel Kiertus admonished, gesturing with his file. "She's helpful and trying to make you happy. She doesn't know what qualifies as a good object. You need to carry toys or candy bars to reward her for her gifts, even if you plan to recycle them immediately."

Sol was fascinated and disturbed. "Or bury them in a hazardous waste site! Uranium, sirs, really?"

The captain's sense of humor soaked in the stale urine of defeat. "Wash your hair and butt out, astrum."

"Yes, sir!"

Valdieren strode deeper in the warm saline water, toward the middle of one end of the figure-8 pool. "It's just, dammit, Curly brings Cheldyne electronics and gear. Nova brings you medals and jewelry! I get rocks and cocks." The last word was mumbled as he sank, rather like his bug a short while before.

Again Sol failed at not laughing and received a nudge with a scary foot and a head shake from the colonel. " Astrum Solvreyil, you have barely taken Ozlietsin out of training zones. You have no idea what she will decide is 'special'. You could well be eating that laughter."

"Yeah, Astrum Pants."

Sol ignored the comment, figuring if he got out of the situation with only a new nickname, he was lucky. As he scrubbed his naked torso, he kept casting his eyes on Kiertus. The older man's plug-grafts were uncovered, since there was no risk of them becoming dry here; the upper one on his left arm was surrounded by a tattooed armband of red and gold feathers which seemed to spell something out in arcane glyphs. Beneath it was a symbol made up of lines and circles which Sol had seen before; it was on a patch adorning an old jacket that hung in his mother's closet. He just now noticed that the circles were a solar system - planets of descending size with a blazing sun in the rear, a harpoon impaled through the largest one. The cable end of the spear made up the old Shandrian rune *mai*, "honor". The same rune was also inked onto Kiertus' left breast, highly visible on the pale flesh near his sternum. It was nested with *vah-shaatu*, "sacrifice". He remembered his father demonstrating the characters and how they evolved from interpretations of fish hooks, wind gusts, and lightning, so fascinated by this magical language not taught in school Sol never asked how he knew so much about it. He splashed his face, then turned to Valdieren.

"Trade me places, captain? Water's a little too shallow here."

They swapped spots and Vald swam over to lean on the side of the pool with his elbows. "Ozzie's pretty close in breed-class to Harmony. What's the worst thing Harmony ever brought to Colonel Ferrox?"

Amused, admiring his shining, sharpened nails, Kiertus reported, "He might disagree with me on this, but I'd have to say the terrapod."

324

"No shit, sir!" Sol exclaimed. "A live one, colonel?"

"Yes indeed." Kiertus stood and stretched his impressive old body, deftly holding the towel in place.

Captain Valdieren's already large eyes were wide under the wet, two-toned locks into which he rubbed gen wax. "What'd he do with that, anyway, sir? Eat it?"

"His other more notorious culinary habits aside," a glacial glance fell on the captain from one baleful yellow and grey orb, "he's rather fond of the legged land mollusks and has a respect for their protected status. It lives aboard his ship, and provides Harmony with a durable playmate by which she can wreak havoc day and night." The inflection dried to exasperation somewhere on the border of disgust. "'Poggo', I believe he calls it."

Sol's face paled and fell. He was less than thrilled about his vision of the future: mucus-covered and pantsless, coaxing radioactive, disgusting, or endangered presents out of the mouth of his new best friend.

A low "murr-rup" came from behind Valdieren, who turned to see Squeak's emerald green head, feelers lowered, gently drop his abducted leggings on the edge of the pool. "Aw, thanks honey. You even rolled them up first." He reached over to pet her. "You're a good bug. I'm sorry I'm a squeamish whiner."

The gen, not entirely sure of her standing, softly head-butted her partner and burbled. Feelers perked tentatively. Valdieren kissed the small end of her head between the infrared-range set of eyes. Squeak tapped all four of her scythe-like legs in a strange little rhythm then leaned against her bond-mate.

"Captain, I know you told me to butt out, but aren't you supposed to meet with Major Parthenos?"

A look of consternation crossed Valdieren's face. "Yes, astrum, thank you for reminding me. Fortunately, it's just up in the lounge." He pointed to the observation window on the far end of the chamber, about a storey from the floor, then climbed from the pool and stood by an air vent in his soggy shirt and briefs. Grabbing his slate from the 'dry basket', he motioned to Sol. "And you should get into kit. You're going to be on my drop team today. Central starboard pipes, 09:00."

The astrum's eyes widened and he climbed from the pool to dry off. His gear was in his bunk locker, and C Pipes were off the opposite hall. He needed to get moving if he wanted to avoid a run through the retriever wing. *Rapid reassignment, indeed.*

Sol had only been aboard about two and a half weeks since his mission to 'reassign' his mother. He met back up with the crew at Todekki Station after leave and shipped off promptly. He was not informed and did not ask why the vessel had unparked from Orminos – the station that served Holtiin's system - and forced him to take a transit from there to another system. Utterly broke from the trip, he was thrilled the flight was free, although he had to stop by the dispensary and plead rations out of Onzillora for the layover. Shortly after his returning to the ship, on the heels of his last tea with Kiertus, they jumped into 'hostile intent' proximity of Kourhos and the entire ship went into a 'critical silence' mode. This meant no one spoke to anyone else unless they were required, curfews were strictly enforced, and half the ship normally accessible to him was off-limits due to 'increased security'. The restrictions were lifted about forty-eight hours later, and they pulled back to orbit one of the planet's tiny moons. He received a terse email – copied to all the paratrooper officers – from Parthenos to 'familiarize yourselves with Verraken and the post-atomic environment of Kourhos' during downtime.

It had hardly been downtime for Sol. Several transfer recruits had been acquired at Todekki and Uayavu and he had been put to work on behalf of Cheldyne and the perpetually overbooked Doctor Laathas. With Laathas' snotty young assistant Gronney, he doled out dosages of combat drugs and double-checked immunizations and charts.

Apparently irked at Parthenos switching Sol's trainer from Val to Myshkor without permission, Kiertus had included breakfast with Val on his schedule. Through the disappointingly professional conversations, he learned that Gyrfru and Val were charged with passing out uniforms to new recruits and assigning people to training simulators. He envied this easier sounding work and the better-humored company, but Sol decided he could not complain about Gronney's lousy attitude or back-breaking hours. At least he was not stuck helping poor Mysh 'training up the sacrificial meat puppets', as Parthenos so grimly put it.

Sol cultivated more sympathy for the major while researching his mother's and master's involvement in the last intergalactic wars. The attack on Ruahanu by Ilv'xukzuiy forces fully re-ignited long dormant hostility between saurtzek and kaffir. Independent of the Archon Empire at the time, the Ruhn begged for protection when an Ilu force amassed in the asteroid belt between their world and the gas giant, Mior. Ambassadorial negotiations were still underway when the raid began. The *Ishulya* was in the area, and took matters into their own hands, orders from the Council be damned. By the time 23rd Strikeforce finally re-captured the largest settlement, Triotos, the surviving POWs were so infested with disease and parasites or gruesomely tortured by Ilu 'scientists' that every last one was mercifully killed. While most history books omitted gory details, the legend of 'two teenage boys and a handful of children escaping the burning city in a barely-functional commercial jumpliner' was retold everywhere.

Other than Ruhn mercenaries or émigrés already working or living within the Archon Empire, only thirty two children were recorded as survivors. Parthenos appeared by name in much documentation and a photograph of him as an adolescent, just a hair younger than Sol, graced one article. The youngster's broken look touched him so deeply he almost failed to notice the absence of the other teenaged pilot's name and image. This led Sol to finally approach the colonel to borrow the relevant volumes from his private collection. "Those don't leave my room," Kiertus responded, buried in a distraction of digital notes. "I allow perusal of those only to men who spend the night."

That invitation was somewhat more daunting than spending training time with Major Parthenos and his gruesome, haunted past. Getting to know these men better only cemented his apprehensions; every trapping of culture, sensitivity, or education that came to light represented to Sol a horrific equal weight in darkness somewhere else in their characters.

My own road in life is strongly influenced by the steps I make in their presence. I have to remember that even when they are being kind to me.

XV. Between Monsters and Holy Men

Damn chromatophore panels, Sol thought, looking down in frustrated amusement at the high-tech multi-use suit of armor clinging to his slender body. His mop-like mud locks flopped into his face, exaggerating the unfortunate comedic effect. *One of the most state-of-the-art personnel items in our military, capable of an array of offensive, defensive, and surveillance functions… aesthetically designed to resemble its traditional historic countpart, the armor of the elite Shandrian Gen-Knights. And I look like a casino clown in it.*

Still, he looked forward to working with Valdieren and had high hopes for the day. He almost vibrated with anticipation, so excited, in fact, he could not keep his armor at default coloration. Every time his mind wandered, it responded to his mood with elaborate luminescent patterns. This was only acceptable during special parade displays, so he fought to control it.

A mission alone with Captain V would be cool. We haven't had a real chat since we parted ways on Holtiin. I wonder if he broke his vow with that IGN lady?

His hopes were partially crushed by the appearance of Astrum Gronney, sans bug and carrying a small chemical kit of some sort. Sol scowled at the man's bright colored dye-job. That was cheating, to the red-haired haki. *If you had a full head of locks it wouldn't look bad, the blue and lilac, but with the sides shaved, and that top knot? You look more of a fuckknob than I do. And I was born a freak. Douche. Not everyone with long ears has class, I guess. The sad part is I wouldn't even care if you weren't so half-assed about your work…*

"I hope I don't get paired with you," the slight-framed pureblood sneered, flipping his top-knot in an emphatically dismissive manner.

Sol did not break his proper regimental posture; the smooth parts of his body armor displayed a simple, lustrous black. "The feeling is utterly mutual, I assure you, Astrum Gronney." Further words were spared as a couple newbie paratroopers with analog 'chutes walked into the hangar. They saluted the glowering men and took up waiting positions alongside.

What remained of his poor suffering hope peeled up and blew away as Captain Valdieren strode in with 1.98 meters of sour-tempered, furry Ruhn behind him.

To add insult to injury, the major jabbed a finger precisely into the unarmored section of his chest and growled, "Well hello, Red. You're with me today."

"Sir, yes, sir! It'll be an honor, sir!" *Jerk sometimes or not, he's a war hero, and I can learn a lot from him. I just have to police every little gesture and every last word out of my damn mouth. And this armor!*

Behind Parthenos' back, Valdieren assumed a rigid posture, faced the line and stamped an armored boot, barking, "Attention!"

The major's malicious smirk continued as he stepped backwards to stand authoritatively beside the captain, back straight and thick arms crossed. Sol wanted to shave the smug, hairy bastard in his sleep, then concentrated back the rusty color creeping up from the corners of his panels. *It's all calculated to slip me up, to test my fitness as the colonel's astrum. I can't spend energy being angry at him.*

Sol settled his eyes on his superiors. Both were armored, although the major's outfit lacked a panel kilt so all could see he spent the exorbitant amount on a Vektaar Syherion codpiece instead of a standard Vsorb. This optional armor item became available at the rank of lieutenant but ordering it required an application process and sucked down a good two month's wages. The Sypherion, a piece of semi-sentient bio-armor, had a number of peculiar properties aside from genital protection. Cheldyne had one which he claimed he received 'when leaving Exo Corps'. He attempted to explain its interface and conduction capabilities, something about 'pulse storage', 'backup weaponry', and 'hands free interaction with any military vehicle', but utterly lost the boy when he casually mentioned, "And if you're bored, you can fuck it!"

Images of Parthenos growling and writhing around in nothing but his Sypherion filled Sol's mind. The only thing that suppressed a kaleidoscope across his uniform was the desire to puke. He feigned a cough-sneeze and received a quiet, polite, "Take care" from the captain before Val launched into briefing.

"Alright, troops. We're jumping into airspace in what is not technically Imperial domain. Make sure your slates and helmets are sync'd, log in, and download the info file linked from your inboxes." Val waited while they fiddled with devices. "Astrum Solvreyil will help you on the Dash if you have any problems."

Me? Am I senior jumper in this group? Guess I am. Weird. Gronney had been in the unit a year longer than Sol, but he was abandoned by his first bug and generally kept to the pharm lab. He learned to jump on a non-sentient parachute when need be, but Laathas, Wyvern, or Cheldyne usually went instead when a medic was needed on field operations. Gronney admitted he was more of a science officer; he was in Star Assault for a short-cut to full citizenship to attend Ryzaa University and work for Vektaar Corp. Even wealthy pure-bloods born off-world had trouble getting citizenship on the home world, which pretty much annihilated the one conspiracy theory Sol ever believed. Gronney wanted it badly enough to be sterilized and face a 22 month chance at getting blown to essential salts over three to five years of dreary but safe rotting on an IGN research ship.

One hell of a short-cut, thought Sol as he tested equipment links. Mysh had walked him through the suit's 're/com' system; it recorded shots fired and kills through his rifle, images or heat signatures through his goggles, the voices of people standing near him via a clever system scattered through the helmet and armor. Mysh also taught how to switch said system to a sonic weapon. Even with the surgical enhancement to his ears, Sol thought it sounded unpleasant, so he preferred the vibration field. This disturbed light and sound around the wearer, creating an illusion of multiple targets for anyone attempting to attack. This plus the passive chromatophoric camouflage (turned off for the briefing) made Archon paratroopers difficult to target. *Or so they tell me…*

"Are we all squared away, folks? Good enough? OK. Here are the bare bones: the planet we're visiting today has beseeched Archos for protection from encroaching Ilu operations. However, the terms of their treaty include a stipulation that their theocracy stays in place and they hold relative autonomy, similar to the nation Mantzaar on the homeworld."

The four men cast looks at one another, shrugged and nodded. Seemed fair. Val paused before continuing. "However. The Kourhonoi government is controlled by a strongly pro-human faction; we've received consistent intelligence they mistreat the small groups of kaffa and haki who remain in their dominion."

Yeah, I remember. I hope Celita is doing okay…

Major Parthenos made a nasty face and interjected, "You're welcome to some of the reports, if you care. But that's not actually why we're here today."

Captain Valdieren nodded. "The territory of Oun'a-akal has been unoccupied by Kourhonoi for about five centuries, since a nuclear exchange between warring

330

factions cleared it. This also threw civilization on Kourhos back to the Dark Ages; they've been struggling ever since. The Theocrat declared it 'haunted land', claiming the, ahem, 'spirits of elves', who made up the bulk of the population there, would destroy anyone who entered. The Archon Empire has been secretly using this wasteland for training and testing for the past few centuries, including small bases by which to observe Ilu operations in that sector of space. The ruling faction seems none the wiser."

"Recently, however, intelligence has reported unusual sightings in the wasteland. While I would like each of you to treat this as a simple training run, keep your eyes and ears open and be prepared to use your cameras." Valdieren tapped his goggles emphatically. "You'll basically be playing tag; you are paired to another member of the team. Once you land, make your way to that individual using your tracker. You'll be timed, but if your route yields photographs useful to intel, points will be added to your overall score."

Only Gronney seemed interested in the scoring part. "Excuse me, captain, sir, but, what do we win, sir?"

Valdieren chuckled.

"Good question, Astrum Gronney," answered Parthenos. "Two alcohol ration coupons and a potential for career advancement… but I'm sure most of you only care about the first part. You assholes board the fuckin' drop ship already and let's get this party started."

A chorus of "Yes, sirs!" was lost in the scramble. Ozzie hopped on Sol's back and he heaved into the Dash. He guided the rookies – Seamus and Hamusi - through adjusting their seat niches and locking in. Both needed assistance with their injections. Many officers preferred not to self-inject but it had more to do with a kaffir ideal of camaraderie than any revulsion over the process. These two were outright uncomfortable with the way the syrigun entered their grafts. After administering to them, he popped his own into his bare, graftless right shoulder, unaffected by their reactions or the pain. *The tattoo was way worse. You are hopeless cannon fodder. Jumpers my ass. No wonder Chel didn't issue you bugs.*

A gruff voice called from the cockpit. "Astrum Solvreyil!" Sol leaned through the opening to see Parthenos in the gunner's seat, interface cabling trailing down his folded arms, a look of condescending approval on his face. He nodded curtly. "Keep up the good work, kid."

331

Demeaning way of saying it or not, he meant that. "Sir! Yes, sir!"

"Astrum, would you do the final briefing once we're in atmosphere?"

Sol had only sat through a few 'drop speeches', and never given one. He felt fortunate for once in not having pretty long ears, because they would have drooped to his shoulders when he saluted and said, "Sir! Certainly, yes,sir!" *No wonder kaffir don't believe in lying; must be tough to fake it with twitchy ears…*

He secured himself and observed an unsettling stillness amid the crew. He petted one of Ozzie's scythes and wondered what was unsaid at the briefing.

The ship's computer spoke in an eerie feminine voice "Jump sequence initiated. Make final preparations."

Valdieren's voice followed. "Astrum Solvreyil. How's it lookin' in the cabin?"

"Sir! Everything is stowed and secure, sir!" The only thing he had to worry about at this point was Ozzie, who was fast asleep in his back harness.

"Excellent and thank you, astrum!"

"Transfer in ten minutes," intoned the ship.

The rookies looked towards the floor and closed their eyes. Gronney was reading something on his slate and cast the nearest speaker a hairy stink-eye.

"Astrum Gronney, I would appreciate if you put that away before the timer gets to three minutes."

Gronney grunted. "Yeah, yeah, I was planning to."

A cough issued from the cockpit. "'Yeah yeah I was planning to' what, astrum?"

"Put away my slate, Major Parthenos?"

"Errrrrrnt", returned Parthenos' best imitation of a game show buzzer. "Wrong."

Gronney seemed annoyed and confused, with a hint of dread. "Excuse me, sir?"

Sol secretly enjoyed the exchange, hands folded peacefully in his lap, face expressionless.

"Who were you addressing, Astrum Gronney? Try again."

The medical assistant made a face as if handed a dung salad. "I was planning on putting away my slate, Astrum Solvreyil."

The major's voice reached a level of singsongy smarminess. He clearly watched a lot of human comvision on his surveillance missions. *It figures, a sadist like him would get off on garbage like that.*

"And he's still getting it wrong, bugs and gentlemen. We're not sure he's going to make it to the final round!"

From what Sol could read on his face, Gronney was not ready to stumble onto Parthenos' shit list, but he objected to what the major indicated.

"Transfer in. Seven. Minutes."

"Time's running out! Would another contestant care to take the answer?"

This brought glee to the larger of the two rookies. "Ooh, sir, I will, I will!"

Valdieren tossed in a "Bzzzt!" He probably needed this interlude of banter. He lacked the enthusiasm for smarmy host voice, but seemed amused. "Contestant Seamus? How should Astrum Gronney have responded?"

Cheerfully the trooper declared, "'Yes, sir, I will do so, Astrum Solvreyil, sir!'"

"Oh! We have a winner!" Major Parthenos called back.

Gronney peevishly regarded the cockpit. "Are you shitting me, sir? We're the same rank."

The funny voice was gone. "While that's technically true, I also put him in charge. So put your fucking slate away and shut your mouth."

"Transfer in. Two. Minutes."

Sol smiled cheerfully at Gronney, not just for the minor victory, but because his combat pharms were kicking in and he had come to enjoy the sensation of 'shift' in this particular state of awareness. He looked forward to the hallucinations. They reminded him of ancient artwork in the tiny Shandrian Heritage Museum at the old Royal Palace. It was taboo to discuss jump hallucinations in any detail, an old pilot's superstition. He did not need to discuss them, though. Just to -

Whoooooooooooooooooooooshhhhh

- everything stretched and bent into tendrils of negative light, ultraviolet, distorted faces, dissolving orbs, the stars exhaled, galaxies sang, and he was reborn -

- feel it. To be there and experience it as had aeons of his ancestors.

It took a second or two for his perception to right itself from the inversion it had just undergone. He stretched his shoulders and Ozzie woke and nipped at him. "Ready to go, girl?"

She chirped affirmatively. He unhooked himself from the alcove and stood, holding onto a rung suspended above him since the craft was in motion, now inside a planetary atmosphere, with full natural gravity. The bug seemed substantially heavier now. He took a spot near the aft hatch and watched the crew come round from their respective shift-dazes.

Astrum Solvreyil bombed public speaking a few times in Framework, but did pretty well at acting courses and stage club, and with a few notes from observing other Star Assault officers, he went with improvisation. *I'm going to need to get over the apprehension for my debate forum anyway.* "Attention!" Sol called as commandingly as he could. Thankfully, his voice did not crack. He pulled down his goggles and tapped the left side. "Please test your altimeters. All should currently read," he paused to check, "'4.42 kilometers'. If you read anything else, recalibrate your slate and reboot your system immediately."

The other three (and out of his sight, Valdieren) checked their gear and nodded, looking around to confirm: yes, everything was cool.

"We'll drop at different spots. Use your trackers to find whomever you're assigned. Test your trackers now by finding unit 'Echo' in this cabin." A show of hands pointed toward Sol. "Great, that's what I wanted to see, boys. Remember, when we leave this ship, we leave our names behind. Out there, it's call signs only. Or numbers, if you're still on the meat rack."

The crew nodded. He felt pretty good about this, but maybe it was just the enhanced boldness from his prescription atquel and vyddarin cocktail.

Ozzie chirruped excitedly, knowing all this gesturing and yelling meant she would get to fly in open air soon. In doing so, she reminded him of something crucial; he thanked her by way of silently squeezing a foreleg.

"Heads up. If you're on an analog 'chute, keep your altimeter app open until you land. When you reach 'optimal', it will flash red. Your smartchute should automatically deploy at that time, but if it does not, you must manually deploy it." He gestured to where said manual pull cord would be were he wearing a parachute instead of a sentient being. *Glad I have you and your instincts and I don't have to worry about my own scatterbrain deploying anything at the right time.* "If for some reason you need to abandon your smartchute, don't worry, just cut the cords with your utility knife, they're biodegradable. Once deployed, they only last about 14 hours tops in the open air. I'm going to dive first; Checkmate will direct the drop order of the rest of you. Honor and Sacrifice!"

He saluted, pulled up his re-breather, and backed towards the exit. Grabbing a rung on either side tightly, rifle compressed on his hip, bug secured, he called, "Ready when you are, Bootstrap!"

Captain Valdieren activated the sphincter-like hatch and Sol felt the suction grab hold. Wind obliterated any other sound. He exhaled, bent his knees, and released the rungs with a spring, repelling himself away from the Dash.

This was his first daytime drop, and the view above the clouds was amazing, a strange fluffy sunlit landscape. He enjoyed the freefall part of jumping; time stopped for a few seconds and he was absolutely free. In a combat drop, one was supposed to focus on the objective, or on ramping up one's Imperial zeal, or something similar that would theoretically increase combat effectiveness. In this case, he cleared his mind and allowed the sky to rush past. Ozlietsin reveled in the gales, spread her wings early to let them be buffeted, diving back toward their intended coordinates when the blasts died down. The behavior startled Sol at first, but realizing she was still on target, he let her go undisciplined. Tzanshidi had shown him how to use his collapsed rifle as a control baton for her, a thing less cruel than it seemed. *Practical, actually. Freefall's too loud for voice commands and teaching a series of reminder taps is way easier than getting your bug to wear a com helmet.*

It was an interesting lesson. To demonstrate to the gen they were not being singled out and abused, he, Okallin, and Tzanshidi took turns hitting one another with partially charged chon-sticks while avoiding vocalization. The exercises were performed near the tower's raucous water processing unit to drive the point home. Other paratroopers and gen trainers could use the backs of their hands or some other, gentler non-verbal command set, but with the omyoi type being so freethinking and stubborn, a slightly more abrupt method was required.

And here I was worried that it would ruin your wonderful spirit, Sol mused as they busted through a cloudbank and rolled.

When Ozzie straightend out and fully spread her wings, Sol noticed his altimeter reading and snapped back to reality. He pressed his left forearm against his dormant rifle and it came alive, extending its grip tendrils and seeking the flesh of his upper arm through his sleeve valves. Pressure, stinging, an electric tingle, and the gun was part of him. He appreciated direct interface with bio-ware and not needing plug-grafts, in spite of everything that accompanied the ability.

Chel told me Parthenos got the bulk of his tattoo work done to conceal scar tissue, mostly what built up from repeated tendril violation. Maybe I'll do something like that, someday, although the scars alone look cool... That however does not.

Without the clouds to conceal it, this place, half the planet away from Tukodok, was the definition of ugly. Rocky terrain was punctuated by grim craters. Dark, cool spots in deeper crevices indicated precipitation at some distant past, but the terrain was otherwise dry. A charitable heart unwise to the ways of humans might chalk it up to volcanic activity at first glance. *Even volcanoes have plants that call them home; only the factories of hate make fire like that.*

Ozzie screeched; Sol felt it in his bones. He braced and unclicked the straps. She continued to hold him, briefly, then released her grip over a stretch of cracked dried mud. Sol slammed onto the ground feet first, grateful for the shock absorption provided by his gear. He straightened his body and surveyed his surroundings, idly fingering his collars.

The 'Missionotes' app opened, superimposed over the transparent goggle display map, highlighting his 'target'. Sol shook his head and commanded the map to zoom out. He compared dismal scenery against the virtual terrain diagram to pick a route. All obstacles seemed abysmal, mostly involving harshly angled climbs. He set his course with an exasperated sigh and trudged towards the massive crater that obviously drained the lake in the first place. *I would get Parthenos, it just figures. I bet this is another test.*

Ozzie shadowed him at a distance, hovering, emitting a low hum. Between her and the sensitive hardware built into his helmet, he would be aware of anything approaching from a good distance. Not like there was anything out here besides the crew of the ship from which he just leapt. He had not seen so much as an insect, although according to his suit, the radiation levels were low and air would be fairly breathable without his mask.

He looked up at his companion. "Place is a shithole, huh?"

The gen returned an affirmative chirp. This place was clearly devoid of snacks.

…

Sol scaled the lake's former shore to an outcropping of sad straggly grass. It was mostly ochre-grey, so he had not recognized it as vegetation from above. It crunched unpleasantly beneath his boots. Parthenos was in a valley 2.8 km beyond the low rocky hills on which Sol now gazed. Dense cloud cover made the place even more dismal. The papery, pathetic grass ended abruptly in a wide, crumbed concrete strip, once a road perhaps, although barren of markings that would have indicated function. The old thoroughfare stretched toward the hills; logic and convenience dictated his path.

The decrepit highway took him past vast fields of crunchy grass strewn with blackened rocks and periodic barren patches. When the wind blew, ash drifted in wavy lines across the road. As they neared the hills, the massive road forked, and his suit's sensors detected mild atmospheric toxins.

Sol was unconcerned about Ozzie; genadri could adapt to a large variety of poisonous substances or even go a good period of time without breathing if the need arose. *I'm not about to remove my mask, so there's no immediate threat to either of us.* Where the road forked, there was a brackish mess; oily fluids and blackened humps of grass and debris surrounded the raised concrete on all sides. Ozzie flew higher, presumably because it smelled revolting. As he chose the right hand fork, something shiny caught his eye and he went to investigate.

The source of the sheen was a small oily pool on the pavement. There was nothing particularly special about that save the question of how it got there. He took a picture; it was probably nothing but it was the most uncharacteristic thing he observed thus far. As he skirted the pool, he noted a regular shape in the dirt and gravel where the concrete reverted to its components. He bent to examine; the far-too-regular rounded depression held an indentation resembling a pointed 'T' roughly his height in length, distinctly moist.

While he stooped there, head tilted, marveling over this strange impression, Ozzie landed nearby and gingerly sidled over on her dainty scythes. She sniffed at the shape, then backed up and assumed what was referred to by gen-handlers as 'Phase One'. Her front end dropped slightly, legs positioned for a pounce as her lower head plates slid back and bunched up and her eyes went from dome-shaped to a more elliptical form. Her feelers lay back across her head and she emitted a low, crackling hiss. This posture sent folks unfamiliar with the creatures running and alerted those who were to take caution.

"Whoa, girl." He looked at the hole again; something was familiar about it but he could not place it. He grabbed another picture and a bit of video of Ozlietsin's actions over the hole. Adding in a scan of the surrounding terrain, he sent the file to Valdieren with a note of 'WTF?'

Sol moved cautiously, scanning for more prints. He spotted what appeared to be half of one down the road embankment not far from the first. He acquired more shots as Ozzie took to the air again, still growly and disconcerted. He knelt by some dark, oily fluid on the broken road and commanded his armor, "Content read." The response was a flurry of chemical names; he recognized a few salts and enzymes which indicated the origin was at least partially living.

Sol hurried to the hills, dredging his memory for that shape. A biotech creature made it, meaning it originated off-world. The surviving kaffir here barely got on in grungy segregated tenements; they did not engineer biotechnological marvels. *Ryzaan historians cite Kourhos as an example why humans shouldn't self-govern; the GPM sites it as to why humans should be food or exterminated. I can't really agree with the GPM but the Ryzaans might have a point.*

The idea was reinforced when he reached the top of the short rocky outcropping. Sol turned around, allowing for a panoramic view of the scene from crater to hills on one side and from hills to distant mountains on the other. Seen from this vantage, he saw these rocky mounds and the land on either side once hosted a good-sized city. He landed on the blast side; little remained but ash-drifted foundations overgrown with anemic dune grass. The far side bore decayed skeletons of eroded stone and bent corroded metal that stretched for several kilometers in all directions, violated periodically by copses of blighted shrubs and further stressed by the grasp of thorny vines. There was little green; all was pallid and deathly. Wind whipped ash into piles in stray corners and buried struggling clumps of weeds.

Atomic weapons. He shook his chitin-armored head. *What a stupid fuckin' idea.*

He proceeded down what remained of the highway, which continued through the hills partially buried by land-slides and rubble. Easy going it was not; he found new appreciation for his kneepads, for the carapace-skirt that covered his crotch and buttocks, and for the underarmor's rubbery resilience. *Guys who skip their undershirts to look intimidating and trust their carapace's self-healing membrane are nuts. I'd rather be modest and non-threatening than be cut to ribbons by sharp rocks,* he mused, inching down a fallen pillar. It abraded the parts of his hands not covered by response-sleeves even though it left his membranous gloves unscathed. *And man, what about wind burn during the drop? What if my bug slipped? She'd gash me. How much can these membranes really take, anyway? Screw that.*

Sol followed the tracker beacon down shadowed, pock-marked side streets, careful of debris, sticking as close to the center as possible in case anything flanking the road collapsed. The path wound down a mild grade and the lower and further he got from the crater, the more intact the ruins. Architecture was a mix of Archon and local styles; hewn stone was combined with cultivated coral, but everything was long dead and beyond repair. Vegetation grew on what remained of the elven-style buildings; the human ones were sterile broken skeletons. His sensors said Ozzie landed behind him; he turned.

She appeared normal again, kind of cute, with her large round shiny eyes and perky little antennae and funny rounded pyramid of a head. "What's up, Oz?" he asked through the mask mic. "Need something?"

Oz tilted her head at the mountains, pressed her antennae together, and clicked.

Sol nodded. "Something you want to look at over there? OK well, stay safe. I need you." *Not that I really want to be alone in this creepy dead city but I'm about to go find the guy you hate most.* He approached and gave her a scratch.

Ozzie chirped, backed up, and launched. Sol watched her fly off before returning to his path. *Chel and Tzanshidi both say bugs can smell us for miles and find us easily, and if there's trouble,, our hardware can track individual gen. I've tested it on the ship, but it seems like a lot of faith to put in a suit of armor, living or otherwise.*

As he rounded a corner, tiny hairs on the back of his neck tickled inside his uniform's thin hood. Sol twitched, checked his equipment; there were no life readings, not even Ozzie returning. He scanned miserable empty buildings and rubble; nothing moved. However, he could not escape the sensation of *company*.

A large, regular pit came into view, possibly the foundation site of an ambitious building never constructed, vegetation creeping up its sides. Sol leaned over the edge; the terrain below was verdant and lush. At the bottom of the eroded embankment to his right was a mostly intact, relatively recent small building. It was partially concealed by wreckage and living trees of a fair age. It seemed of human design, although quaint, humble, encrusted with lichen and moss. Shaded by nearby trees was a healthy-looking pond. He turned communications on as he climbed down. The soles of his armor boots transformed subtly to compensate for the mossy slickness, forcing a sudden pause for stability. His voice warbled. "Come in, Checkmate."

"Bitchin'. Ya found me." *What a weirdo.* "Entrance is behind that metal sheet."

Air in the depression read free of abnormal radiation or dangerous microbes. Sol popped up his goggles and dropped his mask. Between large mossy rocks and the trunk of a decent young tree was enough of an opening to reach a leaning corroded metal sheet, salvaged from somewhere in the city above no doubt. He ducked behind this to a door and entered the little structure, which on closer inspection seemed constructed wholly from salvage.

"Back here," came the familiar voice. The first room was arrayed to look like an abandoned private home; Sol could not tell if it had been once or if it were a ruse. The stories about Archon military intel often included such things. He found another opening, barely visible between two off-kilter bookshelves, stepped over ragged boxes, and around an el-shaped corridor.

Place didn't look this big from outside. We must be inside the hill now. Clever design. Parthenos stood by a panel; when he hit a sequence, a wall slid into place turning the spot behind the book cases back into a storage area at one end

340

of a decaying hovel.

"How was the walk?" the major asked as he led Sol to a room with pale walls, two of which were outfitted with ostrekaal counters. Opposite the entry was high-PSI clarithane opening onto what resembled a hospital ICU. A digital notebook sat open on a simple, clean desk near the entrance. A water heating device sat on the counter nearest the desk; the major poured him a cup of tea.

"This place is disgusting, uh, Checkmate." *I almost said 'sir'; call signs only down here. I'm nervous. It's his fault.* "The planet I mean. This house is kinda cool." *Except why does it have a laboratory hidden in it? I would've thought this room was just for water and soil sampling if it wasn't for that creepy hospital room. Are we researching the diseases?*

Parthenos laughed and sat at the desk, continuing to go through an open folder of paper files and record chips, taking notes on the device. "Yes. Beats what the Ilu do to populated planets but it's still horrible."

"Did Bootstrap forward the images I sent to him?"

Deep indigo orbs gazed up at him. It was difficult to see his pupils aboard the *Sanjeera*; the lighting there turned his irises nearly black. Clear as day, he saw them: triple-lobed like a dashinki. He froze. *Must be the Ruhn heritage. Does he wear contact lenses normally? I don't see the funny glint.* "Yes," said the major icily. "You don't need to worry about what that is yet, Echo."

Sol nodded and gave a sharply abbreviated salute.

"Is there something else?"

"It's going to sound stupid, but I felt like I was being watched in the city above. There were no signs of life, though, on my readers."

The look continued. "Really. Did you happen to mark your coordinates at the time you felt it?"

Aw, shit. "No, but I remember the exact corner, it's the last tall building in the city before the slope into here. 47 degrees and something."

Parthenos nodded. "Right. We have a camera and some reading equipment up there. What you felt was the signature of it's power source. You need an upgrade to identify that stuff from a distance, but you're hyper-sensitive, which will be a boon to you in the long run."

"Uh, gotcha." *Creepy smile. Nasty stare was better. Please turn back around.*

Thankfully, he went back to work. "Get me the locked orange crate over there, Echo." Parthenos did not look up. "I need to get through as much of this as I can, so I need it sooner rather than later."

Sol glowered at the lovely black mane of hair, made a face, and said nothing. A proximity alarm sounded inside his helmet. "What the fuck?"

"It's called an order, you know, orders, those things you take, in the military, when it's your job?"

"No, not that - my proximity sensor just -" The major was armored but his headgear hung off the chair. He shook his head violently and immediately was afoot rectifying the situation as Sol replaced goggles and mask.

"Not ours. Stay alert." He lowered himself slightly, pressed his large, muscular hands before him, and quietly uttered, "Opcam. Full rec."

He's a conduit too but he does that posture Mysh taught me to charge anyway. I've never had to use it; I start charging the moment I put it on… that's probably a bad thing. He looks kinda cool when he does it. I bet I would look like a dork. "Opcam," Sol commanded his armor.

Parthenos flicked switches as they blended into their surroundings. The room was dark and the laptop was stowed. They moved cautiously forward.

Two orange lights moved outside the house on their mini maps. They crept from the secret room and filed through the closet, closing everything behind them. There was a small window, mostly boarded over, in the main room. They flanked it silently; the major nodded at Sol, who leaned slowly toward the time-fogged glass. Vaguely visible in the vale were two humanoid shapes sporting heavy combat gear. A symbol reminiscent of a hammer growing from a globe decorated their shoulders and chests.

Leaning back to his side of the wall, Sol spoke quietly via helmet-to-helmet,

"Theocracy?"

Parthenos peeked through the window and nodded as he returned to the wall. "Holy Order of Okurod. They have a camp about 10 kilometers from here; the Theocracy denies it."

"How did they get so close unnoticed?"

The voice seemed darkly amused. "That's just the question, ain't it?" Parthenos took a deep breath, clenching and unclenching his fists slowly.

We're not supposed to be here either. "Awaiting orders."

"Stay put. I'm going to take care of this. Do not emulate my behavior under any circumstance; I will debrief you later." The major slipped out into broken sunlight. He remained camouflaged until away from the door. They failed to notice him skulking in the moss, creeping up the other side of the pond.

Their armor was either metal or ceramic - Sol could not really tell - over heavy fabric fatigues. They bore rad counters and clunky-looking ballistic weapons. Their heads looked tiny in all the gear, lower half of their faces covered by awkward gas filters and the tops by hat-like helmets with visor eye-shields. Sol turned up his slate mic and set it near a wall crack, hoping to catch the exchange.

Parthenos made his presence known a few leaps from them. He was intimidating, even next to their bulk. Broad-shouldered, tall, clad head to toe in black save the rib-like piping on his armor (trimming the hip and thorax panels, highlighting the overlapping helmet segments, and emphasizing the nasty mandible quality of the re-breather), his goggles like green bug eyes, glittering oddly when light caught them. There was a pulse rifle, uncompressed and massive, on his back, his usual cresc pistol on his hip, but also two large service pistols of the kind MPs wore - cartridge weapons designed to do various damage to people while doing minimal damage to bio-hulls and so forth.

Where'd he get those? It's not like you can walk into a cornershop and get one. With that blue finish, they look like Rim Patrol pounders...

One of the men jumped and pointed his gun at the massive elf. He yelled something in Kourhonoi. *Dammit, of course.*

Parthenos spoke, but he remained calm and was thereby nearly inaudible within the house. Curiosity gnawed at Sol as he watched through the tiny window.

....

"This is Holy Ground! You need to leave at once!" cried the man with the gun, whose insignia indicated the rank of lieutenant.

"You may cease yelling at any time. I can hear you just fine." Parthenos lifted his goggles and unhooked his mask. He smiled, raising his hands.

The gun remained trained on him. The second soldier snarled, "Archon scum. What are you doing here?"

"Investigating reports of Ilu activity in the area, by order of the Peace Council."

The humans looked at one another but the gun stayed stiffly aimed at Parthenos.

"Is that so?"

"You two wouldn't know anything about any saurtzek merchant ships being spotted landing out this way, would you? No, of course not. You believe in human supremacy."

The second soldier, a commandant by his insignia, drew his weapon, visibly angered. He barely held the gun steady. "You need to get off this land. It is sacred and you do not belong here."

I smell guilt mixed with the fear in your sweat. Gotcha, bastards. "To be fair," Parthenos stretched, flexed his thoracic panels. "This land is sacred because it's haunted by vindictive elven spirits, am I correct?"

The human men again exchanged glances. Both seemed profoundly nervous.

"Well, I am elven and quite vindictive." He resumed his surrender posture, palms out, grinning.

.....

Frustrated, Sol inched his way out into the mossy rocks to watch, even though he could understand little. He turned on recording so he could watch later and

344

practice Kourhonoi. *He said I shouldn't emulate him, not that I shouldn't record. If he wants me to destroy it, I will. I'll need it though if I have to call 'distress'.* One man, apparently top brass from the extra insignia on his cap-helmet and breastplate, had his large, ungainly weapon pointed at the major, and the other cast nervous glances around, shifted his feet, held his weapon with both hands but kept it pointed at the ground.

Parthenos grinned, but his hands were up as if he would allow them to take him prisoner. Someone less versed in ma'at-shi and pulse use might have missed the tenseness of the major's back or the pre-combat position of his feet. With goggles set to proper frequency, Sol noted energy pulsing through the black carapace. *He's probably electrifying it in case they try to grab him. Good tactic. Huh… that's a lot of pulse, though; I can feel it from here.*

    ….

"On the contrary, it is you who should get off of my land." For both visual and auditory emphasis, he slid his extended tongue between his unsheathed fangs on the slowly enunciated final syllables.

Furious, the human leader yelled, "You're coming with us for questioning!"

He mocked the man's tone. "Is that so?"

One could almost hear the frantic saliva spattering the inside his mask as he sputtered: "Get on your knees or I'll shoot, you pointy-eared heathen scum!"

His dark, smiling lips formed a single word: "No."

The knight-commandant attempted to pull the trigger, and that was the end of his mortal cares.

    ….

It occurred so fast it was difficult for Sol to follow. The second man to draw his weapon yelled: the Ruhn responded calmly but continued to charge his armor. Things intensified in the dialog; the human shifted to fire but at the same moment, Parthenos made a single, wave-like motion as if rolling something from his left hand, up his arm, across his shoulder, and down the other hand, discharging a massive ball of energy.

The armor's unknown material arced dramatically as the flesh inside reacted as if hit by a speeding train. A spray of blood and fleshy hunks spattered around Parthenos, across trees, rocks, and the man's subordinate. Blasted armor clattered to the ground. Rattled beyond coherence, the other knight dropped his gun and ran. Parthenos, smiling, deftly drew his left pistol and shot a cartridge into the escapee's air tank; he fell convulsing as black vapor emanated from the hole in the tank. He twitched for a bit and then ceased moving entirely.

"Fanatic assholes," spat Parthenos in Unified Archon as he walked to the intact corpse. He kicked it once, then knelt and began an unceremonious examination. Sol crouched, horrified and nauseous, in the rocks.

"Come here, Echo. Don't unmask." The major re-covered his own face.

Sol de-cloaked and approached, carefully stepping over the mess.

Parthenos gestured to the corpse beside which he knelt. "Take me up on a bet?"

Seriously gonna barf, and you want to gamble? "Um. Depends on the wager."

"This body's full of worms. I'll bet you two drinks at the Come Down if we dissect it, it's crawlin'."

"Nasty, man." *Oh, can't say rank or sir, so you say man and dude. I get it!* "How about I buy you two drinks next time we're at Pachar, we don't dissect that, and you tell me how you drew that conclusion."

"Well I'd love to do it your way, but we have to clean up these corpses. I'll still take the drinks, kid, but there's no getting out of this. Text Bootstrap that we need time, I'm giving you a ma'at-shi lesson, okay, and while you're doing that, walk back to the lab and get two green kits from cabinet four and an orange kit from cabinet one. There are carry-alls in the tall locker. Go."

Eyes wide and head full of bad, Sol took out his slate and walked toward the shack. He opened the video folder and saw the new file sitting there staring back at him. He was about to delete it then hit 'send' instead, entering a delicately worded message in the description.

This can't be protocol. I just want to talk to Val about it, that's all. He deleted the sent file and entered the lab. *And don't we have Retrievers for this?*

XVI. Vengeance of the Fallen

"How many times are you going to watch that, sir?" He fidgeted uncomfortably as the long, manicured finger again tapped the symbol for 'Play' on the screen.

"Can't stop. I'm fascinated by his unsettling speed. He pulses off before the trigger is two-thirds depressed. Even with a gun that primitive, it's impressive."

Val looked away. In the process of sitting here, translating, and discussing it with Kiertus, he had seen that poor Templar commandant detonate twenty-two times. That included slow-motion, double speed, and reverse. Reverse was worst, because it made the origin of parts splattered on the deputy inarguable, and clarified what Parthenos stepped over uncaringly as he put down the second.

"And he recovers fast enough to pull and discharge his pistol before the other has run a meter. Simply amazing." He noticed the younger officer's body language. "I'm still not great with spoken Kourhonoi, so I appreciate the subtitles, Val. You're a model member of this division."

I sure don't feel it, sir. If he saw that meaty eruption again, he would vomit. Instead he gazed at the old man's impassive face. Val shifted, wondered if he could leave, cast his eyes to the pretty picture on the wall: a soaking wet, shirtless kaffa with sand-colored ringlets and crimson eyes, leaned against a huge tree, vines gripped one-handed, smiling as if inviting the viewer into his arboreal nest. It had been shot for the Academy Annual but dropped before publication; the charming marine captain it featured was tried and convicted for the murder of every adult human male in a remote village. *I am not like these men. But I don't think they were, once, either. What's going to flip my switch? Or was it already flipped and I just didn't notice? Maybe I am these men...*

Kiertus, almost on cue, leaned forward and tapped the 'Pause' symbol. "Bring Solvreyil here, please." No formality, no rank. A fatherly gentle voice making a simple request. But Colonel Kiertus Sheriden was an officer with nothing to prove and none to impress. The only reason he was not in black armor beside the queen was a badly weighted war-crimes tribunal.

You took a fall, a big one, for the sake of your commander and your people.

That's what a god among men you are. I hope the history books of latter centuries remedy the omissions of my own. Val shook out his half-asleep arms, folded across his chest for nearly two hours to keep his ribs from sympathetic pain. He retrieved his slate from the desk, scrolled to 'Echo', and hit 'call'.

"I appreciate your effort," smiled Kiertus, elegantly poking the 'cancel' button, "but if you would check your locater, you can just walk in and wake him."

...

Roughly nine hours prior, Sol stood, smock over his armor, in a sterile lab watching the major specify evidence of an advanced verchyne infestation in a poisoned corpse. His skin crawled and threw up once; fragments lingered in his mask in spite of clearing it.

Parthenos laughed, scalpel in hand, as he offered a suction collector with the other. He demonstrated on where to hook it through the breathing apparatus before passing it over. "It happens, kid; worms runnin' around inside living people is gnarly, there's just no two ways about that."

Sol tried to laugh, too, puked in mask and all. The rebreather was designed to move fluid away from the nose and mouth and 'digest' it, but the process was uncomfortable and foul-smelling. The vacuum option was preferable when available. *I can't believe these things are real. I thought they were an urban legend. Gods...* "Sorry, just not cut out for surgery or science, I guess."

"Trust me that science, strictly speaking, is furthest from my fields of interest. Eventually you'll get the handbook upgrade with dissection and rendering chapters; it is a good idea to get familiar. You'll see and touch things worse than this." He leaned towards the flayed body, targeted something with his tweezers, and deftly removed it. "We're looking for evidence. Can't wait for Laathas. Advanced decay rate, increased exposure risk, increased security risk, yadda yadda booda booda. Look! A female!"

Parthenos jammed the loaded tweezers in Sol's direction; there was no risk of contact but the boy jumped. The thing's outline was too much, tiny as it was. He fed another stream to the still-attached filter-vac.

The major waited until he had Sol's attention again. "Sorry. Gotta make sure the cameras pick 'em up; autofocus takes a minute." He held the horrid thing stiffly in the air. "They're inert, because of the gas, otherwise they'd be advancing to their final life stage and actively leaving; we'd be at risk of getting bitten and perpetuating the cycle. I'll wait if you have to hurl again, little dude." The goggles regarded him as the few millimeter long parasite sat still in the tool's clutch. "You good? No imagination, then? Oh, yeah, there you go, just chuck it, you'll feel better after some gel. Wanna go for Ryzaan? I could go for some runfi, with extra sauce! Yum."

You are a jerk beyond all jerks. I can't possibly have anything left to barf. My stomach hurts. "Is there any nutrient gel on the Dash, actually?"

Parthenos cheerfully dropped the little worm into a beaker of acid, bobbing his head as if cheering on the hissing dissolution. "Of course. That's our next stop, putting chowder bucket there into the ship." He gestured with one elbow at the heavy bin into which they earlier dumped the fleshy chunks of commandant as they hauled the sections of his armor to the compactor closet.

"But not this guy, right. What do we do with him?"

"The verchyne are incapacitated; we could feed him to the Dash, but we'll slide him into the cooling vat and let this base's processor have the remaining soup."

'Cooling vat'. More prison slang.It's a bad idea to feed really diseased bodies into processors in a closed system, so you purify them first in a series of washes, the last of which is a strong acid. All that's left is clean lipids and a bit of hard matter. "Clothes and all?"

"Yeah, can't be too careful, especially not here. Okurod has some of the best facilities and a lot of money, they're the least diseased faction, but you can only polish a coprolite so much. Shiny, colorful, still crap." Parthenos hefted the bio-skin tarp under the corpse's heels. "Get that end, we just need to slide him like yeah... careful there...got it? Good thought you were going to pass out."

They stopped near an oddly-edged floor panel which the major triggered to reveal a chemical trough. Sol watched, then assisted as Parthenos carefully slid the man's gear into the bath. "Those things carry ichemius, huh?"

"And other things, but ichemius is our biggest concern beyond verch infestation, because it can make us sick, and make us a risk to our human allies." The man's voice was tired, sympathetic, frustrated. "As opposed to guys like this. Don't get me wrong, I feel a bit sorry for them, if they're trading with the Ilu. That doesn't really absolve them of their crimes."

"I read your articles, all the way through, finally. I'm sorry about your friends."

Parthenos shrugged. "We lose people, in this line of work. And sometimes we lose people in ways we didn't think possible. The hardest part sometimes is seeing the bigger picture and not taking it personally. It's not about you, there's a whole empire you serve and protect, even people who might not realize they're under your wing yet. Lot of tough decisions. Gotta keep your heart tied down, even when it's screaming in your chest."

The major closed the floor panel. He squatted there a moment, staring up at Sol. "If you lose sight of the big picture, you can fuck things up for lots of people. The great unsaid of our mandatory sterilization." He stood, maintaining his gaze. "Let's get this other douche in the fuel and get cleaned up. After we disinfect, we can go for a swim. Pond's cold, but it's clean."

....

Without a finger of direct contact, the arms sentinel slammed against the wall from his furious pulse rush. Ferrox cringed at the impact as he launched into lambasting. *I might have hurt the Esimaar!* "Do not fuck with me, Shaan! Spit it all out. Why are you telling me this now?"

I want to tear you apart, so help me, saints of the void, I will destroy you. How many chances have I given you, worthless son of a snake? If I give in, I'll get nothing from you, but it will be so very satisfying...

Shaan regarded his justifiably angry superior with no particular upset. "That's just how it happened, Colonel Ferrox. There's no need to demonstrate your strength. I do not need to be tortured to talk."

Grudgingly, Ferrox withdrew his force tendrils; energy hissed around him as he glared. *You're too calm. As always.* He barely restrained his fury; the blood lust remained tangible in his voice. "Our people are there now. They could be in danger. Do you ever think of anyone but yourself?"

"Of course," Shaan said tensely as he smoothed his wrinkled sleeves. "I think of the Empire that let my people be brutalized in Ilu research centers."

Ferrox shuddered as he drew and exhaled a breath, as much from withholding pulse as from residual anger and the painful recognition of sentinel's truth. "Fine. Your son is among our people there now; do you care about him?"

"That's precisely why I decided to talk. I will reiterate the request for amnesty; simply, please, no further punishments if I present everything in good faith, right now."

Ferrox cracked his shoulder blades in the confines of his brace, shook his tangled sandy-gold hair out to relieve tension, never taking his eyes from Shaan. "How can I trust a man willing to sacrifice my lover and two former lovers of his own to set a trap? You're the biggest bastard that ever breathed, and I have every reason to hate you." *I used to sympathize with your cause, too. You tricked me into caring about you, just like everyone else.* He suppressed again the urge to strike the man. "I still wonder why they didn't just execute your ass when they finally caught you."

Shaan sighed as he stared back at his substantially younger commander, his jailer, the brilliant ma'at-shi student who bested him at every sphere he taught. "They wisely relied on accrued guilt and the bargaining chip of my children. And, much like you, when it comes down to it, no matter what else I may have done, I'm just so very good at what I do."

. . . .

Leaning back on a nearby rock, naked from the waist up minus a black bioware brace, Parthenos scrubbed out his long hair in the sun-speckled water. He flexed his tattooed muscles and let out a sigh, "Nice out here, don't you think?"

Sol felt a little inadequate, a little too young, and tried to ignore the man. *At least he removed the Sypherion.* "Especially compared to the city above." *Nice. Minus the part with the corpses.* He focused on rubbing his feet beneath the water, doing his best not to examine the major's extensive ink. *Probably just the drugs but I feel crawly. Wonder how many centuries-dead people are blowing around in the ash up there and we're breathing down here?* "Are you sure they won't send more people from the camp to look for those guys?"

"Not that I couldn't take an army of those assholes naked, but did you notice the lack of communications devices on those two when we stripped them? Yeah. It will be hours, maybe even a full day, before anyone even becomes worried.

They were carrying tents and food. They were either on a long patrol or they were headed to another facility somewhere. The nearest populated area that we know of, sympathetic to Okurod, is a two day drive from here in an all-terrain vehicle."

"Were those keys to an all-terrain vehicle?"

"A really crappy one. They might have been coming down here to camp." He shrugged. "It's notable they weren't using an aircraft. They really didn't want to be noticed by someone… but they really weren't expecting us."

Parthenos climbed from the water and lay down on the long, flat top of the rock and stretched out to dry a bit. He closed his eyes and rested his head on his arms just as the slate pocket of his belt, beside him on the rock, buzzed and squawked. He opened his eyes to roll them as he flipped open the slate. It was a fancy one, silvery-blue, in the shape of a stylized Haarnsvaar war craft. The thing looked like it might fly from his palm without warning and commit grievous harm. He held the pointy pocket computer above his face and shielded his eyes from the sun with his free hand. "Sharps is ready for pickup." Parthenos snapped the slate shut again and returned it to his belt. "He can wait."

Sharps. *'Use it once and dispose of it safely.' Wonder if he pissed off Laathas or P to get awarded that gem? I'm fortunate with mine, even if I don't really get it.* This dragged his mind to something else he had been avoiding, which seemed not so bad in light of rendering human corpses for fuel.

"Checkmate?"

He sat with his armored knees on the rocks, leaned slightly forward as he squeeze-dried his hair. "Yo."

Sol watched the thorny vines swell and contract over broad shoulders and biceps as Parth wrung out his enviable tresses. Further down his arms, thorns transformed to chains, which extended to shackles that were sealed at his wrists. It seemed true: had Sol not sought interface scars, he never would have seen them amid the elaborate branches and links. He remembered how the one little tattoo on his hip gutter stung and was dumbstruck. *What's physical pain to a man whose entire race was tortured to death?*

Freaky indigo eyes bored into him. "Did you want something, Echo?"

"When I ... when I came back from studying with Whisper, you said you were 'surprised'..."

"I'm surprised you're that rigidly attached to your virginity. To my knowledge, Wyvern and I are the only guys who've ever gotten lessons without getting impaled on his ancient fishing spear. I think Wyvern orally serviced him, but he was Exo before SA. That's how tankers say 'hello'." He demonstratively gestured with hand to mouth, making sure Sol noticed, then roughly shook his long mane. Water droplets splashed over Sol's undershirt and face. The major laughed. "Told ya to take it off and get wet."

"Hey!" protested the astrum, sounding as young as he was.

Another creepy laugh. Wet strands stuck to his grinning face, clung to his sideburns. "Get over this shyness shit or this unit will rape you. Or are you hiding some inappropriate tattoos from me, too?"

Sol scratched the scalp at the base of his skull. Sweaty helmet and membrane hood had led to itchy locks. Parthenos slid over rocks to sit closer. Sol was captivated and horrified by the image inked into the big man's chest: a skull, saurtzek from its length and snake-fangs, shattering as thick, highly-detailed brambles ripped out its jaw and cranium. He swallowed and forced his breathing to regularity. "I'm not attached to it so much as... I feel stupid asking Gunsmoke to ... I'd just hire a prostitute if it weren't for this..." He fingered his second collar.

Parthenos looked oddly off at the trees and devastated city beyond. His mouth twitched. "You shouldn't feel bad about it, kid; you should have gotten sex out of the way before your signal fully manifested." His smile on turning back was surprisingly sympathetic.

"Whisper gave me a list of 'qualified knights'. It was really short. Like, five people."

The major rolled his eyes. "It probably was based on qualifications of who could initiate and train you, not based on who you could safely have a throw with. Whisper is a manipulative bastard who was trying to make you a pet. I can tell you who on the ship can handle your pulse; part of my job is to know everyone's limits." The look was distinctly filthy, wickedly mirthful. "I know I was on his list, and far be it from me to actively decrease my chances, but trust me that you have better than five options for a good first time. This is Star Assault. We have positions for conduits."

"What did it take for you to get the other collar off?"

His jaw tightened for a second before he answered. "A shitload of training, that's the long and short of it. You're doing well; you've already proven you won't just arc civilians even when they piss you off. Better than me at that age." His tone was grim and sorrowful in spite his smile. "I was impressed our first time on Kourhos. The sit-rep from Holtiin amazed me. I know how mean Torchsong can get."

Was that my mother's call sign? "She talks like she wasn't one of us... but she walks through security gates like she doesn't know they're there."

"She wants to forget; maybe she lucked out and finally did. Maybe the illness or pain drugs took that part of her brain. Fucking bliss, is what that sounds like. Being able to forget that fucking war." Parthenos stared into the branches; sun dappled his tattooed shoulders and chest. *The iconic Shandrian soldier: an ideal combination of pain and beauty. When did I start thinking this way? Did I always?* "But more likely, she's just that good of 'one of us', protocol as second nature, so as no one would notice she is what she is."

As much as he tried to swallow it, bitterness flavored his words. "If she's 'one of us', you'd think she wouldn't have been so adamant against having folk for my sister."

"Hm?"

"I couldn't sleep for my parent's arguing; I was seven. I got up and crept to the wall and listened. My father said he had someone he wanted to bring in, that money wouldn't be an issue because favors were owed. And she was furious."

A peculiar look shone through strands of damp hair. "Do you remember what was said, precisely?"

"He said, 'Your feelings notwithstanding – and I know you could use more help around here - we owe it to our daughter. It's tradition.' And she said, 'I won't have that particular history in my house. Get her a prostitute.' I'll never forget it." *My memory is coming back?*

"You realize she probably meant 'the war' or 'some ex-lover of yours I hate', his history, their history, not 'Shandrian history', right?"

His voice sounds like he's going to laugh at me, but his eyes... are those tears? No must just be water from his hair. "I can honestly say that until this exact moment, I never had that frame of reference."

"Dumb ass." Parthenos sighed. "She ran from all of it the moment she found out she had a second chance to play civilian. She wanted to forget. And I don't blame her." He acquired a tone of surprise as the words left his mouth, as if he just happened to find them beneath his tongue.

"You knew her well, I guess? I figured you contributed to the relocation fund and wondered why you were being so kind to me; I am pretty dense. Sorry."

Parthenos snorted and stood, an icy shroud of emotional armor congealed. His voice was empty and distant. "Yes to all of the above." He mades strides toward the camouflaged ship. With more firmness, but without facing Sol, he said, "Pick up, kid. Time to retrieve that fuck-up Sharps and whichever poor newb ended up with him, then meet with Bootstrap and discuss the next half of the mission."

As he watched the major trod into the moss and brush, his slate vibrated. Sol slapped it open to a text message from 'Bootstrap'.

::: He know you sent that? :::

He followed Parthenos slowly. :::No.:::

::: Keep it that way, talk later. Tell him I'm ready but his slate's doing the send back thing again.:::

Sol caught up with the major at the mossy hillock that was in actuality their Dash. He approached cautiously; he did not want to break into whatever mental darkness Parthenos currently experienced. "Bootstrap contacted me. He said your slate is rejecting his texts…"

"D'aw, fuck," laughed the major, a little of his usual flavor flowing back. He leaned forward, one hand on the Dash, about to trigger it to a new mode. His hair hung in his face, hiding most of his expression, but Sol could see fangs and something of a grin. "Thanks. I totally fuckin' forgot I turned him off yesterday. It was either that or go to his cocoon, haul him out, and punch him in the face."

Way to be professional, sir. The craft, still looking like a lot of mossy rock and dirt, albeit shimmering queerly, raised itself up on landing gear. The hatch winked open. "Would I be out of line asking why?"

An incredulous face looked back, one lazy needle-fang overhung his lower lip. "Do you read the forums on SACnet?"

Sol snorted. "Only when I have to look something up. Even then, I search and skim."

"You know, once you're promoted you need to; it keeps you aware of the Empire and the relations of your crew." Parthenos started preflight procedures. "He posted a link to one of those liberal 'free thinker' web sites he likes to read, article from another unrealistic pacifist from some podunk corner of the Empire. Some shit who gets free education but who's never gotten blood on his fuckin' hands you know?" He held his fingers up and wriggled them, brows raised over his alien eyes.

Glowering, Sol began to sit. "Yeah, I know… now."

The major started his tirade but broke it with a slap to Sol's arm before the boy's butt could reach the seat. "Don't sit there." The remark's tone was, *What, you stupid or something?* Parthenos stood and pointed at the pilot's seat, brows furrowed. "There."

This turn of events both stunned and thrilled the astrum. He inched toward the bigger soldier, who was still mostly bare from the waist up. He had only put his sleeves back on. Sol could feel body heat - or at least pulse radiation - as he squeezed by to take the master seat.

"Anyway. Posted some crap about there being a 'historical precedent' for peace with the saurtzek and if we could just look past Mior and Yetzjmaal and 'get over it', we could 'unify all elvenkind'". An array of dismissive hand gestures and tones emphasized how ridiculous those sentiments were to Parthenos.

Sol watched silently. The article in question was over a year old; he read it elsewhere, while in IGN. He thought it was well-written and made many valid points, especially the use of Holtiin as an example of how inter-species peace could work even when it seemed impossible elsewhere in the Empire. *But my family wasn't murdered by the Ilu.*

"I know you know how to hook up. I've seen your scores. Whatcha waitin' for, Red? Engraved invitation? Plug in, fucker!" The major's glee was child-like.

"Ship? Initiate direct interface."

Fleshy wing-like structures unfurled from the sides of the oddly-angled seat, curling to reach around Sol's ribs. However, they touched the bio-fiber of his underarmor and whipped back, hovering and wriggling. The boy made a confused noise. Parthenos laughed.

"What the fuck, ship!" sputtered Sol.

There was a sinister hint to the major's amusement. "Ah ah. You're the one doing it wrong." He waggled a finger, smirking. "Off comes the shirt or we're stuck on the ground."

Bright red washed his cheeks again. Sol pushed on the resisting wings,agitated. "Aw, come on! I have HTS! I can run a ship in the winter uniform!"

"Yeah, if it's calibrated at Val's level, I guess you can force it. You can't tell a ship how it works unless you know how to build the fuckin' things." Parthenos leaned back and let the gun cables plug in to his arms, blending seamlessly, save for color, with the tattooed vines. His smile was huge. "Get naked."

The young officer grumbled incoherently as he stripped off his undershirt. *I look like such a prepubescent kid next to you! Gods. Ugh.* Fleshy membranes encircled his ribs and tightened. Multitudes of tiny, pulsating, mildly stinging, rubbery cups sucked against his bare ribs and abdomen. It was not unpleasant, just peculiar with his skin pharmaceutically over-sensitized. He lowered his head and slunk down the seat. Parthenos continued to laugh, exacerbating Sol's self-consciousness.

"The ship has plenty of fuel, but if you want to run off a batch, I'm sure there's room."

That was not something he needed to hear. He had a trump card, and it would also fix that pesky erection. "So how'd you first meet my mom?"

Laughter ceased. The black brows furrowed. "Mind your own business and fly the ship."

I win, jerk. "Ship. Initiate vertical launch." Simultaneously, he pulled up on a rubbery handle on the end of a long cable, releasing pulse as gradually as he could. *Probably didn't even need the voice command,* he decided as the Dash leapt upward into hover position, expanded its wings over the trees and rotated to follow his coordinates. "Maintain camouflage." With a hand motion, he gradually increased the altitude.

Still visibly annoyed, the major spoke. "You're doing great."

An alarm indicated an urgent call from central command. Sol glanced at Parthenos a second and promptly answered. "Echo here."

"This is Gunsmoke. Have you been offline?"

Parthenos slapped his forehead and mouthed an Archon contraction: '*N'tzidji.*' ("Aw, fuck me.")

Sol shrugged and mouthed, 'What should I tell him?' "Yes, we were cleaning up at the pond, apolo-"

Kiertus was uncharacteristically agitated. "I don't give a shit. Mission aborted. Return to the *Sanjeera* immediately."

"Gotcha, we have a few members to pick up but we're already in the air."

"Great, Echo, you need to hurry. Is Checkmate with you, by any chance?"

Boy he sounds really pissed. Sol gestured at the major, who nodded furiously as he fixed on his helmet and mouthpiece. "He was securing some cargo; want me to switch to single mode?"

"That would be fantastic, Echo."

Sol clicked communications to 'gunner only' and returned his eyes to the monitors, trying to ignore the ensuing one-sided conversation.

"Yes… absolutely… understood… I expect a briefing - yes, of course, I – yes. That is true, Gunsmoke." Out of the corner of his eye, Sol noted Parthenos staring up at the ceiling of the cockpit. "Mm, no he didn't mention… I see… We are on our way, there's no-"

"Holy shit!" Sol automatically exclaimed as his focus returned fully to the monitor and he dipped the Dash to one side as it rapidly sped toward a billowing plume of black smoke and flames.

"There seems to be a fire, sir, edge of the Haunted Zone Forest, yes, um," Parthenos examined the gunner's map screen and made an indescribable face, "approximately in the location of the, ah, 'rat hole'… hm, really? Oh."

He re-routed the ship, allowing curiosity to divert his attention to Parth's finger tapping on the map. "OKU. BASE" was marked where the major pointed with a symbol that meant "Avoid Area".

"Yes, understood. We'll speak with you when we return. Checkmate, out." Parthenos reached over and killed the communicator, saying to his pilot, "We didn't do that."

"Didn't do what, sir?"

"No one from the *Sanjeera* is responsible for that fire. It wasn't us. Which begs some questions…" He slipped the helmet off to rub his temples. "Remember the rings I showed you, that both men carried?"

"You said they were tabs from timed incendiary devices, sometimes kept as souvenirs…"

"Right. Souvenirs, or they were trying to get the evidence far from the scene. There are a lot of possibilities, but those men probably blew up their own base, fleeing from a crime, from unpleasant orders and returning to another base, probably? Impossible to say, now… I only sort of wish I'd reversed the hostage situation and asked a few questions."

"Only sort of?"

"I knew the one was worm-ridden. I'd have had to kill him anyway. That would have increased potential communication difficulty." The major shook his head.

"Why would fleeing men try to take a hostage?"

"Fear and desperation, maybe? How did you know he was wormy, anyway?"

The map flashed Sharps' location. Sol entered landing procedures as Parthenos explained. "When the infestation is advanced it fucks up the nerves, so they shake."

"Worm shakes is a real thing? Like in video games?"

Parthenos snort-laughed. "Yeah, not as dramatic, but quite distinctive. Change the subject, kiddies boarding."

Well this is the furthest thing from appropriate, but it's also the furthest thing from the other topic. "Pardon me if this is out of line, but were you coming on to me back at the pond?"

Lashes lowered over indigo orbs; the tone mocked. "Were you interested?"

Valid question. Sol saw via external camera the craft found a suitable spot, near where Gronney and Ramusi sat on a rock. This conversation needed to end. "I think, in different circumstances I would have been, yes."

The major's eyebrows raised and mouth opened, but the other two men boarded, chit chatting. They seemed to have bonded. To Sol's surprise, Parthenos smiled and said in clean, unaccented Archaic Shandrian, "Situations like that always get me hard. Nothing like being elbow deep in Death to make me want to get up to my hips in life."

The men in the crew compartment took no notice. Sol went through the liftoff sequence, more baffled by the language change than disgusted by Parthenos' frank admission. *You speak Archon so slangy and Shandrian like a noble gentleman... there is no end to your oddness.*

"What is with that look every time I speak the holy tongue? Ruhn has its roots in Shandrian. It was easy for me to learn. Not like Ryzaan or that chaotic ape-garble from Sheriden's homeworld."

Sol pretended he had not heard the technical insubordination. He wondered abstractly if letting Parthenos take his virginity would atone on some level for secretly passing off the video. Val was in charge of this mission and was Sol's immediate superior, so there was no inherent wrong doing. The apparent animosity between them that he potentially fueled was more his concern.

On the other hand, I'm not sure I could give it up to the sort that shot a fleeing man in the back, wormy or not. Cap'n V seems like the more respectable option, although I don't know what his vow covers so I'd never ask. Kiertus is a good man, he's certainly attractive, he's just so… old. And Wyvern scares me, but, if he's serious, he'd be ending his vows with me? Not sure how I feel about that.

"I was caught up in the moment, really," Parthenos spoke softly as the ship flew, his usually abrasive mannerisms once again temporarily replaced by a real gentleman. "I figured you would say no, which was ideal. You are technically Gunsmoke's 'property', and he is no one to challenge."

As this information sank in for Sol, the major spoke in Archon again, to the ship PA. "Anyone have anything to immediately report?"

"Fine with waiting until the rendezvous, Checkmate."

"There's been a change of plans, men; we're returning to the cruiser immediately upon picking up the others. Orders from central."

"I have no questions, then, Checkmate."

The regular major returned with a flourish. "Fantastic, Sharps. I note you still haven't been safely disposed!" He clicked the PA off. Sol withheld laughter as he assisted the ship at the final pick-up.

Here they found Valdieren, Airman Seamus, Squeak, and Ozzie; the latter three boarded the ship in a noisy tumble. The captain's boarded with a disparaging expression; they came to guilty-faced order.

"What's with you guys," Sol heard Ramusi say quietly as Val ordered a cringing Squeak into an empty seating alcove.

Subdued but smug, he replied, "I totally got in trouble for playin' with the bugs." Seamus waited for the captain to pass into the cockpit and whispered, "It was so much fun! Squeak is hilarious!"

361

"Gentlemen," breathed the young captain, now standing between the seats. "There is profound evidence of human activity in this corner of Oun'a-akal. I don't know what they're doing here, but they're clearly transporting something in and out with some frequency." He held up three tiny memory cards. "Each of these is 42 hours. It's gonna take me a while on this; we suddenly don't have that kinda time anymore."

"Give some of it to Wrasse and Mimic; Wyvern can take some when he gets back. I'll take the rest." The major was absolutely emotionless, detached, almost as if he was doing math problems in his head. "Now I wish we'd kept Wisp a bit longer. Who else is fluent?"

"What about Sharps?"

"No. And that's my final answer."

Valdieren pursed his lips. "Clear."

"I learn languages really fast," offered Sol helpfully. "Maybe - "

The major and captain exchanged glances; Parthenos made a gesture and the captain turned back to his young charge. "You're not cleared for this yet, but I'll give you some training apps. Kourhonoi is rapidly becoming a language we all need to speak." With an odd face, Valdieren swiveled on one boot, returning to crew cabin to settle into the niche with his (yet again) repentant bug. Ozzie had been waiting her turn and nearly knocked the captain down as she shoved past to get to her bond-mate.

Seamus whispered, "Hey girl. You forgetting somethin'?"

She chirped and reared, balancing her pointy legs on the edge of Seamus' seat. Lowering her head, she used her mouth to unsnap a compartment on his utility belt, pulled something out and clip-clopped perkily toward the cockpit. He grinned at the annoyed captain and said, "They don't shut things, really, do they?"

Ozzie peered in cautiously, keeping to the left so she was further from Parthenos. He avoided looking at her, concentrating on the view screen and being alert.

"Hey bugbutt, long time no see. What's up?" Sol, keeping his eyes on the console, switched his steering hand and gave her a scratch. He noted her head jerk just at the bottom of his vision and felt something fall in his lap. "Oh! What'd ya bring me?"

Parthenos glanced over, one eyebrow raised but otherwise at least feigning disinterest. His expression shifted to an appreciative nod as he returned his full attention to the view screen. "Damn. Good score."

Sol picked up the hard, cold, clearly machined object. It was a solid metal emblem, with little bolt holes at either end, scratched and scuffed, but definitely an Okurod soldier's holy symbol. He twitched a little, having just compacted pieces of armor decorated with enameled versions of the same, but encouraged his proud gen profusely. "Thank you, Ozzie! You're such a nice bug!"

Screwing up his mouth, he asked the the major, "Should I turn this in as evidence?"

Parthenos shrugged. "Put it in your written report and have Airmen Seamus explain where he found it if he can. But unless the colonel says otherwise, I say you can keep it after a trip through quarantine." The fuzzy-faced veteran produced his syrigun and popped a dose. "Don't forget your shift dose, kid. You really need that up here. And don't accidentally shoot the combat dose unless you got a fuck buddy waitin' on the ship."

Part of Sol's mind was still a few sentences behind as Ozzie crushed herself up next to his seat and went to sleep on the floor. *Wrasse is Liesh's call sign, but who's Mimic?*

"Alright, astrum. Get us home." Sol nodded affirmatively to Parthenos' orders as he returned the syrigun to his belt. "I'll walk you through the docking process."

He didn't say 'Walk you through the shift'. Wow, he thinks that highly of my skills? Maybe I am the jerk. "I think I've got it, major. Thank you, sir."

Lights flashed and the strange voice said, "Approaching. Shiftpoint." Sol decreased speed and hit the PA.

"Captain Valdieren. Are we jump secure, sir?"

"Solid as it gets, astrum." He sounded a little pissy and distant still, but otherwise his kind-hearted, patient self. "Get us home in one piece; we have a lot to do."

This is for real. Sol took a deep breath. "Ship. Initiate shift sequence." The Dash counted down. No one spoke. As the count got closer, he noted via the observation cam that everyone in the crew area had their eyes closed. Up in the cockpit, however, one pair stormy hazel eyes and one pair broody indigo stared at the external view screen. The only closed pairs were the four black shiny domes on the alien arthropod snoring beside him. "You too, huh, sir?" Sol quietly asked of Parthenos.

"Fighter pilots never close their eyes."

I think I get it now. Scattered stars became ribbons, the cockpit a photo-negative and then a rainbow blur. This was expected. He was up front once for a jump, but Captain Valdieren ordered him to close his eyes. *"You're too young. That drives men insane. Close 'em. I won't hear it."* But Sol was not prone to listening to hyperbolic advice if there was not someone watching.

Amidst the rushing of speed beyond form, time seemed to stop, and the only thing of which the body that normally housed Solvreyil Yenraziir was aware was an army of mouthless, huge-eyed kaffoid forms whose appendages melted and changed as they slipped through one another to examine him. He realized he had no body, that flesh was meaningless, that Nothing was Everything, Everything was Nothing. He was Them, and They had been here Always. Then they scattered, like fish from a rock in a pond; there was a brief, horrifying glimpse of something made of no color he could name, pulsing centrally, dragging in and crushing all around it, spitting forth things beyond description; a heaving mass of unnamable organs and tendrils that howled with a sound that tore planets apart as they unfurled... then the rushing resumed and the process reversed, rainbows, photonegative, ribbons, strangely haloed cockpit in a small bio-craft, floating along in space.

"You got some fuckin' eggs, Red."

Sol blinked. The ship jarred sharply; a gen bark pierced the air. Parthenos was punching him in the arm.

"Hey! Holtiini! Fuckin' *Sanjeera*!? Right in front of us?" Punch, punch.

Growling. "Stop it, bug, he's gonna fuckin' crash us into the hull!"

Red mudlocks shook with a feathery slapping. "Shit!" He veered the Dash sharply toward the pipes. "Ship! Initiate docking sequence." There was a large commotion beside him. "Ozzie! Get down! Sorry, sir. Sorry. Down, bug! Bad bug!"

"Command not valid. Please try again."

"I'm used to it," the major said coldly as Ozzie squatted nearby, glowering at the Ruhn with black shiny balls of hate. "OK. We're set up for docking. But, we're a hair off course and still have to make the *Sanjeera* aware of our presence and coordinates. Procedure?"

He struggled with his hallucination-fogged brain. *That's all they are. Hallucinations.* Sol tapped a contact sequence on the mini-screen.

"Contact: successful. Main engines cycling down. Preparing for catch."

A large, elliptical, subtly glowing hole slowly opened in one of the series of wide, crooked tubes that lined either side of the cruiser. More than anything, they resembled the perelopods of a crustacean, albeit a crustacean the size of a small city. A long, corrugated tendril extended from the opening and encircled the comparatively dainty bio-craft, dragging it inside.

A strange sound rose behind him. Sol glanced at the crew cam; Captain Valdieren clapped and nodded. Gradually, the other three men, even Gronney, followed suit, and Squeak whistle-warbled. Parthenos turned and smiled. "Thanks for not killing us. Do it better next time or I'll punch you a lot harder."

Ozzie growled.

"Enough of that, Ozlietsin." She crushed her feelers to her head and looked up at Sol, silenced.

"Powering down," noted the ship's dreamy, effeminate voice.

Once released from the tendril and the airlocks sealed behind them, Valdieren stood and announced, "Debriefing will be at 08:00 tomorrow. Take notes on anything you intend to bring up in the morning before you start drinking tonight." He saluted stiffly. "Follow me to inoculation, then you're dismissed."

Sol looked after him as he opened the hatch and hopped out. *Is it what's on those memory cards? Or what I sent him? Something's really wrong.*

Parthenos leaned back in his seat as Val filed everyone to the disinfecting kiosk. "Stick here with me, kid. Colonel's got us on a different detail." He gestured casually with his pointy slate.

"Will we disinfect afterwards?"

"Naw, we'll be inspecting the ship when it gets sprayed, conveniently. What? Won't hurt us. Same shit, OK yeah and some ship lube but we'll be in armor; just don't swallow any, right? Here, drink some gel and get that barf smell off your face." As he handed off the tube of drink, he checked his locater. "Take your fucking time, Val, it was just emergency orders, after all, little prick… there you go. OK, kid, come on. Get that down before the spraying starts."

The casual attitude shattered as Parthenos hopped out. Before his feet even touched the hangar floor, he was yelling at the pilots and techs. "What are you fuckers doing!? Spearhead, Cloudbreak, get this bay secured, what're you waiting for, engraved invitations? Me and the kid got lifts four and five you all get the rest. Hurricane, what does that look like to you? Well it looks like a jump countdown to me! We have less than twenty five minutes to secure these pipes! Step on it!"

Sol tried to tune out the furious rattle of names and orders and turn down his agitated brain. As he initiated the internal rinse procedure for the Dash and launched into vent inspection, he heard from the other side of the craft, "Major, what are you doing down here, sir? No disrespect intended, but where is Master Wyvern?" He peered around the forward guns to see if he knew the speaker; he recognized the face from his first day of work in the pipes.

Parthenos glowered at the brown-suited technician and snidely responded, "Houseboy's not comin' home tonight, kids; you gotta deal with me."

….

Why are we meeting in A-1? High tier briefings are always in the lounge. What's going on? Val broke his run and took a breath as he rounded the corner into the open door. His eyes bugged. *The last time I saw all these guys in uniform was Ajshunejol's memorial service… and I'm late, and very short on friends… no Freyr, where the fuck is he? Gods, Gyrf, could have saved me a spot, you bastard… I refuse to believe the only open spaces are by Syavrasky Kahner and that one jump-tech who hates me.*

Val tried to keep his cool as he saluted Kiertus – waiting stiffly with a thermos of coffee at the head of the room- and scanned the walls for a seat. A slightly-too-pretty man with Ryzaan bone structure, sitting centrally on the floor in an immaculate command jacket, glanced over his shoulder. He slid closer to his greyer companion and patted the empty area to his left.

Who? Oh fuck me, Jady's back. And that's Chel sitting beside him, with Laathas behind them, and they're all dressed up, this is bad. This is really bad. He took the open spot on the training room floor, oddly more uncomfortable for having been invited to sit with the highest-ranking officers. Shandrian-style, honored guests and nobility sat on the floor towards the middle, with beverages and open floor space between them and the host. Lower-ranking officers – the rest of the captains in the room and a few sentinels – clustered the integral benches and in corners. Respectful distance was maintained between superiors at center and men about the perimeter; Val might as well have stood with the colonel as far as visibility was concerned. *At least this can't get more awkward cuz Parth is on wing duty right now…*

Without looking Val's direction, Chel passed a cup of coffee across Jady. Colonel Kiertus began to speak, so Val tapped the man beside him with a Ryzaan hand-sign of gratitude; it was silently passed to the beverage provider.

"Gentlemen, I regret to inform you all attempts by intel and advance scouts to prevent our initiative have been withdrawn, due to no error on their part. We are returning to the original plan for Operation: Wormbait after receiving last-minute intelligence confirming an agent supposedly working on our behalf negotiated an arms deal between Shuuv-Enk'raath agents and the Kourhonoi Theocracy."

Shuuv-Enk'raath? They're the militant division of the Cult of the Devourer. The worst of the Ilu's worst. The room buzzed; Kiertus gestured for stillness. Val wiped the coffee he had choked through his nose off on his hand, accepting a rag from Jady to blow out the rest of his now flavorful snot. *One of ours? Why would someone do that? That's insane; of course those weapons are intended to be used on us! What were they thinking? Double crossing bastards!*

"As such we are heading to Pachar immediately, which we will protect as we wait for the 89th to take a first run over Verraken. We will trade places as they head to Kourhos and the ICSM and Flamethrowers will head up the rear. Changes to operation are, as of a half hour ago, official from the Haarnsvaar."

Val recognized a twinge of pain on the colonel's face in spite the stoic pose and emotionless voice. Operation: Wormbait, as Val remembered the briefings, had initially only been the 89th with 17th on clean-up and only IGN Rehab to make amends on their tails. *You hate giving this news as much or more than we hate hearing it. Sorry, sir.*

Kiertus checked his slate and returned his attention to the group. "I have just received from Councilor Therek a message of thanks for attempting to resolve the situation more peacefully; all of your efforts are appreciated and he expressed that he would thank you each in person should the universe permit." He cleared his throat quietly as the combined weight of hearts in the room threatened to draw in passing satellites. "We should have about a week of stand-by depending on the efficiency of our Air Shark brethren. Make use of that time by stepping up training. Further, if you have any promotion suggestions, now is the time to submit them. Updated instructions regarding operation procedures will be individually emailed. Honor and sacrifice!"

The colonel saluted rigidly; the crowd rose and responded as a single unit. *Sometimes I forget that we are capable of this level of 'together'*, Val thought, more than a little impressed. The jump alarm blared over his half-formed thoughts of fraternal adoration.

"If you can reach securing stations, you are dismissed; if not you are welcome to stay here." The colonel delivered a final salute before he joined the dispersing crowd. Val stepped in behind him, toward the bridge. "Are you concerned about the future, Captain Valdieren?" Kiertus asked over his shoulder.

"Not as long as you're giving the orders, sir."

...

Although they successfully secured the starboard pipes, Sol and Parthenos weathered the transfer in crew alcoves with the hangar staff. The major seemed displeased about it but at least the work was done. Sol followed him to the lounge to check out lap tops to more easily file their mission reports.

"Sir, does 'incidents' in section four refer to 'encountered' units? Seems redundant to section three."

The major's casually informative response did not detract from his own typing. "That would refer to interpersonnel incidents in your own unit. For example you could report me blocking Val or failing to pick up a ship alert, but I'd just include that I sexually harassed you, if I was an astrum writing a report about –" His slate played a snippet of music Sol attempted to identify. "Yo. Yes, sir? Oh I'd love to do that, sir, but I don't see how I can brief your astrum when I haven't been properly briefed. Sounds like a great idea, please do, sir. Over."

Sol cocked an eyebrow at Parthenos, who stared at his closed slate and shook his head. *I know that song; it was popular with the kids in the costume club, can't even the artis's name. I remember she was haki. It's about a jilted lover who manages to get the new lovers of their old flame on a transit craft and crashes it into a lunar base and she's explaining to the Rim Patrol as she dies, 'I did it for us, you can't understand, my unshared love, was bigger than life'... That's the ring tone he has set for the colonel?*

"What? He's emailing you the overview he gave the officers assembly. Yeah you should make *that* face; it's a huge deal for you to get that. Remember the no chatter rules. You can talk to me but if anyone walks in here under the rank of captain, shut yer fuckin' mouth, got it, Red?"

His admonitions were drowned out part way by the proximity alarm's howl. They cringed; Sol made to jump up but noticed his superior simply staring, slit eyed and peevish, at the PA, gesturing with his slate in hand as if he expected what was coming next.

"Attention, crew. Please disregard the previous alarm." Sol did not recognize the voice. The accent was Ryzaan and sarcastic. "It seems some hot shot dropped a Kimetj class cruiser into our radius. Carry on with regular duties; we are in no danger. I repeat: disregard, we are in no danger." The PA sounded like it was clicking off and then the voice returned hurriedly, snapping out, "That's right, crew, we've been Ezzimarr'd. Over!"

Parthenos rolled his eyes. "Fucking dildo."

"Sir, who was that?" Sol was still tilting his head at the speaker. *'Ezzimarr'? Is that how you actually pronounce the characters 'Esimaar'? I thought it was more like 'Essya'mair'? Shandrian name, though, so maybe the Ryzaan said it wrong.*

"Huh? Sorry, I didn't mean Jady on the com, there. Ferrox Ya'miro, the colonel of the 89th."

"Why is he allowed to fly the ship if he's that dangerous of a pilot?"

"He's an excellent pilot, Sol; I'm confident he can jump a Dash in and out of a crowded space station shopping center without killing anyone." He downloaded the file Kiertus had just mailed; Sol followed suit but continued to listen. "He's just doing that to annoy the big K. Childish, really."

I totally don't understand this, but this is the first I've heard anything about the guy other than that he's this man-eating cold-hearted monster. "What do you mean? Do they have a problem with one another?"

"A chronic one, like 25 years worth?" Parthenos laughed but was still visibly annoyed. "Terms of Ferrox's sentencing keep them from meeting in person, especially right now. So he pulls stupid stunts to make sure his lover still thinks of him. I don't think they had to pass us at all, but I had a feeling he'd do that since we have to be in the same system." He caught Sol's expression. "I also shouldn't shit talk the man. He'd be brigadier of SA today if he'd knock shit like that off; his irresponsible showing off fucks him more than it annoys us. Read the mail and ignore me."

Both read their slates in silence. As they did, Laathas shuffled in, just noisily enough to be sure they noticed, with Cheldyne behind. Chel tapped Sol as he passed to the sterilizer with a few thermoses. "Hey," he said gruffly.

"Oh, uh, hi, Chel." Sol was horrified by the overview. Parthenos, likewise, was absorbed, frown increasing exponentially as he re-read. The astrum looked up at him and the other two men in turn. "I... I... this is... sirs, this is terrible."

Laathas had his hair tendrils arranged carefully away from his eyes, giving a sense of austerity he usually lacked. He raised a brow at the scowling major then the casually-attired bug sarge beside him. "It is, unfortunately, understandable. We can't wish away the monster we created."

"Who would do such a thing, though? To his own people?"

"Ah," Chel interjected. "That is the thing. He does not identify most Archons as his people and honestly, had we not incidentally been holding a thing of great value to him, we would have sailed right into it unaware." He held a hand up in the direction of Parthenos, whose now-open mouth prepared to launch rage. "I am glad we removed you two alive, and feel it unwise to displace any anger."

Just us? Not the rest of the team? That's not nice. Laathas? He just implied we could have left your astrum to die. I don't like the guy, but say something...

"At any rate, that's not what I came here to discuss." Laathas acquired a cup of coffee, showing no interest in Cheldyne's statement. "I'm ordering both of you and the colonel to bed rest. One of the two of you should accompany Kiertus; decide amongst yourselves. There are beds open in sick bay in case you don't feel like a hike back when the next round of meetings starts; Kiertus says they'll all be held up here, and you'll both variously be required at them."

Parthenos snorted. "Well, Astrum Solvreyil, I concede if you're feeling up to it."

Cheldyne watched, amused, as Sol made a variety of faces and exchanged looks with the major. "No one's ordering sex, of course, it just wouldn't be polite of us to order him to sleep alone. Jady volunteered if you're both prickly. You are required to sleep regardless. It's going to be a long day."

"I'll do it, sirs." Sol managed not to stutter in spite of self-consciousness. To his surprise, Cheldyne walked over and unlocked the door to Kiertus' private office.

"Wait for him here." Chel saluted and walked away. Laathas thanked the boy in a friendly manner before disappearing himself. Parthenos remained seated in the lounge, chuckling, as Sol carried the laptop with him into the office.

Stopping to salute him on the way, Sol requested, "Why are you laughing, sir?"

Strands of black hair tangled in his brows and sideburns as the chuckle turned to an uproarious cackle. He wiped tears from his eyes and exhaled to reply, "You have no idea how fucked up that just was, kid. Get some sleep before the shit hits the intake." He gave a smirking salute. "Honor and sacrifice. Dismissed!"

XVII Dust and Shadows

A peculiar mix of shyness and guilt confronted Sol as the gory dream startled him awake and the reality of his surroundings replaced the fire and screams. Amidst comfortable drifts of silky bedding and substantial pillows of varying pliability, he faced the taut, naked chest of his commander. He observed on the man's face emotionless serenity that was somehow sadder than a frown. This detail swayed him to stay in spite the sense he had no place here, that he was deeply out of his element.

I don't even remember getting in bed. Did I finish my report? Yes, I fell asleep re-reading Parthenos' horrible report on Verraken or… was it the account of Triotos? I don't remember. Something horrible, I was flipping through the cross-referenced stuff. Sol shuddered then self-consciously stilled as the body beside him shifted minutely. *We didn't do anything? No. Nothing. He escorted me from the chair to here. I think he went back to the office to talk to someone afterward. I'm sleeping in my clothes. Oh man, Yen, you're a piece of work.*

The only light came from luminescent emergency strips that marked the way to safety gear and exits. His eyes, were kaffa enough that the so-called darkness presented little obstacle. The difference in color range took some getting used to; he generally preferred to see the world the "human" way.

Sol blinked at the torso before him. It was a thing he had seen enough to memorize the tattoos and scars. He was fond of them, even: Shandrian runes where the rifle strap would fall near the left clavicle; a polite but faded setting sun on the left hip; a bizarre stylized winged creature on his right shoulder, its tapered tail coiled into a loose spiral; the decorative band of feathers and glyphs integrated with gun grafts on his left shoulder with the invasion unit logo beneath; plug grafts up his forearms for firing ship to ship guns; faint burn and shrapnel scars over the right set of ribs; and the 'mystery scar' that fascinated Sol. Between his lowest rib and the top of his left pelvic bone, a few inches to the right of his navel, sat an old, straight, white ridged gash, which had a mate on the other side, indicating whatever penetrated the old scrapper made it all the way through.

Normally, this scar would hold all his attention, but as he worked his way to maximum focus, he picked up something else on the colonel's chest. He assumed his eyes played tricks on him at first, but there was no mistaking it: a faintly glowing pair of wings lay evenly over his pectorals. Their qualities reminded him of the method by which call numbers were tattooed on bio-ships; Cheldyne mentioned that via a grafting process, a version of that living colony of material could be inserted into the carapaces of gen and the skin of people, creating 'tattoos' only visible under certain conditions. He hazily recalled childhood reading of an elite, secretive order of religious knights in Eshandir who did such a thing to themselves; he had dismissed it as exaggerated romanticism at the time. *'Unable to speak of their calling,'* the prosaic old book explained, *'they laced their skins with the echoes of stars. By these traces they recognized and spared one another their blades.'*

What were they called ... Sol softly traced the right wing, delicately avoiding the nipple, coming to rest flat-palmed against his master's chest. *I remember you can't ask them directly, but I can't remember the words to ask, the little code. I am just enough of a Shandrian to know I make a very bad one.*

A warm hand pressed against his, forcing him to feel the sturdy old heart beating in the sturdy old chest. The eyes remained closed but the blank face shifted to a smile. The colonel's soothing voice was barely above a whisper. "To the brave and strong fall the universe, and thereby the responsibility of its care."

There was no chance to question the statement; he was asleep again immediately following the last consonant, almost as if he spoke it without waking. The hand remained in place. Sol followed him slowly back to the dream side, lulled by the steady breathing, heartbeat, and strange comfort of something unsaid and unacted but still shared between them which transcended age, time, and hardship.

My ancestors would say I am 'recognizing my star-blood', he noted with groggy amusement, the trauma of earlier nightmares fading. *Funnier still that I know I've felt this before and told myself it was something else…Where is Wyvern, anyway, with his bothersome poetry about purposeful killing? 'Saal n'aven, aven'Aur', 'My wings are mercy, mercy Itself'… Itself being the name of 'god'… in a sense, since the mountain cults personified consciousness as a divine entity manifested in the best examples of 'life'… the watchers, or knights preserved the dignity of consciousness, seeking to end undue suffering… mercy soldiers, mostly… surgeons, field medics… Novamauri? Oh, I see… I think…*

His associative loop lulled as sleep, this time tranquil, graciously swallowed him.

...

"Astrum? I hate to wake you, you seem so peaceful. The colonel demands your presence."

Huh? I'm... OK I'm still in my clothes. Ack but Val's still seeing me in the colonel's bed. I guess... I guess it's to be expected, I think? He doesn't look thrilled. "Greetings, captain." Sol straightened his locks and gave a half-awake salute. "What time is it?"

"Damned early o'clock, Sol, you don't even want to know. I'll let you hit the head if you need and I'll be in the office with the big K." Valdieren yawned and strode from the bedroom.

Sol rose resistantly from the lavish bed with its silky draperies, and crossed to where he felt the nook should be located, stopping a moment to catch himself on a shelf. *I'm really light-headed. Did we jump again while I was asleep?*

The layout was similar to Okallin's, as he suspected, sans the additional room with rock garden and salt shower. Embedded in the wall was a bas relief, ostrekaal, apparently, featuring what at first Sol read as an abstract design. As he studied, however, it became a being, or some arrangement of overlaid outlines of creatures to make one whole entity that was not quite a gen, not quite a kaffa, not quite a droka, and not quite a dashinki. The creature's distinctly kaffir eyes looked down on him, judged him passively as he pissed. *Damn, you're kind of creepy, thing. Beautiful, but creepy. Are you 'God'?*

As he crossed to the office door, he groggily looked around, having no conscious memory of being in this part of the ship. It was gorgeously appointed, decorated with tasteful, exotic artifacts from many worlds and decades. Thick, beautiful tapestries – the silky curtains were quite elaborate on the non-sleeping side - surrounded the large bed. Shelves of hardbound books – restrained by long rigid bands just in case – framed the sleeping area. Nova had her own bed which resembled a miniature hive structure with a wide opening and huge squishy cushion within. She dozed inside, undisturbed by his presence.

Where is Ozzie? Did she follow me in here or follow Chel back to the hive? She gets so quiet and weird when Parthenos is around. It's bad of me to lose track of her like that...

"Hello, sirs, sorry to have kept you waiting." One of the big squishy chairs had been unbolted from the floor and moved over to the desk where colonel and captain sat with a laptop. It was paused on what Sol recognized as a freeze frame of the detonated Okurod Templar. *Oh, gross, I did not need to look at that again just now… Where's the intake in here, just incase? Side of K's desk? I think…?*

"It's quite alright," Kiertus gestured to the open chair. "I want to speak to you about this…"

Sol meant his response to sound comical, but it came out rather nervously. "Ah, about blood, sir?"

"Well, that too, astrum."

Strong coffee permeated the air. Each exhausted-looking man had an open mug of the stuff – not low-grav-safe thermoses - sitting on decorative coasters on either side of the colonel's computer. Something about the room just felt off, though, in spite of its ordered, sensible décor. Perhaps it was the draft…

No, there's someone else in here, someone I can't see, doing that thing Wyvern does, but it's not him. Sol sat cautiously, attempting to remain inconspicuous as he sought to pick up vibrations. His eyes fell on three framed images on the wall to the right of the colonel's desk. One was a scenic view of a sculptural monument Sol recognized from books as the Honor Memorial of Eshandir and the other two attractively posed but quite different shots of a young, annoyingly pretty Islander man. *I bet that's Ferrox…*

The chair's vat-grown upholstery responded to his body weight by warming up, inviting his achy joints to fall back asleep. *This borders on cruelty*, Sol mused. *Oh, there's one of those jam cakes left, that's what I was doing before I passed out in the chair before; I had a couple of those and some… tea…*

Strong, tapered fingers tapped the laptop to attract the weary youth's attention as he struggled against maliciously cuddly furnishings. The jerky, slightly fuzzy recording playing on it was a flashback from Sol's afternoon, now captioned. "Astrum, what should proper engagement protocol be in this situation?"

"I was not briefed, specifically, regarding encounters with humans on that soil. I assume we should have observed them, written a report, and left, only engaging

375

if discovered." He shifted his legs and shivered. *Huh, I'm cold. Really cold.* "In light of the major's correct assumption the subordinate was worm-ridden, I'm not sure letting them get back to a population center would have been the right thing to do, either."

Kiertus regarded Val a moment then inexplicably glanced at the couch against the far wall. "True; knowingly allowing an infected person to enter a human population would have constituted biological warfare. Did you acquire footage of the dissection?"

"I was hoping that would be in Parthenos' report, sir. I just puked a lot."

Val made a horrible face and looked as if he might perform a reenactment on Sol's behalf. The colonel tilted his head sympathetically. "Valdieren. I believe your bed needs you more than I at this point. I've got it from here. You are dismissed."

"Appreciated, sir," said the exhausted man quietly as he stood and performed a round of salutes, then exited. *He just honored the couch. He's either hallucinating or I was right.*

The laptop rotated away from Sol. Rhythmic, rapid touch-typing followed. "Captain Valdieren showed me some photographs you took on Kourhos."

"The major said I shouldn't concern myself with those."

"Did he? Hm. That's interesting. I'll ask him what he meant by that, since he most certainly submitted a request to promote you to lieutenant prior to this mission."

"He what?" *I'm freezing. Why aren't my ladders working? And I'm nauseous again. Motion sickness?*

"We'll discuss that later." Kiertus messed with his computer a bit more. "That triple-spoked footprint is a trademark of Myzhanzi Offensive Biotechnology."

Once more, the laptop turned so that the screen faced him. A new video rolled, with identical image and sound quality to the last. There was a lot of movement and mostly incoherent noise.

Didn't we destroy all their production facilities? Didn't you supervise that operation? Sol strained to make something out on the screen. He rubbed his biceps and shivered. His mouth opened, but his attempt at speech was aborted by Kiertus' crisp, peculiar voice. *Smoke in cold air...*

"It was likely made by something like this."

More blurry movement and loud noises. The camera panned between open air and towers of rock, fire, dark smoke, what appeared to be distant lightning. Odd shapes were lit up by flashes; slowly it occurred to Sol he was looking at a land-coral village built into the sides of a valley. He heard three voices, two men and one woman, over whistles, cracks, and explosions. There was an awful hum to as well, which with the shakiness made it very difficult to look at directly. Occasionally one man would be in view; the other man's voice must have been the trooper wearing the camera. The woman he only saw as the top of a head here, a shoulder there. One man spoke Archon; the woman screamed frantically in an unfamiliar language. The second man translated between the two, although for obvious reasons once he made it out, he was not translating her to the other soldier as much as the other way around.

"You have to move! Get up!" More scrambling. More screaming. "Come on!"

"Her children..."

"Tell her we have someone on it. She has to come with us. Come with us, you hear me? Right now!"

There was more of the strange language, which struck Sol as oddly-accented saurtaf. The man giving the orders tried to carry or help the woman along. Then the translator, the one who was not the camera, started screaming in Archon, "Fuck! Fuck what is that! Captain – what the fuck is that!"

"Where!" The camera moved, and moved again. "Oh shit. Shit!" The humming whine amplified, accompanied by a booming, creaking cacophony, a powerful and unpleasant winding noise. "Grab her and run, Stormcrow. Run as fast as you can, get out of here."

"Captain!"

The voice roared: "That's an order! Get out of here!"

Through all this, the woman screamed. Then she was silent. The man –
Stormcrow - was visible on camera now. His features were obscured by full Star
Assault kit, albeit a slightly older version, and the elvish-looking woman was
unconscious, thrown over his shoulders. He said something Sol could not make
out, and scrambled down the cliff with the woman's limp body strapped
awkwardly to his gen harness. The camera turned, and the source of the noise
could be seen: trailing smoke, roughly five meters tall, an impossible
contraption clambered over the rocks and coral towards the captain. It was
something like a stubby anemone grafted to a sea star over a mechanical base,
with five rotten legs that seemed to be made of bone or chitin and heavy,
dripping hydraulic tubes. When it lifted its feet, the pads were *that shape*.

From the shift in camera, the captain crouched, propping his rifle on his knee.
The contraption lowered itself as well, and it was easier to see that the pumping
disc-like structure in the center had a pivoting skeletal domed cap, a circle of
inward-curving ribs with loose, stretchy membranes between. A huge,
irregularly patterned cylinder rose from the middle of this, also hooked to loose
translucent hoses. The tapered cylinder swung to a new angle, pressing down
into a membrane wall, as the whole assembly shuddered and made more
horrifying noises.

The captain spoke quietly in a soft repetitive way. Sol focused; Archaic
Shandrian. He made out, "… and I fear nothing… for I am above the sun… I am
beyond harm…" and something that sounded like, "I am a part of everything."

The cylinder pumped in a revolting, fleshy way, like a massive penile sea
creature ejaculating. A reddish orange object hurtled from the tip and fell with a
visceral slap on the rocks near the captain, who fired his pulse rifle into the
bulging, stressed hoses on the front side of the crouching craft. Fluid exploded
out; the device creaked and rattled. He backed up and the camera turned to the
orange thing on the ground.

An oily, rubbery ball with five spindly, writhing, spine-covered tendrils twitched
and vibrated, slowly approaching. "Fuck fuck fuck," he mumbled as he backed
against the cliff. He sought a way away from it, down rather than up, but it
obstructed passage. He was cornered. The arms swelled and throbbed as it oozed
inexorably over the boulders. It stopped, shuddered, and launched its spines, all
at once; a rough sound escaped the captain. He did not say whether he was hit.

Instead the man prayed again. "Aur, take my sacrifice unto yourself, and spare my tribe. Initiate self – "

Suddenly a scree, a flurry of bone-yellow scythes, and the captain was off the ground. "Emily! Emily! You're alive! Let's go, go go!"

Massive wings flapped upward as the camera caught the wretched thing below swelling further, discoloring to a hot, red-laced white, then exploding in a ball of fire that rolled up toward the camera, which went dark. The captain screamed.

Kiertus, now standing beside the desk, looking down at Sol's mortified face, hit the symbol for 'Stop'.

"Sir. What the fuck was that?"

"Footage my men shot about 25 years ago." Yellow and grey irises continued to stare into him under long dark lashes. "We call that walking device a 'Stalker'; that particular one already had most of its external armor burned off by troops further down the pass who did not survive. The projectile is a 'pyrovite'"

The weaponized reconstruction of an echosangia that Bacharanzin obsesses over. Fucking sick.

"Did... did they survive, sir?"

"Stormcrow and the refugee were taken prisoner. The captain died in the infirmary. His bug went mad and Aurgaia had to put her down before she took all the others with her. Fortunately for my crew, he only had to take out Emily, and his own gen, Joyelle. He refused to bond again and became a D-7 pilot."

Sol turned from the pained look in his master's eyes. He thought of Ozzie and huddled. *He killed his own gen, with his own hands?* When he looked up, the colonel squatted before him with a hand on his chair. "Aurgaia, ah, Major Parthenos, is a broken man. Do not hate him; he does a fine job of that himself."

Meekly the boy asked, "Do you know where Ozlietsin is?"

"She's asleep under my desk." The desk 'murp'ed affirmatively as Kiertus put a hand to Sol's forehead. "Are you feeling alright?"

"Kind of feverish and ill, since you mention it." *Oh fuck, no, I was working on those corpses, what if...*

The colonel examined his eyes, gently turned his head left, then right and felt the nodes behind Sol's ears. He smiled. "You didn't drink one of those blue tea bags with the pretty Saurtaf script on it, did you?"

What did I... I remember, flavor choices in the guest basket were horrible so I went with a bag I couldn't read. The only Archon script on it was tiny, 'Made in Uayavu, Avenaur' and a little logo. "Uh, yes, sir."

"Sorry I left those out. Oh my, you probably feel awful. My apologies. Those are a prescription narcotic blend for people suffering from extreme illness. I'll get you some ginger…"

"We make stuff for the saurtzek market still? Even with the trade embargo?" Sol realized he was shaking when the colonel returned to pass him a drink bag.

"That batch was printed for a refugee colony. The colony didn't make it, so I took the shipment since it's my prescription." He sat on the chair arm and smiled down at his astrum.

"Are you ill, sir?"

"Technically, yes. I carry a potentially dangerous infection in my blood. We've successfully kept it suppressed thus far with experimental treatments. Other men in my crew aren't quite as fortunate so I share my stash, as it were." He shrugged. "No need to be concerned; they would be up front with you if there were any risk of contraction. We're all professionals and quite careful."

Sol felt something that might have been anger if he were not so drugged. "You have a blood borne disease and took a virgin astrum?"

"Whoa there, partner." The colonel neatly popped up and dropped into a crouch next to the chair, leaning his forearms on the arm beside Sol's face. "First, the standard procedures of the methods I prefer for initiation are not risky for exposure to my particular passenger, but had you requested that sort of 'instruction', I'd have explained the score and let you make the call. Second, I rather expected that due to my age you'd go for Valdieren or Wyvern rather than me." Kiertus winked with a little smirk, then his face went cold and impassive again. "Third, you run the risk of dying horribly in combat daily in Star Assault; is the slight risk of sexual infection more intimidating than the footage I just showed you?"

Huh. When you put it like that...

"The years after Third Mior were bad for all of us, Yenraziir. I contracted this rotten thing serving my people, and I willingly subject my body as a research vessel to find a cure for it for the same. Every part of me is devoted, every aspect of my life."

"Strain four ichemius, then?" *I can't remember if that's the one that mutates into a killer epidemic if it gets in humans or saurtzek, is that four or two? Oh wait, maybe it's strain one that does that, the one you get if you eat genadri eggs or chrysalises? Yeah that's the one that gets in water supplies and mutates and went rampant all over Archos... and two is the one the worms carry, I think? I don't want to read that file again, it's so nasty...*

Kiertus nodded. "Do you mind if I call you by your given name? Solvreyil is your mother to me, still."

"No, sir. Er, Sheriden." Sol tried to smile. The ginger drink was helping his nausea but his mind was a gruesome montage. "You once said, my mother, she was good at hitting those machines..."

A short laugh issued from the old, tired elf, crouching balanced on the balls of his long feet. "Oh, yes. The Ilu started using Stalkers about 60 years ago; at least, that's when we started seeing them, during the siege of Triotos. Pyrovites are a relatively new development; they've been a hot topic of research for the past three decades, no intention of pun." He took Sol's hand in both of his, and said in a fatherly story-telling tone, "Niarri served on General Oraska's ship, the *Lorelei*. But she was in love with a young Ruhn on my ship, a paratrooper, my very first astrum, in fact. She made it her personal mission to turn every Stalker she saw into a smoldering scrapheap, and she would keep a little tally of them, taking screen caps of her observation monitor, sending them to him with little notes. 'This one's for you, Auri.' And he'd show them to me, laughing, 'That crazy haki girl is sending me notes again'. But he lived for it, and eventually, they were lovers. She transferred to my ship to be with him. She took the oath of knighthood so they could be together."

Ice water poured into his heart from some extra-dimensional flood gate. *I guess I should have seen this coming.* "Parthenos... and my mom?"

"His obsession with revenge and pursuit of his career eventually turned her away. But due to a little fuck up by the *Vol Hryzrmyr*'s medical wing, a portion of my crew, Parthenos and the Lady Solvreyil included, were improperly staged. The Haarnsvaar stationed aboard my ship took his second collar and expunged the record of him being a conduit; I ordered him to start a family. He went straight for Niarri, rejected or not. She had already hooked up with a chubby red haired tech liaison from her old post."

"My dad." Sol shivered.

"The biggest insult for Parthenos came later, after he chose to be surgically sterilized and returned to my crew... but that ties in with a historical issue of security clearance. Trust me when I say, his wounds run deep; your presence has been a challenge for him."

Sol stared at his feet. "Why didn't he find someone else?"

Kiertus sighed. "Aurgaia felt he could never find someone who not only had seen what he had seen and survived the hell of that war, but someone who saw right through him and was never afraid to say so. Your mother was – is – one of a kind. He said if he couldn't have her, then being with Joyelle and myself for the rest of his life would be enough."

Ouch. Every part of his slender body ached in tune with his heart.

"I need to call him up next, and part of our meeting will involve you. Don't bring any of what I just told you up; I simply felt you needed the perspective." He stood and tapped his slate. "You're welcome to go to your coffin when dismissed, or the infirmary, but you are also welcome to stay here. I appreciate sleeping next to a warm body and not waking up with spunk all over my back."

Thankfully I swallowed that last slurp of ginger drink. "Excuse me, colonel?"

In a straight-forward manner, Kiertus explained, "Just between astrum and master, when I bed the top brass on this ship, I inevitably wake up to them frosting my spine. Wyvern is the only one who's willing to just cuddle, and he's assigned elsewhere for a time. I understand their frustrations on all levels but

I've also considered training Nova to bite. As such, I usually sleep alone."

Your life sounds difficult. I don't envy you at all, wealthy star ship commander or not. You have a lover you never see and your partners of convenience are a bunch of dickbags. You're ill but you never really take days off. You spend a lot of time getting to know people who could die at any second. Is religion required to rationalize that shit? I'd need invincible imaginary friends at that point, too.

The colonel offered him a fuzzy bundle. He eyed his master and the squishy lump, then unfolded it. It was an oversized fluffy dark brown sweater of unknown manufacture. Sol gratefully slipped it on. "Thanks, sir. Does this ... tea stuff... break the way the ladders function?"

"Not precisely. You're currently feeling with your ladders instead of being insulated by them; side effect of the pseuvarsine; the fenatja is making you notice the ambient temperature more. It's possible to get used to working with your pulse on those chemicals, but that combo was originally designed by the saurtzek to impair kaffir troops. Turns out, it works much better the other way around, and it works to suppress both active ichemius symptoms as well as keep a verchyne infestation dormant."

As Parthenos strode in, he smiled oddly and squeezed Sol's shoulder. "Goin' native, eh?"

"Excuse me, sir?"

The major tugged demonstratively on the sleeve of his own sweater. Kiertus interjected, "My astrum inadvertently consumed a bag of my *nudj't*."

Sadistic amusement lit the Ruhn. "Man, with your genetics, you have to be miserable right now. Didn't you puke enough for one day? You look like an anti-drug leaflet. Sheriden, look at his eyes."

"I know, poor thing." The colonel regarded Parthenos chastisingly. "So, Auri, I'd love to hear your theories on that torched Okurod facility."

"What'd I do? I know you're pissed because you didn't offer me a drink first."

"Oh. Where are my manners." Kiertus' voice was flat, unamused. "Tea and coffee are on the sideboard, as always. It's serve yourself this morning." The colonel sat back down at his desk.

Parthenos acquired a thermos of coffee and gestured at Sol before taking a seat. "Have you adjusted his clearance yet?"

"Let's do that now, shall we?" Kiertus fidgeted with his slate again. Sol felt a tap on his knee and looked up at the grumpy side-burned face leaning in towards his.

"Hey, kid, gimme your slate, this'll go faster. Thanks." He swiped it from the astrum's hand the moment it was produced and returned to his seat. "Congratulations on your promotion."

"Huh?"

The colonel acknowledged, "Lieutenant Astra, GC3."

Sol was stunned; he wished to say something, express his surprise and gratitude, but Parthenos talked over him. "He's got substantial gaps in his training, still. You're overbooked this week. Who do you want me to put him with?"

"Jaahyden," Kiertus said decisively, without even a pause.

As Parthenos updated schedules, he glanced at Sol dubiously, and exhaled a small, "Whoa. If you insist."

Jaahyden? Wasn't he one of the wing commanders Val warned me about? What is that face *Parthenos is making? There's someone that freaks* him *out?*

"I have a number of theories, colonel, but I'm not really sure how I would verify them without violating our non-intervention policy…"

Sol enjoyed the perturbed parent expression Kiertus made as he grimly quipped, "Well I think it's pretty safe to say we done spread that policy over toast and fucked it black and blue at this point."

Non-chalantly reorganizing his pony tail and smoothing his sideburns, Parthenos remained unflustered. "I disagree. I think we could still hide the gun at its back, say it fell down the stairs, and keep pretending we give a shit." He stretched. "My number one assumption is the verchyne infestation was an unwanted gift from the Baalphae scum, I mean, the arms dealers, they discovered it, flipped, and burned the base. Possibly under orders. The fact one escapee was infected was just ironic, although the way the verchyne hive mind operates under normal circumstances, a dormant carrier is usually a failsafe for perpetuation. Other possibilities include that other factions caught on to the illegal operations and Okurod main HQ ordered the facility destroyed. In that case, the infection was likely incidental; the lucky worms were just hitchhiking to fertile new ground, probably picked up handling black market goods from an unregulated factory or contaminated storage facility."

Parthenos caught Sol's expression and turned to explain, "We're not talking imperially sponsored agents, here; we're talking a criminal faction of Shuv'Enkraath, a group only peripherally associated with the Ilv'xukzuiy government – tough to distinguish sometimes, I know, but as hard as you may find it to believe, the Ilu are rigidly structured people; they take bureaucracy to maddening heights. They like a certain degree of purity in the production of their monstrosities."

"I had the distinctly unpleasant experience of touring a Myzhanzi production facility a few years before I was ordered to annihilate every one we could locate. Parthenos speaks the truth. Whether we agree with their practices regarding the value of life or not, minute details are highly regulated in Ilu society; a saurtzek designer, regardless of religious or political standing, is a saurtzek designer. They take pride in their craft and specificity of purpose."

I get it, I guess. I don't want to grasp that better, at the moment, really. I guess they're saying a professional and regulated Ilu weapons facility would strictly control possible contamination vectors in their abominable sadistic war machines. Yeah, gotta stop thinking about that. Pretty, pretty Honor Memorial, pretty, pretty flags on the wall... Scythes of Mercy... My side is better because it's not as grody, la la la... Yen, you're really high, don't laugh, don't laugh.

"The recordings Val has may hold a key. We may find that the 'heavy activity' in the area included other factions discovering the base. Or we may find the Okurod were there investigating the actions of another faction, that the Okurod were not involved in the trades, in which case, well I apologize for blowing that Templar to shit." He shrugged at Kiertus, whose eyes were slits.

His right arm is twitching. I think he's going to – no, no, he's getting his coffee. I was sure he would back hand the major for a second. Hey colonel, it's cool,

I'd want to slap the sideburns off that smug face, too. Does he jerk off on your back when you sleep? I could imagine that. Don't laugh.

Tension in Kiertus' jaw made his crisp words crack like tiny whips. "You are implying to me that you let your personal hatred of the Okurod potentially interfere with the clarity of our investigation. We very likely should have been attempting to work with them this entire time to uncover the threat to their planet, and, in the long run, to Verraken and to us."

If it was me, my pulse would have exploded that coffee cup by now. Maybe that's why he's not using a closed one; less chance of a steam build up.

"Obviously, this situation requires rectification." The voice, crystalline and pure, like a subterranean waterfall, trickled from an unseen source. The smugness evaporated from the major's countenance but he set his coffee down with a surprising amount of delicacy.

Parthenos calmly returned, "The 89th is on its way. We can easily delegate a few of their advance craft to examining the base wreckage. I have in mind a few 'volunteers' from their crew, even."

"Is that so, Cadet Parthenos?"

He flinched that time. Cadet? Like … Imperial Guild Cadet? That's… odd…

Colonel Kiertus began to speak, then cast exasperated eyes toward the couch. "Master, would you please uncloak? I do so tire of addressing my sofa."

The black form faded into view slowly. Before it fully materialized, both Sol and Parthenos were out of their chairs, kneeling, faced toward the floor. An approving split-second glance from the major confirmed Sol's response as appropriate.

The plated visor rose as horn-like structures on the head lowered, revealing a beautiful, ageless, fine-boned kaffa face. He pressed a hand to either side of his neck, just below his skull, and the helmet collapsed with a chitinous rustle into a cowl against his tendril-covered back. Wavy, silvery hair spilled over his cheeks and shoulders and a precisely trimmed streak of silver fluff hung down from his pale rose pink lips. His skin resembled yellowed ivory with a near luminescent quality; the tone was common in pure north Shandrians and nocturnal mountainfolk, often referred to as 'moon tan'. He shook the shape back into his hair with a toss of his elegant head. "You may return to your seats," he remarked to the kneeling men as he rose. Sol noted the voice had a similar reverberant quality as that of Parthenos, although musical rather than gruff. The crystal clarity of each word was an intentional work-around to combat both his massive fangs and whatever throat structure created the minute but tangible echo.

"*Gen-sheid, Immada,*" Parthenos breathed as he rose; Sol was short of this only by a few seconds, stunned as he was by the man on which he looked. They settled into their seats as the Haarnsvaar officer drifted ghost-like toward the side board. His motions were as fluid as his eerie voice and his feet silent as he stepped nearly on the tips of his pointy armored toes. He was taller than Parthenos, slender and serpentine. Even in his twitching, writhing blue-black armor, which added dimension to all his joints with angular shell-like outcroppings and flanges, he was disturbingly thin.

The officer opened the cabinet beneath the coffee and, using a tendril of his armor, acquired the bottle of luret Kiertus stored there. His arms remained crossed over his chest as his armor poured a glass. "You will lead the advanced detachment at Kourhos, ahead of even the 89th, Parthenos Aurgaia of Triotos. You will personally supervise the operation, answering to me. You will not be working from this cruiser, so I hope that Kiertus can replace you rapidly."

He sipped, staring at Parthenos with pale grey eyes.

"It should not present a serious issue, Master Thiel," the colonel responded with a quarter bow.

Master Thiel. Thielassian Zhemhiir. I'm looking at a several hundred year old dead man. I looked him up after I found his name in the Mior documents and his face is unmistakable. He was an IGN officer who became commander of the Haarnsvaar after an impressive campaign in First Mior, but a series of articles trashing his pre-Imperial background in the press led to his demotion and rumored suicide before the second war. He was the first commander in centuries born in non-imperial territory; a Ruhn who supported Ruahanu joining the Empire and avidly fought for an alternative to execution for HTS sufferers; his detractors successfully used a few youthful acts of piracy against him. They say Queen Aphoisia loved him dearly; it's a shame the public did not.

Sol had not meant to stare, but he found his gaze met by the exquisitely preserved living historical artifact. "Greetings, Solarum Solvreyil Yenraziir of West Asria. It is delightful to finally meet you in person. It is true what they have told me; your resemblance to Myentrios is remarkable." He held an armored hand out to the stunned young officer. "We hope it stops at the physical traits."

'Solarum' is the archaic term for 'Lieutenant Astra' – a man who is on the path of command but is still training as a Holy Knight. What's the protocol? The handbook said to keep our eyes down until they speak to us and I wasn't even doing that much. How did Knights of the Sun greet masters in that book? Here goes nothing... Sol took the offered hand in both of his and bowed his head, almost touching his forehead to the forbiddingly sharp joints of the glove. "*Gensheid*. I am unsure who this Myentrios is or was, but I apologize if my appearance brings unfortunate memories, sir."

That was pretty slick. I sounded all officer-ly. Who's a squire? I'm a squire! Booyah. Man I really want some ice cream.

Celestial grey eyes squinted and waves of silver hair bounced as the man regarded Sol and then the other men, not moving his outstretched arm. Sol was distracted by the joints of the glove softening as the armored hand clasped his left. "You mean to tell me you scoundrels have told this poor boy nothing?"

Kiertus sipped his coffee at the edge of Sol's vision. "Simple enough, Thiel, he was not cleared to know. We could amend that, now, sir, if you wish to do so."

"I left that fixer in Sheriden's garage, sir," Parthenos shrugged haplessly. "I did not wish my personal sentiments to color the facts."

Holding his hand, sympathetically examining the young red-head's drugged eyes and confused expression, the ancient officer quietly reported, "Myentrios Hyrshaanziir was the other hero of Ruahanu. He was a notable officer of 23rd Star Assault and a respected member of the Imperial Guild, destined to wear the black armor." Thiel sipped his luret, casually observing Sol's slowed reaction. "After a public statement by Marsura regarding the genocide of the Ruhn people as 'no particular loss', however, he vanished. Several of us believed him dead, but he had cleverly assumed a new identity and been hiding in IGN. We did not find him again until well after he married and had children."

Sol stared incredulously back. *Was he somehow in the same mix up as mom and*

Parthenos? "Excuse me, sir? How could an officer of the 23rd have children?"

A strange, appreciative smile lit Master Thiel's face for a split second. If Sol assumed correctly, he was appreciating his cover in front of Parthenos, having witnessed Sheriden telling him the other half of the story. "Aurian blood was rare enough traditionally in the military that we did not really understand that Aurians require different chemicals for the staging process; the Ruhn – your father in particular, but many Ruhn – have more Aurian blood than even the most red-headed Holtiini. Combine that with the occasional wild saurtzek gene and you create men who may even regenerate a surgical vasectomy."

Holding his coffee up aloft, Parthenos mocked a toast. "Behold, the Ruhn will to survive."

"That said, we would appreciate if you would voluntarily submit a quantity of semen to Laathas for the Department of Species Preservation. Ah, for research purposes only, of course." Finally retracting his hand, Thiel finished his glass and regarded Sol over the empty container.

His eyes and his mind were as glazed over as the colonel's back after a night of drinking. A bright red mudlock slid as he shifted, falling square into his line of sight. The attempt to suppress a wave of mad giggling was noticed by all present.

"Master Thiel, with the pseuvarsine in that tea, that boy couldn't squeeze half a drop from his melted cannon." The major set his coffee cup down and cracked his knuckles. "Could we get back to discussing this mission you're sticking me on?"

"Hm, well, I suppose that's true, but a week with Jaahyden and he probably won't have a problem with that anymore!" The Haarnsvaar turned with a flourish and drifted back to the sideboard for a refill. "And yes, Parthenos, let's address that matter once I have fixed this lonely container." He hummed the Imperial Anthem as he poured.

Lips pursed between perfectly trimmed streams of black fluff, brows knitted, Parthenos interrupted the musical accompaniment with barely-concealed annoyance, "Sir, am I understanding correctly that you're assigning me to the 89th for the purpose of carrying out a covert exercise?"

"Oh, not at all, my dear cadet. Put you with Ferrox? I love my ships too much to do that. You already destroyed one over far less." Thiel rolled his eyes as he sipped. "I pulled a ship out of Fenrir for you and had it modified months ago, I just was deliberating over which scripture to name the new unit after."

Parthenos stared at Thiel, his expression indescribable. "Excuse me?"

"The *Yetzjmaal*. I'm sure you remember touring last time I saw you? She has been troubleshot to my satisfaction, now."

"Well, yes, I didn't expect you to rebuild the *Ishulya*, but that's not what I meant. How are we even staffing a new Star Assault ship?"

"Ah, you see, this is where we have to dismiss our young friend; this is GC4 business." Thiel smiled broadly, his large fangs escaping a little as he did so. They exchanged salutes as Kiertus assisted the boy out of his chair. "Goodnight, Solarum Solvreyil. Sleep well."

. . . .

Sol made the morning briefing just barely; it consisted of a heavily edited rundown of the information he learned the day prior: last minute intelligence changed plans, the ship would be stationed near Pachar for a time awaiting word from the 89th at Verraken, and Parthenos departed to do a specialist mission with another unit. It was repeatedly stated that chatter regarding their current situation must remain null. In the last minutes of the meeting, a string of promotions were hurriedly announced, including Sol's. The last one surprised him, though. *Val is going to sit in as major prime for a while? There have to be more experienced and qualified people. If I ask, it would be both insubordinate and count as chatter...*

Examining his slate as he approached the lounge, Sol sighed. Sheridan's affectionate voice approached from behind; they were headed the same direction. "What seems to be the trouble, squire?"

Sol blushed a little, even though their physical contact had been limited to sleeping closely for a few scattered hours. He cleared his mind and addressed his superior. "Colonel, what's this Captain Jaahyden's specialty, may I ask, or perhaps I should ask, what sort of job I'm going to be doing, sir?"

Genuine surprise crossed the often-inscrutable countenance. "He flies combat ships, Yenraziir. He used to be XO of the *Ishulya*. Did Teshkanzin or Cheldyne not mention him to you?"

"Several people have mentioned him, sir, but his file is locked up as tight as a monk's ass."

This elicited an inappropriate laugh. "Maybe I should not have increased your time around Val." Kiertus coughed. "Jaahyden came aboard as a navigation engineer, quite a story there; you'll have to wait until he permits you to learn it. He was a troublemaker, though; getting bored was bad for him, very bright boy. Tzan, who was arms sentinel then, armed him and we trained him to fight and fly, because I was going to kill him with my bare hands if someone didn't make him useful. Surprisingly, he took to it like a fish to water; he excelled at everything he tried as long as he was allowed to do it his own way. He was rapidly scaling his way to command when I was given my own vessel again." He rubbed the nearest wall.

"So, he's going to give me more jet training? Or is this about something else?"

A feline eye fell on Sol although the head did not turn. "Solvreyil, I felt it time to expand your scope of knowledge regarding the function and operation of this particular unit. Seeing things from more than one side builds character and disperses the tendency towards factionalisation and, ah, ill-considered habits within this crew." Kiertus sighed, seeming to puzzle his words before speaking again. The final statement came rushed: "I apologize for refusing Parthenos' request to take you as astrum."

Sol was more than happy Kiertus could not see the look on his face. *Weird old man! What a dumb thing to apologize for!* "Did you suppose he would mistreat me because of his relationsip with my parents?"

"Ah. Yes and no. You likely would have been safe from sexual or physical abuse, at least for a time, as he has deep empathy with virginal and confused young men. Much as he is extraordinarily kind and polite to women and animals – as if they are sacred and holy. His time on the refugee ship, as a boy, was rough. Even with therapy, with good masters, he is still scarred in a way that he sometimes… turns out."

"I heard, about Wyvern…"

"I care for Auri, but I am glad he is off my ship. And now you will answer to Jaahyden as your direct supervisor, and myself as your mentor. This will remain true until our next operation, at least. You may wish to consider your initiatory options during this time."

"Initiatory? That means it hurts, right?" Sol was half joking, half genuinely concerned.

Before Kiertus could answer, the doors squelched open and the air was filled with excited bug-sounds and the laughter and chatter of bathing officers. The colonel hurried on towards his office saluting hellos to the crowd as Sol was dragged aside by Bacharanzin to verify anecdotal information – and settle a monetary bet – regarding the frequency of volcanic activity on Holtiin.

"Once a month if not more, a mountain explodes or a new one comes up out of the water or one sinks. It's why no one lives in the southern hemisphere. Man you people sometimes, I swear. How do you go to the Academy and not know this?" Faces fell. Most of the currently assembled had not bothered with formal education in spite of their opportunity to get it for free. *Glad Aukaldir isn't here; I'd be 'Mr Privileged Jerk' for the rest of the day.*

"See? See? I told you. Hah! In your face." Bachi did a little dance on the pool edge in his underwear. "You can all just instant transfer me when you get your slates at the lockers, swabs." A damp hand grabbed Sol's shoulder. "You gonna grace us with your sainted presence, Lieutenant Space-monk?"

And that's why our slates have credit readers. Go Star Assault. "I'd love to stick around but I've gotta go meet with Captain Jaahyden, apparently."

The remark was aimed at Bacharanzin and spoken with no particular volume, but every two-legged individual in earshot went silent. When the gen noticed, they clammed up, too. Sol looked around uncomfortably, saluted, and marched on towards the lounge.

His immediate view of the room included no occupants, though his slate showed a purple dot with no call sign. An agitated voice came from the Casualty Couch (the nickname for the lounge's legendary, much abused sofa; Cheldyne claimed it 'got more post-combat action than any bed on the ship').

"Come on, little fuckers!" It was a thick Ryzaan accent, all the 'i' sounds were long 'e's and the 'e' s were long 'a's, and the consonants had a bite. "Goblin scum! Eat astral whip. How do you like me now, eh!"

Sol walked around to the front of the sofa. The man on the couch, lying on his back in disarrayed casual clothing, glaring up at his slate (held in both hands) took no notice. He had sharp facial features, protruding cheekbones that would have given him a completely triangular countenance if his chin had been even slightly more pointed. Thin black mudlocks flopped in all directions as he animatedly played his game. *He doesn't even know I'm standing here.* Sol checked the map and verified that, yes, this was the unspecified purple dot.

Here goes nothing. "Lieutenant Solvreyil Yenraziir reporting for duty, sir!"

The head turned with a snap, tossing locks into a new configuration. Wide eyes accented by enormous pupils bored into him; little fangs peeked in his peculiar smile. "*Cho wahd'tze,*" he drawled.

Ryzaan slang, means something like, 'How is life, brother?' Weird. I didn't know people really talked like that. He's like a bad stereotype. Is that mascara or does he just have dark eyes? Ryzaan guys wear make up when they go out on the town, tourists back home did it all the time, but that's not appropriate for a starship officer, is it?

Since the locks moved, Sol could now see a swirly design tattooed above the man's left eye. He was trying not to stare conspicuously and saluted to have an excuse to look at the ceiling instead.

"At ease. We're in the lounge for fuck's sake." The man returned to his game. "Almost to a save cube, have a seat."

You are kidding me. "Yes, sir." Sol sat at a nearby table, checking the time on his slate before shutting off its non-essential functions and storing it. He noticed no motion, but the officer was standing right beside him when he looked up. *And that's how Ryzaa enslaved humanity and conquered Eshandir.*

A hand extended. "Captain Jaahyden Iloquarri, DSC, MPR, NFS."

'DSC' is 'Dash Superior Command', meaning he can supervise and train wing commanders; 'MPR' is something like 'Master Pilot, Regal' meaning he's qualified to fly any of the Royalty Class cruisers and command them in combat. He shook Jaahyden's unpleasantly drug-sweaty hand. "NFS, Sir?"

"That would be 'No Fuckin' Shit', lieutenant." The cheerful demeanor did not abate, but the tone was downright snotty. "Stand up for a proper greeting; I hate this New Civility shit."

Oh hell, what's a proper Ryzaan folk greeting consist of? Why can't I remember? Think back to the etiquette course. Maybe he'll lead? Jaahyden stepped forward, clasped both Sol's hands, and sniffed the young lieutenant deeply. Sol followed suit; the man reeked of synthensin and pseuvarsine, a rarely prescribed drug based on an exceedingly addictive, often lethal, Ilu intoxicant. *Navigator's Sap,* Sol thought with a twinge of nausea, having just ridden the last of a dose from his system. *How does he maintain that level of fine coordination on that crap?*

The captain stood a little too close, continued to sniff. Before he let go and stepped back, he purred, "Mmm. Virgin." The boy hopped back a hair, much to Jaahyden's amusement.

"How..." Sol glared. *Maybe Parthenos told him?*

A stretch, a shrug, a neck scratch. "Hard to hide things like who you're fucking on a ship with no showers. All you smell like is gun oil, bugs, and drugs. You're too young to be a monk, boy. I hear you trained with Teshkanzin though..." He tossed himself onto the sofa, sitting up somewhat properly this time. "If you kept your ass one-way through that, you are one tough little fucker. I applaud."

Disregarding that. "Colonel Kiertus said you had some work for me, sir."

The voice was genuine but the face mocked. Long brows knitted over half-closed eyes and a devious smirk. "He wants me to teach you to fly a ship old-style, of course. With your orgone output."

Sol stared then saluted. "Yes sir. Do you intend to stick your cock in me, sir?"

"Naw, thanks for the invite, but I'm at the tail end of a five year vaccine research study and I can't fuck it up, no pun meant." Jaahyden hooked his thumbs in the belt that was not really holding up his trousers. In fact, the only thing that seemed to keep them in place was their snugness, and this gesture furthered their journey down his hips. "If we're going to spend a week floating around Pachar jerking off while the 89th does all the work, you might as well do it literally, huh? Beats bayonet practice, I guess. Follow me to C-2; I'll show you how to solo on the main console of a cruiser."

"I'm going to learn to fly the *Sanjeera*?"

"Or any ship just like it. It's easier to learn the Ryzaan method on a cruiser console; less potential distractions even though you're surrounded by other people. Say goodbye to shame and hello to a long and prosperous career, brother."

XVIII. Dutiful Satellites

"Oh, it's just you. For a second I thought it was Ferrox coming to unleash a font of Hell on me." He turned back to the console, unconcerned in his smoke cloud.

Shaan planted his muscular rear in the communications seat. "Lucky you, it's just Sentinel Shame." He stretched his legs and leaned his coppery locks back on his well-honed arms. "Smells like a fuckin' mine in here. You just starin' at that fuckhole chain smokin'?"

"Yes, actually." Ulissarian 'Stormcrow' Mavarakki rolled the fenny between his fingers before replacing it between his dark lips. They stared at the image of Verraken on the view screen.

"Please tell me we're sittin' here waitin for a Rec cruiser so we can ash that piece of shit."

One white eyebrow (all he had to speak of, as the location of the other was covered by a partially fused prosthetic eye/patch/harness arrangement) rose as the old major issued something that could have been a laugh. "According to Ferrox, that's not included in the Haarnsvaar orders." He jiggled his slate at Shaan. "Or did you not notice we had a Razor in the aft pipe?"

"Fuck. Still here?"

"Yeah. Orders dispensed. Been assigning units for two hours. Wasn't going to start raids until after your shift started. Surprised to see you up, really."

"Mighty polite of ya, major." Lines creased his face as Shaan smiled. "Let me guess; I'm issuing because Ferrox won't let me go to the surface." After the colonel's utterly justified tirade a few days prior, Shaan was surprised he was not pinched and floating in hard freeze.

Ulissarian handlessly rolled the cigarette to one edge of his mouth and did not remove it to say, "No, we're short of D-7 pilots. You're leading a team with Ratya; you'll be gunning after you lose the cargo."

"Why not just solo me in a D-7?"

Ulissarian's partially mechanical glare could have stopped the hearts of smaller beasts. "How 'bout, 'not only no, but fuck no'?"

"Fine." Shaan unrelaxed, logging in to the computer before him with a swipe of his hand-tag. "Is Ratya picking our team or can I?"

"You're stuck with a bunch of airmen. Sterzin took the worthy officers. Sorry."

This elicited an eyeroll from Sentinel Kvatchkiir. "Figures." *I have no room to protest a damned thing just now.* "Low-risk mission, I take it?"

Smoke swirled as Major Ulissarian shook his head. "You'll laugh at the mission plan. We'd have to work at it for more than a handful of friendly fire casualties."

"You're fucking kidding me!" exclaimed Shaan as he scrolled the info on his terminal. "This is almost better than atmosphere flambé."

"I understand the reasons for your feelings, but there are kaffir there…"

"Yeah. Guys like Ledo. That's a model for society."

"Fair enough." Ulissarian offered the butt of his fennie to the sentinel.

"I want to, but I'd rather lose a hand than explain to monk-boy why I'm vomiting in our cockpit."

"How about a shot, then? That'll wear off before you have to jump."

"Excellent." The coppery mane flipped as he opened a door under the console. A tray bearing a crystal kolzhi set slid out. "Let's toast to regime change."

….

"Orange and grey? That's no color for a sea! You're joking right?"

The entire bridge laughed. Since they often laughed at things he said (the pilots and chief nav laughed at farts, it was no achievement) Sol ignored it and awaited a serious answer.

Colonel Kiertus did not look up from petting Nova. He seemed queerly delighted. "No one is messing with you, lieutenant. That is a sea. Or was, before an earthquake upset a fossil fuel retrieval device and contaminated it beyond the capacity of most life forms."

"Orange is, in fact no color for a sea." Jaahyden alone found no humor in Sol's exclamation. It was his way to swing from buffoonery to sober discussion in a heartbeat. In the past week, Sol watched him swap demeanors like an actor changing between scenes. "Rather than plug or fix the leaking device, they squabbled over responsibility and money until that little sea and several nearby waterways were poisoned. There are spots like this all over their planet, and they are being cornered into little arable terrain through misuse of their environment. Just like Kourhos. Now they beg for help, 'Come, elves, from heaven, do your magic and save us,' but only if we disregard the enslavement of the remaining kaffir on their soil, for which they claim religious justification." He spat into a suction tube (if Kiertus was not a-bridge, it would have been the floor). "These are the people we are dealing with, Sol, look hard and remember."

Parthenos' voice echoed in his head, *"Try not to hate your ancestors when you see it."* He hoped to see the *Esimaar*; the 89th was performing an 'operation' on the other side as of 24 hours prior. Their ship was cloaked or obstructed so the only visual was an environmentally devastated ash trap and its squalid moon.

Cassami, one of the two pilots required to keep the ship in a stable orbit, cheerfully piped up in his typically drug-hazy voice. "Welcome to Verraken. Population: Fucked. Recommended course of action: 10 EOS cannons into stratosphere. Bake until done."

"Poof, no eyebrows!" chimed in Utjyra, beside him, equally drugged up and additionally, half dressed. They fell into fits of giggling in spite of holding their arms still against the pulse-responsive panels to which they were pressed.

Nutty chews. That's what Val calls them. It's been affecting my ability to eat my favorite snack, thinking of them every single time I open one. What a pair. And Jaahyden says they make them like this on purpose. What the Hell, Archos. Thinking of Valdieren bummed him out a little; Val was extra moody and short lately. Whether it was one of their promotions, his assignment change, or something else, the temperature lowered when Val entered a room with him.

"BCSO. Let's just do it already, I'm sick of lookin' at that thing. Where's IGN? Can we HT the *Kelmia*?"

Sol would have been appalled beyond belief a few weeks prior. 'HT' stood for 'Hostile Takeover' and 'BCSO' stood for 'Burn Clear, Start Over'. Lashniel, the navigator, was a doped up but still furious man. He served with Kiertus in at least two wars, but was moved to this position 'because it has no authority and no fucking guns', according to Jaahyden. 'Navigator' seemed like a dangerous position of power to Sol, although watching Lash absorbed in the calculations of ship movement, he saw the butterfly at the center of the cyclone. Somehow, in numbers, the man found peace.

"Lash," Kiertus said gingerly, "there are at least fifty thousand kaffir left there, of which we are aware, purebloods not counting possibly haki and saurka. They would love to be Imperial citizens. We would like to liberate them. Should that number dwindle sharply, I'm sure there's a case for negotiation."

'We don't burn anymore.' That's what everyone in IGN says. But you talk to Star Assault guys, they say 'IGN doesn't train people to fire cannons anymore. We still do.' Surprise! We just have to take over a vessel with enough big guns for long enough, then a few of our brass eat it in prison for a while. As Kiertus says, 'It is a dirty job, but someone must do it.' Why isn't that one of our glorious mottos? Sol was, thanks to his most recent boss, well-educated in what was quaintly termed 'Last Resort Protocol'. LRPs were a grim, secret priority of Star Assault. While 'We get there first' was usually true, 'We show up after the party to clean' seemed more accurate for the 17th. 'Leave no trace'.

Jaahyden took the empty seat behind the pilots. Sol took a position near this seat and took an interest in the console, aware who was about to enter. The bridge doors opened with a little 'slurp' and Valdieren appeared. As expected, the ambient temperature fell approximately ten degrees as the captain-temporarily-major caught sight of the fresh lieutenant and his boss.

'The Third Seat' as it was often referred, was that of the M-prime, although Jaahyden explained that he, not Val, would take that seat if there were any incidences of ship-to-ship confrontation until someone named 'Tyrnan' came aboard. Otherwise it would fall to Kiertus, whom everyone swore could both fly a ship and fire the forward guns while commanding its men solo. The selection of Val as prime had more to do with his ma'at-shi abilities and respect-based relationship with the colonel. Mysh explained during a training break that the second in command of a Kimetj cruiser needed not only the usual authoritarian streak and attention to detail one would expect, but the ability to take down the chief in hand-to-hand combat. *"The hope is the prime stays on the Empire's side in case of coup,"* Myshkor remarked. *"Which is why it'll never be Jady again."*

Val and the colonel spoke in hushed tones. Try as he might not to look, Sol noticed agitation on the face of the younger officer. He could not make out words per se, but there was strain in Valdieren's voice. Finally they nodded at one another, and Val approached the communications console. No one manned it currently, as the only full-time communications guy, Alanso, had been on a 25-hour shift up until a few hours ago. Toshogar ('Toshi', to everyone), who was trained to replace him, was now being aggressively trained up as a trooper by Kahner and Myshkor. *This ship's staffing situation is unbelievable. I hate to think like this, but what keeps us from rebellion and piracy?*

Turning not to catch Val's eyes, Sol noticed Jaahyden playing with a figurine that had been on the console. Something Parthenos left behind, no doubt; a limitedly poseable statuette of a busty woman clad in improbable clubwear. It embarrassed him to look at, but his new captain flailed her little arms at him. "This is how humans on Curtis' homeworld see elves. Look at her pouty lips. Can you imagine Eavrellene making a face like this? I'd piss myself."

"Why are you so inappropriate, sir?"

"Does that massive stick in your tiny ass hurt, lieutenant?" Jaahyden 'ran' the little elf woman across his console, 'pursued' by a rubber dragon. "Rarrrgh."

I work for you. You have medals. You are paid to fly star ships into combat. I cry for the Empire. "Do they think elven women need rescuing from anyone but themselves, sir?" Sol asked, settling his posterior on the portion of the console usually reserved for drinks. "How the hell did he grow up on a human colony without getting murdered? Or do you know?"

Sol was correct he would incur no wrath for his drop in formality. Jaahyden was not prone to giving a fuck. "Well," the captain said with a quick glance back at Kiertus, who petted the sleeping gen draping his lap and both arms of his command chair, "I guess he found a tribe of humans he convinced to accept him, because he was tough enough to take bullets from the men they were fighting. That's the story, anyway. Would explain why he's such a hard bastard, huh?"

Val's voice crisply broke the air. "Attention. I'm going to do that thing you all hate. I apologize in advance."

Even with earplugs, the 'all hands' triple-alarm was obnoxious. It roused attention, even from deep sleep or a dead drunk. The sound silenced even the gen, who would all turn their heads quizzically up at the nearest PA system.

"Attention crew, this is Officer Valdieren speaking. This is a mandatory announcement. It will repeat at 02.25 and 02.55. No excuses will be accepted; failure to acknowledge will result in severe disciplinary action." He turned off the PA to collect himself. Kiertus nodded, eyes closed, and Val continued. "We are currently orbiting Verraken. The 89th has just warped out and it is now our turn. Starting on the hour, I will dispense missions. Assignments are classified. Chatter regarding target information is strictly forbidden. If not called to the bridge, your assignment will be dispensed via slate from your commanding officer. If you do not hear from anyone specifically by 0400, report immediately to your commanding officer. Honor and sacrifice. Over."

He slumped into his chair, looking paler and thinner than usual. Sol wondered when he last slept. There were no runners on the bridge. "Captain Jaahyden, permission to get Captain Valdieren some coffee?"

"Go ahead. Kid's a wreck." Jaahyden cleaned his nails with a tiny plastic sword. He held it before him and remarked, "That's where that went!" before returning it to the figurine. "Only maker's in the lounge though, now. He'll call you back to the bridge the moment you leave, you just watch."

"That's OK. I have a plan." Sol produced his slate and texted Cheldyne. In twenty minutes, Ozzie appeared at the bridge door with a no-spill thermal mug.

The colonel was impressed. "I never thought of training Nova to do that." He scratched his chin. "Does she operate the coffee maker by herself, too?"

"No, sir. Cheldyne does, sir. We've made some attempts, but so far Minerva is the only bug who can make coffee or tea by herself, and she does make quite a mess doing so, sir." Sol was proud of their experimental training all the same. He suspected Tracy would be best at it. Since his slate abduction, Sol witnessed her using the vending machine, using Jady's slate to prank call Aukaldir, and doing pre-flight manual prep in a Dash. However, she could not be bothered to stop playing virtual card games with Lep to learn the coffee process. *She's just as weird and unruly as he is; 'every knight has his mirror', indeed.*

"Thanks for the coffee, Ozzie, Lieutenant Sol. Deeply appreciated." Val held the mug tightly in his tired hands. "Captain Jaahyden, step out with me a moment. Sol, don't go anywhere; you're next."

Jaahyden rose from his seat, gesturing Sol to take it. He did so, expecting the collar-reading device to yell at him, since it previously was programmed to accept Val, Jaahyden, Parthenos, or Kiertus, and to Sol's knowledge, no one else. Silence. A couple others on the bridge clapped or gave a "Whoo!"

Sol chucked the rubber dragon and caught pilot #2 up side the head, quite on purpose. He hissed, "Don't 'whoo' me, Utjrya. Now I actually have to pay attention when Jady runs his scary potty mouth."

"Now Sol. Don't be insubordinate. That's Captain Jady and that potty mouth is respectably decorated."

Lash seemed impressed. "Colonel, be honest, do you have amplifiers in those things? He barely spoke loud enough for me to hear him."

Kiertus' smile was genuine. He wiggled his ears emphatically. "My only amplification devices are the ones with which I was born, I'm afraid."

Huh… what's this? That's a ship, off to our side. It displays on Jady's screen but not the main monitor? Is it the Esimaar? *I want to see it! I hear it's an older model of Kimetj than the* Sanjeera. *That seems too big though, but too small to be an IG ship. Why doesn't it have a label? I wonder…*

The door slurped. Sol abandoned the console as a hand fell on his shoulder. "Your presence is requested outside. Congratulations on your first leading mission. Get out of my seat."

Leading? Aw, what the… dammit. "Yes, Captain Jaahyden, sir!" The lieutenant rose, saluted, and walked out to meet Val. He leaned on the wall, drinking his coffee calmly. He looked beyond exhausted. Sol bowed and saluted.

Even his voice was tired. "How are you doing, Sol? It's been a while since we've had a chance to talk."

"Alright, I guess, sir. Busy, you know, but, as things go, can't complain." That was not quite a lie; Sol never had an opportunity to complain to people about being lonely and feeling left out. *I've had so few friends, I wouldn't know from 'normal'. And I'm certainly not going to complain about it to a superior officer who's far more put upon than I. We're both busy and he's been stressed out, and*

I'm sure Kiertus putting me with Jady wounded his pride. "I hope you are well, too, all things considered, captain."

Val shrug-nodded, almost as if to say, "It could be worse." "You've trained intensively and you've done well, so I've put you in charge of your own Dash for this. You'll be able to select a small team; I've emailed you a list of available men. I'm afraid a few others got first pick, but you're early enough in the rosters that your team won't have to be total newbs."

"Thank you, captain. I really appreciate that, sir."

"Do you want some of this coffee? I'm not in the shape to drink it all, but it's nice and strong the way Chel always makes it." Solvreyil accepted the cup gratefully. "Your target information is in a double-secured file attached to the mail. You'll need to feed it to your Dash and log in twice and answer a question to get it. Short form, the 89th, while they were disabling power and ... acquiring incidental supplies, I guess ... confirmed locations of some suspected religious extremists and their training compounds and munitions stores. Your coordinates are specific so as to avoid civilians. If you veer off them, you'll have additional collateral clean up to preserve mission security. Am I making myself clear?"

"Sir. Yes, sir." *Just like the simulation we did competitively this week. I came in second to Val for 'fewest innocent casualties' and won extra rations because I was in the top ten for mission completion efficiency. Jaahyden schooled everyone, though, in spite of a 50% civie casualty rate, he aced the mission in twenty minutes with an uninjured crew with two handicaps working against him. You'd never tell by just hanging out with him, but that freak is a bad ass.*

"I have a lot of other appointments today, Sol. Any further questions?"

Fanging his lower lip, he asked, "Am I doing this from air or ground, sir?"

"You have a crew and ship and are familiar with protocol. We trust you to decide what's best in a given situation." He saluted, a little too stiffly, as if unhappy with formality. "Honor and sacrifice, lieutenant."

Solvreyil returned the gesture. "Honor and sacrifice, captain."

...

His crew were assembled and seated aboard the Dash when Sol and Ozzie boarded. He gave his men an abbreviated rundown, reminding them of the recommended combo dosage then took his own before he swung into the cockpit. Bacharanzin sat in a relaxed manner in the master seat until Sol issued an exaggerated cough in his direction.

"Welcome, lieutenant!"

I'll count that as a salute and not give him a hard time for now. Sol synched his slate to the vehicle and opened Missionnotes. As it loaded, Bachi began pre-flight procedures while Sol scanned the Dash's documentation. "Eek?" he said aloud, without meaning to, referring to their craft's release signature.

Bacharanzin nodded affirmatively as he continued his tasks, taxiing up to the launch bay. "Yeah. There was a pilot meeting two days ago, I was surprised to not see you at it, what with you working with Trauma and all." He shrugged. "He's sitting in as wing commander for starboard, right now, while Wyvern's doing… whatever he's doing."

Iekierpin is stand-in commander? Knew I should have gone to that meeting even though Jady said it was optional for paratrooper officers. "Not Spearhead?"

The response was quiet, almost under the astrum's breath. "Yeah. People aren't really happy about that."

That had the tone of a 'we're not supposed to discuss this' issue. Digitally paging through the maps for their mission, Sol remained silent as Bachi launched their vessel from the *Sanjeera*.

"Hey, swing the main view screen to the right in about… now."

"Huh?" Sol switched the monitors and sputtered. "What the hell is that?"

Bacharanzin laughed. "I have a good guess, but I couldn't actually tell you. I got a text from Checkmate last night to look out the starboard observation deck, 'to see something you've never seen'."

That must be the Yetzjmaal*; it's that new class, the Triotine, it must be.* It vaguely resembled the *Sanjeera*, although wider and longer with more head-like projections. There were a second set of heavier-looking pipes arranged beneath the 'regular' pipes. *Exo launchers? Wow. Is Parthenos on a ship full of armored or marines? Those clusters of oblong things, if they're the same on that as on ours... Holy fuck. We don't need to HT anything if Star Assault has a full set of planet burners again.*

"It's rad. I want on it. I keep hoping they'll restation me, nothing yet." Bachi seemed upset, then returned to flying as if nothing was out of the ordinary.

"I'd take the fact that you're not assigned to a new master yet as a good sign, Wildfire." *For him and you; I kind of assumed this was a suicide mission for him. He's probably too valuable for that. Ugh I hope I am, too.* "Tossing a map on main with our sites on it, still picking who to drop where but you can get us through the atmosphere and to the location without further assistance, I trust?"

"What I'm best at; apparently even my bug doesn't want me to jump." Rocket had gotten in a fight with 'another gen' (Chel would not say whom) and was in the infirmary. His frustrated face lit up as he scanned the map. "Hey, Echo. There 'Incidental Supplies' tag on mission." He said it in his hacked up, hodge-podge version of Holtiini, presumably to keep the conversation private.

Sol continued to examine maps, mentally allocating the man and bug power they carried. "What's that one mean, anyway? Couldn't find it in the handbook."

Childlike glee resonated in the deeply accented voice. "Requisitioning allowed. Um looting, basically."

"Are you for real, Wildfire?"

Bacharanzin nodded furiously. "Totes serious. There bunch of rules and everything we take has be inspected by chiefs, but can score pretty cool shit."

"Like what sort of rules?" Sol double-checked the coordinates and gestured to Bachi and the mini-yun controls. Switching to Universal Archon, he said over the PA, "About to shift into the atmosphere, everyone fueled and secure?"

A loose chorus of affirmatives and bug chirps issued from the crew cabin.

"Like we can't strip our own guys – leave 'em for Retrievers - we're not supposed to bring back food unless it's still crated in the original packaging and it's from inside the Empire, and absolutely no saurtzek stuff at all unless there's a Haarnsvaar-certified expert in your drop team. But that still leaves books, non-Baalphae jewelry, flags, household stuff as long as it doesn't have an illegal fuel supply still in, sometimes clothing, weapons… Checks has impressive collection; boxed it all up for him."

His room's been reassigned? This is not looking good for you, Bachi…Probably much better for me, though. Sol braced for the transfer and said nothing.

….

Where is this captain? I thought this kid was the best they had. Parthenos cracked his knuckles impatiently behind his back as he stored his slate. *Hurry up you little shit, I don't have all day.*

The man skidded into the room, clearly having used his pulse to propel him. He saluted with his longish black hair half scrambled from its pony tail. "Sir! Major Parthenos, sir! Apologies for my tardiness, sir!"

Wonder if he remembers me from that time when his little girlfriend smashed Val's nuts? The major remained perfectly calm and straight faced, displaying neither his anger nor amusement. "Can you explain said tardiness, Captain Tauverius?"

"Sir! Yes, sir. I was going over final training with Master Wyvern before he returns to the *Sanjeera*, sir."

Major Parthenos licked the sheathes of his currently retracted fangs. *As much as I'd like to rip him for it, that training is crucial to the effectiveness of this team. Clearly in need of some humility, though.* "Well, in that case, I hope it was a fantastic blow job."

The young captain did not skip a beat. "Sir, yes, sir. It was just a hand job, sir."

Surprise, surprise, little rich boy is as Shandrian as he looks. He'll be tough to fuck with. "Shake me with the other one, then." Parthenos extended his arm with one raised eyebrow. He guessed right about which palm had been used and Tauverius was forced into an awkward hand shake. "At ease, I'm happy to have you in my crew. Hope you're ready to work your ass off."

"Thank you, sir." He took a second to fix his hair and smooth his oddly shimmering violet uniform now. "Is that a Ruhn custom, sir?"

Eumelje was right; he's very attractive with his hair grown out. If I didn't out rank him, I'd be unable to get a woman on my cock for the duration. "Hand shake? No it's an Yrthyi thing. My first master's homeworld. Follow me."

"Yes sir!" Tauverius kept pace beside the major. Out of the corner of his eye, Parthenos noticed the man scrutinizing his face.

Ah, think I'm going to get my opportunity now. "Something wrong, captain?"

"I apologize, sir, I did not recognize you without your facial mane."

"Yeah, Commander Brinsanjin made me shave it." *I'm still furious about it. One day, I will ruin him. My potential to do that is quite expanded with this ship. Thiel said Brin was essentially tricked into signing off on this mission plan... whatever it takes, at this point, or this whole Empire will go down in flames.*

Tauverius stopped in the hall, frozen in place, as Parthenos walked ahead a bit before realizing it and turned around. "I am sorry, but I assumed the commander of the Haarnsvaar would have more respect for a Tetrarch, sir. I am floored by this information, sir."

"He doesn't like Star Assault, especially not me. He was overjoyed to invoke his power to order me to remove my mane for a mission. I will not speak of this further." *Welcome to reality, kid; your hero is a shithead who pisses on your religion and hates his own men.*

The captain's pace slowed, but he caught up shortly. "Apologies, sir." He paused, the cheerfully said, "I suppose it's no comfort, but they are quite beautiful, sir."

Parthenos glowered at the young man and requested with some dubiousness, "What are quite beautiful, Captain Tauverius?"

He smiled nervously. "Your stripes, sir. I've never seen a set in quite that lovely of a color, sir."

I remember how hard I tried to scrub them off when they first started to show, and how Sheriden tried to make me feel better by saying almost the same thing.

"Thanks but I've never been a fan." Facial striping was a mark of sexual maturity in saurtzek, the absolute confirmation of his lineage, of the real mother he never met. He had been able to deny it to himself even having such unusual fangs and pupils for a kaffir – after all, Felsetti and Aurians were both sometimes born with such - but the week of his twenty-fifth naming day had been one of tears and self-hatred. He thought of his step-mother shoving him through the door without a goodbye as she prepped her rifle to cover their escape from the city and of the report of her mutilated body when he was allowed to return. Parthenos ground his molars together.

"I understand, sir. He can take your mane but can't take who you are, right, sir?"

Funny way of putting that after complimenting the stripes. "That is correct, Tauverius; my position in the Trench and my training cannot be removed by a razor. I hope the same thing is true of yours."

Quite intentionally, he let the young captain walk ahead this time. Tauverius turned to see him with the refresher mask up by his face. *With the stripes exposed, this doesn't look strange to anyone, at least there's that.* The man turned back and waited patiently as the major deftly slid out both contact lenses and clasped them into the custom compartment within his mask.

"General Eumelje told me a lot about you; have to admit I figured her exaggerating to convince me to hire you because of *that* incident. You didn't have *that* when I first met you." He emphatically tweaked Tauverius' left ear, which bore a fairly recent, relatively faint microbial tattoo of the Wing of Aur, as he briskly caught up. *Without my natural eyes, I would never have seen it.*

"Sir, no sir," remarked the captain quietly.

He knows I didn't mean that earring. "Did you have that when you last stood before Brinsanjin?"

He swallowed and hesitated. "Sir, no sir." Tauverius altered his vocal inflection rapidly to sound less nervous. "I got my ear pierced when I joined the Fangs, Samsvargyr did it, tradition and all."

Savvy, just in case we're being recorded. "Please, by all means, dispense with the pony tail or wear a hood for the rest of your time aboard this ship. No one needs to see that except Eumelje and I, and in a few days, other men will board this ship with eyes like mine." *When she said she was paying me back for that time I saved her life on Naahiljir, I thought she meant by fucking me, not by giving me the exact tool for my revenge. See, Kanzi, I told you I would find a way without turning Star Assault's guns on their own people... just a little bit longer, now. I hope I live to see it.*

…..

"Ready when you are, lieutenant!" came a voice from their rear.

Sol readied the hatch. "Counting on you to knock out that generator, Gargoyle. Then keep us covered the best you can."

"Will do, Echo! Want me to disable these trucks?" Trazaal held up his slate, displaying the map of his drop site. He was an air sergeant; he had more than enough merits to be a true officer, but according to his 'officers only' note file, lacked patience for people or paperwork. In spite his rank, he was the most skilled man on Sol's team, and his gen, 'Poppy', was high on Cheldyne's list of 'model symbiotes'.

"Trooks? What the fuck are trooks?"

Bachi cackled briefly and Sol punched him in the shoulder just out of view of the crew cabin as Trazaal responded in plain but not condescending Archon. "Echo, a truck is a motorized vehicle for carrying cargo, something like a non-living *penjaahrdu*. These dots along the entry road are parked trucks, probably run on vegetable fuel but could be flammable fossil fuel. I won't set them on fire either way."

Poppy chirped from his back as if to say, "You can trust us, sir!"

Aren't those called 'lorrida'? Whoever heard the word 'trook'? "Alright, Gargoyle. Good thinking. Don't go outside your original target area, though; if there are more alert whoever is closest because I might need you when I drop in." *I always wondered what her bond was like because he doesn't hang out with anyone in my rank class. She came alone to Chel's 'step synchro' demo and marched with a trainee who didn't have a bug yet. Trazaal I met for the first time when he reported en route to the pipes. He seems really professional, just like Parthenos noted on his file... and just like his bug.* "Honor and sacrifice!"

"Honor and sacrifice, Echo!" An anticipatory chill ran through Sol's body as he watched the sergeant and Poppy leap from the opening into the roaring wind. Ozzie burbled a stream of little noises beside him. He patted her head. "We're going last, bugbutt. You just have to wait."

"You sure you wanna jump today?" Bachi asked hopefully.

Rolling his eyes, Sol returned, "Yes, and I'm even more sure I want you and your analog chute to stay in this Dash." *That sounded harsh. I'm not trying to be.* "You're the only person I trust to keep this thing in the air and follow coordinates if I'm not in it. You'll have other chances when Rocket's better."

Bachi grimaced again, fourth attempt to get out of the cockpit quashed. "Fine."

"You're good at it, shut up," Sol reassured with a growl. "The political climate sucks a hairy ball sac right now; I'm certain you'll get a go way too soon."

"Fair enough, Echo," mumbled the pilot. He positioned the Dash for the next drop. On behalf of the guy's amazing attention to detail, Sol had decided to set Toshi out toward the main roadway to serve as scout. Bachi took the PA. "You're up, Songbird. Make sure none get in or out without Echo's approval."

After Toshi jumped, Bacharanzin returned to Holtiini again. "So, we clear these missions fast enough, we probably camp here day or two before shoreleave. That usually how done; Gunsmoke makes use of our time. Sometimes we recon, sometimes drill…"

"You mean camping, planetside?" *We actually use those tents in the storage compartments?* "That sounds kind of nice." The only thing on Missionnotes was a post action rendezvous at a specific point, genadri were 'to stay controlled or stay a-ship', and 'uniforms required'.

Bachi laughed. "Marines, IGN get mingle with locals after take a place, we not allowed, security reasons. We no barracks this rock." His voice quieted, not that anyone else on the Dash could understand this conversation in the first place. "So, uh, there probably enough tents, but I volunteer share you… uh, sir."

They dropped the next two men. It was almost Sol's turn before he finished mulling the proposition in his head. "Are you offering me a warmer tent or something else?"

He shrugged and switched back to Archon. "I haven't had sex since Checkmate left. So either."

Sol looked forward, his tone very serious. He knew one thing about Bachi's sex life: the guy liked to be on the bottom. Minus one consideration, he was willing to give that a try. "Aren't you afraid of me losing control of my pulse?"

"Naw! I can think of worse ways to go then being blown apart by an orgasm."

The lieutenant stood with a laugh, gripping his seat for balance as he shooed Ozzie from the cockpit in advance. "You are one fucked up little jam cake."

There was silence except for periodic bug chirps and coordinate updates from the ship. Sol was fully suited and waiting at the hatch with Ozzie on his back. "Do you have me into position yet, Wildfire?"

"I dunno, I'm still hoping you say yes!"

Sol summoned up his best command voice. "For the jump, Wildfire!"

The return call came back in Holtiini, low country fruit farmer patois in full-effect. "Aye! Show 'em fuggs nae mercy, Red."

"You ready, Oz? Let's do it." They hurled into the dark and windy night.

He could see neither massive ship orbiting Verraken from within the atmosphere. Sol pondered the terror that less advanced cultures felt when elves and genadri came pouring from the sky in waves. *It must be something else, monsters materializing from the air before you… I suppose I am fortunate I grew up in a position to envy and admire Archons rather than fear them.*

They approached their target, an old, isolated estate built on a Ryzaan ruin. He made out the signature of it through his goggles as the coordinate map in the corner began to flash. The plan was to land in the wooded area up hill from the manor house; Sol had shown Ozzie aerial photographs of the location and he counted on her to pick the best contact point.

She chose a small clearing within the gutted outline of the ruin, just outside the radius of the remaining external lights of the main buildings. As they set down and Sol adjusted his equipment, there was a blast from the southwest and the lights went out. Ozzie lowered herself automatically at the sound, but Sol gave her a pat on the head. *Good shooting, Trazaal. Must have been a second generator.*

Scrawy trees dotted the hillside, although here within the ruin were weathered stumps in which four Sols could have stood comfortably, shorn cleanly away about a metre from the ground. Sadly, he touched one with a gloved hand. The material identifier application popped up the species name, rattled off properties of the wood, then gave the approximate age and date of the tree's demise.

At one time, these trees were an integrated part of the structure that stood here. That looks like a wall section, thought it was a dead tree too at first. Sol approached and touched the ragged, thin, tall fragment. Bits of brittle material crumbled away at the contact as the reader identified ostrekaal, of Ryzaan construction, several hundred years old. He imagined from the scattered remnants here the elaborateness of what once stood in the spot; it stretched up the hills and down, trees growing through, in, and around it; it likely housed apartments, a school, and shopping plaza for people working for Ravasich Corp. Ryzaan weather was terrible enough of the year that they preferred covered structures connecting all 'important' facilities, building up as much as possible to preserve natural beauty and use the least amount of land. *I wonder if the humans didn't understand how to care for it, or if it followed its original occupants to death when they weren't around to maintain it, and the humans came and took the trees then, or if the humans willfully destroyed it so as not to let it remind them of their former masters? Oh well, one of the things we get back if we take these places is archaeological rights to our own sites; regardless of anything else that gets under my skin about this invasion, I support reclaiming history before zealots erase it.*

Sol crept through the trees toward a set of out buildings of human construction, cautious in spite of the fact that his sensors showed no indication of enemies. Ozzie kept close, using her natural camoflauge talents and staying low to the ground. Trazaal had already dispatched any exterior guards along with the lights and the 'trooks'. The generator's impressive explosion would doubtlessly draw attention, though.

Maybe I should have left the power on. Our guns are silent. Didn't even occur to me these are diurnal people... we could have crept right in and aced them in their sleep. He cringed. *How unsporting. What was it mom liked to say when she and pa were arguing? 'That's the trouble with elves, they fight dirty.' Ironic she didn't even realize he was Ruhn, ergo one of the dirtiest fighters of all.*

Two orange indicators moved in the nearest intact building. Sol was camouflaged and not particularly worried, but kept to the best cover anyway. He turned up his helmet amplifier to pick up voices in the shed. From what he understood of the language, they discussed the power outage, although specifics were lost on him. Antennae indicated the shed contained some form of radio equipment. The two men seemed to argue in low voices, becoming increasingly upset. Finally one cracked the door and slipped through.

Sol did not wait for him to get both feet out the door before discharging rifle bolt. The body jerked, slumped, and slid down the door frame, thumping limply to the ground. *He didn't even see it coming. Oh, whoa, fuck, I just killed a person, a real person.*

Movement within the shed became frantic; Sol charged his rifle more and aimed a blast straight through the wall, leaving a gaping, smouldering hole. *He might still be alive; bayonet him or let Ozzie do him? The notes say 'leave no adult human males alive within compound', that any women, kaffir, haki, or children found will be slaves or prisoners.*

He approached the shed, stepping over the first corpse to enter the cluttered edifice. There was a man on the ground in agony, clutching at his side where his clothes and armored vest were singed. He looked up as Sol materialized, eyes widening in terror. "Dear God, no," the man gasped in Kouronoi.

He's not looking at me. What – oh, Ozlietsin must be sniffing his friend's body. Sol marshaled up his phrase book memorizations. "What are you doing here?"

Blood mixed with the saliva that dripped as the cringing man squeezed out, "Please, do whatever, take whatever, kill me, but do not let that thing touch us!"

"Deal," Sol said. He turned to his symbiote, who appeared to be digging in the dead man's jacket for something, and ordered her to sit watch in Shandrian then brought his attention back to the wounded man as Ozzie dejectedly slunk back outside. "What is this?"

"Ah... how we communicate, without power."

Sol looked about the shed; there were many devices he did not recognize, most built from aging metal. Cables ran out the walls from these, into the ground. There were piles of books, papers, magazines, some kind of small printing press device, remains of partially finished dinners, and a cot. The lieutenant lamented his lack of fluency; this dying man could probably answer quite a few questions if he could ask them. He nodded a thank you then mercifully dispatched his victim with a low-pulse shot to the head, pulling a blanket from the cot to cover the body.

Rummaging through papers, Sol found mostly what appeared to be anti-Archon propaganda, much of it illustrated with vile, exaggerated caricatures of kaffir and genadri; bloody fangs, dripping ovipositors, piles of human corpses littered all around. There was a small, hand printed leaflet containing some very strange imagery; the most striking page depicted two men holding hands and looking at one another tenderly with large angry looking text, of which the only line he could read contained "abomination before God". Amidst the magazines were pornographic picture books of men being abusive to women, many of them haki and obviously drugged and uncomfortable. Suddenly, he had no regrets, and wanted to kill both men a second time.

Sol tossed the porn aside after allowing residual pulse in his gloves to singe it, then confiscated some of the posters, pamphlets, and leaflets as evidence. He came across a stack of papers clipped together, all text save the symbol of the Ilu government; there were hand written notes on different colored scraps of paper sorted in, apparently in some sort of shorthand. *This is important, it has to be; maybe it's the answer to 'who sold what to whom'? I'll take this, too.* As he passed through the door, Sol kicked the corpse. "Fuck you for not having anything cool in here, douche," he mumbled into his mask, noting the kick thunked and probably would have hurt if not for his armored boot. He knelt, patted down the thick coat the body wore, discovering a small ballistic firearm, fully loaded. "Pardon me, fuck you for only having one cool thing. You won't need this anymore."

Ozzie perked and hopped over as he figured out his bearings and faced the manor below. "Come on, we have to go down and wipe up the rest of these shit bags, girl. You wanna kill some? They drew horrible pictures of you, too. Follow me."

XIX. Maalek's Blood

Sol pondered what to include in his report as he swapped attention between vague crew supervision and watching the sky for the inevitable appearance of his superiors. Among the papers in his pouch was a shipping manifest with his father's hand writing unmistakably all over it. The items described on the manifest were 'self-composting planters' and 'purifying rain barrels', corresponding to similarly labeled crates full of weaponry he photographed and left in the manor house.

I can almost understand it, why a Ruhn would want to re-start war between the Ilu and Archons, but why were you selling our weapons to a human faction that hated us? And everything, including themselves, apparently... If I ever see you again, will I ask you, or will I just slug you in the face?

His tent was up with Ozzie passed out and snoring within; Sol elected to take first watch and be immediately present for the rendezvous since his pharms were not wearing off enough to permit sleep. He was embarrassed at the men failing to pitch a tiny camp a few metres away. In the speed drills performed in the pipes and on Summit Island, genadri had not been present and the tents seemed simple enough to trigger and stabilize. The gen, as it turned out, found great interest in pop-up tents, mostly in cowering playfully as the tent expanded, then leaping atop to cause its collapse.

Bacharanzin approached Sol cautiously, chewing dried fish from his rations, watching the other three men (they left Trazaal stationed at the manor) wrestle with two tents and three excited bugs. "Makes me glad Rocket's laid-up. She'd be wrestling with Ozzie and we'd be out a tent in no time..."

"Yeah, seriously." Sol removed his goggles and shook out his locks. He caught out of the corner of his eye the helmet inching over to snuggle up to Ozlietsin. *That's a first. Maybe I should forcibly turn it off.*

"Whoa, Dash incoming." The words were uttered around a mouthful of chewy fish as Bachi jumped to his feet. He swallowed as he pointed. "See it yet?"

Sol followed the finger, made out vague atmospheric haze. "How do you do that without a helmet, man?"

"Flight school," grinned the freckled pilot. "Don't get me wrong, you get a good education in this unit. But you might consider the Air Defense Intensive at the Holtiini barracks if you get a chance."

"Huh, yeah... I'm definitely curious." He watched the craft land in the rock-strewn meadow, still deciding if the fact he recognized his dad's writing was going in the report.

Bachi finished his fish, talking while chewing as he approached the Dash with Sol. "Improves chances of 'retiring' into Air Defense, too, rather than being exiled for life to tiny cruisers hopping around the perimeter." He stopped, swallowed, and eyed the landing vessel. "Air Defenders get the best, stablest house folk jobs or teach at the academy on the side; good life if you're cleared for it."

"Do you think you'll ever be clear?"

"Man, I don't know. There's an exponential risk of going insane for every five years you spend as a star pilot, if you don't straight up get blown to essential salts. Then you can just end up pissing someone off and losing your house clearance forever to some petty argument, like Checkmate." He shrugged. "But that motherfucker's got a degree collection, right, guess he doesn't really let it stop him."

Laughing at 'motherfucker' with no interest in explaining why, Sol noted, "I've seen he had at least two graduate-level degrees, among other things; his full documentation is alphabet soup."

"Colonial history, military tech, and a law degree. He's like, I dunno, a few credits short of a doctorate in law. Pretty nuts, huh? I must be an embarrassment to him, as an apprentice."

The Dash's upper hatch opened. Bachi scarfed down the rice-based fish wrapper and wiped his hands on his ladders. A few armored men and bugs climbed out and assumed orderly positions to either side of the opening. "Oh, looks like we got us a senior officer comin' right up. Make with the givin' a fuck, oy."

"Nice Checkmate impression. You practice that shit or what?" They straightened their posture as Jaahyden and Cheldyne dropped from the opening one after the other.

Sol and Bachi snapped to salutes. "Greetings, Trauma and Serum!"

Curly ran to stuff her head under Sol's free hand. "Easy, boys. No need," Captain Jaahyden smiled. The new crew's bugs broke rank to cavort in the meadow.

"We're joining your camp, eh," Cheldyne said, eying the frustrated team struggling with the remaining two pop-ups. "Been having some trouble, I see?"

Of all the people to show up... "Yes, uh, the gen seem to make a game of tent smashing." To save face he threw in a gesture to his tent: "Except Ozzie!"

With the gen distracted by their frolick, however, both crews' tents were quickly managed. Noticing a beckoning hand on the part of Cheldyne, Sol left Bachi and approached the captain and sentinel.

"Gunsmoke'll be around shortly for a report," Jaahyden informed. "Anything prepared?"

Sol took a deep breath and produced the loose papers. "I have a few more things in my tent, including a long document that seems to be a copy of a treaty agreement with the Ilu."

"These are telegraphs here, mostly work orders to print and distribute other documents. Good score on those, and these propaganda leaflets... I collect these, you know." Jaahyden smiled as he flipped through the gruesome, bizarre imagery.

"Your interest in such negativity confounds me, Trauma," Cheldyne remarked with a frown.

Jaahyden chuckled. "Negativity? More like 'high comedy'. I mean, listen to this one: 'Broadsheet leaflet must explain monstrous nature of parasitic mega-insect stop be sure to mention violently exploded corpses in graphic detail stop.'"

"What the fuck?" Sol glanced at the paper and the captain, then to Chel, who rolled his eyes. There were no pictures, just a page of unpunctuated text in weirdly interpreted characters. As Jady laughed, Cheldyne broke into a less-than-dignified snicker, causing Jady to laugh even harder, further confusing the young lieutenant. "Will someone please explain why that's funny?"

"They think the gen carry terrible diseases and lay their eggs in living people." Cheldyne wiped laughter tears away. "Granted, the disease part is true, for humans, if they're stupid enough to eat the eggs or drink water where they've been breeding. The egg-laying paranoia is just a crazy urban myth. Stupid yabbos."

'Yabbo' was a Ryzaan colloquialism from the root, 'laakyavet', 'to go backwards'. The word was used to describe colonists who reverted to primitivity or to label people deemed uneducated and brutish. It could be used on any sentient people, but was most frequently applied to humans since elvish reversion tended to be more harmonious and practical. When kaffir suffered a violent regression, the expression 'ylph' was usually used instead, implying savagery such as consumption of human flesh. Sol found his usual knee-jerk offense at human-specific phrases lacking. He scratched his locks with a silly grin. "They sit around fantasizing that baby bugs are going to grow inside them and eat their way out like predatory wasps do to taba-droka? What a bunch of sick bastards."

"Oh yes, funny image though, no?" Jaahyden smiled as he scanned the overcast sky. The sun was mostly up now. Everyone seemed tired. "Little cute buglings, pushing their way out of some screaming fuck, 'Murp? Murp?' Tell me that's not funny."

"I think their interpretations of gen in these leaflets are more hideous than they look in combat mode though; this is how they see us and our friends... horrible monsters from outer space, coming to rape them and eat their hearts." Cheldyne joined the captain in watching the sky.

"This manifest... what's up with this? The one in Archon..."

"Uh, yeah, Trauma, that... all the entries correspond with boxes of Archon manufactured weaponry sitting in the manor house. I have Trazaal watching it all. They inspected it, but nothing was moved or missing... like they were putting it on, um, trooks, to move it elsewhere?"

Jaahyden turned sharply towards him as another Dash appeared above. It circled the meadow before settling near Sol's camoflauged vessel at the other end. The craft had been customized with two lurid blue stripes and the Scythes of Mercy. Sol tensed, scrambling his fragmented thoughts. Men and bugs came to attention. The hatch slid open and out hopped Nova, proudly carrying a tent sack in her mouth. Colonel Kiertus followed but there was no one else.

He kept his eyes on his commander rather than gawk at Nova. She dropped the sack with a flourish, tugged off the sheath, unrolled the tent and popped it up. When another bug broke rank and crept over to leap, she soundly whacked the offender on her snout.

All saluted Colonel Kiertus, but many incredulous, shameful eyes wandered toward the tent-erecting gen. Kiertus coughed, saluted, and placed his hands behind his back, nodding at the crowd. Everyone relaxed a little. His helmet was still on, but re-breather and goggles were pushed out of the way. His sticky, dripping armor glinted in the sun in a less than pleasant manner. *He dropped? Who's flying his ship?*

"Feel free to go about your business, gentlemen. I'll summon you one by one for the usual. Carry on."

This buys me time to think a bit more. Sol relaxed just a little. *I need something to say outlined before I sleep and lose pertinent details...* He wandered back to his crew, mentally re-enacting a few hours prior through exhaustion and lingering combat pharm-fog.

...

"Gargoyle, did you shoot all these people?"

"Yes, Echo, well, no, Poppy got a few."

Sol stepped over yet another body as he wound down the hill, where the manor road curved up around a rocky outcropping and the hill leveled to an open clearing. "Any left in the house?"

"By my readings, about five. Mmm, uh, yeah, make that four. And you're approaching one now; I couldn't get a good bead on him earlier, he's checking the trucks. You see his signature yet?"

"Yeah, I got him. Keep Poppy up there with you for now. Echo, out."

Trazaal's voice was amused. "Gotcha. When you get visual, watch this dude around the trucks, it's pretty funny. Gargoyle, over."

What? Sol made his way through scrubby under brush and sad, frail excuses for trees and picked out a line of blocky shapes along the road's curve. He walked parallel to them, just off the poorly maintained pavement, staying camoflauged, low, and silent. The man's heat signature slowly became a shape with a small, periodically flickering hand-held electric torch. He seemed to be checking one of the trucks, then swore loudly. He jumped suddenly and looked around while waving a pistol with the other hand.

Ozzie started forward; Sol grabbed her neck. She eyed him curiously then sat. The man approached the next truck, hopped in but almost immediately devolved into frantic cursing rage. He jumped out, flipped a frontal panel, and shone his light within only to have it go out. This caused more cursing and Sol laughed. His helmet and rebreather dampened the sound, but unfortunately, he stepped backwards and broke a dry branch. The man swung around and fired a shot into the darkness.

The projectile splintered chunks of wood from the trunk of a small tree nearby. *Fucker! That was close!*

He lost hold of Ozlietsin, who leapt from the woods and half-flew, half-bounded onto the stranger's shoulders. The electric torch clattered to the pavement. More shots went wide into the night sky as he struggled back into the side of the truck from the creature's weight. She deftly swung up her rear end and jammed her hind scythes cris-crossed into the space between his hip bones and armored vest. With a flutter and heave, she swung them out like massive scissors. Ozzie took wing, releasing his upper body as gore splattered pavement and truck; his legs fell first followed shortly by his chest, still attached to his screaming head and the arm flailing, firing impotently into the buzzing sky.

"Fuck!" Sol exclaimed with disgust, inadvertently re-opening his channel with Trazaal. He positioned his rifle, determined to finish off the howling, bleeding wreckage on the ground.

Trazaal's laughter came to his ears. "Echo, don't miss, that truck has flammable fuel!" He chuckled quietly. "Wish I'd filmed that. Damn the look on his face…"

Sick bastard! Agh! So nasty. "Warning appreciated, Gargoyle." Sol quickly crossed the road, stepped on the man's arm, pierced bayonette through shoulder, and released a low pulse blast; agonized screams terminated with cardiac arrest. He sighed and looked away, tried to ignore warm blood spattering his armor from residual systolic pressure in the fallen legs. *That never happens in the sim... Kiertus told me I might have to do that some time, and Jaahyden showed me by demonstrating on Gyrf. Scared the shit out of Gyrfru, threw him on the floor and mock-stabbed him in the middle of Sim-2. I wished he was joking. That's why they transferred me from Val; he won't use his bayonette and he won't train bayonette skills. I thought it was over sex; I'm such an idiot.*

Ozzie hovered and swayed in the air, face contorted into 'combat mode' configuration, scythes unsheathed and deathly sharp. Gore pitter-patted the ground as Sol gently coaxed her down. "It's OK, you did well, you saved me, good girl. *Shu, avaak'ja...*"

Cautiously, she settled. Her face softened, her jaw extension retracted, but the 'foreskin' of her legs did not ease down; fluid throbbed in vein-like structures along them. They glistened with natural moisture and chunks of insurgent.

I want to wipe her off, but Chel said to leave it for her pride and to 'increases her intimidation factor'. My job is gross. Sol fished out a treat for his symbiotic guardian. "That was pretty stupid, firing at something he couldn't see, huh, Oz? Hey, Gargoyle; how's the movement inside?"

"They're laying low; think that scream put the fear into 'em. If they've half a brain to share, they're not mo- um, one down. Think they're offing themselves."

"Understood. Moving in. Hold position 'til I signal. Echo out." Sol trudged across cracked pavement away from the trucks and over broken, decaying remains of a long neglected garden fountain. Burned out sodium lamps leaned crookedly along the path to the entrance. *This place is in terrible disrepair, too. Don't they even respect the ancestors who didn't keep them as slaves?*

Light flickered in the manor; the windows were mostly covered but the door wide open. Sol approached cautiously; Ozzie flew silently to his rear. He read three signatures within; one very faint, from the ground diagonally beneath his feet to the front. *In a cellar, maybe?* His goggles adjusted for the light, Sol slipped inside.

Water-damaged fissures split plaster-frosted walls in the foyer. Pockmarks and stains indicated where furnishings once stood. Sol silently moved along the wall; Ozlietsin landed to tip-toe behind. Two live people were indicated in the next room. Increasing his external mic amplification, he listened closely.

Kourhonoi? Or something else? Arguing, though. No, one person yelling, the other one... As rapidly as possible without making noise, Sol slipped around the corner and through the archway into the large open room beyond. Lanterns fluttered weakly upon a few scattered crates, one human male stood, yelling, his gun pointed at another on the ground. Blood trickled from the half-sprawled man's nose and lips. He wiped blood from his face to yell back, a desperate sound; Sol could not make sense of the words.

The standing man fired as Sol intervened, knocking him across the floor with a blast of pulse from his armor. Oddly, the seated man only watched as the pistol spun away on the scarred stone tiles. Sol allowed his concealment to fade, materializing above the man he now held in place with his rifle.

He was older, grey in his beard, balding. His eyes squinted and brows creased in anger, attempting to mask the fear his sweat revealed. "Elven filth," he sneered in queerly accented Archon. "Fuck you."

"Unbind," Sol softly commanded Vtek, flipping the rifle around once it pulled free of his bicep, whipping the unretracted fleshy tendril of the butt hard across the human man's face and torso. "We'll see who's fucked, old man." He stepped aside, snapped with his free hand. "*Jytrirt'k.*"

Further words were not exchanged in Archon, although it was clear the last thing he wanted to see – and the last thing he did see – was an irate genadri. Sol turned away from the carnage to the prone man. This one was young, with thick dark brown hair and a thin, juvenile beard. He cringed as Sol knelt and looked him over. *Lot of blood. He's been shot, in the leg? Or the side?*

"I won't hurt you," Sol spoke through the mask mic, inexpertly in Kourhonoi. "Can you stand?"

"No... it does not matter, now." His face swung to the floor as he mumbled again. His body shuddered, although whether from shock, fear, or suppressedweeping could not be discerned.

Sol switched to Archon on internal com. "Gargoyle? How's your Kourhonoi? Can you get down here?"

"Probably not better than yours. On my way."

Sol unclipped a hydro-cartridge from his belt and handed it to the man. "Water," he informed.

Hesitantly, the shaking man took but did not open it. "We will not... survive..."

Trazaal skidded to a stop on the stones. "That is a fucking mess, dude," he gestured at the old pieces Ozzie left of the old man. She sat on a large crate labeled 'ORGANIC POTTERY – HANDLE WITH CARE' in Unified Archon, which she sniffed curiously.

"Help me figure out what this guy is saying."

The man on the floor looked at them as blood seeped from his swollen, discolored nose, tears from his blue eyes. He mumbled in Kourhonoi between gasps of pain.

Trazaal haltingly spoke with him, slowly translating for Sol.

"He says there's no hope for the humans of Verraken... they were fools, they never ... never should have tried ... we can't ... I don't understand this part, but he is saying the same thing over and over..."

Sol began to record, wondering why the person below had not yet surfaced. He set Ozzie at the top of the stairs and returned to Trazaal and the incidental captive.

"He says, 'No chance, no hope, we were fools'. I asked him why; from what I get, his faction caught a splinter cell of their group here, and they'd dealt 'with elves', and elves started... taking their families? Something about how he wanted to see his 'wife and kids, one last time'. I don't get it. All these crates are actually full of weapons, to kill humans, an enemy faction, I guess?"

"Take over recording; I'm going to the basement, alert me if anything happens." Sol wished not to convey his upset with the situation to Trazaal. *I don't want to kill this guy, not just because I want him to talk, but my immediate commander on this mission is Mr. Fifty Per Cent Civie Casualties, the fuck he's going to say anything other than 'no' if I ask permission to spare an enemy.*

He had not fully descended the rickety stairs before it became obvious what was afoot. A man sat in dirty clothes, a water-damaged book open before him, tools and wires spread out from a small box, with a bundle of cables running from another, more compact box to a stack of tubes bearing Ravisch stencils: DANGER! EXPLOSIVE!

Son of a fuck! He intends to blow the whole house! If I fire a pulse blast in here, what if it deflected and...

Sol silently laid his rifle on the stair and stretched his arms, flexed his fingers, timing himself in his head before he sprang. Tools clattered as the man struggled, but thanks to several hundred years of bio-technological armor design, the would-be bomber was no match for the scrawny mixed blooded boy a good two weight classes beneath him. Sol had not fully considered his plan; reaching for his knife would cost his advantage. Thinking quickly, he snatched a spanner as they rolled and crushed it into the big man's throat with both hands until movement ceasesd. Sol hopped backwards to avoid being trapped beneath the unconscious body then drew his utility knife and guaranteed no rematch.

A shot was fired upstairs; Sol unleashed a painful, frustrated sigh before racing back up. Trazaal stood next to an open crate. Poppy and Ozzy beside him peered and sniffed at the contents. The human lay lifeless, a recently discharged pistol in his limp left hand, blood spread slowly over the tiles.

"Sorry, sir." Trazaal said with his natural voice; his goggles were up and his mask down. "Letting him end his own life seemed like the kindest thing. Even if he could have made it with that wound, even if he could get off this land without one of our guys plugging him, there's no guarantee his wife and kids are still alive. He said they were in Buonfaddek..."

Sol nodded. *A bunch of our ships went that way, odds aren't good.* "Did you learn anything else?"

"I couldn't understand the last part at all; something about the saurtzek being under something; mind you, my directions are bad, he might have said 'behind' but he said it over and over. I got it all committed." He tapped his armor. "I'll forward it to you. But look it all this: KSaGs, twitch cans, blood poison, I don't even know what this is, nerve agent of some kind? Can we take some of this? I want some foamers if we're going to fight saurtzek."

Sol rotated one of the small cylinders in his hand. "This isn't that kind of foaming agent, is it? Aren't these that banned gas that turns out to kill human beings dead as shit?"

"Right, but see that? It's an intake valve. Put a bit of ship drainage in that, instant foamers. You gotta do it real careful or the whole thing explodes and everything's covered in it. Or you can explode it on purpose, if surrounded, shouldn't hurt an armored kaffa too much. Kinda rollie way to do it, but works in a pinch."

Hey, I grew up in a rollie! That totally sounds like something dad would do, though. The lieutenant remained dubious of improvised chemical warfare. "Have you seen it work?"

"Not personally, it's in Checkmate's vid tutorial for surviving saurtzek attacks."

My dad probably invented that trick. "Yeah, yeah, I hear you..." Subtly pushing Trazaal away from the crate as he spoke, Sol put the canisters back in place and shut the lid. "We'll talk to Jaahyden about that at the rendezvous. Don't touch these until then, that's an order."

...

Still poking notes into his slate, Solvreyil noticed Airman Vanden, the youngest, newest member of his team. *We picked him back up at the end of things, when I was already emotionally numb. Talking to him will jog my memory and help me focus, I hope.* He pocketed his slate and approached the shady spot where Vanden traded off meat components from his ration pack to an airman from Jady's team. Vanden looked up and saluted as the lieutenant approached.

"At ease," Sol said quietly, taking a seat on a nearby rock. He smiled patiently at the other until Jady's airman wised up and left.

"How are you doing?"

"Alright, I guess. Never done anything quite like that. A all very educational." He inspected his assortment of dried fruit and biscuits. There was no surprise meat had lost appeal. "I expected to kill, when I joined... it's not like..."

425

Sol nodded. "Yeah, I don't think anyone signs on expecting salvage, but it's part of what we do. Old style ships, not a lot of refuel stops, low crew numbers; you're going to cut up bodies now and then."

Vanden poked at his food. "I get that, Echo." He turned toward his squad leader. "Is it ironic I didn't go to medical school like my parents, because I didn't want to put my hands in dead bodies? First mission, what do I do? Hand in a dead body." He smiled as he stuck a piece of fruit in his mouth and chewed.

Songbird intercepted a slaver caravan on the main road, that's important; we saved two haki women, they should definitely go in the report. Kiertus probably won't care about the fact we had to hack up all of the incidental kills to refuel our Dash. I'll make sure to note Vanden did most of the work on that with me so maybe he can lose that number and get a call sign. "Grossed me out the first time, too." Sol stood and stretched. He felt sun and wanted to go nap. *Probably shouldn't spend much time in it. They've critically fucked their UV protection.* Smiling back at the striking, sienna-skinned airman, he noted, "Well, you're on third watch, just keep that in mind."

"Under control, Echo."

When he returned to their tent, Bacharanzin sat outside, playing with Ozzie in the grass. Sol shoved Bachi aside as he crawled in to the flap. "I'm pretty sure I said you were on second watch."

Bachi righted himself with a lost look. "Right. Wasn't sure when exactly it started."

The lieutenant barely raised his face from the lightly cushioned floor of the tent to snap, "It starts now. And take her with you." Exhaustion robbed him of any further derision aimed at his lazy subordinate.

An annoying vibration roused him from his slumber. Sol fumbled at his belt for his slate. He noticed, as he checked it, he had acquired a thin blanket from somewhere. Huddling with this, he blinked at the screen. The message was from 'Gunsmoke'.

"Of course you want to meet now," Sol mumbled aloud at the device. He was still fully dressed minus his harness so he straightened his locks and crawled out into the meadow.

It was past mid-day. Aside from himself and the watchmen, there seemed no one awake. Bugs slept under sad trees near Kiertus's Dash. Ozzie was not among them. He finally spotted her heading back with Bachi from the watch point and gave a wave as he climbed the concealed vessel and into the hatch.

To his left, a man in pilot's webbing slept awkwardly across three of the troop seats. Sol began to step very carefully, but his internal tracks were skipping over the clingy fluid-like bio fabric of the uniform and the gorgeous, oddly familiar symmetrical tattoos over the man's shoulders. Both man and conductive material glistened; at first he assumed from sweat, but he realized the bottle knocked over on the seat beside the pilot was an expensive grade of 'calming toner'. *Soothes and cleans the grafts and that eerily sexy second-skin uniform. The vets call it 'combat lingerie'. Pretty apt description. It doesn't look that erotic in the catalog... Then again, this guy's body is amazing, like, calendar model sexy...if I was put together like that, I'd never need porn, I'd just touch myself in front of a mirror.*

In a deep sleep twitch, the man's right arm flopped weirdly over and his head half-shook. Ratted, sweaty black hair shifted and the face became clear. *Wyvern! The fuck? Oh, uh, wow. Why do I know those tattoos? I can't believe I'm standing here staring at –*

A firm hand pressed gently against Sol's shoulder. He started and turned, facing the less than cheerful countenance of his knight-sire.

"Ah!" Sol quieted himself immediately. "Sorry, master."

Eternally polite but clearly annoyed, the colonel smiled. "Could you step out, lieutenant?"

Sol scrabbled backwards out the hatch and down the ship's simulated 'moss' texture. He waited in the Dash's shade as Kiertus gracefully swung down, spill-proof thermal mug in hand.

"When I said 'at my Dash', I meant to meet you outside. The warmer took longer than expected."

Sol felt guilty and out of place. He shuffled. "Apologies, Gunsmoke." *Why does*

427

it not surprise me that you have a plug in water heater for your Dash cockpit?
"Did I wake him?"

Sipping his tea, eyes closed, Kiertus made it clear that was not the issue. "He's on enough pseuvarsine to sleep through a nuclear strike. It'll take a defrost shot to wake him before tomorrow." Up close in the sun, the blood slowly absorbing into his armor was fully visible. His helmet was off, but the goggles and breather remained. Sol observed the combat drugs gave youth to his countenance, but every inch of the colonel's body vibrated, radiating an aura of destructive power.

Sol did not know what to say. Embarrassing as the thought was, part of his mind was stuck on the slight sheen of recently rubbed in salve over Wyvern's barely covered torso. And now he was dumbstruck in his master's aura, heart pounding, thigh veins throbbing; blood was not making it properly to his brain.

"Tell me, Echo, about your first mission, as a leader." Yellow irises were dominated by dilated pupils. Blood grimed his hair and was caked in his ears.

How did he manage that? Did he salvage with his gear off? He doesn't look injured... "All enemy combatants were destroyed, Gunsmoke. Songbird rescued two slaves; I had Wildfire give them a lift toward the desert, they said there was a settlement there."

Kiertus nodded, still not looking terribly pleased. "That is true; of the kaffir settlements on this world, Shap-Tishara is probably the safest."

Tjaptjara? Isn't that what the Aurmalki called Heaven? Stolen from Shandrian, 'Shaav Tvara', 'garden of glory'. Strange hearing it squeezed into Ryzaan consonants. "I wish I could have taken them all the way, but the city described was not on our map. I thought perhaps they were confused, but they were insistent not to go to Kuuln-kuog. They gave me verbal directions, but I did not wish to challenge them against our fuel supply." Sol straightened up, producing his slate as Kiertus nodded affirmatively. "214 assisted me in refueling our ship from hostile salvage. I already turned over confiscated documents to Trauma for translation. There are boxes of our weaponry, described in the short hand email I sent you, at the manor house. Gargoyle and Poppy are still there keeping watch; I sent you a copy of the recordings he and I took of the hostile we questioned."

"Is that everything, Echo?" the colonel asked as he downloaded the file.

Sol considered things a moment, then added, "I would like to propose the call sign, 'Lunchbox' for 214 if no one else has a better handle selected. Beyond that, I've provided you with everything of import."

"Well, then, it is as I suspected." Kiertus leaned against the Dash, keeping his dilated eyes from the breaking sun. "You're a natural for command."

Inspite of attempts otherwise, Sol's frustrated sigh was audible. "Yes. Thank you, Gunsmoke."

"G some rest, Echo. You have an assignment after dark falls." There was an odd look in the man's eyes. Perhaps it was the drugs? "You'll be flying with me to Shap-Tishara to deliver supplies. Maybe we can find your rescues on the way and help them along, hm?"

"If it's really the glorious garden, do they need supplies?"

This amused Kiertus. "Amidst the ironic naming conventions signature to this planet, I find this one makes the most sense. I'll page you after the evening drill." The colonel took a sip of tea and saluted with a click of his armored heels.

En route to his tent, Sol checked his slate. There was a message from roughly an hour prior, from Chel, saying he should come by for a drink. He turned on his personnel locater, hoping the offer was still good. *Alcohol might take the edge off... this... Otherwise I need to kick Bachi out of the tent for twenty minutes so I can dump the main cannon into a rag.*

According to the locater, Chel and Jady were both awake and moving aboard Jaahyden's Dash. The hatch was wide open; he heard laughter. He braced himself for old, drunk, inappropriate military elves and abusive language and climbed up. *It'll be worth it for a drink and probably funny. I guess Jady's not that old, really, he's like what, fifty seven cycles? He just talks like someone's nasty pervy old uncle.*

Had the scene he walked in on been a picture stumbled across in a magazine, Sol would have turned it over for several minutes trying to figure out the physics, blushed, and put it away for later. But coming face to face with that much heretofore-unknown intimate detail of the bodies and lives of two men with whom he worked regularly was a bit much for the poor boy. Sol issued a sound like, "Wuaawoaa!" and recoiled rapidly out the hatch.

429

"Shit! Shit! Ach, sorry Quarri… Echo?"

There was drunken mumbling and shuffling. "Was that Sholvryll? What the…"

"I invited him for drinks. A while ago. You left the fucking hatch open, dildo."

There was laughter. Cheldyne climbed out and dropped down in the grass to where Sol sat in a daze. "Hey, um, really sorry about that…"

"No, I'm sorry. Seriously, I should have messaged you first. I didn't even…" Sol shook his locks out. "I had no idea. It didn't even occur to me. I'm an ass. You both have my apologies. I need to go. Take care."

Cheldyne watched the lieutenant stumble off toward his tent. "Fuck."

"Sure! Up here waiting, yesh." Jaahyden hung part way out the hatch, grinning drunkenly, bottle in hand.

"Bah! Not you, Trauma. Haven't you had enough?" Once far enough up the ladder he yanked the booze away from his companion.

"No, misther bug stharjint, no I haffn't. Givvat back."

Cheldyne shoved the captain easily out of the way. "Go to bed, child."

….

In the tent, Bachi was out cold. Sol shook him but received nothing more than a shift in snore for his efforts. *I can't jerk off like this, but this isn't going to just go away on its own. Fucking drugs.* He considered the earlier invitation, examining the syrigun and drained ampule that were likely responsible for the astrum's current condition. *He shouldn't even be on something like this right now. We're on duty.*

Sol yanked down Bacharanzin's ladders with little difficulty. Snoring continued unabated, as did the irrepressible erection. His intention had simply been to empty his extra weight over the back and ass of his subordinate and leave him thus, but in his overwrought state, something else took over. *This is neither ethical nor friendly, but Bachi's a little shit, and at least I'm thoughtful enough*

430

to wear a sack. Take this!

The violation, however, woke Bachi up. His eyes flew open, hands dug for purchase on the tent floor, startled cursing erupted forth. "Auri!? Fuck!"

It had taken little time in the tight warmth of his unconscious teammate before he was ready, and Sol was already coming. The mistaken identity threw him for a bit of a loop. "Auri!?"

He pulled out in annoyance, at precisely the moment to leave the condom and make a mess all over Bachi, his clothes, and the tent.

"Oh, holy fuck, Sol!" Laughing, the astrum rolled over, a relieved hand to his forehead. "I'm so sorry I was out... I ... was I good?"

An indescribable noise escaped the lieutenant as he fixed his now oversensitive gear into his uniform. "You were a log, with a hole."

"I am really sorry." The man continued to laugh.

Sol sat awkwardly, stared at his friend, eyebrows knotted. "I just raped you, and you're apologizing?"

"That's not rape. I invited you. I just didn't mean to be out cold for it." He yawned and blinked as he extracted the condom and deposited it and the empty ampule into a little paper fold-up box. "Laathas keeps changing my pharms because I can't adjust to the difference in driving a Dash versus a D-7. The energy exchange is weird. Hurts afterward, in a really no fun way."

"Sucky, I'd never considered that; Wyvern had me stay on the paratrooper schedule during my training so it wouldn't fuck with my suppression treatment. But I mixed pilot pharms for the rack a few times. Sorry man, it's gotta be rough."

"Everything's all different – all the people in my day to day life, the missions, the expectations of the brass... And man, interacting with civilians is alien to me. I guess you and Bootstrap are right; I'm not ready for ground service yet. I still think like a pilot; everything's a target." Bachi blinked and yawned more, stretching his tense jaw until it cracked.

You know, I've never asked this, all the times we'ver hung out. "Why'd you switch, anyway?"

"Honestly?" A little chuckle escaped as Bachi wiped fugitive semen from the rear of the tent. "You got everywhere… I can't believe you frosted me. Trauma clearly is a stellar influence on you."

Oh man… he's right. Sol laughed. "Yeah, honestly. I'd really like to know why you traded having your own jet for a bug and a rifle, especially when you're as good a pilot and mechanic as you are."

"Checks and I were screwing, I'm sure you knew about that, I know you worked with Mouthy. Was no big deal to either of us but Wyvern started fucking with me. Singled out and humiliated me at every opportunity. I made the mistake of standing up for myself and got schooled." Leaning back on his arms, he closed his eyes and shook his head at the memory. "Gunsmoke transferred me while I was unconscious in the infirmary. Went down a pilot, woke up a paratrooper."

"Dude. Fuck." *I've never seen Wyvern mess with someone for no reason, not that way. Wonder what you have to bring up to get him to blow a gasket and kick your ass? I got some guesses, especially with you.* "That must have had an impact on your relationship with Checkmate, huh?"

"You can say that again. I miss just being fuck buddies; this is a lot more difficult. By the way, sorry I called you Auri. You're bigger than him. I just… I think I was dreaming…"

Bigger …? But … Sol's eyes went wide when he realized what Bachi meant. There were proportions to his anatomy he never previously considered. Suddenly, he felt quite self-conscious.

The tired smile was mischievous in its sea of freckles. "If you ever wanna do that when I'm awake…"

Sol grunted. "Enough of that. We need more sleep. There are drills and assignments tonight. Trauma's in charge and I don't want to know his disciplinarian side. Ever." Sol wriggled from his armor and piled it at the deep end of the tent to use as a pillow. "Stay on your side. I'm so not cuddly right now."

"Yes, sir." Bachi's tone was respectful, but he grinned and laughed to himself as he rolled over.

Sol realized Bachi had probably won some kind of bet, and fell asleep even more irritated than before.

....

In light of his condition a handful of hours prior, Jady seemed in remarkable shape. He jogged briskly up and down the lines, barking at the assembled crew. Everyone short of the colonel, including Wyvern and Cheldyne, were put through the ringers; he followed a synchronized facing drill, complete with rifle spins, with thirty push-ups. Other than sweating profusely, he did not seem the least bit under the weather.

"Twenty-eight! Twenty-nine! And, thirty! If you dropped your rifle during the first drill you have fifteen more push-ups to do! Everyone else may take a bow and go for breakfast."

Sol bowed and walked towards Chel's Dash. The sentinel texted just before the drills started to meet there after. He turned back and watched Bachi knock out the next fifteen, shook his head, and swung himself onto a wing lump. Chel was not far behind; he stopped to talk to Kiertus, who was in full kit but seemed back to his usual gentle demeanor otherwise.

"Hey. Let's go have a chat, shall we?" The hatch opened in response to Chel's remote sequence. Sol followed him inside.

"Do you mind if I have my breakfast? I'm starving."

"Not at all. Having some myself." Chel shook a ration pack at him. As he opened it, he spoke earnestly. "So, about what happened earlier today. I have been wanting to tell you some things that –"

The hatch opened. They looked back in startled annoyance. Jady's pupils were pinpoints; he reeled. Chel moved to speak but was interrupted by the captain vomiting violently into an available processor intake.

"Do you have to do that here, now?"

A finger flew up dramatically demanding their patience. Sol was impressed. *I didn't think veteran drinkers ever made that much noise puking.*

Jady gripped the wall, wiping his lips with his free hand. "After yesterday, we need to replenish the reserve on all these ships." He paused to expel again. "All of that is getting terraformed so I'm not wasting this on plants that are going to get recycled anyway."

"All of it? I didn't get that out of what Oscar said." Chel waited irritably for the next round of squealing and hurling to be done.

"That meadow is a goner. Bunch of dead oil tanks underneath it. All has to come up. 'Swhy we were told not to bathe in the water blah blah…" Non-productive, painful wretching wracked his frame.

During a short briefing before the drills, Kiertus explained that Archos officially took back this region for the Empire as of the previous night. A unit of 'Specials' would be here soon to fully secure and hold it, then Mobilife, Vektaar, and other concerns would arrive to work on reversing damage done by generations of greed and ignorance. He vanished and Jady started yelling out his hangover.

The colonel appeared, as if summoned by Sol's mind, hopping gracefully through the hatch. "Well, suppose that answers question number one," he said, watching Jady wipe his pale face and trembling hands with a sanitary cloth. Kiertus handed the captain some ginger candies. "Fix that. We need you later. Fortunately for you, this was a non-essential and private mission on my part."

Chel leaned back and stared at the ceiling, exasperated. "I'm saluting; you just can't see it, Sheriden."

Oh, I guess we're off mission protocol now, since we're technically occupying. Now I have to remember to 'sir' and 'master' all over the place…

Abandoning rations on the seat, Sol rose and saluted the colonel, who raised a dismissive hand. "At ease. Eat, by all means. I can't afford what few men I have to be complete wrecks." Kiertus swung a sharp sideways kick into Jady's shin. "Solvreyil, accompany me to the desert to bring gifts to the loyalists. Chel, I'd love it if you'd fly so Wyvern can have a day off. This isn't mandatory. I can do it with just Nova."

Curly perked up from her nap at the sound of 'gifts'. She was up, chirping and nosing around the colonel's legs before Cheldyne could swallow his fish and issue a protest.

"Ah, well you know, if you don't want to go, Chel, may I just take the little miss, here? She's so good with civilians, just like my Nova. She can air drop presents without you. Can't you, Curly?"

"Dammit. Fine. I'll fly. Where can I put him to sleep it off?"

Kiertus held stiff as a happy bug aggressively licked his face. "Commandeer a tent, Chel. It's really not my problem. Honestly, it shouldn't be yours, either."

…

When they originally dropped the refugees at the canyon head, Sol had only glimpsed a corner of its vastness. Staring now into its forbidding, rocky maw on the console monitor, he was glad he chose to spare fuel previously. "Damn, that is… is it bigger than that horrible trench on Gravian?"

"Syrvaak is longer and wider, not deeper than the Aprian Rift. It's easier to get a Dash down into the Rift by far – more erosion, less of these pokey towers of crumbly stone to hit." Chel gestured at the formations below. "The winds here aren't as potentially destructive, though, so at least there's that. Hey, think these two life forms are your girls?"

Sol fixed up his mask. "Yeah, almost certainly."

Chel nodded. "Great. I'll drop you here, and bring the ship to this nook; meet up with us there."

"No, that is exactly what I'm telling you… Yes. Right." Sol looked confused until Kiertus held up a finger and continued his conference call as the lieutenant approached the exit. "Given that, I would like to proceed with evac. Yes once I'm done with this we'll head back in that direction and assist. I see no issue in starting without me." The colonel sat in the passenger cabin, legs crossed, petting Nova as he chatted.

Evacuation? He's so calm about it. Sol saluted as Ozzie boarded his back and they prepped to jump.

Kiertus stood, still talking into his helmet mouthpiece, and moved towards the cockpit. "I'll be certain to keep an eye out for them... hm? Is he? How long ago? No, he has not. Interesting." As he passed, Kiertus brushed against Sol with a sideways smile and wink, still talking as if nothing significant was up.

He totally could have passed me without contact. Strange man. He felt awkward, and even guiltier about the situation with Bachi earlier. *I don't think he'd be proud of that if he found out; I have a feeling I might get punished a great deal... especially if... man I hope Parthenos is permanently reassigned.*

Wind roared behind him as he counted down in his head; Ozzie clung tight to the harness. Sol could no longer hear Kiertus's conversational phone voice as he let Nova before him into the cockpit. Just as Sol's count hit 'one' and he released the rungs, Kiertus spun around and yelled "Echo! Abort mission!"

Sol attempted a 'return to ship' command with Ozzie but the wind already had her; he would have to hit ground before he tried again. "She won't go back yet! Suggest course of action!" he pleaded frantically.

"Get the refugees out of the open! We'll cover as best we – Serum! Cloak! Gunsmoke out."

The ship vanished from Sol's ordinary field of vision but was a shadow in his goggles as it zipped away from the drop site and he sailed down amidst the jagged rocks.

I don't know what's going on. I've got orders, though, so... Urging Ozzie towards the two 'non hostile' traces on the overview, Sol braced for the hit and began to charge. *I haven't taken a combat shot. I don't know if I even have time. Them first, then me...*

They were startled to see the trooper and bug materialize out of the sky. Sol gestured with his rifle at a crevice in the canyon wall, not too far from where they walked. Ozzie dropped him, dove toward the pair, grabbed the limping one and hauled her to the niche. Her companion ran behind; Sol brought up the rear.

Now the alarms went off in his ears; there were hostile craft in the air above the canyon, two, then three, then five. The two women crouched into the crack as Ozzie returned to the air and Sol began to run down amidst the rocky towers to get a bead on the enemy craft.

Verties! Fuck. Was this a trap?

They did not immediately seem interested in the individuals below, instead splitting their formation to pursue the Dash. Sol heard shots and saw a vertie explode in air some distance away, raining over the canyon in smoking shards.

"Echo, if any of that falls near you, keep it away from the refugees and burn it."

"Understood, Serum."

Sol took this opportunity to inject a round of combat pharms. He checked the monitor for Ozzie's signal then turned back to the refugees hiding in the crack. "Don't worry, we'll get them and get you to safety."

The taller of the two held her injured friend protectively, eying the sky with concern. "What are those?"

"Ilu ships, our enemies. Everyone's enemies."

Kiertus' voice crackled into his helmet. "There's one coming your way, Echo; make sure your surface to air trajectory calculator's on. Start charging now and you might avoid shrapnel. Gunsmoke out."

"Copy. Echo out." The moment their communication channel closed, he ordered his displacement field on. He ran low, zig-zagged about the columns of stone, took a position with the best mix of cover and visibility he could assess. Sol hunkered down, pouring the fire of his soul into his VTek. Via monitor and the corner of his eye, he watched as Ozzie took his place at the crevice, angling her wings forward to maintain cover.

The velocity of its passage pulverized the peaks of intervening rock formations. The Ilu V-Craft was every bit as intimidating in real life as in simulation. Sol barely had time to think, *I'm so fucked if I miss...*

Projectiles howled as they fired from both sides of the craft, winding not towards him, but at the walls of the canyon. Sol fired his first shot as the vertie swooped suddenly upward. Rock and debris showered down toward him; he ran forward, composing impromptu obscene poetry as he dodged and skidded behind a rock wall.

Unforseen but smart tactic. Hope the ladies are OK. Sol glanced right and discerned Ozzie and two non-hostile dots beyond swirling dust and clattering clods of crumbled rock. *Might have to dig 'em out later.*

"Good shot Echo, you left him smoking, now he's mine." An explosion lit the sky off to the left, disturbing the readings within Sol's helmet for a moment.

Funny, that wasn't Kiertus or Chel. Wonder who joined us? Another ally vessel was read in the vicinity, although he had no visual and it lacked a tag.

Another explosion, to the upper right of the canyon. "Whoa-hoa, check that shit out. Nice of you to show up, Trauma."

"I never miss a party, Checkmate." In its bedraggled state, his Ryzaan drawl was heavier than usual. "Echo, get your friends away from where that vertie fired. I'll drop lines for 'em, not landing though."

"On it, Trauma." *Parthenos is here? I hope he doesn't have free time to chat with Bachi.* Sol navigated through loose shale and broken chunks carefully. The projectiles did not seem to have left contaminants, but he was in no mood to take chances. When the crevice was within view, he motioned for them to follow the wall and avoid debris, joining the group at the most convenient point.

Elsham, the wounded refugee, had too much trouble with the lift cable, so Ozzie took matters into her own scythes and grabbed the slight woman, yanking her aboard the Dash. Elsham yelped and Sol admonished his symbiote from the ground as he assisted the other.

"Ozzie! Don't grab unarmored people with your bare feet! You'll hurt them!"

Oz peered from the portal down at her bond, feelers back, face dour as Jady defended, "Hey, scratches beat exposure to Baalphae toxins. I'm sure she'll be fine once we get her to civilization."

Once Sol was aboard, they lifted from the canyon as he checked Elsham for further injuries. Jady was correct; the scratches were minor, all things considered. Sol dug salve from the med bin and handed it to her. "Sorry about that."

Dark hair hung in her face as she applied the crème. "It…it is all right, made me very scared though."

Sol leaned into the cockpit as they sped on toward the destination. "Hey, Wildfire…"

"Dude I shot a vertie! A real vertie! Did you see that? Shit blew right the fuck up!"

"Well who's cleaning up the mess, then?"

"Serum and Checkmate, I guess. We've got to get back to our mission but we'll leave you with the girls at paradise." Jaahyden scratched his chin thoughtfully. "Doesn't sound so bad. I wanna switch now."

Tracey, heretofore squatting silently on the floor, nipped him on the thigh.

"Ow! Hey. I was joking! Joke! Joke!"

"Dude Echo did you see what Checkmate is flying?"

"No fuckin' chatter, Wildfire." Jady's voice was icily serious; Bachi cringed and returned to silently analyzing the monitors.

Shaking his head, Sol returned to the crew cabin to check on the refugees and Ozzie. *Something serious is happening…it's definitely not over yet.*

Elsham and Teja seemed a little concerned yet hopeful as Jady's voice came over the PA. In surprisingly elegant Ravasich, he announced something to the effect of, "This is the place for which you hoped?" The monitor came on, displaying a city built straight in to the steep walls of the deepest part of the canyon.

The ladies gasped, squeezing one another's arms. Elsham winced and her friend apologized. Ozzie deemed the excitement important so she jumped up and trotted a wobbly lap around the cabin, leaping over people where necessary.

"Sit down, bug," commanded Sol, making an effort not to laugh. "Don't hurt anyone more than you already have." He stared in amazement at the impressive integrated construction on the screen.

"Ah, Echo? Trade places with Wildfire, please."

Huh? Bachi made a funny face as he passed, holding his bare palm in Sol's direction. He laughed as Sol slipped into the cockpit and sat. "What's the problem, Trauma?"

"You're frying so hard you don't even notice. That's funny."

What's funny? Oh, crap, I'm arcing all over the place. Bad timing on the drugs. Right. I'm a dumbass. "It was not my intention to endanger the lives of civilians."

"Of course it wasn't." Jady seemed tired more than annoyed. "Ah, shit, it gets worse. We can't take those two with us to the rendezvous." He tapped the screen, indicating Sol should not speak as he called back to the cabin. "Wildfire, I'm dropping a rope near that plaza to our left; escort the refugees and assist them down. Might be a little tricky but I trust you."

"Sure, Trauma. Where do I take them, though?"

"Follow the carved stairs down to the west. Council hall is the building with flags outside."

Sol, still mentally registering the number of blue bars and craft sitting at the proposed rendezvous site, cast a dubious expression at his boss and quietly asked, "Does he even speak any Ravasich?"

This amused Jady. "Fuck no. It'll give the locals a chance to practice their Archon."

They watched as Bachi helped Elsham and Teja out then released himself to the carved tier below. As the hatch shut, Sol asked, "Where'd all those Guildsmen come from? What is all that?"

"Pretty intimidating, huh? Blue aren't Guildsmen. They're Haarnsvaar. Guildsmen are purple bars."

Sol sat staring at the purple-barred name in front of him, 'Trauma'. He swallowed hard. "I suppose I mis-read that section of the protocol guide."

"It's easy enough to misunderstand," came the exhausted smile as Jady angled the Dash toward the plateau edge. There was a Razor in addition to the Dashes already parked there. One appeared to be the marine troop transport version, a D-10. "Try to reign in that aura, kid. Seriously."

Easy for you to say. "I don't think I've ever seen the gold color used, so my mind swapped gold for purple. Maybe my gold is broken, I mean, Wyvern's always grey, he's supposed to be gold, right?" *No, my gold's not broken; Okallin and Tzanshidi both read as gold. Val reads as gold now instead of brown. Grey isn't even in the handbook, though.*

Jady just blinked. "No, he sets it that way, same way as Serum and … you have a lot to learn. Not a time to stress about it, just remember how to present yourself and pull that field in."

They simultaneously took deep breaths, filed onto the plateau, leaving Tracey and Ozzie aboard. The sense of ultra-awareness from combat pharms and his apprehension over standing before so many powerful soldiers combined to make Sol's head swim. He looked to the right of their landing spot, out into the vast, steep canyon, at the small city built dizzyingly into the vertical walls. Looking up into the sky at the moon, he realized he could see the *Yetzjmaal* in orbit; superiority was achieved, apparently, and stealth no longer a requirement.

I note the Sanjeera *remains cloaked. And we're still in 'no chatter'. And then there's all this.* Sol faced the curiously spaced group, respectfully lowered his head and saluted, hoping the stiffness of his arms compensated for the full-body vibration of holding back intense energy. *Wow that must be the full guild uniform on that purple bar there…*

Kiertus, showing as a nameless blue bar as opposed to his usual purple call sign, returned salute first. "Greetings, Trauma, Echo."

"Greetings," said Jady with an unusually formal salute.

Why do some of them have their names off? Maybe I can't see them with my clearance? This is creepy.

"At ease, Echo," said the fully-uniformed Guildsman in a nearly sarcastic tone.

Easy for you to say! Here are a bunch of uber-brass – now relax, lieutenant!

The soldier approached, a towering being clad in scintillating tentacles and chitinous plates. The full uniform clung at points, but eliminated most potentially distinguishing features. He turned his blank, sharp mask toward Kiertus and Chel (showing as a nameless purple bar), then to the masked, fully armored Haarnsvaar near them. "I'll take him for the mission, as well."

The Haarnsvaar and Kiertus both nodded softly. Another purple bar stepped forward, this one reading 'Wyvern'. He wore the embarrassingly sexy pilot uniform with a threadbare wreck of a sweater thrown over and a pilot's breathing mask, unhooked and dangling off his tired face. "I suppose that means I'm trading places with you, then, Checkmate?"

"Yes." The response came eerily from the uniformed Haarnsvaar officer; the man was broad chested but shorter in stature than anyone present. His uniform had the appearance of an icthyoid or draconic creature covered in oily black metallic scales and long, sharp spines, giving him a much larger presence. The mask was equally monstrous, displaying multiple eyes rather than a single set of goggles or the blank mirror-like surface of the Guildsman's mask. Defraying some of the intimidation factor of the uniform was a tessellation of variously sized, intricately detailed shorelings at the hips and crotch, diminishing in number and size as they ascended towards the vicinity of the officer's navel.

I'm not sure if that's the cutest or creepiest thing I've ever seen…

"C'mon, guys. This way." Tendrils flicked as the Guildsman gestured at Sol and vaguely at Cheldyne. Chel briskly walked towards the modified Dash-10, which bore an Armored Corps logo.

Sol was confused. "Aw, darnn, not the Razor?" He jumped and cringed; he had not meant to say it out loud. *Damn drugs slaughtering my inhibitions.*

"No, he wishes," said Wyvern, Cheldyne, and Jaahyden simultaneously.

I don't see the third blue bar now. Did someone lower their status for some reason or – is it the Razor itself that reads as a Haarnsvaar? Or … is there someone else here? This is no end of spooky.

As they prepared to enter the D-10, a man in a full exo suit with additional marine armor atop it, in a pilot's mask, hopped out, saluted the uniformed Guildsman and Cheldyne, and said, "All ready to go, Checkmate, Gunsmoke. What's my next assignment?" His call sign read in gold: 'Acolyte'.

Chel looked to the Guildsman and nodded. "Figure out which of these gentlemen is Trauma. He'll take you to your next position."

The man called 'Acolyte' saluted Cheld again, although his uncovered, large, dark blue eyes were on Sol. "Aye, will do, Gunsmoke."

Cheldyne coughed. "I understand ogling my astrum, trust me, but try to be more professional."

The tanker coughed, wheeled, and headed toward the other men. Sol followed his superiors aboard.

"I apologize but, what the fuck is going on?"

Parthenos triggered the release on his mask with a long sigh. "More than I'd really care to explain, Echo."

"At least you're you. Nice uniform." Sol saluted. *Um, nice stripes too, but I'm not gonna say it. Where did his mane go?*

"Kiertus is a wanted man in this system; to make a long story less complicated, let's say we're keeping the heat off a little town that doesn't deserve any pain." Parthenos sat at the console, in the gunner's seat.

Chel took the master seat. "It was a mistake to not switch back at the camp and insist you fly. Rectified."

Wait, that means they think he's with us. I don't like where this is going!

As Chel started the ship, he leaned back toward Sol. "That gentleman you questioned at the manor was just saying something we already figured out: that an Ilu renegade faction established a facility beneath the ground. Mind you, he was under the paranoid delusion they were under every city and town; the reality is, they're only under Kuuln-Kuog. That factory is the source of most if not all the war-creatures we know to have been sold on Kourhos. We've been evacuating since yesterday, trying to move fast, but we need to … get rid of the facility, sooner rather than later."

"Executive decisions have been made," Parthenos said softly, not looking anyone in the eye.

Sol swallowed, trying to comprehend the situation. "We're going to the *Yetzjmaal* to fire cannons from the atmosphere, even if the city's not fully evacuated, huh?"

"We can't simply fire into the atmosphere of a friendly populated planet with even a single incinerator; it's far too risky. We don't have those kind of gunners, anymore." Parthenos' voice was distant and cold. "Our men – my exo unit, led by Acolyte, that is, and the 17th's air units, led by Trauma and Wyvern - are congregating in the vicinity; nothing will escape what we're about to do."

Looking back and forth between the two men, Sol attempted to quell the taste of terror franticly climbing toward his brain. "W-where's Curly?"

"Safe. She doesn't need to be part of this."

Sol exhaled into his mask, hoping the sound of his shuddering was not obvious outside it. "Please brief me on the mission, then."

Parthenos pulled up a map, his face expressionless and movements stiff. "We'll set down the Dash here. There's a vent out of the production facility's nitro unit here. It isn't well-guarded from the outside. Mostly because this area," he gestured with a gloved finger around the perimeter, "is an old toxic waste zone from an abandoned human settlement."

"It… it's so close to Kuuln-kuog…"

"Yeah, the kaffir here were willing to put up with that to live away from humans." Save for a tiny hint of bitterness, Chel's voice was also flat and distant. "It's that or the risk of starvation and exposure in the desert. Hell of a choice, huh?"

"We're going to change that, right? That's the point of all this, right?"

Parthenos looked at the monitor and took notes on his slate. "That was the point of forcefully taking Buonfaddek and ripping out the heart of those who opposed us. This is older business."

"So, what do we do once we're inside?"

"Facilities like this are macro-organisms, somewhat like our star vessels. Mechanistically different, of course; the immune system, for example, is a bit less subtle and more..." Parthenos glanced over at Chel.

"Mono-focused, maybe is the descriptor you're looking for?"

He shrugged. "There are too many I could use, ironically. Anyway, if wounded harshly enough, it will commit all its immediately available resources to ridding itself of the threat and repairing the damage. Our job is to get far enough in and hurt it badly enough that it can't or won't adequately fight off any external threat. If we do our job right, by the time it realizes the trap and starts fighting back, it'll just be a matter of putting some salve on a scar."

The bug sergeant activated his handle; it read as that of Kiertus Sheriden and was purple in color. He smiled strangely as he banked down towards the edge of the contaminated wetland that was their destination. "For obvious reasons, we won't be discussing our plans once on the ground. Ignore colors and follow my lead. Should I be out of contact, Checkmate is in command."

"Understood."

Parthenos stood and stretched, the tendrils of his armor scintillated from violet to viridian in hypnotic waves. "Pay very close attention to the readings your armor gives you, and maintain maximum defense as necessary. This may require some of the less aesthetic modes..."

"Mucus barrier?"

"Great, you paid attention." The creepy reflective face plate was in place, returning a distorted vision of Sol in the cockpit doorway. "Your armor knows better than you most of the time what to do in places like this, this is what it's designed for... but you will want to turn 'pheromone' way up."

I've never even turned that one on before... "Pheromone, sir? Am I trying to get a date?"

445

Clearing his throat, Chel scratched the side of his face and explained matter-of-factly, "This bio system is designed not to immediately defend against saurtzek and it's not cutting edge... it can't distinguish a kaffa walking along with two Ruhns from two Ilu with an Archon prisoner."

"But it reads our insignia? That's why you turned your call sign on, right?"

"Well, some of their guards can," said Parthenos, angling his slate at Sol's still-exposed collar. "Hold still… welcome to the holy anonymity."

I want to know how that one works but I know it's some Guild shit; if I ask I'll get religious mumbo jumbo… or 'you're not cleared for that'. "I get kind of what we're doing now, but how do we get rid of guards without alerting the system that we're here? Visually, it's obvious what we are, isn't it?"

"That's the part where you'll follow our leads. Don't use your external communicator unless cleared. Don't touch anything, don't open anything, and don't activate your pulse without our say so." Chel finished suiting up in paratrooper field gear. "You ready, then?"

"Aye." Parthenos saluted. "For the empire."

That's the Haarnsvaar salute. I don't think I'm supposed to do it; only Guildsmen and their masters are… right? I'll go with the default. "Honor and sacrifice."

"For the empire," Chel returned, handing his rifle to Parthenos. He held his hands up. "Come on, boys, time to bring a little sunshine to your long-lost cousins."

XX. Executive Decision

Discolored muck sucked at their boots as they crossed the bog. Readings displayed the toxicity of air and earth, listing chemical compounds present. Cheldyne, walking with hands zip-tied above his head, leaned back towards Sol. "Whattya think of this as a vacation spot? Everything you could ask for, flammable *and* carcinogenic!"

"Shut the fuck up," Parthenos said with a snarl. "Just because you're playing the part doesn't mean you have to perform his jerk-ass version of comedy, too."

"I assure you I developed this sense of humor well before I met him."

"Whatever. Prisoners should be quiet or they might get hit by rifle butts."

They ascended a hump that had likely been a pile of refuse that accrued sand, mud, plant debris, and other detritus over time to become a landform. Two humanoid shapes moved in the distance near a similar hump and a disturbance in the air was visible near them.

"Those are our guards, and the vent," Parthenos noted. "There will be a third guard on patrol around the perimeter; by my guess from earlier readings, he'll be rejoining them in the next fifteen minutes." He carefully descended the rubbish hillock and onto a hump of struggling vegetation which began a dry-ish path through the unpleasant looking tarry pools.

Cheldyne looked down and tilted his head back and forth then cleared the uneven territory between the top of the heap and the weedy path in one graceful leap, hands still above his head. Sol and Parthenos whistled appreciatively.

"Old, fat, sick, still Haarnsvaar," Chel remarked quietly as he caught up. Sol would not have heard it had they not been using their helmet communicators. "Armor isn't everything."

The Guildsman said nothing, turned, and cloaked, vanishing from view save for a nameless trace on the overlay map in Sol's goggles. As the lieutenant caught up to his faux captive, the trace faded. Parthenos' voice materialized in Sol's ears like mist, coming from nowhere in specific, distant and strange.

"When you get to the guards, I will override your microphone; I will speak for you. Don't worry too much about your gestures; hit the captive with the barrel of your VTek a couple times for emphasis if you want. I'll handle the rest. Our only goal here is getting inside; these men are no threat to us."

Chel proceeded, leading in spite the fact that Sol held his weapon so as to appear he pushed the prisoner along. Eventually, one of the guards noticed them and guns were pointed their direction.

"Hail them. The override starts … now."

Sol waved his free hand, keeping the VTek pressed against Cheldyne's arm. Parthenos' voice, speaking clearly in Saurtaf, broadcast from Sol's external speakers.

I don't understand a word of what I'm 'saying'. I hope this works…

The two men standing at the vent exchanged glaces, then gestured Sol to approach. As he moved forward, a bark in Saurtaf came from him and Chel dropped to his knees. Sol followed him with the rifle and gave him a whack, trying not to openly cringe at hitting his friend and mentor.

Was that believable? I think it was. Who knew acting classes could pay off so well in an assault squad?

One of the guards approached, his weapon half-lowered. He was tall, pure saurtzek from the dark blue-green flesh around his exposed eyes. Sol surmised he was from a lower caste; the kind of unfortunate sort who would be given an incredibly crappy job patrolling an exhalation vent in a toxic swamp.

Although the soldier was clearly unsettled – shaking, even – he was conversational as he stepped over. He did not want to be anywhere near Cheldyne, though. Gingerly, he reached for the barrel of the VTek, shook his head, wide-eyed, almost afraid to touch it. He withdrew before actually contact, looking at Sol with big shiny black eyes. He had undergone several modifications; his airmask was welded to his face. It periodically misted his eyes, which seeped a little; lines around them displayed physical stress. Finally, he touched the gun, shuddered and stepped back, laughing uncomfortably. Looking at his fellow guard, he made a remark that sounded a bit to Sol like a nervous wisecrack.

The other guard approached. Parthenos spoke through Sol's speaker with a friendlier tone. He was similar in appearance, with a lighter skin tone and pronounced dark stripes to his eyes. Again, his mask seemed fused. As he stepped around Chel he sneered and made an unpleasant, hissing comment in the man's direction. When he bravely touched the VTek, however, an alarm symbol flashed on Sol's goggles:

VERCHYNE INFESTATION PRESENT

The misty voice returned, audible only to the lieutenant, "Step back slowly, Echo. It's probably true of both but that one's very sick if your gun can detect it on your current settings."

At this point, the wandering patrol returned, obviously demanding to know what was up. There were many hand gestures and some explaining from the two previous guards, then Parthenos broadcast out of Sol again. The third guard wore the armor Sol had seen many times in military guide books – the oily brownish leathery suit that went only up to the nipples and a decorative yoke hung with reddish-orange cabochons down the chest.

He's someone in a low level of power, but I couldn't say what. The ranking system the Ilu use is ludicrously micro-managing; their hard-on for bureaucracy makes Ryzaans look uncivilized.

"Three fingers on your free hand, up quickly at a quarter angle from your face. Good. That looked properly casual." Parthenos switched to broadcast again; this conversation was longer and Sol got twitchy, unsure of what to do with his body. Almost as if reading his mind, Chel shifted a little, inviting another rifle slap from the lieutenant.

Sol understood from the discussion this man's name was 'Izzaryu', a fairly common name for Saurtaf speakers, although some vowels were weakly pronounced and it came out more like 'Izz-roo' the way Parthenos said it. The officer had a sleazy manner, peering creepily into Sol's mask and standing a little too close. Suddenly, he backed up, fierce anger on what was visible of his face. He turned to the infected guard and yelled; the other guard went wide-eyed and scrambled backward, looking about for cover.

Izzru made a head gesture at Sol and said something vile from the way the other guards cringed. The infected one dropped his weapon and backed away from the vent, holding his hands - dramatically vibrating now – and moving his head strangely.

"Fry him, Sol."

"Ahm…"

Parthenos hissed, sounding more saurtzek than kaffir. "That's a fucking order. Fry that wormbait now."

Aur, have mercy. And don't let any of that get on me. His rifle was charged enough for a few good bolts, but Sol dumped extra energy into the blast – ending the beat of one heart was easy; guaranteeing the deaths of an unknown quantity of contagious parasitic life forms was something else entirely.

Right before he unleashed the charge into the cringing guard, he heard Parthenos' disembodied voice whisper, "Look hard, that's the face that killed your father's people."

Sol recognized terror on the cowering man's face; he gritted his teeth and fired. The force of the bolt left little more than a gory fog and a few hunks of sizzled meat. A soul-chillingly foul sound came from somewhere to his right; Sol, still heaving and shuddering from the discharge, turned to see the other guard attempting to be unobtrusive and disinterested on the far side of the vent and Izzru laughing with his entire body. He made what must have been amusing comments to which Parthenos responded in kind, but Sol was repulsed and fought not to display so in his body language.

You enjoyed me killing one of your own men like that? What the fuck is wrong with you?

"Clean up residuals; some verch still moving… arcing field or web, try not to hit Izzru or the prisoner."

Ugh. Sol crouched and threw out a net-like field, sizzling stray bits around him. Izzru's eyes widened and he backed up further, regarding Sol as if he might be dangerous to him as well.

Parthenos laughed softly, only for Sol's benefit. "Not now, kid, and I know exactly how you feel." He tossed off a snide remark in Saurtaf through the lieutenant's speakers as Sol stood back up.

Izzru laughed again, uncomfortably this time. He addressed the remaining guard without taking his eyes off the unpredictable Ruhn warrior and gestured at the vent. Sol roughly grabbed a knobby bit on the back of Chel's armor and shoved him forward. Both saurtzek moved away from the old Archon, who leered at Izzru and said, "Boo."

They entered the vent and descended out of visual contact with the saurtzek shortly. Sol glanced around the moist, fleshy walls and bony steps leading down the faintly lit passage. Gusts of air, exhaust from the system that kept the atmosphere comfortably breathable for workers below, pumped rhythmically through it every few minutes.

Chel kept his transmission between them. "We've got a long way to go. He'll catch up with us."

"Understood." Sol had a preponderance of questions, but remembered his orders and remained silent.

"You can take the gun off my back, Echo."

Sol shouldered the VTek rapidly. "Er, uh, sorry."

"No cameras down this tube. Just kinda low-tech life form sensors. Could probably talk without masks if we wanted to breathe the air." He paused as if reading his mask. "Which I for one would rather not."

I can't stand it anymore. If I get in trouble, I just do. "Can I ask how you know that?"

"These facilities are all the same in design, some have better resources, but our agents got blueprints to this one specifically. This was built on a pant lace budget with handicapping factors." Chel shrugged.

"I'd say their biggest handicapping factor was the double-crossing shitsack arms dealer who set this whole rig up." Parthenos faded in as he dropped from the ceiling of the passage. His tendrils flicked goo to the sides. "He's off to safety now. More guards may come; we should be prepared for that eventuality."

"That guy was on our side?"

The other men stopped and exchanged glances as much as their masks allowed. Parthenos spoke. "He's on no one's side but his own. I would never say 'you can trust Izzru', but it'll serve us to let him keep living for now."

"The truth can be such an ugly thing," Cheldyne uttered quietly.

I wonder if he actually meant to broadcast that…

Parthenos stopped in the gradually widening passage and put his arms slowly out at his sides. Chel stopped first, putting a hand on Sol's arm as the Guildsman informed, "Replacements en route. They expect to see two men in Archon uniforms. See ya."

"Gods he is an extra cock in that armor."

"Do you mean to have your broadcast on?"

"It's only on for you, Echo."

Three guards ascended toward them, two more surgically modified and one donning his mask, apparently attempting to joke with the others, who seemed to have no sense of humor. Sol employed the barrel of his rifle to press on Chel's chest, forcing him against the wall to allow the new guards passage. They were on their way again with about three body lengths of distance between one another when one of the modified guards turned and yelled.

"Shit," Sol heard Chel whisper.

Parthenos immediately overrode Sol's speaker from wherever he hid and Saurtaf flowed forth. The unmodified saurtzek came back down to converse.

Cheldyne nodded and pushed up his goggles with thumbs and elbows. He shrugged and waved his bound wrists at the expectant guard.

"Remove his helmet, and then you need to do it too, Echo. Now."

He did not have the time to be upset about how this would interfere with transmission reception. Without lowering his rifle from Chel's back, Sol unhooked and took his faux prisoner's helmet. He then removed his own and pushed his goggles up. As the red locks fell around his face, the saurtzek guard backed up, raising his hands. He bowed once and said something that included the name 'Myentrios'. The guards turned and continued up the shaft.

Sol returned Chel's helmet and refixed his, remarking via internal communicator, "They thought I was…"

Chel cut him off without hesitation. "Yes. Best not to think about it; it saved your ass just now."

Moving on in awkward silence, they approached a split in the tube. The right fork opened into a circular passage and the other sloped down into a large, membranous structure which opened to release the gusts of air they walked against along the way. Ambient temperature increased by another 15 degrees just beyond this, and Sol made a noise of disgust as it became clear it was their destination.

"That hallway's patrolled," came Parthenos' floating voice. "Trust your mucus barrier and follow us."

I can't even see you, you jerk.

Beyond the puffing, sticky flaps was a corridor of strands the three men studiously avoided as Parthenos, visible as a purple signature on their monitors, led them to a hole down into darkness.

Chel waited at the opening, holding out his still tied wrists. He coughed conspicuously, and Sol reached over and slit the ties with his utility knife. "It's serious from here, kid. Stay strong." Then he dropped into the hole to whatever lay beneath.

They hopped off the chute (having not reached the bottom) into a chamber with sticky, striated, fleshy walls, a spongy floor, and a central cluster of rhythmically pumping, bulging tubes running between floor and ceiling. As Sol's boots contacted the soft, moist matter of the room, a warning flashed in his helmet and his armor immediately produced a defensive layer of mucus.

SENSITIVITY AMPLIFIED. TOLERANCE DECREASED, read Sol's personal monitor.

The whole place read as life-forms, although neutral or non-intelligent. One darker dot moved around it, but it read only as 'questionable' rather than 'hostile'.

Sol automatically swung his rifle against Cheldyne's back as the entity came round the pumping central unit and into view. It appeared saurtzek, worn and tired, perma-grafted mask on its face, methodically checking valves on the wall and tubes. It froze and looked in their direction, eyes red and lined, then continued its assigned task.

A warning flashed again. *VERCHYNE INFESTATION. ICHEMIUS HAZARD. AVOID CONTACT.*

"That…that has to be a misreading," remarked the lieutenant in mild distress. "Run diag, expedite, sen-"

Chel's shoulders slumped. "Aw, fuck, am I reading as infested?"

Parthenos, examing tubes in plain sight, twitched. "Son of a bitch."

Cheldyne raised his goggles and removed his mask, his face chagrinned and perspiring beneath. He shrugged and faced Sol, sounding quite apologetic. "True story. I'm worm-ridden as they come. I'll suppress 'em back down, trouble not." He removed a pack of fenerettes from his belt and tapped one out. Rolling it in his fingers a moment, he remarked to Parthenos in Shandrian, "Get that one's attention; he gets a new job probably for the first time in his miserable existence."

"I know what you're about to do and it violates the accord," admonished the Guildsman.

"This base violates the accord." Chel manifested a tiny fire orb between the thumb and forefinger of his right hand, cigarette in his mouth.

"That's not the point."

The man hiding under the identity of Kiertus looked highly perturbed. "Then mercifully off the little fuck, I guess. I'm lighting this either way."

Sol, not understanding the exchange, approached the laboring, broken old saurtzek and attempted to get their attention. The being nearly stumbled over him, then continued on their way. "What the…"

"They're brainwashed, Echo. They can only perform the functions they're designed to and will only change functions at the proper signal." Parthenos seemed very tense. "Exposure to fenatja, even via skin and eyes, could radically interrupt that programming, possibly harming them a great deal."

You hate these people, don't you? Sol turned to Cheldyne. "And you wanted to do what then?"

Chel lit the cigarette. "I was going to blow smoke in their face and push them down the hall with a new command string. Fenatja does some interesting things to full-blooded saurtzek, even the non-brainwashed ones. See also the way you throw up every time you smell it, Ruhn."

I refuse to believe I have that much saurtzek blood even if this … whatever the fuck this is we're inside identifies me as one! "I figured that was my human side, it's a narcotic to humans, you know?"

Parthenos was deeply annoyed; he drew a device from a concealed leg sheath and approached the worker drone. "In saurtzek, it's a delirient that potentially induces traumatic mania or violent psychosis."

As Sol turned to Chel to see if he had anything to say, Parthenos grabbed the drone by the neck, from behind, and jammed the weapon in. As they slid to the floor, the exhausted eyes expressed peaceful relief.

Why is he looking at me? Was I supposed to do something?

A similar expression of relief lit Chel's face as he puffed on the fennie. "Don't start, Checks. He's probably not even initiated yet."

"Then why the fuck did you pick him for this?"

"I needed another person of the right blood rating; that leaves so few people who will even be in the same room with the other person I needed for the mission… hm. Funny, that."

The Guildsman growled and headed for a wound-like opening in the opposite wall. "I'm implementing phase three. I'll be in touch. Stay on ready, Echo." He dissipated from view. The membranes spread and then flexed back to their original position, swallowing his invisible shape.

"Hey, we finally get a chance to talk." Chel exhaled into a meshy opening along a pumping structure and shook his head. "It really shouldn't be that difficult. Maalek's got a shitty sense of humor, sometimes."

The room was loud, but Sol managed to filter Chel's voice out of all the heaving, squeaking, and gasping. "What … is this place, anyway?"

"Part of the air filtration system. It's pumping air from outside down into the nitrogen isolator. The air's scrubbed just above us, so this is clean oxygenated air. You don't want to touch the walls, but if your mask broke, you could theoretically survive… I mean, minus the obvious." He waited until the meshy part opened enough and blew rings of bluish smoke into the gap.

Sol double checked his readings; this was, so far, the best air he had encountered on Verraken. His suit continued to produce its extra viscous protective layer, however, which he tried not to think about. *I'm covered in snot. Snot snot snot. Hey, ladies…have I mentioned… I'm single?* "How long, um, it's not my business I guess… but…"

"The verch? Eh. Many many years." He smiled broadly, in the manner that caused his scar to wrinkle comically. "The worst part was they came with the big prize. I'm sure you were warned, by your armor, if not your boss."

"This was the first time, actually. I guess it makes sense though, what he said about the vaccine study." Sol smiled too, sad for his friends and commanders, but strangely proud of them. "I guess you were under cover or something?"

An eyebrow rose. "Oh, you mean the title? Not exactly. My choice to grey bar myself was based on interpersonal relations with crew on the *Sanj*, nothing else. You'll understand in time." He lowered his goggles and looked up thoughtfully as he took a drag. "Make sure your multi-level reader is on and recalibrate it until you can tune out the pump. Got it? You'll get a better view of incoming hostiles. Checkmate's bringing us some. Don't stress, we'll have plenty of prep time."

"But you're not faceless, then?"

"Funny way to put it. Yes and no, I just haven't lived in the palace in a long time." Shrugging, he blew smoke down the pump again. "I should be dead. They usually don't let men who insult the queen walk. This was my souvenir…" Chel gestured to the scar gracing the bridge of his nose. "Brinsanjin gave me that; can't say I didn't deserve it, either."

The commander of the Haarnsvaar hit you in the face? "You don't sound regretful, though."

The smile was huge. "Not a thing. Not a goddamn thing. They took my armor and shipped me straight into Hell itself." He gestured with both hands, last dregs of his fennie still clasped, at the length of his body. "Couldn't take me down. Still here. My death is still my choice, and my life up until then, still lived on my own terms. Note not one of them had the heart to kill me or take my rank even after all that, just the armor and my right to go home. I did fine, all the same." Chel killed the butt on his boot, putting it in a pouch instead of throwing it on the floor.

"Wasn't living in the palace a dream for you though?"

"Sure, and then it was a dream I didn't care to have, and I took a chance and moved on."

Moving hostiles were visible on Sol's reader, distantly below; from Chel's movements, they were for him as well. Sol charged his rifle and Chel his armor.

"Just because a knight's oath is for life doesn't mean he's got a solitary predestined path. You still have the say in how you live within the oath. Some men forget and imprison themselves on paths that make them bitter and vindictive…"

The hostile mass rose slowly. Sol followed it with his rifle, aiming through walls and floor as it moved. "Is it just attitude that makes you different?"

Chel chuckled. "No, Echo, it's simple: I don't believe in single-purpose entities. I hate societies that try to manufacture them. If some god has a destiny they picked for you, they'll handle that; any mortal telling you they know your destiny, or that you only get one chance to pick it, is manipulative or mad." He

457

raised his mask and turned to his young friend. "When Parthenos gets here, follow him. Unless he goes back down... in that case, you're ordered to go up that –"

Sol followed the pointing gloved finger to a slit up the wall, near the ceiling, that could be climbed to using vents as footholds. He was hesitant about the order; he did not like the sound of it.

"It'll be a squeeze, and a wet one; your armor will keep you safe, as long as you grab some oxygen into your reservoirs before you jump in. Climb in there dripping mucus and it will identify you as something it shouldn't digest, and you'll be ejected from here like a big old –"

The hostiles were close. Parthenos hopped through the slit, thumping onto the spongy tissue of the floor. "Man you are a dick, Yndel."

"What, should I have saved you a drag, too?"

"Seriously, fuck you." Parthenos unhooked and expanded the weapon that clung to his other thigh – a VTek 440, the Haarnsvaar sidearm, a thing Sol knew only from vague diagrams. It resembled a big, angry armored fish hand puppet. He focused charge into it as he braced, aiming for the door.

"Checks, knock it off. Get the fuck out."

The hostile mass was close. "If we kill these, more will come, best use of our resources, I thought. Sol, fire through the wall in four, three, two – now!"

Fleshy walls ruptured and sizzled and an intense alarm sounded, punctuated by screams from the other side. The hostile mass dwindled as the dripping, seered hole gaped wider.

"Now get the fuck out, alright? I can take it from here."

Parthenos turned to Chel. "Are you serious?"

"Thanks for your help? Is that what you want me to say?"

"Are you waiting for me to volunteer? What kind of trick is this?"

"It was no trick, fuckface, it was an order. Check your updated stats, by the way, and if you don't take my order now, I'm going to make sure your Guild call sign is 'Fuckface', fuckface! Get out!" Chel gestured emphatically at the digestive slit. He spoke something into his mask.

The others froze in horror as Chel's – Kiertus Sheriden's – on-screen tag began to intermittently flash orange. The warning read, "*ESDD, ACTIVATED.*"

Parthenos lowered his gun. His shoulders sagged; he stared at the bug sergeant, his voice sad. "Yndel…"

"What. You thought I was going to make you or the kid do it?"

Looking back and forth at them, a mix of emotions washed over Sol. He backed toward the slit, hesitating a little. "I understand the order, but… is there a protocol for 'goodbye'?"

Chel raised his goggles, creases indicating a smile under his mask. "'Goodbye' usually works, I find."

Parthenos moved toward the slit. "You don't have to do this… we could…"

"Silence. I've lived 106 fucking amazing years, kid. There's only a matter of time before my body breaks down too much to keep fighting this shit inside me. I'd like to end things on a strong note, not in an isolation room at the Fenrir ICU." He lowered his mask and lit another cigarette. "And, really, I'd like to think Trauma will move on and have a life again, and one of you has to go remind him he can. I mean, the big K will be too drunk for a while, pretty sure."

106? I'd swear his record says 77 cycles. Sol stopped climbing to retract and secure his rifle and oxygenate the reservoirs that would provide emergency air during his time in the grisly tube. He struggled against tears to sound genuinely regal as he saluted. "Goodbye, sir. I am glad I got to work with you."

Cheld took the fennie from his mouth to return the salute, winking as he gestured with it. "No problem, kid. May you always shine brighter than the shadow that haunts you. Keep an eye on those ol' bastards for me, will ya?"

"Will do, sir!" With this final honor, Sol squeezed into the oppressive, dark, fleshy space beyond, cringing a bit as his instruments went rampant and froth formed around him. Whether it came from the tube wall or a reaction between tube and mucus, he could not tell; he simply pressed forward so Parthenos could enter. He could still hear the other men talking, presumably through the Guildsman's suit.

"Well, this is it. I don't know what to say."

"I have some thoughts for you, Auri; most of them start with you apologizing to Wyvern."

There was an uncomfortable pause. "I paid his freedom price. Isn't that enough?"

"Just because a man's been property since he was a boy doesn't mean he's got no feelings. I can't order you to do it, it's your life, you'll figure out what you want out of it. Just go live it, that's all I ask. My turn to die today; yours will come another time."

"Goddammit."

"I'll accept that."

From the readings, Parthenos was behind him on the wall, almost in the tube.

"Hey, Auri…"

"Yes, sir?"

"One last thing." There was a pause. "Kdjek." Then Chel was laughing.

"Gods! Fuck you, you have the worst sense of humor!"

"Goodbye, Auri. I love you, too!"

The foam became dreadfully thick; the walls of the passage spasmed and churned as Sol continued to force his way. Shortly they seemed to propel him, undulating to move him along, up and out towards the surface. Convulsions increased until he was hurtling in a mass of fluid and froth; he struggled to enter the fetal position, bracing...

He launched forcefully from the ground in a jet of thick fluids, tumbling, readings scrambled as he flew. He was aware of a cacophony, of lights, of far too much motion. Fortunately, his armor processed information a little more efficiently than he, and it expended its remaining stored charge on a barrier of pulse that broke Sol's fall onto the hard, cracked mesa above the toxic swamp. Readings remained chaotic; there were incoming non hostiles from a few directions, but the fast-moving one behind him made him roll and crawl rapidly to the right.

Parthenos had been propelled a bit further and harder, but came down with more grace, on his feet, body low and arms half-outstretched, like a bird sailing in for a landing. As Sol stood, they both looked up and swore at the same time. From their vantage point above the swamp and the decrepit, sad city of Kuuln-kuog, they saw incoming jets and exoskeletal units swarming in, surrounding the area.

"As much as I hate to give this order, Echo – run!"

They headed away from the city, toward the encroaching Cyvaxes, cursing a little as the firing had already started and clearly no one had picked up their readings yet.

"My tag! Make me visible!"

Parthenos skidded to a stop in the dirt, turning with a snap, slate held out. "I can't believe I for-"

A massive blast from the direction they came sent both men sprawling. Before Sol recovered, Parthenos held the slate to his neck again, terminating his invisibility. With better chances of discovery, they resumed running, Sol cringing periodically at the Dash mini-cannons sighing behind. Other sounds became audible as the initial blast's ringing faded; the creaks and rustles of Archon armored vehicles, the thundering ground beneath, and a horrible whistling he remembered from somewhere...

"Don't turn around, just keep running!"

Sol had no interest in disobeying this order. Parthenos initiated a distress sequence when they were knocked down again by a monstrous thing resembling a two story bipedal cockroach landing in their path. With its upward set of spikey arms, it plucked them from the ground and swung them to its armored chest as bolts of fire tore the earth to pieces where they had lain.

A hatch opened; Sol was closest and slid in first, followed closely by his superior.

"Get in, get in – good, now hold on, we're getting out of here!"

Sol could not see the voice's source; it was female and originated somewhere above. They were in a storage or maintenance compartment; it was tight but there were plenty of things to cling to as the roach-droid crouched and then launched into the air.

As the craft stabilized, Parthenos swung himself up a small ladder toward the voice. Sol followed enough to peer into the cockpit, which seemed a single-person operation; Parthenos was wedged, half crouched, behind the pilot's seat.

"Shard, you are the last person I thought I'd see today. Not to imply unhappiness. Thank you."

"Wyvern told me the rest of the plan at the last minute; I couldn't just sit there… I decided I'd come get you if I had to punch through that swampy shit and find you by feel." The woman's tone hinted both relief and aggravation. They flew in silence for a time before she said, "Let me guess – that wasn't actually Curtis down there, huh?"

Parthenos very clearly did not wish to answer. "No…"

"Please tell me it was Okie."

"Gods I wish."

There was more silence. Sol cringed at the awkwardness, dropping back down the ladder into the cargo pocket. Things were rocky for a moment and he returned to clinging for life against the side of the compartment, wondering where they were flying and how fast. A recorded announcement explained they were incoming to the *Yetzjmaal*. The craft parked in a hangar and went through shut down procedures, and still no words were spoken. Parthenos dropped down the ladder and out the hatch; Sol followed. Shortly, a kaffir woman of smallish stature in an exo pilot uniform with a marine's armored vest and the logo of the Fangs hopped out behind. After a cursory examination of the vehicle, she signaled to some techs in the hangar and approached them.

Parthenos regarded her with his head tilted slightly. His mask remained on, so his expression was unreadable. Sol looked over the woman – a violet bar, call sign of 'Shard' - briefly as she pulled down her hood and unhooked her breathing mask. She had grey-streaked brown hair and strange orange eyes. Her staged face bore a few signs of age but she had excellent poise combined with a combat build; older than his mother, he guessed, but still really something. He even blushed a little when she looked up, huge weird eyes open wide and seeping a little, horrified realization spreading on her face as her mask and tube dangled over her chest.

"Oh, no... Yndel?"

"I'm sorry, Eumelje. I tried to get him to change his – "

She buried her face against the Guildsman, who said into his mask, only for Sol's benefit, "Dismiss anyone who doesn't out-color you in this hangar."

To Sol's surprise, not a single technician did. He cleared the area rapidly, amazed at his power. *Maybe everyone with real rank is on the ground or on the bridge?* He took in a shuddering breath as he watched Parthenos raise his mask and let his suit go limp and non-threatening to embrace the crying woman. He noted he was still amped, vibrating slightly, itching to kick the crap out of something. He could not accept the reality of earlier events. *When these drugs wear off, I'll be a wreck; they have to be the only thing keeping me going at this point... wonder how much longer I have?*

Parthenos' voice was surprisingly tender, although Sol could tell his physical state was similar: righteously charged and wired to kill. "What did Wyvern tell you, Mel?"

How can he keep himself so cool and collected? I think the act of trying to reassure someone else would send me over the edge right now. I can't even think about it...

Restraining her soft sobbing, she lifted her head from his chest. "That three people were going into the factory, and my unit, led by Acolyte, was to join his and we were to come in and wait. That all of us were to fire and not stop firing the moment that the ground blew open…" She took in a rough breath and released it, straightening her hair as she stepped back from Parthenos. "A few hours later, he finally told me you were one of the men in the hole. Forgive him for the protocol violation, please."

The Guildsman shrugged. "In this case, I haven't any authority over him; the breach harmed no one; your decision to put yourself in danger was your own."

As she undid the last strap on her mask and removed it from her neck, Sol noticed the pin that declared her a general, immediately saluting and apologizing.

She nodded and half-saluted in return. "I'll forgive you the transgression if you forget you saw a general crying, Red. Deal? Deal."

Somehow when she calls me 'Red', it's cute. People say such mean things about tankers. She seems sweet, honestly… but then again… Parthenos can play sweet and gentle, too.

"Lieutenant Solvreyil?"

"Yes, sir!"

"I need to return you to your station." He eyed Sol sternly. "But off the record, I'd like to take the long way back and waste some Stalkers as they emerge. Just to make the effort go smoothly, of course. We wouldn't be tagged for general view so you wouldn't be violating direct orders… Got any pulse left?"

"Enough for a few good mini-cannon blasts, sir."

Parthenos turned and saluted his friend. "General Eumelje! Do you have a vessel I can commandeer?"

"Absolutely, Master Parthenos! Take that Dash there… I'll be cheering you on from the bridge." She saluted with a flourish.

Parthenos cast a glance about the hangar, still devoid of mechanics after Sol's purge. He stole a kiss like a striking snake then returned to salute as if nothing happened. "See you at the funeral."

"Aye. And I'll act professional. Happy hunting, gentlemen!"

As they climbed aboard the Dash, they worked together to calibrate it for maximum efficiency before take off. Parthenos seemed overjoyed to remember Sol's rating compatibility.

"This will be cake... we'll barely need to charge if we set this thing right." He sat back with a satisfied smirk as Sol checked the supplies and fuel reserves.

"We're good to go as soon as that's all set up, sir."

"It'll take a few minutes at least; just have a seat."

Sol tried not to think about other things. "Where do you suppose Ozlietsin got off to, sir?"

"Staring impatiently at Jady or Wyvern from the back of a Dash somewhere... wondering the same thing about you, probably." The big Ruhn shrugged. "If people were smart, they'd have handed her off to Kiertus before the fire exchange. But we are talking military here, and some really drug-buggered mils at that; I won't make excuses for 'em."

His mind kept wandering to Chel's final words and any number of other things he did not want to consider. "Sir, how do you do it?"

"Do what?"

"Keep fighting, when shit around you breaks your heart?"

For the first time since their original encounter that day, Parthenos dropped his hood, running his hand through his thick black hair. "Most importantly, don't think about the hard shit until you're out of combat. When that simple act seems completely out of your league, and I know, you get in the wrong headspace and it's like you're trapped, right? When you just can't do that, try and remember your reasons to fight."

"Can I ask you what yours are, sir?"

He stretched; tendrils wiggled and ran through a range of colors. "Depends on the day; today it's because what I'm doing, what we're doing, is right. Because we have to, because it needs to be done. In the long run, things will improve. The sooner it's done, the sooner we get shore leave, which we need, some more than I do." Putting his hands behind his head, he closed his eyes. Sol looked at the calibration monitor as Parthenos continued. "Some days it's because I hear the ghosts of my family crying for retribution, crying for the children I never will have, warning me that a universe of unending pain awaits all living beings if I don't stand up to it. And some days I fight because there are people like Eumelje who look to me as a hero, a guardian, a friend, a lover, who make me feel less alone, who somehow, in spite of everything I've been through, can drive away all my darkness in a moment of closeness."

I can't believe I've ever thought poorly of you... But I also can't apologize.

"Have you figured out what you fight for, Yenraziir?"

"I don't know. I've never had lovers, I mean, yet; fighting for the admiration of great men seems a little shallow to me at the moment. I suppose I fight for my mother, but realistically, I know she's probably not long for this reality, and I don't know where I am, then."

The big dark eyes bored into him. "Really? That's all?"

"I apologize if I missed something obvious, sir. I've had to accept some pretty heavy things today; my mind is throwing up walls everywhere, I ..."

"Your older sister, is, to my knowledge, one of the last viable members of our tribe, Yenraziir. She is married and planning children, is she not? And the people who hate Ruhn are none the wiser, no? For on her records, does it not say, she was the child of two Holtiini, one human, one haki?"

Sol blinked as a psychological wall shattered from the force of truth he had failed to assemble on his own.

"If you don't fight on behalf of her, I will."

"But will she stay undetected, living on Archos, using Ryzaan hospitals?"

Gentle but sneaky laughter issued from the Guildsman. "She married a Khemiir,

Yen. All children she has share his protected status in spite of anomalous blood. It's part of the Compensation Provision Act, to make up for colonial Ryzaan behavior. Anyone coming between her and them would be asking for a lot of attention, which those little execution groups aren't usually so into." Sorrow tinged his otherwise smug expression. "Even if Marsura never truly offered us amnesty, the previous queen and the laws of the people did; if only more Ruhn realized Archos was a haven when the rest of the Empire was risky; lesson learned, I suppose. Difficult to imagine what you've never seen, hm?"

I guess someone from the 17th can speak motivationally after all.

"One more thing, Yen, maybe not as bright a light for your heart. I know the current queen pisses you off. Remember that Star Assault is a foot in the door of the Imperial Guild; the Haarnsvaar have the right to invoke Section 12 and bring her to trial should a majority of the armored deem fit."

The ship uttered a satisfied, "Calibration: complete. All functions operable."

"Well, sir, I guess that's our cue…"

"Indeed. Do you still feel up to it?"

Sol smiled, peculiarly warmed by his renewed sense of purpose. "Without a doubt, Master Parthenos. For the Empire!"

"Damn straight, Red."

ABOUT THE AUTHOR

A Koi lives in a boggy den at the south end of the Puget Sound. This fish does not self-describe with gendered pronouns (having the unpleasant luck of being born chimaeric), has survived longer than expected in spite of dark prognostications by both clergy and medical professionals, and is willfully unmarried to anything besides the divine will of creation itself.

45930021R00264

Made in the USA
Middletown, DE
17 July 2017